# A BLIGHT OF MAGES

The five sigils flared, garish, like fire fanned by a wild wind. Barl Lindin gasped, her slight body shocked rigid. A heartbeat later she started trembling. Then the incants melted one into the next, began rising and falling and spinning, the circle shrinking . . . shrinking . . .

The melded sigils touched her shaking shoulders and swiftly sank into her flesh.

'Oh,' she whispered. 'Oh no . . . please, no . . .'

Morgan caught her as she crumpled, and lowered her gently to the floor.

*I'm sorry. Forgive me. You must have seen I had no choice.*

But he couldn't see how she would, when he doubted he'd ever forgive himself.

# By Karen Miller

A Blight of Mages

*Kingmaker, Kingbreaker*
The Innocent Mage
The Awakened Mage

*Godspeaker*
Empress
The Riven Kingdom
Hammer of God

*Fisherman's Children*
The Prodigal Mage
The Reluctant Mage

*Rogue Agent (writing as K. E. Mills)*
The Accidental Sorcerer
Witches Incorporated
Wizard Squared
Wizard Undercover

# A BLIGHT OF MAGES

## KAREN MILLER

www.orbitbooks.net

ORBIT

First published in Great Britain in 2011 by Orbit
This paperback edition published in 2012 by Orbit

A CIP catalogue record for this book
is available from the British Library.

ISBN 978-1-84149-750-1

Typeset in Sabon LT Std by Palimpsest Book Production Limited,
Falkirk, Stirlingshire
Printed and bound in Great Britain by CPI Group (UK) Ltd,
Croydon, CR0 4YY

Papers used by Orbit are from well-managed forests
and other responsible sources.

MIX
Paper from
responsible sources
FSC® C104740

Orbit
An imprint of
Little, Brown Book Group
100 VictoriaEmbankment
London EC4Y 0DY

An Hachette UK Company
www.hachette.co.uk

www.orbitbooks.net

*Dedicated to*
*All the readers who love The Mage books.*
*Thank you.*

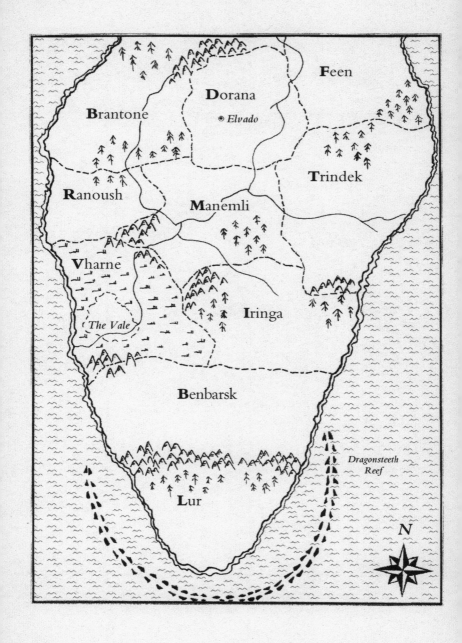

# CHAPTER ONE

There were times – many times – when Barl thought the sound of ticking clocks would drive her mad.

Not that the clocks ticked while they were being created, of course. And once they were completed they ticked just long enough to prove they were in perfect working order, and not a moment longer. After that they were warded between tick and tock and remained hushed as midnight until they reached their destination, so that the artisanry's wealthy patron had the privilege of setting his or her ruinously expensive purchase into motion.

But even so, she could still hear the wretched things.

*Or perhaps what I'm hearing is the rest of my life ticking into oblivion, into obscurity, into nothing but eventual, echoing silence.*

Before her, on the sturdy workbench that had become almost her whole world, sat her partly completed current work piece. This time she was creating a journey clock for Lord Artur Traint, Mage Inspector of the Eleventh district. At the tender age of twenty-two she was the youngest, least experienced clock mage in the artisanry. According to her self-appointed betters that meant she should be flattered and honoured and humbled by this task.

1

Instead, she was offended.

A mole had more artistic integrity in its whiskers than Lord Traint did in all his overweening body. If only he could be guided toward a more daring construction. If only someone would listen when she pointed out the neglected opportunities in the district inspector's humdrum design. But no, he was a great lord, born to one of the seventy First Families' upper ranks, so she must defer to his lack of taste and daring, she must abase herself before his withered imagination, she must –

'Barl Lindin! Do you work or do you frabble?'

*Both*, she wanted to say. But Artisan Master Arndel, owner of the artisanry, was a stickler for the courtesies and the scourge of any mage who idled time. Hiding the impatience that would get her in trouble, she looked into the bony face looming above her on the other side of her bench.

'Master, I thought to revisit the question of Lord Traint's clock design. Perhaps if we—'

'Revisit?' Arndel's wide brow creased with his displeasure. 'Mage Lindin, if you raise the topic again we will revisit the question of your suitability for this task. Our duty is to fulfil the patron's expectations, not indulge our own whims.'

'I'm sorry,' she said stiffly. 'I thought our duty was to exceed expectations. If a patron can be shown a better way to—'

'Better?' Up went Arndel's scraggly eyebrows. 'By whose lights, Mage Lindin? Do you suggest I substitute your judgement for Lord Traint's?'

When his lordship's judgement was lacking? Yes. Of course. But she couldn't say that. Not exactly. 'I was only thinking that—'

Arndel narrowed his muddy green eyes. 'Mage Lindin, as I have told you already, there is more to being a clock mage in my artisanry than a desirable bent for the magic. It would seem, however, that my wise words fall upon stony ground.'

Barl felt her cheeks warm, knowing too well how her fellow mages were enjoying the Artisan Master's displeasure. Every reproof she earned from stolid Arndel was a carelessly tossed gift to those who resented her for being who and what she was: the best mage they would likely see in their lifetimes.

'No, Master Arndel,' she said, and lowered her gaze that he might not see her hot resentment. 'I understand perfectly.'

'Yes?' Arndel's voice was soaked in skepticism. 'Then it is past time you proved it.' His severe finger lifted in warning. 'Mage Lindin, you are a young woman with some talent, I allow, but not the wit or the wisdom that will permit me to permit you to override a loyal patron's wishes. You are required to create the clock as Lord Traint has envisioned it. Are your skills unequal to the task?'

*No, you prosing fool, my skills are wasted!*

She wanted to shout the words loudly enough to raise the artisanry roof. But if she did, she'd only be rewarded with dismissal. She couldn't do that to Remmie. He'd sacrificed far too much for her to throw this position aside, no matter how confining she found it.

'Mage Lindin?' Arndel rapped out her name as though he were striking his knuckles to the bench. 'Do you attend me?'

Staring at the inked design for Lord Traint's tedious journey clock, she took a moment to be certain her voice and face were schooled to repressed obedience. Then she looked up again.

'Master, I apologise. I thought only to surprise Lord Traint with a small and unexpected delight.'

A soft snort from Ibbitha Rannis sounded from the artisan bench beside her, as Arndel's creased brow creased a little deeper.

'Mage Lindin, you must curb your unfortunate tendency toward fancy. A precocious mage is a dangerous mage. Think upon that, rather than the unrequested rearrangements of a patron's commission.'

'Master,' she said, lowering her gaze a second time. She felt so hot with anger now she thought she might easily ignite the fool. Which would well serve him right, but . . .

*Bear with it, Barl. You must bear with it.*

Arndel nodded, not entirely convinced by her show of meek acceptance. One of the other mages raised a hand, desiring his

3

assistance. With a final, critical glance he answered the call for help, leaving her to fume at the various components neatly arrayed on the bench, and the clear crystal shell of the prosaic clock she was being forced to complete. What it could be, what it should be, sang in her blood.

*Traint is an idiot. And so is Arndel.*

With the Artisan Master occupied elsewhere, Ibbitha shifted along her bench seat until she was close enough for whispering.

'Truly, Barl. You never learn, do you?'

Not counting Remmie, Ibbitha was the nearest thing she had to a friend. Talented enough, in a mundane sort of way, her fellow clock mage lacked energetic imagination or ambition and was a stickler for convention, uninterested in challenging a single rule or restriction handed down by Dorana's Council of Mages or the Guild of Artisans or Artisan Master Arndel. *Staid.* That was Ibbitha. A friend of convenience, not of the heart.

She'd never had much luck when it came to making friends.

Mindful of their irascible employer, Barl risked a sidelong glance. 'Nonsense,' she whispered back. 'I'm learning every day.'

'Yes, but what?' said Ibbitha. 'You—'

Daggered looks from the diligent mages around them killed what remained of Ibbitha's scolding lecture. Not mourning its death, Barl returned to her clock-making, hardly needing to think about each incant and counter-ward as, with scant effort, she continued to build Lord Traint's lamentable timepiece.

*I am bored. I am so bored. I deserve much more than this.*

Later, when the artisanry emptied for the midday meal break and they were sitting alone on a stone bench in the sunshine, Ibbitha resurrected her scold.

'You must be more careful, Barl,' she said, dabbing a napkin daintily to her lips. 'And you mustn't be greedy. It was nearly two years before I was permitted to create commissioned clocks. And you? Why, you were accorded that privilege after a mere seven months! Why can't you be satisfied with that?'

Roaming her gaze around the other mages in the garden, lunch box on the bench beside her, Barl polished a plum on her green linen skirt. 'Why is a babe not satisfied with crawling? Why does it struggle to first stand on its own feet, then walk, and then run?'

Ibbitha wrinkled her snub nose. 'You *are* a babe if you think rubbing Arndel across his grain will get you what you want. Besides, there is nothing wrong with Lord Traint's clock design.'

Barl looked at her in wonder. 'You truly believe that, don't you?'

'Yes,' said Ibbitha, prickling. 'Why would I say it if I didn't believe it?'

'You wouldn't,' she said, and took a bite of plum. Rich purple juice tickled down her chin. Another bite splashed more juice to her skirt. She vanished it with a thought and a flutter of her fingers, then nibbled the rest of the plum's sweet flesh off its stone.

'I'll never understand you, Barl,' said Ibbitha, staring. 'Why can't you accept things the way they are? Given your family background . . .' She trailed away, uncomfortable. As a rule, such things weren't discussed. Everybody knew what rank everybody else's family was and how they fitted into the wider tapestry of Doranen society, and that was enough. Gossip on the subject was keenly discouraged. 'Well. You know.'

Barl swallowed a bitter laugh. Oh, yes, she knew. Didn't she beat her fists every day against the constraints of family and her proper place and what was and was not acceptable when one hadn't been born with the right pedigree?

'Anyway,' Ibbitha added. 'What is so terrible about Lord Traint's clock design?'

'Ibbitha . . .' She sighed. 'If I have to explain it then you'll never understand.'

Cheeks pink, grey eyes bright, Ibbitha folded her napkin with quick, overprecise little movements. 'I see.'

Bother. Her impatience had landed her in trouble yet again. Remmie was forever taking her to task over it. *A little kindness never goes astray, Barl. Nobody likes to be thought a fool, even if they are one.* Not that Ibbitha was a fool, exactly. She was simply prosaic.

Around the garden, their fellow artisans were collecting themselves in dribs and drabs, the brief midday break coming to an end, a long afternoon of clockworking and leadlighting and ceramics and weaving and glassmaking ahead of them.

'Ibbitha, I'm sorry,' she said, and touched placating fingers to her sort-of friend's arm. 'I didn't mean it like that. What I meant to say was—'

Ibbitha patted the napkin into her emptied lunch box. 'Please don't, Barl. You said precisely what you meant, so don't insult me further by trying to pretend otherwise.'

'Fine. I won't,' she said, lobbing her plum stone into the garden's fringing of flowers. 'Instead I'll say that Lord Traint's clock will keep perfect time with all the grace of a farm hog trying to run on ice. The man is a boor, Ibbitha, lacking any hint of imagination. He understands function, I grant you, but has no comprehension of beauty or elegance.' A chance here to mend fences a little, so she took it. 'Not like you, for instance.'

Ibbitha was too shocked to notice the compliment. '*Barl*, how can you *say* such things? Lord Traint has a second cousin whose wife was considered for the Council of Mages. His third cousin designed *two* fountains in Elvado. And his grandfather submitted a new incant for ratification and patent. True, it was rejected, but even so, he submitted. And you call him a *boor*?'

Simmering with frustration, Barl warded shut her own lunch box then translocated it home with an impatient finger-snap.

'What does any of that have to do with his talent? None of those achievements belong to him, Ibbitha.'

'He's a district inspector!'

'Only because he's a Traint. If he wasn't I'll wager he'd not lay one finger on an inspector's seal. Artur Traint is living proof that family connections count for more than talent. And why should that be? Why should you, or I, or any mage in Dorana be denied opportunities, denied *anything,* simply because we weren't lucky enough to be born into a First Family?'

'I declare, Barl, sometimes you talk the most arrant nonsense,' Ibbitha retorted. 'How can you claim that you or I have been denied opportunity when every day we are free to create mageworks that are the envy of Dorana's magickless neighbours? The least of our clocks are admired in Trindek and Feen and Manemli, oh, *everywhere.* This artisanry is becoming famous. And if you think Master Arndel would risk its reputation on a mage whose background is little more than adequate, who has flitted from calling to calling, as feckless as a bee, and who is *never* satisfied no matter how much favour is shown her, well – Barl, if I have to explain your situation then I don't suppose you'll ever understand.'

It was the worst scold Ibbitha had ever given her, and mostly it stung because it was true.

*Which it shouldn't be. Every word she utters only goes to prove I'm right about how unjust things are.*

But when it came to mage rankings, it seemed there was no justice. There were rules and protocols and dictates and *acceptable*. And because the rules had held sway for so long, because certain important people made sure they continued to hold sway, nothing changed.

*Why won't Ibbitha see it? Why doesn't she rile up when she's told by the Council of Mages what she is and isn't permitted to do and to be? And for no better reason than a family name? Why should that handful of men and women decide our fates?*

'I understand well enough, Ibbitha. The wrong blood is flowing through my veins. What *you* don't seem to understand is that I don't care, and I don't see why anyone else should care either. Nor do I see why my family tree, however stunted some may call it, should be the yardstick by which I am judged as a mage.'

'Oh, Barl.' Tartly sympathetic, Ibbitha shook her head. 'Life will seem far less harsh once you stop kicking against it. If only you'd accept things as they are, if you'd stop rubbing Artisan Master Arndel against his grain, he might let you create a little mantel clock of your own to sell through the artisanry shop. He

7

doesn't deny your talent. Nobody could. It's your temperament that's questioned, and not without cause. What a pity it would be if your own stubborn pride should make you stumble when the path before you was always clear.'

The path before her had been laid with bricks not of her choosing and meandered pointlessly toward a future littered with opportunities denied. But if she flew at Ibbitha for reminding her of that unpalatable truth then likely she'd lose the woman's shallow friendship, and she didn't want that. So she sighed and nodded, making sure Ibbitha would think her scolding was welcome.

'You're right. Patience and I aren't well enough acquainted. And of course the journey clock's design isn't anywhere near as bad as I complain.'

'I should say it's not!' said Ibbitha, taking a suggestive step toward the garden gate. Tardiness was deeply frowned upon by Master Arndel. 'Lord Traint's taste is the very definition of elegantly refined simplicity.'

No, it was the manifestation of a stunted mind, but there was no use in saying so to Ibbitha, who was forever dazzled by a mage's social standing. As for Arndel, he was just as bad. Artur Traint was a lord, he was a district inspector, and his purse was full of coin. The man's dull sensibilities counted for nothing compared to those useful attributes.

Defeated, Barl walked with Ibbitha back to their workroom. There she spent the afternoon finishing what she'd begun, and before the day was over Lord Traint had his lacklustre journey clock.

Called to inspect it, Artisan Master Arndel walked round her bench, lips pursed as he considered the completed piece. Standing well to one side, giving him free rein to examine her work for nonexistent defects, Barl felt the hard stares of her fellow mages. Not a one of them could complete even a simple clock like this so swiftly or so well, even though they'd been artisans here for three years or more and came from families twice as illustrious as her own.

*You see? Talent does count for something. It can't always be about the family name stitched to our heels.*

'Hmm,' Artisan Master Arndel grunted at last, halting. 'I can detect no flaw in the piece, Mage Lindin. Your incants and counter-wards mesh smoothly, and your crystal work is pleasing.'

Her crystal work was magnificent, but Arndel would never admit it. Not only was it better than the work of every other artisan whose talents he employed, it was better than his own – and he wasn't a man to take pride in the achievement of a mage who stood below him. Take credit for it, yes. He was more than willing to do that and would, when Lord Traint came to collect his clock. Not claim the piece was of his making, of course. But he would suggest and imply and hint and wink that without his constant oversight the finished clock would have been sadly inferior.

And because this was his artisanry she had no choice but to let him. So she feigned gratification.

'Thank you, Artisan Master.'

Arndel's flickering glance was suspicious, seeking insincerity or sarcasm. Detecting none, for he was nowhere near as clever as he imagined himself to be, he nodded.

'Therefore let this be a salutary lesson, Mage Lindin. When one remains constrained by the limits of design, one is free to perform such work as may be pleasing. Shall we hear the tick of Lord Traint's new clock?'

As clock mage, it was her final task to release the clock's temporary warding so that its voice might be tested for precision and a certain sweetness in the air. In this, and only this, was an artisan permitted to indulge his or her individual whim. A clock's tick belonged to no-one but its maker.

Barl stepped to the bench. Looking down at this thing that she had, with despair and contempt, created for a man whose ordinary mind could envisage nothing more daring than a square crystal box touched here and there with gold, she heard the caged mage within herself wail.

*It could've been so beautiful. Given the chance I'd have created a clock to make the sky weep for days.*

With a whisper, she set the ugly thing's voice free.

'Very nice,' Artisan Master Arndel said, grudging, as the sweet tick-tock-tick echoed through the workroom in harmony and counter-harmony, doubled and trebled notes shivering the air.

Barl looked down, outwardly modest, inwardly seething. *Nice? Nice? You cantankerous old mole.* 'Thank you, Artisan Master.'

With a snap of her fingers Lord Traint's clock sounded the hour, and even the most unfriendly artisan in the workroom smiled to hear the lilting carillon of notes. Watching Arndel from beneath her lowered lashes, Barl saw a spasm of jealousy clench his face for a heartbeat, then let go.

'Yes, that will do,' he said, as though she'd presented him with a correctly salted boiled egg. 'Step back, Mage Lindin.'

So she stepped back and waited for him to master ward the new clock between ticks. That was his right, as Master of the artisanry. The balance of the clock's purchase price bought the sigil that would unward it. Assuming Lord Traint accepted his finished commission, and he would, she had no doubt of that, she'd receive a token payment on top of her weekly artisan's wage.

But for all her work it was Arndel who'd emerge the richer, in both purse and reputation.

*Which is theft, pure and simple.*

The injustice of it burned.

As soon as he'd departed, taking Lord Traint's warded clock and the inked design with him, Barl began the methodical task of clearing her workbench.

First, the emptying of the sand trays. Since Dorana had no fine sand fields of its own, sand for crystal alchemy was imported at great expense from Feen and Brantone and Iringa. With the unused sand returned to its stone jars in the storeroom, next she had to collect the unused gold in its nuggets, shavings and dust, for there again was Dorana a pauper. One gold mine only within its jealously guarded borders, and that did not yield the finest red gold found beyond them. Silver and copper of its own Dorana possessed, and in plenty, but every remaining skerrick of those elements she also had to collect for later use. Artisan Master Arndel treated all his supplies as though they were sand and gold. Next she took the gemstones not used for the clock's inner workings, rubies and emeralds and topaz, and saw them stowed safe in the artisanry gem drawers. Last of all she purged the workbench with a cleansing incant. That made sure no lingering memory of Lord Traint's journey clock could catch in the next working she undertook and spoil its unique design.

By that time the work day had drawn to a close and the artisanry's other clock mages were leaving. With her own piece still only three-quarters completed, Ibbitha warded her bench.

'Barl, are you coming?'

She opened her mouth to say yes, then abruptly changed her mind. *I shouldn't. It's madness. If I'm found out I'll be dismissed.* But even as her heart leapt at the terrible thought, she knew she was about to be reckless.

'I can't,' she said, pretending irritation. 'The cleansing incant hasn't taken properly. Finishing Lord Traint's clock tired me more than I realised.'

'It's beautiful work, Barl,' said Ibbitha. For all her prosy scoldings, she could be generous. 'You should be proud.'

In moments like this she felt sick with the need to pretend that her caging didn't chafe. 'I am. You were right, I'm lucky to be shown such trust by Artisan Master Arndel.'

A small, pleased smile softened Ibbitha's habitually disapproving face. 'I'm glad you see it. Can I help you with a stronger cleansing incant?'

'No, I'll manage. I'd not keep you from Arno's eager embrace.'

A faint blush. Newly wed Ibbitha was so terribly *proper.* 'Well, if you're sure, I'll see you on the morrow, Barl.'

Barl watched the workroom door shut behind her, then pretended to fuss over her bench as the last three artisan mages departed, bidding her a disinterested farewell. As soon as she was alone she leapt back from her bench. *Excellent*. Now she could play.

Although, to be clever, she should wait a little while to make certain Arndel didn't return. To pass the time, she gave Ibbitha's work in progress a cursory inspection. A betrothal clock for Lady Isolte's eldest daughter. Ho hum. Oh, the actual design was pretty enough, but as a clock mage Ibbitha was hardly *inspired*. There were so many ways she could stamp herself onto this clock, lift it from *pretty enough* into the realm of *magnificent,* and she'd not taken advantage of even one. Ibbitha's problem was that she had no vision. She never looked past the confines of an inked design to the hinted possibilities that lay between and beyond the lines.

*I don't think it would even occur to her to try. I could make Lady Isolte's girl a glorious betrothal clock. Given the chance, I could make it sing.*

Instead she was lumbered with journey clocks, shackled to the parched imagination of patrons like Artur Traint. What she was doing now was barely a step up from where she'd started in the artisanry, making the cheaper, less fastidious trade clocks that were sold throughout Dorana and into its neighbouring lands.

*Arndel is a nubbin. Why won't he admit my true worth? He has to know it would only enhance his reputation.*

There was still no sign of the Artisan Master. Surely she'd be safe now. Heart skittishly thudding, she withdrew to the storeroom. Just this once she would craft a clock worthy of her gifts.

A trickle of nervous sweat tickled her spine. Hurrying, she tipped the raw ingredients for her dream clock onto the floor. Three types of rare sand, pink and silver and blue, gemstones for weight and counterweight, gold and silver and copper for pendulum and cradles. She didn't need Lord Traint's inked parchment to guide her, the journey clock's design was etched in her memory. Squat and uninspired, functional, *plain*. And all the incants needed was a little tweak here, a twist there, a subtle realignment in this note and that one. So simple. So elegant. How could Traint not *see*?

Sigil by sigil, breath by breath, the journey clock she'd longed to create grew beneath her sure, steady fingers. Not a slow process this time, since she'd created it once already. But now the clock's sheer crystal housing glowed, alive with a pearlescent sheen. It rose swiftly before her, slender and strong, not squat, not merely functional, but a tender, eloquent expression of hope. Journey clocks were made for travelling, and here was a clock to travel full of dreams and possibilities. Created to echo the dreams of the traveller who carried it.

When the clock was finished she knelt gasping, close to tears. If only she could show this piece to Lord Traint, instead of the spiritless lump of crystal Arndel had taken away with him. That clock was correct in all its particulars, scrupulously accurate, possessing no soul. But *this* clock?

*This is the clock that deserves my beautiful chiming. This is the clock that should sing with my voice.*

And no mage could ever see it.

She sketched a warding sigil, then uttered a harsh unmaking incant to collapse the reimagined clock into sand and gold and gemstones. Did weep, just a little, seeing it destroyed. And then she returned each individual component to its proper place so that Artisan Master Arndel would be none the wiser for her meddling.

She nearly ran into him as she came out of the storeroom.

'Mage Lindin!' he said, surprised and not pleased. 'Why do you tarry here? Your fellow artisan mages are long departed.'

'I know, Artisan Master,' she murmured. 'I'm sorry. I had some little difficulty cleansing my bench.'

His eyes slitted, as though he were reluctant to believe her. 'You did? That seems . . . out of character.'

'I was weary,' she said, holding his suspicious stare without flinching. 'But the bench is cleansed now. Would you care to inspect it?'

His gaze shifted to her empty workbench then back again. 'No. Such matters are your responsibility, Mage Lindin. If your cleansing incant was inadequate, your next commission will tell the tale.'

'Has the commission been decided upon, Artisan Master?'

Now he looked her up and down, his resentment of her gifts, that added coin to his treasury, clear in his face.

'You are impertinent. It is for me to broach such matters, not you. Be gone.'

'Artisan Master,' she said, bowing her head, and escaped the workroom before he did something disastrous like banish her back to the making of ordinary clocks.

The late summer light was fading, but that didn't matter. There was glimfire to guide her way, should she need to conjure it. Or she could do what every other artisan mage did and translocate herself home. Only she didn't care for travelling magics. She rarely admitted it but they made her feel weak and unsteady. Besides, they denied her the pleasure of the sweetly scented fresh air. Arndel's artisanry sat on the greenly grassy outskirts of Batava hamlet, where she and Remmie lived, at least for the moment. Her solitary walks to and from work each day helped clear her mind of leftover clock maging and gave her precious time to herself for dreams.

*Not that there's much use in dreaming. Dreams won't change what's wrong in Dorana. Only the Council of Mages can change the rules and it won't. Not until it's made to, anyway.*

And there was wickedly little hope of that. The General Council was too busy with day-to-day concerns, collecting taxes and enforcing the mundane rules and dealing with Dorana's neighbours and the complicated trading arrangements they made with the outside world. Its members seemed perfectly happy to leave the intricate laws of magework to their sister council. Sometimes she thought she was the only mage breathing who cared for what was right and just. Everyone else she knew was like Ibbitha, content to settle for the crumbs dropped careless at her feet by Dorana's supremely selfish First Families.

Even Remmie.

*I love him to pieces, I do, but sometimes I can't believe we're related.*

The laneways she walked were bordered each side by flower-straggled hedgerows. Fireflies danced above them, glimmering brightly in the lowering dusk. Tonight, though, not even their whimsical beauty soothed her. Rankled still by the loss of that other clock, the clock Arndel should have let her create, that he'd as good as *stolen* from her, she stamped the damp grass underfoot and with each step imagined Lord Traint's inferior clock smashed to shards beneath her heels.

*I'm glad no-one will ever know I made it. Let every mage who sees it think Traint's journey clock is Arndel's monstrosity. He deserves to be tarred with that brush. My day will come. In time the whole world will know my name. It will see what I've created and be dumbstruck with awe.*

It was almost properly dark by the time she reached home. Stars pricked overhead, and glimfire lamps burned in the unshuttered windows of the hamlet schoolmaster's cottage.

'There you are!' said Remmie, turning from the sink as she entered the kitchen. 'I was about to do a searching for you.'

Though she was tired and disgruntled, she couldn't not smile at her brother as she sniffed the fragrant air. 'Yes, here I am, you fussy old mother hen.'

'Hen yourself,' he said, shoulders hunching. He didn't much care for that kind of teasing. 'Do you think I don't have enough to contend with, that I need fears for you rattling round in my head?'

The mood she was in, it would be far too easy to strike sparks with him. She took a deep breath and after a heart-thumping moment let go of her peppery temper, along with all her bitter thoughts. Remmie was the soft, kindly one, and always had been. The boy in him still felt the too-soon loss of their parents, was quick to dark imaginings and leaping to the worst conclusions. With her own scars from that wounding long since healed, she found it easy to forget.

'I tarried at the artisanry,' she said, her voice deliberately gentle. 'Not thinking. I'm sorry. Is that mutton-and-barley stew on the hob?'

'Not that you deserve any,' he said. 'Why did you tarry? There's no trouble at Arndel's, I hope.'

His question stung, but it wasn't entirely unfair. They were each other's only family and he had picked up and moved with her every time her restless impatience caused her to fall foul of an employer, or abandon one position in search of the next. And if she fell foul of Artisan Master Arndel, or lost patience entirely with working in his artisanry, her brother would follow her again.

Which was why she strove so hard to stay sweet with Arndel, to not care so much that she wasn't properly appreciated. Remmie wanted to stay in Batava. Teaching in its little school pleased him, deeply. He never would listen when she wailed that he wasted himself on other people's offspring.

'Not the kind of trouble you're imagining,' she said, sliding into one of the two chairs at the small kitchen's table. 'My work for Arndel is well-prized. He knows he'll suffer if he dismisses me.'

'Good,' Remmie said, turning to face her, and not even trying to hide his relief. 'But still, since I'm neither blind nor doltish, I know something's fretting you. What's wrong?'

# CHAPTER TWO

He always knew. Even when she did her best to hide her feelings, even when any other person in the world would never suspect she was churned on the inside, where it didn't show, Remmie could tell.

Sometimes it was irritating, having a twin.

Remmie was staring at her, his blue eyes alight now with a rueful, affectionate resignation. She looked away from him.

He sighed. 'Barl . . .'

By rights she should be setting the table for supper. He liked to cook and she didn't, so he cooked and she set the table and helped clean up after. But instead of doing her part she sat where she was, thoughts tumbling like leaves in an autumn bluster.

Abandoning the sink, leaving his stew to simmer fragrantly on the hob, her brother crossed to the table and slid into its other chair.

'Come on, Barl. You know I'll have the problem out of you in the end.'

She shrugged, one-shouldered. 'It's nothing.'

'It's not. It never is,' he said kindly. He was so patient, little wonder he made a good schoolteacher. 'Is it Arndel again? Has he done or said something to tweak your nose?'

'I'd like to tweak his nose,' she muttered. 'His *and* Lord Traint's.'

Remmie laughed, but there was a groan inside it. 'Why? What have they done now?'

Since she'd get no peace until she answered, she told him how she'd been tasked to create Traint's tedious journey clock. Her brother listened carefully, like always, no interruptions, and when she'd finished her tale of woe he sat back in his chair, his arms folded and his chin sunk to his chest.

'Well, you know what they say, Barl. He who pays the piper calls the tune.'

'Perhaps they do, but I don't need you to say it. I need *you* to say I'm right and that old snicket Arndel is wrong!'

'Oh, *Barl*.' Remmie's fingers tightened. 'What difference would that make? For better or worse, Arndel pays your wage which means you're beholden to his wishes. I know you don't want to be, but that's the way it is.'

What a pity she hadn't laid the table. If she had, she could throw a spoon at him. 'You're supposed to be on my side.'

'And so I am! You know I am. Always. I don't mean to nag or sound unsympathetic. I just hate to see you fretted.'

'You'd be fretted too, if you'd been forced to make such a clodhopping clock.' She blinked hard against a sudden sting of tears. 'I wish you could've seen the one I made after. Remmie, it was *beautiful*.'

'Yes, I'm sure it was,' he said, his face shadowing. 'Only . . .'

'Only it was a foolish risk,' she said, impatiently contrite. 'Yes. I know. I won't do it again.' She pulled a face. 'At least I'll try not to. But Remmie—'

His lips tugged into a wry smile. 'It was make the clock your way, just once, or burst.'

She'd feel less guilty if he didn't understand. If he blustered and railed at her she wouldn't feel so selfish. If once, just *once*, he'd properly lose his temper with her, scold her for being high-handed and thoughtless, then she'd not have to feel so mean. But he never did. It just wasn't Remmie.

18

As she frowned at him, vexed by his unnatural niceness, he shoved his chair back. 'Any measure, what's done is done and no harm done. This time. Now do set the table, would you? Supper's ready.'

So she set the table and he filled two stoneware bowls with the rich mutton and barley he'd cooked. Fresh, cool cider and thickly buttered bread rounded out the meal. Halfway through his tale of the day's classroom antics he interrupted himself, his expression comical.

'Oh, I nearly forgot! Word came from Elvado this morning. The Council of Mages has ratified four new incants, and there's to be a public demonstration of them to mark the occasion. I'm asked to take my pupils to see it. Will you come?'

Belly griping, Barl bit her lip. Doubtless it was petty, the urge to refuse her brother because she resented those unknown mages whom the Council had decided to honour. But she felt what she felt. There was no point denying it.

'I can't go if it's a working day,' she said, poking her spoon through her stew, pretending interest in food so Remmie might not see what raged beneath her indifferent surface. 'Arndel would never give me leave.'

'There's no need to ask, for it's not,' Remmie said, cheerful. Either she'd fooled him, for once, or he was choosing to ignore her rewoken ill temper. 'The demonstration's to be held next Winsun. In the plaza outside Elvado's Hall of Knowledge, no less.'

The Hall, yes. Of course. That fabled place of breathtaking beauty, where Dorana's vastly powerful Council of Mages laid down the rules of magework by which everyone else had to live.

*Still, it could be worse. They could hold the ceremony at the College. I don't think I could bear that.*

'There'll be a terrible crowd,' she said, hunting for a cloud to dim Remmie's smile. 'We'll not see a thing.'

'Ah, but we will,' he said, unclouded. 'On account of being with the children. The Council made sure to mention there'd be a special place reserved for all attending students and their teachers.'

19

Well, didn't he just have an answer for everything?

'Elvado's too far from here to ride in carriages. We'll have to translocate.'

'You can chew on some runip berries before we leave. They'll settle your stomach well enough.' Remmie pushed his emptied bowl away, the faintest hint of irritation shading his voice. 'Or you could not come.'

That would be the easiest answer, certainly. Let Remmie herd his little flock, leaving her to dream alone of beautiful, mageworked things, and how one day she'd escape the confines of Arndel's artisanry. Besides, it would only be a torment to her, visiting Elvado. There were excellent reasons why she'd stayed away.

'Please, Barl,' her brother said, wheedling. 'We can throw a coin in the plaza's great fountain for Mama and Pa. Didn't we promise we'd do that one day? But we never have. And it's bad luck not to keep that kind of promise.'

Oh, well, now *that* was playing dirty. 'One day, yes,' she muttered. 'But does it have to be next Winsun?'

'Surely next Winsun's as good a day as any.'

Of course it was. Staring at the blue-and-yellow checked tablecloth, she swallowed a resentful sigh. She'd have to say yes. If she didn't, she'd give Remmie pause for thought. She'd have him fretting and nagging and niggling . . .

'Fine,' she said crossly, lifting her gaze. 'I'll come, but only so we can toss the remembrance coin. Oh, and so I can laugh myself sick watching you chase after your gaggle of school brats like a three-legged sheepdog.' She raised a warning finger. 'But don't you even *think* of asking me for help herding them. Other people's snotty-nosed children are your delight, not mine.'

Remmie was grinning. 'Don't fret. Barton's coming too, with his class. He'll help me keep order.'

'Barton Haye?' Her heart sank. 'Oh.'

His grin turning sly, Remmie reached for the last piece of buttered bread. 'Of course Barton's coming. I think he's more

20

excited than the children. He'll be tickled even pinker when I tell him you're joining us.'

She wrinkled her nose. 'Yes, well, while you're at it you can tell him I'm walking out with one of the mages from the artisanry.'

'Tell him yourself,' he retorted, around a crammed mouthful. 'Barton's a good fellow. I'll not fib to him on your account.'

'It would be a kindness if you did, Remmie. Coming from me it'll only prick his pride worse. Besides, I don't want to lie to his face.'

'But you've no trouble asking *me* to?' Finished eating, he began collecting his plate and bowl and cutlery. 'You steal my breath, Barl. You truly do.'

She handed him her own bowl and spoon, balanced on her crumb-strewn plate. 'I don't see why. Since you've such a fondness for him I'm surprised you didn't offer.'

Remmie clattered their used dishes into the sink. 'Look. I know Barton isn't your dash of salt but—'

'Is he anyone's?' She laughed. 'I can't see it. He's short and skinny and his ears stick out. And when he laughs he—'

'Don't!' Remmie said, turning. 'Why must you be unkind? What do a man's looks count for? Barton Haye has a good heart, he's gentle and patient and a gifted teacher. If he's not as handsome as you'd have him, how is that a crime? You'd best believe you could do far worse!'

Taken aback, Barl blinked at him. 'I had no idea you'd appointed yourself Barton Haye's champion. Perhaps you ought to walk out with him yourself, if he's such a catch.'

And that, of course, was *exactly* the wrong thing to say . . . for last year, abandoning the Eighth district's village of Granley out of loyalty to her, Remmie had left behind a young woman who might have become more than merely the sister of someone he taught school with.

Her contrition heartfelt this time, she reached out a hand. 'I'm sorry. Truly. That was a heedless jibe to make.'

'I'm not trying to push Barton onto you,' Remmie said, calm

21

as buttermilk now, as though she'd not hurt him or apologised. 'Only you never seem taken with anyone. Perhaps if you did . . .' He shrugged. 'But you don't. I worry you'll end up old and alone.'

Probably that was true. But she thought he also worried *he'd* end up old and alone, from staying loyal to her. It wasn't something they talked of. She wouldn't know where or how to start. But after Granley she'd not been able to pretend so easily that what she did made little difference to her loyal, long-suffering brother.

'I won't be unkind to Barton,' she said, subdued. 'I won't walk out with him, but I'll not make you ashamed of me.'

Remmie's lips curved a little, but the smile didn't reach his eyes. 'Be sure I'll hold you to that. It's a small school, Barl, and we teach cheek by jowl together in it. I don't want my peace with Barton cut up.'

'It won't be. I promise. Please, Remmie, don't be cross.'

'I'm not,' he sighed. He was far too nice a man for grudges. 'Though doubtless I should be.'

Relieved, she bounced to her feet. 'It's because you're not that I love you. Now finish telling me of your day while I do the dishes.'

When the kitchen was clean again they went their separate ways, Remmie to sprawl in the cottage's pocket-sized parlour and read a book, while she retreated to her room to continue her private magework.

During her walks to and from the artisanry, she'd had an idea for a new kind of translucent clock-housing crystal, thinner and lighter and stronger than the crystals Arndel had them use. Those crystals were created with incants of his own devising, and jealously guarded, but her crystal was better than all of his. Or it would be, once she'd perfected the incant for its creation. It called for a tricky marriage of fine Manemlin silver sand with the argumentative grittiness of Brantish coarse black. Nearly five months it had taken her, to scrimp and save enough coin for a small-weight of silver sand. So far the incant's creation had defeated her, but she was undaunted.

And once she'd perfected the mageworking, once she had a

flawless sheet of crystal as proof, she'd show it to Arndel . . . making sure, of course, to stress how his own incants had inspired her. Then perhaps he'd agree to her crystal's use in the artisanry. He might even sponsor a patent submission to the Artisans' Guild and then the new crystal could be named after her.

*Lindin crystal.*

She didn't care how hard she had to work or what small luxuries she had to give up to make sure she had enough of the costly silver sand. She didn't care how long it took to perfect the incant. What was time? Just another tool.

Settled at her small workbench, she dropped a pinchful of silver sand into a waiting crucible. The promise of success burned bright in her blood.

*This incant is only the beginning. Before I am done I'll be the best artisan mage Dorana has ever seen.*

A day and a half after she'd completed Lord Traint's journey clock, Artisan Master Arndel gave her a new commission, a nursery clock for one Lady Ancilla Grie. Clearly he resented passing her the task, but with no other artisan free or skilled enough and his own time swallowed by an established patron he couldn't afford to offend, he had no choice.

'And let me remind you there can be *no* deviation from the requested design,' the Artisan Master said, scowling. 'Lady Grie is a mage of great reputation and influence. Next to Lord Bren, the greatest in these eastern districts. *Nothing* is more important than pleasing her.'

Or more disastrous than earning her ire. So had their rival artisanry in the Seventh district township of Valdere learned, to its dismay, when its Artisan Master made the mistake of countermanding Lady Grie's specifications.

'Tympanne has all but ruined herself,' said Arndel, thrusting his face close. 'Where Ancilla Grie leads, many lords and ladies follow. Her patronage, added to Lord Bren's, could be the making of this artisanry. Put that in jeopardy, Mage Lindin, and you will rue the day you first drew breath.'

Unmoved by his lip-spittled fervour, Barl nodded. 'I will give Lady Grie no cause for complaint.'

'See that you don't,' Arndel hissed, finger jabbing. 'For you'll not be the only Lindin to suffer from a misstep.'

*Remmie*. The old mole would dare to threaten blameless Remmie? She felt her blood turn molten. *You scabrous toad.* Biting back fury, she bowed her head, showing Arndel only what he wanted to see, an obedient underling.

'Yes, Artisan Master,' she murmured. 'I understand.'

Nearly six days it took her to complete the nursery clock . . . and to her surprise, the work was a pleasure. The artisanry's new patron was no Artur Traint. Lady Grie's design was charming, full of whimsical grace, and challenging enough to keep her mind off dark thoughts of the upcoming trip to Elvado.

*For if I go, it will hurt me. And if I don't go, I'll hurt Remmie. No matter what I do, it seems someone always ends up hurt.*

Those six days were the happiest she'd spent in Arndel's employ, even though she had to attempt the clock's crystal housing twice. The first time she misjudged the crucial balance between the superfine Brantish blue sand and the heavier grey sand from Trindek's Istafarn desert. Moments after coalescence the crystal collapsed into blobs of grainy, useless glass. Shocked speechless, Barl could only stare and nod as Arndel berated her for wasting her time and his jealously guarded supplies.

'I'm sorry, Artisan Master,' she said, once his tirade ended.

'As you should be! Don't make me regret giving you this commission, Mage Lindin.'

Oh, how it galled her to be wrong in front of him. To have failed in a task she'd assumed would be simple. 'I won't, Artisan Master. You have my word.'

Arndel glared, unappeased. 'You have but four more days to complete this clock, Mage Lindin. Do not waste them.'

Spurred mercilessly by such a public failure, the muffled snickers of the other mages burning in her ears, her second attempt at the clock housing succeeded. Shimmering like Lake Nartana, jewel of the Second district, the crystal's flawless beauty stunned her to tears and helped to bolster her shaken confidence.

'Better,' said Arndel, grudging, called to inspect her progress. 'Now get back to work.'

Hunted by a sense of urgency, haunted by the fear of failure, Barl finished Lady Grie's nursery clock eight minutes before midnight on the fourth day following her disastrous mistake.

Alone in the artisanry, driven to sleeping there the past three nights so she might complete her task on time, she let the tears fall as she stared at the beautiful nursery clock.

*I'm not imagining things. I was born for this. For greatness. Now not even Arndel will be able to deny it.*

Next morning, Winsun Eve, Lady Grie herself came to hear the clock's first sounding. Scant weeks from giving birth, her body bursting ripe, she swept into the artisanry's private viewing room in a cloud of rich rose scent. Arndel trailed behind her like a fart.

'And of course, Lady Grie, if the piece does not meet with your approval we will simply begin again,' he declared, with a pained enthusiasm. 'But I think you'll agree that—'

'Hush,' said Lady Grie, one finger imperiously raised. Her sunrise silk gown rustled, murmuring of wealth and authority. 'Incessant chatter bores me.'

Too exhausted to feel nervous, Barl clasped her hands tightly behind her back, kept her face tactfully blank and watched Ancilla Grie as the woman inspected her commission. Roamed her sharp gaze over the nursery clock's arching crystal rainbow, with every bright colour shining, rested it on the small boy quaintly fishing with a rod and line, and then on the pond fringed with nodding bulrushes. Last of all she stared at the leaping crystal fish . . . and smiled.

'Yes,' she said softly. 'I knew I wasn't mistaken. That fool Tympanne said my design could not be executed, but I knew it could be . . . by the right mage.'

Torn between triumph and the importance of never criticising a Guild colleague, Arndel gobbled something in the back of his throat.

Lady Grie's amethyst-blue stare shifted. 'You. Young woman. Why do you stand there pretending servility? What have you to do with the making of my clock?'

Barl looked to Arndel. She knew better than to answer without his permission. The Artisan Master was resentful enough of her already. Offer him the smallest excuse to whet his temper on her, and he'd snatch it.

'This is Mage Lindin,' Arndel croaked. 'She – she—' His larynx convulsed. 'Under my strict and constant supervision, she made your clock.'

'*She* made it?' Lady Grie's finely arched eyebrows echoed her surprise. 'Not you, Master Arndel?'

Clasped fingers tightening to breaking point, Barl took a small step forward. 'It's true I performed the incants and conjurations, Lady Grie. But Artisan Master Arndel made certain of every syllable. Not a single piece in this artisanry is created without his involvement, or released to a patron without his permission. If the clock pleases you, my lady, you have him to thank.'

Arndel cleared his throat. From the look on his face it would be easy to think he'd swallowed a hedgehog.

'Mage Lindin's work is of the highest standard, Lady Grie. There isn't another mage in my artisanry I'd have trusted with your design.'

'I'm sure,' said Lady Grie, pettish. 'But why did you trust her with it at all? For the exorbitant fee I'm paying I expected *you* to make my nursery clock.'

'Lady Grie, it would've been my great pleasure to do so,' said Arndel, chin lifted. He was astonishingly close to looking down his nose. 'But I had already undertaken a commission from Lord Bren. You were unwilling to wait and I was unwilling to inconvenience a patron who has shown this artisanry much grace these past two years.'

Barl held her breath. That was more spice than she'd ever

thought was in the old trout. She might not like him but she could respect him for that much, at least.

'Indeed?' Unexpectedly, Lady Grie laughed. 'A proper answer, Artisan Master. I will expect no less a defence of me in the future.'

Arndel's thin lips stretched wide in a smile. 'The future? Most certainly, Lady Grie.'

'Not so fast, Artisan Master. There are conditions.' Lady Grie smoothed the vastly curved front of her glorious dress. 'Firstly, I must be satisfied with the clock's sounding. And secondly—'

'Yes, Lady Grie?' Arndel prompted, after a moment.

Ignoring him, Lady Grie shifted round. 'You. Mage Lindin. What does your family call you?'

Barl loosened her clasping fingers, making sure to keep her gaze far from Arndel. 'Barl, Lady Grie.'

'Hmm.' Lady Grie sniffed. 'Odd name for a girl, isn't it?'

'Perhaps, but I find myself content.'

'And if I tell Artisan Master Arndel that should my first condition be met, my second condition is that you, and only you, are to execute my commissions? Would *that* content you, too?'

Barl felt her heart stutter within its cage of curved bone. Moistening her lips, she risked a glance at Arndel. His eyes bulged at her in a face now flushed dusky red.

'My feelings in the matter are of no import, my lady. But should Artisan Master Arndel agree to such an arrangement, I would of course be honoured.'

'Ha!' said Lady Grie, trenchantly amused. 'And I suppose butter wouldn't melt in your mouth, either.' She turned back. 'Well, Arndel?'

'This artisanry would be pleased and proud to serve you, Lady Grie,' Arndel replied. Only someone who knew him well, who worked with him day in and day out, would hear the lemon tang in his voice. 'And of course I will assign your commissions to any mage whose work you find pleasing.'

'And you'll agree never to argue with me when it comes to what I want?'

27

Arndel bowed. 'Of course, Lady Grie. She who pays, says.'

'What about you, Mage Lindin?' Lady Grie demanded. 'Do you agree, as well?'

'Certainly not,' she said, and met Lady Grie's challenging stare with a challenge of her own. 'If I believe you're mistaken in your desire or design, I'll tell you. I could hardly call myself an artisan mage and lie to you, could I? That would be disrespectful to both of us.'

'*Mage Lindin*!' Arndel's voice exploded the silence. 'You stand too high in your own esteem! Please, Lady Grie, I beg you, accept my most—'

But Lady Grie laughed again. 'Restrain yourself, Arndel. Begging is so unattractive. Mage Lindin, it seems you have fire in your belly. I like that.' Her gaze flickered to Arndel. 'It makes a nice change from being fawned over.'

Wary, Barl offered the woman a slight bow. 'It's not in my nature to fawn, Lady Grie. All I can promise you is my best work and my honesty.'

'And I'll take them both, gladly,' Lady Grie replied. 'Provided I'm thoroughly satisfied with my clock. Let me hear its tick and chime.'

A catch in her breathing. A hitch in the steady beating of her heart. She'd spent nearly eleven hours perfecting the nursery clock's voice. If Lady Grie should find it displeasing . . .

*But she won't. She can't. She doesn't seem a lackwit.*

Arndel was glaring, daring her to fail. If Lady Grie was displeased there was no doubt Mage Lindin would be held responsible and cast into the cold.

On a breath, in a whisper, she released the nursery clock's voice. A ticktock of silence . . . and then the steady, rhythmic sound of a horse's hooves on beaten earth filled the private viewing room. *Clop-clop-clop-clop,* ticking time with a jaunty air.

'Oh!' Lady Grie clapped her hands once, delighted. 'How diverting. And the chime?'

Smothering her own pleasure, Barl silenced the tick-tock. Then, her heart hitching again, she sketched the brief sigil that would set free the nursery clock's chime.

'Beautiful,' whispered Lady Grie, as the liquid music of a marsh warbler's cry softened to silence. 'Mage Lindin, that was beautiful.'

Yes. And so difficult to recreate with an incant that she'd thought until the last moment the task would defeat her.

'Thank you, Lady Grie,' she murmured. Relief and the crushing fatigue she'd been fending off combined to make her head swim and her eyes blur. 'I'm very happy you like it.'

Lady Grie nodded to Arndel. 'Mage Lindin is a credit to you, Artisan Master. I look forward to seeing what she creates for me next. Now, shall we discuss the particulars of our arrangement?'

Barl didn't need the Artisan Master's quirked eyebrow to tell her that here was her cue to depart the viewing room. Somehow, she managed a bow to Lady Grie without falling over. Another bow to Arndel, because he'd feel the slight if she didn't. Then she escaped to the artisanry garden, where the sun shone unhindered by cloud and a riot of flowers scented the warm air. Safely alone, she folded to the short, sweet grass, pressed her palms to her face and let the joy bubble free.

*No more tedious journey clocks. No more being tethered to someone else's inferior imagination. At last . . . at last . . . I have the chance to become the mage I was born to be.*

'Barl!' Remmie's face lit up like a solstice lantern. 'That's *wonderful*! Ancilla Grie is the oldest daughter of the highest ranked First Family in the district. There's *nobody* she doesn't know. Once she starts talking about you, showing off the clock you made her, your name will become a byword in some of the most important houses in all of eastern Dorana. Perhaps even all the way to Elvado!'

Sent home an hour early by Arndel, which was his notion of a substantial reward, Barl sprawled in the cottage parlour's saggy-bottomed armchair and grinned at her brother, who perched on the windowsill like a cheerful cockadiddy.

29

'You're just relieved this means I'll have no want to move on in another month or three.'

Remmie reddened, as she knew he would. 'It's true I'm not afflicted with wanderlust, like some people, but that doesn't mean I'm not truly pleased for you. Barl—'

'Sorry,' she said, hands lifting. 'I know you are. *I'm* pleased for me too, I suppose. And you're right. If this arrangement goes well, if Lady Grie doesn't interfere with my work, I'm sure the itch will die out of my heels. Once I'm happy, Remmie, once I know I'm where I'm meant to be, I'll have no need to move on.'

'You say that now,' he muttered. 'And I'm sure you mean it. But you're a restless spirit, Barl. You're so eager to see what's over the horizon that you can't see what's right under your nose.'

Startled, she stared at her brother. He sounded almost *bitter*. And that wasn't like him. He was all sunshine, where she was dappled shadow. Had she so badly misread him, then? Had she completely mistaken how deep his feelings had run for that girl in Granley?

*I must have. He's not said as much, never mentioned her since we left there, but . . .*

She wasn't used to misreading Remmie. Shaken, she slid from the armchair to the carpet and knelt earnestly at her brother's feet. If she didn't make this right, convince him she did appreciate his love and loyalty, the matter would rub and rub between them until the festered wound hurt them both.

'Would it help if I promised, Remmie? I will.' She crossed her palms over her heart. 'I promise I'll not drag you harum-scarum across the country again.'

Remmie drummed his fingers on the windowsill, restless. 'You shouldn't make a promise you know you can't – you won't – keep.'

'I will keep it!' she insisted, indignant. Hurt that he would doubt her word. 'How can you fling it in my face I wouldn't?'

He groaned. 'Because I know you, Barl. You mean well, you always do. But something will happen, you'll fall into one

30

of your snits, Lady Grie won't pay you enough respect, or she'll *interfere,* and you'll storm out of the artisanry in a raging temper swearing you'll never, never, *never* go back, and—'

Barl pushed off her heels and rested her hands on her agitated brother's knees. 'No, Remmie. *I won't.* Do you hear me? This is my word to you, my solemn unflinching word. Batava is your home, now. I'll not ask you to leave it.'

Arms folded, he stared over his shoulder at the majestically sinking sun. Its mellow rose-gold light set his pale hair afire. A muscle leapt along his jaw.

'I know you'll not stay with Arndel forever,' he said at last, his voice low. 'You're ambitious, and you'll outgrow him. I do understand that. But if you mean what you say . . . at least for now . . . if you promise that what Lady Grie is offering is enough to keep you content a while longer, then I'll believe you. And I won't pretend I'm not well pleased for it.'

'I never asked you to pretend,' she said, still stinging.

He shrugged. 'Yes, you did. But that's neither here nor there. If it's been hard for me, it's not been easy for you either. I do know that, Barl.'

For all their closeness, their easy camaraderie, she and Remmie rarely bared their tender hearts to each other. She liked to tell herself it was because twins had no need of cumbersome words but that wasn't entirely true, and she knew it. If they never spoke honestly of how her restless nature affected him, then she was spared discomfort.

And that was a prickling thing to know of oneself.

'I'm content enough at the artisanry,' she said firmly. 'I moan about Arndel, but in truth I know full well I'm lucky to be there. And now, with this chance to make beautiful things for Lady Grie, my fortune is even brighter. I've no need to look toward the horizon, Remmie.'

'I must get supper started,' he said, almost smiling, and slid off the windowsill. 'Come and peel potatoes, and tell me incant by incant how you made Lady Grie's nursery clock. Since you always find an excuse not to come and talk to my pupils, a second-hand accounting will have to do.'

'I'm not a teacher,' she protested, guilt-seared, and clambered to her feet. 'Or a storyteller. You wouldn't have me embarrass you in front of your flock, would you?'

That made Remmie laugh. 'For an arrogant woman, Barl, you have the oddest notions.'

'Arrogant? *Arrogant?*' Outraged, she stared after him. 'Would an arrogant women peel potatoes? I hardly think so!'

'You haven't peeled anything yet,' he said, heading for the kitchen. 'So come along and prove me wrong!'

Oh, he was impossible. But he was her brother, and she loved him, and she owed him for the loss of that insipid girl in Granley.

'I'm coming, I'm coming,' she said, and followed him out.

# CHAPTER THREE

*E*lvado.

Staring around her at the fabled city, Barl pressed a fist to her roiling midriff.

*I should've eaten more runip berries. Heaving scrambled eggs over the cobblestones would hardly be polite.*

'Mage Lindin! You look unwell, is aught amiss?'

Swallowing a groan along with her travel sickness, she turned to Remmie's inconvenient friend, Barton. 'Naught, Mage Haye. Thank you.'

His overhelpful expression collapsed in the face of her briskness. 'Oh.'

Remmie looked up from his goggling, giggling, pointing pupils. So *many* of them, bobbing about like corks in a stream. It was a wonder he could keep their names straight.

'My sister doesn't translocate well.'

'What a shame,' Barton Haye said again, annoyingly sympathetic. 'Then perhaps, Mage Lindin, you could try—'

*Hold your tongue, Remmie.* 'Runip berries, yes, I know,' she said, smiling tightly at Barton Haye. 'Thank you.'

Remmie's lips pinched. He didn't care for her manner in front of his pupils. But for one thing the wide-eyed school children were too distracted by Elvado's glorious Hall of Knowledge, towering over them, and for another, well, Barton had brought it upon himself.

*He's no business being solicitous with me.*

Barton turned aside. 'We should discern where the Council desires us to stand for the demonstration.'

'Agreed,' said Remmie. 'We're here in plenty of time, but doubtless there'll be crowds arriving within the hour. We want to find the best vantage point before giving the children a chance to explore.'

Hearing that, the chattering horde of pupils broke into a louder clamour. Barl stepped well back, leaving Remmie and Barton Haye to their self-inflicted task of calming them. When that was done, and Barton had launched into a lecture about Elvado's central plaza, she tugged her brother several prudent steps sideways.

'I think I'll take a wander elsewhere until the Council deigns to grace us with its presence.'

Remmie started to object, then changed his mind. 'If you like. Don't get lost. We'll look for you in a little under an hour's time.'

As always, he'd taken great pains with his appearance, wearing silk for the occasion instead of his customary linen and wool, with a gold and carnelian stud in his right ear. His long hair was intricately braided, a thin, bright blue ribbon threaded sinuously through it. He was so fine she had to smile.

'What?' said Remmie, suspicious. 'Barl, what mischief are you—'

'None!' she protested, and patted his brocade weskit with its bold emerald and purple stripes. 'What a mind you've got, always seeking the nefarious. I was only thinking I have a very dashing brother. A compliment I think I regret, now.'

'A pity I can't return the sentiment,' he said, grinning. He was forever twitting her about wrinkled tunics and flyaway hair. 'Still, I suppose I should be grateful that at least your stockings match.'

*Wretch.* To say such a thing, with Barton Haye listening! She'd have to devise a suitable revenge for when they were alone.

34

'I'll see you presently, Mage Lindin,' she said, repressive. 'Mage Haye.'

Barton nodded, very formal. 'Mage Lindin.'

So that was *him* discouraged, any road. Good.

Abandoning Remmie to his child-ridden fate, Barl turned her back on the plaza with its magnificent fountain, mosaicked with unicorns and mermaids and dolphins and eagles, and made her way along the nearest of the wide, crowded thoroughfares leading away from the city centre.

Elvado was so full of ambient magic that she felt like a lute plucked from every direction. Blood and bones thrumming, she threaded a path between the pedestrians jostling around her. So much noise, after sleepy Batava and the disciplined artisanry. So much colour and movement. And all the tall, beautiful buildings, pane after pane of stained glass struck by sunlight into fiery, living jewels. Gold and silver and the blue-grey ores of Brantone and Ranoush, worked with skilled hands and magic into shimmering spires.

*We are such a clever, colourful people. No wonder we're gazed upon with envious eyes.*

Not that there was cause for concern in that. As the only mage race in the world, they had nothing to fear. Not even Vharne's best swordsmen or Iringa's famed horse warriors or the singing assassins of Feen could cost the mages of Dorana a single night of sleep. Let them squabble amongst themselves. Dorana was safe and always would be.

One advantage of being a gifted clockmaker was that she needed no help to feel the steady passing of time. The sense of it lived inside her, sitting lightly behind her eyes. So with no fear of provoking Remmie by returning tardy to the plaza, she walked the wide streets of Elvado. A city not simply beautiful, but gracious, its sunlit air sweetened by an abundance of fresh flowers, its sunlit streets thoughtfully shaded with wide-branched, lacy-leafed foiuta trees. In the scattered pocket-sized parks she wandered by, djelbas heavy with blossom towered above the neat grass, haughty as the potentates of Trindek.

As she walked she passed herbal shops and alchemists, medicinals and a library. In Artisan Row she lingered before each immaculate window, marvelling at the beauty of the tapestries, the weavings, the wood turnings and the musical instruments stringed and fretted and ivory-keyed. A good thing the only businesses permitted to trade on Winsun sold food, else she'd be leaving Elvado with an empty purse and so many purchases she'd need to hire a carriage to get home.

She lingered longest before a clockmaker's workshop. Forehead pressed to its cool, clean glass she stared at the journey clocks, the bedside ticktockers, the grand vestibule clock, nearly tall as a tree, and the whimsical wedding clock with its stiffly dancing bride and groom. The gilded name above the workshop's warded door read *Markus Stokely, Artisan Mage*. She'd never heard Arndel mention him. His clocks were passable. Pleasant, even. But they weren't anywhere near as good as hers.

Cheerful, she kept walking.

Beyond Artisan Row was the fabric district, and there she sighed over silks and velvets and brocades and satins, over beads and buttons and lush furs imported from the brutish Iringan wilderness and beyond. On Bakers' Square she bought a sweet mouthful of cherry pie, its buttery crust and fruity filling a symphony on her tongue. Whoever had baked it was a true artisan.

She walked on again, licking her lips. Everywhere she stepped, everywhere she looked, Elvado's grandeur stole her breath. Yes, oh, yes, it was a beautiful city. And so long as the First Families ruled in Dorana, she would never call it her own.

Without warning a swift rush of resentment stung her, so sharp she had to reach out a hand to the yellow wall beside her. The injustice of her plight closed her throat and blurred her vision. Killed the memory of that cherry pie and the lingering pleasure of the fabulous nursery clock she'd made. What she could learn here, at the College of Mages. Given the chance, what could she become?

*But I'll never know, will I? I won't be given that chance.*
She could hear Remmie's voice scolding her.

*Count your blessings, Barl. You have Ancilla Grie and her patronage, which is more than most unranked mages can even dream of.*

And though that was true, it wasn't enough. Besides, what was true today might not be true tomorrow. Who knew how long Lady Grie's approval would last? A week ago it had been Tympanne Ranett perched on her ladyship's silken shoulder . . . and now the celebrated Master Artisan was spurned.

*Only a fool trusts in the whims of a spoiled First Family mage. The only mage I can rely upon is myself.*

She straightened and took a proper look around. She'd walked a goodly distance from Elvado's central plaza. Here was a hushed residential district, gaily painted houses pressed shoulder to shoulder along a much narrower flagstoned side street, with window boxes and polished brass door-knockers and curtains drawn to keep the world at a polite distance. Some wardings here and there, too, put in place by mages not inclined to trust human nature.

How very wise of them.

She'd wanted to find the College of Mages, to stand before its open gates and dream, but if she didn't start back to the plaza now she'd be tardy. And that would leave Remmie in a stew of worry and he'd likely scold her in front of Barton Haye.

So she retraced her steps, pushing her way through and around the throng of mages heading for the plaza. Reaching it, she sighed. An hour ago it had been merely dotted with people. Now the plaza was crowded, all but the spouting tip of its fountain hidden by town dwellers and visitors eager to witness the day's so-called *historic events*.

'There you are!' Remmie said, pleased, as she elbowed the last few gawkers aside to join him in the Hall of Knowledge's beautifully tiled forecourt. 'They haven't started yet.'

'So I see,' she replied, looking at the imposing dais that had been set up directly before them. 'It seems I rushed back for nothing.'

Remmie rolled his eyes. 'Did you have a good wander?'

'I wasn't bored,' she said, shrugging. More than that she'd no intention of sharing, not with Barton Haye's sticking-out ears so close by and flapping.

'Well, we had a delightful adventure,' said Remmie, not in the least fooled by her show of indifference. 'Over there, not too far away—' He pointed eastward across the crowded plaza. '—there's a maze, where you must decipher a slew of clues to discover the incants that will let you find your way out again. Without the right incant in the right place you can't escape. Very clever, it was.'

'And highly entertaining,' added Barton, turning. 'Your brother and I left our fates up to the children.'

'Luckily for us,' said Remmie, mock pompous, 'we're excellent teachers.'

One of his students, short and chubby with a splotch of ink on his collar, looked up and grinned. 'Lucky we're excellent pupils, you mean.'

As the other Batava children collapsed into giggles, Remmie reached out a finger and flicked the plump boy's nose. 'Instead of congratulating yourself, Rine, why don't you take care of that blot on your shirt? Or do you want these fancy-pants township children to think mages from the Eleventh district don't know how to look smart?'

'Blot?' The boy half-strangled himself trying to see. 'Oh. Sorry.'

Glancing around the specially roped-off student area, Barl saw that quite a lot of the gathered children were flashily dressed and possessed a certain polished sophistication that spoke of lives lived without benefit of seeing cows through the kitchen window. And then she saw that some of those polished children were flicking supercilious looks toward Remmie's plainly-garbed pupils. Little nudges, hurried whispers, sly smiles hinting at unkindness and an unearned superiority. First Family brats every one of them, she had no doubt, and dearly deserving of more than a flick on the nose.

38

'Never you mind, Rine,' she said to the boy, surprising herself. 'There's more to magework than clothing. A clean collar wouldn't have whisked you out of that maze.'

'Oh!' said the boy, caught between pleasure and uncertainty. He wasn't used to hearing his teacher contradicted. 'No. I s'pose not.'

'*But*—' said Remmie, his voice heavy with warning, 'a neat mage is a careful mage, and a careful mage is a mage less likely to do himself or anybody else a mischief. Don't you agree, Mage Lindin?'

If she didn't say yes, Remmie would punish her with cold leftovers for a week. Or worse, make her cook for herself.

'Yes, of course. It's very important.'

'*Very* important,' Remmie repeated, staring at the boy Rine. 'And don't—'

Interrupted by a tuneful fanfare, he shifted his teacherly gaze to the Hall of Knowledge's grand entrance. The fanfare played again and the jumble of conversations around the plaza died down. Cutting through the ringing silence, the sound of Elvado's grand clock tolling the hour. Barl closed her eyes, touched to stillness by its deep, solemn chime. Sudden excitement rippling through the crowd broke her reverie. Looking for its cause, she saw a procession of men and women emerge from the Hall of Knowledge and make their stately, gold-and-brocade way to the dais.

Dorana's revered and feared Council of Mages.

Barl felt her jaw tighten. She knew the Council's leader was one Lord Varen, but had no idea who the rest of them were. Didn't care. What did it matter which First Family claimed them? All that mattered was that by their arrogant decree she must forever believe herself to be *inferior*, just because she was unranked. Was supposed to accept her secondary status, uncomplaining, and forget stillborn dreams of attending the College.

She turned as Remmie's hand came to rest lightly on her shoulder. In his eyes she saw a sorrow that drifted perilously close to pity. But she didn't want his pity. She wanted him angry, sharing her outrage, her burning desire to right what was wrong in Dorana.

*How can he be my brother, my other half, and be so complacent?*

She saw him hear the unspoken question, but before she could speak he shook his head. 'Not now. The children. Barton.'

And he was right, about that, anyway. Not about anything else. About everything else he couldn't be more mistaken. She shrugged his hand away and turned back to the dais.

The Council's members had climbed to its top and now stood neatly arranged, the three men and two women staring over the crowd. A pace back and to one side stood the last three mages, all women, each one dressed in silks, decorated with jewels, trembling with ill-concealed excitement and pride. But there were four new incants approved, so where was the fourth mage to be honoured? Surely he or she wouldn't risk insulting the Council by not attending?

Lord Varen, a man well past his seventieth year if the lines in his face spoke the truth, stepped to the edge of the dais and raised his hands.

'*Winsun greetings to all. The Council of Mages welcomes you on this auspicious occasion.*'

An enhancement incant carried his melodious voice to every mage in the plaza.

'*With us this day stand three talented mages,*' Varen continued, '*who by virtue of their diligence and creative vision have created new incants for our lexicon of knowledge, and in doing so further burnish the lustre of Dorana's magical heritage. Mage Lakewell . . . Mage Tranter . . . Mage Folet—*' One by one, the women stepped forward as their names were called. '*Dorana thanks you for your service to our arcane lore.*'

As applause rippled through the audience gathered in the plaza, enthusiastic from the gathered school children, more polite and restrained from everyone else, each of the three acknowledged mages pressed a hand to her heart and lowered her head in humble appreciation . . . or an excellent imitation of it.

Watching them closely, Barl felt a pang of envy so sharp she had to swallow. That Mage Folet was so *young,* a mere handful of years older than she and Remmie. Yet there the woman stood, elevated to the status of an Incant Mage, her name to be recorded for all time in the Council register.

For one terrible moment, she thought she might weep.

'*Alas,*' said Lord Varen, his expression darkening, '*magic is not without its dangers. Today we mourn the loss of Mage Brahn Sorvold. Two days ago, emboldened by his recent success, he attempted an even more daring incant . . . and paid for his ambition with his life.*'

Shocked gasps from the crowd. Remmie and Barton murmured to their students, patting heads, whispering reassurances. Barl frowned, disapproving. They might be children, but they were mages first. There was no such thing as being too young for the truth. But if she opened her mouth on that score Remmie would be furious.

Again, Lord Varen raised his hands. The agitated crowd hushed.

'*But this is not the time or place for grief,*' he said, his green gaze steady. '*We are gathered here to celebrate new magic. Mage Lakewell?*'

The oldest of the three honoured mages took another step forward. Lord Varen nodded at her, then joined his fellow councillors. Excitement thrummed through the waiting crowd.

Mage Lakewell's lips moved as she silently recited a short incant. Next she sketched a sigil on the air, where it glowed molten gold. In her outstretched left hand appeared a small flowerpot, but instead of a ripe bloom it contained a single stalk of renna, rotting with grain blight.

Those mages close enough to clearly see the pot and its contents sighed. Grain blight was a curse gifted them by the careless farmers of Feen, who three summers before had failed to purge their own crops of the disease before its spores blew over the border into Dorana. Used in ale-making and baking a sour, nourishing bread, renna grain was highly prized. Being a fickle crop it grew grudgingly elsewhere, which meant importing the grain was difficult and ruinously expensive. All of Dorana was pinched by the shortage.

Barl felt her fingers curl, nails biting her palm. So, had Mage Lakewell defeated renna blight? For if that was her achievement . . .

Another sigil burned the air, this time the bright crimson of fresh blood. Another sigil, dark green, then one of sky blue, and finally a fifth of storm-cloud purple. The plaza's air crackled, prickling bare skin and stirring unbound hair. Mage Lakewell recited a second silent incant, her lips moving too quickly for the syllables to be discerned. Her right hand hovered above the blighted stalk of grain, outstretched fingers slightly hooked. In her face, a fierce concentration.

With a shudder that shook the plaza's cobblestones and splashed the water in its fountain, the incant ignited. Remmie and Barton's transfixed pupils squealed. Even the fancy-pants First Family children cried out, and more than a few of the adult mages behind them. Barl caught her breath as the magic's power surged through her, searing nerve and bone and muscle.

Now the potted stalk of grain was obscured by a thick greenish haze. There was sweat on Mage Lakewell's face and she breathed deep and hard. The incant was costing her.

'*A'bar'at!*' she said, the command bursting from her in a grunting of pain.

A flash of light. A roar of discharged power. The greenish haze vanished to reveal a *healthy* stalk of renna.

Cries of joy. Rapturous applause. With a careless wave of her hand Mage Lakewell returned the pot to wherever it belonged and waited for the acclaim to subside. Her lips were curved in the merest hint of a smile.

Remmie turned, his face alight with admiration. '*Remarkable.* Don't you think so, Barl?'

'It was well done,' she admitted, because it was, and she couldn't with honesty say otherwise.

Mage Lakewell stepped back, and into her place stepped Mage

Tranter. Her great achievement was an incant to render harmless any poison brewed, on purpose or by accident, from the fruit of the yababi bush. Since yababi was the favoured poison of certain warlike Ranoushi clans, and a crucial ingredient of extensively popular yababi paste, which had been known to turn rancid and kill by mistake, thanks to Mage Tranter Dorana stood to make a good deal of coin.

Remmie and Barton and a few of their pupils were distressed by Tranter's use of live rabbits to demonstrate both poison and cure but really, what did they expect? Volunteers from the audience? Rabbit served up in a stew or used to demonstrate magework, there was no difference, surely. Dead was dead.

Mage Folet's newly patented incant was far less bloody. She'd devised a method of showing where an object had been in the previous nine hours.

'Nine hours?' Barl muttered to Remmie, under cover of the resulting applause. 'Make it a full day and perhaps there'd be some use to it.'

'Doubtless that will be her next achievement,' Remmie replied. 'In the meantime, petty pilferers far and wide will think twice before taking what doesn't belong to them. There'll be a market for that incant well beyond our borders.'

Which meant more riches for Dorana, with every sale tariffed by the General Council.

A nod from Lord Varen had Mage Folet rejoining her companions. Then, at another nod, the youngest councillor stepped forward. Brahn Sorvold might have succumbed to his own arrogant ambition, but it seemed his final achievement would still be honoured.

Tall and pleasingly lithe, his golden hair pleated away from a hawkishly handsome face, the councillor lifted one graceful, beringed hand. Seeing him properly, Barl blinked.

*Oh, my.*

With careless authority the councillor summoned to himself the items required for dead Mage Sorvold's incant. Looking past his striking appearance, she saw that just like every First Family mage she'd ever encountered there was a haughty arrogance to the man.

But despite the knot of old, cold anger tangled in her chest, she couldn't help admiring the way his long fingers danced their way through a complicated sequence of sigils. The way his molasses voice caressed the incant's syllables. The gleam of unbridled pleasure in his piercing blue eyes as he caused first unrefined gold, then silver, to melt into crude, formless liquids. The councillor smiled to see their destruction, smiled wider still as his audience gasped and groaned. Barl bit her lip, staring.

*There's so much power in him. Can't anyone else feel it? Is the whole world made of straw, that no-one else feels it?*

His seamed face impassive, Lord Varen was watching with no more anxiety than if he waited for a kettle to boil. Surely *he* must feel the beautiful mage's power. But if he did, he gave no outward hint.

Remmie could feel it. There was tension in the back of his neck, in the way his hands were thrust deep in his pockets. The corners of his mouth were tucked deep, betraying his unease. Barl frowned.

*Don't be a fool, Remmie. Power should be embraced, not feared.*

The powerful mage on the dais held the glass vial of liquid gold in his left hand, the vial of silver in his right. Steadily he emptied them into the shallow glass bowl he'd summoned and set before him on a conjured stand. Hot metal kissed hot metal, hissing, breathing out pungent steam. Finished, he tossed the vials into nothingness then spread his arms wide and drew fresh sigils to left and right, so swiftly she couldn't keep track of their shapes. The air sizzled and smoked, bright jewel colours blinding.

Not a sound in the plaza. Even the children were struck dumb.

With a joy that was almost like laughter, the councillor sang out the syllables of dead Sorvold's incant. They ignited the shimmering air and set the melted gold and silver in the glass bowl to wild swirling. Round and round they whirled, melding and muddling into one gleaming silver-gold mass.

The councillor clapped his hands sharply. Whispered a single word under his breath. His fingers traced two final sigils. Barl felt the pull of them, felt the punch through her ribcage and the burn in her blood. Her heart leapt as she was trapped in the power of the incant, the power of raw power, the glory of great work. She nearly cried her heartache aloud.

*Me. Me. That should be me.*

Now the councillor was muttering more swift syllables. The newly melded precious metals rose in a slender column, as lithe and elegant as the mage who created it. Like a weaver with his spindle he coaxed the blended gold and silver higher, then higher still, his planed and angled face alight with pleasure. The column caught the sunlight and blazed fire. Around the plaza, mages broke into fresh applause. Children squealed.

Barl closed her eyes, fighting tears.

*Me. Me. That should be me.*

When she could bear to lift her eyelids, she saw the glorious silver-gold column suspended in the air, caught fast in a web of magic. It looked like a frozen flame, a captured sunspark.

It looked like magic brought to life.

The councillor raised his right hand, fingers clenched to a fist . . . and Barl knew, she *knew,* what he was going to do.

*An unmaking? With no safeguards? You can't be so rash!*

'Ri'ga!' commanded the councillor. 'Ba'vek!'

She gasped as the unmaking incant punched through her. Beside her Remmie flinched, feeling it just as keenly, but he ignored his own pain to care for Batava's frightened children. So did Barton. Every mage in the plaza was distressed to some degree. Unmaking incants of that strength were restricted, their use almost never approved. Too much could go wrong with them. And this one was brutal. Why would the Council countenance its use when –

And then Barl turned back to the magic-melded gold and silver column . . . and saw exactly why.

'Remmie,' she whispered, reaching for him. '*Look.*'

Distracted by upset children, he started to scold her for

bothering him. But Barton Haye choked and pointed, forestalling him. And then the plaza was full of pointing, gasping mages.

'That's not possible,' said Remmie. 'Is it?'

The powerful unmaking incant had failed.

'It was once,' she breathed. 'But not any more.'

Somehow, incredibly, Brahn Sorvold had created a fusing incant that could not be destroyed.

With a careless snap of his fingers, the councillor vanished the unharmed gold and silver column, then returned to his fellow councillors. Lord Varen stepped forward, hands raised, and waited for the excitement in the plaza to subside.

'*The Council of Mages thanks you for attending this Winsun demonstration. And, in memory of Mage Sorvold, opens the Hall of Knowledge to public enjoyment for the next three hours.*'

'Did you hear that?' Barton demanded of Batava's pupils. 'What an honour. The Hall is hardly ever open to the public.'

As the children set up a clamour, Barl frowned at Remmie. 'So we're to feel *grateful*? When magic is a birthright belonging to all Doranen, and the Hall of Knowledge is—'

'Please, Barl,' her brother sighed. 'Don't spoil this for the children.'

She felt her eyes sting. *I knew this was a mistake. I knew I shouldn't have come.* 'Fine. I'll not say another word.'

And she didn't. Not while she loitered behind her brother and Barton and their goggling pupils as they shuffled their way through the Hall of Knowledge, into its lofty workrooms and hushed libraries, up its majestically spiralling staircases and along its wide corridors lined with glorious stained-glass windows. Not while they crowded onto its broad balconies and squealed to see sun-kissed Elvado spread far and wide below them. Instead she feasted her hungry gaze on every locked door and barred passageway. Stared after the Hall's resident mages, who threaded their purposeful way through the crowding gawkers and whose shuttered gazes hinted at magics held aloof from those deemed unworthy of their grace. Closed her eyes and breathed in the

Hall's power, felt it chime through her, making promises it could not keep.

Heartsick, she folded her arms so tight her ribs threatened to break.

*I deserve to be here. This wondrous city should be my home.*

Not wanting to waste a rare opportunity, after the Hall was again closed to public scrutiny Remmie and Barton let their pupils explore the plaza's surrounding streets, keeping them in Elvado as late as they dared. By the time they finally returned to Batava's schoolhouse and saw the weary children into the keeping of their parents, the late afternoon was fast surrendering to dusk.

'Is something wrong?' said Remmie. 'You've not said a word for hours.'

Walking beside him back to their cottage, Barl shrugged. 'You're the one who told me to be quiet.'

'True. But I only meant—'

'I know what you meant.'

'I'm sorry we didn't get a chance to toss that coin for Mama and Pa.'

'I'm not,' she said. 'It's a private matter. As if I'd want Barton Haye gawking.'

Remmie sighed. 'I knew you were cross.'

'I'm not cross! I'm thinking.'

'Barl.' Remmie's fingers caught her elbow, tugging her to a halt. 'I know that look, too. What are you plotting?'

She winced at the scarcely muffled despair in his voice. 'Nothing you need worry about.'

Even in the dim, dusking light, though no anger showed in his narrow face or gentle eyes she could tell he was angered by her reply.

'I mean it, Remmie,' she insisted. 'What I choose to do doesn't change anything for you.'

He shook his head. 'That's not true and you know it. How can I be happy when you aren't? Barl, you promised, and now—'

47

'I promised I'd not drag you with me, and I won't!' she said, struggling not to shout. 'The truth is I never have done. Following me has always been your idea. Admit it.'

'Don't change the subject,' he muttered. 'We're not talking about me, we're talking about how you won't – you never—' He shook his head, torn between frustration and bafflement. 'Why can't you stay satisfied for more than five minutes? I thought you *liked* making clocks.'

'I like it well enough,' she said, shrugging again. 'But I want more than clocks.'

'And you'll have more, won't you? With Lady Grie as your patron, you'll have—'

Remmie wasn't a nubbin, he was just being contrary. 'With Lady Grie as my patron I'll do what Lady Grie wants. It won't be about what *I* want.' Defiant, she stared at her brother. 'And I want Elvado.'

'Oh, *Barl*.' Turning away, Remmie took hold of his long, ribbon-threaded braid and tugged. 'I thought you'd abandoned that idea.'

'I did,' she said, glowering. 'But now I've come to my senses.'

He rounded on her. 'No, you've *lost* your senses. The College of Mages is out of your reach.'

She stamped her foot, as though they were both five again. 'Says who? Remmie, three hundred years ago only First Family members were allowed to be mages. Would *that* have changed if someone like me had given up her dream as hopeless?'

'I'm not saying it's fair,' said Remmie. 'There's no just reason for you to be kept from studying in Elvado.'

'No, and no hard-and-fast written rule, either. Under the College's code, Remmie, which I've studied back to front and sideways, I have every right to be admitted as a student there.'

'I *know*,' he said, his voice tight with frustration. 'But Dorana is governed by *un*written rules too. Like it or not, Barl, First Families make the important decisions and that means no unranked mage will ever be recognised as worthy of a College place.'

She could hate him for being so easily cowed. 'Remmie, you know my gifts. They're your gifts too, if only you'd stretch yourself to use them. I *am* worthy of College acceptance. And if I have to shout until every stained-glass window in Elvado shatters, the mages who gatekeep the College will hear me. There's greatness in me and I won't let them ignore it.'

'There's something in you. And all I can say for certain is it's not modesty.' He turned away again, fingers linked around the back of his neck. 'Barl, I wish you'd think about this.'

'I have. I'm going to petition the College to reconsider my application. I've got more experience now. Nearly three years worth.'

Remmie glared at her over his shoulder. 'If you had *ten* years more experience, it still wouldn't matter. You were foolish to apply the first time, and you'll be just as foolish to apply again.'

He wasn't going to talk her out of it. 'So you say.'

'And I'm *right*. You're being hopelessly naïve, Barl. This is all moonbeams and dreamdust. And when you're turned down again? How long before you let the disappointment goad you into some foolish loss of temper? How long before you're dismissed from the artisanry and we're homeless again and traipsing from district to district in search of work you'll accept?'

Guilt-struck, resentful, she stared at her brother. 'You're so sure they'll reject me.'

Instead of answering, he scuffed his booted toe through the lush grass verging Crackbone Lane. Then he sighed.

'I'm sorry, Barl. I just don't want you hurt.'

'I won't be.'

Remmie frowned, his eyes chilling. 'In other words, you'll do what you want, like always. Fine. Write to the College. Ask them to admit you. But when your heart's broken for good this time, Barl, don't say I didn't warn you.'

# CHAPTER FOUR

'No,' said the old man, querulous, his voice a disgruntled wheeze. 'Morgan, what is this nonsense? Are you fevered? Are you deaf? The energies as they exist, as you have combined them, are not compatible. They must be balanced *counter*clockwise, else the sigils, once confirmed, will not support the connecting incantation.'

Morgan looked down so his father wouldn't see how close he was to saying something unwise. A cutting retort danced on his tongue. The need to lash out, to remind his father he was a man, not a boy to be commanded or treated like an ignorant student, was almost overpowering.

But he stayed silent. There'd be no profit in indulging his sorely tried temper. Hold tongue and endure: this was his life now and had been, almost without respite, for the past stifling eleven weeks. How much longer it would last he could not tell, nor could his father's pother advise. Since his heart seizure, and the attack of palsy that followed it, Lord Danfey's health had been gravely uncertain. His faculties were like a tide now at ebb, now on the rise, and while relieving his own feelings with an acidic retort might briefly satisfy, such self-indulgence would end only in estrangement . . . or worse.

'Well?' his father demanded. 'Do you understand what I am telling you, or must we return to the schoolroom so I might refresh your memory on the basics of sigil creation?'

'No, my lord,' he said, and clasped his betraying hands behind his back. 'I need no reminding. But if I might be permitted to explain—'

'What?' His father glared. 'School me, would you? When I was creating sigils at half your age?'

'No, my lord. Of course not. But I fear I have not made clear my—'

'School *and* condescend to me! And this is the conduct of a dutiful son, is it?'

Morgan stared at his experiment. Cupped in their crucibles, the three barely coalesced sigils he struggled to confirm glittered in the intermittent sunlight shafting through his attic workroom's plain round window. He could feel the latent power in them, feel the warp and weft of competing energies alternate hot then cold against his skin. The sigils would collapse soon, undone by the fragility of their incomplete creation.

*And I will lose near a whole month's work, see Dorana creep closer to danger, for no other reason than a sick old man's pique.*

He looked up. 'My lord, if you would hear me out?'

That same intermittent sunlight played across his father's sunken, sallow cheeks and for a moment bleached the shadows beneath his bloodshot eyes. His drooping left eyelid twitched, an echo of past trouble. Perhaps a harbinger of more trouble to come. But to suggest as much would provoke a storm of abuse.

'Do I hear you aright?' said his father, derisive. 'You'll stand there and tell me, in the face of all accepted practice, that a *clockwise* balancing must be pursued?'

'In this instance, yes,' he replied. 'Since I am attempting to reconfigure a basic transmutation incant I must redistribute the energies antithetically, or risk—'

'Risk blowing the roof off this mansion!' his father shouted. A thread of spittle glistened on his too-pale lips. 'And you cannot expect me to remain sanguine about *that*.'

'I admit the incant is volatile,' he said, choosing his words with continued care. 'But worthwhile, I am convinced.'

His father grimaced. 'Worthwhile for what purpose? Do you say there is a sudden, overwhelming need for a new transmutation incant? No matter of urgency has reached my ears and reach me it would, though I am ridiculously confined to this estate.'

'My lord . . .' Morgan swallowed a groan. *Why must you turn this into an argument? Would you have me bar you from my work?* 'There is no immediate crisis, it's true, but—'

'But you will not accept constraint.' Pinching the bridge of his beakish nose, a familiar gesture of goaded self-control, his father breathed out hard. 'And so we come to it. This new incantation, is it commissioned by the Council?'

Telling his father a point-blank lie was out of the question. 'No.'

'Sanctioned, at least?'

'No.'

Heart seizure and palsy had left his father weakened, but still he managed to stamp about the attic with his fingers fisted. 'Morgan, what are you thinking? There are *prohibitions.*'

'That do not apply to me,' he pointed out. 'As a member of the Council, I—'

'Its junior member!' his father said, turning. 'And newly seated. Do not let being chosen to demonstrate Sorvold's confounded incant go to your head! If Brice Varen should learn of your *experimenting* I cannot imagine he will salute your daring. Rather he'll wonder if the Council's choice of you to replace Andwin Bellem was rash.'

'That is your opinion, my lord,' he said, unable to keep the stiff offence from his tone. 'I choose to see the matter differently.'

'Yes, of course you do,' his father muttered. 'And so leave me wondering if it's any great surprise I am plagued by pothers when you persist in such reckless pursuits.'

With a sigh of released energies, the crucible-cradled sigils on the cluttered workbench collapsed in a flare of blue light.

'There!' said his father, triumphant. 'You see? They did not hold, Morgan, and it was folly to dream they would. As my son, you should know better. As your father I expect better. You are a Danfey. There are standards to maintain.'

Making sure to hide his dismay, and his resentment at being held accountable for his father's ill health, Morgan looked away from the emptied crucibles with their faint blue smears of dissipated energy.

'Forgive me,' he said, his throat tight. 'I intended to please, not disappoint.'

With halting, shuffled steps and a rustle of silk tunic, his father came close and tapped a finger to his cheek. 'Perfect your magecraft within the bounds of law and I *will* be pleased.'

A fresh prickle of resentment. 'The law must bend itself to the weakest amongst us, not taking into account the strengths of greater mages.'

'Mages such as yourself?'

'*Yes!*' Morgan waved his hand across the emptied crucibles. 'My lord, the choice is plain. Either we remain mired in the familiar, dooming ourselves to stagnation, or we accept the challenge of the unfamiliar and push ourselves to greater heights.'

*Heights that will save us when the need arises.*

'Morgan—' His father pinched the bridge of his nose again. 'Brahn Sorvold thought like that.'

'I am not Brahn Sorvold!' he snapped, then took a deep breath to subdue his own temper. 'My lord, I know what I'm doing.'

'As do I!' said his father. 'You tempt fate.'

'No, my lord. I simply encourage it to smile on me. I am a councillor, it's true, but the Danfey name can rise higher.'

'And it can fall,' his father retorted. 'Or be pushed, by those who do not relish your achievements. By mages who wait in the shadows for the chance to see you eclipsed.'

He shook his head. 'Small mages, my lord. Jealous and spiteful. As a Danfey should I fear them?'

'As a Danfey you should fear *nothing*,' said his father, with all the strength left to him. 'But prudence is a survival trait,

Morgan, not a fault. Dorana's mages are bound by rules for good reason. Magework kills the careless without compunction! And a father should not be asked to bury his only son.'

He had to harden his heart against the pain in his father's voice. But even as he felt that echo of distress, he felt a fresh wash of resentment drown it.

*Perhaps not, my lord. But should an only son be held prisoner by his father's unfounded fears?*

And they were unfounded. Magework might well be dangerous, but he was not that overpraised sot Brahn Sorvold. Besides, success and timidity could not leap to achievement's summit hand in hand. His father should know that it was unjust of him, to demand in one breath that he bring honour to the Danfey name, then in the next berate him for being too bold.

'Morgan . . .' Lord Danfey's clawed left hand gestured at the roomy attic. 'Why do you lock yourself away in here for days on end, in pursuit of new incants, when those you've already perfected still await Council ratification? You wish to impress me? Get your patents and you can be sure, I will be impressed!'

'I assure *you,* my lord,' he said, wincing, 'I have done all within my power on that score. Now I must wait. And in the meantime—'

'Yes, Morgan, I know! In the meantime you are determined to pursue these new incantations, these – these *experiments* of yours – to whatever end awaits you. A father's broken heart is no counterweight to your ambition.'

And that was a monstrously unfair thing to say.

'My lord, you wrong me. Did I care for you as little as you seem to think, would I have remained on this estate these past weeks of your confinement? Would I have abandoned the Council duties so recently placed upon me, risking censure? Risking worse?'

His father plucked a kerchief from his sleeve and dabbed his loosened lips dry of spittle. 'No.'

'Indeed, no. And you're peevish to say otherwise.'

'*Peevish*?' His father's eyes narrowed. 'That's a word for a dutiful son to use against his father, is it?'

Of course not, but of a sudden he was in a mood to be contrary. 'It is when a dutiful son is smarting.'

Instead of answering that, his father picked up the nearest emptied crucible and trailed a fingertip through its blue smear of wasted power. After a long silence, he put it down and frowned at his stained skin.

'Why do you want to create a new transmutation incant, Morgan?'

He answered readily, but not entirely honestly. He had to. Presented with the whole truth, Greve Danfey would mock and scold.

'To see if I can.'

'To see if you can,' his father murmured, looking up. Not even the after effects of recent illness could dull the sharpness of his regard. 'And what manner of difference would it make, did you succeed?'

It wasn't only mockery and criticism that concerned him. His father was weakened, wandering in purpose, and might easily betray a confidence. That would likely see him ruined.

'I don't know, my lord. I won't, until I've succeeded.'

*And I will succeed, you may be sure of that.*

Harsh glare softening, his father wiped his finger free of blue residue then tucked the stained kerchief back into his sleeve. 'Even as a child, Morgan, you were never satisfied. You were born hungry, not for the wetnurse's milk but for every experience to be wrung from the world.'

He couldn't fathom if that was compliment or complaint. Wary, he made sure to remain dutifully deferential.

'Do you say that is a fault, my lord?'

'I say what I said before,' his father replied. 'A prudent man is not to be despised. You may run to your destination, or you may walk. Running is faster but in walking one has time to see the journey's pitfalls. To notice those traps laid for the unwary.'

Morgan hid his growing irritation behind a smile. 'True. But will you accuse me of arrogance if I say I can avoid pitfalls and leap traps as I run?'

'Accuse?' His father laughed, the sound slurred with weariness. 'No. To accuse implies the chance of innocence. In this case I must declare it, for you are guilty through and through.'

'And is *that* a fault?'

Another slurred laugh. 'Show me a modest mage and I'll show you a charlatan. Arrogance a fault? Never. Without arrogance no mage would cast his first incantation.'

'And yet you are displeased with me.'

'Not for this,' his father said, jerking his chin at the workbench and the stained crucibles. 'Though I do question your flouting of the rules. No, your magework could never displease me, Morgan. But it can frighten me. It *does* frighten me.'

'My lord—' He stepped closer. 'There is nothing to fear. My skills are more than equal to this small task.'

His father raised an eyebrow. 'Or so you believe.'

'My lord, belief implies uncertainty. I have no doubts.'

'And perhaps I would be less frightened if you did.'

With an effort Morgan kept himself relaxed. *This is his weakness talking. He has grown an old man before my eyes.* 'If you are unsettled, my lord, I suspect there is more than magework to blame. It is past time we sat down to luncheon. Ranmer was most particular that you pay close attention to your belly.'

'My belly is my business,' his father said, scowling. 'None of yours, nor of any meddling pother.'

'Meddling Ranmer saved your life, my lord. We would both be well-served did you not forget that.'

His father grunted, not liking the reproof but knowing better than to contradict bald fact.

'Besides,' he added, coaxing, 'if your private belly is not growling, mine is. And I would not sit at the table in solitary splendour. Shall we adjourn to the dining room?'

He braced himself for a tart reply, but instead his father looked around the attic workroom. 'You are a fine mage, Morgan. I expect you will achieve feats no other mage in our history has even dreamed of attempting. But you would do well not to dismiss my call for caution as the ramblings of a decrepit.'

'My lord, I do not,' he said, prepared to tell that one lie. 'Your advice is always welcome.'

His father sniffed. 'But rarely heeded.'

And there was the tartness he'd been expecting. Best sweeten the old man before their relationship soured entirely. 'If you're in the mood for dispensing advice, my lord, I would appreciate your wisdom regarding my work here. After luncheon, perhaps?'

'Perhaps,' said his father, grudging. Pretending indifference, though the gleam of pleasure in his eye said otherwise. 'If you are determined to chart this course.'

'I am,' he said, pretending apology. 'I must, if I would stay true to myself as a man and a mage.'

'Yes,' his father said, with a heavy sigh. 'That would be the crux of it . . . and on that head I cannot complain.'

So in better accord they made their way downstairs to the dining room, where servants brought them their delayed midday repast. Scarcely tasting his own meal of cold chicken and dressed greens, from the corner of his eye Morgan watched his father's half-hearted attempt to empty his bowl. Watched the old man's shaking hand spill the soup from his spoon onto the tablecloth and down the broad napkin tucked into his padded brocade tunic.

It was a painful sight but he could not spare himself, no matter how much he might wish to or how deeply he ached for even a single day's respite. He could not hand his father's care to another. Lord Danfey's dignity would not permit it. And in truth, neither would his own. Pother Ranmer he could trust never to speak of his father's weakened condition, the occasional instability of intellect, but no other man or woman than that.

It wasn't only a question of dignity. Greve Danfey had enemies, and his plight could be – would be – used against him, to hurt him and his son. Only a fool handed an adversary a weapon.

*And of all the things I am, a fool is not amongst them.*

With an exclamation of disgust his father let the spoon drop, plucked the napkin free and hurled it to the floor, then slumped in dour, frustrated silence. Knowing that to speak now would do no good, Morgan finished his own meal, drained his goblet of wine, dabbed his lips clean and pushed his emptied plate away. Only then did he look to his morose father.

The unconsumed pea and ham soup was growing cold, a thin skin congealing across its porridgy green surface. Already today Lord Danfey had refused his breakfast. He could not be permitted to refuse luncheon as well, for beneath his padded tunic he was close to skin and bone. So if he must once again be fed like a babe, so be it. No loving son could sit idly by as his father will-fully starved.

'Perhaps one more mouthful, my lord,' he murmured, picking up the spoon and dipping it into the bowl. 'So I can make a good report to Pother Ranmer when next he visits.'

With a feeble wave of one hand his father sent bowl and spoon flying across the chamber. The heavily aromatic soup splashed tablecloth, wall, floor and Feenish rug indiscriminately, painting Lord Danfey's displeasure wide for all Dorana to see.

'My lord . . .' Morgan frowned at his pea-stained sleeve. 'You must eat.'

His father sneered. 'I'd eat if those cursed servants brought me food. That's not food. It's slop.'

'Ranmer said—'

'By the scales of *justice*!' his father bellowed. 'Do not prate to me of pothers! Do not task me with soup! Do not – do not—' He broke off, gasping, the stubborn phlegm curdling noisily in his chest. One frail fist beat at his breastbone, forcing more angry words into his throat. 'You say you regret displeasing me, Morgan, yet what do you do but find ways to salt my wounds? You look to feed me as though I was an infant, you dismiss my concerns about your magework, and you refuse to pay attention to your single most pressing duty.'

Stung by the attack, Morgan sat back in his chair. *He lashes out because he's shamed. Because he cannot reconcile himself to what he's become.* But understanding why his father railed at him didn't mean he wasn't hurt.

'My lord, you speak in riddles. I have shirked no duty.'

'No?' His father stabbed at the dining room's frescoed ceiling with one pointed finger. 'Then instead of locking yourself away in that attic of yours, *experimenting,* why are you not busy finding yourself a wife? How little you must truly care for the Danfey name and legacy, to leave me languishing with no hope of our future! Are you so eager to call this mansion and my title your own that you'd seek to kill me with despair?'

Jaw tight, temper freshly woken, Morgan summoned his will and whispered an incant. The soup stain on his sleeve vanished. With another harshly breathed incant he translocated soup bowl and spoon to the kitchens. That left the stains on tablecloth, wall, floor and Feenish rug. He raised a hand to banish them, but his father snatched at his forearm.

'*Leave be*!' he said, savage. 'Am I a tit-sucking babe, that I can't attend to my own mess?'

Morgan folded his hands on the dining table. It was a matter of pride that they did not clench to show white knuckles.

'No, my lord.'

'No,' his father echoed, bitter. 'Then keep your incants to yourself.'

Greve Danfey had never been a robust man. In his childhood there were fevers. His prime had lasted but four years and after that had come a slow descent into bouts of haggard ill-health. For many years he'd managed to keep his weakness at bay, but no longer. Twice in the past year he'd flirted with dying and twice Ranmer had pulled him back from the brink. Morgan was loath to admit it, but the truth could no longer be denied: a third reprieve seemed unlikely.

Watching his father sweat over a simple cleansing incant hurt him in ways the shouted, intemperate words never could.

'There,' his father said at last, rheumy, tear-filled eyes defiant. 'You see? I'm not dead yet.'

He forced a smile. 'I know you're not, my lord.'

'*My lord.*' Glowering, his father blotted his forehead dry of sweat with the napkin. 'A lip-service respect. That's all you have for me.'

And that hurt, too. 'No, my lord. You have from me all the honour due to you.'

'It *is* so,' his father said, stubbled chin trembling. 'One son, I have. One son.' He was staring through the chamber's windows now, communing with the clouds and the afternoon sun dipping in and out between them. 'And in him resides all hope for our proud family. But will he marry? Will he sire a son who'll carry the Danfey name stitched to a broad and alabaster brow? He will not. He dallies with incants nobody needs, instead of with a woman.'

Morgan slid from the chair to the floor beside his father, bruising his knees even though there was a rug beneath them. 'Please, my lord. You mustn't distress yourself. We can talk of my marriage another time. For now, bend your thoughts toward regaining your strength. How many more days do you want to spend prisoned within this mansion? You must eat, you must rest, you mustn't fret yourself with my future.'

'Your future?' His father snatched up the crumpled napkin and threw it in his face. 'Have a care for your future, should I? When you care naught for the Danfey legacy?'

He was a fool to persist, but the injustice here was untenable. 'How can you accuse me of not caring? Am I not the first Danfey to earn a seat on the Council of Mages?'

His father flinched at the question. Appointment to the Council had been Greve Danfey's ambition, denied him due to a misstep in his youth. Never reconciled to the blunder, he was both proud and resentful of his son's success.

*He'll not admit it, but I've surpassed him. Therein lies the seed of all his caution and rancour. And were he not my father I would rip out his meanness by its roots.*

'My lord?' he persisted. 'Have I not honoured you with that?'

'Yes, and I've already praised you for it,' his father muttered. 'Don't look for me to repeat myself. Besides, it would be of more use if you'd barter the honour into a taking of marriage vows. Perhaps I'd live longer if I had before me the timely prospect of your heir.'

Morgan bit his lip. Unkindness piled upon unkindness, and no way to portion all blame to his father's poor health. This was an old wound rubbed to new rawness by recent events.

'My lord, I but learn the lessons you would teach,' he said, goaded enough to indulge in a little unkindness of his own. 'Fathers with eligible daughters do not care to be flattered into submission. Nor are they vulnerable to the demands of a man so lately come into Council prominence. Given past Danfey indiscretions, a touch of circumspection cannot go astray.'

Another flinch as his father noted the barb. 'And too much circumspection can run you to ground. In learning from my mistake, best you not make one all your own.'

'My lord—'

'Morgan,' said his father, fastening thin fingers to his shoulder. 'You are thirty-six, unmarried, and you have no son. Yet here you kneel claiming you respect me. What am I to make of that, when words and deeds stand so far apart?'

The grip on his shoulder was painful, but he made no attempt to shrug his father's hand free. If Greve Danfey chose to see his only child's unwed, childless state as a mark of disrespect then what could he say to the complaint? The only answer to satisfy was a wife with a belly full of grandson.

'Morgan, Morgan . . .' With a sigh, his father released his shoulder and patted his cheek instead. 'The girl died fourteen years ago. Will you mourn me as long?'

Luzena, his youthful passion. Eternally preserved in a stone coffin, her beauty arrested out of time. A flower he'd been too reverent to pluck before she was formally his to touch. He'd loved her, brutally. Her death had marred him. His father was cruel to beat him with her memory, but there was no use saying so. In this instance Greve Danfey was the one who'd been ill-used . . . or so the old man felt.

'Don't speak of mourning, my lord. Such talk is nonsense.'

'Another insult,' his father said, sour as stale milk. 'You're in fine fettle today, Morgan. But you're wrong and I'm right and I think I'd rather you smothered me in my sleep and had done with it. A slow death by disappointment is little to my taste.'

At times like this love was hard to find. 'If I answered that charge as it deserved, my lord, *then* you would have cause to accuse me of disrespect.'

A flicker of shame in the old man's eyes, quickly extinguished. 'If you're so shy of facing facts then it could be I'm mistaken and you're not fit for marriage.'

'And it profits us how, my lord, to bandy words of your dying?' Morgan retorted, uncoiling to his feet. 'You might chafe me with this carping on marriage and sons but the fault isn't so great that I'd repay it by describing your funeral long before you've drawn your last breath!'

'*Carping?*' His father slapped the table. 'What right have you to throw such a word in my face?'

'And what right have *you*, my lord, to call into question my duty to you and this family? There is time for me to sire a son. *I* am not a dying old man!'

'So you admit my decline at last.' His father smiled, revealing loosened teeth and pale gums pinpricked with blood. 'That's progress, of a sort.'

Pained by the words, by his father's grotesque physical decline, Morgan retreated to the dining room's wide windows and stared across his family's estate toward distant, sun-glittered Elvado.

'Why are we wasting precious time with harsh words?' he said at last. 'Have I ever said I wouldn't marry? Have I ever said I would let this family die when I die?'

'No,' his father admitted. 'But Morgan, who knows better than you that life is unpredictable? If it weren't you'd be a husband with sons enough to carry their grandfather's body in solemn procession to the family crypt.'

'Yes, my lord. I would,' he said, and thought he heard the ghost of Luzena's sweet laughter. 'But I had a wake, not a wedding.

How unnatural a man your son would be if he did not grieve the loss of his unconsummated bride.'

'Grieving for one year is natural. Grieving for fourteen is unbecoming. Morgan, it's unmanly. And yes, it is disrespectful to me. It is past time that you chose another bride.'

He turned away from the window. 'You think because I don't speak of this that I've given it no thought. You're wrong. But the plain fact is, my affections are not engaged. You'd have me court an eligible young woman with false coin?'

'Affections are like the moon!' said his father. 'They wax and they wane. You fancied yourself in love with Luzena Talth and perhaps you were, greenly. But had she lived you might well despise her today. It happens. Affections have no place in this business. When you choose a wife you do not ask *Do I love this girl? You ask Is she born of a First Family? Can her bloodline strengthen our own? Has she enough to recommend her that I'll stiffen when it's needful she be planted with my son?* Those are the questions you must ask. Tell me that love answers any of them and then I'll listen to talk of *affections.*'

Morgan stared at his father. As well as stripping his flesh, illness had caused much of the old man's hair to shed, leaving him bald in spreading patches. His scalp was scaled and oozing, the rot defying Ranmer's many ointments. Even so, he'd refused to have his remaining hair clipped close. As though surrendering to the scissors was the same as surrendering to death.

'Did you ever love my mother?' he said, almost whispering.

'She stiffened me. It amounts to the same thing.'

He continued to stare, torn between revulsion and fascination.

*I loved my mother. I loved Luzena. I do not count that as a weakness. Did I never see this in you before, this cool, cruel detachment?*

No. Because not even one day in his life was he given cause to doubt his father's fervent love for him.

*And if you can love me, how could you not love the woman who birthed me?*

63

'You never remarried,' he said, cautious. 'I would ask you why not.'

His father shrugged. 'I had no need of a second wife. I had you.'

There was flattery in that, even though he was still disconcerted. 'And if I, like Luzena, had died untimely?'

'If that had happened I would have found another woman to bear me another son,' said his father. And then he frowned. 'Morgan, enough. You are years too old for giddy romanticism. Breeding the next generation of mages is a serious matter. Perhaps with Luzena you could indulge whimsy, but that time is gone. Let me speak plain: I want your word given to me, here and now, that aside from your Council duties your only concern will be the finding of your unborn son's mother.'

Before he could stop himself, his gaze flicked up as though it could penetrate every chamber between this dining room and his attic workroom.

'Your *experiments*?' With a grunting effort, his father levered himself to standing. 'Morgan, I *forbid* your experiments! Until I see you wed, and hard on your vow's heels learn of a son in the woman's belly, I tell you there will be no more magework in this house.'

'And I tell you there will be, my lord. When I was that green youth promised to Luzena then perhaps you could forbid me. But like Luzena, those days are long dead. You are my father and I honour you but do not presume to—'

'*Presume*?' Fresh spittle flecked his father's blanched lips. 'When I house you? Feed you? If there is presumption to speak of, Morgan, of a surety it is yours.'

'And there's a calumny, my lord,' he retorted. 'When I stay because you beg me not to leave, because you will not hear of me finding rooms in Elvado, when I stay because—'

'Because this is your home!' said his father, and thudded back into his chair. 'Where else would you live?'

Heart pounding, Morgan glared at him. 'I would live where no man thinks to forbid me my life's work.'

'Morgan . . . Morgan . . .' His father clasped trembling hands, each breath a wet whistling in and out of his soft lungs. His eyes were teary again. 'I spoke hastily.'

'My lord, you spoke from your heart.'

'Hastily and from my heart, yes,' his father admitted. 'I would not deny you your life's work, Morgan. Therein lies Danfey glory. But in pursuing it, would you deny me your heir?'

*How can I deny him anything when he looks so pale and poorly?*

'Of course not.'

'Then let us not quarrel,' his father said, beseeching. 'Let us instead make our own vows. You will choose yourself a wife before the leaves fall, and I will not plague you about antithetical incantations.'

He returned to the dinner table. 'Almost, but not quite. I will choose a wife, and you will *aid* me with my antithetical incantations. My lord, this quarrel started because I asked you to be my second set of eyes. Let us end it with you helping me put a finger on where my reworking of the transmutation sigils went awry.'

His father coughed, trying to hide his feelings. 'You would trust me so far?'

'My lord . . .' Morgan kissed his father's forehead. 'Talk nonsense like that and you'll have us quarrelling again.'

'No, no,' said his father hastily. 'That's behind us. Come. You can show me these newfangled sigils from the beginning.'

'Now? Perhaps now is too soon. Perhaps you should rest, then—'

'Talk nonsense like that and *you'll* have us quarrelling again,' said his father, mock-scolding this time. 'Enough, Morgan. I am not dying quite yet. Let us return to your attic and do magework together.'

# CHAPTER FIVE

But his father's strength was short-lived. Morgan was scarcely halfway through his explanation of the theory underpinning his brand new sigil and incant, being careful to gloss over certain aspects he knew would cause dismay, when the tremor marring the old man's hands spread throughout his frail body.

He set down his fresh crucible with its burden of rare and costly powdered *azafris*.

'My lord, perhaps we might continue this discourse on the morrow? Your lack of enthusiasm reproaches me for failing to remember that most basic rule: simplicity must form the foundation of all magework.'

A muted gleam in his father's eye told him the ruse was noted . . . and appreciated.

After escorting him back down the mansion's narrow attic staircase to the third floor landing, and from there to his privy suite of apartments, and seeing him reposed once more in the bed he should not have abandoned, Morgan made his way outside to clear his mind with fresh air.

*Why* had his reworking of Hartigan's sigil failed?

Strolling the mansion's immaculate garden, aware of servants' raised voices in the stables, of the temperature falling as rain clouds gathered overhead like a frown, of the fear he felt for his father ever-simmering beneath the surface, he dismantled his work step by painstaking step.

And could find no reason to explain the sigil's collapse.

*Which means what, exactly? That my father is right and there can be no compatible clockwise construction of the energies?*

No. He refused to accept that. Reversal of the primary energy conduits was key to his new transmutation incant. An incant that would make Sorvold's triumph seem paltry child's play. Only by *reversing* the natural inclination of the matrix's coherence could he hope to expand the effect of the transmutation itself. He was seeking to undo nature, after all. No timid tinkering would answer his need.

*Perhaps the fault lies in my choice of catalyst. Perhaps* azafris *does not best serve my purpose.*

And that would be unfortunate. Not only had he risked his standing on the Council to procure, by illicitly roundabout means, more than the sanctioned amount of the mineral, he'd been forced to sell his second-best horse to cover the cost. Besides, he was certain that *azafris* was the key ingredient in his new sigil's creation. Which could only mean that his error was in combining it with oil of *atlar.*

*Very well. A mistake easily unmade. But if not* atlar, *then what –*

A spit of water on his face. Startled, he looked up to see that the frown of clouds had become a black scowl. Thunder rumbled, shivering the chill, lightless air. Moments later a predatory wind roared through the dense woodland belting the family mansion's cultivated grounds. Branches whipped, leaves tore, and a few moments after that the neatly tended flowerbeds thrashed beneath the onslaught. Morgan laughed at the elemental savagery, the sudden raw, crackling power surrounding him.

And then the skies opened, pouring water, and he ran. Still laughing.

A simple incant took care of his rain-soaked attire. Returned to his attic workroom, with freshly conjured glimfire banishing the gloom, he again brooded over the question of his elusive new sigil as he took a soft cloth and wiped the three used crucibles clean of failure's blue smears. With that done, he cleansed them further with a neutralising incant.

*Balance. The catalyst and its counter-catalyst must balance. They must clear a path for the energies to combine. To overturn nature, first I must master it.*

At length he sighed, and nodded. So. He was ready.

A pinch of precious, dwindling *azafris*. No oil of *atlar* this time, but two meagre drops of *tilatantin*. The stink of it had him recoiling. He paused, then, to make certain his decision wasn't about to catch fire in his face. When there was no untoward reaction he continued, adding a pinch of powdered bone and finally a shaving of *urvil* root.

Nothing. Nothing. Then a shiver in each crucible as the catalytic ingredients began to interact.

Morgan closed his eyes, feeling the ecstatic tremble in his blood, that caress of power more seductive than a woman's touch. Trembling on his tongue, the harmonic syllables he'd devised to bridge the gap between dream and reality. To ignite creation.

'*Ravak tokai,*' he whispered, slowly dragging his fingertips through the quivering air above the crucibles. '*Ravak hinmish. Ravak vant*—'

A soundless boom. A flash of light. The catalytic inversion extinguished his glimfire, shattered the glass in the storm-lashed attic window and flung him into the far wall.

Sprawled on the floor with his dignity in tatters, blood trickling from his nose and his head ringing like a thousand hammered bells, he blinked into the attic's storm-wracked darkness.

'So,' he said, sounding as wheezy as his afflicted father. 'Not *tilatantin*. That's useful to know.'

When he could trust that his bones wouldn't splinter if he moved, he groped his way to sitting and conjured more glimfire. Even such a small burst of power flooded fresh blood from his nose. Relief gave way to anger.

*I am Morgan Danfey. I am better than this.*

He looked at his workbench, where all three crucibles lay in jagged pieces and his carefully hoarded supply of *azafris* smoked gently, perfuming the air.

Anger surrendered to despair.

*I might as well have broken the damned horse's neck.*

He kept the attic well warded, so no hint of the disaster had been felt in the mansion below. And the servants knew better than to disturb him while he worked. It meant he could protest his latest failure as loudly as he liked for as long as he liked.

And he did.

By the time he'd recovered his composure the wild storm had passed too, dissolving into a steady, reasonable fall of rain. Before he left the attic, he saw his notes on the working updated, the window repaired and the floor dried.

The mansion's discreet master servant greeted him at the foot of the central staircase. 'Sir,' Rumm murmured, proffering a folded parchment. 'This arrived while you were occupied above stairs.'

He knew what the message was, and who it was from, before he broke the plain wax seal and unfolded it.

*'Lord Greve Danfey's delicate condition notwithstanding, your presence is required in Council on the morrow.'*

The curt missive was signed only with an elaborate 'V.' Brice Varen, head of Dorana's Council of Mages, disdained any signature more elaborate, confident that all the world would know who he was by a single inked flourish. Morgan felt his lip curl.

*Such pretension.*

But pretentious or not, he was answerable to the man. And in truth he'd been expecting such a summons. He'd not set foot in the Hall of Knowledge since Winsun, the rippled consequences of Brahn Sorvold's untimely death handled without him. All of Dorana's recent mage business handled without him. The neglect couldn't continue. Any mage invited to sit on the Council accepted the appointment knowing full well that every other consideration must take a backwards step thereafter. In putting his father first for so many weeks he was trying not only Varen's limited patience, but the goodwill of his fellow councillors.

And with one exception, he'd not had much of that to start with.

'Has his lordship stirred, Rumm?' he said, refolding the note.

'He has not, sir.'

'Be attentive. I would be informed the instant he does.'

Rumm bowed. 'Sir.'

'I'll be in the library.'

Another bow. 'Shall I bring supper to you there?'

Morgan hesitated, then nodded. 'Something light. With a jug of strong red wine.' Because his nerves were still unsettled from his mishap with the *tilatantin*. 'In an hour.'

'One hour,' said Rumm, with a third and final punctilious bow. 'Yes, sir.'

His attic and the library: the two rooms of the mansion where he felt truly at home. The rest might as well not exist, were needed only to satisfy base, begrudged human urges for sleep, food and bathing.

Only his mansion of the mind had real value.

Slouched deep in a leather chair, surrounded by the collection of books he was transforming into the greatest arcane library in Dorana, he studied again the inflammatory words of Rubin Cylte.

*And if no way of doing a thing can be seen, still let the thing be attempted, that the way might be found. For many things done easily now were counted a challenge in their time. And many things done commonplace were once new and despised.*

Not a popular arcane philosopher, Cylte. Every so often there was a call to gather his books and pamphlets and treatises and have done with them once and for all. *Not bred in a First Family* was one popular refrain. *Unorthodox* was another. Both accusations were true. Cylte had been common and outrageous and had paid the price for both crimes, eventually. But in the sixty-odd years that had passed since the controversial mage's downfall, Morgan had found no greater voice lifted in praise of experimental magics. His father was unaware he'd purchased one of Cylte's rare books. There was no need for him to know, especially since knowing might well hasten him into the family crypt.

It was Cylte's ruminations on the reconfiguring of sigils that had inspired him to exchange dreaming for daring, and undertake a reworking of Hartigan's transmutation incant.

*For many things done easily now were counted a challenge in their time.*

Words to provide comfort when the work was not going as planned.

Cheered a little by the dead mage's encouragement, Morgan put that book aside and turned to his *Compendium of Catalysts*. Therein must lie the answer to his collapsing sigils. He had to find it. His was a First Family, but it wasn't first amongst the First. There were more illustrious names in Dorana than his. To be recognised, to become one day head of the Council, Dorana's most eminent mage, he had to make his mark. He had to be *seen* as the peerless mage he knew himself to be, no matter what more highly ranked mages hinted and winked at.

*I must be known as the greatest innovator in our history . . . and protect it from the dangers I alone seem to see.*

When Rumm brought him his supper he put aside the *Compendium* and ate, distracted, as he examined the question of the recalcitrant sigil. He remained convinced that *azafris* was the correct central catalyst. Very well, if oil of *atlar* was an incompatible counter-catalyst, and *tilatantin* was combustible, and *urvil* root wasn't strong enough to be effective, what did that leave him? *Frill* root, perhaps. Or possibly *susquinel*. Though that was a dangerous notion. The wretched stuff was almost as bad as *azafris*. Mishandled, it could do a careless mage real harm.

'I should leave the problem aside until the morrow, sir,' said Rumm, abruptly at his elbow. 'There's very little a sound night's sleep can't solve or mend.'

The man prowled like a cat, curse him. It would be unforgivable if he weren't indispensable. A Doranen like Rumm, born with little or no mage ability, was a sorry creature, forced into manual labours, farming and animal husbandry and cartering and the like, or to the serving of his betters. But by virtue of his dignity and wholly discreet efficiency, Rumm managed to serve yet still command a modicum of respect.

Morgan smiled at him. 'Perhaps you're right.'

'I have looked in on his lordship, sir,' said Rumm. 'He's sleeping comfortably enough. Though the hour advances, I am loath to wake him for a meal, most especially since his appetite today has been finicky. I expect it will be more robust come breakfast.'

'Do you?' he said, ready to rap the man's knuckles for lecturing. But the reprimand withered when he saw the sympathy in his servant's steady gaze. 'Yes. Well, if it's not, we must send to Ranmer for a remedy and let Lord Danfey kick as he will.'

Rumm collected the used plates and cutlery, the emptied wine jug and goblet. 'A note for the pother is already written, sir. But I trust it will not be required. Shall I bring you a brandy nightcap, or do you now retire?'

'What time is it?' he said, glancing at the betrothal clock on the library fireplace mantel. A gift from Luzena, dainty and delicate, as she had been. 'Not so very late. I have an hour's more reading in me.'

'An hour's extra rest would be more to the purpose,' said Rumm, blunter than usual. 'Or when next I send to Ranmer he'll be coming to tend you. Sir.'

'I see.' Prickled between amusement and offence, Morgan raised an eyebrow. 'You presume to order my affairs, Rumm?'

'Sir, I presume to do my duty,' Rumm replied, unmoved. 'I serve the Danfey family in all things.'

He waved a hand. 'Then serve it now by bringing me a snifter of brandy.'

'Sir.'

But Rumm was right. With the brandy glowing in his belly, and the relentless anxiety for his father joining with his day's arcane failures to brew a pain behind his eyes, Morgan found the words of the *Compendium* swimming like fish on the pages. Defeated, he closed the book. But before retiring, he stopped to check on his father. The old man's wheezing filled his bedchamber with a bitter song of slow decay.

Stranded in the open doorway, summoned glimfire showing him the truth he'd pretended to accept and now couldn't escape, Morgan felt a wave of grief crash over him, stripping him of years. He was a small boy again, losing his mother, adrift in a world grown cold and cruel. His heart boomed in his chest like a tolling funeral bell. Greve Danfey was yet a young man, as the mages of Dorana counted time. Brice Varen could give him ten years and he remained hale, hearty and spry. Why should that not be so for the sleeping man before him?

*Lord Danfey wants a grandson? Very well. I shall give him one. Then he'll have no reason to die.*

On the morrow, leaving Rumm with strict instructions to keep a close eye on his lordship, who was yet to wake, he rode to Elvado. Of course he could have used a travel incant. Doubtless someone on the Council would say he should have, but the simple fact was that he enjoyed riding in the open air. His stallion was blood-bred and spirited, the sky brightly blue, the rain-washed fields beyond the estate's woodland fragrant with hedge flowers. The country road he travelled was empty, save for himself, its sun-warmed solitude welcome. It was a glorious morning, and in its glory he could forget, for a short time, the shadow-filled mansion behind him, forget yesterday's arcane disappointments, and think instead of the solemn vow that he'd taken. That he meant to keep, on his honour.

Only to give his father a grandson he must first take a wife, and quickly. But Luzena was the only wife he'd ever wanted. Could some other girl's pretty face and pleasing body obliterate enough of her memory that he would stiffen, as his father crudely put it, to the purpose of making a son?

*It will have to. Or else I will have to alchemy Luzena out of memory and into my bed even as my yet-unchosen wife lies beneath me.*

A repugnant thought. Sullied by the prospect, he felt his spirits sink. His blood-bred stallion shied at shadows, feeling the shift in his temper. With an effort he banished misgivings. His father was right: the Danfey name must live on.

'Forgive me,' he said to the warm, fresh air, and touched fingertips to the gold locket he wore always, next to his skin. It contained his love's portrait, her likeness to the life. 'But I have a duty and an oath to uphold.'

He thought he heard her voice in the up-springing breeze. Thought he felt her lips in the sunlight kissing his face.

*Luzena.*

Elvado was an hour's brisk ride from the Danfey mansion's front door. Clattering along the bustling city's wide, central thoroughfare, his stallion's shod hooves cheerful on the cobbles, Morgan felt his mood lift again. Home to every brilliant mage ever born, Elvado was the gentle, genteel beating heart of magic. The safekeeping and pursuit of arcane knowledge was its purpose. Magic was soaked into the beautiful city's bones. He loved it as passionately as ever he loved Luzena.

There was no stabling at the Hall of Knowledge, so he left his stallion in a private livery yard and completed his journey on foot. Every passerby who noticed the Council insignia pinned to his blue silk brocade lapel acknowledged his authority with a bow or a smile. He recognised them with a raised eyebrow, nothing more. Dignity and distance were the hallmarks of the Council. The insignia ensured no conversation occurred without he was the instigator, an arrangement that could be trusted to prevent any public unpleasantness.

Reaching the central plaza, he paused before its beautiful fountain and laughed without restraint at the day's water-trickery, rainbowed dolphins leaping and dancing. Childishly entranced, he lingered longer than he should. But then the sonorous chiming of the city's grand clock recalled him to his obligations.

'Morgan,' said Brice Varen, glancing up from the scattering of papers and unrolled parchment on the Council chamber's table. 'How does your father prosper?'

74

'Well enough, my lord,' he replied, waving the imposing door closed behind him. Councillor or not, he wasn't free to make free with Varen's given name. He was not yet a lord himself and was decades too young, besides. 'My thanks to you for asking.'

Varen indicated the Council table's last empty chair. 'Sit. As you can see we have been waiting for you.'

The words were said mildly enough, but beneath them he felt the slap of censure. So he humbly took his seat beside Venette Martain, nodded to Sallis Arkley and Shari Frieden, and with his fellow councillors waited at Varen's pleasure. Stained-glass light washed over table and floor, painting their faces motley and turning their soberly rich clothes garish.

'First order of business,' Varen said, his spine straight, his hands neatly folded, 'is a matter referred to us by the General Council. Do we sanction the establishment of a second trade fair?'

'And the request comes from . . .?' said Shari, slender fingers idly playing with her long blonde plait.

As usual, she sat beside Sallis. Two mages, one thought . . . and never was it friendly. Not where Morgan Danfey was concerned.

'The Iringans,' said Varen. He half smiled, his seamed face wolfish. 'They claim Brantone is too great a distance to travel for those not blessed with mage powers.'

'It is a goodly distance from Iringa to Brantone,' Sallis agreed. 'And in principle I have no objection to the notion of further commerce. Any expansion of trade must benefit our coffers.'

Morgan hesitated, then raised a cautioning hand. 'Unless there are those behind the request who would halve our profits by doubling the availability of what we sell. We should remember, Lord Arkley, that our neighbours love our magework. They do not love us.'

'How cynical you are, Morgan,' said Venette, slyly grinning. 'Mind you, I'd trust my housemaid with the key to my treasury box before an Iringan with a small purse only part-full of cuicks.'

'Cynical or not, Morgan is correct,' said Shari, and looked unhappy admitting it. 'Don't forget that only last month the

General Council had to impose sanctions on Feen for attempting to evade tariff collections. If we let them, these magickless nations will ride over us roughshod.'

'But if it can be shown that a second trade fair would benefit Dorana,' Sallis said, 'then the General Council can tell the Iringans we'll approve one in Manemli, say, provided certain fiscal conditions are met.'

Venette's nose wrinkled. 'Not Manemli. They have unsavoury practices.'

'So do others we truck with,' said Shari. 'But I haven't noticed any taint on their coin. Have you?'

At fifty-two, Venette was some nine years younger than Shari Frieden, but that never stopped her from standing her ground.

'If this is to be a unanimous decision, it won't be reached with my vote if Manemli is not discarded.'

All eyes turned to Varen. He rubbed a finger across his age-pinched lips, in no hurry to offer an opinion. But at length he swept the table with his cool grey gaze.

'You bicker particulars while o'erleaping the first hurdle. The question before us is whether a second trade fair is desirable at all. Brantone will not want it.'

Morgan sat back. 'I don't support a second trade fair, but nor do I think we can bend our knee to Brantone. We must not be trammelled by our inferiors.'

Varen's stare was dispassionate. 'Brantone is a loyal friend to Dorana. It hosts the summer trade fair to our great advantage. A second fair would trammel them, Morgan.'

'My lord, we speak of Dorana's sovereignty. Nothing is more important than that.'

Beneath the table, Venette pressed her foot to his in warning. In the five months since his elevation to the Council she had more than once slipped a steadying hand beneath his elbow. Such a shame she had no daughter to tempt him. Her bloodline was exemplary, but she'd failed to produce children.

'I fear you betray your greenness, Morgan,' said Varen, disapproving. 'To be magickless is not to be without value entirely.

For myself, I have no interest in pandering to the Iringans. They spend nowhere near enough at the summer trade fair for us to risk slighting Brantone. Let them prove with plentiful coin their great need of Doranen magework, and then we might consider another fair. Agreed?'

One by one the others nodded. But did they truly agree or did they only pander to Varen? Looking at their faces, Morgan couldn't tell. But, mindful of his precarious position, reluctantly he nodded too.

'Excellent,' said Varen. 'I shall so inform Chief Councillor Lady Brislyn.' He glanced at his notes. 'She also made mention of trouble brewing between Manemli and Ranoush. It seems the dispute is seeded in our trade route, which travels to Ranoush first, by way of Brantone. Manemli is claiming we give preference to both Brantone and Ranoush, meaning they are left to pick over the leavings. This is making them openly resentful. A handful of our trader-mages have reported Manemlin hostility.'

Venette looked at Shari. 'I told you Manemli was trouble.'

'Hostility, my lord?' Morgan frowned. 'Do you mean bloodletting?'

'Between Manemli and Ranoush, yes,' said Varen. 'Our traders have been jeered at, nothing more.'

Chilled with apprehension, he shifted in his chair. 'Nothing more yet. But—'

'*But?*' Sallis laughed, scornful. 'What's wrong with you, Morgan? You can't be suggesting any mage of Dorana is in peril from a Manemlin!'

'From anyone,' said Shari, just as scornful. 'We are *mages*, Morgan. Inviolate.'

There was no use pursuing the matter. Even if he tried to explain his growing unease, a sense that some danger crept closer to Dorana, his fellow councillors would never believe him.

*But I trust that feeling. I know I am right.*

'True, Shari,' said Varen, 'but I'll inform the General Council we will permit Dorana's trader-mages stronger wardings, should tensions rise. Now, to the question of age limits with regards to tertiary-level incantations . . .'

The meeting continued. Not the smallest question of complaint or clarification regarding magework in Dorana failed to be considered by the Council of Mages. Let the General Council truck with commonplace laws and tax collection and civil infringements and foreign ructions and the like. The Council of Mages dealt with far loftier matters.

They confirmed the tertiary-level incant age at twelve; amended the statute dealing with legal recourse for non-Doranen individuals suffering hardship as a result of magework; approved in principle the new syllabus for parochial mage education – pending commentary from the College of Mages, which was jealous of its private educational purviews; extended the temporary prohibition placed upon the sale of mage-enhanced fireworks until the investigation into the destruction of the artisanry at Nyecroft was completed; and drafted a formal letter of censure to one Marale Chasin, an unranked mage who was overheard by four witnesses criticising the Council's recent decision to deny marriage rights to those unfortunate Doranen afflicted with a lack of mage talent.

'And so to our last item of business,' said Varen. 'The College's proctor has received a letter regarding student admission. Given the sensitive nature of this request, he referred the matter to Lord Hahren and Hahren is now referring it to us.'

'Sensitive how?' said Sallis, stifling a yawn. He was only a year or three behind Varen, and lacking in stamina.

Varen consulted his notes. 'The mage in question, one Barl Lindin, is unranked. She's a clock mage in the Eleventh district hamlet of Batava.'

Venette snorted. 'She's an optimist, you mean.'

'So it would seem. She applied to the College several years ago and was refused. According to Hahren she now says—' Again, Varen consulted his notes. '"I am sure that once the College is made familiar with my mageworking abilities it will reconsider my application and offer me a place."'

'I take it back,' said Venette, laughing. 'She's not an optimist, she's an upstart. Tell Hahren to tell her to seek a parochial remedy for her woes. There are mage schools aplenty for the unranked of Dorana. They can't possibly begrudge us a single school of our own.'

'And if they do complain, that's no cause for us to listen,' Shari added. 'Jealousy's not to be rewarded.'

Muttered agreement from Sallis Arkley. With a slight, appreciative smile, Varen shifted his gaze. 'Your thoughts, Morgan?'

He shrugged. 'I think this young woman must be touched in the head. *Lindin.* Have we even heard of the family?'

'No,' Sallis said briskly. 'And after today never shall again.' He pushed to his feet. 'I have my own business with Hahren. Shall I tender him our opinion?'

Varen's pale eyebrows lifted. 'You think to withdraw?'

'We're done here, aren't we?'

'I have not formally said so.'

'Then formally say so, Brice. Or continue without me. I cannot tarry.'

'We are concluded,' said Varen, after the briefest hesitation. 'And by all means, Lord Arkley, inform Hahren of our decision.'

'You should excuse him,' said Shari Frieden, once Sallis was safely out of hearing. 'There's trouble with his youngest.'

Nodding, Varen collected his various papers. 'I have heard something of it. He'd do well to curb the boy. First Family or not, Peynten will be brought before a justice if he cannot control his wayward impulse to wreak havoc.'

'I've heard none of this,' said Morgan to Venette, his voice lowered, while Varen and Shari widened their censure of Dorana's youth. 'Enlighten me.'

Venette's rings flashed in the sunlight as she playfully tapped his forearm. 'A regrettable prank run out of hand. A boy from an unranked family is left disfigured, and the father is making a great deal of fuss.'

'Is he not entitled to?'

'Of course,' said Venette. 'But whether it's wise is another matter. After all, the boy's not dead. Tell me, Morgan dear, if you've unburied yourself from the Danfey estate does that mean I can entice you to an informal dinner party this evening? Excellent food and wine, pleasing company.' Her flashing fingers stroked his sleeve. 'Say you'll come.'

He thought of his ailing father and opened his mouth to refuse. Then he recalled, again, his promise.

*No grandson to give him, without first I find a wife.*

'Informal, you say?'

Venette smiled, revealing wicked dimples. Unlike most Doranen women she wore her hair cropped daringly short. She'd even been known to streak strands of copper colour through it, though today it was uniformly gold.

'Just a few friends. We serve drinks at seven, and after dinner there'll be dancing. Do come. You deserve a little respite from care.'

Having abandoned their disapproving duet, Lord Varen and Shari Frieden were looking ready to depart the chamber. Morgan slid from his chair and offered Venette a flourishing bow.

'My lady, I shall attend with pleasure.'

'Morgan,' said Varen, his papers and parchments tucked under one arm. 'You'd do well to convey my best wishes to Lord Danfey.'

This time his bow was much more restrained. Brice Varen was largely the reason for his father being denied a place on the Council of Mages. Sentiments like that flirted with hypocrisy.

'My lord, he'll be heartened to know you're thinking of him.'

A glitter in Varen's eyes suggested disbelief. 'His illness must be a source of sorrow to all, but you have wider duties, Morgan. It's past time you resumed them.'

'I assure you, my lord, I am ready to play my part in Council matters.'

'Indeed,' said Varen, with the thinnest of smiles. 'Then I shall give close thought to how best we can use you.'

He offered another bow. 'My lord, I serve at your pleasure.'

'And you do, you know, Morgan,' said Venette, once they were alone. 'You should also know that two days ago, Shari and Sallis argued for your suspension.'

The news made him stare. 'On what grounds?'

'Dereliction, of course,' she said, sighing. 'But Brice saved you.'

*Varen* did? He found that surprising.

'My dear,' Venette added, shaking her head. 'For a brilliant man you can be tiresomely obtuse. They hide it well because they have to, but there's no love lost between Sallis and Shari and Brice. Did you think our esteemed Council leader feuded only with your father?'

'I had my suspicions. But as you say, there are many hidden truths in Doranen society.'

She tapped his arm again. 'Well, here's one truth that should be apparent. Brice has decided to shield you, a little, doubtless out of guilt for the damage done to Greve when they were both much younger men. But if you think he'll go on shielding you while you blatantly ignore your duties then you are *so* obtuse you're long past saving.'

Venette knew the story? How unfortunate. 'I didn't realise that sorry tale was bandied about as common knowledge.'

Venette's lips pursed. 'Climb down, Morgan. It's not. All I know is that many years ago, Brice behaved badly, Greve was unwise in his response, and so found himself in no position to quibble when he was slighted. But Brice's lingering guilt won't prick him much deeper. So take heed, my dear. How far you rise now is up to you. And when the day comes that you're the next Lord Danfey there'll be no excuses made for you by anyone.'

He raised an eyebrow. 'Not even you?'

'Not even me. I have my own family to consider.'

'I see,' he said, feeling his temper stir. 'My thanks, Venette, for your solicitous care.'

'Now, now, Morgan.' She patted his cheek, her fingers cool, her smile not quite touching her violet eyes. 'Are there so many brilliant, handsome young mages in Elvado that I would wish to see one retire to the country in disgrace? Hardly. For if you are disgraced, who will I turn to when I'm pining for company at dinner?'

Taking her hand lightly in his, he kissed the soft, scented skin over her knuckles. 'Your husband?'

'Ah.' Now her smile was pouting. 'It seems I've irked you.'

'Not at all, Lady Martain,' he said, releasing her. 'Forgive me if I made you think otherwise.'

'That means I shall still see you tonight?'

Of course, if there was any way he could use her to his advantage. 'Yes.'

This time she kissed his cheek. Her breath fanned his skin, warmly. 'Until seven, then.'

'Venette,' he said, as she reached the chamber door. 'One last thing. Your advice on a matter of magework.'

She turned in a swirl of crimson velvet skirt. 'Certainly.'

'What would you say is the most effective counter-catalyst in sigil working?'

'*Tilatantin*,' she said, without hesitation.

'And the second?'

A small line appeared between her brows as she thought. '*Risill*. Or possibly *urvil*.'

'Not *susquinel*?'

Venette frowned a little deeper. 'Only were I working with *azafris*. Morgan, you're not thinking to work with *azafris*, are you? Legal or not, the stuff is frowned upon, you know, and quite ruinously expensive. Not to mention easily offended. As for *susquinel*, it's nearly as tricky. I'd not see you hurt, my dear, nor your Council standing diminished. Not for the purpose of impressing Sallis and Shari.'

He laughed. 'Venette, the notion of impressing them could not be further from my mind.'

'Well, good,' she said, uncertain. 'But do think twice before you dance with dangerous catalysts. I enjoy your company and would not be deprived of it betimes.'

And on that gently scolding note, she slipped from the room.

As a member of the Council he was entitled to remain in its privy chamber for as long as he liked, in or out of company. So he moved to the nearest intricate stained-glass window and stared down into the plaza, then out across the city. Feeling an odd sense of ownership, as though Elvado had been built for him . . . and him alone. A shiver whispered over his skin, hinting at shadows and peril, at dark days yet to come. He felt his heart thud, felt his body brace as though expecting a blow.

*Never fear, my beloved city. So long as I am breathing, no harm shall come to you.*

# CHAPTER SIX

'She's rather pretty, isn't she?'

Caught staring at the young mage on the far side of the dance floor, Morgan shrugged to hide his irritation. Took a restrained sip of icewine. 'She's acceptable.'

Venette plucked a glass of icewine for herself from a passing servant's tray. Though she claimed the evening was informal, she'd taken great pains with her appearance. But then she always did, being gloriously vain and unashamed of her wealth. The rubies bound to her brow were the finest Trindek would part with, their hue the rich red of heart's blood. Her flowing tunic was fashioned from Feenish gossamer silk, its myriad shades of green vibrant as new spring.

'Acceptable?' she said. 'That's a trifle ungenerous, Morgan.'

What game was Venette playing now? 'You asked my opinion, and I gave it.'

Standing by his side, fingers lightly touching his elbow, Venette leaned closer. 'My dear . . .' Her voice was lowered, even though the ballroom musicians in their gallery were playing loudly enough to mask her words. 'You are too particular. Maris Garrick is entirely presentable.'

He spared Venette a tight smile. 'I must bow to your superior judgement, since ogling women is not a regular pastime with me.'

'Now you're being deliberately unpleasant,' she said, pouting, and pinched him. 'Stop it.'

Dinner concluded, Venette and her stolid husband Orwin had invited their guests to the ballroom, where they might continue the evening's entertainment and make amends for the sumptuous five-course meal they'd so eagerly consumed.

Having eaten sparingly, in no mood to dance, Morgan had flirted with the notion of excusing himself for home. There was just enough *azafris* left for him to make one last attempt at creating his new sigil, this time using *susquinel* as the primary catalyst. With such a momentous achievement in the balance, the thought of wasting the rest of the night in empty frivolity grated.

But then Venette had looked at him, eyebrows raised. *Leaving, Morgan? I don't think so.* Which, of course, meant he'd stayed. It would have been impolitic to do anything else.

On the dance floor, four glimlit couples swirled through the lilting music. Their constant motion meant he played hide-and-seek with demure Maris Garrick, neatly wrapped in cream and gold brocade and slender as a lily. He thought her shy smile hinted at secrets. Intriguing.

'She's scarcely more than a child, Venette,' he said, angry with himself for being stirred. 'She's escorted here by her parents, for pity's sake. Do you think I'm a cradle-snatcher?'

'No, my dear,' said Venette, serene. 'I think you're a man in search of a wife.'

Like the Garricks, her husband stood on the far side of the dance floor. Since he was in close conversation with Stim and Harele Boqur, it was safe to show a snarling face to Orwin's bride.

'Venette, I'll thank you to mind your business while I mind mine. Indeed, if Maris Garrick is to be so highly recommended, allow me to recommend that you snare her for your eldest nephew.'

Instead of scolding, or taking offence, Venette laughed then swallowed a generous mouthful of wine. 'My dear, you snap at flies. Tobe was matched before he learned to walk. Now do stop being tiresome. I know how much you resent anyone dabbling in your privy affairs but I don't do it to hurt you. I'm your friend, and you should listen to my excellent advice.'

'Your excellent nagging,' he muttered, and emptied his own glass. He wanted to glare at her, but found his gaze tugged back to Maris Garrick. Even as he stared at the girl, his fingers found the shape of his locket, buttoned safe beneath his dark purple brocade tunic. 'Why should I think this Garrick daughter will suit me?'

'Aside from the fact that I tell you she will?' Venette sighed. 'Morgan, if I weren't so fond of you I believe I'd be quite cross. Maris has exemplary magework, she is sweet and biddable, and her family is more highly ranked than yours. Indeed, my dear, for those very reasons were she not a pretty girl I would still push you toward her.'

But Maris Garrick was pretty, he couldn't deny it. There'd be no hardship in bedding her. Add that to her social standing and surely his father would approve.

'You think my place on the Council overcomes the delicate matter of unequal family ranking?'

'That, and the fact you'll soon enough be Lord Danfey,' said Venette, her painted lips curved in a small cat smile. Then she raised a finger. 'No biting, Morgan. Palatable or not, it's the truth. Turn down your suit and she'll be some years waiting for another chance to become Lady Maris. The marriage market is at present scanty.'

It was also humiliating.

*I can't do this. Am I stallion for parading? Is that girl a mare in heat? There is no dignity here, no honour. We barter titles and fertility like hawkers from Ranoush.*

Sickened, he turned away from the dance floor where six couples now jigged like giggling children set free from the nursery. No dignity there, either.

'Morgan.' Venette's scolding tone was softened. 'This distresses you. I am sorry. I know you long for Luzena by your side and your father hale and hearty, no thought of crypting him for years. Alas, like poor Luzena, that dream is dead. My dear, let it go.'

He looked at the hand she'd let rest on his arm. 'Why do you embroil yourself in my troubles?'

'Because your mother was like a sister to me,' she said simply, and let her hand drop. 'Besides. If I don't, who will?'

'I can find my own wife.'

'I never said you couldn't. But isn't my way more convenient? Why quibble over *fribbles*, Morgan?'

'Because I've learned that little in our magic-charmed lives is free,' he said, prepared for once to let her see behind his careful mask. 'Everything I've achieved I have worked for, very hard. I've had to. The Danfeys are only ranked middling high. In the past year I've submitted six incants for Council ratification. The one I've had sanctioned I was forced to resubmit twice, three were dismissed out of hand and two are yet pending, even now.'

The musicians in the gallery finished their jig with a lively flourish, then shifted smoothly into the warning *ta-ta-ta* that heralded a rantina, the stately, patterned measure taught to every child old enough to walk without a nurse. On the dance floor the smiling, breathless guests broke out of their close couplings and took their places. Abandoning Venette's husband, Stim and Harele Boqur joined them.

'I hope,' said Venette, as the musicians launched into the rantina proper, 'you don't blame me for that. I am no paragon of virtue, nor have ever claimed to be, but not for any reason, petty or grand, do I play parlour games with another mage's lifework.'

She sounded genuinely hurt, and it wasn't what he'd intended. 'Of course I don't. You've always been my steadfast supporter. It's Sallis Arkley and Shari Frieden behind it, I know.'

'Morgan . . .' Venette stared at him, frowning. 'You do

understand *why* Sallis and Shari delay a decision on your patents? They seek to keep you uncertain, and in doing so control you. Because your talent is such that once it has fully flowered, your ranking won't matter.'

It was odd, hearing his suspicions confirmed. 'And how do you suggest I counter their strategy?'

'With patience, of course,' she said, impatient, glass lifted to her lips. 'You seem to have forgotten that time is on your side.'

No, he'd not forgotten. He was just tired of waiting.

'I'm sorry,' he said, forcing a smile. 'I thought I was fit for polite company, but clearly my temper remains uncertain. I'll excuse myself to Orwin and—'

'No, you won't,' she said, catching his sleeve. 'Not when the Garricks promised to be here in the hope I'd convinced you to come.'

Surprised, he let her keep hold of him. 'Maris's parents pursue the match?'

She made no effort to hide her gently scornful amusement. 'Morgan, don't pretend to a modesty we both know you lack. You're not unwed because you're unweddable. You might only be singly patented, but that's more than most mages will ever achieve. Add to that your Council appointment and the fact you were chosen to stand in for Brahn Sorvold at Winsun and, well, take my word for it. You are eminently eligible. So ask Maris to dance. If you should take her in dislike there's no need to think of her further. But if she doesn't instantly repel you, then perhaps tonight might be the start of a new and happier chapter in your life.'

'A life in which I find myself in your debt?'

'I don't recall claiming to be an *altruist*, Morgan,' she said, with her sly grin. 'I'm expecting you to name at least *one* child after me.'

She was beautiful and polished, like the rubies bound to her brow. He shook his head, smiling. 'Without considering my wife-to-be's opinion on the matter?'

'Naturally.' She plucked his empty glass from his fingers then gave him a little push. 'Now off you go, and don't stint on your charm. Because you can be terribly charming when it suits you, Morgan.'

The rantina was drawing to its elegant conclusion. Making his way around the edge of the dance floor, watching the dancers dip and sidestep and turn, he was jolted by a memory. The night he'd asked Luzena to wed him. They'd attended the new year's ball in Elvado, with the city's central plaza glimlit and turned into a fantastic outdoor ballroom. Deeply in love, they'd danced the rantina around the fountain with two hundred other ranked mages. He could still feel her hand in his, see the delight in her as the mageworked water formed itself into a couple and danced the rantina with them. He remembered her joyous laughter, and then the warm press of her lips on his as she breathed *yes* into his soul.

Maris Garrick was watching him. Not boldly, she wasn't brazen, but her gaze was on him just the same. Her softly rounded cheeks were tinted becomingly pink. Some womanly art had touched colour to her lips, to her eyelids, and darkened her long lashes. Her silver-gilt hair was coaxed into shining waves, fixed with jewel-studded gold pins. She was more than acceptable, more than merely pretty. She wasn't Luzena, but he couldn't blame her for that.

Halting before her, he bowed. 'Mage Garrick. I must remember to scold Venette later. She neglected to seat us side by side at dinner.'

The glint in her eye suggested that Maris Garrick only pretended primness. 'Am I to be flattered, Councillor Danfey, or defend our hostess?'

He glanced across the dance floor to Venette, who was flirting now with Illim Terenz. He and his sister, Jeen, who'd been dancing with Reb Flory, weren't First Family, but their theatre works were renowned throughout Dorana and even in Brantone. Such success made it possible to wink at their lack of ranking, justify their inclusion at the most exclusive gatherings . . . and excuse their occasional, inevitable social lapses.

'Venette needs no defending by anyone, Mage Garrick,' he said, faintly smiling. 'And I am more likely to need protection from her.'

'In that case, I'll be flattered,' said Maris Garrick. 'Lady Martain told you my name?'

'She told me if I came to dinner this evening I'd not be disappointed. She was right.' He looked at the girl's parents, discreetly watching from a distance. 'This is an informal gathering. How strict should I be in observing the protocols?'

'I think you might now call me Maris. And I will call you Morgan.' Maris Garrick's gaze lowered, modestly. 'Unless of course you'd find such familiarity offensive.'

Having taken a short break after the rantina, the musicians were returned to their pipes and drums and strings. A brief trill announced the next dance, a leisurely glide.

Morgan held out his hand. 'On the contrary. It delights me. Maris, shall we dance?'

They joined another five couples and let the music sweep them in lazy circles across the ballroom floor. Blotting out memory, he held Maris close, but not too close, and was pleased to find that she was graceful on her feet.

'How old are you?' he said, breathing in her floral perfume.

She had the palest green eyes, like rain-washed peridot. They narrowed, just a little. 'Old enough that I'm ready to submit my first incant to the Council.'

Disappointment pricked. 'And is that why you dance with me? You wish to dance me into sanctioning an incant of your devising?'

'If you thought me that kind of girl,' she said, comfortable in his arms, 'you never would've asked me to dance.'

'My dear Maris.' He gave her a bladed smile. 'I have no idea what kind of girl you are. Until tonight I never knew you existed.'

Which wasn't entirely true, since he'd long since made it his business to know a little of every First Family who lived in Elvado. But it was true enough. Beyond the fact of her existence, she was a complete stranger.

Now there was a combative tilt to the girl's chin. 'I am

nineteen, sir. But do not be deceived by my tender years. Though I do not attend the College I am yet counted a talent and will receive my Council patent with or without your vote on the matter. You should also know that I am sound in mind and limb and understand that you are on the hunt for a wife.'

He felt a pang of unease. *Nineteen. So young. She is almost half my age.* And she knew he needed to marry. Curse Venette and her meddling.

'I see. Tell me, Maris, are you on the hunt for a husband?'

She shrugged. 'My parents want me to be. For myself, I am . . . open to possibilities.'

A saucy answer. Sweet and biddable? This girl had the world hoodwinked. Interested almost despite himself he smiled again, more warmly. 'Are you ambitious?'

'Yes,' she said, bluntly unapologetic as they glided around the dance floor. 'Does that offend you?'

'I'd be offended if you weren't. What is it you want out of life, Maris?'

This time she smiled at him, brilliantly. 'Everything. Don't you?'

The music ended, ending their dance. When the musicians struck up again, he frowned. 'Do you care to jig?'

'Not particularly,' she said, careless. 'Disappointed?'

Raising her hand, he touched his lips to her skin, lightly, making sure to look directly into her eyes.

'No.'

She smiled again, cattish, like Venette. 'Neither am I.'

To his surprise, her parents took to the dance floor as he and Maris abandoned it. Noticing, she laughed.

'I made them promise not to haunt me. You should know the prospect of your interest has them all aflutter.'

'And you, Maris? Are you aflutter too?'

'I am flattered, Morgan,' she said, after a moment. 'And not displeased. If you feel we have made a promising start, and would like to see me again, then arrangements can be made. Through my parents, of course.'

He started to give Maris the answer she was expecting, then stopped. Of a sudden he felt crowded. Manipulated. From the corner of his eye he could see Venette, watching them, an almost smugly satisfied look on her face.

'Maris—'

'The decision's not entirely yours, you know,' she said sharply. 'It's not enough that you find me acceptable. I must be sure about you as well. But if you're already convinced that we could never suit, then this was an amusing diversion and nothing more.'

Her self-possession was attractive. Women who clung and simpered annoyed him. 'I would not make any important decision based upon one dance and a little banter. If I said the prospect of another encounter was not unpleasant, would that please you?'

Maris's eyes warmed. 'How could it not?'

He couldn't deny it felt good to be desired. A long time had passed since he'd held a woman so close, breathed in her scent, seen attraction in her eyes.

*All the more reason to tread with care.*

He shifted backwards, just slightly. 'It is only fair to caution you, though, Maris. My father, Lord Danfey, is not well. In doing my duty to him I have been forced to set aside important Council matters, which must now be addressed.'

'I understand,' she said, nodding. 'And I would not presume to make demands. Shall we agree that we might fall once more into company some time within the next week or two?'

He kissed her hand again. 'That sounds most agreeable. I look forward to getting to know you better, Maris, as soon as my duties permit. Now, alas, I must depart.'

She curtsied. He bowed. Then he watched her retreat to the ballroom's elegant sideboard of refreshments.

'Well?' said Venette, as he joined her. 'Did I not say you'd be well entertained?' She smoothed his sleeve. 'Shall you be seeing Maris again?'

Remembering that smug look, he decided to punish her a little. 'Perhaps.'

She pouted, knowing full well what he was doing. 'I give you fair warning, Morgan. The Garricks and I are friends. So don't dally with the girl. If you find your heart's engaged, or even if you think it might be, well and good. But if you think to wed her falsely, then I shall be most unamused.'

As if he would, knowing how poorly Luzena would count him for trifling with an innocent, no matter how saucy she might play herself.

'And I consider myself warned,' he said, with a pretended lightness. 'Thank you for tonight, Venette. Though it pains me to admit it, you weren't wrong. I did need a light-hearted evening.'

'I know you did,' she retorted. 'I'm a mage with two eyes and I see clearly with both of them. Morgan—' She frowned, ill at ease. 'You're not really troubled by those pending incants, are you?'

It had been a mistake to let the mask slip. 'I scarcely think of them.'

'Good. Because you shouldn't. Besides, Sallis and Shari are the past. Young mages like you and Maris are our future. Remember that. And remember what I said about *azafris* and *susquinel*. After what happened to Brahn Sorvold, I don't like to think of you experimenting. The risk is hardly worth it. I know you're ambitious, Morgan. It's not a bad thing. But you mustn't be greedy, or take unnecessary chances. Dorana needs you.'

She had irked and humiliated him this night, though she'd meant to do neither. But any lingering resentment he felt faded in the face of her genuine concern. Leaning close, he kissed her cheek.

'You have my word, Venette, that my eyes shall never grow larger than my appetite. Nor shall ambition leap me into danger. And on that note, I bid you farewell. Enjoy what remains of your party. And don't trouble yourself. I can find my own way out.'

Although Venette's husband was still present, and in theory his host, he felt no need to do more than nod and smile at Orwin as he departed. He could feel Maris Garrick's following gaze on him, but he didn't look back.

Reaching the street on which stood Venette and Orwin's town house, he paused to breathe in the cool, sweet night air. The hour was late, with the moon risen high and distant amid a beguiling scatter of stars. Not even the lampposts with their small glimfire crowns could dim the diamond-bright vista. Much of Elvado's most exclusive residential district was sleeping. He listened, but could hear no carrying voices or creak of carriage wheels with clattering hooves on the cobbles. Faint strains of dance music drifted from Venette's ballroom. Fainter still, he caught a hint of other music playing. Perhaps it came from the concert hall. Was there a performance tonight? He had no idea. He'd long ago lost track of such transitory diversions, though once he'd enjoyed them very much.

*And will I enjoy them again, with Maris Garrick beside me? Or am I doomed to play the gallant husband with some other acceptable girl?*

Assuming, of course, that one could be found. He had no idea of that, either, and abruptly realised he didn't care. He was tired of thinking about it. He'd do what he must, for his father, for their family, but for now he'd done more than enough fretting over women.

As easily as breathing, he ignited three sigils, spoke the required words of power, stepped through his conjured portal . . . and out again, at the mansion.

'Welcome home, sir,' said Rumm, punctilious in the glimlit foyer. 'I trust you passed a pleasant evening?'

'Pleasant enough,' Morgan replied, heading for the mansion's sweeping staircase.

Though he could easily have manifested directly in his attic workroom, his father did not care for such casual comings and goings. A man of breeding, he said, considered the master servant's position. In any good establishment the master servant was at all times kept apprised of his gentlemen's whereabouts.

'I'll be upstairs, Rumm,' he added. 'And I don't wish to be disturbed.'

'No, sir,' said Rumm. 'But I'm asked to ask you to stop by his lordship's room upon your return.'

Hand on the staircase's carved banister, he hesitated. 'It's late. I'll see him in the morning, and be sure to let him know you passed on his request.'

'Less a request, sir, than a command,' said Rumm, taking a step after him. 'If you'll forgive my plain speaking.'

Morgan watched his fingers tighten on the polished wood. 'Of course.'

His father should have long since been sleeping, but instead he was sitting up against a raft of pillows, reading a book.

'My lord, it's late. You shouldn't stint your sleep.'

Setting the book aside, his father looked him up and down. 'So, Morgan. I'm to learn of your whereabouts from a servant, am I? That's how I taught you to show proper respect?'

*Oh, Father.* Waving the door closed, he approached the vast, high bed. 'You were resting when I returned from Elvado. Venette's invitation was last minute. I had no time to wait.'

'And resting's the same as dead, is it, that you couldn't bestir me and let me know you'd be out for the night?'

'Without you get your proper rest you *will* be dead,' he snapped. 'And what then? You'd prefer I make haste for the crypt to tell you of my business?'

'You take a tone with me?' said his father, slapping the bedspread. 'I'll have no tone taken beneath my own roof, Morgan. And I'll know what you're doing. As Lord Danfey, that's my right. Your business *is* my business.'

'No, my lord,' he said, struggling to keep his voice even. 'A man's business is his own.'

Another slap to the bedspread. A thread of spittle on the lips. 'You're not a man, you're my son! You're not a man until you've *bred* a son. Turn your buttocks to leather sitting in a Council seat, Morgan, and you still won't be a man until there's a boy calling you father.'

Morgan stared at him, any thought of mentioning Maris Garrick killed stone dead. He'd die himself before giving the old man such satisfaction.

'Enjoy your book, sir,' he said at last, cool and impersonal. 'If you're stirring by the time I take breakfast, perhaps if you've the appetite we can eat together. Otherwise I shall doubtless see you in between my Council duties, which resume now with some urgency. Good evening.'

'You're walking out?' said his father, incredulous. 'I'll not have it! Stand where you are and give an account of your night's doings. Morgan! Do you hear me? Morgan—'

He closed the chamber door on his father's hoarse fury. Made his way to the attic with his own burden of temper, which he could not drive out no matter how hard his heels thudded on the stairs.

*You're not a man, you're my son.*

Close to weeping his rage and frustration, he summoned glimfire then raggedly paced his workroom floor. The air trapped inside the attic still reeked of burned *azafris*. It stank of his failure. His heart ached as it drubbed his ribs. One incant ratified, two more to come, and it wasn't enough. A seat on the revered Council of Mages, and it wasn't enough.

He'd have a son of his own by now, he'd be a man in his father's eyes, if Luzena hadn't died. So what was his remedy? Should he paper over any cracks of doubt, crush all his bitter-sweet memories and woo Maris Garrick until either he loved her or could live the lie? Wed her and bed her until she birthed him a son? Trembling, he staggered then dropped to his knees. Dropped again, to his hands, to his forearms, and bowed his spine until his forehead touched the floor. His unsteady fingers found the locket and gripped it to hurting.

*If I have to, I'll do it. Luzena, I'll have to. And you'll have to forgive me. You're the one who left.*

Eventually he unbent himself. Found his feet and stood like a man, like a proud mage of Dorana. And he was a man, no matter what his father said. It was foolish of him to set so much store by intemperate accusations.

'And I'll not fall into that trap again,' he said, out loud so he could hear himself make the promise. 'Let him rail, let him bluster, let him flog me with words. It's only air. Greve Danfey does not define who I am.'

The glimfire he'd summoned showed him his workbench with its three new crucibles and its pots and jars of base elements and catalysts. Showed him his tiny store of remaining *azafris,* salvaged against all hope. No matter what it cost him, or the risks involved, he'd have to procure more. In the small, wax-sealed glass vial beside it there was drab brown *susquinel,* his last, best chance of success.

Spurred into action, Morgan assembled the components of the incant he was trying to create. Into each waiting crucible he dropped the *azafris,* the powdered bone, a smidgin more this time of shaved *urvil.* It was a neutral ingredient, a bonding agent. Using *susquinel* he needed more of it, but not too much more. The balance was delicate. Crucial.

Last of all, he unstoppered the vial of *susquinel.* The distilled tincture was acrid, viciously stinging his eyes. A glass dropper-rod dipped into it, one miserly drop for each crucible . . .

The catalytic reaction was almost immediate. Stoppering the vial again, hastily shoving it out of the way, he took a precious moment to calm himself, banish the lingering remnants of his anger, and recall the words of the incant.

'*Ravak tokai.*'

The glimlit air above the crucibles shivered awake.

'*Ravak hinmish.*'

He felt a tremor pass through him, waking echoes in his bones.

'*Ravak vanteri.*'

A change in the atmosphere, like the looming promise of a storm. He held his breath. This moment had been his undoing last time.

*But not now. I cannot fail again.*

Avidly he stared into the crucibles, feeling the laboured drub of his heart. Watched the *azafris* and *susquinel* melt and meld and transmute. Bright blue turned dark green then grew brighter, and brighter again. Astonished, he felt an answering glow beneath his skin, power calling to power. The green substance in the crucibles began to bubble and seethe.

And now he was come to the knife-edge instant of creation, to the calling forth of the recrafted sigil at the heart of his new incant. Once, he'd done this . . . but the sigils hadn't held.

*They'll hold this time. They will. They must.*

His eyes were burning. Sweat, not *susquinel*. He dragged his embroidered sleeve across them, heedless of stains. A small part of him wanted to shout down the stairs, shout for Rumm to rouse Lord Danfey and haul the sick old man out of his bed and up to the attic so he could see the kind of mage his son was. Because he knew, he *knew*, that this time was different. He could feel it, he could taste it.

Slowly, so very slowly, he traced the shape of the sigil onto the shimmering air above the first crucible. Antithetical. Clockwise. The very opposite of what was known. And then he watched, teeth sunk into his lower lip, as the green substance within the crucible spun itself into a thin thread, idly at first and then picking up speed. It spun and spun itself into the air, spun itself into an echo of that slowly traced sigil. Became the sigil, green and glowing, crucible-cradled and strong.

If he smiled any wider his face would tear in two.

Carefully, for overconfidence would undo him, he traced the second sigil and after it the third. Then he stood back from the workbench and savoured the sight of all three glowing sigils. No sign of inconstancy. No hint of poor cohesion. No teetering on the brink of pathetic collapse. Laughter bubbled through him, washing away what remained of fear and doubt and pain.

*Venette's right. I am the future. And I will keep Dorana safe.*

Of course, this was but the first step in the creation of his new transmutation incant. The next step was to transform the sigil into a malleable part of the recrafted working, something that could be called and used and banished at will. In many ways that was as tricky as the creation of the sigil itself. Mages had died, or been ruinously injured, attempting such a feat. Brahn Sorvold had died attempting it, slowly and in great pain.

*But not me. I won't die.*

Only first, the sigil had to prove itself stable.

Waiting, he paced the attic again. At last he halted before the window and stared into the night. Rested his hot forehead against the cool glass and could have wept for wanting.

*Let them hold. Let them hold. Let this be the moment of my making.*

Time dragged by, slow as a hobbled horse. He kept his back turned, knowing he'd feel the first instant of disaster. But the sigils held. At last he swung round.

Green and glowing and sturdy, each sigil sat in its crucible. Their extravagant, cursive signatures were imprinted on his eyes. They lived in his fingers. They dwelled in his mind. Let him see one hundred summers, he would never forget them.

Fresh sweat slicking his skin, Morgan undertook the next step: confirming the sigils. No *azafris* or *susquinel* or *tilatantin* for this task. Requiring pure and simple magework, it was a test in the blood. One breath too much power, one breath too little, a moment too long or too short, and the sigils would destroy themselves and most likely him as well.

Breathing rigorously controlled, he spread his fingers wide. Felt for the weft and warp of magic, for the power and glory in the air. The peoples beyond Dorana's borders lived in kingdoms of the blind, the deaf, the dumb and the lame. They could no more see or feel the magic surrounding them than a stone could drink soup.

*Poor wretches. Pitiful paupers. They might as well be dead.*

He focused on the first sigil. Eased his mind around its trembling edges, feeling for any weakness in its fabric. Found none, and softly laughed.

'Belemi. Belemi. Ra'tu. De'sak.'

Slowly, so slowly, the sigil's trembling stopped. It flared once, sun bright, then it settled to a mellow glow, green like new grass.

Morgan felt himself blink. Felt more laughter bubble into

his throat. He swallowed it, swiftly. That was only one sigil. Two remained that could kill him.

But they didn't.

It wasn't until the third and final sigil firmed into permanence that he allowed himself to acknowledge his ruthlessly strangled fear. Shaking like a virgin facing her wedding bed, he felt his legs give way. Felt himself thud to the attic's floorboards, his vision swimming with tears and relief and triumph.

*Luzena. Luzena. I wish you were here.*

# CHAPTER SEVEN

It was agony, waiting for a reply from the College of Mages. Not even a second commission from Lady Grie, a natal clock for her aged mother, could ease the churning in her belly.

'Barl, you have to be patient,' Remmie said, sounding impatient himself. 'Two weeks isn't so long. Do you think you're the only mage in Dorana with a question for the College?'

Elbows braced on the kitchen table, Barl glared. 'This isn't a question, Remmie. This is my *life*.'

'Your life,' he said, under his breath. 'Barl, you have a life already, a good one, and—'

'So *you* say!' she retorted. 'But *I* decide the quality of my life. If you choose to squander your gifts in some obscure little hamlet schoolhouse, well, that's your choice. But I won't make the same mistake and I won't sit around hoping for scattered crumbs from the great mages' table. I'm not stupid. I know what they're doing. They think if they ignore me for long enough I'll give up and go away. Well, I won't. Not this time.'

Instead of answering, Remmie took his emptied plate and used cutlery and clattered them into the sink. Then he stood there, head lowered. She'd hurt his feelings, disparaging his precious little school. Disparaging him. Well, she was sorry for that, but she was right. And she was tired of him refusing to admit it.

'You should've let me mention you, too,' she said, slumping in her chair. Her sausages and green beans were hardly touched. She wasn't hungry. 'In a pinch they might be able to ignore one exceptional mage, but two? I swear, Remmie, if they turn me down because – because—'

'Because why?' he demanded, turning. 'Because I'm content with my life? Because I'm not obsessed with becoming a famous mage?'

'Neither am I obsessed!'

He laughed at her, scornful. 'Of course you are. And because I'm not, because I believe in teaching, in helping children who'll never be great mages, because I don't care about fame, you think I'm a failure.'

Oh, he was so stubborn. He understood perfectly well what she meant.

'It's not about *fame,* Remmie! It's about making a *real* difference. I can make a real difference and so can you. Schoolteachers are as common as daisies in a field.'

His fist thumped the sink's draining board. 'So I'm common now, am I? In that case, Barl, I'm surprised you don't want to hide me away somewhere I'll not be an embarrassment!'

Well, he was just determined to misread everything she said, wasn't he? Because he didn't approve of her dreams, thought she should be satisfied with a life spent at the beck and call of mages like Lady Grie and Artisan Master Arndel, he was going to twist every word she uttered into something mean and hateful, as though *she* were mean and hateful.

*And I'm not. I just want a chance to spread my wings. Why is that so wrong?*

Remmie was still glaring, his dark blue eyes hot and hurt. She couldn't remember the last time she and her brother had been so much at odds.

*And it's his fault. Never once have I stood in his way, but now he thinks to stand in mine?*

102

Torn between misery and her own resentful anger, she leaned across the table. 'Of course you don't embarrass me, Rem. But if you had a student who wanted to make a difference, who you *knew* could make a difference, wouldn't you do everything in your power to help him make his dreams come true?'

'Barl . . .' Folding his arms, Remmie leaned against the sink. 'You know I would.'

'Yes, I do,' she said, fighting the urge to shout. 'So why won't you do the same for me? Why would you do it for a stranger and not your own flesh and blood?'

Now his eyes were sullen. 'You like to pretend that what you're after is simple, but it's not. You're one mage, Barl. You can't unmake centuries of history.'

'Who says I can't? The greatest flood starts with a single drop of rain.'

'Perhaps it does, but floods are destructive! If you want to make a difference, invent a new incant, one that will change lives for the better, like Mage Lakewell did. And don't tell me you can't because the Lindin name's not ranked. Plenty of unranked mages have been patented and celebrated ever after for their work.'

'*Plenty?*' she said, incredulous. 'You call twelve mages *plenty*? In three centuries of trying? Remmie—'

'At least it's not none!' he said, goaded. 'At least you must admit you could be considered. But you won't have even that chance, Barl, not if you persist in—'

'In what?' she said, longing to shake him. 'Pointing out how wrong it is that a handful of men and women on the Council of Mages hold sway over so many? That the finest education Dorana has to offer is denied to all but a select, self-appointed few? Remmie, you're a teacher! How can you *defend* that?'

'I don't!' he retorted. 'I'm not blind, I can see where Dorana could do with some changing. But you can't *make* people change, Barl. Not when the change you want means upsetting the way they live. You have to be careful. You have to be tactful.'

She leapt to her feet. 'How can you be so staid, so prosaic?

*Careful. Tactful.* Next you'll be saying I should apologise for being angry!'

'I'd never say that,' he snapped. 'But this isn't about what you feel, Barl, it's about—'

'I'll tell you what it's about!' she said, riding roughshod, because give him half a chance and he'd prose on at her like a teacher until first light had every cockerel in the lane crowing. 'Dorana is hidebound, Remmie, *that's* what this is about. And the mages on the Council are keeping it hidebound, for no better reason than to protect their own precious superiority! It's wicked, you *know* it is. If there's you and there's me with our true potential unexplored, how many other mages are there who could make the most amazing discoveries, but who'll never get the chance because the First Families keep them in their place?'

Remmie rarely lost his temper, but when he did his face went pale. It was milk-white now. He shoved away from the sink, hands fisted by his sides.

'You call me staid and prosaic, and maybe I am,' he said. His voice was coldly distant, hardly sounding like Remmie at all. 'But when was the last time a staid, prosaic mage hurt someone? Barl, you're so arrogant. And it's the arrogant mages who do the damage.'

'No, Remmie. It's the cowards who hurt us,' she said, desperate for him to see things her way. 'They see what's wrong in the world, they see its injustices and they do nothing to fight them because they're afraid of being noticed and losing what precious little importance they might have.'

'So by your lights I'm a staid, prosaic coward?' He looked away, as though the sight of her pained him. 'That's quite a list of accomplishments.'

'Remmie, no . . . wait . . .' she said, as he headed for the kitchen door. 'I didn't mean you're a coward, I didn't—'

'Yes, you did,' he said, over his shoulder, not pausing. 'You meant every word. And now I know what you really think of me.'

Staring after him, she felt a wave of furious grief crash over her.

*Oh, Remmie.* If only he'd be reasonable, if only he'd climb down off his high horse and admit she was right. Then they wouldn't have to argue and say hurtful things to each other.

Well, she certainly wasn't going after him. He was wrong. He thought her fight for recognition and acceptance had nothing to do with him because he was safe and happy in his little hamlet schoolhouse.

*But that's only because the Council of Mages, or someone from a First Family, has no desire to interfere. If ever that changes he'll swiftly learn how little he and his life and his pupils matter to them.*

Disconsolate, she collected her plate from the table, scraped her unwanted dinner into the pail for scraps, then turned her attention to the sink. Often, Remmie would stay and dry the dishes as she washed them and they'd good-naturedly argue various points of mage lore. Laugh at each other's foolishness. Play *do you remember* with tales of their dead parents, keeping them alive, even though some memories hurt.

But there'd be no companionable laughing or sweetly painful memories tonight.

Sighing, she plugged the sink and turned on the taps. Washing dishes by hand never failed to soothe her. She knew Ibbitha thought her very odd for it. But it was like walking home from the artisanry instead of using a travel incant. Magework was too important for frivolous usage. A mage who lost touch with the earthy reality of life was in danger of becoming so detached from the world that remembering the impact magic had on it became harder and harder until it was never remembered at all.

*Remmie couldn't be more mistaken. I'm not careless of my actions. Someone's got to hold the Council of Mages and the First Families accountable. And if I don't, who will? Nobody else seems to care.*

As she scrubbed the plates and pans and cutlery, then towelled them dry and put them away, and after that cleaned the hob and the kitchen table, she waited for the sound of her mistaken brother's footsteps in the corridor. It didn't come. *He* didn't come.

She couldn't remember him ever walking away from her with such anger and hurt in his face.

*But then, I can't remember being so mean to him, either.*

Their whole lives they'd never let their resentments fester. He was her shadow and she was his. She'd have to swallow her pride, it seemed, and go after him. However would they be able to look at each other over their boiled morning eggs if she'd slammed her door and he'd slammed his without this upset put to rights?

After hunting through every empty room in the cottage she found him outside, beside his beloved vegetable patch, recreating the night's constellations with little glimfire stars.

'That's pretty,' she said, smiling to cover the ache in her heart. 'Is it for a lesson?'

At eight and nine, his pupils were still young enough to be enchanted by magic, to be taught with games and laughter. The harder, solemn lessons were yet to come. He could have taught those too, easily, sought out older students, like Barton Haye had, but he didn't want to. Though he was a grown man there remained something boyish about him. It was why the children loved him. Why he was so good at his job.

With a gentle snap of his fingers, Remmie extinguished the glimfire. His face plunged into darkness. 'Yes. What do you want?'

*For you to admit that I'm right! For you to fight with me, not against me, and accept you could be so much more than a teacher.*

She sighed. 'To say sorry.'

'I'd rather you didn't. Not when you don't mean it.'

The unfriendliness in his voice was like a slap. 'I do mean it!'

'Then show me, Barl.' Now he sounded weary, and as sad as she felt. 'Convince me.'

'Or what?'

He shrugged. 'Or we'll stay at odds. I don't want that. Do you?'

No. But she didn't want to be bullied into submission, either. Irritated, she conjured glimfire so she could see him properly.

'And I suppose the only proof you'll accept is if I give up my dream?'

'The world's full of dreams,' he said softly. 'Please, Barl? When the College proctor finally writes back to tell you no, *please*, accept the decision. Throw your energy and passion into clock-making. You're so good at it. In a year or two, with Lady Grie's help, you'll be a master artisan in your own right. You'll be renowned, I have no doubt. There's honour and prestige in that. Don't provoke the anger of mages we can never hope to best. Seek fame where it won't hurt you. Or me.'

Hugging herself, she looked at the stars. They were a blurred dazzle through her tears. 'Why won't you believe I'm not interested in fame?'

'Because I *know* you, Barl!' Remmie said, his voice tight with frustration. 'You love praise. You live for it. Growing up you were never happier than when Pa called you his best and brightest little mage.'

'You're *jealous*?' Shocked, she stared at him. 'Is this why you begrudge me wanting acceptance to the College? Because Pa used to praise me? He praised you too! He praised you always!'

'*No.*' Remmie half-turned away from her, one hand dragging down his face. The face that looked so much like hers, its beauty masculine, its planes and angles so well-known and beloved. His pale golden hair was pulled back into a braid and tied with a neat twist of red ribbon. 'Barl, if I begrudge you I promise, that's not the reason.'

'Then what is?'

'You want so much,' he said, sad again. As though all his temper had burned out. 'I'm afraid for you. 'Til the day he died, Pa filled you full of fire. And whenever Mama tried to tell you be careful, fire burns, he hushed her.'

'So I'm Pa and you're Mama, is that it?'

'Perhaps.' He laughed, the sound despairing, not amused. 'She always was the practical one.'

The one who'd died of a broken heart, scant weeks after their father succumbed to a Feenish fever. How she'd surprised them. How she'd left them bereft.

'Nonsense,' she said. 'I'm very practical. And wanting more for myself isn't *im*practical. It's not foolish or greedy or selfish, either. I'm not asking you to live my life, Remmie. All I'm asking is that you let me live mine.'

A cool breeze sprang up, scented with late-blooming innis. The evening was so quiet they could hear a distant owl, hooting. Winking through the weeping grobe trees, glimlamps in their closest neighbour's window.

'I know,' Remmie said, still sad. 'But it's not in me to watch you run pell-mell for a cliff and not try to stop you from tumbling over the edge.'

She felt another sting of tears. 'I thought you had more faith in me than that.'

'It's not faith in you I'm lacking. You are as great a mage as you dream. That's why I'm afraid, Barl. The mages you look to for recognition won't welcome your brilliance. Do you think those haughty First Families will be pleased to find themselves cast in the shade by some unranked nobody from the Eleventh district?'

'I'm well used to jealousy,' she said slowly. 'It's everywhere, Remmie. Even in the artisanry. But the College of Mages is dedicated to learning and great achievements in magework. You're a teacher. Do *you* resent a gifted student?'

'You know full well I don't,' he said. 'But then I'm a nobody too, aren't I? The College of Mages is revered throughout Dorana. Name me one First Family that would welcome a son or daughter being shown up by the likes of us.'

'Remmie—' She slapped her palms to his chest, exasperated. 'I'm not talking about First Families, I'm talking about the College tutors!'

'Who are First Family members,' he retorted. 'You can't be so clod-headed as to think it's not the same thing!'

Uncertain, she stared at him. 'You want me to believe the

honour and integrity of both College and Council are so paltry they'd risk Dorana's future out of spite?'

'I thought you already believed it!'

'I believe they're selfish and short-sighted. I believe they've been allowed to have their own way for too long. But that's not the same as thinking they'd rather see ignorance trump knowledge than reconsider my request!'

The glimlight she'd conjured showed Remmie's surprise and resignation and a rueful affection.

'You really do believe that, don't you?'

Sometimes the urge to slap him made her hand itch. '*Yes.* Why do you sound so surprised? When do I ever say things I don't believe?'

'Never.' He shook his head. 'You're right. I shouldn't be surprised at all. You're being exactly yourself.'

'Well, then?'

'Well, then—' Remmie let out a gusty sigh. 'I suppose I've been wearing out my tongue for no good purpose. I can't imagine why I thought you'd ever listen to me.'

'Remmie.' She threw her arms around him and held on tight. 'I was afraid you might never forgive me.'

His hand rubbed her shoulder. 'Who says I've forgiven you?'

'Ha.' She swallowed relieved, tearful laughter. 'You have.'

'I've stopped fighting. I'm not sure that's the same thing.'

'*Remmie.*' Letting go of him, she stepped back. 'Can we only be friends if I agree to do as you say?'

He tucked a strand of hair behind her ear. 'Can we only be friends if I never question your choices?'

Their parents were dead. They had no other family. And if they turned their backs on each other . . .

'Say we're friends, Rem,' she whispered. 'Say we're friends even if I think you're wrong and you think I'm wrong and we could stamp and shout our disagreements 'til sunrise. Please. Just say it.'

After a long silence, Remmie nodded. 'We're friends.'

She hugged him again, then tugged his loose linen sleeve. 'It's getting late. Come inside.'

'Not yet,' he said, glancing at the star-bright sky. 'I've got to finish preparing tomorrow's class.'

'Your glimfire constellations? I can help. Let me help.'

'I thought you wanted to finish your new crystal? Isn't it nearly ready to show Arndel?'

'It is.' Surging beneath her unhappiness, a warm glow of pride. 'But it can wait one more night, Remmie. I'd rather—'

'I wouldn't,' he said, and flicked her nose. 'It'll only confuse the children if they sense your incant signature and mine. Go and finish your crystal, Barl.'

So, reluctant, she left him to his constellation and shut herself in her room. Eventually the quiet joy of magic soothed her bruised feelings, eased the belly-tightness of nerves. She forgot her resentment of the College, her frustration with Remmie, and instead laughed as the shimmering crystal she'd imagined sprang to life at her command . . . and at last, at long last, held its delicate, deceptively fragile form.

*I'll show it to Arndel in the morning, before I finish Lady Grie's natal clock. He'll be so impressed. And he'll have no choice but to sponsor the crystal's submission to the Artisans' Guild.*

And surely the Guild would have no choice but to approve. It would make her the second-youngest artisan mage ever to be honoured with artisanwork named after them.

'You see, Remmie?' she whispered, the tip of one finger gently stroking her beautiful creation. 'Dreams do come true. If I can do this . . . I can do anything. You'll see.'

So precious was the crystal she'd created that she didn't dare risk it by walking to the artisanry. Instead she swallowed a handful of runip berries and used a hated travel incant to make the journey safely.

She found Artisan Master Arndel in his privy workroom, squeezed behind his crowded bench and reading a letter. At her confident rap-rap-rap on the open door he looked up.

Just to be safe, she offered him a shallow bow. 'Good morning, Artisan Master.'

His eyes widened, then narrowed with familiar ill-temper. 'Mage Lindin.' The letter dropped from his hand. 'A curious coincidence. I was about to send for you.'

Taking that as an invitation, she entered the room. Her cloth-wrapped crystal was cradled against her chest. She thought she could feel it thrumming in time with her heart.

'I'm sorry to disturb you, Artisan Master, but—'

'Disturb?' He snorted. 'Yes, indeed, Mage Lindin. You disturb me to no end. Sit.'

Gently she lowered herself to the chamber's sole uncluttered chair. It was wooden, splintered and uncomfortable. He couldn't receive new patrons in this room, they'd run from it screaming with their hands clutched to their purses.

'Artisan Master—'

'Mage Lindin.' Arndel flicked the sheet of paper he'd been reading. 'I have before me a most unwelcome letter.'

Clearly she wasn't to be permitted to speak. At least not until he'd unburdened himself of whatever had curdled his mood this time.

'Oh,' she said. 'Yes, Artisan Master?'

He frowned at the letter in question. 'It seems that in a fit of madness, Mage Lindin, you wrote to the College of Mages demanding they admit you as a student.' His gaze lifted. 'Is this true? Or has the College somehow mixed you up with some other presumptuous, deluded young mage?'

Shocked, for a moment she could only stare. And then she found her voice. 'I'm sorry, Artisan Master? How do you – why would they – are you saying they wrote to you? About me? About my request?'

'Deluded, but not deaf,' said Arndel, scathing. 'Mage Lindin, I—'

'This is wrong,' Barl said, and pushed to her feet. Now her sheet of crystal was clutched to her chest like a shield. 'They had no business writing to you, Artisan Master. It's none of your affair if I—'

Both his fists crashed onto the desk, leaping letter and

111

quills, splashing ink, scattering random crystal droplets and shards.

'*None of my affair?*' he shouted. 'When you are *my artisan?* When your services are promised to Lady Ancilla Grie? When I am bluntly told by an advisor to the Council of Mages – *the Council* – that as your Artisan Master it is my duty to keep your mind on your work so it might not lead you into giving grave offence? *None of my affair?* Mage Lindin, what were you *thinking?*'

Her knees were trembling. If she didn't sit again they'd give way, and she'd be humiliated. So she folded back to the chair and tried to gather her disordered wits. When she could trust herself, she looked up and met Arndel's glare.

'I was thinking, Artisan Master, that no mage in Dorana should be denied an education.'

'No mage is!'

'That's not true, Artisan Master. Every day the College of Mages—'

'Enough about the College! There are scores of mage schools in Dorana, Mage Lindin.'

With difficulty, she kept a precarious hold of her temper. 'Yes, Artisan Master. But only one College.'

Arndel's nostrils pinched, then flared. 'Which is free to admit or deny whatever students it likes! And it should come as no surprise, Mage Lindin, that it does not like *you!*'

She blinked. 'I don't understand.'

'Then you must be far more stupid than even this nonsense suggests.'

'Master Arndel, are you saying I'm turned down?'

'Of course you're turned down! Don't tell me you thought the College would *accept* you?'

Nausea churned through her, burning her throat with bile. 'And the proctor wrote to *you* of the decision? Not me?'

'No, Mage Lindin.' Arndel's eyes gleamed with a nasty satisfaction, seeing her distress. 'Are you even listening? The letter writer was one Lord Hahren, who advises both the proctor and

112

the Council on College matters. He felt I had the right to know what one of my artisans has been up to behind my back.'

Pushing nausea aside, Barl took a deep breath to steady her voice. 'I came here a Guild-lettered mage, Artisan Master Arndel. I am not 'prenticed to this artisanry. You don't own me.'

She had him there, and he knew it. His lips thinned. 'By the strict letter of Guild law, Mage Lindin, that is true. But do not pretend to be more than you are, or brush aside inconvenient facts. Despite your unsteady past I made a place for you here. I gave you the benefit of my knowledge, my experience. I taught you the art of clock-maging, I—'

'And I have more than earned my keep, Artisan Master!' she said, abandoning prudence. That he'd dare to censure her. That he would *dare*. 'I have repaid you thrice over for your investment. I call it churlish that you would complain of a little time spent in schooling me when the rewards I've earned you come in thick and fast.'

Arndel lurched to his feet. 'And *I* call it churlish that you would abandon this artisanry, abandon *me,* to pursue such folly, to pound your fists against a door locked for good reason! And why? Because your talent is o'ermatched only by your profligate pride!'

Heart thudding, the cramped chamber's air raw in her throat, Barl stood to face him. 'Was there no letter from this Lord Hahren included for me?'

'No,' he said, curt. 'I was requested to inform you of the College's decision, and I have done so. But just in case you remain in any doubt, Mage Lindin, let me spell it out for you most plainly. You are not the kind of student candidate the College desires. Furthermore, I will give you a timely warning. With this display of arrogance, you have brought yourself to the Council of Mages' attention. That was not wise. The Council has a long memory and tends to hold a grudge.'

So he was pretending to *care* for her now? 'And you, Artisan Master? Do you hold a grudge?'

He sniffed. 'I suppose that is your disrespectful way of asking

113

if I intend to dismiss you? The answer is no, you are not dismissed. At least not permanently. But neither are you required here today. Go home, Mage Lindin. Reflect upon your poor choices . . . and the very dim prospects you may expect to enjoy should you so trespass upon the Council's goodwill ever again. Or mine.'

She tried, but she couldn't mask her surprise. 'You still want me?'

'Mage Lindin, you are young,' Arndel said, condescending now. 'And in this matter you have shown a deplorable lack of judgement. Let its outcome be a lesson to you. *Learn* from your mistake.' His lips pinched. 'Yes, I still want you. But understand that even my patience has limits.'

The expectant gleam in his eye told her he now waited for a humbled gushing of gratitude. She felt her spine stiffen. *I'd rather drop dead.* The wrapped crystal in her arms weighed heavy as lead. He'd not even glanced at it, let alone asked what it was or why she'd brought it to him. And there'd be no point trying to tell him. Her small triumph would have to wait.

She bowed her head, just far enough that he couldn't again accuse her of insufficient courtesy. 'Artisan Master.'

'But you'll return to the workroom tomorrow,' he said sharply. 'Lady Grie expects her clock completed upon the agreed date.'

Another careful nod. 'Of course, Artisan Master. I'll not disappoint her.'

Escaped from his privy chamber, she took a moment to catch her breath. As she stood in a pool of shadow within the artisanry's central courtyard, its chivvying clock chimed the hour. Time to start work. Scurrying footsteps had her turning. It was one of the 'prentice mages late to her place. Lucky for her, Arndel remained in his chamber, still fuming, else she'd have to endure a lecture on tardiness. The trade artisanry's workroom door slammed shut, then all was silence.

Too angry yet for tears, her belly still roiling, Barl hefted the marvellous crystal she'd created. It was too heavy for carrying home, and she desperately needed to walk. So she translocated it to the cottage ahead of her, briefly pressed cold palms to her

still-flushed cheeks, willing her face not to betray her . . . then
marched out of the artisanry with her head defiantly high.

That anger carried her more than half the way home. Arms
swinging, heels thudding against the beaten earth track, she felt
it burn through her, setting her blood alight. Write to Arndel?
Turn him against her? What gave them the right? And what right
had *he*, that prosing, selfish old mole, to read her a lecture,
presume to admonish her, when it was none of his business! All
she owed him was the time and effort that he paid for. Not so
generously, either. He wasn't making her rich.

Temper goading her, she walked faster and faster as the litany
of injustices chased themselves dizzy inside her head.

'I do all he asks, and better than he could ever hope for!' she
shouted at a startled crow, when she couldn't keep silent any
more. 'He has no cause for complaint, no grounds to criticise.
If I turned around right now and gave him notice he'd have no
power to stop me! And he knows it!'

Perched on a fence post, raucously derisive, the crow ruffled
its glossy black feathers. Then it flapped away, leisurely, and she
was left to shout at thin air.

'I've a good mind to do just that,' she muttered, slowing.
Abruptly weary. Beads of sweat rolled in thin lines down her
ribs and back. 'Wouldn't that make him look a fool to Lady
Grie? Wouldn't she be slighted?'

Yes, indeed. And slighted, she'd make sure to inform every
mage of her acquaintance, so many of them ranked First Family,
that Arndel's artisanry was – was – *unreliable*.

'That's the word, unreliable!' she told a sleepy spotted milch
cow, chewing its cud beneath a bulbin tree on the other side of
the fence. 'And wouldn't *that* serve him right?'

Yes. Only . . . damage to his reputation would hurt the artisanry, which meant hurting the mages who toiled there beneath
Arndel's interfering, unforgiving rule.

Halting, she frowned at the cow. 'And while I'm not fussed
for most of them, I can't knowingly do them such a bad turn.

It's the College at fault here, and this Lord Hahren, not Ibbitha and the rest.'

The cow blinked at her, its mild brown eyes incurious.

'Besides.' She rested her forearms along the fence's highest wooden rail and let her forehead drop. 'There's Remmie, isn't there?'

She dreaded to think what he'd say if she told him she'd abandoned the artisanry, not to attend the College, which of course he'd understand, but because she'd flown into a temper at Arndel.

'So I'm trapped here,' she said to the cow. 'Aren't I? Fenced in just like you.'

A sting of tears extinguished the embers of her rage. All the strength drained out of her and the misery held at bay by fury rose to swamp her. Knees buckling, she sank to the cool, damp grass.

Over her aching head, the cloudless sky vaulted sunlit and blue. She heard a whisper of wings and a chattering cry as a flock of pink-and-white dibbydabs rushed through the warm air. Tickling her nose, the scent of newly bloomed frasfras threading through the earthier pungency of fresh cow pats. Somewhere out of sight a creek chuckled between its banks. It was a beautiful day. This was a beautiful part of Dorana. Who couldn't be happy here?

*Me. I'm not, and I doubt I ever will be. I want more. I can't help it.*

'Remmie, I'm sorry,' she whispered. 'I just can't.'

But he'd never understand that. So easily content himself, he found her restlessness and hungry ambition baffling.

*If only I'd never gone to Elvado. I knew it would hurt me, seeing it. Oh, I'm a fool.*

Regrets were useless, though, weren't they? The damage was done. She knew exactly what it was she was missing, now, living her quiet Batava life. Hedgerows instead of cobblestones, the schoolmaster's cottage in place of the College and that grand Hall of Knowledge. A small life filled with clock magic. Filled with sand and glass.

116

It would never be enough . . . but she'd have to make do. Find a way to live with it. For Remmie's sake, if not her own.

With a deep sigh, almost a groan, she took hold of the fence and pulled herself back to her feet. It would be easy, too easy, to sit here the rest of the day with the silent cow for company. But she had to face her brother. Watch him pretend he wasn't pleased the College of Mages had rejected her. Pretend she didn't care.

Heavy-hearted, she continued for home.

# CHAPTER EIGHT

Hiding a smile, Remmie watched his small collection of pupils perform their final exercise of the day. With creased brows and poked tongue-tips and even some laboured breathing, they worked in groups of three to recreate with glimfire the glorious Waterfall constellation: a cascade of brilliant stars that centuries-worth of Doranen travellers had used to guide them home.

It was a tricky incant. Doubtless some teachers, and maybe some parents, would chide him for expecting too much but he knew his students. They relished a challenge . . . and because he'd always been careful, even the most limited mage amongst them was made to feel useful. Just as the best mages were praised, but never lauded so high they became arrogant.

*If only Barl's teachers had troubled to do the same.*

Though he loved his sister dearly, the bald truth was that a sound dose of humility would have served her well. But she'd not received it, which meant she had to learn her lessons the hard way.

Just like some of his pupils, as it happened.

Over by the window, Jossie Tindel, a clever mage and a pert little minx, was busily contradicting her team mates. She was wrong and they were right, but Kinthy Scobie and Bedel Royce barely possessed one strong spine between them. And so, by letting Jossie rumble right over their timid suggestions, they were condemning themselves to share her fate. A harsh lesson, but a useful one, assuming they took it to heart.

*And will Barl take hers to heart, when it comes?*

He was horribly afraid she wouldn't. There was a wildness in her, a reckless refusal to accept any hand on her bridle. And he was beginning to think he'd never find a way to change that.

His other pupils were faring better, at least so far as teamwork was concerned. Sadly, only Rine Grovsik and his two best friends had managed to recreate the constellation incant correctly. They'd carry the class honours today. But at least the rest would fail harmoniously, and not because they'd let themselves be bossed down the wrong path.

*Unlike Kinthy and Bedel. Poor little mites.*

He couldn't help feeling sorry for them as Jossie's unbalanced incant fell apart, taking the rest of their Waterfall constellation with it. And he ignored the tears and tantrums and cries of dismay until Jossie decided to start laying blame.

'That's enough,' he said, and was rewarded with immediate silence. 'You're all three of you at fault. Jossie, your mistake was in the rhythm and pronunciation of the incant. You should have listened to Bedel. And Kinthy, you should've insisted on drawing the second sigil your way.' He raised an eyebrow at them, letting his admonitions sink in. 'When you know you're right, stand your ground. And you, Jossie, need to remember that you *aren't* always right.' Kinthy and Bedel exchanged glances muddled with pleasure and mortification. Jossie's cheeks turned pink with resentful shame.

'Can we try again?' said Kinthy, fingers twisting in her pretty cotton dress.

He shook his head. 'I'm sorry. The day's nearly over.'

Her face fell, tears brimming.

'But if your parents don't mind, you can practise the conjuration by yourself this eve and show me before lessons start on the morrow,' he added.

Kinthy lit up with pleasure. 'Really?'

'You all can,' he said, looking at Jossie and Bedel. 'I must still record a fail in the class book, but I'd like you to get it right for yourselves. Now take your seats while I see how the others are faring.'

Kinthy and Bedel scampered to their desks, a little cheered despite their failure.

'Jossie,' he said, as the girl turned away slowly, ready to sulk.

She turned back, still pouting. Her dark green eyes were angry. 'Yes, Master?'

'There's more to magery than having the loudest voice. The best mages listen and aren't too proud to admit a fault. Remember that.'

'I will, Master,' she muttered.

But would she? Watching her stomp back to her desk, he had his doubts. She could go either way, Jossie Tindel, and on days like this he had his own doubts on whether he could keep her safe from self-made trouble.

*Especially since I can't save my own sister from herself.*

'Master!' piped Rine Grovsik. 'We're finished!'

A good teacher never showed favouritism, so he didn't rush to the classroom's far side. He wandered over, circumspect, making sure to pause and offer encouragement to Bril Coop, Henne Chatsik and Tyne Yolen. Their magery was about to fall apart too, bless them, but they'd done their best. They nearly had it.

Of course, Rine and his friends Ullie Michin and Ebie Droft did have it. He praised the three boys, and promised himself that next time he'd make certain Rine worked with Jossie. He was a match for her, talent-wise, and more than a match when it came to rumbling.

*It'll do her good to be taken down a peg.*

Bril's team cried out with disappointment as their constellation disintegrated into sparks. Moments later the others did too, and he had to wait while his chastened pupils moaned and commiserated and argued the whys and wherefores of their failure. After that he spoke to each group, explaining what went wrong. The one successfully completed constellation he bound in a holding incant and placed on the classroom's display shelf, a reward for success.

On his desk, the day clock Barl had made for him chimed the late hour. At least, not *chimed*. Letting her giddy sense of humour hold sway, Barl had crafted his class clock so it honked like a goose on the hour, every hour. And on the hour, every hour, hearing it, his pupils dissolved into giggles.

'Take your seats!' he said, over their hilarity. Discipline was important. His children were never permitted to bolt from the room like startled rabbits. 'Take your seats for the Oath of Mages.'

It was how they began and ended each day: with the solemn recitation of that most sacred of vows. Scuffled to their rightful places, heads bowed, hands clasped before them on their child-sized wooden desks, even sulking Jossie joined in the careful chant.

'*By the scales of justice we do properly swear that no harm shall be done, no darkness shall guide us, for we are Dorana's mages, humble and true.*'

Remmie swept his gaze across every small, trusting face in his classroom. '*We are Dorana's mages, humble and true.* And let that be true of us, every day of our lives. Class is dismissed.'

Their self-control lasted until they crossed the room's threshold. And then, because they were children, they ran and squealed and shoved their way outside into the afternoon sunshine. Because it was safe now, he laughed. Barl never understood his delight in teaching, in children. He couldn't understand her lack of it.

Relishing the quiet, he entered his thoughts in the class book, noting who had passed the day's mage tests and who had not, and a few little comments here and there. He'd be meeting with his pupils' parents soon, and they were a useful reminder.

With the class book completed, that was almost his day over. Last of all he doused the room in a powerful cleansing incant, washing away the remnants of his pupils' failed constellations. When that was done, he breathed a sigh of relief. The children's poorly constructed energies never failed to distress him. It was the only sorrowful part of teaching. Well . . . that, and whenever he felt he'd failed to do his best by a child.

Like his temperamental sister, he preferred to walk home. Of course for him the journey was short, since their rented cottage and his classroom were both in Batava hamlet. There was no denying Barl's eccentricity, that she took pleasure in walking nearly an hour to the artisanry and home again. And not just in summer, either. She walked everywhere in winter too, bundled warm in a coat. She even walked in pouring rain, protected by a repelling incant. Small wonder so many mages looked at her askance.

But she wouldn't be Barl if she wasn't raising eyebrows.

Barton and his students were out in the school's little flower-strewn field, practising inanimate translocations. Batava's older pupils stayed in class a full hour later, which meant Barton had the longer working day. Waving his friend a cheerful farewell, Remmie headed for the laneway and home, by way of the poulterer. Herbed chicken for dinner. His belly rumbled, anticipating. And there was another eccentricity, that Barl left him to cook. What woman didn't like cooking? Did his sister hope to marry some day? He'd never asked her, but he thought she must. All women did, didn't they?

*So she'll have to find a way to love cooking, or else a husband who'll cook for her. Justice knows I'll not be her cook forever.*

And he was sure she would marry, sooner or later. Beautiful and talented as she was, how could she not? Though she'd never admit it aloud, she knew her quest for a place in the College of Mages was nonsense. It was only visiting Elvado that had stirred her up. Let that memory fade, let her come to fully appreciate her good fortune at the artisanry, accept it as both home and future, begin to trust and enjoy Lady Grie's patronage, and she'd not give two hoots about the College. Instead she'd let herself relax and join the local community, make friends, learn to play. Then she'd lose her heart to some man and wed him and that would tame her restless spirit once and for all.

122

*And then, at last, I'll be free to think of myself.*

A prickle of guilt followed hard on the heels of pleasure. But he had no cause for self-reproach. Never once had he abandoned his sister, no matter what it cost him. It was the last thing he'd promised his dying mother. *'Take care of Barl, Remmie. You know how she is.'* And of course he'd promised. How could he refuse?

But he did wonder, sometimes, if his mother would have asked for his word if she'd known the price he'd pay for keeping it.

*Irielle.*

Nearly a year now, but he'd not forgotten her. She was the sweetest, most beautiful girl he'd ever known. From time to time he toyed with the notion of returning to Granley, seeing if she was still there, still unspoken for. He dreamed there was a chance they could rekindle what his sister's impetuous temper had doused.

*Provided she's forgiven me for putting Barl ahead of her.*

He had to believe he still had the hope of making a family of his own, having a loving, normal life. Because promise or no promise, he couldn't live the rest of his days in Barl's restless shadow.

But a wife and children of his own would never happen until his sister found her peace. Until then, no matter what he threatened, no matter how it hurt, he couldn't leave Barl to fend for herself. He didn't dare think of the strife she'd fall into if he wasn't at hand to keep her feet on the ground.

*I just hope she finds that peace soon. Before I start resenting her for the promise I made.*

Unsettled, he shook himself. It was far too lovely an afternoon to be dwelling on such melancholy thoughts. Besides, here was the poultery. It wouldn't do to walk in there showing a thundercloud face. Everyone in Batava knew him. Tongues would wag.

With a plump, freshly killed and plucked chicken paid for and wrapped in a length of cheesecloth, he wandered the rest of his way home planning supper. Herbed chicken, yes, with buttery green beans and some baked baby carrots. Strawberries with clotted cream for after. His mouth watered. Oh, he did love to cook.

Gaddie Larken from the top of their lane had let her tamest milch cow out to graze the lush verges. He paused a moment to chat with the beast, rub the nub of bone between her gently waving ears and give her glossy flank a pat. Gaddie sold him butter and cream when she had some to spare. Come to think of it, he was running low. And he needed more eggs, too. But there was no time to duck in to see Gaddie now, he'd have to remember on the morrow.

It wasn't until he walked into his small, tidy kitchen that he realised he wasn't the first one home. The bread board, the bread knife and the raggedly remains of a crusty brown loaf had been left on the table. The butter was out, uncovered, with a yellow-smeared knife beside it. The honey pot, too, without its lid, an invitation to flies.

Barl.

Heart thudding, he put the chicken into the sink. She was hours early. And the only time she *ever* came home early was when there'd been some personal disaster. Fear and grief flooded heat throughout his body. He could feel himself trembling. His fingers were clenched into fists.

*I don't want to leave.*

There'd been other classrooms, other pupils, but the little hamlet school of Batava touched him to his heart. He belonged here. He was *needed*.

A tiny groan escaped him. How many times was this, that his sister had been dismissed or walked away over some insult, some hot-tempered falling out? Four times? No, five. Five upheavals of his life, and in only three years.

For the longest time he stood beside the kitchen table, breathing in and breathing out. If his impossible sister was in the cottage somewhere, he had no desire to find her. And if she was in the garden she could stay there. Lay eyes on her now and he'd say things they'd never forget . . . or forgive.

124

He'd not intended to start dinner yet, but he needed a distraction. So he fired up the oven's heat bricks then pulled out the baking dish and set it on the hob. Unwrapped the chicken and placed it breast-up in the dish. Next he took scissors and snipped fresh herbs in their windowsill pots. Retrieved the butter, beat the herbs into three generous, softened spoonfuls, carefully inserted the mix between the chicken's skin and its flesh. All the while his thoughts seethed.

*Any other artisan mage in Dorana would tie himself in knots to earn a place in an esteemed artisanry like Arndel's, to be granted the honour of Ancilla Grie's patronage. But not the great Barl Lindin. Oh, no.*

He could feel his embered temper stirring to flames.

*When you were busy asking for promises, Mama, I wish you'd thought to ask one of her. I wish you'd made her promise to think of me, now and then.*

The last touch for roasting the chicken was onions, peeled and quartered and pushed inside. If his eyes stung, if tears slid down his cheeks, that was the reason. It was the onions. Nothing else.

He shoved the chicken into the oven and stood back.

'Vegetables,' he said to the silent kitchen.

And that meant the garden. If his sister was in the cottage he'd have seen or heard her by now. She never could keep her furious misery to herself. So most likely he'd stumble across her on his way to the bean patch. Was he ready? Could he face her? Would he be able to hold his tongue? He didn't know. Uncertain, he hesitated.

A good cook was also a tidy cook. He couldn't go outside leaving a mess behind him. So he cleaned up after himself, washed his hands even though they'd soon get dirty enough, pulling carrots, and splashed some water onto his face. Wretched onions. Someone should invent an onion that didn't make a grown man cry.

*If Barl is so set upon changing the world, that would be an excellent place to start.*

Adrift between the sink and the table, he chewed his lip. There was no good reason to tarry any longer. Besides, he needed those carrots and beans.

Stupidly nervous, he went outside. When he didn't find his sister skulking amongst the vegetables, for a handful of heartbeats he felt a vast relief. And then he breathed out a resigned sigh and went looking for her.

The schoolmaster's cottage had a duck pond, right at the bottom of the garden. Fringed with rushes and drooping fenna trees, home to deep-voiced green frogs and water newts and one solitary drake, a rickety old wooden bench invited taradiddlers to stay a while and twiddle their thumbs in repose.

That was where he found his sister, on the bench beside the still, deep pond, kept company by the drake who swam round and round.

'That's me, you know,' Barl said, as he hesitantly approached. 'I'm that stupid old duck. Swimming and swimming, going nowhere at all.'

'I've often thought you walk like a duck,' he said, and stopped at the other end of the bench.

Her face was mostly turned away from him. What he could see of her mouth twisted in a brief, wry smile. 'Ha ha.'

Whatever he'd expected to find, it wasn't this. Not Barl subdued and sorrowful, all the fight drained out of her. Every other time she'd stormed away from a position, or been dismissed, he'd found her feisty and spoiling for a brangle, fired up to defend herself and justify her actions.

But this time? This time, for the first time, she looked . . . *defeated.*

'I'm roasting herbed chicken for supper,' he said, because he couldn't think of anything else. Because all the hot words he'd had for her were cold now, and too unkind.

She shrugged, listless. 'That sounds nice.'

'I've come out to pick beans and baby carrots. Want to help?'

'Not really.'

'Barl.' Feeling defeated himself, he sank to the other end of the bench. It wobbled a little then steadied under his weight. He kept meaning to fix it, but always forgot. 'I'm sorry. But perhaps it's not too late. Whatever's gone wrong, I'm sure it can be put right. Even if *you* were right, perhaps if you swallowed your pride, just this once, if you begged Arndel for another chance – or if it was Lady Grie who upset you, enough that you lost your temper and – well, I'm sure if you explained about artistic temperaments, then – only you shouldn't give up so easily, you really shouldn't.'

'Remmie—' Barl was staring at him. 'What are you talking about?'

He stared back. 'What am I – what do you *think* I'm talking about?'

'You think I've been dismissed again? Or that I've flounced off in high dudgeon after some imagined slight?'

Amazing. She actually sounded *offended*. 'What else should I think? It's nowhere near close to sunset and here you are, at home before me, and—' He shoved his hands in his pockets. 'And it wouldn't be the first time. And every *other* time—'

'Oh, Remmie.' Barl shook her head. There were tears in her eyes. 'Of course that's what you thought. I should have realised.'

A tiny, warm flush of hope. 'So you're not dismissed? You haven't stormed out of the artisanry in a huff?'

Her chin lifted. 'Remmie Lindin. Never in my whole life have I stormed *anywhere* in a *huff*!'

He could argue that, easily, but this probably wasn't the best time. 'Then what's happened? Are you ill? Oh, justice. You're ill. Have you sent for a pother?' He leapt up. 'I'll send for a pother. What are you doing out here? Go to bed!'

'No, Remmie, no . . .' She pressed her hands to her face. 'Do stop fussing. I'm not ill.'

'Then what—' And then he realised, because only one other catastrophe could have sent her home to hide. *The College.* He sank back to the wobbly bench. 'Oh. Oh, I see. You've heard.'

Hands lowered again, Barl stared at the idly paddling drake.

'I honestly can't decide which is worse. That they turned me down a second time . . . or that they had Arndel deliver the blow.'

*'Arndel?'*

'Yes. So now I'm twice scolded. Properly put in my unranked place.'

He'd not expected that. 'It's poorly done, I think. They could have refused you kindly. There's no need for unkindness, or disrespect.'

'No need?' She laughed, scornful. 'Don't be a fool, Remmie. They wanted to hurt me. To teach me a lesson. Why else make me wait so long for an answer? Why else seek to cause trouble between me and Arndel?'

And she was right, of course. There could be no other reason. But it made him uncomfortable, that the greatest mages in Dorana could be so vindictive. So petty. Barl was no threat to them. Such behaviour made them look small.

'I suppose,' he said, hating to admit it. 'And what of Arndel? Is he very displeased with you?'

She shrugged. 'What do you think?'

*I think all this misery could've been avoided if only, for once, you'd listened to me.*

But he couldn't say that. 'I think he's probably fuming.'

'And you'd be right. But he's not angry enough to dismiss me.' A sideways glance. 'So you can breathe easy.'

'I'll never breathe easy, Barl,' he retorted. 'Not so long as you persist in arrogantly tempting fate like this.'

He'd thought – hoped – she'd snap back at him for that. But she didn't. Aching, he watched as she slid from the bench and walked to the duck pond's soggy, weed-frilled edge. There she stood with her back to him, her head lifted defiantly . . . and with her arms hugged tight to her ribs, holding herself against the angry grief he could feel churning through her in enormous, sickening waves.

'Barl.' He bit his lip. 'Tell me the truth. Did you really think they would let you in?'

'I don't know,' she said, after a long silence. 'I wanted to. Honestly, I thought they might. I thought there was a chance they'd see past themselves and do the right thing. For the College. For Dorana.'

In that case, she truly had been living in a dream. 'I know how much you wanted this. I'm so sorry.'

'Really?' she said, not turning. 'I'd have thought you'd want to gloat. Prance about shouting *I told you so*.'

And that hurt. 'How can you say that?'

'Easily,' she said, shrugging again. 'I've always been nastier than you, Remmie.'

'Then you can bite your nasty tongue,' he snapped. 'Just because this has fallen out the way I always thought it would doesn't mean I'm pleased you've been slapped down.'

'But you're pleased I'm not leaving Batava, aren't you? Pleased you're not being dragged along at my heels again.'

'And what if I am? Does that mean I can't be genuinely sorry you're disappointed?'

She flicked him a darkly sardonic glance. 'Do you know what I think? I think you'd have sulked a while, and then fallen in love with Elvado. I think you tell yourself you love Batava because it's easier, it's less painful, than admitting the truth.'

His fingers were clenching again. With an effort he relaxed them. 'And what truth would that be?'

'That you wish as much as I do you had the chance to live there. To maybe get yourself noticed by some of the greatest mages in all Dorana.'

Shocked, he felt the hard thud of his heart. *She doesn't mean it. She can't. She's hurt, and she's lashing out.* But even though he knew that, he couldn't stop himself from lashing back.

'I don't know why it is you *never* believe what I say. What will it take to convince you I'm not interested in being noticed? I couldn't care less for your *great mages*, Barl. Most everything I need to make me happy is here in Batava. And no matter what you say, no matter how hard you try to tell yourself, and me, that you know my heart better than I do? You don't.'

129

Silence, as his sister watched the drake dabble and splash in the pond's murky water. And then she heaved a great sigh.

'Anyway, it hardly matters. You were right and I was wrong. I can't change anything. I've no power at all.'

She'd hurt him with her waspish tongue. She often did. More often than he liked to admit, or ever told her. But it wasn't in him to further twist the knife that the College had plunged through her heart.

'You're mistaken, Barl,' he said quietly. 'You have the power to make beautiful things. Not just clocks. I think clocks are just the beginning. In time I've no doubt you'll become Dorana's greatest artisan mage. I think you'll make things other mages can only dream of.'

Barl laughed, the sound breathy and shaken. 'You don't need to flatter me, Remmie. I've no intention of casting myself into the pond.'

'It's not flattery. I mean it.'

'I know,' she said, and turned. The lowering sun glittered the tears on her cheeks. 'But please, don't say anything more. Let's just go pick your wretched beans and carrots.'

Nodding, he stood. Hurting miserably for her, knowing there was nothing he could say or do to make this better. In her own time, in her own way, she'd have to come to acceptance. Find a way to ease the disappointment, a reason to laugh and smile.

'Yes. All right.'

'Barl!' Ibbitha hurried to meet her halfway to her workbench. 'Should you be here? Master Arndel told us yesterday you were taken poorly. I must say, you look peaked. Perhaps you should take another day in bed.'

The concern was meant kindly, but it set her teeth on edge. Easing her hands free of Ibbitha's solicitous clutchings, Barl smiled then edged sideways toward her bench.

'I'm fine,' she said. 'It was only a megrim. Besides, if I'd stayed abed again today I'd only have fretted over Lady Grie's clock.

Master Arndel is very anxious it be finished, since he promised her delivery of it this afternoon.'

'Oh,' said Ibbitha, following. Her lips thinned. 'Yes. Of course. We mustn't upset Lady Grie.'

So, there was still a lingering resentment over that, was there? She shouldn't be surprised. There were artisans here who'd had worked years for Arndel and never attracted the attention of an influential First Family mage. And while she and Ibbitha might be friendly, their bond wasn't near deep enough to overcome the perceived slight.

*She can't bring herself to admit that on my worst day I'm twice the mage she'll ever be. None of them can. But it's not my fault and I won't feel guilty for it.*

Especially since not one of them, aside from Ibbitha, bothered to ask after her health or even glance up as she slid onto her workbench's stool. Doubtless they were sorry she didn't lie at death's door. Doubtless they'd spent all yesterday coveting the natal clock she'd almost finished, hoping, dreaming, that she was gone for good and that Arndel would point them out to Lady Grie and that Lady Grie, forgetting her, would show them favour instead.

*Dream on,* she thought, sneering on the inside where they couldn't see. *Dead or alive, Arndel's favourite new patron won't forget me.*

The natal clock for Ancilla Grie's mother was close to complete. Oblivious to her fellow artisans and their occasional hushed to-and-fro comments, ignoring Ibbitha, whose frequent glances suggested she had more to say, not even acknowledging Arndel when he entered the workroom to count heads and issue orders, Barl poured herself into the final, exacting incants that would see her latest commission a success. Lady Grie's design this time featured a full moon and the rising sun, sharing a starless sky. So for the clock's steady tick she wove an incant echoing the hoots of an owl, that popular symbol of wisdom . . . and for its hourly chime a brash cockerel's crow, optimistic herald of the new day. Both incants were a challenge, but there was no chance she would fail.

Finished at last, the incants warded safe within the glossy clock, she slid off her wooden stool and slipped out of the workroom for a few precious moments, to breathe in some fresh air and wriggle the kinks out of her spine. The late morning sky was beginning to gauze over with high cloud, and it was cooler than it had been when she'd left Remmie brooding over his morning poached egg and brown toast. She thought she could taste the promise of rain.

Wandering the outside of the artisanry, arms folded against the slight chill, she felt the day before's bruised feeling return as her glow of success faded. Her eyes were scratchy and tired. Tormented by failure, she'd not passed a restful night. And though, for Remmie's sake, she'd tried hard to show a careless face at breakfast, she'd not managed to fool him . . . and his concern was another burden wearing her down.

*He'd be better off if I wasn't around. I think it's time he lived his own life, and stopped fretting about mine. We've been in each other's pockets ever since Mama and Pa died. That's long enough.*

Not that he'd agree. Remmie was convinced she couldn't manage without him. And though she'd told him and told him he was very much mistaken, he wouldn't listen. Which meant he left her with no choice: she'd have to convince him the hard way, by deed instead of word.

*But not yet. Let the dust settle on this College business. Let him see I've not fallen into a heartbroken decline. And then, once he's stopped hovering . . .*

She'd thought about little else most of the night, and while she walked to the artisanry. Six more months, she'd decided. That was all she needed. Six months taking advantage of Lady Ancilla Grie's patronage and learning what little there remained for Arndel to teach her. Then she'd look for a new artisanry, in the northern or western districts, say. A goodly distance from Batava, at any rate. An artisanry that would appreciate her talents, that would pay her what she was truly worth and give her room to grow.

And when she found it, she wouldn't tell Remmie. She'd slip out of their cottage in the dead of night, leaving an apologetic note and a promise she'd be fine. So he could live his life, and she could live hers, and they could care for each other from a sensible distance.

*He deserves to be happy, to have a family, not struggle along always caught in my wake. And since he won't free himself, I have to do it for him.*

He'd be furious, of course. He might even, for once, hold a genuine grudge. But she'd rather live with him angry than go on watching him deny his own happiness for her sake.

*If I don't do this, I'll start to hate him for caring.*

And if that ever happened, her heart really would break.

Drifting to a halt she closed her eyes and tilted her face to the sun. Still bruised, still shaken, but at the same time oddly at peace.

'Mage Lindin? *Mage Lindin!*'

So much for peace. Breathing out her resentment, beating down her stubborn pride, Barl schooled her expression to polite enquiry and turned.

'Yes, Artisan Master?'

Arndel was wearing his swallowed-hedgehog face. 'What are you doing out here?' he demanded, striding across the grass toward her. 'Have you finished Lady Grie's clock?'

'I have, Artisan Master.'

'Then why did you not—'

'Master Arndel, I was just coming to fetch you.'

Halting, he snorted. 'Indeed.' His face pinched even tighter. 'You're to take the clock to Lady Grie. She is sending a carriage. Come now and show me it won't disgrace the artisanry.'

*She* was to take the clock? By herself? But before she could ask, Arndel marched off toward the workroom, and all she could do was hurry after him, perplexed.

# CHAPTER NINE

'I'm told your brother is a man for whom teaching is a passion, Mage Lindin. Would you agree?'

Barl took her time turning away from the picture window in Lady Grie's grand parlour. The comment was an odd way for the woman to announce her presence. Did she think complimenting Remmie would set an unranked mage at ease? Or was her intent more sinister?

*I know who your family is. And if you displease me, who can say what I might do?*

She didn't know Lady Grie well enough to be certain. Best to be cautious, then, and remain on her guard.

'Lady Grie,' she said, nodding respectfully. 'Artisan Master Arndel asks me to convey his best wishes, and his hope that you find your clock satisfactory.'

Today Lady Grie was dressed in blue silk, her hair pinned with sapphires, her slender throat captured by gold. She closed the parlour doors, then flicked a careless glance at the gift for her mother, covered and placed on the carved wooden sideboard by a servant.

'I've no doubt I shall.' One eyebrow arched. 'You haven't assuaged my curiosity.'

And nor did she want to. Remmie had nothing to do with this woman. His pupils were unranked, his world far removed from hers.

*But I don't dare displease her.*

Resenting that, she forced a polite smile. 'Remmie's a fine teacher, yes. His students care for him very much.'

'But do they learn?'

'He says they do.'

Lady Grie arched both her eyebrow. 'And what do you say?'

'I say he's right, but you can hardly count me disinterested. He's my brother.'

'I have two brothers,' said Lady Grie. 'I never compliment them, nor do they compliment me. Our loathing is mutual. Such is the joy of family.'

Barl linked her fingers behind her back. All this pointless chitchat, and if she was late returning to the artisanry Arndel would blame her.

'Lady Grie—'

Waving a hand for silence, Lady Grie crossed the plush cream carpet to a silk-striped, plumply cushioned armchair and lowered herself into it with a groaning sigh. She looked monstrously uncomfortable, a life-sized discouragement to any woman contemplating a child.

'I'm curious about your brother, Mage Lindin, because I'm curious about you. So much talent in an unranked mage, it's not . . . usual. I'm intrigued.'

Barl blinked. 'Oh.'

Lady Grie rubbed a smooth, slender hand over her distended belly. The blue silk rustled, whispering of wealth. 'And because I'm intrigued, I made some inquiries. It seems you've ruffled feathers in the College of Mages. And the Hall of Knowledge.'

Hearing that was like being doused with ice water. Before she could stop herself, Barl took a step forward, her temper woken and seething. 'The Council's told tales of me? To *you?* Lady Grie—'

'No, no, not the Council,' the woman said. 'Your Guild. So

many important people upset with you, Mage Lindin. I have to say, I'm surprised. I thought you were clever.'

And what did that mean? Had Lady Grie changed her mind? Did she not want Barl Lindin's exclusive services any more?

*If that's so, then Arndel will surely dismiss me. The blow to his pride won't permit anything less.*

And if she was dismissed . . .

No reputable artisanry took on a mage without first checking that mage's standing with the Guild. Her standing was precarious now, thanks to the College proctor and interfering Lord Hahren. More than likely she'd be disparaged. Recommended against.

*If my life falls to pieces, and takes Remmie down with it, I doubt he'll forgive me. Not this time.*

'Mage Lindin—' Lady Grie leaned forward as far as her belly would allow. 'You've gone quite pale. Are you unwell?'

Upset, she answered without thinking. 'No, I'm *angry*. The Guild had no right to talk of me. What business is it of theirs if I choose to further my studies?'

'I think you'll find it's where you want to further them that's caused the consternation.'

And now Lady Grie sounded exactly like Remmie. '*Why?* Because it's the College and my family is unranked?' She folded her arms tight across her aching stomach. 'I tell you I am sick to death of this nonsense. By what right do ranked mages trample my dreams? I am no criminal, I do not seek to use magic in any unlawful way. All I want is a chance to test the length and breadth and depth of my talent in the best school Dorana has to offer. There is no good reason for that chance to be denied me. My rejection by the College is nothing but a conspiracy of pettiness.'

'Well, well, well.' Lady Grie laughed. 'You're quite the firebrand, aren't you?'

Silenced, Barl let her arms fall by her sides. *Oh, my wretched temper.* 'I'm sorry, Lady Grie. I forgot myself. It won't happen again.'

'That would be for the best,' said Lady Grie, eyebrows raised again. 'Now show me my new clock. I've told my mother

I have a wonderful surprise for her. I'm keen to know you've not made a liar of me.'

So her foolishness was to be swept under the fine cream carpet, was it? Soundlessly sighing, Barl relaxed her tight fingers.

*I'll not complain. I'll even wield the broom myself if it keeps me safe in the artisanry.*

'Of course, my lady.'

She removed the warded cloth from the clock, hefted her heavy crystal creation from the sideboard to the small round table Lady Grie indicated, then stood back.

*Like it. Please like it. You have to like it. It's beautiful.*

'Hmmm,' said Lady Grie, roaming her sharp gaze over each twist and curve of the clock's crystal housing. 'Let me hear it.'

A whispered incant released the clock's tick and chime. Lady Grie smiled at the owl hoots, then clapped her hands in delight as the raucous cock-crow chime faded into silence.

'Wonderful! I adore it. Better yet, my mother will be most diverted. And I assure you, Mage Lindin, such a feat is not easily achieved.'

'*Remember,*' Artisan Master Arndel had warned her before she left the artisanry. '*If Lady Grie should compliment your work, you are to take no credit, is that clear? The design was hers, you but followed her lead. Her taste is exquisite. The clock's success is her own.*'

Mindful of her precarious position, Barl pasted a modest smile to her lips. 'The clock practically made itself, Lady Grie, so wonderful was your original design.'

Lady Grie snorted. 'Arndel told you to say that, did he? Well, you've done as you were bid. But know that *I* know how much is due to you.'

Barl felt a warm flush of pleasure. Immediately resenting it, she returned the clock to the sideboard. If only the woman's approval didn't mean so much. If only she could prove Remmie wrong, and be indifferent to praise. But she couldn't. When she was sure her expression was once more blandly polite, she turned to Lady Grie.

'Master Arndel hopes you know that his door remains open to you always, my lady.'

Another snort. 'In the hope that my purse remains open to him. And so it shall, Mage Lindin, provided you are here to turn my idle dreams into reality.'

'Of course, Lady Grie.'

*Where else would I be but in Batava, since I'm denied a privilege that you take for granted?*

Lady Grie tapped her fingertips on the arm of her chair. 'Your expression tells me plainly you think I am ignorant of your plight. You're mistaken. I may be a First Family mage, Barl, but we are not all of us equal. I could yearn for a place on the Council of Mages, but I would yearn in vain. As you vainly yearn for a place in the College.' Her lips curved into an edged smile. 'I tell you this so you'll know I understand your frustrations. And because I understand them, I shall protect you as best I can, and see you are well treated by Master Arndel.'

'Oh.' Surprised almost speechless, Barl nodded. 'That is kind of you, Lady Grie.'

'Not really. I don't wish to lose your magework.'

At least the woman was honest. 'As I don't wish to lose your patronage, my lady.'

Lady Grie shrugged. 'Continue making beautiful things for me and you won't.' With a grimace, she shifted in her chair. 'You can collect payment for my mother's gift from Dassett on your way out. The carriage will return you to the artisanry. Tell your esteemed Artisan Master I'll have another commission for you soon.'

She was dismissed. Bowing, one hand pressed to her heart so Lady Grie might not doubt her sincerity, Barl took her leave.

On his knees in his vegetable patch, weeding, Remmie glanced up. 'You're lucky Lady Grie is so understanding. If she'd taken offence at your outburst . . .'

'Well, she didn't,' Barl said, snappish, and brushed damp dirt from a filched baby carrot. 'Besides, she's the lucky one. That clock will have her mother in raptures. Which works well for me,

I must say.' She crunched the carrot. 'Her approval of my work will keep me sweet with Arndel.'

'In other words, you're using her.'

She wriggled a little, trying to get comfortable on the upturned tin bucket she was using for a seat. 'We're using each other. And what does that matter, if we both get what we want?'

Dubious, Remmie sat back on his heels. 'And what is it you want, Barl?'

'To put this upset behind me.' And while it wasn't the whole truth, it was still true. She wasn't lying to Remmie. He'd never be able to throw that accusation in her face. 'For Arndel to recognise my worth to him. To have my crystal acknowledged by the Guild.' But that would have to wait until the College's kicked-up dust settled. '*And* I want to explore my gifts as an artisan.'

Remmie plucked another weed and shredded it. 'So. You really are taking no for an answer, this time? You've not got some mad scheme tucked up your sleeve?'

'The only thing tucked up my sleeve is my arm.' At his look, she shook her head. 'You don't believe me?'

'I want to,' he said slowly. 'Only . . . Barl, I know how much you want to attend the College.'

'And if wanting meant having then I'd not be here, would I? But it doesn't, and I am, and now you've got what *you* wanted.' She shoved off the old bucket, nearly tipping it over. 'I'm not stupid, Remmie. I know when I'm beaten.'

'Sorry,' he said. 'I didn't mean to—' He rubbed the back of his hand along his jaw, smearing dirt. 'Sorry. Let's talk about something else. Does Lady Grie want you to make her another clock?'

She dug her heel into the edge of the vegetable patch. 'Not yet. But soon, she said. She'll have something for me soon.'

'There you go,' he said, smiling. 'See? Things are looking up.'

Dear Remmie. He did try but, really, he'd never understand.

'Now make yourself useful,' he added, 'and help me with these weeds.'

She hated weeding. She wasn't a gardener. She loathed the damp, musty smell of compost and the scratchiness of dirt beneath her nails. But the time was fast approaching when she'd be leaving him behind.

She helped Remmie with his weeds.

The next morning, Arndel sent her back to the trade workroom.

'Mage Egin has the gripe,' he said. The glint in his eye dared her to complain. 'And there are trade clocks for export to Brantone that must be done by week's end.'

'Of course, Artisan Master,' she said, compliant. There was her Lindin crystal at home, waiting for his submission to the Guild. Give him the smallest excuse and he'd likely smash it instead. 'I'll get started right away.'

And with gritted teeth she filled in for hapless Tagget Egin.

Four days he was absent from the artisanry, him and his inconvenient gripe. Every time the trade workroom doors opened during those long four days she looked around, hoping it was Arndel with a new commission from Lady Grie. But though he often came to supervise, he always came empty-handed. On the fifth day Tagget Egin sheepishly reappeared. With scarcely concealed relief she gave him back his trade workbench and returned to her place in the smaller, specialist artisan room.

'That's good timing,' Ibbitha greeted her. 'We've some new commissions coming today. Master Arndel told us last night.'

*New commissions*. Barl felt her heart double-thud. She was so tired of trade clocks she could easily scream. Her fingers itched to make something fabulous, something beautiful. Something for Ancilla Grie. If she never again saw the makings for another tedious trade clock, she'd die happy.

Not long after the artisanry clock finished chiming the work day's start, Arndel entered with a sheaf of papers tucked under his arm. Designs for their latest commissioned pieces. One by one he handed them out, to Ada Mortyn and Nyn Bardulf and Ibbitha. Last of all he stopped before her bench.

'Mage Lindin,' he said, and handed her the final design.

Staring at it, she felt an unpleasant jolt beneath her ribs. 'It's a journey clock.'

'Indeed it is,' said Arndel. 'How perceptive of you.'

She scarcely noticed his dry sarcasm, too overwhelmed by the larger insult of the commission.

'It's for Lady Lassifer,' Arndel added. 'Her nephew travels soon to an appointed position in the Seventh district.'

Another unpleasant jolt. 'Lady Lassifer? But—'

'That's correct. Why?' Arndel raised an eyebrow. 'With Mage Egin recovered, did you think I would pay you to sit idle until Lady Grie dreams up something else for you to make?'

She bit her lip. 'Of course not, Artisan Master. But it's a *journey* clock. With a design so simple it makes Lord Traint's piece seem a miracle of complexity. The least accomplished mage in the artisanry could create it with his eyes shut. I am worthy of a greater challenge than *this*.'

A sudden hush in the workroom. Feeling her fellow artisans' disparaging stares, Barl curled her fingers to fists beneath the cover of her bench.

'Indeed?' Arndel's eyebrow lifted higher. 'Well, Mage Lindin, that is your opinion. *My* opinion is that you are employed to undertake whatever task I deem suitable. Are you refusing the commission?'

A paltry journey clock. Oh, how she ached to snatch up the inked design, scrunch it into a ball and throw it in his face.

*Why would you do this, Arndel? Why would you waste me? You know what I am!*

There was an odd look on the Artisan Master's face, as though he both wanted and dreaded her making even more of a scene. In his eyes, that familiar, curdled resentment. How petty. Whatever she achieved only made him and his artisanry stand higher.

*His meanness blinds him. But if I push him any further he'll find a way to punish me, out of spite.*

So she surrendered, the effort nearly breaking something

inside her. 'I'm sorry, Artisan Master,' she murmured. 'I was . . . taken aback. Of course I'll make Lady Lassifer her journey clock.'

'How very obliging of you, Mage Lindin,' Arndel sneered. 'You render me almost speechless with gratitude. Now get to work. I shall return in due course to see how you progress.'

'Artisan Master,' she said, keeping her gaze pinned to the design on the bench.

As Arndel slammed the workroom door shut behind him, a hissing babble of whispers broke out. Ibbitha actually left her own bench for a scolding confrontation.

'Barl! Are you truly so arrogant you think you can get away with such outrageous behaviour? And that no-one, not even Master Arndel, will call you to account for it?'

There was that ugly word again. *Arrogant.* First Remmie, now Ibbitha. And from the corner of her eye she saw the other mages nodding, agreeing with her so-called friend's stringent accusation.

And oh, she was *tired* of being called that ugly name.

'Why is it, Ibbitha, that confidence is so quickly smeared into something unpleasant?' she demanded. 'Why is it wrong for me to believe in myself? Why is it desirable that I apologise for being *good*?'

'Nobody's asking you to apologise, Barl,' said Ibbitha, still rankled. 'We'd just like you to appreciate that you're not the only talented mage working here.'

*Perhaps not, but I'm the most talented.*

Only if she said that, though they all knew it, the fuss would take a week to die down. There might even be a formal complaint lodged, which would be all the excuse Arndel needed to exact a painful revenge for the wrongs he believed she'd done him by simply existing.

'You're right, Ibbitha. I'm sorry.' She looked around the workroom. 'I didn't mean to offend.'

Ibbitha sniffed. 'Perhaps not, Barl, but you do. And I tell you plainly, we're sick to death of it.'

And on that flouncing note, Ibbitha returned to her workbench.

Uncomfortably aware of the other mages and their unfriendly glances, Barl pushed her feelings deep inside and looked more closely at the journey clock's design.

*Brantish green sand. Three topaz. One emerald. Copper wire. Gold wire. Two gold drop weights.*

Stifling a sigh, she fetched the necessary supplies and settled down to work. Breathed out her own lingering resentment and sank herself into magic's welcome embrace.

First, the journey clock's heart, its time-telling centre. Spin and thin the gold wire, spin the copper wire to match it and meld the two into one coppery gold conductor. Twist it, shape it, let the magic mould it into a cradle for the incant that would tell time until the end of time itself. Suspend it between the two gold drop weights. Infuse the topaz and emerald with the counter-balancing incants. Set them in their gentle orbit, round and round the coppery gold cradle. Swiftly working, Barl felt the building tension . . . felt the power rise . . . and though she despised the clock for its unimaginative simplicity, still she felt herself fall in love, because the magic was never anything less than wondrous.

That done, she transmuted the Brantish green sand into shimmering green crystal for the clock's housing. Not satisfied with the resulting flat leafish tint, she breathed the merest hint of lake blue into the glass. Not enough to darken it, wanting only to enhance the clear colour's depth. *Perfect.*

And now to the crystal's shaping. The clock's design called for a sphere, inside which the time-piece workings would be infinitely suspended. Delicately, Barl laid the flat sheet of greeny-blue crystal across her workbench's padded support stands. Slid her right hand beneath it, palm up and fingers spread, and with her left hand traced a careful sigil on the air. It ignited dark crimson. The next sigil burned bright blue. The third and final sigil shone a dull, burnished gold. Power shivered across her skin.

'*Rondolo.*'

The air above the crystal sheet shimmered. A single sweet note sang out of the glass . . . and it began to writhe and melt, forming into a perfect orb.

'That's it,' she crooned, as the power in her right hand kept the growing sphere aloft. 'Dance for me.'

With a snap of her fingers, she halted the transmutation just before the crystal sphere sealed itself shut. Then, holding her breath, she guided the gold-and-copper cradle, with its gold drop weights and orbiting gemstones, inside the crystal sphere. *Exactly.* Another finger-snap restarted the transmutation. Four steady heartbeats later, and the sphere was sealed shut.

Now the timepiece incant, so familiar she could create it in her sleep. Fourteen syllables, three sigils, and it was done. The clock's inner workings accepted it without complaint.

As she smiled, ridiculously pleased, the artisanry clock sounded the luncheon break. Ibbitha and the others abandoned their clock-maging, but she stayed. She wasn't hungry. Besides, she wanted to finish the clock within a day, faster than any other mage here could complete it. Just to remind Arndel of how good she was.

The final touch for Lady Lassifer's piece was its chime and tick and toll. For Lord Traint's journey clock, since he was a district inspector, she'd created a deep, custodial sound, ripe with undertones of authority. But she knew nothing of Lady Lassifer or her nephew, and she wasn't inclined to go chasing after Arndel to find out.

*Birdsong. Everybody loves birdsong. And from the look of this design Lady Lassifer has as much originality as a hen.*

But her fresh irritation faded as she crafted the incant that would give a sweet voice to the green crystal clock. When it was finished she smiled again, then put the incanted crystal aside so the delicate energies could settle before it was melded into the clock.

Abruptly aware of stiff muscles, Barl took advantage of the brief respite and wandered around the quiet workroom. She was curious to see what her fellow mages were creating. And yes, just as she'd expected, everyone else's tasks were far more alluring than her own.

*One day I shall make Arndel sorry for wasting me like this.*

She gasped a little, seeing Nyn Bardulf's fantastic piece. It

144

was a rearing winged horse, front hooves striking the air. To get that pulsing, heartsblood crimson he must have used the mortally expensive firesands from Manemli. Whoever could afford such extravagance for a clock?

*Of course,* she thought, looking at the inked design. *The Tarkalin of Ranoush. Only a fabulously wealthy ruler would have the coin for a clock like this.*

A wave of violent envy flooded through her. Why should Nyn Bardulf be singled out for such an honour? She could have crafted this clock as well as he. Better. There was the tiniest flaw in his crystal, she could feel it. A clumsiness in the transmuting of the sand. Probably the clock would keep time all right, wouldn't shatter. Nyn wasn't a bad mage. He had a certain gift.

*But I'd have made this clock without flaw.*

Aching, she crossed to the next bench. It was Ada Mortyn's, whose crystal-work was bound to be little better than adequate. Prepared to be offended, instead she felt a warning prickle stand the hair on the nape of her neck.

*Trouble.*

But the warning didn't come from Ada Mortyn's partially completed crystal sphere. Uncertain, Barl looked around. There was an off-kilter incant here somewhere, she was certain. Squibs of pain were bursting behind her eyes now, half-blinding her. But she couldn't put her finger on which –

The workroom doors opened, and her fellow artisans jostled in.

'What are you doing, Barl?' Ada Mortyn demanded. 'Leave my work alone!'

'Oh, be quiet, Ada,' she said, impatient. 'I'm not touching it. Look—' She pressed the heel of her hand to her temple, wincing. 'Something's wrong. Can't you feel it?'

'No,' said Nyn Bardulf. 'You're imagining things.'

She wasn't. Frustrated, she watched Ibbitha and the others return to their benches, oblivious to the danger. The pain behind her eyes was pulsing . . . pulsing . . .

'Barl!' Ibbitha protested. 'What are you doing? Stop it! Put that down!'

'I'm fetching Arndel!' somebody else shouted, but she didn't care about them either. Eyes closed, she clutched Ibbitha's silver incant cradle, but couldn't feel anything wrong. The problem wasn't here. Tossing it aside she leapt next to Baret Ventin's bench. He tried to block her, but she was so angry, so desperate, she nearly pushed him to the floor.

And there it was, the source of the danger. The unravelling incant was in the central timepiece of Baret's exquisitely opulent funeral clock. Commissioned by Lord and Lady Somerfell to honour his late father, it was worth even more than the Tarkalin of Ranoush's extravagance.

And it was about to blow apart, and take the artisanry with it.

'Baret, you snivelling idiot, *what did you do?*'

Deaf to his ranting, to her shouting fellow artisans, she snatched up the clock. The unstable incant hammered against her mage-sense, throbbing pain through every bone and muscle. Fighting the urge to run, she opened herself to the twisting mayhem of Baret's mistake.

Except it wasn't a mistake. He'd done this on purpose.

*What was he thinking? You can't thread the central helix counterclockwise! All that does is unravel the incant's foundations. Baret, you – you jigget!*

His misguided attempt to treble the clock's natural life span had resulted in a fatal torquing of the incant. Like beads popping off a broken string, each of its elements was springing free of alignment, tearing the delicate magework's balance to shreds. And if she didn't reverse its wild unravelling –

On a sob, she plunged her mage-sense into the heart of Baret's chaos. Cried out as she felt the distortions of power lash at her. The incant was almost entirely unravelled now, a rope of fire with its strands cut nearly all the way through. Acting on desperate instinct and arrogant faith, she wrapped her mage-sense around the unstable incant and sank to her knees. Sought to smother the flames and undo the damage.

*Hamina. Leba'cek. Nusti. Ach'ara. Dolni. Dolni.*

They were words of command to halt stupid, ignorant Baret's

unravelling incant in its tracks. She felt them clash with his robust magework, sizzle and spark and shiver through the workroom. Crying out at the pain, she thought she might be catching fire. Wasn't sure if she cared, though it hurt so much . . .

But that didn't matter. All that mattered was averting disaster. Except she wasn't averting it. She'd slowed it down a little but the incant was still unravelling.

*No!*

She plunged herself deeper still into the maelstrom. And this was dangerous, this was reckless. Clock mages played with elemental forces, with *time*. And Baret might be a jigget but he was a powerful mage, too. In twisting this incant he'd not just captured one of the natural world's greatest impulses, he'd imposed his will on it. Clock magery was about working in harmony with the elements, but *stupid* Baret Ventin had attempted domination.

*Now this is arrogance, Ibbitha. This is a mage with more power than sense.*

And now nature, resentful of Baret taking such liberties, was fighting back . . . and if she wasn't careful it would beat her to a pulp even though she was doing her best to put things right.

The funeral clock's rising heat scorched through her lightly padded green linen tunic. Its crystal carapace was thrumming a rising song of distress. Tears pricked her closed eyes in desperate sympathy. Her bones began to hum in counterpoint to its violent tune.

If she was going to stop this, she had to stop it now.

*Dolni. Dolni. Trinta'da. Va'rai.*

But the words of power weren't enough.

With a wailing cry she lifted her right hand against the fiery mayhem. Uncrooked a clawed finger, eyes screwed tight shut, and drew a dangerous sigil in the dark. *Rantiracek*. The sigil of endings. It was a crazy gamble. Undoing another mage's work was crushingly difficult at the best of times.

The sigil's power ripped through her, sundering her flesh from bone. Or so it felt. Curled onto her side, shuddering, she could only breathe and hope. Though she lay utterly unmoving, it seemed the artisanry rocked around her, rippled beneath her, torn free from solid earth. The clock in her gasping embrace burned as hot as the sun.

*Please, please, oh please . . .*

Breath by breath the roiling chaos subsided. She could hear her heartbeat again, feel the air rasping in and out of her lungs. She could feel Baret's incant, frozen in time. Harmless now, and the artisanry saved. Slowly, she rolled onto her back and prised open her eyes.

*Justice preserve me. It worked.*

'And what is the meaning of *this*, Mage Lindin?'

Artisan Master Arndel, glaring down at her, his bony face flushed hectic with anger and shock. Crowded at his back, Baret Ventin and Ibbitha and the others.

'Look what she's done to the Somerfell commission,' said Baret, pointing. 'Artisan Master, she's *ruined* it.'

Her head hurt so much her vision was blurred red around the edges. Blinking, she looked down at the clock still clutched to her chest.

*Oh.*

The Somerfell funeral clock was indeed ruined, its glorious gold and peacock blue crystal smoked black and distorted into an ugly, misshapen lump of dead glass.

Artisan Master Arndel narrowed his eyes. 'On your feet, Mage Lindin.'

Awkwardly, Barl set the funeral clock on the floor. But as soon as she let go it toppled, and shattered. Everyone gasped. Sorry for the ruination of beauty, she clambered herself upright. Nobody offered a hand to help her. Every muscle hurt, her head pounded as though it would split apart, and her blistered palms stung from the heat of Baret's warped creation.

Even so, she met Arndel's frigid glare unflinching. 'This isn't my fault. That funeral clock was doomed the moment Baret meddled with the timepiece incant.'

'How *dare* you blame me for this?' said Baret, everything

about him savage. Of course he was desperate now to save his own skin. 'This is your mischief! You thought you could do a better job of the clock, because you're Barl Lindin, the greatest mage ever born. So you interfered and this is the result!'

Stunned, Barl turned on him. 'How can you stand there and tell such *lies*? You tried to force the timepiece's incant into an unnatural extension!'

Baret's gaze flicked to the pieces of smashed crystal, scattered across the floor between them. The central timepiece had rolled free, a sad, melted lump of gold and silver wiring. The incant it had contained, that Baret had toyed with, was extinguished. No proof remained of what rules he'd broken. The danger he'd put all of them in.

He looked to Arndel. 'I don't know what she's talking about, Artisan Master. I would never attempt anything so foolhardy.'

No. No. Not even Baret could be this craven. 'Yes, you did. You *know* you did.' She took a step toward Arndel, her outstretched fingers trembling. 'Artisan Master, please, you must believe me. And if I hadn't overriden Baret's meddling this artisanry would be nothing but a smoking hole in the ground! I—'

'*Enough*!' said Arndel, knocking her hand aside. 'Are you mad? Do you expect me to believe you could override Baret Ventin's magework? Mage Lindin, from the day you set foot in my artisanry you have been a disruptive presence. Until now I chose to overlook that, because your work has been satisfactory and because you pleased Lady Grie. Clearly I was in error. Clearly all I did was encourage your obstreperous arrogance. I shall do so no longer. You're dismissed.'

Barl blinked at him, stunned.

*But you can't dismiss me. Not for this. You can't.*

'Master Arndel, you're being unjust.' Her voice was thin and shaking. 'I might be outspoken, but I have never been untruthful. You won't find anyone who can claim they ever caught me in a lie. Baret Ventin's the liar here, not me.'

Arndel's lips pressed so tight they all but vanished. 'Mage Ventin has been with me for nine years. *You* have worked here less than one. And you think I should discard my good opinion of him on your unproven say-so? Give credence to your outlandish claims?'

'*Yes!* Master Arndel, you *can't* make me pay for Baret's mistake!'

'No, Mage Lindin,' said Arndel. His cold voice cut as deep as a plunged knife. 'The mistake was mine, in appointing you to this artisanry. I have rectified it. Leave. And you can be sure a report on this disgraceful affair will be sent forthwith to the Guild.'

The workroom was so hushed Barl thought she could hear every watching mage's heartbeat. Light-headed with pain and disbelief, she searched Baret Ventin's face for any hint of shame. His blank eyes stared back at her. On his lips a small, derisive smile.

*You bastard.*

Arndel pointed to the workroom door. 'Will you leave, Mage Lindin? Or must I have you removed by rough handling? If so I will make sure you cannot find magework anywhere in Dorana!'

Did he have so much influence? Perhaps. His client list was impressive. Most likely Lord Bren or Lady Grie or another of his patrons would see her ruined in return for a lifetime of generous considerations.

Barl made herself smile. 'You're a fool, Arndel. If you'd given me the chance I'd have made clocks to make you famous. I would have made you renowned throughout the known world. Now all you have is Baret Ventin. And I promise . . . before either of you is much older he'll bring this artisanry down around your foolish ears.'

And on that parting note, she walked from the workroom. Every step was a torment, her magic-battered body a shouting of pain. She welcomed it. Her bruises and scorch marks were her badge of honour. She'd done what was needful. She'd done nothing wrong.

And now she knew what it was she had to do next.

*The question is, will Remmie forgive me?*

# CHAPTER TEN

Troubled, Venette tapped her neat fingernails to the table. The sound rattled loud in the hushed Council chamber.

Brice frowned. 'You wish to say something, Lady Martain?'

He only ever called her that when he was vexed. But she wasn't the one who'd requested this urgent meeting. That was Sallis Arkley's doing. With Shari's connivance, of course. Thick as Feenish thieves, those two.

'I fail to see why this matter couldn't wait,' she said, letting her own vexation show. 'Without Morgan we can hardly claim a united stance, can we?'

Shari Frieden grimaced. 'True enough, which is why he should be here. His absence reflects poorly upon his dedication.'

'He has personal business this morning, Shari, that couldn't be postponed.'

'*Personal business.*' Shari sniffed, disapproving. 'I tell you, once Greve finally expires, Morgan will be hard-pressed to justify his lacksadaisical attitude.'

Shari Frieden really was a miserable sow. *Morgan, you idiot, why won't you be more careful?* 'You're too harsh.'

'And you, Venette, are too lenient!' Sallis said. 'But I didn't request this meeting to discuss your shortcomings.'

'Which is just as well for you, Sallis, since I would then feel obliged to point out a few of *your* flaws, such as how it came about that Morgan's pending incants were not presented for patenting with Brahn Sorvold's, and the rest!'

'*What*?' said Sallis, flushing dark red. 'Do you imply my conduct has been somehow *improper*?'

'Imply? No. I claim it as fact. Both you *and* Shari have deliberately obstructed Morgan's progress.'

Shari gasped. 'That is untrue!'

'I beg to differ.'

Shari turned to Brice. 'This is outrageous! Lord Varen, you are derelict in your duty. Will you sit there saying *nothing* while Lady Martain questions not only my integrity, but—'

'Enough,' Brice said, his eyes hooded and cold. 'Another word, Lady Frieden, and I will censure you. Lady Martain, have you proof to support such a grave accusation?'

'She does not,' said Sallis, white about the mouth. 'For there is none.'

Brice folded his hands upon the table. 'I will decide that. Lady Martain?'

Taking a moment to choose the approach that would best suit her ends, Venette looked through the nearest window at the morning's damp, cloudy sky. Elvado in the rain had a different, paler kind of beauty, like a watercolour painting trapped under glass.

*Morgan won't thank me for this. But I can't let Sallis and Shari think they play their petty games unnoticed. I promised Haeth I'd look out for her son.*

Besides. Brice should know how his Council was conducting itself. Or, if he already knew, must be made to show his hand. Either his support of Morgan was genuine, or it wasn't. It was time she knew which.

'*Lady Martain*.'

She'd tried Brice's patience far enough. Looking back, she made no effort to hide her disdain for Shari and Sallis. 'Morgan's pending incants should've been considered for a full Council vote. They were not, even though they were submitted long before those other mages' work came to our attention. That they weren't is a travesty and—'

Shari slapped the table. 'That is a *lie*! Sallis and I did consider them, and found them unsatisfactory.'

And that was too easy. 'When, Shari? Not during the one patent meeting I couldn't attend, by any chance?'

'Is that true?' said Brice, deceptively mild, as Shari and Sallis sat uncomfortably silent. 'Did you wait until Venette was absent before discounting Morgan's incants?'

So. He wasn't aware? Or was he simply playing some deep game of his own? It didn't matter. Not yet. All that mattered was pushing Sallis and Shari off-stride.

'Of course they did, Brice,' she said. 'Because they knew I'd insist on his work being placed before you. That they weren't is naught but petty politicking and bigotry.'

'Bigotry?' Sallis looked close to choking. 'Withdraw that remark, Venette. I am an honourable man.'

'In most things you are, Sallis,' she agreed. 'But when it comes to Family rankings you've a blind spot the size of the sun.'

'And you lack discrimination!' said Shari. 'Besides, it is not *petty politicking* to be mindful of appearances. Had we granted Morgan another patent so soon after his Council appointment we'd have been accused of favouritism. *Especially* since the incants he submitted weren't perfect.'

'No incant is perfect, Shari.'

'Brahn Sorvold's was.'

'We're not discussing Brahn Sorvold! Morgan's incants might benefit from a little refining, but we have in the past patented less polished work.'

Brice sighed. 'True. But like it or not, Venette, appearances do matter. Ratifying the magework of a fellow councillor has ever been a tricky business. It's Morgan's misfortune that in this instance, the timing was . . . delicate.'

'Perhaps,' she said, reluctant. 'But I'd be less worried were I not aware that Sallis and Shari have taken Morgan in strong dislike.'

'I don't see it as a problem,' said Shari, shrugging. 'You seem to like him well enough for all of us.'

Venette looked at her. 'If you think I will tolerate the slightest suggestion that an unsavoury affection exists between myself and Morgan Danfey—'

Brice pushed to his feet. *'Enough!'* Glaring, he dared them to speak. 'Venette, your concern for Morgan is commendable but misplaced. He is not slighted. I'll allow that, given his position, he is at a disadvantage but there are many mages who'd be most pleased to be as burdened as he.'

'Indeed,' Sallis muttered. 'I wonder how many accolades must be heaped on him before the young man is satisfied.'

'Given,' Brice continued, with a repressive look at Sallis, 'that he'll be a lord soon, lack of privilege is hardly Morgan's complaint. Nor does it reflect well upon him, that he would—'

'Brice, I don't raise the matter on his behalf,' Venette said swiftly. 'Believe me, if he knew I'd spoken of this he'd be furious. But I'll happily chance that. Morgan is a friend.' She glanced at Shari, a warning. 'And, I think, a great mage who hasn't begun to fulfil his potential. I simply wanted to be sure he's not being held back due to . . . irrelevant personal considerations.'

Brice sat again, slowly. 'And if that were the case, Venette, do you think I'd not know it? Do you think I'd stand idly by while the power of this Council was so blatantly misused?'

And now, it seemed, he was calling her bluff. Daring her to openly accuse him of negligence or worse. She wouldn't, of course. It was enough that she'd reminded him not to underestimate her.

'Of course not, Brice,' she said, conciliatory. 'I am sorry if my concerns gave you that impression.'

Brice accepted the apology with an ice-edged smile. 'As it happens, Venette, I've examined Morgan's submitted incants and I agree with both you and Shari. While his attention to detail isn't what it might be, Morgan is without doubt an exceptional mage. But he needs tempering. He needs to slow down. It will do him no harm to cool his heels for a time, and learn to exercise restraint of his ambition.'

As Sallis and Shari muttered their passionate agreement, Venette could not bring herself to argue Brice's point. Hadn't she said the same thing to Morgan herself, more than once? And didn't she despair, sometimes, that he'd never heed her sage advice?

*I just wish I could believe the same sentiments drove Sallis and Shari.*

But if she started another squabble she'd put herself at outs with Brice, and that would be a stupid thing to do.

'No, my lord,' she said, accepting temporary defeat. 'I doubt it will do him any harm at all.'

'I'm flattered you agree,' said Brice. 'And I charge all of you not to repeat this conversation, most especially to Morgan. Now then, Lord Arkley, might we at last touch upon the matter that brings us here?'

'Two matters,' said Sallis, his self-impressed expression sobering. 'Firstly, I would draw this Council's attention to a tempest brewing in the College.'

Venette looked down her nose at him. While she might tread warily with Brice, Sallis Arkley gave her no pause at all. 'It's Voln Hahren's job to oversee the College. Is this another matter he feels unable to address without running to us for advice? Perhaps we should be looking for a more confident mage to take his place.'

Sallis looked at Brice, as though they were comfortably alone. 'I believe Hahren is unaware of the problem. I was approached directly, by a friend. It's a delicate business. Handled clumsily, I fear there could be unfortunate repercussions.'

'And does your troubled friend have a name, Sallis?' said Brice. 'Or do you expect us to guess whose cause we are expected to champion?'

Sallow cheeks staining red, Sallis cleared his throat. 'Nevin Jordane.'

'Ah.' Brice's fingernails tap-tap-tapped on the table as he contemplated the rain running down the chamber's windows. 'So in truth we are speaking of his daughter. Yes?'

'In truth we are speaking of a mage who by rights should not have been appointed tutor at the College,' Sallis replied, his voice clipped with distaste. A vein pulsed at his temple. 'I'm sure you'll recall I had my doubts at the time.'

'And you aired them, Sallis,' said Brice. 'Comprehensively. I certainly recall that.'

Shari's lips thinned. 'Sallis was right. Bellamie Ranowen's appointment was a mistake. The woman comes from some nothing and nobody family in the Seventh district. Her appointment flies in the face of all tradition and undermines the exclusivity of the College. Furthermore, her ideas are contradictory. They challenge *years* of accepted wisdom. And now she is threatening the daughter of a highly ranked First Family. The entire situation is unacceptable!'

'Ranowen has launched some kind of vendetta against Nevin's daughter,' said Sallis. 'If she's not stopped she'll single-handedly destroy the girl's future.'

Brice's stilled fingers drummed again once, slowly. 'Vendetta? That is a very serious accusation.'

'And I make it very seriously,' Sallis replied, brows pulled low. 'Nevin's daughter is failing Ranowen's class. A vendetta is the only explanation.'

'It's my understanding,' Brice said at length, 'that, contradictory or not, unranked or not, Mage Ranowen has proven herself a gifted tutor. In the field of transmutation I've heard her expertise is unrivalled.'

Sallis shook his head. 'That's hardly the point.'

'Given that she's the girl's tutor, I feel it is a little to the point,' said Brice. 'Has Lord Jordane taken his concerns to the College proctor? Has he spoken to Mage Ranowen himself about his daughter's progress, or lack of it?'

'Or did he simply run to his good friend, the councillor?' Venette asked. 'Assuming that with his influence, this inconvenient, unranked tutor would be dismissed out of hand?'

Sallis shifted to stare at her. 'Perhaps I imagined it, Venette, but I seem to recall you were also vocal in your opposition to

Bellamie Ranowen's appointment.' His expression twisted. 'Or is the problem that Nevin Jordane is my friend?'

Caught hypocrite, she willed herself to hold Sallis's taunting gaze. 'Your friendships aren't the point, Sallis. And yes, I expressed reservations at Bellamie Ranowen's appointment. I don't make any apology for that. But as Brice rightly points out, it seems she has proven her worth. To every rule it appears there is an exception.'

'*Seems. Appears.*' Sallis sneered. 'For myself, I prefer evidence to supposition.'

'Except you don't have any evidence,' she retorted. 'You have the wild accusations of a biased father. And you'd destroy a woman's career on no more than that? Shame on you, Sallis. Be they ranked or unranked, Dorana's mages deserve a fair hearing.'

'Agreed,' said Brice, before Sallis could gather himself for an angry reply. 'And it is this Council's responsibility to see that justice is done.'

'Then have the College proctor investigate,' she said. 'This Council cannot be seen o'erstepping its mark, Brice. You know how fiercely Hahren defends the College's independence. It occurs to me that had we not so vigorously objected to Bellamie Ranowen's appointment she might never have been taken on as a tutor in the first place.'

'So this is *our* fault?' Shari laughed, disbelieving. 'Venette, you never cease to astound me.'

'Enough!' Brice snapped. 'What's done is done. I suggest we concern ourselves with what must be done next. Sallis, am I right in thinking you've already assured Lord Jordane of our support?'

Sallis had the grace to look abashed. 'Well, yes. As it happens. Nevin was most distressed and—'

Brice lowered his hand. 'Which means a proctorial investigation is out of the question. Your presumption is noted, Lord Arkley. As for Jordane's claim, I shall instruct Morgan to investigate.'

'Morgan?' Sallis shifted again, displeased. 'Brice, I don't think—'

'I do,' Brice said flatly. 'He wasn't part of this Council when

Mage Ranowen was appointed. As far as I'm aware he does not socialise with the Jordanes. And since he's absent this morning, he's not privy to the circumstances of the complaint. That renders him impartial. You said there were two matters you wished to discuss, Sallis?'

Venette was hard put not to laugh out loud at the look on Sallis's face. Biting the inside of her cheek, she shifted her gaze to the still-weeping sky and wondered what Morgan would make of being given such a task.

*It will do him good, I think. He needs to believe he's valued. He needs to trust that Brice sees him as – well, not an equal, but not as an afterthought either.*

Dear Morgan. So proud and so prickly. Not a comfortable combination.

'I did,' said Sallis at last, his temper recovered. 'As you all know, I keep my ear close to the ground when it comes to certain . . . foreign purveyors of catalytic supplies. Not all of our neighbours are diligent when it comes to observing the relevant restrictions. Word's reached me from a reliable source that someone of late has purchased a good deal of *azafris*.'

Brice sat a little straighter, his own ill-temper forgotten. 'And when you say *a good deal*?'

'More than the law permits. It's a clear violation.'

'This purchaser's name? You have it?'

Sallis shook his head. 'Alas.'

'Perhaps now, Brice, you'll revisit the question of keeping a tighter rein on such items,' said Shari. 'Freedom is all very well, but when unscrupulous mages seek to circumvent the law, freedom must be held forfeit – for everyone's sake.'

'The penalties for illegal catalytic import are already severe, Shari.'

'And what good is that, I ask you, when we lack reliable means of identifying rule breakers?' she retorted. 'I say we must establish a register so that every transaction of dangerous substances, not just *azafris*, but *liggsinth* and *Cordett's fire* and Nantari spine-seeds and the like, is on record. Clearly, Brice, we can no longer trust that the mages of Dorana will do the right thing unprompted.'

'Nor can we expect those foreigners who sell such items to cut a hole in their own purses by informing on their customers,' Sallis added. 'They'd not stay in business long if that were their practice. And since Dorana's laws stop at its borders and the banning of such substances failed once, and will surely fail again, Shari's suggestion is the only answer.'

Brice's sigh was close to a growl. 'Shari's suggestion, like outright banning, will cause more trouble than it prevents. Sallis, I do not dismiss the gravity of this news. Far from it. But nor do I think that—'

Frozen where she sat, barely listening to Brice and Sallis brangle, Venette smoothed her face to a safe blankness. She could feel her heart thudding hard against her ribs. *Azafris.* That cursed stuff. A pity its efficacy was ever discovered. A greater pity that when its meagre source played out in Dorana, some clever Trindeki trader found it elsewhere and failed to keep his mouth shut.

Briefly closing her eyes, she saw again the look on Morgan's face as he asked her, so casually, about working with the terrible stuff. She'd known then, in her bones, that though he denied it he was about to do something rash. And now every instinct she possessed told her he had.

*You fool, my dear. You silly boy. How often do you expect me to save you from yourself?*

'Do you have an opinion, Venette?'

With a wrenching effort she forced herself to look properly interested, before Sallis or Shari noticed she felt ill enough to weep.

'I always have an opinion, Brice,' she said, pretending lightness. 'In this case, I agree with you. An overreaction to one incident will do more harm than good. But should we uncover further transgressions, I think we must seriously consider adopting Shari's suggestion.' She nodded at the woman. 'It's not that you're wrong. But I don't believe we're quite there yet.'

Brice was frowning at his steepled fingers, lips pursed as he thought through the disturbing news. 'Regardless of how we proceed in the long term, it is the short term with which we must concern ourselves now. We need a name, Sallis.'

'And if I had a name I'd provide it,' Sallis replied, shrugging. 'But these matters are kept clandestine. Names are not bruited about. I consider it fortunate that even this much information found its way to me.'

'Sallis . . .' Brice looked up, his stare forbidding. 'There are ways to encourage volubility.'

'And if I thought they'd be useful, Brice, I'd have used them. But you must trust my judgement in this.'

'Must I?'

'Yes, if you've not taken leave of your senses.'

And clearly, Brice did not care for that reply. 'Lord Arkley, is it possible you've forgotten what happened the last time *azafris* found its way to the wrong mage?'

Venette shuddered. If Sallis had, she certainly had not. Even with the strongest banishing incants, the stench of charred flesh had sullied Elvado for near a week.

Shari touched a diffident hand to Sallis's arm. 'I know you guard your sources most jealously, but given the dangers here, perhaps—'

He shook her off. 'No. I worked too long and too hard to cultivate this connection. I won't put it at risk when I've been told all there is of use. Credit me with some acumen. I don't burn bridges before I'm sure I'll not need them again. There's still some hope of more information to come.'

With another sigh, Brice accepted defeat. 'Very well, Sallis. Pursue this matter as far as you can, would you, with all possible alacrity. If some ambitious, unprepared young mage is in possession of *azafris* in a copious quantity, we could be facing a crisis. The Council's authority might well be at risk.'

'I appreciate that,' said Sallis, just as grim. 'Never fear, I'll do my best to uncover the whole truth as quickly and discreetly as I can.'

'And is that all the bad news you have for us today?' Brice said, heavily sardonic. 'For I'm not certain my spirits can withstand another blow.'

'I'm done,' said Sallis. 'But having said that, I must say again that with regards to the Jordane matter—'

Venette leaned forward a little, engaging Brice's attention. 'I'll tell Morgan what's happened, and that he's to look into it. I'd already intended to visit the Danfey estate today and see how Greve goes on. Shall I carry him your best wishes, Brice?'

'Yes,' said Brice, after the briefest hesitation. 'I would know the truth of his condition. Morgan puts a good face on it, I'd not expect anything less, but I suspect his father's health is more precarious than he's shared with us.'

So did she. And with Maris Garrick's interest in Morgan now well and truly caught, the thought of him wantonly dabbling with *azafris* was enough to drive her into hysterics. She had to dissuade him, and quickly.

'Then I won't dally,' she said, and stood. 'How soon do you want Morgan to visit the College?'

'Today!' Sallis snapped. 'It must be today. Nevin waits on tenterhooks for the matter to be resolved. This calumnious cloud over his daughter's future must be dispersed with all haste.'

Seemingly placid, Brice smiled. 'Tomorrow will be soon enough, Venette. Or even the next day. This Council does not leap to any mage's finger-snap.'

'Brice—'

Not placid at all now, Brice silenced Sallis with a look. 'I warn you, Lord Arkley, do not further presume upon my forbearance. It was improper of Nevin Jordane to approach you, and ill-advised for you to promise anything on this Council's behalf. Be satisfied I've agreed to investigate the matter. And should your friend mislike the way it's being handled, by all means refer him to me.'

Leaving Brice and Sallis to their fuming, and Shari to murmur anxiously impartial support, Venette departed the Council chamber. Someone called her name as she hurried toward the Hall's imposing entrance, but she didn't stop. Whoever it was would

161

have to wait. Outside, paused by the fountain, she tipped her face to the cool rain and let it wash the heated flush from her cheeks.

*Morgan, I swear, I'm going to kill you.*

Trembling, but not from a chill, she recited a travel incant and let it carry her out of Elvado.

'Lady Martain.' One flickering glance at the foyer ceiling, then the Danfeys' master servant executed a punctilious bow. 'Forgive me, my lady. Were we expecting you?'

'No,' she said shortly. Oh, what was the wretched man's name? Something to do with whiskey, wasn't it? Ah, yes. 'Nevertheless, Rumm, I must ask you to disturb Councillor Danfey on my behalf. Council business, you understand. Although, before I deal with that, I would like a moment with his lordship. Lord Varen has asked me to convey his respects.'

Another ceilingwards glance. 'Of course,' said Rumm, exquisitely polite. 'That is most kind of his lordship. However, Lord Danfey has yet to rise this morning. Might I prevail upon you to take some refreshment in the parlour while I make certain he is able to receive you?'

Nearly midday and Greve was still abed? So, things were gone downhill as far as that, were they? Worse and worse. *Morgan, you should have told me.* 'That would be lovely, Rumm,' she said, smiling through her temper. 'Thank you.'

By the time the servant returned with the news that Lord Danfey would be only too pleased to entertain a visit from her ladyship, she'd accounted for two cups of tea and three small cakes.

'I take it Morgan is at home?' she said, following Rumm up the stairs to the mansion's third floor.

The servant nodded. 'Indeed, my lady. He is working, at present, with the Danfey estate manager expected within the hour.'

In other words, she should keep her unexpected visit short and sweet. 'Don't fret, Rumm. What I've come to say won't take long at all.'

162

'Very good, my lady,' Rumm replied, with just the right amount of deferential approval. The man was a marvel.

*I wonder if I can entice him to the town house? I've never met a servant who wasn't keen to improve his situation, and Jarman's not as young as he was.*

And it wasn't as though Morgan and his dying father led any kind of exciting life . . .

Reaching an imposing set of closed double doors, bound in polished brass and beautifully carved, Rumm halted and turned. 'Am I correct in surmising her ladyship has not enjoyed Lord Danfey's company for some little time?'

He was taking it upon himself to prepare her? Oh. *Morgan, my dear. I am so very sorry.* 'Yes, Rumm, you're quite correct.'

Looking discomfited, his washy blue eyes eloquent, the servant closed his fingers on the brass doorknob. 'In that case, Lady Martain,' he said, his voice hushed, 'I would ask you to . . . school yourself. It pains me to say that his lordship is very much changed.'

He opened the doors and preceded her, saying in a clear and carrying voice: 'Lady Venette Martain to see you, my lord.'

The privy apartment's outer chamber was a charmingly decorated sitting room. Glancing around, Venette noted the pleasing touches of fresh flowers, a wide bowl of sweet scented herbs, the windows cracked a scarce finger-width to admit a breath of fresh air. In the generously proportioned fireplace a cheerful fire leapt and crackled. Morgan's father sat propped in a shabbily imposing wingback chair, his feet on a padded rest, wrapped in a dark blue quilted satin dressing gown, his lap and legs draped in an expensive Feenish blanket.

He looked like a living corpse.

*School yourself,* the servant had told her . . . but the warning hadn't been nearly stern enough.

Greve Danfey took one look at her face and barked his amusement. 'Justice be thanked you're not forced to look at me every day, eh, Venette?'

'Greve,' she said faintly, and drifted to a halt.

She'd used him as an excuse to come here, so she could accost Morgan and bully sense into his stubborn head before he brought himself undone. And once here of course she'd had to see Morgan's ailing father, because Brice would enquire after him and know if she prevaricated. And now that she'd seen him –

'Greve,' she said again. 'I am so very sorry. I had no idea.'

'Which is precisely as I planned it,' he replied, and feebly snapped his painfully twisted fingers. 'That'll do, Rumm. There must be a maid somewhere for you to harangue.'

Rumm bowed. 'Always, my lord.'

'Morgan's shut up in his attic, I take it?' Greve added, as the servant retreated to the apartment door.

'Yes, my lord.'

He grunted. 'My son,' he said sourly, watching the door close. 'Hardly lay eyes on him from dawn to dusk, these days. Got some twittish notion about a new incant. Won't leave it alone.'

The warm room whirled around her. *I was right,* she thought, anguished, and would have sworn she could smell *azafris*. 'I see.'

'Every time I turn around, Rumm's telling me he's locked himself away under the roof,' Greve added, and jerked a thumb toward the ceiling. 'I tell him he'll get to greatness walking, that he don't need to run, but what do I know, eh? I've only got three score years of maging experience. Won't listen to me. My own son. Don't suppose you can talk sense to him, can you, girl?'

*Girl.* So impolite. So typically Greve. 'I can try,' she said, stepping closer. It was a battle to keep the horrified pity from her face. 'This mysterious incant he's working on. Have you any idea what it's for?'

His clouded eyes, nastily crusted and sunken, gleamed at her. 'If I've an inkling, I'll not share it. Best he tells you himself, if he wants to. He'll not thank me for interfering. How's that husband of yours?'

Fear had its claws sunk deep in her chest. And there were tears for the sick old man before her, burning and crowding and blurring her vision. A mercy. She didn't begin to know how Morgan could bear looking at this travesty day after day.

'Orwin?' She had to clear her throat. 'Orwin is well. He sends you his kindest wishes, as does Brice Varen. I'm instructed particularly to convey them.'

Greve snorted. 'That old goat. Runs his precious Council of Mages with an iron fist, does he? Morgan won't tell me much of that, either. Far too nice to gossip, my son.'

'Brice is a stickler for the protocols, it's true,' she said, cautious. 'But he's fair-minded with it, Greve. I know you and he have had your differences, but he is a good man.'

Greve opened his mouth to answer, but began coughing instead. As he pressed a kerchief to his mouth, muffling the tearing sounds of distress, she looked around for some water. Greve shook his hand toward the furthest of the sitting room's three windows. A filled pitcher and a glass sat there, on the sill. Hurrying, she fetched him a drink and helped him swallow.

'You should have that beside you, Greve,' she scolded, when he'd sipped his fill. 'What use is it to you all the way over there?'

He rolled his oozing, scabbed head against the back of the chair. 'Blame my pother for that,' he croaked. 'Says I need a reason to get up and use my legs.'

'Pothers,' she said, scornful. 'They might mean well, but I've no time for them, myself.'

Chuckling, he patted her hand. 'It's a shame our stars weren't better aligned, Venette. I doubt I'd have minded being married to you.'

What could she say to that? 'Ah, Greve, you flatter me. And if it weren't for my dear Orwin . . .'

'Venette.' Sobering, Greve wrapped his fingers around hers. His skin felt like sunburned paper. 'This girl Morgan's looking at. Maris Garrick. Family ranking aside, she's good enough for him, is she?'

'I'd not have pushed them together if I didn't think so.'

'She'll not hurt him?'

'If you're asking whether her interest is genuine, then yes, Greve. I believe it is.' She hesitated, then added, 'But can you say the same of his? I'd not have Maris bruised.'

165

'As to that, I couldn't give you a firm answer,' Greve said, his gaze shifting. 'He's not spoken of her to me. Thinks I'm too old and sickly to know that in the past three weeks he's twice escorted her to a dance *and* taken her on a horseback jaunt to Knucklebone Hill.'

How aggravating. And how typically close-mouthed of Morgan. 'I think it's a good match, Greve. And we both agree it's time Morgan moved on from the past . . . don't we?'

Greve pressed the kerchief back to his lips. His fingers were trembling, and a raw wheeze rattled in his chest. 'I was a fool to indulge him,' he muttered. 'Should've pushed him to the purpose years before this. But that other girl, dying—' He looked up, his eyes frightened. 'I thought I'd lose him over it, y'know. I thought he'd break his heart and follow after her.'

'I know,' she said, gently. 'But you needn't worry now.'

'Needn't I?' Again, Greve looked to the ceiling. 'You talk to him, Venette. Make him leave this incanting nonsense alone. He's got to be married, to the Garrick girl or some other chit. Can't say I much care who he weds, provided his pick is suitable. He's patented once *and* on the Council. He's got no business—' He caught himself, lips pinching shut. 'He won't listen to me. You talk to him, Venette.'

*Azafris,* she thought, wincing, and patted Greve's unsteady hand. 'I will. Please, you mustn't fret. It's not good for you.'

He wasn't listening. 'Morgan's all right, on the Council? Holding his own, is he?'

'Very much so,' she said. 'In fact, I've come to give him a task Brice wants him to undertake. Very delicate, very sensitive, and he'd not have anyone but Morgan looking into it.'

Which wasn't a lie. She wasn't lying to a man more than three-quarters dead.

Greve's grey face lit up. 'Chosen specific by Brice Varen, is he? Well, well. There's a thing.'

'Yes,' she said. 'And I'm sorry to cut our visit short, Greve, but I really must speak to Morgan about the problem. There is some urgency to bear in mind. So if you'll excuse me . . .'

'Yes, you go, girl. I'll not have that goat Varen blaming Morgan for my dallying. Only – Venette—'

She looked down at his shrivelled claw of a hand, its twisted fingers clutching. 'Greve?'

'Get my son out of that attic,' he whispered. 'He won't listen to me.'

'I'll do my best,' she promised. 'But you ought to know, my lord, he doesn't always listen to me either.'

'Doesn't listen to anyone! Headstrong. Reckless. Always has been.'

'I used to think you encouraged him.'

'I had to,' Greve said, defensive. 'His mother was soft.'

Morgan's mother had been the sweetest soul. Her husband's iron will had broken her spirit. 'Don't fret, my lord. I'll not let any harm come to him.'

'Fond of him, aren't you?'

'Very fond. And proud, as you should be.'

Greve grunted. 'I am.'

'Does Morgan know it?'

Another grunt. '*I* know it. That's enough.'

Staring down at him, she thought of everything she should say to that. Only why bother? Morgan wasn't the only Danfey who sometimes refused to listen.

'I'll visit you again soon, Greve,' she said, and kissed his scabbed cheek. 'You rest, and get well.'

His scornful amusement followed her out of the chamber. Standing in the corridor, shaking, fingers pressing back the tears, it was some time before she could trust herself to speak. Rumm, ever-attentive, waited, holding his tongue.

'Take me to Morgan,' she said at last, her voice rough.

Rumm bowed. 'Of course, your ladyship. Please, follow me.'

# CHAPTER ELEVEN

Sweating like some brute Feenish farm hand, stripped to bare chest and *azafris*-singed trousers, Morgan roamed his smoky attic and sucked on his burned hand.

'Do your worst!' he snarled at the incant-cradle on his main workbench, where the charred remains of failed magic pungently smoked. 'I *will* have this incant!'

And to think he'd assumed that with the sigils confirmed, his troubles were over. But no, far from it, thanks to the intransigence of Hartigan's original transmutation matrix.

Cursing, he returned to his bench. Surely he'd not been misled by Rubin Cylte. The man had been a genius in the deconstruction of incants. What was it he'd written about the spliced reversal of energies?

'For pity's sake, I read it not an hour ago,' he muttered, roughly flipping the book's fragile pages in search of the relevant passage. '*And* I understood it. I'm not a dolt.'

The thought of failure was a sharpened spur dug deep in his pride. He was a Danfey, born to succeed. And if he did not . . .

*Then Dorana will pay the price.*

Which meant it was imperative that this incant did not defeat him.

Still searching Cylte's book, he felt a warning thrum through the warded attic door a breath before Rumm's diffident voice sounded on its other side.

'Sir? Councillor Danfey?'

His father's health was too precarious for him to ignore the master servant. Feeling vicious, Morgan disengaged the ward and flung the door open.

'This had better be important, Rumm, or I'll—'

The rest of his intended threat he swallowed, unspoken. Rumm wasn't alone. Behind him stood Venette, violet eyes glittering, her finely drawn jaw clenched tight.

Trouble.

Rumm bowed. 'Forgive me, sir, but Lady Martain claims to be here on Council business.'

*Claims.* That was a nice touch. It placed the blame for this unwelcome interruption square on Venette's silk-clad shoulders.

'Fine, Rumm. You can go.'

'Sir,' Rumm murmured, and left Venette to her fate.

Her chin was up, combative. 'You'd best ask me in, Morgan. This isn't a conversation you'll want to have in the corridor.'

'*Fine,*' he said again, stepping back. 'But don't think to make yourself comfortable. I'm busy.'

She swept past him. 'Never fear. We're in no danger of comfort.'

Impossible woman, treating the Danfey mansion as though it were her town house. Talking to him like he was no better than Rumm. He slammed the attic door and reignited his privacy ward.

'Council business?'

The thudding of her heels on the floorboards sounded loud and full of temper. Her turquoise Ranoushi silk tunic swirled around her as she paced. 'That's right.'

He hitched his hip onto the end of his workbench. 'You mean Sallis wasn't wasting everyone's time? Behold me amazed.'

'Sallis?' She turned on him. 'Sallis, you *arrogant* fool, knows someone has been diddling the rules of purchase for *azafris*. And

169

do not sit there smirking at me, Morgan, when I can smell the stinking stuff in the air!'

He felt the words like a hard punch, under his ribs. 'How would Sallis know about recent sales of *azafris*?'

'Oh, how does Sallis know anything? He's a skinny little spider with a far-flung web! He knows people who know people who know peddlers who know thieves. No scrap of gossip is too small for Sallis Arkley to notice. For pity's sake, Morgan, what do you need with so much of the stuff? What do you need with even a *pinch* of it?'

Did she truly expect him to tell her? A mage's privy workings were precisely that. *Privy*. To ask, no – *demand* – that he divulge the details of his work to her was the grossest of insults. Not even his father had crossed that line.

'Don't think you'll intimidate me with that haughty Danfey stare,' Venette said, scornful. 'I've been stared down by stronger mages than you.'

He slapped a hand to his heart. 'Lady Martain, you wound me!'

Still pacing, she glowered. 'Morgan, this is serious. Brice was talking of *coercion* to force Sallis's tattletale to tattle all!'

Another punch, as hard as the first. 'And did he prevail?'

Fetching up at the attic window, she turned. 'No. At least not yet. Morgan—'

'You've nothing to fear, Venette,' he said, unhitching himself from the bench. 'I'm done working with *azafris* for now. And what I have left will serve my purpose for some time.'

'Which would be what? What are you *doing* with it?'

He let his eyes and voice chill. 'Mind your manners.'

'If I could trust you weren't dancing a jig with danger, Morgan, I would!' she retorted. 'But how can I trust that when Greve *begs* me to drag you by the scruff of your neck out of this attic?'

*Now that does cross the line.*

'You've no business bothering my father. He's unwell. I won't have him upset.'

'Then stop gambling your life on *azafris*!'

170

Needing a moment to regain control of his temper, he pulled his tunic back on. Pushing its buttons through their holes, he saw his fingers were trembling . . . and felt his belly roil.

*Pestilent, pestilent Sallis Arkley. What I wouldn't give to snap my fingers and ruin him.*

'Morgan . . .' Venette's scolding tone was softened to a wheedling. 'I know you think you need to prove yourself. You don't. Not like this. Not with *azafris*. My dear, you're no longer an ordinary mage. You're a *councillor*. You have obligations.'

He gave her a swift and brittle smile. 'Really? I had no idea.'

'Oh, it pleases you to be flippant,' she said. 'Well, if you won't think of yourself, Morgan, then at least think of Maris!'

'Maris Garrick has nothing to do with this.'

'She has *everything* to do with it!' Venette took a step toward him, jewelled fingers tightening to fists. 'She has *feelings* for you, Morgan. And she believes they are reciprocated. If this goes badly she will be hurt.'

'So I'm answerable to you for her feelings, am I?'

'You must be answerable to someone!'

'Maris's parents, surely. Was she suddenly orphaned today, Venette, that you feel the need to play at being her mother?'

'Oh, *Morgan* . . .' Lips tight, Venette turned away. 'I think you must have breathed in too much of that cursed *azafris*. I have never known you so contrary.'

'And I have never known you so determined to meddle in things that are not your concern!'

She raised a finger at him. 'Maris *is* my concern. If you pursue her to an understanding and then tumble yourself into strife with your magework, you'll tumble her with you! Have you even bothered to think of that, Morgan? To think of *her*? Or does your selfish ambition blind you entirely?'

How galling, to realise that shrewish Venette was right. 'I've no intention of tumbling anywhere,' he said curtly. 'Nor am I in the habit of harming the innocent. Whatever I do, Venette, Maris Garrick will not suffer for it. You have my word.'

'Which I'll hold you to. Believe me. But Morgan, what about you? My dear—'

'Your dear Morgan can take care of himself. There's no need to fret. I am not a child.'

'There's every need,' Venette retorted. 'I can't do nothing as you wantonly chart a course toward self-destruction. Whatever magework you're pursuing here, Morgan, please, you must *stop*. Sallis and Shari would love nothing more than to tear you down. Don't tell me you want to *help* them!'

For all the difference in their ages, she was his closest friend. But even so he could not trust her with the truth, any more than he could confide in his father. She'd give no credence to his misgivings for Dorana's future. Not when he had no proof. And, being Venette, for his own good she might easily try to thwart him.

'Of course I don't want to help them,' he said. 'But neither will I live in fear of what they, or any other mage, might say or do.'

Venette sighed. 'I'm wasting my breath, aren't I? You have no intention of heeding me.'

There were tears in her eyes, and on her cheeks. She was weeping for him. No-one else he knew would do that. No-one living, at least.

'You mustn't think me ungrateful,' he said, his insulted anger doused. 'Your friendship means a great deal, Venette. Your advice and guidance too. I might not always do what you wish but I promise you, I listen.'

The look she gave him then was equal parts affection and doubt. 'And drive me to distraction. Don't forget that. Morgan, I would ask you something . . . and I need an honest answer.'

He felt his muscles tense. 'All right.'

'Do you court Maris for yourself, or to please your father?'

He hesitated, then shrugged. 'Both.'

'I thought so,' she murmured. 'And I'm sorry.'

'I've displeased you.'

'By being honest? Never.' She summoned a smile. 'But Morgan,

I'd counsel you to give your own feelings the greater weight. To be brutally frank, my dear, you're the one who'll have to live with Maris. That is, if you wed her. Your father . . .'

A different punch to the heart, this time. But there was no use dissembling, not with Venette. 'My father won't. Yes. I know.'

She knew better than to soothe him with platitudes. 'Sallis didn't call the meeting only because of *azafris*,' she said, her eyes dark with pained sympathy. 'There's trouble brewing at the College. Brice wants you to look into it.'

And that surprised him. 'Really?'

'Yes, really. Which is another reason why all *this*—' Venette waved her hand at his laden workbenches. '—is so hazardous to your political health. Handle the College's problem deftly, my dear, and you'll go a long way to earning Brice's genuine approval. Not to mention put Sallis in your debt.'

'I like the sound of that. Best you give me the details.'

When she'd finished explaining the crisis and his task, he shook his head.

'Arkley is a fool. He should've told Jordane to take his concerns direct to the proctor, or to Hahren if he thought the proctor of no use.'

Venette rolled her eyes. 'Yes, well, you know that, and I know that, but Nevin Jordane has made it his life's work to use people.'

'Hahren has no inkling of this?'

'Apparently not. You'll involve him?'

'If it's warranted.'

'Well, I'm sure you'll do what's best,' Venette said. 'Just don't be tempted to put your thumb in Sallis's eye, just because you can. The welfare of the College must come first.'

'Agreed,' he said, nodding. 'Which is why I shall look into the matter as soon as I've met with our man of business. It won't do me any harm to treat the problem with more urgency than our esteemed Lord Varen suggests.'

Venette laughed. 'How devious of you, my dear. Sallis won't know whether to smile or spit.' Crossing to him, she laid a hand on his arm. 'I'll be about my own affairs, now. Don't rail too much at Rumm after I'm gone. He really had no choice but to let me up here, you know.'

'I know,' he said, and kissed her cheek. 'Besides, it would take a man made of sterner stuff than Rumm to resist the formidable Lady Martain.'

'Ha!' she said, stepping back. 'Which makes you made of what, I wonder? Solid granite?' Then she stilled, her gaze fallen upon the open book beside him on the bench. '*Rubin Cylte?*' Her voice was a shocked gasp. She looked at him, her violet eyes dismayed. 'Oh, my dear. My dear. I hope you know what you're doing.'

Not replying, he unwarded the door and watched her walk out of his attic, her head high, her shoulders slumping.

'Believe me, Venette,' he said into the silence. 'So do I.'

Though Pother Ranmer severely disapproved, Lord Danfey insisted upon leaving his privy apartments to attend the monthly meeting with the family's man of business.

'I'm not crypted yet, Morgan!' he snapped, wheezing as he fastened the buttons on his shirt. He was perched on the edge of his bed, his legs not steady enough to hold him upright while his fingers fumbled a task any child would find simple. 'And I'll know the standing of this family's monies and interests before I am.'

Waiting ready with his father's blue velvet long coat, Morgan stifled a sigh. 'Yes, my lord. But I could just as easily bring the accounts to you after I've gone through them with Nydd and then—'

'*No,*' his father said, glowering. 'So long as I breathe, I'm still the master here. I won't have this coddling, Morgan, d'you hear me? I've already given Rumm fair warning. I'll dismiss him out of hand if I have to complain of it again.'

Intemperate or not, he had to counter that. 'My lord, you are not going to dismiss Rumm,' he said, trying to keep his voice light. Almost playful. 'And even if you did, I'd reinstate him in the next breath.'

'Would you indeed?' His father's jaw worked, bristled eyebrows jutting. 'So you'd lord it over me while there remains a beating heart in my breast?'

'Lord it over you? Never. But I would save you from making a grave mistake. What kind of a son would I be if I didn't?'

'What kind of a son spits in his father's eye and declares he'll overrule him in his own house?'

Morgan bit his tongue on all the things he wanted to say. They'd achieve him nothing, serve only to worsen his father's increasingly cantankerous mood.

*He's alive to bite your nose off. Remember that and be grateful.*

'I am sorry, my lord,' he said, dipping his head in contrition. 'I chose my response poorly. Better I should beg your indulgence not to dismiss Rumm. He does me good service, and I would miss him very much.'

*Even if he does let Venette trample all over him.*

Shirt buttoned, finally, his father let his hands fall to his lap. So small a task as pushing buttons through buttonholes nearly defeated the old man's strength these days.

'You make a great fuss over nothing, Morgan,' he said, retreating. 'I did not say I had dismissed him, only that I take his mumblings against my grain.'

'Then again the fault is mine, for placing more weight on your words than was warranted. I hope Rumm knows his place here is in no real danger?'

'He knows what I want him to know!' his father retorted. 'So don't you go cozening him behind my back, for I'll know if you do and I'll not thank you for it.'

Best they step aside this topic altogether. 'Your coat, my lord?'

'Yes, yes, I can see it. Wanting to accuse me of blindness now, too, are you?'

If he could keep his temper with Sallis Arkley, he could keep it with his father. 'Of course not. But Nydd will be here soon, and I know how much you mislike keeping anyone waiting.'

His father snorted. 'So now you're cozening me, Morgan. Think you're quite the clever one, don't you?'

'Clever enough, my lord, but on my best day not near to touching you,' he said, and smiled again, hoping his sweetness would take the sting from the old man's tongue. Conversing with him had of late become like playing hide and seek with a hornet. 'My lord—'

'I know, I know!' his father said, still stinging. 'Not that letting Nydd twiddle his thumbs is such a bad thing. It does no good to let these fellows think too highly of their importance.' He wagged a gnarled finger. 'Heed that, my clever son. And don't claim I never gave you a smatter of good advice in your life.'

Since most anything he said would be taken as argumentative, Morgan simply nodded. 'No, my lord.'

His father grunted. 'And don't you forget it. Now why are you standing about like a coat rack, Morgan? You look no better than a servant, standing there like that.'

*He's an old man, and he's dying. Nothing else matters.* 'Sorry, my lord.'

More than anything he wanted to cast the velvet coat aside and help his father off the bed, but that would cause such grave offence they'd go without speaking for days after. So he stood and watched in pained silence as his father tried to stand and stay standing. Not 'til his third attempt was the old man successful. To save them both, he had to pretend the other tries were figments of his imagination. Risking censure, he stepped to meet his father midway across the chamber's carpet with the velvet coat outstretched, and then eased him gently into it without revealing the care he took or that he knew full well his father could do little more than hold out one half-lifted arm after the other.

*It never should've come to this. He should've gone to meet death a whole man, in his prime. This slow decay is an undeserved punishment.*

For both of them.

Gentled into his blue velvet finery, Lord Danfey suffered to have the old-fashioned coat's buttons fastened for him, and even permitted his upstart son to rearrange his lace cravat. Its gold-mounted firestone pin flashed in the chamber's glimlight, a rare display of vanity.

Morgan smiled yet again, hoping his grief was well-disguised. 'As ever, my lord, you are the epitome of elegance.'

Halfway down the staircase, his father nudged an elbow to his ribs. 'You're paying close attention to the Garrick girl, I'm told. That is, when you're not hiding upstairs in your attic.'

And who'd told him? Venette? She simply couldn't help herself, could she? If she weren't careful, his interfering friend would soon find herself on the receiving end of his considerable ire.

'Don't blame the lovely Lady Martain,' his father added. 'I wrangled the truth out of Rumm. Had to, didn't I? You didn't see fit to tell me.'

The jibe was intended to make him feel guilty, but he had no intention of it. 'I didn't want to get your hopes up, my lord.'

'You're going to wed her?'

'I am . . . exploring possibilities,' he said, very careful. 'As you requested.' *Demanded. But by all means, let us not quibble over semantics.* 'Why, my lord? Do you mislike the connection?'

His father paused to catch his breath at the next twist of the staircase. 'I mislike learning of my son's courting from a servant.'

*Not as much as I do. Believe me.*

'I was going to tell you. I was only waiting until you were feeling a little stronger. Ranmer doesn't want you excited.'

The comment earned him a hot glare. 'Don't think to play this off to my confounded health. I'll crack you across the ear if you try.'

And his father would, too. In fairness, Greve Danfey could not be called a brutal parent but he had no qualms about raising his fist when provoked.

The glare faded into something less easily withstood. 'You should've spoken up, Morgan. I've been waiting some days for you to confide in me.'

A shade of hurt in his father's voice. 'I am sorry.'

177

'Well? Do you want the girl or don't you? A plain answer, this time.'

If only it were as simple as his father imagined. 'Maris is young, attractive, unattached and the only daughter of a First Family ranked more highly than ours. I'd be a fool to discount her.'

His father flicked him a look. 'But?'

'But every family has its secrets. What do you know of the Garricks?'

'Venette hasn't given you chapter and verse?'

'I haven't asked her to. When it comes to Maris Garrick she's not what you'd call unbiased.'

His father frowned, thinking. 'For all their high ranking they're good mages, but not brilliant. As a family they're proud. Too proud, to my mind. There's a son. Ehrig. Six years your senior. Started at the College but was invited to leave before the end of his first year. You won't remember that. Too young, and it was kept quiet. Caught cheating. A bad business. The wife's nothing out of the ordinary. Parnel Garrick's stiff-necked but honest. The son's misconduct nearly broke him. Some cut him for it. I never did, the rare times I saw him after. Only been in Elvado two years. They started off in the north, you know. The Fifth district.'

Morgan stifled amusement. Trust his father to have a comprehensive knowledge of the Garricks' history. And it was typically contrary and kind of him, too, not to bruise Parnel Garrick over the actions of his wayward heir. For all he was often a hard man, there could be found in Greve Danfey the occasional impulse toward softness.

'What do you make of the girl's people?' his father added. 'Can you stomach them?'

'I can't say,' he said. 'So far Lord and Lady Garrick have taken great pains to stay mostly in the background. But it is a mark in their favour that they were granted permission to take up residence in Elvado. The honour's not lightly come by. As for Maris's brother . . .' He shrugged. 'I've not met him.'

178

His father raked him with a sharp, considering look. 'And still you step sideways around my question.'

'Because I don't have an easy answer for you, my lord. The best I can say is that I find Maris to be a not unpleasant proposition.'

Which was simply another way of saying that despite the girl's suitability and charms, on a personal level he felt . . . indifferent.

His father smoothed the nap of one blue velvet sleeve. 'You haven't made a formal declaration to her?'

And that question stung. 'No, my lord. Nor would I without consulting you first. I don't believe I am that unwieldy a son.'

His father grunted. 'As I recall, you rode your horse before the hounds when it came to the Talth girl.'

'Luzena was different,' he said stiffly. 'I will not compare her to Maris Garrick.'

There came the sound of footsteps on the staircase below them. Then Rumm's neatly trimmed head came into sight. Looking up, seeing them, he paused. 'My lord, Nydd has arrived.'

Another dyspeptic grunt. 'Show him to the library, Rumm. Offer him refreshment. Tea, not sherry. I'll be there directly.'

Noting that his father's breathing had eased a little, and that some fresh colour had washed into his cheeks, Morgan took a suggestive step down the staircase. His father's clawed fingers took him by the forearm, halting him. The old man's eyes were unnervingly anxious.

'Morgan, can you see yourself abiding with this Maris Garrick?'

'That depends, my lord,' he said, taken aback. In general his father never worried overmuch about his feelings. 'Can you? I'd not handfast with any woman of whom you could not approve.'

'The brother's still distasteful,' said his father, after a thoughtful pause. 'But the mother's inoffensive, and I know far trickier mages than Parnel. You could do a deal worse than his daughter, Morgan. Bring the girl to supper. Let me see her for myself.'

179

He bowed. 'My lord, I shall invite her . . . but perhaps not too soon. I would not overplay my hand, nor give her permission to indulge in hasty speculation.'

'When do you see her again?'

'Tonight, as it happens. We dine at The Opal.'

That made his father stare. 'The Opal's expensive, Morgan. You don't think dipping so deep in your purse isn't overplaying your hand?'

'If I am to wed her, I must court her in some style.'

'Woo her as you see fit, then,' said his father. Deep in his chest, that ominous wheeze. 'But if you think she'll suit, don't take too long to speak up.'

'My lord,' he said, hiding all distress. 'As always, I'll follow your excellent advice.'

Two hours, just over, it took them to plough through the Danfey accounts and estates. All in all their prospects continued comfortable, was Nydd's conclusion. Farms, crops, livestock and trading ventures prospered as well as could be expected, the vagaries of life notwithstanding. The three-way trouble with Brantone, Manemli and Ranoush was unfortunate, but none of their traders was in trouble over it, at least. Still, the rumblings would bear close watching. Banditry in Trindek and a long spell of foul weather in Feen had taken a toll on their pressed suswill oil and mageworked leather goods, it was true, but those losses were neatly offset by the new strike of firestones in their Ranoush mine holding. Demand for the gems in Dorana was not likely to fade, at least not in the next several years. And this year's icewine vintage promised to be exceptional, as did their Brantish oldberry harvest. They could look forward to much success in both cases. The furs they procured in Iringa were also turning a tidy profit, though they should be warned there was a looming danger of the rare Iringan snowcat being hunted to extinction.

'If they could be bred in captivity I'd suggest it,' Nydd sighed. 'But they can't. And since restraint by other hunters is unlikely, my advice is to make a push to take as many of what's left of the beast as we can, hoard the pelts until they're all gone, and watch the prices shoot skyward.'

'And sound advice it is,' said Morgan. 'See to it, Nydd.' He turned. 'Unless you have any objection, my lord?'

His father waved a hand. 'None.'

Nydd made a note. 'Very good, my lord. And that just leaves the Second district horse farms . . .'

The discussion of which didn't take long. The meeting concluded, Morgan left his father to gossip with Nydd and withdrew from the library to find Rumm.

'Sir?' said the master servant, looking up from a saucepan. He was in the kitchen, tasting a sauce. The cook looked nervous, awaiting his verdict. 'Is there a problem?'

His polite way of asking *Is His Lordship in distress?* Rumm was nothing if not a monument to tact.

'A word, Rumm,' he said, with a jerk of his head.

Rumm put down the spoon. 'Sir.'

Discreetly distant from the cook, whose back was now turned as he prudently sharpened a carving knife, Morgan folded his arms. 'You discussed me with Lord Danfey.'

'Yes.' Rumm blinked. 'In the course of my duties I do sometimes make reference to you, sir. Was there something in particular that—'

'*In particular,*' he said, in no mood for arch games, 'you discussed me and my—' *Stud duty negotiations.* '—relationship with Maris Garrick.'

This time Rumm moistened his lips. 'Ah.'

'Yes, Rumm. *Ah.*'

'Sir—' Sighing, Rumm dropped his gaze to the kitchen's beautifully scrubbed flagstones. 'I apologise.'

'That's a start, certainly. And now you can explain why I shouldn't show you the door.'

Rumm's gaze jerked up. 'If I'm to be shown the door, sir, better it be for obeying his lordship than for openly defying him.'

That gave him pause. 'You're saying Lord Danfey *ordered* you

181

to discuss my privy business with him? It wasn't a case of him dropping a hint and you picking it up?'

Another sigh. 'No, sir. The afternoon you and Mage Garrick went riding, his lordship woke from his restitutional and wanted to know where you were. I did try to be vague, sir, as you requested. Unfortunately I was not vague enough, and so was forced to reveal more than either of us would wish.'

Clasping his hands behind his back, not wanting Rumm to see his white-knuckled anger, Morgan nodded. 'I see.'

'Sir, I would have told you – *warned* you—' Rumm said, his expression earnest. 'But his lordship bade me hold my tongue on pain of dismissal.'

So he could sit back and brood and fester on the impertinence of a grown son keeping his personal business to himself.

*Greve Danfey, sometimes you are a most unreasonable man.*

'Sir . . .' Rumm's voice was lowered. 'If I might speak my mind freely?'

He snorted. 'As far as I can tell, you always do.'

The master servant flicked a glance at the cook, still industriously knife-sharpening, and took a small step closer. 'I understand your feelings in this, sir. Marriage is a delicate business, especially where a prominent family is concerned. And when a man has had his heart broken once already . . .'

Morgan stepped back. 'That's enough.'

'His lordship crowds you out of fear, sir,' said Rumm, heedless of his danger. 'I know it seems he has no care for your sensibilities, but the truth is he cares so much it chokes him to a standstill. Don't fault him for that, sir, don't—'

'*I said that's enough!*'

A gasp and a clatter, as the cook dropped his sharpened knife.

'Sir,' said Rumm, and stood there, a stubborn pride in him that did not belong in a servant, be he a master of the breed or no.

Waiting till he could trust himself, Morgan stared at the man. What age was Rumm? He didn't know. He'd never asked. Perhaps some ten years older than himself? He wasn't married. Never

182

had been. And thanks to the Council's recent ruling never would be, now. But had he loved? Had he lived through a heartbreak? Had his arms held the woman he adored as she lay dying in slow agony? Had he breathed in her final, shuddering sigh?

*It doesn't matter if he has. That still wouldn't give him the right to –*

'You're angry,' Rumm said, stating the obvious with such aplomb it was almost amusing. 'I'm sorry. But sir, you have to know it's not easy walking the line between yourself and your father.'

*You're not paid for easy, Rumm. You're paid to do as you're told.*

And wasn't that the problem? Rumm had done precisely as he was told. Indeed, if he'd not answered Lord Danfey honestly he'd be held gravely at fault.

Muscle by taut muscle, Morgan made himself relax. 'Very well, Rumm. I'll overlook it, this once. But don't think I'll be so forgiving again. Now you can take sherry to the library. But his lordship is not to have more than one glass. In fact, don't take a bottle. Take two glasses on a tray, in which case give Nydd the Ospia. That's good enough for him. His lordship will of course imbibe only the dry Tartaffe.'

Rumm nodded. His face was sober but his eyes were relieved. 'Of course, sir.'

'And you can tell his lordship I've gone into Elvado,' he added. 'I've Council business at the College and then I'm staying in town to dine. You can reach me at The Opal, should anything – should I be required. Reassure Lord Danfey that I'll not be home late.'

'Very good, sir,' Rumm murmured, bowing, once more the perfect, self-contained servant.

Leaving the kitchen, Morgan heard him say to the cook, in a tone he reserved for his own servant underlings, 'Mosson, this sauce is rubbish. Did you trip and drop the salt cellar into the pot, you ramshackle spoon bender? Throw it out and do it over. And you can be sure the cost will come out of your too-generous wages.'

Morgan grinned, his good temper abruptly restored. Dismiss Rumm? No. He couldn't do that, no matter how provoking his behaviour.

*But I will have a pointed word with his lordship. If he wants to know something, let him ask me. I'll not be the fodder for a servant's speculation . . . no, not even for Rumm.*

# CHAPTER TWELVE

Morgan returned to the College amidst a confusion of feelings. His years spent studying within its ivy-clad walls hadn't been a misery . . . but they'd not been an undiluted delight, either. As ever, ranking counted. The fact that in raw talent he'd outstripped nearly every son and daughter from the more prestigious First Families could not make up for his less illustrious name.

In many ways, his talent had only made things worse.

The other boys from Dorana's lower-ranked families had formed a little herd that kept them safe from the worst of the subtle sneering by those students, like Brahn Sorvold, who were born to greater privilege. They'd made a few tentative overtures in his direction, but he'd spurned them. The thought of hiding amongst that mediocre gaggle had sickened him.

And so his years in the College were spent mostly solitary. He was noticed, of course. The quality of his magework couldn't be denied. But when it came down to *choices,* to the tutors favouring this student and not that one, he'd spent four years more often than not being *that one.*

The sting had never quite faded. Which was why he took Sallis and Shari's disparagements so amiss, of course. He wasn't a fool. He knew that inside Councillor Danfey still lived the shade of his younger, student-mage self.

'Sir? Sir, is something amiss?'

Startled out of melancholy thought, he stared at the youth who had so intemperately plucked at his elbow.

'Are you blind?' he demanded, and flicked the Council insignia pinned to his pearl-embroidered, blue velvet tunic. 'Is it censure you're seeking?'

The student opened his amberish eyes wide and let his small, wet mouth fall open. From the look of his merely serviceable attire, he was the offspring of a *very* lowly placed First Family. The upper ranks dressed their sons and daughters in brocades and velvets, not hardy linen. To be sure the boy's tunic was dyed a rich forest green, and stitched here and there with gold thread, but at the end of the day it was linen. And that was that.

'Councillor!' he gasped. 'Forgive me. You looked stricken and I thought – I thought—'

Morgan cuffed the gibbering fool on the side of his unkempt head. *If you can't afford a decent haircut, dolt, what are you doing here?* 'No, you *failed* to think or pay attention. And you would be a mage in the world beyond this College? *Numbskull.*' Another cuff. 'Name?'

The student blinked. 'My name, sir?'

'No, *pibble!* The name of my wet nurse's big left toe!'

Shuddering, the boy gathered his wandering wits. 'Werik Gowen, sir.'

Gowen? Yes indeed, a most lowly ranked First Family. If he'd been admitted as a student then he had to have talent, but talent wasn't enough. When would people learn?

'And is there a reason, Student Gowen, why I should not make complaint of you to the proctor?'

Werik Gowen swallowed a sob. Hovering at a safe distance, three more students. Avid and peering, horrified by their friend's predicament, relieved it was his and not theirs. The absence of other students roaming the College grounds suggested that all four of them were late to their next class.

186

'Please, sir, please . . .' The boy's voice had sunk to a near whisper. His damp, mortified gaze was trained on the grass. 'I humbly beg your pardon. I meant no offence.'

Morgan considered him. The afternoon was fast dwindling. He had no more time to waste. 'You are pardoned. But should you again come to my attention, Student Gowen, you can be sure the repercussions will not be to your liking. Now get to class. Quickly!'

'Sir!' the boy gasped. 'Thank you, sir!'

Shaking, Werik Gowen retreated to the safety of his goggling fellow students. With a final scorching stare Morgan continued down the tree-shaded brickwork pathway that led from the College's front gates to its sprawling complex of lecture halls, staff offices and heavily warded practical application workrooms. As he walked, he repinned his Council insignia to the inside of his tunic. His purpose was to assess the situation here discreetly. When that was done he'd once again identify himself.

Though years had passed since he'd breathed College air, he recalled every twist and turn of its central thoroughfare, every sinuous side path, every ancient, flowering tree. The lecture hall he sought sat in the furthest north-east corner of the College grounds, shrouded in ferns and rambling hancinthia vines. He'd timed his arrival so he could slip into the hall while the students were getting settled for Bellamie Ranowen's last class of the day. Their bustle and flurry meant he'd go unnoticed, and once the lecture began he'd observe, unnoticed, and so be perfectly poised to deliver an accounting of his findings to Lord Varen. Though in truth, whatever he said would be aimed at Sallis Arkley.

*And what Sallis will do with it, or make of Varen's insistence on involving me in Nevin Jordane's crisis, justice alone knows.*

For himself, he didn't care. For now it was enough to know that Arkley could only be lemon-sour knowing he'd have to abide by Morgan Danfey's recommendations.

Stepping softly through the lecture hall's doors, left ajar, Morgan hid himself in the shadows that blurred the furthest edges of the large room. The tutor's podium was glimlit, but yet unoccupied. Ranowen's whispering students, some thirty of them by his rough head-count, prepared themselves to work, tugging ink and pen and paper from their satchels, igniting the tiny balls of glimfire that would illuminate their note-taking. Though these were the College's senior residents, they were not permitted the use of transcribing incants. It was thought, perhaps not without merit, that the act of putting pen to paper helped ink the lesson into a student's labouring brain.

A door behind the tutor's podium opened and Bellamie Ranowen entered the hall. Short for a Doranen, she was more muscular and broader in the frame than most. Not beautiful at all. As she closed the door her students sank into a respectful hush, which spoke well of her discipline if nothing else. Intrigued, Morgan eased sideways until he was fetched up against the wall, where the hall's deepest shadows lay, and considered his quarry.

She was a rare creature, this Bellamie Ranowen. The only College lecturer to teach here who'd not sprung from a First Family. Her unremarkable appearance was sharply at odds with what had been reported of her, that she swam in dangerously unorthodox and reckless waters. But no mage worth his magic judged another mage by appearance alone.

*And if she's to be condemned, she'll condemn herself by her own words and actions.*

Should Nevin Jordane's accusation be proven, if this unlikely College tutor did indeed overreach her authority while conducting a vendetta against his daughter, she'd pay the price . . . and payment would not be pretty. A prominent family, the Jordanes. Sixth-generation Elvadians, and in the first rank of First Families. Nevin's younger brother had also been considered for the Council seat rendered vacant by Andwin Bellem's untimely death.

Venette had refused to divulge why it was that Greve Danfey's son had defeated Arnulf Jordane for the honour, and he'd not pressed her to break silence. Sometimes it was wiser not to question a victory.

*But while I question the wisdom of Mage Ranowen's appointment, and likely would have voted against it had I been on the*

*Council then, what does it say about me that I hope I can prove Sallis Arkley's friend wrong?*

No doubt that he was petty. Incapable of rising above the personal, of leaving his complaints about Sallis to one side.

*Fine. Then I'm petty. I don't intend to lose sleep over that.*

Comfortable behind the dais's tall wooden lectern now, her opening remarks concluded, Bellamie Ranowen launched into the meat and drink of her lecture. Within moments she revealed herself to be an indisputable expert on the subject of advanced transmutations, and not unfamiliar with Rubin Cylte's theories. Eyebrows raised, Morgan listened as she deftly worked the least controversial of Cylte's notions into her deconstruction of transmutational harmonics.

*Interesting. One could call it simple erudition . . . or dangerous unorthodoxy, if there was a personal score to settle. But I wonder how it is that Nevin Jordane knows Cylte's work?*

A question he might well ask of Sallis Arkley.

Twice, Ranowen paused her lecturing to call forth a student to help her illustrate a point. In neither instance did she mock or belittle, even though both young mages made stupid mistakes.

Morgan began to feel a stirring of temper.

*Ranked or not, she's an exemplary tutor. That more than makes up for her unfortunate family. What we have here is an abuse of Council power. Arkley sides with Jordane to punish a mage who dares look upward, toward the next rung of Dorana's ladder.*

Well, he'd not be a party to that. Not when Sallis was doing his best to keep Morgan Danfey pinned in his place. But as he turned to leave, Bellamie Ranowen rapped her knuckles to the lectern.

'Student Jordane! I'm sorry, do I bore you?'

He stopped. Turned back. Drifted once more into the shadows.

'I'm so pleased, Student Jordane,' Bellamie Ranowen added, pleasantly mellow, 'that your grasp of these principles is so perfect you can find time for idle gossip. Come. Join me on the dais and help me illustrate an important point.'

A frozen moment, then a student slowly stood. Jordane's daughter had chosen to sit as far as she could from her tutor, but that hadn't saved her. So either she was careless, or Bellamie Ranowen had been lying in wait.

*Curse it. If it turns out Sallis was right . . .*

As the girl picked her reluctant way to the front of the hall, Ranowen continued her lecture.

'And so we must conclude that the key component of any successful transmutation lies not in the balance and counter-balance of sigil and incant, as received wisdom would have it, but in the specific syllabic stressors contained *within* the incant itself as it particularly relates to the boisterous give-and-take of the incantic excitation at the moment of completion. In other words, if transmutation is your weakness it is not because you can't juggle, it's because you have a tin ear for rhythm! In which case neither take a young lady dancing, gentlemen, nor accept a dancing invitation from a handsome young man, ladies. Because as sure as glimfire vanishes in sunshine it'll be bruised toes and bruised hearts and no stolen kisses for you!'

A gentle chorus of chuckling broke out amongst the students. Smiling, Bellamie Ranowen waited for the amusement to die down, then nodded at Student Jordane as she stepped up to the lectern. The girl knew better than to openly defy her tutor, but there was a curl to her lips that suggested an imperfectly veiled contempt.

Morgan frowned. *Like father, like daughter.* The girl should be disciplined for that disrespect alone. Once appointed a College tutor, Ranowen's lack of ranking had been rendered moot.

Bellamie Ranowen pretended not to notice her student's mutinous expression. Instead, with effortless expertise, she trans-located a slender crystal bud-vase from elsewhere to balance on her outstretched palm.

'Student Jordane. Be so good as to take possession of this vase.'

With poor grace, Nevin Jordane's daughter did as she was told.

The set of her elegant jaw said she wanted to hurl the vase to the very back of the hall.

'Excellent,' said Bellamie Ranowen, approving. 'Now, transform it into a crystal flower. Nothing too elaborate. A single-stem budded nartani, perhaps.'

'Yes, Tutor Ranowen,' the girl murmured, pretending dutiful compliance . . . but if her fingers tightened much more she'd be holding a handful of broken glass.

Still watching closely, Morgan stepped as near to the back row of student seats as he dared. None of Bellamie Ranowen's pupils noticed him. Their attentions were fixed upon the drama playing out before them on the dais.

'Come along, Student Jordane,' said Bellamie Ranowen. 'We're waiting.'

Was it a trick of the hall's atmosphere, or did she now sound a trifle mocking? Morgan thought she did. And with what he could sense . . . or *not* sense . . . in Nevin Jordane's rude daughter, he suspected the truth behind the accusations made against Bellamie Ranowen was far less savoury than Lord Varen was going to like. He stifled a smile.

*Oh dear. Sallis is going to look such a fool.*

Student Jordane flicked a nervous, resentful glance at her watching classmates, then cleared her throat. With the crystal vase held in her left hand, she used her right to trace the transmutation sigil in the air. It burned indigo blue, vibrant with promise.

'Quickly now, the incant,' said Bellamie Ranowen. 'Don't let the sigil's energies go to waste.'

Her tongue stumbling, Nevin Jordane's daughter recited the transmutation incant's nine lilting syllables. Three words into her casting, Morgan felt his skin begin to crawl.

So his suspicion was correct, and Bellamie Ranowen knew it too. Nevin's daughter had a tin ear. She was mangling the incant. Even as she reached its painful end, the crystal vase she was holding collapsed into glassy dust.

Bellamie Ranowen sighed, and with another flourish produced a second vase. 'Try again, Student Jordane.'

Cheeks burned dull red, pretending not to hear the whisperings of her peers, the girl took the second vase and ignited a second sigil.

'Now,' said Bellamie Ranowen, who'd made no attempt to silence the whisperers, 'repeat the incant after me, exactly as I pronounce it. Understood?'

The girl nodded, bottom lip caught between her small, perfectly even teeth. Even wreathed in embarrassment, she was beautiful, this Jordane daughter. But then why wouldn't she be? Doubtless she took after her mother. Sons born into the best First Families had the pick of prospective wives, after all.

Since the power and energy of the sigil belonged to Student Jordane, Bellamie Ranowen's recitation of the incant could not trigger the transmutation. Woodenly, the Jordane girl repeated the incant. Even with help her cadences were stiffly imposed. The girl was a blockhead. However had she managed to stay in College this long?

But then, the answer was obvious, wasn't it? Morgan shook his head, disgusted.

*Family. Connections. Always, always, it comes down to that.*

Unsurprised, he watched the shuddering transformation of the crystal vase into a sprig of nartani. The incant worked well enough this time, but the change was laborious and the finished crystal flower looked oddly deformed.

More whispers and murmurs from the watching students. Scarcely seeming to notice, Student Jordane stared at her creation as though it were poison, or might spring to life and bite her.

Bellamie Ranowen parted her lips, seemingly on the point of asking the girl a question. Then she changed her mind. 'Thank you, Student Jordane,' she said, nodding. 'Although I think you'll agree you don't yet grasp the task's subtleties. Less gossip and more practice, perhaps? You have until the morrow to muse on what you've just done. We'll talk on it then.'

'Tutor Ranowen,' said the girl, a breath away now from open defiance.

'Good,' said Bellamie Ranowen, with a thin, restrained smile. 'Take your seat.'

As she returned to her place, the girl's furious, unsavoury thoughts were shockingly clear in her face. Morgan felt his hands itch to slap her free of them.

'And in case the rest of you are congratulating yourselves for escaping this little exercise,' Bellamie Ranowen added, frowning at the hall's sea of student faces, 'you will all be doing the same task in your own time, making sure, on the morrow, to present me with your transmuted crystal so I might gauge the effectiveness of your syllabic rhythms and incantic prowess. Now. Turning to the question of harmonically linked sigils . . .'

Even though he was sure he'd reached the correct conclusion, Morgan stayed to hear nearly all that remained of Bellamie Ranowen's lecture. Nevin Jordane's daughter was not called upon a second time. Three more students were singled out to perform exercises designed to illuminate the subject. All three easily outstripped Student Jordane.

Before the lecture concluded, while the hall was still mostly dark, he slipped out and made his way to the College proctor's domain. There he closed the door to Mage Lowyn's chamber, explained enough of his presence to receive an alarmed surety of discretion, and skimmed through Student Jordane's privy records.

Finished, setting them aside, he kept his expression sternly noncommittal, but on the inside he was laughing. There was no pleasure quite so exquisite as being proven right.

After a sharp conversation with hapless, chagrined Proctor Lowyn, he made his way to the Hall of Knowledge. The afternoon was fast drawing to a close, dusk creeping in, wreathed in purplish shadows. Provided there were no last minute, unpleasant surprises, like running into Sallis Arkley, he'd have this matter dealt with in plenty of time to meet Maris Garrick for dinner at The Opal.

Voln Hahren was in his privy chamber on the Hall's seventh floor, reading from a haphazard pile of correspondence.

'Yes?' he said, looking up. There was a vague impatience in his voice, as though College matters were tiresome, even though their oversight was entirely his responsibility. 'Can I help you, Councillor Danfey?'

Morgan closed the door and sat in a chair, uninvited. 'Have you been made aware of the complaint lodged against Bellamie Ranowen?'

Hahren dropped the letter he was reading and sat back, the corners of his mouth turned down. He was a proud man with finicking standards, quick to take offence at visitors to his privy chamber *taking liberties*. Most particularly he was jealous of his position as College overseer, but if he resented Councillor Danfey's investigation of this matter, he was wise enough not to show it.

'Yes, Councillor,' he said, very civil. 'Lord Varen informed me. You've looked into it?'

'I have. The complaint is spurious.'

Hahren stared. '*Spurious?*'

'Voln . . .' Enjoying himself, Morgan drummed his fingers on the arm of the chair. 'I am more likely to suggest a censure against Lord Nevin Jordane than I am to approve Bellamie Ranowen's dismissal from the College.'

Nonplussed, Hahren fidgeted behind his desk, pushing bits of paper around while he ordered his thoughts.

'I'm not sure I find your conclusion satisfactory,' he said at last, eyebrows pulled low over his unpleasantly deep-set eyes. 'I think you should return to the College and—'

Not so wise after all. Morgan stood, a single, swift movement explosive with power. 'Did I hear you aright, Lord Hahren? Did you just *contradict* me?'

'Councillor Danfey—' Swallowing, with difficulty, Hahren collected his wits. 'No. Of course not. I'm sorry if I gave that impression. It's just—'

'Believe me, Hahren, I know perfectly what it's *just*,' he said, unleashing his temper. 'It's just you bowing and scraping with no thought beyond ingratiating yourself with Nevin Jordane.'

Hahren's mouth open and closed. He swallowed again, convulsive. 'But don't you see? To call the complaint spurious is to question Lord Jordane's veracity. And he is a mage of impeccable lineage and social standing while *she*—'

'Is a College tutor. Which you know full well renders her social ranking irrelevant.' Letting the reminder sink in, Morgan sat again, slowly. 'Lack of rank is not her crime. Have you any idea what is?'

Voln Hahren shook his head. 'None.'

'Then I'll enlighten you. Bellamie Ranowen is guilty of placing integrity above ingratiation, which is more than I can say for every other College tutor who has had the dubious pleasure of Tinette Jordane's company in class.'

'Councillor?' Hahren's cheeks paled. 'I'm afraid I don't follow your meaning.'

*Oh, I think you do.* 'Lord Hahren, the Jordane girl's magework is rudimentary at best. Certainly it's not of the quality we expect in a highly ranked First Family's offspring.'

Hahren indulged in more fish-like gaping. 'What are you saying?'

'I'm saying Jordane's daughter is a throwback! A cripple!' *You bleating fool.* 'I'm saying there has been a deliberate – let's call it *embellishment* – of her scholarly achievements.' *Because calling this what it is, outright fraud, would likely provoke you to spasms.* 'And it's only come to light because Bellamie Ranowen, unlike her colleagues, is refusing to compromise her standards.'

Hahren looked close to vomiting. 'Councillor, you *can't* intend saying as much to Lord Jordane!'

'Why can't I?'

'Because – because—' Hahren spluttered, close to incoherent. 'He is one of the College's most generous benefactors!'

'I know,' Morgan said, sneering. 'And the reason why is now apparent. Coin-clinking Nevin Jordane thinks to purchase his daughter's passage through the College. This complaint he's lodged against Bellamie Ranowen is a base calumny designed to deflect attention from his profitless child. If it becomes common knowledge the useless girl's a throwback, no Family will sanction marriage with her. The Jordane name will be sullied for generations to come.'

'You have no proof of this,' Hahren muttered, trembling fingers smoothing his lank hair. 'And to make such a bold accusation outside this chamber—'

He smiled. 'I see no need for the Jordanes to be publicly humiliated, provided there is no interference with my handling of the matter.'

'Meaning?'

'Meaning that Proctor Lowyn is on notice . . . and so are you. There'll be no further gilding of Tinette Jordane's wilted lily. Bellamie Ranowen is but one of the girl's tutors. The rest will be privily advised that they can rank her according to her true skills with no eyebrow being raised or else face a summons to the Council, where they will be asked many inconvenient questions.'

'I see,' said Hahren, faintly. A patina of sweat gleamed on his brow. 'And you think Lord Jordane will curtsy to this, do you?'

Morgan frowned at Hahren, loathing the man. Where was his outrage on behalf of the College? Where was his disgust over Nevin Jordane's dynastic selfishness? By comparison, Bellamie Ranowen's lack of ranking was *harmless*. That Jordane would foist his abomination of a child upon the unsuspecting young men of Dorana, corrupt good mages to his cause, undermine the College's revered reputation . . . did all of that mean *nothing* to Voln Hahren?

*The man's not fit for his position. When the Jordane dust has settled, I'll see him removed.*

'I think Lord Jordane is clever enough to cut his losses,' he said mildly. No point in revealing to Hahren his true feelings. 'While he still can.'

A vein was throbbing in Hahren's right temple. The patina of sweat was a trickle now, sliding down his colourless cheeks like tears. Indeed, the despicable craven did look close to weeping.

'Councillor Danfey, I fear you cannot conceive of what you're asking.'

'You mean I cannot conceive of what doing your duty will cost you. Hahren, do you imagine that I care?'

'No, Councillor Danfey,' Hahren muttered, as sweat stained his fine silk tunic. 'I see plainly that you don't.'

'Good,' Morgan said, and rapped his knuckles once to Hahren's cluttered desk. 'Then we understand each other. See this sordid matter settled. I'll look for your report to the Council when next it formally meets.'

Hahren groped inside his tunic for a kerchief and dragged it over his face. 'And what of Lord Arkley?'

Ah. So Hahren knew of that connection, did he? 'You can leave Lord Arkley to me. Be assured you'll not be hindered in the execution of your duties.'

Leaving Hahren to gape after him, Morgan withdrew from the chamber. As he closed its door behind him, thoughts bending toward Maris Garrick, he glanced casually around the antechamber – and felt his heart stop, his blood seize. He forgot how to breathe.

A young mage, fine-boned and slender, untidily dressed in shabby blue linen. Her golden hair was braided like a crown. She sat on the edge of a bench pushed against the small room's far wall, hands pressed between her knees, gaze fixed to the tiled floor. He'd never seen her before, and yet he was certain he knew her. Lost in her own thoughts, she didn't look up, or even realise she was no longer alone.

Mouth dry, palms sweating, he feasted his eyes upon her. This girl, this stranger, made the air dance against his tingling skin. Who *was* she? Why did she strike him like lightning from a clear sky? He didn't know. All he knew was that she stirred him. *Deeply* stirred him. In a way no woman had since – since –

Profoundly unsettled, he withdrew before she noticed him. He was expected at The Opal. Maris would be waiting, and it wouldn't be wise to make her feel neglected.

The girl's face haunted him every step of the way.

\* \* \*

Sick with nerves, with a dread she resented more than she could say, Barl sat in the Hall of Knowledge, outside Lord Voln Hahren's privy chamber, and waited for him to honour her with his presence.

He'd known for nearly five hours that she was there, because one of the Hall's disapproving mages had told him. And then she'd told her to '*Sit there. Lord Hahren will see you when he has a moment free.*'

So she'd sat. And now she waited. And while she waited, tried not to think about her last conversation with Remmie. But that was proving impossible. Over and over and over it sounded, trudging the confines of her skull like a Brantish mill-house donkey hitched to a grindstone.

'*What?*' he'd said blankly, after she'd told him her plan. '*Barl, have you lost your mind?*'

She'd stared back at him, just as angry.

'*Remmie, I know it's outrageous, but I have to at least try. If I don't, then Arndel's won. And I won't let him have this victory. My whole future hangs in the balance. If he has his way I'll be taken on as a milkmaid before ever I'm allowed near magework again.*'

But Remmie hadn't wanted to hear her. '*Don't talk nonsense. Of course you'll find other magework.*'

'*It's not nonsense!*' she'd shouted at him. '*You weren't there, Remmie. You didn't see Arndel's face, or hear the gloating satisfaction in his voice.*'

'*Yes, all right, he was angry. But that was two days ago, Barl.*'

'*Two days, two weeks, two months, it won't matter!*'

'*You don't know that,*' he'd said, so stubborn. '*For all you know, Arndel's repented of his hasty action and now he's waiting for you to come back.*'

She'd laughed, incredulous. '*Arndel? Really? Now who's lost his mind? Remmie—*'

But he'd trampled all over her. Gentle Remmie, throwing words at her like stones. '*I'm telling you, Barl, if you go to Elvado, try to force a meeting with this Lord Hahren, with the*

198

Council, try to – to bully them into admitting you to the College? You'll regret it. When are you going to face the facts? Mages like us don't make the rules. You've only got one choice. You'll have to wait a few days more so you can be certain Arndel has calmed down, and then go to see him. Plead your case. Or go to Lady Grie and ask her to plead it for you. She values you. Surely she'll help.'

She'd never been so close to despising her brother. '*I won't trust my future to any hands but my own. And if you honestly think I would, Remmie, then you don't know me at all.*'

That was when he walked away from her. She hadn't gone after him. And that morning, when she left the cottage, she didn't say goodbye.

Stirring out of bleak memory, aware once more of her surroundings, she breathed out a shuddering sigh. The intricately woven artisan carpet beneath her feet blurred as her stinging eyes filled with tears. She blinked them away, a swift fluttering of lashes. They came back. She blinked again. Something warm and wet trickled down her cheek. She smeared it to nothingness with her fingertips, then sank her teeth into her bottom lip.

*I'm not weeping. I'm not.*

She couldn't. If she didn't face Lord Hahren fiercely her cause would be lost before she'd struck the first blow.

Footsteps, approaching. Hurriedly straightening, pressing her back to the wall, she clasped her hands loosely in her lap and rearranged her expression into a mask of serene indifference.

A moment, then the mage who'd abandoned her in this ante-chamber marched back through the open, arched doorway, crossed to Hahren's closed chamber door and knocked. Another moment, then she opened it. She must've been invited to enter. Without glancing over, the mage went inside. The door thudded softly closed behind her.

Slumping again, Barl rubbed at her temples. A vicious headache was brewing, she could feel the promise of its teeth and talons pounding through her blood. How long would Hahren make her wait, then? Another hour? Another two? The whole night?

199

*Fine. If I have to, I'll wait the whole night. I'll wait longer, as long as he likes. He won't drive me away. I'm not leaving Elvado until I get what I came for.*

Time dragged its heels, and she dawdled along with it. The pounding in her blood, in her head, grew steadily worse. And then Hahren's chamber door opened and the summoned mage came out. This time she looked over.

'You can go in.'

Standing, Barl smoothed the front of her sadly wrinkled tunic. The mage looked her up and down, disapproving, shook her head, then departed.

'Close the door,' Hahren snapped, glaring at a letter on the desk before him. 'And don't sit.'

Barl closed the door, heart sickly thudding, then positioned herself directly in front of the imposing desk. Head up, shoulders back, hands tightly held behind her back. No blinking. No weeping. No losing her temper. Wooing this man to her cause was vital.

'Lord Hahren—'

'Did I give you leave to speak?'

'No, my lord.'

'Then hold your tongue.'

He'd spoken without lifting his gaze, but she stared at the polished timber floor anyway so he wouldn't see the resentment in her eyes.

At last the arrogant wurzle looked up. 'So. You are Barl Lindin.'

'I am, Lord Hahren. My lord, I'm here to—'

'Do you know what this is?' he said, tapping fingers to the letter he'd been reading. 'Do you know what it says?'

She hesitated, then shook her head. 'How can I, my lord?'

'Do not think to be clever with me, Mage Lindin,' he growled. 'I am in no mood for that.'

Lord Hahren was handsome, in a hatchet-faced fashion. But his hair looked faintly tarnished and his thin lips were bracketed with deep lines of aggravation. His storm-grey eyes were sunk a shade too deep, his thin nose thrusting sharply between them. Nothing about him suggested sympathy or softness. He looked the kind of man who'd gladly kick an opponent already brought to his knees.

*So I'd best not kneel before him, had I?*

'This,' Hahren said, brandishing the letter before her, 'is an almost incoherent rant from Artisan Master Arndel, regarding your recent disgrace and dismissal. And *this*—' Dropping that letter, he rummaged for a different one and brandished it instead. '—is a copy of the rant he sent to the Artisan's Guild. And now here *you* are, doubtless wishing to add your voice to this tedious chorus. But why *I* am being dragged into your petty dispute is beyond my understanding.'

So, it wasn't enough to dismiss her. Arndel had run bleating to the most powerful mage he knew, hoping to hurt her further. She felt hatred for him flash through her, so swift and white-hot it stole her breath.

'There is no dispute, my lord. Master Arndel and I have no business together. I'm here to speak to you of my acceptance into the College.'

Eyes wide, Hahren sat back in his ornately-tapestried chair. 'I think you must be addled, Mage Lindin. That question has already been asked and answered. Now get out. I have no more time for you.'

*Get out?* Head pounding beyond bearing, her vision misted red, all thought of temperate good sense vanished, Barl leapt toward Hahren and with one wild sweep of her arm sent his paperwork flying, ink pot and ink flying, glimlamp flying.

'Then you can *make* time, my lord!' she shouted. 'I might be unranked, but my talent is prodigious and you will *recognise* that! Or history will record you as the greatest fool ever born!'

# CHAPTER THIRTEEN

'My dear sir, you are most *elsewhere* this evening,' said Maris Garrick, as she dipped her soup spoon into her bowl. 'Should you be troubled, perhaps you might wish to discuss the problem?' Her artfully tinted lips curved. 'I thought I'd proven myself a comfortable listener.'

With an effort he found difficult to conceal, which was almost as disturbing as the girl in Hahren's antechamber, Morgan wrenched his thoughts to the here-and-now. Maris was looking magnificent, wrapped in sheer, shimmering peach-pink silk lavishly embroidered with gold thread and crystal beading. The dress was a shade too low-cut, her breasts swelling invitingly, provocatively, above its scalloped, crystal-edged neckline.

*She baits her trap with care, this Garrick daughter. Were I a callow youth I might well tumble into it without a second thought.*

But he wasn't callow. He never had been. And since Venette's dinner party he'd had his suspicions confirmed. Maris Garrick might be young, but she wasn't entirely an innocent. His shifting gaze touched on the woman sitting alone at the table beside them. Maris's companion, her silent shadow. Though Lord and Lady Garrick were anxious to see their daughter well wed, they weren't entirely reckless.

*Or perhaps they know she cares less for propriety than a proper young mage should.*

'Morgan?'

Maris was staring at him, a light frown creasing her fair brow. She had the palest, most translucent skin. It was beautiful. She was beautiful.

*But not as beautiful as the girl waiting for Hahren.*

Another wrenching effort, and the girl's face was banished. He dredged up an apologetic smile.

'Forgive me. There is certain Council business weighing on my mind. You'll understand if I cannot say any more than that.'

'Of course,' Maris replied, and took more soup. 'I understand perfectly.'

But did she? Was that a shadow of displeasure darkening her lustrous eyes? He thought it was. So what, then, was Maris Garrick thinking? That she should be privy to his discreet Council business? That marriage to Morgan Danfey would see the Garrick family gain some roundabout, backhanded Council influence? Even power?

*If so, my dear, you are sorely mistaken.*

Busy this evening, as usual, The Opal's warm air glowed with the rustic novelty of Brantish beeswax candles. Their sweet scent mingled with the aromas of fine food. In the gallery above the dining area musicians serenaded the guests with soft, elegant music. A haven of luxurious gentility, The Opal, where supremely gifted food mages slaved to provide sumptuous repasts for wealthy and discriminating palates.

Appetite quite fled, Morgan stared at his opening course of tender rabbit loin stuffed with prune and wrapped in salt bacon. No matter his efforts, the girl in Hahren's antechamber would not be dismissed.

*Though she hid it well, she was distressed. What brings her to Elvado? She was dressed in linen. That makes her either unranked, or so lowly placed she might as well be. But there's power in her, as belongs in the best First Family blood. That's why my skin danced. Power calling to power.*

203

Justice be damned, who *was* she?

'Dear sir, I have something to ask you,' said Maris, setting aside her spoon. Intruding again. 'If I may?'

In emptying her bowl she'd splashed soup on the immaculate white tablecloth. Was the woman a boor? How could he invite her to dine at the Danfey mansion if she was incapable of keeping her soup safe in its spoon?

'Of course,' he said, smothering irritation with pleasantry. 'There is no need to ask my permission.'

Maris laughed. The sound grated. 'As you know, though we are well established in Elvado, the Garrick estate still flourishes in the verdant beauty of Dorana's Fifth district. My parents look to host a house party there next week, and would be honoured to receive you as a guest.'

A house party? And what was this, a ploy to secure his interest? A way for Lord Parnel Garrick to insinuate himself into a prospective goodson's good graces? A Councillor's good graces?

*They are not subtle, these Garricks. Their idea of stealth is to gaily blow trumpets as they blunder through the woods in search of their fox.*

But he was no man's fox. Though he might play at being the quarry, he was the true hunter here. He would catch Maris Garrick in his own time, and keep her on his own terms.

*Provided I want her. And that is yet to be settled.*

'A house party sounds delightful,' he said, being sure to sound sincere. 'Alas, I am reluctant to travel so far from home. Lord Danfey, you understand. His health continues precarious.'

'Oh,' Maris said, all sweet concern and, heedless of her watching companion, reached across the table to press fingers to his arm. Her wrist was laden with a gold and ruby bracelet. A vulgar, boastful thing. Luzena would never have worn it. 'Oh, of course. You worry for him. No wonder your palate is jaded.'

Reminded, he looked at his burdened plate. If he did not eat all but a mouthful of his rabbit, word would go back to the kitchen and dismay would ensue. Furthermore, it would be noted by The Opal's other diners. He was known here, his every smile and swallow and sigh avidly noted. If his demeanour so much as hinted at dissatisfaction, gossiping tongues would wag until they fell out entirely.

*'Did you hear? Councillor Danfey was indifferent toward his dinner at The Opal. I wonder if there is some magery trouble in the place?'*

And that would hardly be fair to Harlim Seffley, The Opal's proprietor and senior mage. Harlim's establishment wasn't to blame for Councillor Danfey's distracted thoughts.

Lifting his knife and fork, Morgan shook his head. 'Jaded? Not at all, Maris. I am merely distracted.'

She pouted. 'By me a little, I hope, as well as your mysterious Council business!'

No mention of his father. But then, Greve Danfey was nothing more than an obstacle, was he?

'Of course,' he replied, forcing another smile. 'My dear, you must not entertain any doubt on it, or fear that kind of distraction could be considered unpleasant.'

As Maris simpered at the compliment he relieved his feelings by shoving rabbit, prune and bacon between his teeth. Never once in her too-short life had Luzena simpered. Nor could he imagine the young mage in Hahren's antechamber simpering. No. He'd seen too much strength in her fine-boned face for that. Who was she? Who *was* she?

'Perhaps,' Maris said, slender fingers caressing the stem of her wineglass, 'Lord Danfey would care to join us? At the house party, I mean. As it happens my mother's cousin is an exceptional pother. I'm sure—'

'Maris,' he said, and lowered his hand. Try as he might, he could not smile this time. 'It's a kind thought, but I cannot entertain it. My father's recovery is much slower than I would like. Subjecting him to a long journey, and then so much social excitement, well, I'm afraid that's out of the question. But do extend my appreciation to your parents for the invitation.'

'The invitation is mine, Morgan.' There was now the hint of

an edge to her playful voice. 'As for your dear father, perhaps he should be permitted to accept or decline for himself.'

And now she far overstepped the mark. A curt reproof trembled on his tongue. But indulging it would not be wise. Everywhere he turned, it seemed, he was trammelled.

'Of course, Maris,' he said smoothly, the salty sweetness of the rabbit turned rancid. 'And I shall be sure to mention it to him on the morrow. If I seem ungrateful, I apologise. Knowing my father's health as I do, and knowing too how Pother Ranmer so jealously guards his patient's frail condition, I simply leapt ahead to voice his most likely opinion. An opinion I am bound to respect, for my father's sake.'

'Morgan . . .' Maris's eyelashes fluttered. 'Your loving loyalty quite steals my breath.'

And there she was, simpering again. It turned his stomach. She smiled, expecting a compliment in kind. If he disappointed her, if he spurned her, she might well slip from his grasp.

The truth was he didn't want her . . . but he didn't want to lose her, either.

Taking her left hand, he turned it over and caressed the soft inside of her wrist. Her warm, rapid pulse thundered against his fingertips.

'I think you'll find, Maris, that I have many ways of stealing your breath.'

'Morgan!' She feigned shock, pulling her hand from his, but her cheeks were pink with pleasure. A discreet flick of her fingers kept the alerted companion in her seat. 'How bold you are, sir.'

*And what a hypocrite you are, my lady. Oh, Luzena. She's so petty. So small, and obvious. How can I think of shackling myself to her . . . after you?*

It was almost impossible to keep the thought from his face.

Maris was pouting again. 'Well, I suppose if you can't attend the house party, we must think of something else to do. You work so terribly hard, Morgan. You need to take care of yourself. And if you won't, then your friends must do the caring for you.'

Friends? He and Maris weren't friends. He'd been friends with Luzena. Could he even imagine that kind of friendship with Maris Garrick?

*Perhaps. I don't know. But if I'm to do this, I must find a way. The thought of spending the rest of my life tied to a woman I can neither like nor respect is enough to freeze my blood. Father, Father . . . what you ask me to do!*

Maris still watched him, like a cat waiting for cream. He offered her another hard-fought smile. 'You think to spoil me, my lady Garrick?'

More eyelash fluttering. 'Well, of course! In fact—'

He was saved from her fawning by the return of their table attendant. 'Forgive me, Lord Danfey,' the man murmured, bending low, 'but an urgent message has arrived for you.'

Mouth dry, aware of Maris's ill-concealed pique, he took the folded note. 'Thank you.'

'Is something amiss?' said Maris. 'Please don't say you have to go!'

'I'm sorry,' he said, light-headed after a glance at the brief message. *Return to the Council chamber. V.* 'A councillor cannot safely call his time his own. But you should stay, Maris. I see no reason for us both to have dinner spoiled.'

She wanted to complain, he could see it, but she wanted to be Lady Danfey more. So she sighed instead, and offered him an understanding smile.

'I suppose I shall have to get used to these interruptions. Perhaps we can dine again properly another night this week?'

He pushed his chair back and stood. 'Perhaps. Let us hope so.' Taking her hand, he kissed it. Perfume breathed from her skin. 'I am truly sorry. I'd looked forward to seeing you.'

She smiled again, and for a moment seemed genuinely sweet. Seemed an innocent young girl, disappointed, and not the simpering, calculating woman on the hunt for a lord. Perhaps if he could be sure *that* was the Maris Garrick he'd be marrying . . .

'Good night, Morgan,' she said softly. 'Whatever calls you

back to the Council, I do hope it's resolved soon and to your satisfaction.'

Nodding, Morgan signalled to their attendant. 'See to my guest and her companion. Anything they desire. Tell Harlim I'll settle with him on the morrow.'

The attendant bowed. 'Of course, Councillor Danfey. Good evening, sir.'

Escaped outside to the street, he took a moment to steady himself. For one terrible moment, before he'd read Varen's note, he'd thought the message was from Rumm. He'd thought –

Angry, he shook his head. *I must stop borrowing grief. Justice knows it will come for me soon enough.* Then, breathing deep of the cool night air, fingers wrapped painfully tight about his locket, about Luzena, he made his brisk way back to the Hall.

When he saw Voln Hahren standing in the Council chamber he came dangerously close to breaking stride. *This* was why he'd been summoned? The nonsense over Lord Jordane's useless daughter?

*If Hahren has dared lay complaint against me, I shall make him rue this day.*

'Lord Varen, I apologise,' he said, glaring at Hahren. 'I made it plain to Lord Hahren that I would keep the Council informed of how things stood with Nevin Jordane and his concerns. If he has—'

'He hasn't,' Varen said curtly, as though the man wasn't standing in their midst. 'We don't know what he wants. We've been waiting for you.'

As Venette rolled her eyes at Brice Varen's testiness, Sallis Arkley cleared his throat. 'But, since you touch upon the subject, Morgan, what have you—'

If he smiled, there would be trouble. Morgan kept his face severe. 'In a nutshell? Bellamie Ranowen is blameless. The fault lies with Jordane's daughter. She is insolent, and her lack of aptitude makes her unfit for her place in the College. Proctor Lowyn and Lord Hahren, here, are looking more deeply into the matter. I'll have a full report for the Council soon.'

Varen tapped his steepled fingers, unhappy. 'You're sure of this, Morgan? There can be no mistake?'

'None, my lord,' he said, taking his seat at the table. 'But I'm confident we can prevent an open scandal.'

'Yes, that would be preferable,' said Varen, very dry. He looked at Sallis. 'I don't want the matter discussed beyond this chamber. If Jordane should press you, Sallis, I expect you to put him in his place.'

Sallis was looking shaken. Beside him, Shari Frieden shifted her hand slightly toward his.

'Of course,' he said, subdued. 'But I confess, I find Morgan's conclusion difficult to accept.'

'Doubtless you do, Sallis,' said Varen, dismissive. 'But accept it you will. Unless you wish to contend he's made the whole thing up out of spite?'

Sallis Arkley would like nothing better, but not even he would go so far. 'Of course not,' he muttered.

'Good,' said Varen, and slapped his palms to the table. 'Hahren, you'll be equally discreet, is that clear? And you'll warn Proctor Lowyn, though I suspect he's already stitched his lips shut. Now does that conclude our business?'

'I'm afraid not, Lord Varen. And I'm sorry to have summoned you, but I felt it was imperative.'

'Let's hope your feelings haven't led you astray,' said Venette. 'Because I, for one, could have done without traipsing back here.'

'And I,' said Sallis, scowling. 'If it turns out this would've kept till the morrow, Hahren, you'll have cause for regret. The Council of Mages isn't your tame dog to be summoned at a whistle.'

As Hahren stumbled over a more fulsome apology, Morgan noticed he had a bruise blooming over his left cheekbone. And there was – yes! – a hint of dried blood in his nostrils. Which hadn't been the case when he left the man before joining Maris for dinner.

*The girl in his antechamber? Surely she's not responsible.*
Remembering her, he felt his heart leap.

'*Enough*, Hahren,' said Lord Varen, with an impatient glance at Sallis Arkley. 'You can be sure we know you've an understanding of what is important, and what isn't.'

Sallis folded his arms, resenting the unsubtle rebuke.

'Yes, Lord Varen,' said Hahren, not quite wise enough to hide all his triumph. 'My lord, I – *we* – have a problem that I feel must be dealt with by the Council. If you recall some weeks ago I passed on to you a request for College admission from one Mage Barl Lindin?'

'Vaguely,' said Venette, not waiting for Varen to speak. She was the only one of them who could get away with such impertinence. 'A little nobody from an outlying district, isn't she?'

Hahren's cheeks reddened, making the bruise stand out more starkly. 'The Eleventh district, yes. But she is far from a nobody, my lady. She's a proven troublemaker. I've received warnings of her from the artisan mage who recently dismissed her for knavery, and from the Artisan's Guild.'

'Is that so?' said Shari Frieden, her lips pleated with distaste. 'Hahren, you appear a trifle the worse for wear. Do you claim this Mage Lindin has attacked you? With magic? And you were unable to defend yourself?'

Caught between humiliation and outrage, Hahren hemmed and hawed, then nodded. 'She turned up without warning, demanding to see me. I thought it best she be dealt with once and for all, so I gave her a few minutes. When I didn't say what she wanted to hear, she lost her temper. And when I attempted to remove her from my office . . .'

'She attacked you?' Lord Varen leaned forward, fingers drumming the Council table. 'Hahren, this is a grave charge indeed.'

'When you say you attempted to remove her,' Morgan added before Hahren could reply, risking censure and not caring, 'do you mean you laid hands on her?'

Hahren's eyes glittered with woken fury. 'She wouldn't leave when I told her to! She stood there, in my office, and *defied* me!'

'So you did lay hands on her. In effect, you attacked her first.'

'Councillor Danfey, I did no such thing!' Hahren snapped. 'I

210

told her she had no claim for a dispensation, that the College's decision was final, and instructed her to leave. Instead of obeying me, she threw a tantrum! Said she'd go nowhere without first speaking to the Council of Mages. I told her that was out of the question. That's when she called me a spruling jigget.'

Venette muffled a snort of laughter. 'Indeed. How very provoking.'

'And then, when I ordered her yet again to leave, and still she wouldn't, I took her by the arm. Just by the arm, mind you, and not roughly. There was no violence about it. Certainly no magic. All I did was try to escort her from the room.'

'She took exception?' said Venette.

'*Exception*?' Hahren's chest heaved. 'Lady Martain, she hurled me across my own chamber with a repulsion incant!'

Morgan sat back in his chair. 'Because you attacked her.'

'How many times must I say it?' said Hahren, close to spluttering. 'I did no such thing!'

'Care to explain why you're defending this unranked upstart, Morgan?' said Sallis Arkley. 'Seems to me you should be spitting fire at her temerity.'

Yes. He should be, shouldn't he? But all he could do was smother the smile that threatened to ruin his Council career. This unranked girl, this *Barl Lindin*, she of the strong, beautiful face and plain linen tunic and shimmering promise of power, in the Hall of Knowledge itself dared to challenge Lord Voln Hahren.

*What an extraordinary young woman.*

'I defend nothing and no-one, Lord Arkley. I merely suggest that we give the girl a chance to explain herself.'

'Really, Morgan?' Venette considered him. 'What further explanation do we need? This Barl Lindin used magic against a Council-appointed official who was merely doing his duty. A trifle crudely, perhaps, but that's neither here nor there. The *point* is—'

'*I* think, Lady Martain, the point is that she might have thought herself in real danger,' he said, meeting Venette's unsympathetic stare. 'Would you punish her for being afraid? That's harsh, even for you.'

Lord Varen forestalled Venette's heated reply with a raised hand. 'Hahren, where is Mage Lindin now?'

'Outside this chamber, my lord,' said Hahren, with a jerk of his chin. 'Held in close custody and awaiting your pleasure.'

'There's no pleasure in this,' Shari complained. 'I have the megrim. I want my bed.'

'Bring the woman in,' said Varen, ignoring her. 'And we shall decide what the consequence of this hubble-bubble shall be.'

Looking pleased, Hahren retreated to the chamber door, tugged it ajar then beckoned into the antechamber beyond. A moment later the girl entered, flanked by two of the Hall's duty mages. Her colour was high, her linen tunic dishevelled. Her clear blue eyes were alight with defiance. Acutely aware of Venette's speculative scrutiny, that in Shari Frieden and Sallis Arkley he had enemies, not allies, Morgan kept himself strictly in hand.

And then Barl Lindin's blue gaze fell on him . . . and she faltered. Her shock, seeing him, was shocking.

*She feels it, just as I do. What does this mean?*

He knew what he wanted it to mean, even as he knew such a thing was impossible. She was unranked, and brought before the Council on the most serious of charges. But how could he not think of it? Even as her beauty beat through his blood, her breathtaking power lit a flame in his heart.

'Well, well,' Venette said under breath. 'Nobody or not, she has a surfeit of aptitude.'

From the looks on their faces, the others could feel it too. Varen, who never slumped, somehow managed to sit even straighter in his chair.

'You may leave us, Lord Hahren. Take the duty mages with you. They can wait outside.'

Hahren hesitated longer than was wise, then nodded. His eyes raged with disappointment. He'd wanted to see the girl punished. 'My lord. Councillors,' he murmured, then withdrew, the duty mages silently obedient at his heels.

As the chamber door closed behind them, Varen drummed his fingers on the table. 'Very well, Mage Lindin. Account for yourself.'

'Is there any point?' the girl asked. Her chin was up, her expression defiant. 'Surely you've already decided to condemn me.'

'Tread carefully, Mage Lindin,' Sallis snapped. 'You are in perilous straits.'

A faint flush of colour touched the girl's cheeks. 'What did Lord Hahren tell you?'

'We aren't interested in his tale,' said Venette. 'We want to hear yours.'

'You didn't before,' the girl said. Beneath her defiance she was frightened. 'You dismissed me before, without giving me the chance to prove myself worthy of a place in the College.'

Varen's drumming fingers drummed louder. Then he slapped the table. 'Enough posturing, Mage Lindin. You do not impress.'

Barl Lindin stared at the floor. Watching her closely, Morgan thought she was making a deliberate effort not to look at him. And he thought that effort cost her something. Still aware of too-perceptive Venette beside him, he did his utmost to show the girl nothing but indifference.

'I'm sorry, Lord Varen,' she said, not looking up. 'I don't mean to be rude.'

Venette snorted. 'And yet you are. Can it be you're *trying* to give us a bad impression of you?'

The girl lifted her gaze, stricken. 'No!'

'Then tell us what happened.'

'Lord Hahren tried to lay hands on me. I was afraid. I lashed out.'

'With magic,' said Shari, unmoved. 'Even a rustic from the Eleventh district must know that is a crime.'

'It wouldn't have happened if he hadn't tried to snatch at me!'

'It wouldn't have happened,' Varen countered coldly, 'if you'd taken no for an answer.'

And that was indisputably true. The look on the girl's face was as good as a confession.

Idly, Venette smoothed a wrinkle in her mauve silk sleeve. 'Why didn't you?'

The girl's cheeks pinked again. 'Because I dispute the notion that only those mages born to a First Family are worthy enough to study in the College.'

'Mage Lindin, we are not interested in your opinions,' said Varen, brusque with impatience. 'You are not standing here because we want you to air them. We understand you've been dismissed from your employment.'

'I recently left Master Arndel's artisanry,' the girl said, wary now. 'Yes.'

'Stop prevaricating!' said Sallis. 'You were dismissed.'

'Unfairly! My lord, I prevented a terrible accident and saved the artisanry. But the mage at fault lied. Arndel took his word over mine because he doesn't like me.'

And that was the truth. They could all hear it. But instead of expressing sympathy, Varen shook his head. 'It seems you find trouble at every turn, Barl Lindin. It seems you are a mage who has yet to learn her place.'

'My place is in the College,' the girl said, no longer defiant. Almost beseeching. '*Look!*'

Without asking permission, she summoned a paperweight from somewhere. Hahren's chamber, perhaps? Then, even as Sallis and Shari protested, with astonishing ease she transmuted the clear crystal globe into a perfect porum blossom. A whispered incant, a swift sigil, and the crystal flower flooded blue, flooded emerald, flooded violet, flooded gold, the rainbow colours cascading, the girl's mastery complete. Another incant, another sigil, and the flower transmuted into an eagle, fluid and effortless, snatched timeless out of flight.

Morgan felt his breath catch. Barl Lindin's command and artistry were flawless.

Unimpressed, Varen surged to his feet. '*Enough!* You are not brought before us to perform parlour tricks.'

A flash of desolate fury, then Barl Lindin lowered her head.

'We succeed as a society *not* because we are mages,' Varen

continued, implacable, 'but because we understand the limits of our power. We understand there must be restraint, and balance, a careful order maintained that we might not be overcome. Your indiscipline, Barl Lindin, is a threat to that order.'

The girl's head lifted sharply. 'And do you call it *indiscipline* when a ranked mage—'

'Hold your tongue, Mage Lindin! This is not a debate!'

She wanted to argue that, but wisely refrained.

'With the exception of this Council,' Varen said, 'it is a capital crime for a mage to use magic on another. Barl Lindin, do you claim ignorance of that fact?'

'My lord—' The girl swallowed. 'I was protecting myself.'

'*Do you claim ignorance?*'

'No.' She swallowed again. 'My lord.'

There was courage in the answer . . . and beneath that, despair. As though the enormity of her predicament had finally struck home. Staring at her, Morgan saw her brilliant blue eyes fill with tears.

*If I don't speak up, they'll slay her. And if I do . . .*

If he didn't he would find it hard to live with himself.

'Lord Varen, I think perhaps it's an overstatement to call this a capital crime,' he said, striving to sound indifferent. 'I say we bind the insolent child so she cannot bloody anyone else's nose while contemplating the manifest error of her ways.'

Sallis slewed round in his chair. 'Are you addled, Danfey? Binding is for misdemeanours.'

'You'd put her to death, Lord Arkley? For doing no more harm to Hahren than if she'd slapped him across the face?'

'But she didn't slap him, did she?' Shari said, vicious. 'She used an incant. She broke the law.'

'If her intent had been to kill, Lord Hahren would surely be dead. So it's my contention there was no murderous intent, in which case this is *not* a capital crime, therefore—'

'Start down that road and we will reach no helpful destination,' said Sallis. 'Bend the law for this unruly girl and I tell you, the day will come when we'll regret our foolish leniency!'

Hating him, Morgan glared. 'I prefer to think of it as mercy.'

'Word games!' Sallis snarled. 'I'll not play them. Besides, the end result will be the same, as Lord Varen rightly points out. Chaos. Lawlessness. An overturning of the social order, which has served us for centuries. And I for one will not abide by—'

'Actually?' Venette's mild voice halted the tirade. 'I feel Morgan has a valid point. I'm sorry.' She flicked Varen a look. 'But if you mean to sit there, Sallis, and deny all knowledge of magical dust-ups caused by hot-blooded young bucks in any number of First Families, then although it would pain me, I'd have to call you a liar.'

Sallis Arkley drew back as though she'd spat on him. 'That's different, Venette, and you know it!'

'Really?' she said, still mild. 'Lord Arkley, just recently your son was involved in an unfortunate situation, and he was given the benefit of the doubt. Are you saying that if the prank had run the contrary way you'd be baying for that other young man's blood? For no better reason than his family is unranked?'

Morgan held his breath. *Of course he would.* But how could Arkley admit it and not brand himself unfit for the Council? Unfit for any power at all? He risked a glance at Barl Lindin. She stood before them as though carved from alabaster, her linen-covered breasts scarcely lifting as she breathed. Did she realise her brimming tears had spilled onto her pale cheeks?

'We stray far from the purpose,' said Varen, his tone and stare quelling. 'Given the facts before us, I concur with Councillor Danfey. Binding is a sufficient punishment. This time.'

'Binding for how long?' said Shari. She sounded disappointed, as though the shedding of blood would have cured her of megrim. 'This was no harmless prank.'

'Until we are satisfied that the lesson has been learned,' said Varen. 'I see no need to place a limit on its term.'

At that, the girl stirred. 'You'd bind me for *life*?'

Varen's lips thinned into an austere smile. 'That will be your choice, Mage Lindin. Not ours.'

216

'Have Morgan do it,' Venette suggested. 'We've all of us done a judicial binding. We shouldn't deprive him of the experience.'

'Agreed,' said Varen, and resumed his seat. 'Morgan?'

Stupidly, he felt as though Venette had somehow betrayed him. He looked at her, and she looked back, her neatly plucked eyebrows arched, a challenging glitter in her eyes. So. Though he'd surely tried, he'd failed to hide his visceral reaction to Barl Lindin. And Venette, who'd appointed herself matchmaker for Maris Garrick, had decided to take it as a personal affront.

*Curse you, Venette. I do not deserve this!*

His turn to suffer the glare of full scrutiny. He could no more refuse to do this than Sallis Arkley could admit his unseemly prejudice and hypocrisy.

'My lord,' he said, nodding to Varen, and pushed out of his chair.

To her credit, the girl stood her ground as he approached. She didn't even lean away from him as he took the crystal eagle from her and put it on the Council table, then settled the fingers of his left hand gently on her face.

*Her eyes are so blue. I could drown in them, like a lake.*

'This will hurt,' he said, keeping his tone impersonal. 'Do not fight me. You'll only make things worse.'

She said nothing, only stared at him with her blue, blue lake eyes.

The judicial binding incant was one of several severely restricted magics to which he'd been made privy after his swearing in as a councillor. Once he'd learned its sigils and syllables he'd pushed it far to one side, along with the rest. Its imposition was rare. He'd never thought the day would come when he'd be called upon to use it.

*I do not want to use it now. Barl, I am sorry.*

And why that should be, he couldn't begin to understand. Nothing about this Barl Lindin, or what she stirred in him, made any sense.

Fingertips touching her cheekbones, her brow, he lowered his eyelids to mask her from his sight. He couldn't watch while he hurt her. He wasn't that strong.

His fellow councillors were watching him. He could feel the weight of Varen's cool stare, the heat of Venette's irritated regard. He cared less about Sallis Arkley and Shari Frieden. Nothing he did or could do would ever impress them.

He drew the binding's first sigil on the chamber's still air. Left it there curdling, and spoke the incant's first cruel words. Beneath his fingers, the girl flinched. He heard a breath catch in her throat. But he couldn't let that move him. He couldn't afford to care.

Barl Lindin wasn't the only one on trial.

Five more sigils, five more tongue-twisting parts to the binding incant. Then he had to open his eyes. Even with his back to Varen and the others he didn't dare let the regret show in his face. Her face might reflect it, betray him, and he'd have questions to answer.

But she was too mired in her own distress to be any danger to him.

The five sigils, each one a fiery crimson, surrounded her in a tight circle at shoulder height. They pulsed with the power of the yet-untriggered incant, flickering her with heat and light. The chamber's air was thick with threatening promise, slickly coated with fear and pain. The girl was sickly pallid, her breathing swift and shallow. Her small hands were clenched to fists by her sides. And her eyes – her blue eyes –

*Don't look at me like that, girl! You brought this on yourself. You should've stayed in Batava, where you were safe.*

But if she'd stayed in Batava he'd never have met her.

Those astonishing, pain-filled eyes narrowed. 'Well, my lord?' she said tightly. 'What are you waiting for? *Do it*!'

Her courage nearly broke him.

'*Takra!*' he said, and triggered the incant.

The five sigils flared, garish, like fire fanned by a wild wind. Barl Lindin gasped, her slight body shocked rigid. A heartbeat later she started trembling. Then the incants melted one into the next, began rising and falling and spinning, the circle shrinking . . . shrinking . . .

The melded sigils touched her shaking shoulders and swiftly sank into her flesh.

'Oh,' she whispered. 'Oh no . . . please, no . . .'

Morgan caught her as she crumpled, and lowered her gently to the floor.

*I'm sorry. Forgive me. You must have seen I had no choice.*

But he couldn't see how she would, when he doubted he'd ever forgive himself.

# CHAPTER FOURTEEN

'Excellent, Councillor Danfey,' said Lord Varen behind him. 'That was neatly done.'

There was bile in his throat, sour and scorching. Staring at the bound girl at his feet, Morgan rose then stepped back. Made himself turn and stare Venette in the face.

She was smiling. 'Yes, indeed. Very neatly, especially for a first attempt. It seems you have a knack for the harsher incants, Morgan.'

On the floor, Barl Lindin was whimpering. The pitiful sound closed his throat. 'The girl was foolish and arrogant. Of course she had to be punished. But if you think I should take pleasure in that, then—'

'No-one here has suggested it,' said Varen, curt. He glanced at their fellow councillors. 'And if I thought anyone did I should be forced to reconsider his or her place on this Council.'

'So, the upstart's bound,' said Shari Frieden. Whatever pleasure *she* felt, to see the girl huddled and hurting, humbled, she made sure to hide it. She wasn't a fool. 'But that still begs the question of what's to be done with her next.'

'Has she family in Batava?' said Venette. 'Does anyone know?'

Varen shook his head. 'I've no idea, but even if she does we can't send her back there. It's too far away for us to judge her contrition. Besides, it's clear her family has been no good influence, else she'd not find herself in this predicament. She'll spend the night here, in the Hall, closely watched. Bindings have been known to go awry.'

'Fine,' said Sallis. 'But what happens tomorrow? The Hall's not a judiciary.'

'One challenge at a time,' said Varen, mildly enough. 'First let us see how Mage Lindin passes the night.' He frowned, considering her. 'Between now and the morning I'll give a measure of thought to how she can best be accommodated in the weeks to come.'

'You may think on her 'til the sun sets in the north,' said Venette. 'But I give you fair warning, Brice. If it's a custodian you're looking for, I'll not be her keeper.'

'Nor I,' said Shari Frieden, eyeing the girl with distasteful contempt. 'I won't abide such a troublemaker under my roof.'

Turning, Morgan looked down at the girl shivering on the chamber's floor. No outward sign was on her, but any mage of talent would know she'd been bound. She felt like the bright sun, shadowed with clouds. Muffled. *Stifled.* He thought that was the reason for her distress. Once the binding was in place, the incant caused a mage no pain.

*Poor thing. Were such a thing done to me, I think I might go mad.*

He turned back to Varen. 'I'll take her, my lord.'

Sallis laughed. '*You*, Morgan?'

'Why not, Lord Arkley? Or are you suggesting that Lord Varen shoulder the burden?'

'Provided she passes the night without incident, she should be consigned to a judiciary,' said Shari, impatient. 'She deserves no more consideration than that.'

'Exactly,' said Venette, nodding approval. 'To dispose of her otherwise would set an unfortunate precedent.'

Frowning, Varen shifted his gaze. 'You disagree, Morgan?'

*Careful . . . careful . . .* 'My lord, the girl might be bound but her tongue is still free to wag. We're all of us agreed she's a troublemaker. Do we really need to chance her causing mischief for the Council?'

'That's easily fixed,' said Sallis. 'Keep her solitary. Keep her drugged. Or is there a binding incant that can be twisted to still her tongue?'

Varen's frown became a scowl. 'Three solutions that would not reflect well upon this Council. We are more civilised, I think, than a Feenish warlord.'

This time Morgan did not hide his feelings. 'I should think so, my lord. The girl's crime was not so great. Kept close at the Danfey estate she won't cause trouble. Our master servant is strict. He can be trusted with her supervision.'

'And she'll do what, precisely, while she's in your tender care?' Venette demanded. 'Twiddle her thumbs and stare out of the nearest window as she plots a revenge against the mages who've dared thwart her ludicrous ambitions?'

Oh, she *was* displeased, wasn't she? Well, it couldn't be helped. *You were my mother's friend, Venette, but that does not make you her replacement.*

'No, Lady Martain,' he said, very cool. 'Mage Lindin will perform whatever menial household tasks Rumm sees fit to assign her.'

'And Lord Danfey will agree to this unusual arrangement?' said Shari, sounding skeptical.

'Lord Danfey does not concern himself with domestic matters,' he replied, and again looked to Varen. 'I've no doubt that a few weeks spent scrubbing floors and kitchen pots and dusting every crevice of the mansion will push home to Mage Lindin the benefits of living an unremarkable, unnoticed life.'

Varen's lips twitched. 'Nor do I doubt it. Very well, Morgan. But since I'd not usurp Lord Danfey's authority, be sure to gain his express permission for this. And come the morning—' He glanced down at Barl Lindin, motionless on the floor. 'We'll see how things stand.'

'With luck,' Sallis added, 'she'll expire through the night, and serve as a warning to other reckless, unranked mages.'

Rage pounding through him, Morgan shifted until his back was turned full upon the man. 'Lord Varen, if we are done with this distasteful business, I'd beg your leave to depart. My father insists on keeping awake until I'm safely home, and I'd not unduly tire him.'

Varen nodded. 'Of course. But I'll see you back here first thing.'

'Yes, my lord.'

'And I want the Jordane matter dealt with on the morrow, as well,' Varen added. 'Discreetly.'

Morgan bowed. 'Yes, my lord.'

Without looking again at Barl Lindin, without bidding farewell to Venette, or offering Sallis and Shari the most cursory good manners, he withdrew from the chamber, and at the first warded alcove he came to, savagely chanted a travel incant . . . and left the Hall behind.

Stepping into the Danfey family crypt, he summoned glimfire. Light and shadow played over smooth walls and flagstoned floor and Luzena's tomb, where she slept instead of in his bed. She had been his chosen wife so he'd claimed the privilege, fiercely. Her family of course had not prevailed against him.

No-one prevailed against him, once his mind was made up.

He stood beside her, his lost love, aching with loss, as his conjured glimfire played over her smooth marble face.

'You understand, Luzena? Don't you? Where else could the girl go where she'd not be abused? A judiciary would've kept her penned like an animal. And with my binding incant on her, how could I allow that? Knowing that she suffered, that I was the cause, and knowing too there'd be scant kindness offered? As for buffeting Hahren—' He had to smile. 'I've often wanted to buffet him myself. But if ever desire did outrun prudence, my Council rank would protect me. Should Barl Lindin be left vulnerable, for no better reason than she's *un*ranked? She made a mistake. There's no shame in showing her mercy.'

Luzena had been tenderhearted, moved to tears by the smallest plight of the least important Doranen mage. For that alone he'd loved her. This foolish young woman from Batava would have stirred her to pity, of that he had no doubt.

'If you were still by my side, where you belong, you'd have insisted that I bring her here. I know it.'

Cold hands framing her cold face, he kissed Luzena's gently parted lips. Her throat. The swell of her sweet breasts. Their warmth had been denied him for the rest of his life. Now all he had was their cold stone comfort.

'My love . . . my love. How I miss you.'

His fingers caressed the curving lines of her face. Her nose had been the tiniest bit crooked. The imperfection had only made her more perfect. Maris Garrick's nose was perfect, her entire beauty beyond dispute. Only he wanted, *needed,* more than beauty. And Maris Garrick did not have it.

*But what do my needs matter? I have a duty, I made a promise, and that must override all.*

He kissed Luzena again, hard enough to bruise lips against teeth. 'Dear one, I can see no way of rebuffing Maris Garrick. In every respect counted important she is, without question, a suitable match.'

Snatching the locket from beneath his tunic, he wrenched it open. His love's painted face smiled back at him, somehow more real, more *Luzena,* than the exquisite marble woman laid out before him.

'Please, my love, I beg you. Forgive me this betrayal. When I bed Maris Garrick there will be no pleasure in it.'

Glimfire in close quarters was warming, but still he shivered. Kind shadows hid the chamber's other occupants, but the crypt was a house of death and it pressed down on him, smothering.

*Father will sleep here soon. With all my mage powers I can't save him. Ranmer with his pills and potions, he can't save him either. Before the year dies I will be Lord Danfey.*

The thought broke him, and he sobbed without restraint on

Luzena's unyielding breast . . . but only for a moment. Such displays of emotion did not become a Danfey or a member of Dorana's Council of Mages. He'd not wept since he lost his beloved, and on that terrible day, when he sought to abandon himself to wild grief, his father had struck him.

'Disgrace me, would you?' he'd demanded. 'Wipe your face, Morgan. You're not a woman, to drown yourself in tears!'

Now, as then, he blotted his eyes dry. Stepped back from Luzena's coffin, his heart pounding, and breathed deep until it slowed.

'You are dead, Luzena, but I yet live. And so long as I live, I must do my duty.'

Glimlight danced across her peaceful stone brow, her cheeks, her lips. He stepped back again, because he wanted to climb onto the coffin beside her and imagine himself safe and loved in her arms.

'Sleep well, my darling,' he whispered, and left her alone in the dark.

Rumm practically pounced on him as he entered the mansion. 'Sir! Thank goodness!'

'What is it?' he said, fighting a fresh wave of dread. 'Lord Danfey? Why did you not—'

'Sir, sir, please, there's no crisis,' Rumm said swiftly. 'But his lordship is restless. In truth, sir, he's been kicking up a right dust. I know you told him you were out to dinner this evening but—' The master servant swallowed hard. 'Sir, he's having some trouble recalling it.'

'I see.' Morgan gave Rumm a curt nod. 'Very well.'

He took the stairs two at a time, his palms suddenly sweaty. Ranmer had warned that his father's lucidity would likely wax and wane. But he'd been himself for such a goodly time, he'd begun to hope –

'Morgan!' his father croaked, as he entered the fire-warmed chamber. 'At last. What's kept you so late?'

Late? Even with that Council business, it was only a whisper past nine. 'I'm sorry, my lord,' he said, taking the chair beside the bed. 'I did not mean to cause concern.'

Hectic colour burned in his father's face. His eyes glittered, overbright. 'Ha! Dallied at dinner, did you? So the Garrick girl's truly to your liking?'

*Luzena.* 'She is most . . . suitable.'

'Then best you snap her up, Morgan, before some other wifeless mage gets wind of her.'

'Yes,' he said, subdued. 'Doubtless that would be wise.'

'And yet you sound doubtful,' his father said, accusing. 'What nonsense is this?'

'My lord, I know nothing of nonsense. But I have been thinking—'

'Then stop it! What good did that ever do a man? You think too much, Morgan. If you'd please me, then *act*.'

Mouth dry, he stared at his slowly dying father. Every time he thought himself reconciled to duty, to Maris Garrick, his misgivings awoke to prick him anew.

*And am I to ignore them, just to keep an old man happy? When he is dying and I'm the one who'll suffer for the mistake?*

'My lord,' he said at last, sick with apprehension, hurt by the rebuke, 'I think of little else but pleasing you. But let me speak plainly now. Let me tell you the truth as it appears to me.'

His father looked offended. If his wits had wandered earlier, they were sharply focused again. 'Did I ever ask for your lies, Morgan?'

Not in so many words, no. Not quite so plainly. Was his father asking for a lie when he expected to hear only what he wished to hear?

*I think he is asking for a lie's kissing cousin. But I need to speak my mind. My heart. There is no-one else to speak it for me.*

'My lord, how pleasing will it be if I choose a wife in haste and in so choosing, choose poorly? Once I handfast with Maris Garrick we are parted only by death. I've known her only a handful of weeks. I knew Luzena for *years*. I—'

226

'*No!* The girl is *dead,* Morgan. Leave her buried.' His father's feeble fist struck the mattress. 'What kind of a son have I raised? One who'd not set a dying man's mind at ease! You care nothing for me or for the Danfey name. If you could fuck a marble statue you'd do it, leaving me to languish my last days in despair!'

He had to blink to clear his vision. 'That is a monstrous thing to say.'

'Ha!' His father punched the mattress again, blood-tinged spittle flecking his greyish lips. 'The monstrous son calls his father monstrous.'

Morgan slid from the chair and retreated to the chamber's fireplace, with its crackling flames. He scarcely felt their fierce heat against his skin. 'I never said I wouldn't marry. I won't deny you my heir. But we talk of my life. My – my *happiness*. Am I no more to you than fertile seed?'

His father had the grace to look taken aback. 'Of course not. How can you ask it? Morgan, you're my son.'

'Then why will you not grant me a moment to *think* before I commit myself to Maris Garrick?'

'To what purpose?' his father demanded, his rheumy eyes blazing. 'Name me one First Family ranked higher than the Garricks in possession of an unmatched beddable daughter!'

Turning, Morgan stared into the fire. 'I can't. But then I've not spent so much as a day looking, have I? Maris Garrick was tossed in my lap, like a ripe peach, and that was that.'

'Tossed by Venette Martain, who seems to care more about the future of this family than you do.'

Another barb, sunk deep into his flesh. 'That's not true.'

Then what? You'd reject the Garrick girl and taint our blood-line by marrying some chit from a Family ranked below our own? Is that it?'

In the leaping flames Morgan saw, leaping, Barl Lindin's striking face. Fear and defiance. Passion and pride. He felt again the pain he'd caused her, and remembered her battle not to break before the indifferent Council's might.

*What a pity she's unranked. There is more power in that girl*

*than was ever dreamt of for Nevin Jordane's crippled embar-
rassment of a daughter. Dorana has need of talent like Barl
Lindin's. If I could match myself with her . . .*

But he couldn't, and he was mad to torment himself with the
thought. Mad to let himself wonder, even briefly, what her lips
might taste like. How it would feel to feel her fingertips on his
skin.

*Fool. You can't have her. Let her go.*

Mingled longing and regret throbbed through his blood. The
woken need was a cruelly taunting pain. *This* was what he should
be feeling for Maris Garrick. The thought of bedding her without
it . . . the thought of bedding her at all . . .

*I am mad. Barl Lindin is so far beneath me I should be
ashamed for even entertaining the notion.*

But he wasn't. Instead he was resentful, not only for himself
but for all of Dorana as well. Barl Lindin had a talent that
defied explanation, that properly trained and channelled might
accomplish astonishing work. Wilfully wasting such a resource
was nothing short of a travesty. Yet the Council was wasting
it. Worse, it had deliberately turned the girl into a cripple.

*And I'm as much to blame as Brice Varen or Sallis Arkley.
I should have refused to bind her. I should have insisted she be
seen as a gift, not a curse. Of course rank matters, of course it
must be considered, but we were wrong about Bellamie Ranowen
and we are wrong this time, too. Surely we cripple ourselves
when we –*

His father's snapping fingers jerked him out of turmoiled
thought.

'*Morgan!* You dare *ignore* me?'

Startled, he looked at the bed. 'No, my lord. I was simply—'

'I do not care about your *simply*. Answer my question! Has
your gaze lit upon a ranked Family that you know I will not like?'

'No, my lord.'

His father coughed wetly, the wheeze in his chest returned
doublefold. 'Then you'd destroy us entirely by marrying out of
the First Families?'

Morgan felt his throat tighten. 'My lord, you have me at a loss. What is it that prompts these wild accusations? Why would you even—'

'I might be dying, Morgan, but I'm not dead yet. No, and I'm not blind either. You were thinking of someone, I could see her in your face!' His father's head fell back against the tumble of pillows. 'Oh, what a son I have. What a glorious son!'

So, in letting his thoughts drift too close to his surface, he'd betrayed himself. He breathed out, suddenly cautious.

'My lord, I *promise* you I wasn't—' But that wouldn't do. Not only would his father never believe him, he couldn't lie to him in cold blood. Not now. Not when—'Forgive me, sir, but I think we speak at cross purposes.' He returned to his chair beside the high bed. 'You are right, after a fashion. I was thinking of an unranked mage. But she's Council business. Naught to do with my marriage though I would discuss her with you.'

His father was frowning. 'I see.'

Smiling again, though his face felt frozen, he took his father's thin, gnarled hands in his. 'My lord, it breaks my heart that we find ourselves so at odds over my marriage, which should be a cause for celebration. If I've grieved you, if I've been selfish, I'm sorry.'

'Morgan . . .' His father sighed. 'This habit you have of harking back to Luzena Talth, measuring all other women against her. It doesn't help.'

He strove to keep his voice mild. 'To me it seems only natural that I would—'

'But that's my point!' his father said, snappish. 'It's *not* natural. Morgan, you have a disposition that will not let go of the past. I am only trying to protect you from that.'

*In other words, forget Luzena ever lived. Forget that I loved her. Do you know me so imperfectly, sir? Is that the kind of man you think I am?*

Yes, and yes. But they had argued around and around this point, never once reaching an amicable understanding, and it was clear to him now that they likely never would. So either they could continue to argue, and make their remaining time together a misery, or . . .

Morgan tightened his fingers on his father's frail hand. 'Perhaps I do dwell too much on Luzena. I shall – I shall—' The words stuck in his throat, threatening to claw his flesh bloody. 'To please you, I shall put her from my mind.'

'Shall you?' said his father, closely watching him. 'Good. I'll help.'

And with a snatch and a twist, more swiftly than his feeble strength should allow, his father tugged Luzena's locket, snapping the chain, and threw the golden treasure into the fire.

'*Leave it there*!' his father commanded, as Morgan tensed himself to leap. 'Let it melt. Let her burn. She is the past. Maris Garrick is your future.'

Half-slid from the chair, stunned, he watched the locket glow, and glow, and then start to buckle.

*Luzena.*

'Morgan—' His father's rough voice dragged his gaze back to the bed. 'That was harsh. I know it. But I'll not beg your pardon. In time you'll come to see I was right.'

Was he angry? Hurt? Or simply . . . unsurprised? He couldn't tell. All he knew was that he felt *diminished,* as though some strange and terrible incant had alchemied him into a child.

'I've been patient long enough, Morgan,' his father said, his blue-tinged lips trembling. 'I can't afford to wait any more. I have to know this business of your marriage is settled.'

The answer to that was obvious. *So you can die happy, my lord, and I can live bereft.* But of course he couldn't say the bitter words out loud. Swallowing them, he looked again to the fire.

His locket was bubbling around its smooth, fragile edges. He'd never warded it. Had never imagined the need. In fourteen years it had never once been unclasped from his neck.

*Luzena . . . Luzena . . .*

Stiff-spined in the bedside chair, Morgan looked at his father. What should he do? Walk out? He was well within his rights.

He was a man, *not* a child, and no man should submit without protest to such rude handling. But if he walked out, his father would suffer. With Lord Danfey's end come so near, could he forgive himself for hastening it? What would Luzena want him to do?

*Stay. Make peace. She would never bear a grudge.*

He needed no locket to remember her. Luzena was engraved on his heart and his soul.

'Then let us be clear about the matter, my lord,' he said. Not warmly, for he still felt frozen. 'You are content that I wed with Maris Garrick? You'll not turn about in a week's time and upbraid me for choosing a girl who, for all her ranking, you suddenly deem stands beneath us?'

'Am I content?' His father, exhausted, rolled his head on the pillows. 'No, Morgan. Maris Garrick lacks Luzena Talth's breeding and background. But she is the only mare to hand and she is not impossible, so I say you will ride her.'

Morgan bowed his head. 'Yes, my lord.'

A lengthy silence, filled with crackling flames and harsh breathing.

'Morgan . . . do not strife yourself over this,' his father murmured, dragging open his half-lidded, cloudy eyes. 'You are a great man who will in time become greater. Once the Garrick bitch has whelped you a son you need not muddy yourself with her after. Most like you'll not have time, your magework and Council duties will take up your days.' He managed the faintest of smiles, as though the locket weren't ruined, as though an only son's happiness had not been sacrificed without a second thought. 'I have no doubt you'll be Council leader within a hand's span of years.'

And what did it say about him, that despite his pain, his anger, his father's praise was welcome and warming?

'Brice Varen will doubtless have an opinion about that.'

His father snorted. 'That old goat. It's true he'll outlive me, but I dare say it won't be by so very many years.'

It cost him, more than he wanted it to, but he once again

231

took his father's wasted, unsteady hand. 'My lord, I have high hopes you will see my first son born.'

'I won't,' his father said roughly. 'Don't talk like a fool, or think I'm to be comforted by flummery.' He tugged his hand free. 'Now, who's this unranked mage you wish to discuss?'

'Her name is Barl Lindin,' he said, after taking a moment to order his thoughts. 'She was brought before the Council tonight as a miscreant. I bound her, and told Varen that from the morrow I'd keep her close here, beneath our roof, while more thought is given to her disposition. She can help Rumm. There's always dusting to be done about the place.'

'You *bound* her?' Wheezing, his father struggled to sit higher against the pillows. 'Morgan—'

'Don't fret, my lord,' he said, and gently eased his father back to the bed. 'I'll not call the experience pleasant, but I took no harm from it.'

'So you might think, but binding magic is not to be trusted,' his father retorted. 'It can strike back at you without warning. I've seen it before, a vile thing. You should send for Ranmer, have him brew you a nossip to ward off an ill flux. I tell you, Morgan, you won't tread careless over this!'

*He does care. I must remember that. Even when he wounds me, he wounds me out of love.*

'My lord, you can be sure I know what signs to look for,' he said, soothing. 'Varen schooled me most carefully when I was taught the binding incant. I feel nothing untoward. But if I do, I promise I will send direct to Ranmer.'

Little by little, his father calmed. 'This bound mage. This *miscreant*. Must you bring her here?'

'She'll make no trouble,' he said, sidestepping the question. 'You have my solemn word on that.'

'Still, the woman gives you pause. Don't try to deny it.'

*My lord, my lord, she gives me more than pause.*

Meeting his father's narrowed gaze, Morgan pretended an indifference he was very far from feeling.

'Any mage who flouts the law is at least a mild cause for

232

concern,' he said. 'But I think her errant ways have been nipped in the bud. She simply needs to learn her place. A week or two of being bound and obeying Rumm should neatly suffice.' He stood. 'And now, sir, I think I must leave you to rest, and take some rest myself. As you say, binding is no easy magic.'

'Yes . . . yes . . .' said his father. 'But Morgan, before you go, why is it I've heard nothing more of this grand experiment of yours?'

The reworked transmutation incant, left to languish uncompleted while he tossed and turned it every which way, seeking to unravel its stubbornly elusive mysteries. The cursed thing haunted him. Taunted him. Racked him with doubt.

But that wasn't something he could share with his father.

'I work on it when I can, my lord. I have had much Council business of late.'

'Indeed?' His father scowled. 'Remember who you're talking to, Morgan. The work falters, am I right?'

Curse it. 'It is a trifle slippery.'

'So you've abandoned it? Do not tell me you are a butterfly mage, Councillor, alighting first on this notion and then flitting to that, no more constant or enduring than a flurry of snow in sunshine!'

'A butterfly mage?' Morgan kept his voice light, even though the accusation stung. 'My lord, you serve me rough justice.'

An unsteady wag of one finger as his father snorted. 'And you cozen me, boy. What, then? Are you truly trammelled?'

*Boy*. Though he longed for the solitude of his own chamber, Morgan sat once more in the chair beside his father's vast, ornate bed. 'I am . . . jiggered,' he admitted. 'But I shall find my way out of the thicket, never fear.'

'On the morrow, Morgan, I shall assist you,' his father declared, his colour ashen, his chest sounding like an old bellows. 'Bound, miscreant mage underfoot or no. Together we shall unjigger you. Not a Danfey born was ever defeated by magic.'

There was no use arguing. 'Indeed, my lord, I would welcome your advice. Provided I am not called once more to the Council.

And I must warn you, I might be. There is an outstanding matter that is not yet put to bed.'

'I see.' His father grunted. 'What's the to-do this time? Or can't you discuss it?'

If it had been anyone other than Nevin Jordane's girl, he'd likely answer and no harm done. But his father and hers were friendly enough that the news would be a cause of pain and even confrontation, and he'd had enough discord for one night.

'I am sorry, my lord, but it's best I err on the side of caution. Be sure I'll tell you everything, just as soon as I can.'

'Morgan—' His father shifted against his pillows. 'Your Council work. Is it everything I imagined?'

Pushing again to his feet, he leaned down and kissed his father's uncomfortably cool, clammy cheek. 'My lord, you would have made an exemplary councillor. And your leadership would have thrown Varen into the shade. It is a wickedness that Dorana was ever denied your wisdom.'

And then he withdrew from his father's chamber, so that they might not be discomfited by the tears in Lord Danfey's grateful eyes.

Alone in his own chamber, no gentle glimfire glowing, he stripped himself naked and dropped haphazard to his bed. Showed the darkness his naked face, showed it the depth of his pain as his fingers touched the naked skin where Luzena's locket used to rest.

And in the midst of anguish, slid into exhausted sleep.

# CHAPTER FIFTEEN

Binding was a *terrible* thing.

Skin crawling, pain simmering in her blood like water on the boil, Barl sat on the floor in the corner of a stone room deep beneath Elvado's soaring Hall of Knowledge. Four blank walls surrounded her. The blank ceiling pressed down on her. Even if she'd had somewhere to run, she couldn't. The same two mages who'd dragged her from Hahren's chamber to face the Council, and then down to this bleak cell, stood sentinel beyond its heavy, brass-bound timber door. She couldn't feel them, because the binding had left her deaf, dumb and blind, or as good as. But they'd marched her down here, ignited one tiny ball of glimfire so they could tell themselves they weren't downright *cruel,* then closed that heavy door on her. And if she listened hard she could hear faint, muffled snatches of their sporadic conversation.

Most likely they were gloating, celebrating how the upstart mage had been so thoroughly chastised.

She couldn't help but wonder what Remmie would say, could he see her now. Would her predicament at last prompt him to an exasperated *I told you so?* Surely he deserved to say it, having yet again been proven right. If just this once she'd listened to him, tempered her outrage with a pinch of his caution, disaster would've been avoided.

'But it's a good thing you can't see me, Rem,' she whispered to the echoing, empty stone room. 'You're far safer where you are. No unranked mage should come to notice by the Council.'

Because Dorana's Council of Mages was a sham. It was meant to protect *every* mage from harm, not just the ranked ones, but if not for Morgan Danfey she'd either be dead now, or waiting to die. She still found it difficult to believe he'd saved her. That haughty mage, who'd stunned her at Winsun with his easy wielding of power?

*Why did he speak for me? It did him no favours. That prune-faced mage, he wanted to see me thrown down. He'll not forget Morgan Danfey's defiance. He's like Arndel, that councillor. He has a mean, shrivelled soul.*

So did the older woman. What a hateful look in her eyes! As for the younger woman, she wasn't sure. There'd been anger at Danfey, that much was clear, but the reason for it was unclear. Something else stirred there.

*And Lord Varen. Why did he support Councillor Danfey? Does he lull me into a false sense of reprieve? Does he hope to catch me law-breaking again, so he can condemn me to death with a clean conscience?*

It seemed more than likely. He'd not be head of the Council if he wasn't first and foremost a champion of Dorana's ranked mages.

*How long do they intend to leave me bound? And after I'm released, if I'm released, what then? Will this binding leave me damaged? Will I live the rest of my days a cripple?*

The thought of that left her almost paralysed with fear. Could even the Council of Mages be so brutal?

*I think they could. I think, given free rein, there is nothing those mages would not dare to do.*

Round and round inside her aching skull the questions marched, so she couldn't find a moment of peace.

*What about Remmie? Is he never to know what's become of me?*

*Will they let me at least write to him? Or would they rather he gave me up for dead and forgot me?*

She'd wanted to ask the Council to at least tell her how long she'd be held on Morgan Danfey's estate, but the binding incant had stolen her voice. It had stolen everything.

Fresh tears slid down her cheeks. She didn't care. There was no-one to see them. How long had she been locked away down here? It could be sunrise outside, or midday, and she wouldn't know it. Thanks to the Council, until the binding was lifted she'd need a clock made by someone else to know what hour it was.

*They've made me no better than a Brantish tramp.*

The injustice of it burned, even hotter than the binding. It felt like every nerve in her body was seared.

*I think they wish I'd never been born. I think it's their hope that this binding will destroy me, so they can pretend Barl Lindin never existed.*

Not just tears now, but whimpers too. She pressed her palms to her face and turned to the stone wall, trying to stifle the sounds of distress. If the mages beyond the door heard her they'd certainly tell the Council. And the Council would rejoice to know how humbled she was.

*Perhaps even Morgan Danfey would enjoy it. How can I trust him? I can't let it matter that he saved me. He's still one of them.*

Somehow she had to find a way to tell Remmie what had happened, warn him that he must leave this mess alone. Though she'd left him hurt and furious behind her, she knew her brother. His anger wouldn't last forever. Knowing Remmie, it wouldn't last past a week.

*And then he'll come to Elvado and raise a ruckus. The Council will see that he loses his position, and probably ensure he's never allowed to teach again. They might even bind him.*

The thought of Remmie bound, and denied his precious schoolhouse, slid more tears down her cheeks, hot and fast.

The sound of the stone chamber's door opening turned her

face from the wall. Had her smearing her wet cheeks dry on her sleeve. And then she was blinking, because her visitor wasn't Morgan Danfey.

'Lady Venette Martain,' the mage said, cool and self-contained, closing the door. 'We met last night, if you recall.'

So. It was morning. Barl nodded. 'My lady.'

With a careless snap of her fingers the woman ignited more glimfire. The jewelled gold clasping her throat and wrists flashed warm fire. The gold threads in her deep-green silk tunic spangled and sparked. She was beautiful and powerful . . . a dangerous combination.

'No, no, Mage Lindin,' she said, her smile swift and sharp. 'It's quite all right. Don't get up.'

Barl matched her smile for smile, feeling reckless. 'I wasn't going to.'

One eyebrow lifted, then Venette Martain began a seemingly aimless wander. 'I'm trying to decide,' she said at last, 'whether you're stupid . . . or deep.'

'Perhaps I'm deeply stupid,' she suggested.

'Yes. Perhaps you are.' Still wandering, Venette Martain folded her arms. 'You're certainly fortunate. If Morgan hadn't spoken up for you when he did . . .'

'You'd have let them do away with me? Thank you, my lady. It's good to know where I stand. Or sit.'

Venette Martain flung out a pointing finger. 'Young woman, you'd be well-advised to mind your manners. If you think binding is the worst thing that can happen to you, trust me when I say you're incorrect.'

'*Trust* you?' Barl laughed. 'Oh, certainly. That would be my first impulse.'

Anger didn't diminish the councillor's beauty. 'You consider yourself hard done by?'

'Trust *me,* Lady Martain. So would you, if our positions were reversed.'

Venette Martain snorted. 'If you're going to talk nonsense, Mage Lindin, I can't see any point continuing this conversation.'

She hadn't yet seen the point of starting it. But she felt certain there was one. 'Nonsense is all that's left to me. The Council's binding took everything else.'

'Except your life,' said Venette Martain, smiling again. 'Remember that.'

As though he sat close beside her, she heard Remmie's whisper. *Careful, Barl. Only a fool pokes a hornet's nest with his finger.* And since that was quite true, she made an effort to smooth her expression into a more pleasing meekness.

'Tell me,' said Venette Martain, halting at the chamber's far wall and swinging round. 'How do you come to know Morgan Danfey?'

'Know him?' She blinked. 'I don't.'

'You must.'

'No, I don't,' she insisted. 'And before you ask, no. I have no idea why he saved me. Do you?'

With an impatient flutter of her fingers, the councillor began wandering again. 'Morgan is subject to fits of sentimentality.'

'You can't expect me to regret that.'

'I expect you to fall face-down before him and weep with gratitude that he saved your life!'

Oh. Breathing carefully, Barl looked at Venette Martain. She was quite a few years older than Morgan Danfey, but that didn't mean they couldn't be . . . involved. So if the councillor had come here to protect what she saw as hers, then –

'Don't be vulgar!' Venette Martain snapped. 'I am many years happily wed, and Morgan is about to make an excellent match that *I* have promoted. Don't think to interfere with it, girl. My voice carries weight on the Council. If I decide I want you locked in a deep, distant cellar, far from Elvado or any other decent-sized town, you will be.' Coming close, she dropped to one knee and leaned forward. 'And if I decide you shouldn't breathe unbound air ever again, *you won't.*'

Barl believed her. Heart thudding, she shook her head. 'I have no interest in Morgan Danfey.'

'Good,' said Venette Martain, and stood. Her smile was keener than a Vharne swordsman's blade. 'It would be most unfortunate if that changed.'

The woman scared her. Resenting that, she folded her arms. 'Lady Martain, I have a brother.'

'Do you?' Venette Martain fiddled with her bracelet. 'Then he has my sympathies.'

'I need to let him know where I am. I need to—'

'Take it up with Morgan,' Venette Martain said, impatient. 'It's none of my concern.'

Was she truly this heartless? Or was she playing some kind of game? 'If I do, will he listen? Will he—'

Hand raised, Venette Martain frowned at her, quelling. 'I expect so. As I said, he's sentimental. Now hold your tongue. You'll shortly be leaving for the Danfey estate. Don't think I won't be kept apprised of your conduct there. Don't think Sallis Arkley isn't itching for an excuse to make a bloodthirsty example of you. Behave yourself, Mage Lindin, and it might be you can escape this regrettable affair unscathed.' Another edged smile. 'Well. Almost.'

As the chamber's heavy door banged shut behind her visitor, Barl pulled her knees tight to her chest and let her aching head drop. The binding incant crawled and burned beneath her skin.

*Oh, Remmie. Remmie. What do I do now?*

Eventually the stone chamber's door opened again, and the sentinel mages escorted her along a maze of glimlit stone corridors and up short flights of stone stairs until, at last, they reached a stout, iron-bound door.

Standing on the other side of it, in a quiet, walled courtyard, Barl saw shimmering in the distance the topmost sunlit spires of Elvado's Hall of Knowledge. So, she'd been spirited away from the town's bustling centre. The Council was making sure there'd be no inconvenient witnesses to her banishment.

'Come along,' her male guard said, touching her arm. 'There's a carriage waiting.'

240

'Why a carriage? Why not just—'

'Bound mages can't use travel incants,' the woman said. 'Now come.'

Both mages turned for the warded door in the wall. Experimenting, Barl stood her ground.

'I don't want to go.'

The male mage turned back to glare at her with slitted grey eyes. 'The Council's not interested in what you want,' he said, and snapped his fingers. '*Come.*'

The binding incant leapt to blazing life beneath her skin. Blinking away tears of pain, Barl tried to resist its implacable compulsion to obey . . . but it hurt too much. Welts were blossoming beneath her crumpled linen tunic, she could feel the hot bite of them like the strike of a poisoned lash.

'Don't be a fool, Mage Lindin,' said the woman. She was young, not much older than her prisoner. If she felt any sympathy, she kept it hidden. 'You're only going to make matters worse.'

'How?' Barl demanded, stumbling forward. 'And how can you *support* this? The Council's as good as *torturing* me. Is this what Dorana's come to? Are we no better than Ranoush?'

'It's not our place to question the Council of Mages,' the woman said. 'Be quiet, Mage Lindin, and do as you're told.'

Forced to obedience, Barl followed the mages out of the courtyard. After a few dragging steps the binding's punishment stopped. The welts faded. Trembling, she climbed into the carriage halted in the narrow laneway beyond the courtyard's door. Her guards climbed in after her, and sat in grim silence facing her as the carriage's driver stirred up the horses.

Neither of them said a word, to her or each other, as the carriage carried them through the outskirts of Elvado then into the surrounding countryside. Its windows were shuttered. A little glimfire leavened the gloom, and a whisper of fresh air seeped in through a small painted grille near the low roof. But the close confinement and steady side-to-side swaying churned her empty belly to miserable nausea.

The least they could've done was give her a few mouthfuls of breakfast. But no, it seemed that as a Council-bound mage, she was to be treated only a little less harshly than if she'd been a sheep-worrying cur.

At long last the carriage slowed and turned, then continued slowly along what sounded like a gravel driveway. The driver's deep voice sounded above them in a soothing *Whoa* and the carriage slowed further until it rolled to a stop.

'Out,' said the mage with grey eyes, his voice clipped with dislike of her. 'Quickly. We've wasted enough time on you.'

She opened the carriage door and clambered to the gravelled ground, clinging to the handle because there was nobody to let the folding step down and she didn't want to fall.

'Barl Lindin.'

Turning, she saw a neatly dressed man some twenty years her senior, with close-cropped hair and measuring eyes. Dressed in plain but immaculate black, hands relaxed by his sides, oddly he reminded her of Remmie. They shared an air of calm authority, a teacherly confidence that they were completely in charge of the situation.

'Where's Councillor Danfey?' her female guard demanded, leaning out of the open carriage door. 'This woman isn't to be left here like a parcel. She's dangerous.'

The man's brow creased in the faintest of frowns. 'Councillor Danfey is otherwise occupied.'

'We've strict instructions. Mage Lindin is to be delivered to the councillor. No-one else.'

'I am Rumm, Lord Danfey's master servant,' the man said, still frowning. 'During her time on the Danfey estate, Mage Lindin will be answerable to me. As for her being a threat, do you tell me Councillor Danfey's binding has been removed?'

Taken aback, the mage shook her head. 'No. Of course not. But—'

'Then I expect the only danger she poses is to the crockery,' said the man, Master Servant Rumm. 'You may return to the Council and assure them you have properly discharged your duty.'

If she hadn't felt so faint, so ill, Barl would have laughed at her erstwhile guard's stunned face. A moment, as the mage pulled back inside the carriage to confer with her fellow guard. Another moment as a hasty, whispered conversation ensued. Then the mage leaned out again.

'Very well. She's your problem now.'

As the carriage door slammed shut, and the driver stirred up his horses, Master Servant Rumm turned on his heel. 'With me, Mage Lindin.'

For the first time since setting foot on the gravel, Barl paid attention to where she'd been abandoned exactly like an unwanted parcel. She stood in the forecourt of an imposing, mellow brick mansion. Ruby ivy climbed its walls and flirted with the sun-sparkled windows. There were neatly tended garden beds, colourful with flowers. The air smelled sweet with them, and with the wilder scent of woodland. A breeze flirted with her hair, limp and unravelling now, and tugged at her woefully rumpled linen tunic. The breeze dropped and suddenly she could smell herself, unwashed, the stink of sweat tainted by the binding incant. A brassy kind of smell, it was, leaving a metallic aftertaste in the mouth.

'*Mage Lindin.*'

Master Servant Rumm had a whipcrack of a voice. She jumped, hearing it, and hurried after him. She didn't want to risk the binding incant lashing her again.

The master servant led her below stairs, down to the mansion's working heart. Since this was a grand house, that meant cellars, a kitchen, a scullery, a laundry room, a dry pantry, a meat larder and a buttery, every chamber cool and shadowy. Well, save for the kitchen when the ovens were going. And the laundry, of course. On washing days that would be clouded with steam. Would she be put to work in there, to wrinkle and scald her skin with soap and hot water? How Arndel would love that. Ibbitha and lying, cowardly Baret Ventin, too. How they'd think she'd been justly served.

'In here,' said Master Servant Rumm, pushing open a green

baize door. 'You'd best sit down before you fall down. But don't think to make a habit of it. You'll be far too busy for sitting, soon enough.'

*In here* was the kitchen, a veritable shrine to cooking that would make Remmie sob with joy, could he see it. A wide wooden table, knife-scarred, in the centre. More vast scrubbed benches against the long, whitewashed stone walls. A roasting alcove complete with turnspit, heavy logs on their grating slowly turning to charcoal. Gleaming pots and pans hanging on hooks overhead, wickedly sharp knives, an enormous, deep triple sink, a full wall of hobs and ovens. Fresh-killed and plucked fowl sat plump on a granite slab, slapped side by side with a rack of bloody beef ribs and a basin of garden peas waiting to be shelled. The fire-warmed air was rich with the yeasty smell of baking bread. Barl felt her mouth flood, and heard her empty belly growl.

A man wrapped in a blue-and-white striped apron stirred a pot on one hot hob. The master servant tapped his shoulder then jerked a thumb. 'See what's low in the flour bins, Biddle. I'll call when you're wanted back.' He glanced in the pot. 'Take that stock off the heat. It can sit a while with no harm.'

'Master Rumm,' the man muttered, dragged the pot aside then scuttled from the kitchen. Not so much as a curious glance at the newcomer. The master servant would likely cuff him for that kind of temerity.

Rumm pointed at a wooden stool set up by the turnspit. 'Sit. Did they feed you, those mages at the Hall?'

'No,' Barl said, cautiously perching on the edge of the stool.

'No, *sir*,' he corrected, scowling. 'You'll mind your manners here, Mage Lindin.'

She bit back a pointless retort. 'No, sir. They did not feed me, or give me drink. If they'd found me dead of hunger this morning they'd have laughed, I think, and counted themselves lucky.'

Rumm grunted. 'There'll be no commenting on the Council under Lord Danfey's roof. Wait there.'

She watched him leave the vast kitchen through the nearest

of its three doors. Waiting, with no-one to gawk at her, she let her spine slump a little. Let the weight of her impossible situation press her closer to the stone floor. Clearly, she was to be put to work here like a servant. Probably this was why Morgan Danfey had offered to house her. Cheap labour. Why pay good money for a housemaid when he could bind himself one for free?

That binding. The incant was quiet again but still, she could feel it. Like a banked fire it burned beneath her skin, its heat as steady as the warmth from the hot coals under the turnspit.

*So I might as well be in that stone cell beneath the Hall. If I were in Brantone, or Vharne, if I fled to Iringa, I'd still be the Council's prisoner. I carry my cage with me.*

And Morgan Danfey held the key. Was there any way to steal it from him? Or to wheedle him into setting her free? She had no idea. But both notions were worth pursuing while she was trapped beneath his roof.

*For I'm only truly a prisoner if I think of myself that way. If I stop fighting, if I surrender to their brute authority, I might as well have bound myself.*

Master Rumm returned, in one hand carrying a heavy stone-ware plate burdened with buttered grain bread and cheese topped with a generous dollop of sharp pickle. In his other hand he held a stone mug.

'Eat,' he said, putting plate and mug on the kitchen's table. 'Then you'll make yourself useful.'

It took every skerrick of self-control she possessed not to fall on the food like a ravenous wolf. 'I can't cook,' she told him, around a glorious mouthful. 'Whatever I set my hand to gets burned to a cinder. If you don't believe me, you can ask my brother.'

Rumm raised his eyebrows. 'You're mad if you think I'd trust you with his lordship's meals. Never fear. I'll find plenty to keep you busy.'

She had no doubt of that. But the warning to Rumm reminded her she had unfinished business. 'Master Rumm, I have to tell my brother what's happened. I'm his only family. I can't leave him to fear for me.'

'If you're his only family, Mage Lindin, and have a care for his feelings, I'd say you've a strange way of showing it.'

The mug was full of sweet cider. Washing down the bread and cheese, Barl made an effort to loosen her clutching fingers. 'Are you going to let me tell him, or aren't you?'

'The decision's not mine,' said Rumm. 'What you can and can't do here is up to Councillor Danfey. And his lordship, of course.'

Of course. With another gut-wrenching effort, she humbled herself. 'I'm sorry. I don't mean to be difficult.'

Another raised-eyebrow look from Rumm. 'Given your current predicament, Mage Lindin, I find that hard to believe.'

She put down the mug of cider. 'Master Rumm, I am not wicked. And no matter what anyone says, I'm not dangerous. All I did was try to set right an injustice. But there are mages in Dorana who take that as a threat. Justice be praised that Councillor Danfey's not one of them. If he hadn't helped me . . .'

'Helped you?' Rumm stared at her, openly skeptical. 'It's my understanding he bound you.'

'He did,' she agreed. 'To stop the others from doing worse. Believe me – *believe me* – I've no grudge against your master.' She managed a small, trembling smile. 'If I did, I wouldn't have warned you I can't cook.'

Rumm didn't smile back, but his gaze softened, just a little. 'You should know I'm a man who puts stock in actions, not words. Behave yourself while you're under his lordship's roof, give me no trouble, cause no mayhem with the other servants, do nothing that reflects poorly on Lord Danfey or the councillor, and you'll have no cause to complain of your treatment. But should you prove mettlesome, should you betray Councillor Danfey's great kindness? Mage Lindin, I will make you rue the day.'

She didn't doubt that for a heartbeat. 'I'll behave myself, Master Rumm.'

He nodded. 'Good. You can start by finishing your repast,

washing that plate and mug, then shelling those peas. There's not much damage you can do to them.'

According to Remmie, in his more irritated moments, she only had to look at food, cooked or uncooked, in order to render it inedible. But with her position so vulnerable, and Master Rumm lord of the mansion's servants, she wasn't about to argue.

He left the kitchen soon after, and the aproned man returned to continue with his aromatic pot-stirring. He scarcely spared her a glance, and said not a word. Either he'd been born taciturn or Master Rumm had warned him to hold his tongue around her. She suspected the latter, and was grateful for it. The last thing she felt like was explaining her presence in the mansion.

Shelling peas proved oddly soothing, a small, manual task that kept her fingers busy and her mind free to absorb and finally accept the bewildering events since she'd stormed to Elvado. As she reached for the last pod, Master Rumm reappeared.

'His lordship will be wanting his morning tea,' he said. 'You'll take it up to him, Mage Lindin.'

She thought, from the hint of constraint in his voice, that Rumm didn't approve of that arrangement. Had he objected and been overruled? The pinching of his lips suggested it. While the master servant made the tea and set out fresh-baked scones, clotted cream and berry jam on a lace-doilied plate, she shelled the last of the peas, disposed of the emptied pods into the kitchen's composting bin, then waited with her hands meekly folded for Rumm to load Lord Danfey's morning tea on a polished silver tray.

'Third floor,' he said curtly. 'The double doors at the end of the corridor. Knock twice, then wait until you're bid enter. And mind your manners.'

She took the heavy tray. 'Yes, Master Rumm.'

'And Mage Lindin?'

'Yes?' she said, looking back.

Rumm's face was severe again. 'You'll set not so much as a toe above the third floor landing. Councillor Danfey's strict instruction.'

247

Oh, yes? And what was hidden up there that he was so eager she didn't see? Magework, most likely.

*As if there's anything I can do about that.*

'Mage Lindin! Is that clear?'

'Quite clear, Master Rumm.'

Climbing the three flights of stairs up to Lord Danfey's domain, she couldn't help but appreciate the mansion's perfect proportions and genteel beauty. Masterful oil paintings marched up the wall beside her, a few landscapes, some faces, each gilt-framed canvas cracked by the passage of time. There was a stained-glass skylight, high overhead. The coloured sunlight filtered down to her, splashing the silver tea tray crimson, azure and gold.

Her insides squeezed tight. It wasn't that she begrudged the likes of Lady Grie and Lord Danfey and those mages on the Council their luxuries. But why did it matter so much, that they make sure the rest of Dorana was denied them?

Upon reaching the doors at the end of the third floor corridor, she followed Rumm's instructions precisely.

'So. Girl. Don't skulk in the shadows,' Lord Danfey barked. 'Let me get a good look at you!'

Barl tightened her hold on the tea tray and took another step into his lordship's privy parlour. 'I wasn't skulking. I was closing the doors.'

Folded into a shabby, wingbacked armchair, the old man snorted. 'And no sass!' His thin hand beckoned, impatient. 'Come *in,* I said! Did my son send you deaf when he bound you?'

'No.'

'No, *my lord.* Dragged up by the scruff of your neck in a cow byre, were you?'

Her fingers tightened again, painful now. 'No. My lord.'

'Then bring me my tea, girl, before it's stone cold. If it's stone cold I'll throw it at you.'

She thought he would. Lord Danfey had that kind of face, austere and intolerant. It wasn't just the grooved lines of long sickness that made Morgan Danfey's father look harsh. Though his blue eyes were clouded, their colour almost obscured, they possessed a hard gleam, searching for a fault to criticise as she approached.

He kicked the leg of the low occasional table beside him. 'Put the tray there.'

She settled the tray safely and waited. He'd been handsome once, she thought. Possibly as handsome as his powerful son. But time and fever had robbed him of all but the vestiges of good looks. Everything about him was sunken now: eyes, cheeks, chest, belly. As though the only thing stopping him from collapsing in on himself was his ample supply of bile and temper.

'Stir up the fire, girl,' the old man said. 'Or are you hoping I'll freeze solid while you stand there and watch?'

A sharp retort burned her tongue, but she swallowed it. 'My lord,' she said, stiffly courteous, no need to give him reason to complain of her, and tended to the fire. As she poked about in the embers then added a fresh, sweetly scented log, she heard the chink and rattle of teaspoon and cup, the soft slosh of tea pouring from pot into cup.

'All right, all right, leave well enough alone,' Lord Danfey commanded. 'Poke a fire too much and you kill it. Never learned that, did you?'

The fire was billowing merrily, resurgent flames greedily feeding. She added one last log and turned.

'Do you require anything else, my lord?'

The old man's pale lips were flour-dusted, smeared sickly red, and he made a wet gobbling sound as his jaw worked an over-large mouthful of scone, cream and jam. His cloudy eyes below their sparse, pale brows glared at her, brimful of suspicion.

'What's your name? My son told me, but I don't remember trivialities.'

She stared back at him. *If I even once show him I'm intimidated, he'll bully me to death.* 'I am Barl Lindin, my lord.'

'Ha.' The old man reached for another scone. 'You say that as though I should be impressed. *Lindin?*' He pushed more lavishly topped scone past his yellowing teeth. 'If you were of consequence I'd have heard of you. I haven't.'

And what did he expect her to say in reply? What *could* she say, that wouldn't land her in even more trouble?

'Lord Danfey—'

'My son risked himself to bind you, Barl Lindin. Risked himself on some upstart, unranked little nobody from nowhere.' The old man raised a crooked, shaking finger. The front of his wine-red velvet jacket was littered with crumbs. 'He's a grown man, a councillor. He can do as he pleases, no need to seek my permission. But you know this, girl. If he had sought it, I'd have denied him. Morgan's a great man. A great mage. He'll grow greater in time. You hobble him, Barl Lindin, and it's me you'll answer to.'

There was genuine menace in him. Beneath his crusting of sickness, a blood-chilling threat. Feeling it, Barl braced her shoulders.

'Do you even know what I did? Why I'm bound? My lord?'

Contemptuous, he glared over the rim of his teacup. 'What do I care for the undisciplined follies of an unranked mage?'

'If justice means anything to you, my lord, you'd care.'

The teacup slammed back in its saucer. 'Did I ask you for a lecture? Get out. Take this tray with you. And tell Rumm there wasn't enough butter in the scones.'

And if she did, would Rumm blame her for the slight?

*Perhaps. But if I don't tell him I'll be caught out in disobedience.*

It seemed she'd have been better off caged at the Hall, after all.

'Well?' said Lord Danfey. 'What are you waiting for, girl? Good thing I'm not being asked to fork over a wage for you. Seems to me you're halfway to being an imbecile. Go on. Get out!'

Rearranging the cup and plates on the tray so they'd not slide as she carried it, she felt a humiliating sting of tears.

*It doesn't matter. It doesn't. What I do in this place doesn't change who I am.*

Who she'd be again one day. They'd not keep her bound forever.

Halfway down the staircase, heading back to the mansion's vast kitchen, she heard swift footfalls behind her. Oddly, they sounded *angry*. Pausing, she turned and looked up the staircase, past the third floor landing.

It was Morgan Danfey.

# CHAPTER SIXTEEN

Staring at her captor as he halted a few steps above her, Barl saw there was a smudge of yellow on the sleeve of his bronze silk brocade tunic. It looked like powdered *gedlef* root. As well, an odour of tinctured *bidaline* clung to his fine clothes. Which must mean he did have his own workroom somewhere upstairs.

*And he's using* gedlef? *He must be mad. Everyone knows it's notoriously unstable.*

Whatever the councillor was doing with it, and the tinctured *bidaline*, she thought the work did not go well. Behind his expression of polite disinterest he was vexed. No, more than that. Distressed.

*Yes, well, so am I.*

So distressed – by her binding, her imprisonment, the Council's arrogant injustice – she wanted to hurl the laden tray she carried over the staircase banister and watch teapot and plates smash to shards on the foyer's splendid marble floor.

But if she did that, well . . .

'Councillor Danfey,' she murmured, and bobbed her head in a servantly show of respect.

He nodded. 'Mage Lindin. Here scarcely an hour, and I see Rumm has already put you to work.'

'Yes, sir. Taking morning tea to Lord Danfey.'

They stood between the third and second floor landings. Councillor Danfey glanced back up the stairs. 'I trust you found his lordship well?'

*Actually, I found him a cantankerous old goat.*

'Yes, sir.'

A hint of warmth crept into his eyes. 'He was peevish? Don't take it to heart. Lord Danfey is weary of being kept close to bed.'

'Yes, sir.'

The councillor stepped one stair tread closer. 'You must have spent an uncomfortable night, prisoned beneath the Hall.'

'I survived.'

'The binding. I hope it doesn't chafe you too badly.'

She shrugged. 'I hardly notice it.'

'You will, Mage Lindin, if you test its limits. Don't.'

'Councillor . . .' It might be foolish, asking him questions, but she had to try. 'How long will the Council keep me bound?'

He stepped closer again, his eyes surprisingly gentle. 'I don't know. I suspect much will depend on my reports of you.'

Of course it would. 'And I suppose your reports will depend on what Master Rumm says of me?'

'Exactly,' he said, very close to a smile. 'My father might be lord here, but it often feels as though it's Rumm who rules the roost.'

Interesting, that he found the notion amusing. She couldn't imagine Lord Varen amused by the bossiness of a servant.

'He is most loyal to the Danfeys, Councillor. I quake in fear lest I offend him, and earn his wrath.'

'Quake in fear, Mage Lindin? You?' Again, that hinting smile. 'I find that idea a nonsense.'

Why was he being so *nice* to her? Why did he care for how she felt, what she thought? Unless . . .

*He finds me appealing? Is that why he's done this? Venette Martain thinks so. She thinks I'm a threat.*

Councillor Danfey frowned. 'What's wrong? Are you in pain? The binding?'

The laden tray was growing heavier by the moment. She tried to ease its weight by shrugging her shoulders a little. 'No, sir. I'm fine.'

He stepped down another tread. Now he was so close she could feel his breath on her cheek. 'That's not true. Tell me what's troubling you. Perhaps I can help.'

She couldn't tell him the truth. Causing trouble between him and Lady Martain would do her no good at all. But if he meant what he said . . .

*Remmie.*

'It's my brother, sir. He's bound to come looking for me, and once he learns what's happened I'm afraid he'll do something rash. Please, will you let me write to him? Will you—' Her voice cracked, because her fear for Remmie wasn't a lie. 'I'd bear my punishment with a far better grace if I could just stop him from getting into trouble because of me.'

Morgan Danfey looked at her, his expression guarded. 'This brother of yours,' he said at last. 'You must love him very much.'

'I do, sir,' she whispered. 'Remmie's a good man. I don't want him touched by my strife.'

'A good man deserves an explanation in person, don't you think? I'll go to him myself. I'll tell him what's happened.'

She almost dropped the tray. 'You'd do that?'

'I've just said so, Mage Lindin. Do you doubt me?'

'No, sir,' she said quickly, and pulled her scattered wits together. 'Of course not.'

This time his faint smile had an edge to it. 'Good. All I need is the incant you'd use to travel home. *Wait*—' he added, as she opened her mouth. 'You mustn't utter it while you're still bound.'

She wasn't certain she could take any more surprises. 'You're going to unbind me?'

'Only for a moment. Now I suggest we're careful, and do this off the stairs.'

Feeling numb, she retreated to the second floor landing. There

254

she put down the tray and waited, docile as a child, for Morgan Danfey to join her.

He rested one elegant hand on her shoulder. 'The unbinding won't hurt you. But when I rebind you—'

It would hurt a great deal. She didn't care. It was for Remmie. 'Go ahead, Councillor. I'm not afraid.'

'I know. Now, you'll need to close your eyes.'

Because he didn't want her to see the sigils that formed the unbinding incant. So. He may be reckless in his magework but he wasn't a fool.

Eyes obediently shut, she listened to him recite six harsh syllables of power. Out of habit, not really out of hope, she bid them sink into her memory. Then she felt the air stir as he inscribed it with two linked sigils. Just in time, she managed to muffle her surprise. She was bound . . . and yet she could see their complex shapes clear in her mind. If he'd asked her to draw them, she knew that she could.

*Is that usual, with a binding? I wish I knew. I can't ask.*

The councillor's fingers tightened. 'Are you all right?'

'Yes, sir. I'm fine.'

'Nearly done.'

One more syllable, swiftly spoken, and she felt his binding incant spring free. Between heartbeats her trammelled mage-senses sprang back to life. The pleasure of it was so great she gasped and opened her eyes. The shock of his power, so close to her, buckled her knees. She would have fallen if he hadn't taken both her arms.

'The incant,' he said, shaking her. 'Quickly. The longer I wait before rebinding you, the worse it will be.'

Desperate, she looked up at him. 'Please, Councillor Danfey, can't you leave me unbound? I won't run away, I won't—'

He shook her again, harder. 'Mage Lindin, don't make me regret my kindness. Give me the travel incant, now, or I'll rebind you and your brother can fend for himself.'

Hating him, hating herself for showing weakness, for giving

in to despair, she told him the incant's syllables and showed him its single sigil. He repeated the words to make sure he had them aright, then used his left hand to sketch the sigil, not quite completed, making sure it didn't engage.

'That's right,' she said. 'You have it.'

His eyes and face lost their fierce coldness. 'Good. Now brace yourself.'

The second binding was even more painful than the first. But only because this time she knew what it meant, what she was losing, how his words would make her cloddish and blind. As the cruel incant sprang closed around her, setting her nerves on fire, she cried out and fell against him. Expected to fall like a witless animal to the floor.

Instead he held her close as she wept.

'I'm sorry,' he murmured. 'I'm so sorry. Be strong, Barl. Be yourself.'

Through the terrible burning, she could feel his heart beneath her cheek. It was pounding like a blacksmith's hammer, his broad chest the anvil, shuddering with her pain. His arms tightened, cradling her. Had she ever felt so safe? Had she ever, in her whole life, felt as *protected* as she did now?

Confused, she struggled free. 'I'm all right.'

His fingers caught her chin, forced her head up so she was looking at him. 'You're certain? If I leave now, for Batava, I'll not find you collapsed when I return?'

There were tears on her face. Humiliated, she brushed them away. 'You can't go now. Remmie's a schoolteacher. At this time of day he'll be in class.'

The councillor shook his head. 'There's no school today.' Releasing her, he retrieved the silver tea tray and held it out. 'Tell Rumm I'll be back before dinner. If his lordship asks after me, I'm about Council business and had to step out betimes.'

'Yes, sir.' She took a deep breath and tightened her cold fingers on the tray. 'Sir, the incant will put you at our front gate. If there's no answer at the door, go round behind. Given half a chance Remmie will spend hours pottering with his vegetables. And sir—'

He raised an eyebrow. 'Yes, Mage Lindin?'

'He'll have to know the truth, there's no avoiding that. But if you could spare him a little, in the telling of it? He's going to take this hard.'

Morgan Danfey nodded, his expression cool and disinterested again. 'I'll do my best, Mage Lindin. Now get back to Rumm, before he comes looking for you.'

'Yes, sir,' she murmured, and even started down the stairs. But then she stopped and waited, watching as he used the incant she gave him . . . and stepped into the air.

Sighing, Remmie held the ravaged carrot-top high enough for the sun's light to lift it from shadow. Frowned at the tiny insects scurrying along the vulnerable green fronds and sighed again.

*Naphins. I knew it.*

'And that means poison,' he said glumly, tossing the ravaged carrot aside. 'Which I hate.' He pulled another carrot from the carefully tended, damp earth. 'But not as much as I hate *you*.'

Indifferent to his enmity, the naphins scurried and chewed.

So much for his plan to take dinner at The Greased Pig, Batava's cosy alehouse, then stay after for Griff Holcomb's fiddle-playing and a game or three of spindle stones with Barton and Hobbie Melton and Mickel Dassify. And he'd been looking forward to it, immensely. An evening with friends was guaranteed to take his mind off his infuriating, terrifying, angrily absent sister.

His heart thudded hard, once. It did that every time he thought of Barl, remembered their last harsh conversation. And now she was run off to Elvado, likely mired to her armpits in trouble by now, and one minute he was all set to chase after her, then the next he dug his heels in and told himself *no*. Because leaving had been her choice. Ignoring him? Her choice. Refusing to admit she might be wrong? Her choice. Proud, stubborn and unreasonable. That was his sister.

Miserable, he slapped at his spoiled carrots. *Curse you, Barl, come home. Or if you won't, at least –*

'Remmie Lindin?'

Startled by the unexpected voice, deep and melodious, he pushed onto his knees and turned. Saw a mage walking down the garden toward him, tall and expensively dressed and oddly familiar.

'Yes, I'm Remmie Lindin,' he said, and got to his feet. Where had he seen this man before? He knew him from somewhere . . . 'Winsun! You're the councillor who demonstrated Mage Sorvold's incant.' Which meant –

*Oh, justice. Barl, what have you done?*

The councillor halted at the edge of the vegetable patch. 'You were there?'

Remmie nodded. 'With my students. I'm sorry, sir, I don't know your name. You were never formally introduced.'

A glitter of amusement in the mage's clear blue eyes. 'I am Morgan Danfey.'

'And you're here because—' He had to clear his throat. Tighten his fingers by his sides, to still their trembling. A mage from the Council was standing in his garden. 'My sister. Barl.'

Councillor Danfey nodded. 'We should go inside. Some discussions are best held privily.'

'Of course,' Remmie said faintly, sweat rolling down his ribs. 'If you'll follow me, sir?'

He escorted Councillor Danfey to the parlour, then excused himself so he could wash clean of garden dirt and sweat. When he returned, the councillor favoured him with a raised-eyebrow look.

'Do you have tea, Mage Lindin? Travel incants wake in me a raging thirst. We could sit in the kitchen and talk.'

In the *kitchen?* So was this an official visit or not?

'Of course, sir,' Remmie said, cautious and confused. 'This way.'

As he took the kettle off the hob and filled it at the sink, Councillor Danfey stared out of the kitchen window.

'I've never been to the Eleventh district before.'

'Nor had I, sir, before I took a place teaching here.' He put the kettle back and fired up the range. 'Batava's very quiet, of course. Not as grand as Elvado. But then, where is?'

Turning, Councillor Danfey smiled. It made him seem friendly. Just a regular mage, no great power at all. But that was an illusion . . . and he'd best not forget it.

'Nowhere,' the councillor said, with a careless shrug. 'But I'd think there'd be worse places to live than this.'

Remmie pulled out a chair at the table. 'Please, sir. Have a seat. Would you care for some cake with your tea? It's baked fresh, and I'm counted a passable cook.'

Another smile, as the councillor dropped neatly into the chair. 'Unlike your sister, or so she says.'

Startled, Remmie almost dropped the tea caddy. 'Sir? Please tell me, where is she? What's happened? I know it's bad. You wouldn't be here if it wasn't. But—'

'Make the tea, Mage Lindin,' said Councillor Danfey, lowering his hand. 'And by all means cut me a slice of cake. I've been working all morning and neglected to take breakfast.'

Oh. So it was *that* bad, was it? Well, yes, of course it was. Barl never did anything in half measures.

He made the tea, poured it into his two best cups, cut the pear and bassiberry cake into generous slices, then laid the hasty feast on the table.

'Don't stint yourself, sir,' he said, sliding into the other chair. 'A cake's easily baked.'

'Perhaps,' said Councillor Danfey, after his first mouthful. 'But rarely so well.'

Remmie tried to smile, but his face had forgotten how. 'Thank you.'

As the councillor continued to eat and drink, he sipped his sugared tea. Didn't dare eat cake, for fear it would choke him. There was a lump in his throat he couldn't swallow away. Any minute now, surely, Councillor Danfey would say what had happened . . . wouldn't he?

259

The answer, it seemed, was no. Another cup of tea. Another slice of cake. No more casual conversation, just a thoughtful stare through the kitchen window, his brow creased into a faint frown. Remmie bit his tongue. They might be in his home but he felt supplanted as its master. Morgan Danfey wore his mantle of authority as comfortably as his fine silk brocade. The rings on his right hand were fashioned from gold and precious jewels. One was even a firestone, worth more than every personal possession in Batava.

So was it some kind of test, making him sit here in silence? And if he didn't pass it, did that mean Barl would suffer? Terrified that it might, he kept on biting his tongue. He'd asked twice now for an explanation. He didn't dare ask again.

At last the councillor sighed, and pushed his emptied cup to one side. 'Mage Lindin, tell me about your sister. The hard truth, mind. No sweetening.'

Remmie blinked. And was this another test? He fought the urge to wipe his damp palms down his shirt front. 'I don't – I'm not sure – sir, what do you want to know?'

'Whatever you wish to tell me.'

*Oh, Barl.* 'She's a brilliant mage,' he said, after a moment. 'Sometimes I think too brilliant for her own good. She has a good heart but she won't suffer jiggets. That's what gets her into strife. Maybe she's not—' He chewed his lip. It felt treacherous, what he intended to say. But Councillor Danfey had said he wanted the hard truth. He'd never believe a gushing of honey, no vinegar. 'My sister isn't overburdened with humility, sir. She makes no apologies for her gifts and doesn't take kindly to those who slight her.'

Councillor Danfey was nodding. 'You'd call her ambitious?'

'I would, sir, yes,' he admitted. 'But not for fame and fortune, Councillor, though I know it might seem so. She's hungry for the work. She always has been. And she frets and chafes herself when she feels she's held back.'

'And that would be why she pressed for entrance to the College?'

Remmie leaned forward. '*Yes,* sir. That's exactly why.'

'And do you understand, Mage Lindin, that there never was a question of her gaining admittance?'

'Because our family's unranked?' he said, and was surprised to feel a twist in his gut. Perhaps it was the way the councillor asked the question, a smooth kind of impatience in him that spoke of unquestioning advantage. 'I did tell her, Councillor Danfey. I told her 'til I was blue in the face. Begged her to abandon such a foolish notion. She wouldn't listen. It was her dream, you see. And Barl never was one for giving up on a dream. *Please,* Councillor. Where is she? Why hasn't she come home?'

Instead of answering, Councillor Danfey uncoiled from his chair and paced to the window. Arms folded, a singing tension in his back, he stared at the garden. 'Your sister's in a great deal of trouble, I'm afraid. Formal complaints of her conduct have been lodged by one Artisan Master Arndel, and the Guild of Artisans. Worse than that, she deliberately used magic against another mage. As you're doubtless aware, that is a privilege reserved to my Council.'

Remmie felt the words strike him like lightning, searing and cruel. *But that's a capital crime.* 'There must be some mistake. Barl's got a temper, I don't deny it, but she would *never*—'

'I'm afraid the facts are not in dispute,' said the councillor. 'Indeed, your sister freely admitted what she'd done.'

'You're saying Barl *killed* someone?'

Councillor Danfey turned, swiftly. 'No. She merely bruised him. But the end result is the same. She raised her hand to harm him.'

Dazed, Remmie pressed a hand to his face. Of all the things he'd imagined, he'd not imagined this. 'Is she condemned?'

'To death? No,' said the councillor. 'She's bound and under house arrest on my family's estate.'

He didn't try to hide his relief. When he could trust himself to speak again, he lowered his hand. 'And is that your doing, sir?'

261

'I spoke for her,' the councillor said, nodding. 'She was foolish, and is certainly misguided. But there are foolish, misguided ranked mages who have found themselves in strife and weren't expected to forfeit their lives. It would not have been justice to expect it of her.'

Remmie found his feet. 'Can I see her?'

'No.'

A cold, curt refusal. He wanted to argue, wanted to call *that* injustice and bully Councillor Danfey into changing his mind. But one look at the ranked mage's hard eyes and he knew he might as well spit into the wind.

'How long must she stay prisoner? How long must she be bound? I've little experience with it, only what most mages know, but I've heard a bound mage left bound for too long is often . . . damaged.' His belly heaved at the thought. A good thing he'd not taken a mouthful of cake. 'If that should happen to Barl, I think she'd rather be dead.'

Behind his set expression, something shifted in Councillor Danfey's face, some kind of revulsion or hint of real pain. 'Don't distress yourself, Mage Lindin. I'll not let that happen.'

Shivering inside, Remmie dragged one sleeve across his wet face. 'You said she's kept confined on your family estate, sir? Is that usual?'

'No,' said the councillor, and almost laughed. 'Far from it. But it was that or see her penned in a judiciary.'

'Sir . . .' He stood, aware of unsteady legs and a heart pounding too hard for his abruptly fragile chest. 'Thank you. My sister and I owe you a great debt. I'd also apologise. You've been put to great trouble. I'm sure there are matters far weightier that the Council must address. I hope you'll believe me when I say Barl wouldn't have meant for this to happen. She's not wicked. She's not dangerous. In speaking up for her, you haven't made a mistake.'

The councillor grimaced. 'So you say, Mage Lindin. But the Council will want more than a brother's assurance. Your sister must prove her contrition to its satisfaction, and I should tell you that so far she is rather lagging behind.'

Remmie swallowed despair. Lagging behind? Barl had thrown herself into a great, gaping hole. If she stood before him right now he'd be hard pressed not to slap her.

'Sir, you say I can't see her and I must accept that, I know. But will you take her a message?'

'Yes,' said Councillor Danfey. 'That I can do.'

'A written note? That's permissible?'

'This once,' the councillor said. 'But after today, Mage Lindin, you'd best accustom yourself to silence.'

Another tremor ran through him. 'For how long? Do you know?'

'That's a question for the Council to decide.'

'And when will it be decided?'

Councillor Danfey raised an eyebrow. 'It's your contention I should discuss privy Council matters with you?'

Remmie felt a rush of heat, and dropped his gaze. 'No, sir.'

'Write your note, Mage Lindin. I've no more time to spare.'

So he fetched ink, paper and quill and scrawled a handful of incoherent thoughts that he hoped would comfort his impossible sister. Since sealing it might be taken as an insult, he merely folded the paper and held it out.

'Thank you, Councillor Danfey. It was good of you to come here, and put my mind at ease.'

The councillor took the note and tucked it inside his sleek tunic. 'Under the circumstances, I thought it was best. You're not to discuss this business with anyone, Mage Lindin. It's the Council's wish that the entire unfortunate imbroglio be kept privy. You understand?'

Only too well. 'Of course. If anyone should ask after her, I'll say she's travelling the Ninth district for a time. That should satisfy the curious.'

Councillor Danfey nodded, his smile thin. 'Indeed it should. As for your sister's future, you'll hear from me when a final decision has been made. Until then, you can trust I'll see she comes to no harm.'

Hesitant, Remmie stared at the man. Morgan Danfey had

wealth, power and high position. In Dorana he was untouchable. One word in the right ear and he could see a lowly schoolteacher dismissed without any hope of redress.

*And I'm to trust him with my sister's life? I'm to believe he'll continue standing for her, an unranked mage, against his fellow councillors? What if she annoys him? What if he grows tired of her being underfoot, or decides she's simply too much trouble?*

And that seemed likely. He could only imagine the state Barl was in, how angry she must be. And when his sister was angry, she rarely schooled her temper. But then, what choice did he have here, save taking the man at his word?

*There's nothing I can do for her. She's made me a prisoner too.*

And sooner or later, he'd have to find a way to forgive her for that.

'Sir,' he said, meeting Councillor Danfey's steady, inscrutable gaze. 'If anything changes, you will tell me?'

'Of course.'

Except there wasn't any *of course*. Not in a situation like this.

A sudden thought occurred. 'Clothes! She'll need clothes. If I throw some together for her, sir, will you take them with you?'

'Yes, but be quick, Mage Lindin. I am a busy man.'

And a kind one, in his haughty, arrogant way. Remmie bolted to the bedroom, ransacked Barl's drawers and cupboard, shoved as much as he could fit into a canvas carryall, added one pair of shoes and one of boots, the book she'd been reading, and hauled everything back to the kitchen.

'Thank you, sir,' he said, handing his visitor the bag. 'This is very good of you.'

Left hand raised to trace the first sigil of his travel incant, Councillor Danfey hesitated. 'One last question, Mage Lindin. Your sister. Should I be wary of an outraged suitor descending upon me to champion her cause?'

'A suitor, sir?' Remmie said, startled. 'No. Barl's never had time for courting. Magic's always come first.'

Another indifferent nod. 'I see.'

And with no more questions, without a word of farewell, Councillor Danfey recited his travel incant, and vanished.

With no heart for harmless carousing down at The Greased Pig, Remmie lost himself in making lesson plans for the upcoming school week. When it was time for supper he made leek and bean soup and forced it down, his appetite half-hearted. A sleepless night followed. The next day he taught class, short-tempered, and when that was done he went to see Master Arndel. The Artisan Master was already mixed up in Barl's dilemma. Surely it couldn't hurt to talk of it with him. Anyway, he had to take the chance.

'Imprisoned?' Arndel sat back in his privy chamber chair, a gloating satisfaction lighting his eyes. 'And how is that my concern, Mage Lindin? Your sister has nothing to do with me any more, and may justice be praised for that.'

'She's not just imprisoned,' Remmie said, fighting to hold onto his temper. He was beginning to see why Barl had loathed the man. 'She's *bound*. Master Arndel, you know what that means.'

Arndel shrugged. 'It means that at long last she's been put in her place.'

Resisting the urge to thump his fist to the man's desk, Remmie instead gentled his tone. 'Sir, there's no need for you to tell me my sister can be aggravating. I grew up with her. But can't you set aside any personal mislikings and remember her talent? Will you sit there and tell me you're willing to see that ruined?' *Out of spite, out of meanness?* 'You can't.'

It was Arndel who thumped the desk. 'Mage Lindin, I'll sit here and tell you that whatever happens to that troublemaker is no trouble of mine. Whatever misery she's in, we both know she's brought it on herself.'

'You're too modest,' Remmie snapped. 'You did your part, in writing to the Council. In complaining of her to the Artisans' Guild. With your weight thrown against her, what chance did she have?'

'You insolent pup!' Arndel leapt to his feet. 'You're as bad as she is. Arrogance is clearly a Lindin family trait. Your sister came within a hair's-breadth of ruining my reputation, my artisanry. I'm glad the Council's bound her. I hope she stays bound the rest of her days. Mages like your sister are a menace to Dorana. Now get out, before I put pen to paper and complain of *you* to the Council.'

And Arndel would, too. He'd trump up some baseless accusation, claim he was threatened, claim the Lindins had a vendetta against him. And with Barl already in trouble, the Council would likely believe him.

Sickened, Remmie shook his head. 'It seems I owe Barl an apology. I told her she was wrong to judge you so harshly. I told her she should be grateful for the chances you gave her. She told me I was talking through my nose. And she was right. Arndel, you're a disgrace.'

Leaving the artisanry behind, he turned next to the only other mage who might be able to help him . . . and Barl.

*'Bound?'* Lady Ancilla Grie pressed a slender white hand to her breast. 'Mage Lindin, I had no idea.'

Invited to sit in her splendid day room, uncomfortably aware of his plain linen and wool in this sumptuously silken place, Remmie struggled to keep all emotion in check.

'The Council doesn't want it widely known, my lady.'

'I'm sure it doesn't. Don't worry, I'll not speak of it.'

He managed a smile. 'I'd be most grateful. Lady Grie, I know my coming here must be counted impertinent. And I know you must be preoccupied with your infant son. But—'

Beautiful, elegant Lady Grie sighed. 'But you want me to help your sister. Mage Lindin, I wish I could. But there's nothing I can do.'

He had to tread carefully. 'Lady Grie, I think I know what Artisan Master Arndel has told you of Barl. If *I* told you that he wasn't being entirely truthful, or was misled, would you be greatly offended?'

'No,' Lady Grie said. 'But even if that's the case, I still can't help you. I have no say in how Master Arndel runs his artisanry.

266

Could you prove your sister unfairly dismissed, it would make no difference. Arndel will never take her back . . . and I think you already know that. As for me interceding on Barl's behalf with the Council, you overestimate my importance. Here in the Eleventh district, I am counted a mage of some influence. But in Elvado? I have none.' Her lips twisted in a wry smile. 'Hard as it may be for you to believe, ranking has its limitations.'

Swallowing hard, Remmie stared at the richly carpeted floor. He'd placed every last hope for Barl in the persuasive powers of this woman . . . and here she was telling him he'd wasted his time.

'I understand, my lady,' he said, fighting to keep his voice steady. Then he stood. 'Thank you for seeing me.'

Lady Grie shook her head. 'Not at all. I only wish I could help. Your sister is a rare talent. I was looking forward to owning more of her marvellous clocks . . . and whatever else she dreamed up.'

And was that all Barl meant to her? Did injustice mean nothing at all? 'My lady.'

'Remmie . . .' Lady Grie smoothed her silk skirts. 'If it should chance I can speak up for her, I promise you I will. But discreetly, you understand. Since the Council wants this kept quiet.'

'My lady,' he said again, and offered her a bow.

Travelled home again, exhausted, Remmie sat in his dimly glimlit kitchen. He didn't have the heart to cook. The cottage felt cold, and desolate, and empty.

'I'm sorry, Barl,' he whispered. 'I did my best. But if you're going to escape this disaster, you'll have to do it alone.'

# CHAPTER SEVENTEEN

Barl broke three plates, waiting for Councillor Danfey to return. Incensed, Rumm banished her outside to the poultry run.

'Keep yourself out of trouble scrubbing perches and putting fresh straw in the nesting boxes,' he said, close to snarling. 'You'll answer to Pagett. And if he has to come inside to tell me you've stepped on a hen and killed it, or smashed so much as *one* egg, Mage Lindin, a binding will be the *least* of your strife!'

It was a relief to escape Rumm's severe scrutiny, even if it meant the mess and stink of poultry. Pagett, she quickly learned, was the Danfey servant who oversaw the estate grounds and all the work of its outbuildings. He was brawny for a Doranen, one of those unfortunates, like Rumm, in whom the talent for magic barely sparked. She had no idea how much the man knew of her. Didn't care. After she explained what Rumm wanted, he grunted then pointed her in the direction of pail, water and scrubbing brush.

The poultry run with its large, attached coop was noisy, the birds free to scratch grass, raise dust and lay eggs, moult feathers, peck each other and drop runny shit wherever and whenever the fancy took them. Stupid creatures, with their constant cackling and beady eyes. Nesting boxes lined the coop's four timber walls, with wooden perches set all over the place at every height imaginable. Trapped beneath its low, sloping roof she had to hunch until her chin was buried in her chest. By the time she'd scrubbed five perches clean of muck her whole body ached. Worse, her nose was clogged with acrid shit stink, and there was shit daubed over her shoes as high as her ankles. It stained her sleeves and spackled her face.

*If Arndel could see me now he'd laugh himself sick. So would Ibbitha, and that jigget Baret Ventin.*

But even though the poultry coop was demeaning, it was still better than slaving in the kitchen. It wasn't just being hounded by Rumm. The kitchen reminded her of Remmie . . . and if she was going to survive this ordeal she had to forget him and what she'd left behind in Batava.

After cleaning ten perches the water was too stinking and filthy to keep using, so she dropped the scrubbing brush and hauled the sloshing pail outside.

And found she wasn't alone.

Councillor Danfey crossed the clipped grass, his long strides swallowing the distance between them. The pail slid from her nerveless grasp, tipping and splashing. Mouth sucked dry, heart thudding, she waited for him to reach her.

With one of those faint, almost mocking smiles, he halted an arm's length away and looked her up and down. 'It's a good thing your brother thought to pack you clean clothes, Mage Lindin. You've reduced what you're wearing to little better than rags.'

She wasn't in the mood for teasing. 'You saw Remmie? Is he – is he very angry with me?'

'Angry?' The councillor shook his head. 'No. He was most grieved.'

And that was worse than anger. *Oh, Remmie, I'm sorry.* Scalded with her own grief, with a throat-closing shame, she blinked back tears.

'What else did he say?'

'He was swift to assure me you are no threat to Dorana.'

Bitterness trampled common sense. 'Not to Dorana, no. But I'm a threat to those mages who would deny others the rights they so heedlessly take for granted. Best you know that about me, before I spend my first night beneath your roof.'

Councillor Danfey's gaze shifted to the woodland beyond his estate's cultivated heart. She found his expression difficult to decipher. There was resignation, and impatience, a grudging sympathy at war with . . . yes, contempt. For her? Or for those mages she railed against to no avail? She didn't know, and didn't dare ask.

'Mage Lindin.' Jaw tight, he looked at her. 'If ever you wish that binding to be lifted, do not say such things where Lord Arkley can hear you.'

'Who?'

'My Council colleague. The one who was keen to see blood spill for your crime.'

Oh, yes. Him. It was good to know the name of a man who so passionately wanted her death.

'He's not the only one, is he? Who was the older woman seated beside him?'

'Lady Frieden.' Councillor Danfey's lips thinned with distaste. 'And you're correct. She is another mage around whom you'd be wise to guard your tongue. Lord Varen, too, though he's not bloodthirsty. And in case you're curious, the final member of the Council, in whose hands your life and liberty rest, is—'

'Lady Martain,' she said. 'I know. She came to see me early this morning.'

And that had his gaze sharpening with suspicion. '*Venette* did?'

Curse it. So much for holding her tongue on that.

'Yes, sir.'

Councillor Danfey's brows were drawn close, the fingers of his right hand drumming his thigh. 'What did she want?'

'To remind me that I was lucky you were there last night.' She shrugged. 'And she's right, of course. I was.'

'What else?'

Should she tell him the rest, after all? That Venette Martain had warned her off as an interloper? Saw her as an obstacle in her plans for the councillor's wedding?

*By all means, if I want to make yet another sworn enemy.*

270

Another shrug. 'It was a general scolding, sir. Lady Martain took me to task for my wickedness.'

For a moment she thought he didn't believe her. Eyes chilly he stared at her, thoughts and suspicions seething. Then he nodded.

'Lady Martain is strict. Your conduct has offended her.'

'But not you, sir?'

His eyes were winter cold now. 'Oh, I am offended. Don't mistake compassion for complicity in your crime.'

'My *crime?*' She felt the word like a slap from a hard, open hand. 'I thought—'

'But you *don't* think, Mage Lindin, do you? You act on impulse, born of rampant emotion. Which is one reason I've brought you here, so you can meditate upon your poor behaviour.'

*Her* poor behaviour? But she was the injured party. Could he really not see that? And if he couldn't, then why had he saved her?

'Remarkable,' the councillor said, still staring. 'You hold yourself blameless.'

Barl felt her face scald with heat. 'I hold myself provoked, sir.'

'But not responsible in any way?'

'I didn't say that,' she muttered. 'It's true I'm bound here, your prisoner, because I lost my temper with Lord Hahren. But if there was equity amongst the mages of Dorana, if the First Families weren't so greedy and selfish, then I never would have argued with him.'

'I see,' the councillor said, musing. 'So I'm greedy and selfish.'

'No! At least—' He was right, curse it. She was stupidly impulsive. 'I'm sorry. I didn't mean to be rude.'

'And yet you were. Again. Rude and ungrateful.' He stepped back. 'Be about your assigned tasks, Mage Lindin. Rumm is not a man you wish to aggravate.'

Rumm was a servant, not much better than herself. But so long as the councillor granted him the authority to order her about, she'd be foolish indeed to needlessly antagonise him.

'Yes, sir,' she said, picking up the abandoned pail. With a curt nod he turned on his heel and walked away. She watched him, just for a moment, torn between resentment and a reluctant admiration of his lithe, easy gait. Then she snorted. 'Don't be a spoggin, Barl. Let an appealing arse distract you, and you'll be a sight sorrier than you already are.'

'She's trouble, that girl,' said Lord Danfey. 'You want my advice, you'll get rid of her.'

It was tempting, but Morgan knew better than to point out that his father's advice was both unwanted and unnecessary. Instead, he pulled back the heavy curtains from the parlour's main window.

'The binding has unsettled her. But of course, if she upset you, my lord, I do apologise.'

His father grunted. 'The day some chit of an upstart young mage upsets me is the day you can measure me for a crypt. And what are you doing with those curtains? Trying to blind me?'

'My lord, of course not. But—'

'It's too bright, I tell you,' his father snapped. 'Close 'em again. If I want the curtains open I can open 'em myself!'

Biting his tongue, Morgan eased the curtains part way across the windows. Ranmer had told him his father needed time in the sun. He'd also cautioned there would come a time when direct light would be painful, but that even so Lord Danfey must not sit in the dark with nothing but a little glimfire to leaven the shadows.

'There, my lord,' he said, turning, feigning a lack of concern while his guts writhed. 'Does that satisfy?'

Irritable, his father plucked at the blanket laid over his legs and lap. 'I'd be satisfied if the Council housed its miscreant somewhere else.'

'I can see that Rumm keeps her downstairs, my lord. It will be as though she's not here.'

'But she *is* here!' His father slapped the arm of his chair. 'And I want to know *why*. What maggot's in your brain, Morgan, that you'd drag us into a nonsense the nearest judiciary should see to?'

How could he answer that when he hardly understood the why of it himself . . . and when what he did grasp would send his father into spasms?

'My lord, do you trust my judgement?'

His father glared. 'Think that's an answer, do you?'

'She's here because I believe it's best,' he said, keeping his voice level and light. 'Which is, you must allow, a question of judgement.'

'I'll allow you're impertinent! I'm still Lord Danfey, or had you forgotten?'

'Never.'

'Then if I told you to get rid of her, you'd do it?'

Morgan crossed to his father's chair and dropped to a crouch beside it. 'Is that what you're telling me?'

Blueish lips slackened, his father plucked again at his blanket. 'The girl's pert, Morgan. She doesn't know her place. Looked me straight in the eye, she did, and answered me back. A cell in the nearest judiciary's too good for her!'

'Well, my lord,' he said, coaxing, 'right now she toils in the poultry run, reeking of bird manure. I think it's fair to say she is suitably humbled.'

'In other words, she's staying, no matter what I want.'

He touched his fingertips to his father's bony wrist. 'My lord, I'd count it a personal favour if you withdrew your objection.'

'Wheedler,' his father muttered, snatching his hand away. 'Very well. She can stay. But whatever strife she causes, I'll hold you accountable. And make sure to tell Rumm *he's* to bring me my trays. I don't like pert young women who answer me back.'

'I shall, my lord,' he said, standing. 'Thank you.'

'If you want to thank me,' his father retorted, 'you can speak of young women more to my taste. How soon before I'm to call the Garrick girl *daughter*?'

*Maris*. Not wanting his father to see his distaste, Morgan wandered back to the window. 'Soon enough, my lord.'

'Sooner than that,' said his father. 'And don't let your eye stray in any other direction.'

He glanced behind him. 'I don't know what you mean.'

'Yes, you do!' Again, his father slapped the arm of his chair. 'You're not blind, Morgan, any more than I am. That Barl Lindin's beautiful. And what you do after you've got yourself a son on the Garrick girl will be no business of mine, seeing as how I'll be dead by then. But you'll not dip your wick in that pert girl's honeypot until there's a Danfey to follow you. Is that clear?'

If he lost his temper, Barl would be sent back to the Council for Sallis Arkley to deal with. He could not, *would* not, let that happen.

'You've nothing to fear, my lord. The girl might be attractive, but my interest is fixed on Maris Garrick.'

Slowly, his father relaxed. 'Good.'

'Now I'm afraid I must excuse myself. I have another Council matter to address, and then I would spend some time in my workroom. Shall we dine together this evening, or do you prefer to dine alone?'

'You should dine with Maris Garrick,' his father said, scowling. 'You shouldn't be letting her out of your sight.'

Without thinking, without blinking, he lied. 'Alas, my lord, Maris is otherwise engaged this evening. A family affair,' he added, when his father's eyes widened with alarm. 'But I shall see her again soon. Can I fetch you a book before I go?'

'Feeble I might be, but I can fetch my own book,' his father said, offended. 'Be off. And mind you tell Rumm what I said!'

He crossed paths with the master servant on the staircase. 'Sir. I was just coming to find you.' Rumm held out a folded note. 'From the Council.'

Morgan slid it unread inside his tunic. 'Lord Danfey prefers not to be waited on by Mage Lindin.'

Rumm nodded. 'Very good, sir.'

'By the way, is there a reason you have her toiling with the poultry?'

'An excellent reason, sir,' said Rumm, his face darkening. 'Do you object?'

Of course, but it would be unwise to say so. 'I was merely curious. I have business with Lady Martain. Expect me back within the hour.'

'Yes, sir.'

Morgan kept on down the stairs, then paused. 'Oh, Rumm. I procured fresh clothes for Mage Lindin.'

'Yes, sir,' Rumm said, his expression rigorously blank. 'Jafe saw that I got them, as you asked. The bag's been put on her bed.'

Hardly a bed. A straw mattress on the floor of the hastily emptied broom and mop closet, which was the only privy place, Rumm claimed, that he could offer at such short notice. Not without crowding the other servants and *that* he wasn't willing to do. Not for a bound mage no better than she had to be.

And what Barl would say when she found out was anybody's guess.

Arriving unexpected at Venette's town house, he was shown into the ornate parlour by her master servant and asked to wait. Declining the offer of wine and wafers, he contented himself with perusing one of Orwin's ponderous books.

'*Morgan*!' Venette exclaimed, sweeping into the parlour almost a quarter of an hour later. She was swathed head to toe in silver-shot mauve silk, violet slippers on her feet and chains of amethysts around her neck and wrists. 'I declare I do *not* understand the game you're playing. How *could* you refuse an invitation to the Garricks' house party?'

Her outrageous demand struck him like spark to tinder. Burning, he tossed Orwin's book onto a nearby table and took a step toward her. Managed to catch himself in time, before he laid hands on her.

'And how could *you*, Venette, insinuate yourself into my privy business? You had the temerity to *interrogate* Barl Lindin? To *discuss* me with her? What gave you the right?'

'Friendship!' she retorted. 'Morgan, you have cast your boat upon perilous waters. Defending that miscreant? Sheltering her in your home? Have you *any* idea how it will look to Maris?'

Nonplussed, he stared at her. 'What I do in my capacity as councillor is no concern of Maris Garrick's! It would not be her concern were we already ratified man and wife.'

'Which you won't be, you fool, if you continue with this madness!' Venette threw up her hands. 'How can you be so brilliant and so *obtuse*? Maris has her pride, Morgan. Do you truly think she'll idly smile and bestow on you her blessing as you insult her in such a savage fashion?'

'How do I insult her? The girl finds me desirable *because* I am a Council mage. How can she possibly be insulted by the performance of my duty?'

Pale with anger, Venette rushed to him and thumped his chest with both her fists. 'Easily! Morgan, it was never your *duty* to take Barl Lindin under your roof. You did that because she *stirs* you! And if you think Maris won't grasp that blindingly obvious fact then truly, I wash my hands of you!'

When she went to thump him again, he caught her wrists hard. Her expensive jewellery bruised his fingers down to the bone.

'By all means, Venette,' he said, as she tried to wrestle free. 'Wash away. Barl Lindin means nothing to me. How could you even imagine I'd consider her? She is unranked, unruly and—'

'Outrageously fair!' Venette was close to panting, her eyes stormy, full of doubt. 'And if you stand there and deny it, Morgan, I'll never believe another word out of your mouth.'

'Why would I deny it?' he said. 'Yes, the girl's beautiful. And that should be enough to overturn my judgement? My sense of what honour is owed my father and our family name? Is *that* your opinion of me, Venette?'

'No, of course it's not, but—'

The parlour door pushed open. 'Venette? Venette, my dear, are you in – oh.' Orwin Martain blinked at them, a tiny frown creasing his brow. 'What's amiss? Venette? Morgan, why are you—'

Letting go of Venette's wrists, stepping back, Morgan cleared his throat. 'I'm sorry, Orwin. I—'

'Oh, Orwin, do go away,' Venette said, flapping her hands at him. 'There's nothing amiss, Morgan and I are simply thrashing out a disagreement. Now off you go. Whatever you want from me will have to wait.'

As the door closed again behind Venette's obedient husband, Morgan turned on her. 'And is *that* what you've told Maris she'll be marrying? A shambling, bumbling—'

'Don't you dare insult Orwin!' Venette cried. 'He's a dear, sweet man whose only care in the world is making sure that I'm happy. And you'd best believe, my dear, that if I could find a man as like him as a twin brother then *that* is the man I'd have recommended to Maris. But my Orwin is one of a kind.'

Though he was still angry, Morgan had to smile. Orwin certainly was that. Besides, though he'd not known Maris Garrick for long, he felt tolerably certain that a man like Orwin Martain would be far too soft-hearted and pliable for her.

'Morgan . . . my dear . . .' Abruptly conciliatory, Venette perched on the arm of the nearest plush sofa. 'If your head's not been turned by that wretched Lindin girl, why would you throw your chances with Maris so up in the air by refusing to attend the Garricks' house party? I don't know if you know it, but it's counted one of the more exclusive social events of the year. Some very useful people will be there. People it will do you no harm to impress.'

He raised an eyebrow. 'Am I not impressive enough already?'

'Oh, *Morgan.*' Venette rolled her eyes. 'There is no such thing as being too impressive.'

'I take it Maris told you I'd refused her invitation?'

'My dear, she was on the doorstep practically at cockcrow, in floods of tears, *convinced* your attentions are fickle! And it didn't help that you bolted from her company before your dinner was half over. Yes, I know, I know—' She waved a hand to forestall his protest. 'And you can be sure I disabused her of any notion that you simply used Council business as an excuse to escape.'

And that had him staring at her, incredulous. 'She thought I – Venette, is the girl unsteady in her wits?'

'No, of course she's not.' Venette shook her head at him, as though he were a wonder. 'If you must know, Morgan – and why I should have to tell you this is a mystery, I declare – Maris has fallen entirely under your spell. To put it plain as I can, she is *enamoured* of you, which is why I am so vexed that you've taken an interest in Barl Lindin. When Maris learns—'

'There is no reason for Maris Garrick to know anything of Barl Lindin,' he said coldly. 'Barl Lindin is a Council matter.'

Her irritated shrug told him he'd scored a point. 'You've still not told me why you won't attend the house party.'

'And you've not told me why it's any of your business.'

Sliding off the sofa's wide, padded armrest, Venette crossed to him with both hands outstretched. 'Oh, come now, Morgan. Let's not fight any more. It's far too exhausting. You know why I'm interested.'

Sighing, Morgan took Venette's hands and held her gently, this time. You've seen my father. You know how feeble he's grown. Every day I watch him lose a little more strength. Do you think I could ever reconcile myself if he should – if something should – while I was carousing at some insipid country gathering?'

Venette slid her hands from his and pressed her palm to his face. Now her eyes were sheened with compassionate tears. 'Oh, Morgan. You *mustn't* look at it like that. If Greve knew you were risking your future with Maris for him, well, I think we both know how angry he'd be. Don't you see? If you go to the house party, you're going for him. Would you really have him die without knowing the Danfey name was secure?'

It was the unkindest of questions, one he'd not tolerate from anyone else. 'You know I wouldn't,' he said, and was shamed to hear his voice break.

She smoothed his cheek. 'Then let me tell Maris you've changed your mind.'

Gently, Morgan slid her hand from his face. 'You're so certain Maris and I will make a good match.'

*How can you be so certain, when I am anything but?*

'Of course I am,' she said, smiling. 'Would I have you wed into misery, Morgan? Would I break a young girl's heart?'

He raised her hand to his lips and kissed it. 'No, Venette. You wouldn't.'

'Then *trust* me,' she urged him softly.

Unbidden, his fingers drifted to the place where his locket had rested. Like a phantom, he could still feel it there, warm against his skin.

'I should go,' he said, releasing her. 'I have work at home, awaiting my attention.'

'Magework?' Venette frowned. 'Morgan—'

He tapped a finger to her lips, lightly pressing. 'I will always have magework, Venette. I am a mage, first and foremost.'

Prettily pouting, she smoothed the front of his tunic. 'And we're friends again?'

'Yes. We are friends.'

'Excellent,' she said, laughing. And do I have your leave to speak to Maris tonight? About the house party?'

More than anything he wanted to say *no*. But how could he? Trapped by his promise to a dying man, he had no choice but to continue down a path he had not looked to tread.

'Yes,' he said, making certain to hide his resentful distaste. 'You have my leave.'

Venette's smile was dazzling. '*Wonderful*. I shall make sure all of Maris's girlish qualms are soothed, I promise. You'll not regret this, Morgan. You'll see.'

He was already regretting it. 'Venette,' he said, and kissed her hand in farewell.

Rumm said nothing beyond a murmured, 'Of course, sir,' after being told Councillor Danfey would be in his workroom until dinner. Which was wise of him, because Venette's impertinent interference still rankled.

An hour later, warded in his attic, Morgan paced from wall to wall. Scattered on his workbench, the remnants of yet another unsuccessful attempt to reconfigure Hartigan's transmutation incant. He couldn't begin to fathom *why* it so stubbornly resisted dissection. If not actually simple, the task should at least be straightforward. All incants operated under the same principle, energies binding each syllable like individually connected links in a chain. Break each connection, break the links into separate component pieces, and a new configuration could be created. Cylte's treatise on the subject was perfectly concise and moreover it *worked*. He'd *proven* that it worked, on a half dozen other incants.

But Hartigan's incant remained recalcitrant.

With a harshly expelled breath, Morgan returned to his copy of Cylte's book. Re-read, yet again, the step-by-step instructions for the dissolution of an incant. Then he gathered together in his scorched and scarred mortar the powdered *gedlef,* the tincture of *gorabim*, a volatile pinch of crystalised *anakaris,* close cousin to *azafris* but not quite so restricted. His supply of all three counter-catalysts was dwindling. And thanks to Sallis Arkley, once he'd emptied his jars he would have to wait a goodly while before daring to purchase more of each ingredient.

Even a councillor had to tread carefully, at times.

Almost more slowly than he could bear, he used his heavy stone pestle to grind the counter-catalysts into a stinking, sloppy paste. But if he tried to rush he'd spoil the concoction. He'd already made that mistake twice. Not again.

At last, satisfied with the counter-catalyst's consistency, he daubed it over seven harmonic prisms, one for each syllable of the incant. The eerily phosphorescent amber crystals pulsed sluggishly beneath their greenish-grey coating. He could feel the latent power stir, like a hunting hound catching its first scent of the prey.

It was time.

Remove the mortar and pestle from the main bench. Tidy away his precious reserves of catalyst ingredient. Take a moment to breathe out all doubt, anxiety and frustration. Then slowly, steadily, recite the seven separate syllables of Hartigan's unco-operative incant.

One by one, the harmonic prisms captured the syllables' raised energies. One by one, they started to hum. To shiver. To burn . . . . . . and burn out.

A heartbeat of shocked dismay gave way to overwhelming rage. Dimly Morgan felt himself snatch up the nearest crystal, heedless of its blackened heat. He shouted, incoherent, and threw it at the wall. Even as it shattered to stinking shards he was snatching up the next, not caring how his fingers blistered, his palm scorched, not caring that he was howling like a crossbowed wolf. In the end all seven crystals burst against the attic wall, scattering his failure over the floor.

Heaving for air, almost sobbing like a child, he collapsed over his workbench and pressed his burned, hurting hands hard to his face.

*How can I fail? This is Dorana's future. And if I do not conquer this incant . . . if I cannot find my way . . .*

Then Dorana would fall.

The binding might have ruined her time-sense, but the pitch dark night outside the Danfey mansion, with its needle-sharp pricking of stars, told Barl that the hour was late.

*And here am I doing the rich lord's dishes, like some magickless skivvy.*

Which of course she was. Up to her elbows in greasy, cooling water, skin wrinkled like ancient prunes, scrubbing charred meat juices and cake crumbs off old, heavy pans.

*At least when I washed dishes at home I'd eaten what was cooked in them first.*

But she'd not touched a mouthful of the Danfeys' rich repast. No, she'd spooned down plain mutton broth and bread that was practically stale. How she missed Remmie's bread. Hot from the oven, full of seeds and honey, soaked through with melted butter, making her smile.

Her fingers clutched the scrubbing brush, painfully tight. No. No. She mustn't think about Remmie.

Brisk footsteps in the corridor beyond the glimlit scullery. She looked up as Master Servant Rumm entered, as neat and tidy now, after the long day, as he'd been when first she laid eyes on him.

'Aren't you finished yet?' he demanded. 'Mage Lindin, dawdling will do you no favours here.'

*Dawdling?* When she could hardly raise her arms above shoulder height after half-killing herself in the poultry coop? And after that with the hoeing of weeds in the horses' carrot patch? And after *that*, helping one of the other servants haul sopping wet sheets out of the laundry tub, wring them free of water, then hang them to dry?

The injustice of Rumm's accusations left her gaping.

'We start our duties early,' he said. 'You'll be roused before dawn. So you decide how much sleep you'd like tonight.'

Teeth sunk into her lower lip, she let him leave without offering a word in her own defence. She didn't dare try. She'd only end up shouting . . . or worse.

Every breath she took, she took afraid she'd wake her binding.

At long last, with the final pot clean and dried, she drained the horrible water from the sink, wiped down every flat surface, bathed in the servants' scullery then staggered off to the pokey little cupboard they'd cleaned out for her to sleep in.

Knowing she had no glimfire, someone had left a lit candle in her tiny room. The small, unexpected kindness touched her on the raw. Then, when she saw her old canvas carryall, stuffed full with clothes to wear in her exile, she had to blink and blink again to clear her blurred vision. And when she found Remmie's hastily scribbled note, and read it, she burst into tears.

*I'm thinking of you every minute. Don't be afraid. I'll find you a way out of this. Remmie.*

Fighting back despair, Barl stripped off her stinking clothes, pulled on her nightshirt, blew out the solitary candle and crawled beneath the blanket on her lumpy, straw-mattress bed.

*Oh, Remmie. Remmie. I'm sorry. Please help me.*

Alone, in the darkness, she shivered herself to sleep.

# CHAPTER EIGHTEEN

*Like a beautiful voice raised in song, the magic lilts through her, making her weep. She feels like a golden fish swimming a river of power. Magic cradles her, carries her sweetly in its golden arms. There is pleasure here, and the glory of serenity. When she swims in magic's river she is entirely herself. Fear is banished, doubt washes away. Surrounded by magic she is strong and sure. She knows who she is, knows what purpose she was born for.*

*She sees the clock in her mind's eye, small and shimmering and perfect. A mystery clock, this one, intended to baffle its beholder. Only the greatest artisans can create such splendour. A mystery clock melts and remoulds itself seemingly on a whim, now a sphere, now a square, one moment green, the next blue. Blink, and it shines scarlet. And when it speaks, it speaks with a panoply of voices. At one o'clock it whispers. At ten o'clock it shouts. It strikes these minutes like drumbeats, and those it tickles like a mother her giggling child.*

*She thinks of herself as a mystery clock. The clock she sees in her mind's eye is herself, Barl Lindin made of magic. Fluid and formless, obedient only to her whim, she confounds expectations, dares what other mages only dream . . . and if a price must be paid for that then she will pay it, with pride.*

*Magic swells within her, demanding release. She feels her blood simmer with power, feels the tingle in her fingertips, the tremble in her tongue. Her tongue is heavy with words of power, words that must be spoken else she burst into flame. There is a clock in her mind's eye, and she has to create it. She opens her mouth to speak the words, quell the fire, create the clock she can see in her mind's eye –*

*– but instead of uttering words, all she can do is scream . . .*

Barl sat bolt upright on her miserly straw mattress, her throat raw, the pain in her so terrible she could hardly breathe. Desperate, she looked at her raised hands but the dreadful burning was only in her mind. Except it felt so real, and now she was weeping as well as screaming.

The door of her tiny prison chamber banged open.

'What is the meaning of this brouhaha?'

And that was Master Servant Rumm, fully dressed, neat as a pin. Did he never go to bed, or was it already a new day?

'Mage Lindin!' Master Rumm dropped to one knee beside her lumpy pallet. 'Enough of this caterwauling! What's amiss?'

How could she answer? She could barely think straight. Morgan Danfey's woken binding had a stranglehold on her throat, had set her bones on fire, threatened to make of her flesh nothing but stinking, bloodied ash.

'*Enough,* I tell you!' Rumm commanded. 'You'll not disrupt the entire household, I won't—'

His fingers closed around her wrists . . . and the flames leapt so high and hot she thought she would die.

'Mage Lindin, *stop*!' Rumm shouted after her, shoved ignominious onto his back. 'Come back here!'

Running almost blindly, Barl smashed her way through the mansion's cavernous kitchen, crashing pots and pans and eggs to the floor, catching hip and shoulder on half-opened doors, scattering startled servants as she banged her way up the stairs. Staggering, she reached the mansion's front door, wrenched it wide enough to slip through and stumbled into the cool, damp dawn beyond. She was still screaming, but on the inside now. Where Morgan Danfey wouldn't hear her.

The binding he'd sunk deep in her flesh was howling for revenge. Sobbing for air, she struck out across the mansion's front lawn, away from the gravelled drive, toward the estate's belting of dense green woodland. She'd be safe in there, with only the deer and the owls and the shadows for company.

Rumm shouted again, not far behind her. Would he get into trouble for this? Most likely. But it was his choice to be her keeper. He could've said no and spared himself the trouble.

A timber fence overgrown with flowering ashlin separated the cultivated estate grounds from the wilderness. There was no gate. Barl flung herself at the top rail and wriggled over it, cursing and coughing as she crushed the yellow blossoms in her haste. The sweet fragrance cloyed in her nose and throat.

As her feet touched the rough ground on the other side her ragged breath was stolen by another shuddering scream. A flare of light. A crack of sound. The Danfey estate's civilised boundary was warded.

*Oh, Remmie. I'm moonstruck. I should've thought of that.*

Her bones had turned to water, and the water was boiling. Graceless on her back, she stared at the distant, cloud-laced sky and heard herself grunting, felt warm spittle oozing onto her chin, as her limbs spasmed and twitched in a parody of running. The pain was unbearable, yet she seemed to be bearing it. Or perhaps she was dying.

*And if I am, do I care?*

Footsteps racing over the grass, coming closer. Someone breathing hard and harsh. '*Mage Lindin!*'

Of course. It was Morgan Danfey. Humiliated, she shivered and twitched and waited.

A rustling of ashlin vine as he vaulted over the fence. A thud she could feel as he landed on both feet, unperturbed by the warding that still battered her watery bones. Another thud as he dropped to his knees beside her.

'You stupid girl. *Look at me.*'

His hand cupped her face, fingers curved and forceful. Furious fear burned in him like a torch.

'Why would you run?' His voice was splintered with feeling. 'Do you want Sallis Arkley to win? And your brother, you'd leave him a grief-stricken wreck?'

She felt tears scald her cold cheeks. Tried to answer, and couldn't.

'Yes, Mage Lindin, you weep,' he said, sneering. His harsh fingers were warm. Branding her. 'Weep for the stubborn pride that will keep you diminished like this *forever* unless you come to your senses and *trust* me.'

The cloud-streaked sky above the fringing woodland was tinting rose and gold. Sunrise, swift and glorious. Deep within the sheltering trees a joyous chorus of birdsong burst forth. For a moment its sweetness dulled the binding that wrapped her tight in streamers of fire.

Morgan Danfey leaned close. 'You're in pain, aren't you? *Good.* Remember it, Mage Lindin. Burn the pain into your memory. Burn it deep so you don't *forget.*'

Helpless, she stared at him as he watched her suffer. And as she stared, his eyes shimmered and sheened. She felt her laboured breath catch.

*He weeps for me? No. He can't be. I'm dreaming.*

He snatched his hand free as though her pain burned his fingers. '*Ba'tari,*' he said, and sketched a swift sigil. '*Nebek tu.*'

Another flare of light, a final pulse of flame, and the worst of the pain fled. He'd deactivated the estate's warding. The relief was enormous.

'Sit up,' he said roughly, then caught her by the elbow and tugged. 'No mage should cower on the ground.'

Struggling, she managed to lift herself. 'But I'm not a mage, am I? Not any more.'

'Don't be foolish. Your binding is temporary.' His fingers still tight around her elbow, he shook her. 'And what were you *thinking*, attempting magic while bound?'

The mystery clock. Remembering it, Barl felt her heart hammer her ribs. She pressed a fist to her chest. 'I didn't.' Dropped to a whisper, her roughened voice broke. 'I was dreaming.' A wonderful, beautiful, impossible dream. She turned on him, lashing out. 'And what kind of man are you, to give me agony in my *sleep*? Is that the Council's justice? Is indiscriminate cruelty all an unranked mage can expect?'

He made no attempt to defend himself. Releasing her elbow, he allowed her to strike him again and again. Let her rage and weep, freshly woken to what she'd lost, what was taken. What *he'd* taken. This was his fault.

*I hate you. I hate you. Stop looking at me like that!*

Why, oh why, was he looking at her like that?

Exhausted and hurting, she let her fists fall. Stared at him, dispirited. 'And now I suppose you'll punish me for hitting you.'

She'd marked his face. A little red smudge high on his cheekbone. His fingers touched the bruise, lightly. She braced herself, expecting retribution.

'I can make you a posset,' he said. 'It will help you sleep more deeply, and most likely stop the dreams.'

The sympathy in his voice was a ruse, it had to be. A cunning strategy to lull her into further personal betrayals.

'Why would you do such a kindness for me?'

'You cannot control your impulses, Mage Lindin. I'd not further inflict your lack of self-discipline upon Rumm. He has enough to do without waiting with bated breath for the next time you put the household in an uproar.'

Her bones still felt watery, but she pushed to her feet regardless. Swaying a little, she glared down at him. 'Anyone would think I woke in torment for no better reason than to inconvenience your servant.'

Lithely, Morgan Danfey rose to face her. Now there was a mocking light in his eyes. 'It would not surprise me. You delight in the discomfort of those you consider inferior.'

And there was just enough truth in *that* to sting. She tilted her chin. 'And you'd know, of course, after our lengthy acquaintance.'

He shrugged, almost smiling. 'Whet your tongue on me if you must. But I do know you . . . and better than you think.'

Her heart was hammering again. 'Is that so?'

'It is,' he said, still with that taunting near-smile. 'And I can prove it.'

He was standing so close she could feel the warmth of his skin, and breathe in a hint of some rich, masculine scent. She fought the impulse to step back.

'Just as I can prove I'm not to be feared, but trusted.'

'How?' he said, one supercilious eyebrow lifting. 'Not that you frighten me.'

She did *something*. A pulse beat fast at the base of his throat, revealed because he'd neglected to properly fasten his hunter-green silk tunic. Seeing that swift pumping of blood beneath his skin, Barl hesitated.

*If it's not fear, then it's an emotion . . . more base. I must use that. I have no other weapon.*

Lifting her gaze, she softened herself. 'Unbind me, sir. You have my word I'll not run. I'll stay on your estate and obey Master Rumm from dawn to dusk, for as long as the Council decrees. I won't complain. I won't cause trouble. Only *please* don't ask me to endure another morning like this.'

'I told you.' Councillor Danfey cleared his throat. 'I will make you a soothing posset.'

'Possets don't agree with me.'

A shadow of distress touched his eyes. 'Mage Lindin, I cannot unbind you.'

'Yes, you can,' she insisted. 'No-one will know, so long as I pretend I'm still bound. You can leave the estate warded. That will keep me your prisoner. That – and my word.' She folded her arms. 'Unless the word of an unranked mage carries no more weight than a promise made by a Feenish mud merchant.'

'Stop harping on this business of being unranked,' he said, turning aside. 'You make the notion of ranking a nonsense.'

She couldn't afford to care for his grudging admiration.

'If that was true, Councillor, I'd not be standing here *bound*. So please don't insult me by—'

'*Insult* you?' Ivory-pale skin flushing, he seized her shoulders. 'From the moment you crossed my path I have done nothing but *protect* you!'

'How?' she demanded, wrenching free of him. 'Like *this*?'

Reckless, she snapped her fingers and tried to summon glimfire. The elementary incant set her on fire instead . . . and even though she'd been expecting it, still the furious pain knocked her to the ground.

Morgan Danfey leapt for her. '*Barl!*'

This time she managed to keep the screams trapped in her throat. Didn't protest as he snatched her close, though his touch was another kind of pain.

'You little fool,' he said, his voice ragged. 'You think to bully me? You think to force my hand by watching you weep?'

Eyes blurred almost blind by tears, she leaned back and looked at him. 'Yes. Is it working?'

One explosive, obscene Trindeki oath – and he snapped free the binding incant.

She flung her arms around his neck, not caring that she looked desperate. Not caring that she wept. 'Thank you. Thank you.'

'Barl . . .' Hesitantly, his arms closed around her. 'Don't thank me. I *can't* leave you unbound.'

'Why not?' she demanded. 'Oh, why not?'

He pushed her away, roughly, then stood and took two staggering steps backwards. Not supercilious now, no. And not haughty. His eyes were anguished, his handsome face ravaged with a resentful, angry grief.

'You know why not! On any day, at any hour, Lord Varen could come here to see how you conduct yourself. Or Sallis Arkley could come. Shari Frieden. Venette. You cannot deceive them!'

He was right. She couldn't. 'Then tell them they aren't welcome!'

'*What?*' He laughed, despairing. 'Barl, have you not grasped the truth of this yet? You are the Council's prisoner, its *property*.'

'And you can stomach that, can you?' she whispered. 'It makes you proud to be a councillor?'

'*Barl*, please, I—'

And then he was looking past her. Turning, she saw that she'd run out of time. Keeping his discreet distance, Rumm was waving his arm.

*Oh, you horrible, inconvenient man.*

Because now she was certain she could break Morgan Danfey. Just a minute or two more . . .

'Barl,' he said again, still pleading. 'You cannot think it amuses me, to see you writhing in pain. That it gives me pleasure knowing how we waste your unique talent. A mage gifted as you are should be celebrated. Not bound. But I cannot sway the Council. Not in this. In my own way, I am as bound as you. And if you think that *delights* me . . .'

Silent, she stared at him. Unbound, so close, she felt his windstorm of power. She felt more than his power, and felt herself shrink. There was no denying the pain in his eyes. Pain for her . . . which hurt him.

Hard on the heels of sympathy came anger.

*Why should I care for his pain? Why should I care that he cares for mine? His caring only goes so far. He's going to bind me again, for no better reason than to protect himself and his ranking. He knows it's wrong but he'll do it anyway. That's who he is. That is Morgan Danfey.*

But this time, when he bound her, as she screamed . . . she thought she heard him screaming with her.


'House party? What house party? You can't mean to go gallivanting now, Morgan. Not when you've dragged that bound troublemaker beneath my roof.'

Knowing that too much would show in his face, Morgan continued to collect his father's scattered breakfast leavings. By rights he should call for a servant to deal with it. If his father weren't so displeased he'd be calling for a servant himself, and berating his son for dallying with a task far beneath him.

'Speaking of the wench, where is she now?' his father added. 'And what mischief is she up to?'

He'd left Barl in Rumm's care, with a stern warning to keep her calm and quiet until the worst of the binding's aftereffects were past. And after that she was to perform light duties only. Rumm had nodded, perfectly obedient, but there'd been questions in his watchful eyes.

*Questions I cannot answer. Questions I do not dare ask myself.*

'No mischief at all, my lord,' he said, at last trusting himself to look round. 'You have my word.'

Lord Danfey was in a quarrelsome mood, with hooded eyes and the corners of his slackened mouth turned down. There were crumbs on his brocade dressing gown, a smear of egg on his chin. Seeing them, Morgan hid a wince. His father was a fastidious man. Such small, seemingly insignificant tells spoke to him of a mind slowly but surely coming to grief.

'And when I'm slaughtered in my bed, Morgan, what will your word do for me then?'

The breakfast leavings tidied, he risked further censure by pulling back the parlour curtains to admit more fresh air and light.

'There'll be no slaughtering, my lord, save of chickens for the pot.'

'Ha! So *you* say!' his father retorted. 'But *I* say I don't want you romping at house parties. What if I should need you? No. You do not have my leave to leave. You'll stay on the estate, where I can easily put a hand on you if it's required.'

The peremptory tone woke memories of stifled childhood. Irritated, Morgan frowned. 'My lord, I must think you weren't listening. I do not go to *romp,* but to make myself amenable to Maris Garrick's family. If I am to tie myself to Maris Garrick, then—'

'If?' His father struggled upright in his wingbacked chair. '*If?*'

*A delicate, beautiful face. Blue eyes that seemed to plumb the depths of his soul. A raging courage that would not admit defeat. Her scream as for the third time he bound her, tearing his newly woken heart in two.*

'A figure of speech,' he said, his lips stiff, his throat tight. 'My choice is made.'

Sighing, his father slumped. 'Very well, then. You may go,' he said, with a petulant shrug of one shoulder. 'Frolic and fill your belly, leaving me to the tender mercies of your bound miscreant. But tell Rumm she's not to set foot anywhere I can see her. And not just while you're away, mind. For as long as she's here. You wanted her, Morgan, you can keep her busy. I don't want Rumm bothered. He's to look after *me*.'

'Yes, my lord.'

'Though how you can stomach the wench,' his father muttered, 'I'll never know.'

Morgan felt his skin crawl with apprehension. If his father knew how his blood burned to hold despised, bound Barl Lindin close to his heart again, feel her hair beneath his cheek again, breathe in her sweet scent as though it were the life-sustaining air, fury would kill him stone dead where he sat.

*So he can never know. And no matter what my heart desires, I can never have her.*

It seemed Barl was right. There was no justice in the world.

'Morgan?' His father thumped the arm of his chair. 'You've got a look on your face that would curdle milk.'

'Hunger,' he said, forcing a smile. 'I must snatch my breakfast from the kitchen before I depart.'

'Where are you going now?'

Surely he was imagining things. His father sounded frightened. 'Not far, my lord . . .' he said, gentling his voice. 'I have a matter to resolve with Sallis Arkley, that I'd like to see put to bed before I attend the Garrick gathering.'

More gnarled than ever, his father's fingers plucked at the blanket covering him, and his gaze, suddenly skittish, darted around the sun-soaked parlour. Rumm had not yet come upstairs to shave him. The bright light glinted on meagre stubble gone tiredly grey.

'I need you here in case you're wanted.'

'And I will be here, once I've spoken with Lord Arkley.'

'For an afternoon, you'll be here,' his father grumbled. 'And then you're leaving me to the silence of servants.'

'Not for two more days, my lord,' he said, pricked with guilt. It was unnerving to hear his father so childishly querulous. Should he mention after all that Maris had also invited Lord Danfey to her house party? Perhaps. But even were his father able to make the journey . . .

*I do not want him there. Bad enough I must sell myself, no better than a Trindeki courtesan. I cannot bear to do it where he is watching.*

'Go and eat,' said his father. 'You looked peaked. Would you have me worrying over your health now?'

Taking up the breakfast tray, Morgan left his father to doze over a favourite book and made his way downstairs. On the second floor landing he glanced through the window and stopped, surprised, to see Barl traipsing toward the poultry coop with an empty pail in her hand. Her halting walk spoke with harsh eloquence of a body still haunted by pain.

For too long he watched her, his father's breakfast tray heavy in his grasp. And watching, found himself hoping that she'd sense his regard and turn. He wanted to see her eyes again. He wanted to feast his gaze on her face. She was a miracle of magic. Though she was bound, he could feel her power in his blood . . . and the empty place beneath his tunic, where for so many years a locket had warmed his cold skin, yearned and burned for her touch.

She didn't feel him, watching her. Instead she let the poultry coop swallow her, and he continued down the stairs.

'My lord, she insisted,' said Rumm, after listening to a trenchant upbraiding. 'And, if you'll permit me to speak bluntly, I see no good coming from cosseting the girl. She is disruptive enough without we give the other servants reason to resent her.'

Morgan shoved the cluttered tray at him. 'You presume to instruct me?'

'No, sir,' said Rumm, very clipped. 'I merely seek to maintain this mansion's orderly atmosphere. Ructions will serve only to distress his lordship.'

And above all else, his lordship must not be distressed.

*As if I need a servant to remind me of that.*

'I have business in Elvado, Rumm,' he said, equally clipped. 'I'll not be absent much above an hour. I trust I can leave you in charge here for such a small space of time?'

Rumm's lips tightened. 'Yes, sir. Of course.'

After changing into a tunic of indigo silk, subtly shot with bronze thread, Morgan incanted himself into the city's eastern quarter. Sallis Arkley was a man of luxurious habit. Every morning, almost without fail, his desiccated lordship indulged himself in the bone-warming heat of a private hot room, part of an exclusive establishment that kept all but the most prestigiously ranked mages at bay.

'Councillor Danfey,' the establishment's gatekeeper murmured. 'Welcome. Your robe . . . your towels . . . would you care for refreshment?'

He took what was proffered. 'Water.'

A wax-sealed bottle joined robe and towels. 'And should you require anything else,' the gatekeeper said, gravely deferential, 'you have but to ask.'

He was interested only if Sallis Arkley were here yet, but had no intention of alerting the man to his business. Instead he withdrew to the inner chambers and took possession of a cubicle, where he stripped himself of his finery and shrugged into the robe. Then he made his way to the communal hot room where Sallis Arkley so enjoyed holding court.

It was empty of all but billows of steam. He was early.

Prepared to wait as long as he had to, unwilling to offer for Parnel Garrick's daughter until this last matter was settled, he loosened his robe, eased himself onto a bench and breathed deep of the heated, damp air. Sweat sprang through his skin within heartbeats. Eyes closed, head resting against the comfortably padded wall, he let the morning's tension seep from his pores.

*If only it were as easy to sweat out Barl Lindin.*

The merest thought of the girl made his pulse race and his muscles contract. Not even the aromatic steam, rich with the healing properties of potent Ranoushi mineral rock, could ease him. Nothing could ease him.

*Nothing save Barl Lindin vanishing from my life. But in binding her I have bound myself, too. It seems I am caught in a snare of my own making.*

And ensnared, he could see no means of escape.

An eddy in the room's clouding vapours as the sealed door opened. Sallis Arkley strode in, trailing four acolyte mages eager to be of use, so that in turn they might boast of it and advance their own causes. Sallis knew that, of course. Which meant either he sought to feed his avaricious appetite for flattery . . . or he was using them, as they thought they used him.

*Most likely it's both. Sallis is devious. Only a fool forgets that.*

The steam billowed again, and Sallis saw him. Only someone who'd sat through a succession of Council meetings with him would see how his confident stride lost its rhythm, just for a moment.

'Danfey.' Because others were watching, Sallis offered a genial smile. At no time could the Council of Mages give a public impression of disharmony. 'It is not usual to see you here.'

Morgan offered his own insincere smile. 'That's true, my lord. But you have a glow of health about you that prompts me to follow your excellent example.'

Eyes glinting, Sallis turned to his companions. 'You would be serving me, my friends, did you retreat a short while to the smaller hot room. As it happens, this chance encounter is most timely. The councillor and I have a privy matter to discuss.'

The acolytes, years younger than Arkley, all of them ranked but not dangerously high, nearly fell over each other to prove their affability. As the door banged shut behind them, Sallis quashed his smile.

'I am not impressed, Morgan.'

And here was another clownish tightrope to walk. Too deferential and Sallis would immediately disbelieve him. Not deferential enough and the man would cut his own throat before granting a hint of consideration.

'My lord, it is unfortunate that I could not find another way to gain your ear,' Morgan said, remaining seated, but lacing his voice with all due deference. 'I'll shortly be absent from Elvado and—'

'The Garrick house party,' Sallis grunted. Without embarrassment he shucked his robe to reveal a decrepit, wrinkled nakedness, and took a seat on the bench opposite. 'Which means you'll be absent another Council meeting.'

A lifetime of circumspection allowed him to mask the surge of anger. *And when will you learn to keep your mouth shut about my doings, Venette?* 'Regrettably, my lord. Yes. But I understand there is nothing of urgency planned for discussion. Should that change, of course I will attend.'

Closing his eyes, Sallis made a show of wafting the billows of pungent steam closer for his inhaling. Even old, even naked and sweating, he posed a threat. The power that slept in him gave off as much heat as the room's heated mineral bricks.

'You know it was a mistake, Morgan, to take that unranked mage into your protection.'

'Not protection. Custody,' he replied, and used his towel to blot stinking sweat from his brow. 'Nor do I hold it a mistake. But we can agree to disagree on that.'

'Can we?' Sallis's eyelids rose, slowly. 'Morgan Danfey, you're a presumptuous man.'

*And you are a man who'd best serve Dorana by dying.*

'Forgive me,' he murmured. 'No presumption was intended.'

With a snap of fingers stripped bare of their customary rings, Sallis caused more water to spill over the steam room's hot mineral bricks. Clouds of heated, healing water swirled between them.

'An unranked mage who knows her place,' he said, when the hissing had died down, 'has a place and a purpose.'

'By which you mean that Barl Lindin has neither?'

Fat drops of sweat rolled indolent down Sallis Arkley's predatory face. 'By which I mean you play a dangerous game. No ranked mage with any pretension to wisdom sports outside the confines of his purview. To do so is to court certain disaster.'

Anger surged again. 'Lord Arkley, I think you are too subtle for me. If you would proffer advice, I beg you, proffer it plainly.'

'Barl Lindin is a menace.' Another smile, this time anything but genial. 'To herself, to Dorana, and to any mage lending her sympathy. I thought you had a greater care for your position. You do know there is precedent for a mage to be dismissed from the Council?'

Morgan let a hint of his own displeasure show. 'My lord, you'd need cause. And since you have none, I see no point to your point. Nor did I disturb you here in order to—'

'Since you have disturbed me, Morgan, I reserve the right to speak as I choose,' said Sallis, his voice cutting. 'And I choose to warn you, not for your sake but for the Council's and the welfare of Dorana. Surrender custody of Barl Lindin, hand her to a judiciary – to be chosen by Brice, I think – and wash your hands of this matter before they are soiled beyond hope.'

His temper, always tightly leashed in the presence of this man, strained – strained – and snapped. He stood, heedless of his gaping robe.

'My lord, it seems to me the presumption here is yours. My conduct is not for your perusal or comment. My conduct in all matters is above reproach. Would that I could claim the same of you.'

Sallis bared his teeth. '*Whelp*. Don't think to cross me. I'll slice your career to ribbons raising less sweat than this hot room. Or did you think your elevation to the Council contained no element of probation within it?'

'You are keen to remind me, yet again, that the mantle of councillor comes with no sinecure!' he retorted. 'Why has it not occurred to you that not even a lord is immune from scrutiny?'

'You *threaten* me?' Sallis laughed. 'Don't think to see me quake with terror, Morgan. You're no more threatening than a moth.'

He stepped closer. 'Threats are for men who have no arrows in their quiver. But I am well armed. You deny my pending incants for no better reason than spite. And if I make a formal complaint, Lord Varen will have to act on it or be held derelict in his duty. That means a formal investigation, and no mage of your affluence and reach can hope to claim his hands are entirely unstained. And if you think Brice Varen will bruise himself for your sake, you are a sadly deluded man . . . *my lord.*'

Sallis glared at him, silenced.

'As I'm sure you already know,' he said softly, 'I attend the Garrick house party to make a change in my status. Should your pettiness damage me in that pursuit, I will have satisfaction. And when I am finished, I won't be the mage who's dismissed from the Council. So my advice to you, Lord Arkley, is this: approve my pending incants, or it will be your career shredded. Not mine.'

# CHAPTER NINETEEN

The mansion felt empty with Morgan Danfey away.

Which was ridiculous, what with Rumm and the other servants underfoot, and his lordship penned on the third floor, reclusive but nonetheless vitally present. Nevertheless . . . it was true.

Rubbing beeswax into the second floor staircase banister, her fingers slick with it, her skin scented like a honeycomb, Barl bit her lip. How was she supposed to wheedle the councillor into unbinding her for good if he wasn't on the estate?

*And I can wheedle him, I know it. All I need is more time.*

But time might well be running out. Because if servant gossip was to be believed, he'd travelled into the countryside to arrange his handfasting with someone called Maris Garrick. Which wouldn't suit her at all. She'd have no hope of wheedling him if he brought a wife back to the estate.

*Of course, the servants could be wrong. Servants frequently are.*

For example, if the councillor's affections were caught by this Maris Garrick, his pulse wouldn't race for Barl Lindin, would it? And she wasn't wrong about that. She knew the effect she often had on men. Barton Haye had been smitten. So had half a dozen other young bucks she'd known in this village, and that one. She wasn't imagining things. Morgan Danfey was not indifferent.

*And neither are you indifferent to him.*

Shocked, she fumbled her beeswax-soaked polishing rag. Where had that thought come from? It was nonsense. *Nonsense.* Morgan Danfey was a councillor, her captor, her prison guard. The enemy.

*And even if he weren't, he's courting this Maris Garrick and ogling me. What a fine, upstanding example of honour that is.*

The man was despicable. So what if he was handsome? What did it matter that when he held her, she felt safe? That was an illusion. She wasn't safe. She never would be, so long as she was bound. Besides . . . he was ranked and she wasn't. There might not be a written law against a ranked mage marrying beneath him, but in Dorana unwritten laws carried the same weight. Sometimes it seemed they carried even more.

*And if I'm clever, I can make sure that for once injustice helps me instead of hurts me. If I'm clever I'll make him feel so guilty for wanting me that he'll do anything to make the discomfort stop.*

Anything like unbind her, or better yet, persuade the Council that she was so repentant it was now safe to send her back to Batava.

Of course, using Morgan Danfey's interest in her against him wasn't precisely honourable. But she couldn't afford to worry about that. She was terrified of dreaming again, of waking the binding fire that slept too lightly beneath her skin. Especially now, with the councillor so far away he'd not be able to rescue her a second time.

*One day I'll see that incant, and all punishing incants like it, declared anathema. Not even the Council of Mages should have so much power.*

With the banisters shining brightly enough to satisfy even fastidious Master Rumm, she trudged to the third floor. There she listened for Lord Danfey stirring behind his closed apartment doors. Not a whisper. She hadn't seen him since the day she'd arrived. Rumm tended to his every need and whim. It was a wonder the master servant wasn't worn to skin and bone with all his running up and down stairs.

Sighing, she started polishing the next stretch of banister. Strictly speaking it was the housemaid's task, only Dilys's mother had taken poorly and Rumm had given the girl leave to go home, because now there was Barl Lindin to take her menial place. But she'd lay a wager that if Remmie were to get sick she'd never even hear of it, let alone be permitted to see him.

She felt her breath catch, imagining. And then it caught again, from temper.

*See what they've done, Remmie? Turned me into a poor, spineless creature leaping at shadows. When they bound my magic, they bound my courage with it. Did they mean to? I think they must have. They know exactly what they've done.*

The pain of that was like a whip's lash, curling round her ribs. She tried to smother her fears with harder polishing, but all that did was remind her of how very far she'd fallen.

Sweeping. Waxing. Dusting nooks and crannies. Washing windows. Wringing out sopping wet clothes and sheets and table linens in the laundry, then lumbering them outside to dry. And of course the poultry coop, which she also had to mind. Rumm was determined to keep her running as hard as he did, from the moment she opened her eyes in the morning until she fell face-first onto her thin, lumpy pillow late at night.

'Idle hands make for mischief,' he'd told her, severe. 'And you, Mage Lindin, are in trouble enough.'

He really was the most disagreeable man.

*From artisan mage to housemaid. If Ibbitha could see me now . . .*

Still, no matter how much she resented all this tedious servant work, she couldn't help admiring the banister's beeswaxed lustre. The elegant staircase, built of rare *anfra*, from Vharne, had been crafted by a mage of real talent. Of particular delight, each landing's newel post was mageworked into a cunningly lifelike beast. Her fingers caressed the antlers on the third floor's magnificent stag.

*Curse it.*

Just when she thought she could endure the misery of her binding, the terrible incompleteness that made her a stranger in her own skin crashed over her yet again. Closing her eyes, she rested her forehead on her outstretched arm.

*I can bear it. I have to. It won't be forever. Not even the Council could be that cruel.*

But what if they were? There was nobody to save her except Morgan Danfey. And if she failed to weaken his resolve . . . if this time next year she was still prisoned in his mansion, still polishing his staircase, still wrapped in the merciless chains of his magic . . .

Breathing hard, she bit her lip and wrestled with the fear. If she wept, if she despaired, it meant the Council had won.

The fragile moment passed. Cautious, she straightened and gave herself a little shake. Then she banished everything but the need to make the next length of banister shine. Oh . . . except she was forbidden to set foot past the third floor landing, wasn't she?

'But Dilys isn't,' she murmured, threading the wax-soaked polishing rag through and through her honey scented fingers. 'And for the moment, I'm her.'

She looked up. The fourth floor was home to Morgan Danfey's apartments. What if she slipped up there now, while she was unwatched? If she could gain entrance to his privy domain she'd be able to catch a glimpse of who he was when he was alone and felt safe. That would be useful. The more she knew of him, the easier it would be to find a way past his defences.

*And I have to break him, before the Council breaks me.*

Holding her breath, she listened again for any hint of Lord Danfey, the slightest creak of stair tread heralding Rumm's approach. Silence. Beyond the third floor landing's intricate stained-glass window, it was a glorious day. Filtered sunlight dappled her emerald and cobalt blue, patchworking the pale yellow linen skirt Remmie had sent her into a stained-glass echo.

*Remmie.*

Imagining her brother's dismay, she pulled a face. 'I have to go up there, Rem. If I don't, just because Morgan Danfey said so, just because I'm afraid, then they really have won.'

If Remmie were here, he'd scold her. Take her elbow and drag her downstairs. But he wasn't. She was alone, and lonely, because the servants didn't dare befriend her and Rumm didn't care. Oh, how she missed her scolding brother. Only now, forbidden to see him, did she realise how much a part of her he'd become since their parents died. Remmie was the light to her shadow, the gentle hand on the string when she was the kite soaring heedless toward the sun.

*I wouldn't be in this mess if I'd listened to him.*

But she hadn't, and she was, and now she had to get herself out of it. Before she changed her mind or Rumm appeared, Barl lightly ran up the stairs.

On the mansion's fourth floor she felt the councillor's absence more keenly than ever. As though he'd imprinted himself upon the unseen air, and now the air was starving for him. Testing the doors to his apartments, she found them both unwarded and unlocked. After one last downward look over the banister, she crept in.

The outer room, his parlour, was ruthlessly neat. Cream walls. Heavy dark red velvet curtains, still drawn. A fireplace, laid with fresh fuel but unlit. Polished *anfra* floors adorned with one enormous green-and-bronze striped Brantish rug. A lamp table with a plain glimlamp on it, still burning. A dark brown leather couch and high-backed armchair, both comfortably battered. Beside the chair a reading table, piled with old, leatherbound books. Tiptoeing, she crossed to them and read their spines, quickly. Magework treatises, all seven, written by mages whose names she'd never heard of. But if she'd studied at the College she had no doubt she'd know them.

Throttling resentment, she looked around the parlour. Neat

and unremarkable, nothing more. If she hadn't known this was the councillor's room she never would have guessed. Perhaps his privy chamber would be more revealing.

Clutching her polishing rag and tin of beeswax, she nudged its unlatched door ajar. Stood on the chamber's threshold, warily listening for the sound of approaching footsteps, and peered through the narrow space between door and jamb.

A sumptuously caparisoned bed, vast and unmade, with a flurry of clothing discarded across its rumpled dark blue counterpane. On the single bedside table an unlit glimlamp, another book and a woman's portrait. She was approaching middle age. His mother, perhaps? There was a resemblance. More dark red velvet curtains, this time flung aside from the windowpanes to spill warm yellow sunlight into the room. Polished floorboards and rich rugs. Against one wall a long, low dresser scattered with papers, ink pots, used quills, an ebony and ivory comb and its matching brush . . . and a man's hair clasp, beautifully enamelled in black and gold.

Staring at it, Barl felt her fingers twitch. Mages imbued their personal possessions with an imprint of their essence, their power. If she had Morgan Danfey's hair clasp, perhaps it could give her some insight into the man. Only . . . if she were caught, the consequences would be dire. They'd call it stealing. They'd label her a thief.

*But I have to risk it. I need every advantage I can find.*

So she darted into the councillor's privy chamber, whisked the hair clasp into her skirt pocket, and fled.

Her heart was beating so hard and fast she had to stop partway down the staircase and sag against the banister until she'd breathed herself calm again. Then she looked and listened down the stairs. Silence, still. A miracle of sorts. Lord Danfey must be sleeping. And perhaps Rumm had gone somewhere on an errand. Prompted by the notion, she looked back up to the fourth floor.

Somewhere above her, beneath the mansion's roof, was Morgan Danfey's attic workroom, where he pursued his mysterious magework. She needed to see it. If she was going to learn the man, what better place to study him?

Motionless as a doe in a thicket when the hounds sniff the air, she waited. Listened. The silence persisted. Not even a servant's drabbling broke the hush. This might be her only chance.

*And if I don't take it, I know I'll be sorry.*

She tucked the tin of beeswax and the polishing rag in a shadowed corner of the third landing, then hurried back up the stairs. The councillor's hair clasp bounced heavy in her pocket. Past the fourth floor landing the stair treads quickly narrowed, plunging into darkness without the smallest flicker of glimfire to light the way.

The landing at the top of the last stair-flight was a miserly disc. Pausing, she listened again then, reassured, continued along the dark corridor. The uncarpeted wooden floor creaked, loud as a purloined shopkeeper's shriek. She paused again, heart lambasting her ribs . . . but no, she was safe. Only the corridor was so gloomy she could hardly make out the wall right beside her, never mind the door that must lie at its end.

Tentative, she walked on, trailing her fingertips at waist height along the old, rustling wallpaper. She felt bumps and blisters, little tears, a few gaps. The plaster beneath the paper was old and dry. Dusty. And then she stopped, abruptly, because in the darkness before her she could feel the attic door, a muffled whisper of power like a faint breeze against her skin. It was warded, which meant she couldn't get into the workroom beyond.

Unbidden, her fingers crept into her pocket to close around Morgan Danfey's enamelled hair clasp. Another muffled whisper, the echo of an echo. Caught between the soundings she closed her eyes and felt his magic . . . even though she wasn't meant to feel anything at all.

*And what does that mean? Why can I feel it? Why can I feel him when his binding won't let me feel anyone or anything else?*

She didn't know. Wasn't even sure the *why* mattered. There might be a way she could use it to her advantage. *That* was what mattered.

Cautious, she reached out her hand, brushed her fingertips against timber – and a crackle of glimfire skittered spider-like in warning. With a startled gasp she leapt back, dazzled by the glimpse of scarred, ancient wood and an age-mellowed brass handle. Raging through her, a chaos of impressions, snatches of magework, the intricate threads of the ward. Beneath her skin the binding shivered, a faint promise of pain.

Spinning round, she bolted.

Returned to the third floor landing, she scrabbled for the beeswax and rag. Safety and sanity lay in the humdrum task of polishing.

Rumm found her there scant minutes later.

'Mage Lindin,' he said, weighed down by a laden tea tray and halting a few stair-treads below her. 'You are slow in your task. Finish it, quickly. Have you forgotten the library must also be tended?'

'No, Master Rumm,' Barl murmured, glancing up, terrified he'd hear how breathless she was, see the guilty flush in her cheeks, and demand that she explain herself forthwith.

But his gaze was pinned sideways to Lord Danfey's closed doors. Behind his frown, the master servant was worried.

'Be sure you're gone when I come out again,' he said, not looking at her. 'Or I'll have to make a dilatory report of you to Councillor Danfey upon his return.'

She hastily burnished the already-waxed newel post. 'Yes, Master Rumm. I'm sorry, Master Rumm.'

Not listening, either, he continued to the closed apartment doors and adroitly let himself in without dropping his lordship's tea and cakes.

As the door clicked shut, Barl thumped her damp forehead to the carved timber.

*Oh, Remmie. That was a near one.*

Mouth dry, palms damp, she wrapped the waxy rag round the tin then made her way on shaking legs down the staircase. In her blood, on her skin, she could still feel the snap and sizzle of Morgan Danfey's magic. What a mercy he'd not barred entry to his workroom with a killing ward. Some mages did. Sometimes there were . . . accidents. Perhaps she should think twice before further meddling, just in case.

Thinking that, she almost missed her footing, nearly tumbled haggy-scaggy down the last few stairs.

*What am I, a coward? If I falter now, if I let danger deter me, then in a few days or a week I'll wake to find myself no better than Dilys the housemaid, magickless and meek.*

Sickened by her moment of weakness, she fetched a duster from the cleaning cupboard, to do sister duty with the beeswax, then hurried to the mansion's ground floor library. This would be first time she was permitted inside.

'*Oh,*' she breathed, in the doorway, staring. '*Oh, Remmie.*'

Reverent as any Brantish priest on a pilgrimage, Barl eased the door closed behind her and stepped further into the room. A well-worn leather reading chair, twin to the chair in Morgan Danfey's privy parlour. Two large reading tables. Two glimlamps, unlit. There was only one window, framed in heavy velvet drapes of dark blue. They were drawn back to let the day spill nowhere but over the polished parquetry.

And *books.*

Shelf after shelf of them, filling all the wall space between the gleaming *anfra* floor and the lofty, corniced ceiling. Leatherbound and loose-leaf, some brass-spined, some plain, stitched and riveted, slender and fat, ancient and youthful. Whispers and chuckles and shouts of precious, wonderful knowledge. Barl felt herself smile for the first time since arriving in Elvado. A proper smile, a *genuine* smile, joy rising within her like sugar sap in the spring. In all her life she'd never seen so many books. She felt like a child again, when all the world was new.

'Oh, Remmie,' she sighed. 'I wish you were here. You'd *love* this library.'

She was meant to be dusting and polishing, and she would, but first . . .

Wandering along the shelves, she kissed the books with her fingertips and feasted her avid gaze on their titles. *Ruminations upon the Philosophy of Magework. Herbal Decoctions. Bilramin's Treatise on Wardings. A Pother's Guide to Elementary Healing. Practical Translocations. The Student's Handbook. Purging Antithetical Energies. Tostig's History of the Sigil.*

The desire to tug one of them free of its brethren and immerse herself in the words had her shivering as hard as Morgan Danfey's attic ward. Even if she couldn't put the words into practice, just to *pretend,* for a moment, that she was still a proper mage . . . She'd denied herself that pleasure in his privy chamber, but she had the time now. She could afford to briefly indulge.

Except what if simply reading about incants triggered her binding?

Scalding resentment stole her sight. On a deep, shuddering breath she looked around at the books.

'One day I will read you,' she murmured. 'One day all of your secrets will belong to me.'

And with the promise made, she started to dust.

After dusting and beeswaxing the library and snatching her servant's lunch – bread, cheese and pickles, how exciting – there were more chores in the kitchen. Carrots and potatoes to peel, pots to scrub. The roasting pit needed emptying of stinking, fatty ash and gobbets of charred meat and splintered bone. She nearly lost her bread, cheese and pickles over that. Once Verrick had done with gutting wild rabbit fresh-caught in the woodland she took the discarded heads and limbs and viscera out to the mansion's kennels so Yan, the kennel man, could boil them up for the councillor's hounds. He took the stripped, bloody pelts too, to turn into winter gloves. Then she scrubbed the kitchen bench from red back to white, pretending not to see how Verrick was delighted to be spared the bloody task.

Morgan Danfey's library seemed an entire world away.

Last task of all, she inspected the poultry coop again. Hens, it seemed, had a habit of dropping eggs wherever and whenever they felt like . . . and of dropping dead without the courtesy of a warning first thing in the day.

She didn't know whether to be relieved or dismayed that the stink of all those chickens didn't seem so bad any more.

Chores completed, her servant's supper of mutton, potato and carrot eaten in solitary silence, she retreated to her cupboard of a room to lose herself in the one book Remmie had managed to squeeze in amongst her clothes. Not a magework book, of course. Just a silly story about a brave Feenish warrior queen fighting to regain her lost throne. Doubtless it was all a nonsense, nothing to do with Feenish history. Since Dorana's mages rarely travelled to other lands, the writer of this tale had most likely relied on wild imagination leavened with generous helpings of trader gossip. It didn't matter. It was only a story, and it helped to pass the time.

But as she read, her fingers strayed to Morgan Danfey's enamelled hair clasp, slipped for safety under her pillow. Letting the book fall open on her chest, she closed her eyes and listened for the councillor's echoes. Waited, her mouth dry, for the waking of his binding. To her great relief the cruel incant stayed asleep . . . even as she felt her bound mage-sense warm to the memory of his magic, trapped within his black and gold trinket.

Subtle, it was, and intricate . . . yet at the same time bold. The councillor painted his power in wide brush strokes, and with delicate finesse. Again she was assailed by that odd sense of the familiar, with the conviction she wasn't encountering anything new, only meeting an old friend. She'd never felt like this before. There was no explaining the mystery. All she knew for certain was it left her feeling . . . less alone.

She fell asleep almost smiling, with the clasp held loosely in her fingers and the oil lamp still burning . . .

. . . and woke out of wild magework dreaming into darkness, consumed by incandescent flame.

The pain was just as bad the second time.

Knowing what it was, Barl managed not to panic. Instead she buried her face in her pillow, sank her teeth into its meagre depths and screamed out her torment as her fingers clutched the sides of her mattress to breaking point.

She didn't call for someone to help her. Lord Danfey was the only mage in the mansion, and he'd never help her. Most likely he'd laugh. Besides, she needed to know how long the binding would punish her and what state she'd be in when the punishment ended. Remaining ignorant was pointless. Only knowledge would set her free.

But the price of gaining that knowledge . . .

Though it felt unending, in truth the pain passed quite swiftly. More swiftly than before, at least, since she'd not set off the Danfey estate's border wards. With one final, vicious stab the binding released her. Whimpering, Barl unclenched her fingers, spat out her horrible mouthful of pillow and, muscle by aching muscle, rolled onto her back. Her ragged breathing filled the small cupboard room. Tears slicked her icy face and her raw throat burned with the memory of screams. She couldn't even comfort herself with a little light. It seemed the oil in the lamp had burned itself up while she slept.

She'd not dreamed of clock-making this time. Instead she'd found herself in the cottage garden with Remmie, down by the duck pond. Together they'd created fantastical, brilliant glimfire constellations for his class. Had played with the magic, the way they'd played when they were children. Laughing. Teasing. No fear. No suffering. Only the pure joy of creation, the splendour of power pouring through them like wine.

For one magical moment, she'd thought the dream was real. Then the binding had woken . . . and plunged her into pain.

Staring at the darkness, she felt her skin crawl. The thought of falling back to sleep was a gibbering fear. But how was she supposed to stay awake for as long as she was kept a prisoner in this place?

'I can't do it, Remmie,' she whispered, too tired now to fight the rising despair. 'I can't endure this torment over and over without end. Because it won't end, I know it. How am I meant to stop dreaming? Does the Council expect me to posset myself into a drooling, mindless stupor?'

310

She didn't know the councillors well enough to be sure, but she thought they might. And she thought Morgan Danfey might stay silent to protect himself from their wrath.

Or perhaps the binding would finish her. If she was kept trammelled long enough, perhaps Morgan Danfey's incant would change her for good. Kill her power, steal her hard-won knowledge, truly make of her another Dilys. And if that were so, there'd be no more fabulous clocks or constellations, no chance to explore the length and breadth of her talent, to become the greatest artisan mage Dorana had ever seen.

Choking, she pressed cold hands to her face as shudder after shudder convulsed through her, the binding's parting slap at a naughty, disobedient child.

*I can't let that happen. I'm no-one, I'm nothing, if I'm not a mage.*

At last the shudders faded. As she dragged her sheet and blanket back up to her shoulders, she heard something clatter to the floor. Morgan Danfey's hair clasp. When her fingers closed around the smooth, cool enamel she gasped, feeling his power call once again to hers.

Call without stirring his binding from sleep.

What was going on? She felt his power in the hair clasp. She'd felt his unbinding incant, seen its sigils, when by rights she should have been numb to it, and blind. Before his ward overcame her she'd felt the shape of that, too. It had to mean something. Something out of the ordinary.

*All right. I can feel Morgan Danfey's magework. What else can I do?*

She could close her eyes. She could breathe out despair. She could open herself to his magic . . . and see what happened next.

The hair clasp felt warm and comfortable against her skin. More than comfortable. *Comforting.* Again the conviction that she wasn't alone. Letting her puzzled mind drift, deliberately not thinking about what *that* might mean, she summoned from memory the shape and sound of the unbinding incant. Heard its

311

sharp syllables. Saw its sigils burn the air. Waited and waited for the binding to wake.

But it didn't.

'Oh, Remmie,' she murmured. 'This is so strange. I'm mad. I must be. But I have to find out.'

She wasn't brave enough to risk speaking the incant's syllables aloud. But she uncrooked one finger . . . and traced its first sigil in the dark. In her tight grasp, the gold and black hair clasp shivered. Caught tight in its binding, her mage-sense shivered in reply. In the air, a flash of crimson. A sigil, that briefly burned then died out.

'It's not possible,' she said, and started at the sound of her own voice. 'It *can't* be. Either I'm bound or I'm not.'

But it seemed she was both, which made no sense at all.

*So does this mean I have a chance to override Morgan Danfey's binding?*

It didn't seem likely. Nor did it seem wise. If somehow, inexplicably, she managed to unbind his binding, what then? How would she explain it when the councillor returned?

*Perhaps I could claim the incant unravelled itself in the midst of my suffering. If I made him feel guilty enough, he might not look too closely at the lie.*

Oh, she was mad to even think of it. Undo Morgan Danfey's magework?

*I can't. How can I? I'm not a tapestry he's stitched, that I can unstitch like a seamstress. Magework has rules. I'm bound. And Morgan Danfey is a powerful mage.*

The most powerful she'd ever met. And what was she?

*Desperate.*

Tapestry. Perhaps that was the key. She wasn't Barl Lindin, a flesh-and-blood woman, she was Barl Lindin's embroidered recreation. Embroidered women weren't afraid. They didn't miss their brothers, or feel their bellies churn because they were weighed down by chains of magic. Chains with barbs in them, that bit, vicious as any hunting hound.

*If I'm a tapestry woman, perhaps the binding won't wake.*

312

A forlorn hope, surely. But it was the only hope she had.

Her breathing unsteady, Barl wriggled until she lay flat on her back, her spine taut as a drawn bowstring. In her fisted hand she felt the hair clasp, warm and somehow alive.

Then, without warning, she was deathly afraid. Only once before had she ever felt this kind of fear. The day her parents died. When she'd realised that aside from Remmie she was alone. For a moment, just a moment, she'd stared into a pitch black abyss. The warm and familiar stolen, her whole world turned to ice. But then Remmie had fallen to pieces, grieving, and there'd been no time for fear or despair. He'd needed her to be strong, so she was strong. And that was that.

*I'm still strong. I am. The binding hasn't ruined me quite yet.*

To prove it, she closed her eyes and went looking for the way to break Morgan Danfey's magework.

*She finds herself in the darkness, in a space of silence between heartbeats. Like thistledown she floats through herself. Like a breeze she hears herself sigh. With her closed eyes opened inwards she sees the binding laid upon her. She sees Morgan Danfey's fingerprints on the needle that against her will has stitched her tight and bound her to pain. There are gold threads wrapped around her. They are beautiful. Like him. In the silence she feels his power. She sees his sigils brightly burning. They are the knots that keep her bound. Magelore states, unequivocal, that the mage who utters the binding incant must be the mage who breaks it. But in this dark, silent place she knows that rule does not rule her. In this place, which is her deepest self, she can unbind his binding, needing neither his help . . . nor his permission. And she wants to. Oh, she wants to. So she becomes the seamstress and she unpicks his golden thread. Stitch by stitch she undoes him until the last stitch is undone. And then lights the darkness with his sigils . . . and sets herself free.*

Was she drowning? She was drowning. There wasn't enough air to breathe. Arms thrashing, lungs heaving, Barl battered her way back to the ugly, cramped cupboard Rumm had shoved her in, like a broom. She dropped the hair clasp, kicked the blanket away, thrust the pillow aside then tumbled half off her uncomfortable pallet, banging knees and elbows in the lightless room.

Without thinking, she summoned glimfire . . . and it chased away the dark.

'Oh, Remmie,' she said, her voice hoarse. 'Remmie . . . what have I done?'

The impossible, it seemed.

Trembling, she called more glimfire in little glowing balls, and set them to dancing just to prove that she could. Pretending magic could only be amusing and beautiful and had never been used against her.

But the pretence wouldn't hold.

Ball by ball she blew on the glimfire until her cramped cupboard of a room plunged back into darkness. In darkness she curled up under her blanket, breathing softly, feeling like herself again. She'd not realised how deeply *altered* she'd been until the ugly alteration was removed.

*Until I removed it. I did it. Me.*

She shouldn't have been able to. Tampering with Morgan Danfey's binding should have left her wracked with pain. Instead, she felt reborn. *No.* Not reborn. Remade. Become a new Barl Lindin, forged in the fires of injustice. The Council's mages in their meanness, in their desire to keep all the best things for themselves and their ranked brethren, had given power to a voice that for too long was kept silent. But she'd stay silent no longer. Someone had to speak for the unranked mages of Dorana.

*I wonder . . . I wonder . . . what else can I do?*

# CHAPTER TWENTY

'Morgan! Morgan, are you in here?'
Finding solace in shadow, Morgan closed his eyes.
*Maris.* Could she not give him even five minutes of peace? Could he not sit in this sadly inadequate Garrick library, far from the muttering intrigues of her father, her brother, her cousins and the family's simpering friends, and nurse a too-early snifter of second-rate brandy without she must pursue him like a cat pouncing a hobbled mouse?

'Morgan?'

No, it seemed she could not.

'Well, *there* you are!' said Maris, finding him, and pressed her hands to her hips as though she meant to scold.

She'd again forsaken her fitted silks and instead wore yet another of her favoured loose, striped cotton gowns which were fashioned after the attire of Ranoushi plainswomen. Quite eccentric. But Venette had assured him a great many of Dorana's young mages were these days adopting fashions with quaint foreign influences. Hadn't he noticed them parading their Trindeki and Manemlin finery through Elvado? Coloured glass and crystal beading, exotic patterns embroidered in silver thread, even the startling hint of feathers in their hair?

No. He hadn't. He had better things to do than ogle strangers in the streets. But if such clothes amused Maris, he'd make no objection . . . at least, not before they were wed. Afterwards he wouldn't tolerate her eccentricity.

*Luzena would never have dressed in such garb.*

Maris was frowning. 'Morgan?'

If he could smile at Sallis Arkley, it was in him to smile at her. 'Forgive me. I was adrift in my thoughts.'

Her lips pouted. 'Oh.'

On arriving at the Garrick estate, knowing he'd leave it bound to this young woman, he'd sworn he'd find a way to make his sacrifice at least *bearable*. And now here was his soon-to-be betrothed, garish and at the same time alluring in her outrageous, faddish costume. The deep rose and grass green hues of the cotton gown suited her gilded prettiness, and the thin fabric clung without fear to her curves. He could see how her long legs flowed into a smooth glide of hip, moulded into a narrow waist, a slender rib cage. How her modestly revealed breasts rose and fell with her breathing.

Desire stirred.

'Morgan?' Maris glanced at the open library door. A wave of her hand closed it. 'My dear, was there something you wanted?'

What he truly wanted he could never have. But did that mean he must live the rest of his days deprived?

He put the dreadful brandy on the small table beside him, and held out his hand to the woman he did not wish to marry. 'I want many things, Maris.'

'As do I,' she said, and went to him. 'Do you suppose you and I might want the same things?'

'Some of the same things.' He laced his fingers with hers and tugged until she tumbled into his lap. 'But what they might be, I think we are yet to discover.'

If his boldness alarmed her, she hid it well behind her smile. With the tips of her fingers she traced a line of fire from his brow to his chin. And then she touched his lips with hers, lightly, the teasing promise of a kiss.

'Do I shock you?' she murmured, her eyes half-lidded and heavy with a rising desire of her own. 'Will you discard me as a wanton if I tell you I've longed to do that since the night of Venette's party?'

*Will you discard me as a wanton?*

When it came to matters of the flesh, there were rules for ranked mages. Bloodlines were jealously guarded, casual couplings strictly discouraged. The power of magic extended only so far. Accidents still happened, despite all the best precautions. Some mages tempted fate, but he doubted Maris was one of them. Luzena had been as careful, even though they were handfasted. Respecting her, loving her, he'd held himself restrained and endured nightly torments, recalling her kisses and caresses that went so far . . . and no further. Since her death, restraint had become a habit . . . but now self-control chafed.

'If feeling desire is wanton, Maris, then must I stand condemned.'

With a shuddering sigh she pressed his hand to her breast. 'I've longed for this, too, Morgan. I want to feel your skin naked against mine. When do you intend to speak with my father?'

This was his fourth day on the Garrick estate. The house party's invitation was for five. 'Tomorrow,' he said, as her heartbeat thudded through his damp palm, his hot blood.

'Not today?' She kissed him, more deeply this time. 'Morgan, why not today?'

*Because today I wish to savour as my last day of freedom.*

He took his hand from her breast. 'Now you sound wanton.' Standing, he tipped her without courtesy from his lap. 'Conduct yourself with more decorum, Maris. As the future Lady Danfey it's the least you can do.'

Her eyes furious, Maris scrambled to her feet. 'Fie, sir! I'm not some unranked doxy to be tossed aside on your whim. I am a Garrick, and this is my future as well as yours. I've a right to know what you'll make of it, and when.'

The only rights she had were the rights he decided to grant her. She was too sure of herself, puffed up in the conceit of her so-called superior ranking. Let her think to browbeat him with that and he would never have a moment's peace.

'Maris, understand this about me,' he said, desire cooling. 'I am—'

They both turned as the library door pushed open. 'Maris? Are you in here?'

Venette. Her carefully plucked eyebrows rose, seeing them. 'Maris, dear, your mother's on the fret for you. Perhaps you ought to see what she wants.'

'Of course, Venette,' said Maris, but instead of instantly withdrawing, she shifted her gaze back to him. 'You think to scold, sir, so I am meek and biddable. But would you breed a son from a woman with blood like watered milk?'

He could feel Venette's intent stare, unwelcome, and made sure not to look at her. 'No.'

Maris smiled. Not sultry now, no banked desire, only anger and pride. 'No. So perhaps you should not be so swift in your temper. This will be a marriage of equals, Morgan, or no marriage at all.'

'I hope,' said Venette, watching Maris leave, 'that you provoke her because you're bored, and for no other reason.'

'I don't provoke her at all,' he said, reaching for his glass of inferior brandy. 'She provokes me.'

'Oh!' Venette laughed. 'Well, then. Good. You sound married already.'

His mood was just sour enough that he could easily start a quarrel with her. Since that wouldn't be wise, he drank the rest of the brandy.

'I know that look, Venette. Say what you came to say and be done.'

While she'd never stoop to striped cotton, Venette had relaxed her standards far enough to wear a luscious silk daffa, patterned after the royal robe favoured by the Iringan court. He had to admit it became her. The abundant fabric rustled richly as she avoided answering him by turning to the nearest bookshelf and inspecting its unexciting contents.

'Venette—'

Her glance was full of censure. 'You shouldn't have threatened Sallis Arkley, Morgan. That was foolish of you. And very clumsy.'

Glass met side table with a crack as he set down the emptied brandy snifter. 'That's not your concern.'

'Don't be stupid,' she snapped, glaring. 'You're my friend.'

'I'm more than happy to relieve you of the burden.'

'And at times like this I'd be more than happy to be relieved! But even were we sworn enemies, I'd still be involved.'

He almost wished he'd never constructed those incants. 'I'm sorry if my personal business interferes with your house party frivolities, Venette.'

She slapped the bookshelf. 'I give you fair warning, Morgan. Continue to treat Sallis like an underling and he will interfere with your Council frivolities! Do you imagine he's toothless, simply because he's old?'

'I imagine it's been too long since someone stood up to his bullying.'

'And you're the mage to make the difference? Oh, Morgan. While I must deplore your lack of tact, I suppose I must also admire your nerve.'

'You're too gracious,' he said, with a mocking bow. 'And how is it you know what transpired between me and Sallis?'

'Parnel told me, just now.'

'And how would Lord Garrick know?'

'Oh, how do you think?' Venette demanded. 'Just because you and Greve hold yourselves aloof, do you suppose the rest of us do? Did you honestly think Sallis wouldn't punish you for that challenge?'

'By attempting to ruin my standing with Maris's father?'

'By any means he can lay hand to! Morgan—' With an effort, Venette calmed herself. 'You really must learn patience. Sallis isn't—'

He lifted his hand. 'Enough, Venette. I don't wish to discuss Sallis Arkley.'

319

'Obviously,' she retorted. 'For if you did, you'd have asked my advice about bearding him in his den.'

'What need of that, my lady, when I already know what you'd advise?'

Giving him another censorious look, she crossed to his abandoned armchair, picked up the emptied brandy glass, sniffed, then grimaced.

'Horrible. I should've warned you to bring a bottle of your own.'

'It would've been the friendly thing to do.'

'Yes,' said Venette after a moment, considering him. 'But these days it's hard to know with you, Morgan, whether friendship will earn a smile or a snarl.'

His turn to walk to a bookshelf and pretend interest in the tired books it contained. 'Don't be foolish. Friends can be friends without they endlessly agree.' He resisted the urge to look at her. 'So. Did you spring to my defence with Parnel?'

'You need to ask?'

'Thank you. It's appreciated.'

But also unnecessary. The Garricks might outrank the Danfeys, but he was a councillor . . . and because of that would forever hold the upper hand.

Venette put down the empty glass. 'You intend to proceed, then? You've not changed your mind?'

If only he could. 'I'm here, aren't I? I'm rehearsing the speech I must make to Maris's lordly father. And when I leave this estate, I'll leave it as a handfasted man.'

Arms folded, she frowned. 'Yes. But will you leave it as a man in love?'

In love? With Maris Garrick? 'She stirs me.'

'Lust is not love, Morgan. Moreover, it is fleeting.'

He turned. 'I have always been a mage before I was a man. Ask me about my magework. I'll show you passion then.'

Another silence, as she looked at him. 'I warned you before, my dear. I'll warn you again. Do not make me regret that I championed you to Maris.'

'She'll have no complaint of me, Venette. I know my duty and the kindness owed to a young girl.'

'Kindness?' Her fingers tightened, as though she longed to slap him. 'When a woman gives herself to a man she is owed a great deal more than *kindness*.'

'Maris Garrick will have all I have to offer. Neither you nor she can ask or expect more than that.'

Sighing, Venette relaxed her fingers. Crossed the distance between them and laid her palm to his cheek. 'Of course we can. What you have and what you offer aren't always the same thing. Did you think we don't know it?'

'How should I know what women know?'

She let her hand fall to her side. 'You realise, of course, that once you've settled terms with Lord Garrick, you must find somewhere else for Mage Lindin to serve her penance.'

*Barl.* He felt his blood leap, swiftly heating. Felt pleasure, and pain. Since leaving home he'd managed to banish all thought of his bound prisoner . . . but with one mention of her name she was summoned instantly to mind. No matter who she was, what she'd done, how disastrous his feelings, those feelings, it seemed, were not to be denied.

With an effort he kept his confusion secret from Venette. Showed her in its place a cool, familiar haughtiness. 'Indeed. Must I?'

'With Greve so uncertain, you won't delay your marriage. You can't think to take Maris home with that dangerously misguided mage still under your roof!'

'Refresh my memory, Venette,' he said, insincerely pleasant. 'When exactly was it I invited you to pass judgement on me?'

Hissing with frustration, Venette took a step back. 'Don't be a fool, Morgan. There are limits.'

'To everything, I know,' he said. 'And you should know, Venette, that you have just found mine.'

Brushing past her, ignoring her exclamation of regret, he left her adrift in the library. With no thought but the need for solitude he turned left along the corridor, intending to seek it in the

321

Garrick mansion's formal gardens – but instead found himself roughly tugged into a closet.

Maris.

'Why do you let her rail at you like that?' the girl demanded, shoving the door shut and calling a teardrop of glimfire to show him her face. 'Venette might mean well, but she's insufferable. I swear she thinks she knows what's best for the whole world.'

In the soft light Maris was luminous, her eyes wide and full of fire. She slid her palms beneath his correct velvet tunic, pressing them hard to his silk-clad chest. Her scent was intoxicating. His head swam, his vision blurred. It had been a long time since he'd let himself feel passion.

'She rails at me over you,' he said, almost whispering. 'She says I must wed you before some other mage notices your charms and attempts to steal you from me. Do you say she's mistaken?'

Maris's fingers moved, lightly caressing. 'Who is Mage Lindin?'

'You were listening?' He pulled back. 'That was impertinent.'

'I didn't hear much,' she said quickly. 'I swear it. Morgan, who is she?'

'Barl Lindin? No-one,' he said . . . and felt his breath catch at the betrayal. Felt a helpless rage that it should strike him as betrayal. Barl Lindin *was* no-one and for the sake of everything he valued she had to *remain* no-one.

'She must be someone,' said Maris. 'Or why would Venette care? What has she done that she should be punished at your estate?'

'Maris, it's Council business. I can't—'

Her lips were sweet, her breath sweeter. She kissed him with ardour, stirring heat to raging flames. Now her breasts pressed against him as her hands slid around his ribcage, tugging them heart to drubbing heart.

'When we are wed,' she breathed, 'we'll be as one. And then you'll tell me everything, Morgan.'

Shuddering, he gasped as her lips found the wild pulse beating at the base of his throat. He raised his hands to push her away, to end this madness, but instead they slid down her back to her cotton-clad buttocks. She laughed as he clutched her, laughed again as he pulled her hard to him.

'I'm not afraid, Morgan. If you want me now, take me. With you I *am* wanton. I'd be no other way!'

The blood was thundering in his ears, lust like a wildfire burning away restraint. Maris was grinding her hips against him, her fingers kneading his buttocks, little mewling cries escaping her lips. The closet's shelves, laden with tablecloths and napkins, tins of polish, spare heavy silver candlesticks and other mansion oddments, pressed across his shoulderblades and into the curve of his lower back. Somehow the pain of it only added to his pleasure. Still mewling, close to sobbing, Maris shifted herself, snatched one of his hands from her clenched buttocks and fumbled his fingers between her legs. He could feel the heat of her through the thin, striped cotton of her dress.

'Morgan,' she groaned, her eyes slitted. 'I'm unbreached, but I know enough to know where I want you to touch me.'

He'd kept himself from Luzena, but before her he'd tempted fate with eager young women. Not many. He'd learned quite young to keep his passions in check. But before the lesson had sunk in he'd played the rutting stallion. He knew what to do. The question was, should he do it?

*If I heed her, there can be no going back. I can't use her and discard her. This act will make me hers.*

Which would be for the best, surely.

Her face flushed, her breathing stormy, Maris unlaced her bodice and bared her breasts for his taking. Crushing her pale flesh in his hands, he stared into her glazed eyes.

'You're certain, Maris? You want this?'

'More than anything,' she said, her voice husky. 'Now, Morgan. *Hurry.*'

He nodded. 'Then ward the door.'

On a gasp she sealed them safely into the closet. There was no time to strip naked, even if it were wise . . . which for certain it was not. Between them they fumbled themselves naked enough to achieve their mating, and when he was sure she could take him in he wrapped her legs about his waist and breached her, and after that did his best to make sure she wasn't sorry. His own release followed soon after hers, years of drought doused in a blinding flood of pleasure.

'Oh . . . oh, Morgan . . .' Sighing, content to have him bear her full weight, Maris dropped her head to his shoulder. 'I've been dreaming of that ever since the night we met. I knew it would be wonderful. No, *glorious*.'

As cold, of a sudden, as he'd been hot moments before, sickened to retching by what he'd just done, Morgan eased apart their sated bodies and set Maris on her feet.

'We must put ourselves to rights. Lace your bodice and smooth your hair.'

'Morgan?' Sounding hurt, she touched her fingers to his face. 'Are you *angry*?'

He had no idea. He felt so much it was the same as feeling nothing. 'Of course not.'

'Then I hope you don't feel guilty,' she said, her voice more sharp than cajoling. 'We're to be handfast. We took our first pleasure a little early. There's no shame in that.'

If he offended her, if he caused her even a moment of doubt, she could cry rape and see him ruined. So he kissed her swollen lips.

'No guilt, Maris. No shame, or regret. I am simply lost for words.'

And that was not a lie.

'Morgan . . .' Smiling now, Maris kissed him. Not ravenous this time, but sweet. Almost chaste. The taste of her did nothing to ease the gripe in his guts. 'We're well suited, you and I. It's good to know such things. And when we can take our pleasure in a bed, and not a closet, can't you imagine how it will be?' Eyes glinting, she nipped his bottom lip with her teeth. '*Exquisite*.'

Even as she stirred him anew, he felt himself recoil. There was something predatory in her passion, an unwelcome greed in the way she danced her fingers over his groin. As though he were her possession. As though he'd just sold himself to her.

'We shouldn't linger, Maris,' he said, capturing her hand in his. 'If it's safe to go, you should go. I'll follow discreetly.'

She pressed her ear to the closet door, waited, then unwarded it and slipped out, extinguishing the glimfire she'd conjured with a careless finger-snap. Plunged into darkness, he let himself sag against the nearest shelf. The lingering remnants of pleasure sparked in his cooling blood, defying his revulsion at such a brute and hasty coupling.

*I'm no better than a Feenish shuckster, a cock-boy, spilling seed for coin with a stranger in a stinking alley, or a ditch.*

He couldn't even find comfort in knowing he'd done it for his father. For the Danfey name, the future and honour of his house.

*Can a man purchase honour by selling his own? I don't think he can. I think –*

But it was best that he didn't think. That way lay despair. So he checked to see if the corridor beyond the closet was empty, then stepped into its deserted silence as though he'd not a care in the world.

The house partyers and their hosts collected in the mansion's conservatory for luncheon. Of the guests, Venette and her husband Orwin were the only mages Morgan knew or cared to know. Maris's three cousins didn't interest him, they were young and flighty, irrelevant to his purpose. As for the other two couples enjoying the Garricks' hospitality, they were provincial mages with sufficient rank to be acceptable, but not enough mage-working talent to have made themselves known in Elvado. Which meant Venette had . . . exaggerated . . . to get him here. Another mark against her.

For this meal, Lord Garrick's son Ehrig was playing the jovial host. Ehrig's wife, quiet and colourless for all she was a strong enough mage, tended to their three children and left the talking to him. Apparently he'd married a copy of his mother.

'Wine, Councillor?' Ehrig said, lifting a bottle.

He'd happily dive into a vat of the stuff. Though she was demurely seated beside her mother at the other end of the table, he could feel the gloating heat in Maris's glances. She'd changed out of her cotton dress into silk tunic and leggings for the afternoon's lawn games. She looked the perfect model of a gentle, well-behaved and unbreached ranked family daughter.

Remembering her lush body, her urgent, pleasured whispers, the way she'd abandoned herself to him and screamed her violent climax into his mouth, he felt a wave of heat scorch through his blood.

'Morgan?' Seated at his left hand, Venette touched his wrist. 'Are you well?'

'Of course,' he said, hiding curtness inside a smile. *Be quiet, Venette. You've meddled more than enough.* 'A trifle weary, perhaps. No doubt due to all the fresh country air.'

Finished pouring icewine for his parents' guests, Ehrig laughed. 'Are you certain? Your estate's in the country, isn't it, Morgan?'

He'd not given Ehrig permission to use his given name. Maris's horse-breeding brother had simply assumed the right, adopting a presumptuous demeanour within five minutes of their meeting. And what could he say against it? Both he and the Garricks knew why he had come. To insist that he should be addressed otherwise was out of the question.

So he endured.

'After a fashion, Ehrig,' he said, shrugging. 'But the Danfey estate lies in sight of Elvado. Here we are surrounded by vast tracts of—' *Nothing.* 'Delightful farmland. I do promise you, there's a difference.'

'Of course there's a difference!' said Ehrig's mother, close to tittering. 'Silly boy. Now do take your seat, Ehrig, so the servants can fill our plates.'

Parnel Garrick darted a quelling look at his son, then followed his wife's lead and laughed. 'He's a prankster, is Ehrig. Full of youth's juices. Always has been.'

Ehrig Garrick was past thirty. If he knew what was good for

him, he'd dry up his youthful juices and conduct himself like a sober man.

*Once I'm married to his sister I'll give him no choice in that. I won't have my reputation harmed by the likes of Ehrig Garrick.*

Morgan smiled again. 'And why not? How dull life would be without a dash of levity.'

Little sighs of relief from Parnel Garrick and his wife, Beys. Beside him, Venette drowned dry amusement in a mouthful of wine. She knew him too well. He must strive to remember that.

Parnel Garrick nodded to his senior dining servant, and a few moments later a parade of lesser servants filed into the conservatory, burdened with plates and tureens and bowls of sauced and spiced meat, fish and fowl. The Garricks' cook prided himself on his wide knowledge of foreign foodery, and so inflicted upon them dishes inspired by Dorana's mostly uncivilised neighbours.

'Eat hearty, Morgan. There's plenty more where that came from.'

But he'd not taken his first mouthful of pungently spiced fish when the Garricks' master servant slipped into the conservatory and bent to whisper in Parnel's surprised ear.

'Morgan—' Deliberately, Maris's father set down his knife and fork. 'There is news.'

He knew the tidings before being told. Felt Venette's hand come to rest on his shoulder. Though he was out of charity with her, still . . . the comforting touch was welcome.

'Lord Danfey,' he said, his voice steady. 'He's—'

'Not dead,' Parnel Garrick said quickly. 'But he's taken a bad turn.'

'Oh, Morgan!' Maris slid from her chair and hurried to his side, as presumptuous as her brother. 'I'm so sorry. Tell me, what can I do?'

*You can at least pretend you're not seeing yourself as Lady Danfey, my dear.*

He pressed her forearm, a neatly correct gesture. 'Hold a good thought for him, Maris. Though my father is not a man to give up without a fight, this enemy is fearsome.'

'You'll go to him, of course?' said Venette. 'Morgan, if you're not properly satisfied with his pother, you need only say so. I'll have—'

'I will,' he said, turning to her. The sincerity of her concern for him stole his voice, for a moment. 'Thank you.'

'Let us know how he goes on,' Orwin added. 'And whatever Venette and I can do . . .'

Venette's husband was a good-natured clodwit, but despite that Orwin was still a decent man. 'I'll not hesitate to ask, my lord.'

Parnel Garrick stood. 'We won't think to see you return to us, Morgan, obviously. It's been an honour to host you here these few days, and a great pity we must lose your company before time. Don't fret about your belongings, I'll see them safely returned. You'll take our hopes for a speedy recovery to Lord Danfey?'

'Of course,' he said, pushing his own chair back. 'And while I must immediately depart, my lord, if you could spare me a moment?'

'Certainly,' said Parnel Garrick, very formal. Seated beside him, his wife remembered to breathe and Maris, clever enough to present a shy and properly innocent demeanour, slipped back to her place.

Leaving the conservatory, Maris's father silent by his side, Morgan willed the churning in his guts to abate.

*I might as well declare myself now. If I can tell my father the marriage is agreed upon, if I can promise him a grandson within the year, then he'll rally. It might even be enough to forestall his leaving.*

And that was more than worth the price he'd have to pay.

'My lord,' he said, slowing, as they reached the country house's spacious foyer. 'I think you must know what it is I wish to say.'

'I do,' said Parnel Garrick. 'So I'll invite you to call me Parnel.'

He nodded. 'Parnel. I would offer myself as a husband for your daughter. But before I do, I must set things straight. I'm told Lord Arkley has spoken slightingly of me.'

'Ah.' Maris's father cleared his throat. 'Yes. As to that—'

'You should know, Parnel, there is no love lost between Sallis and I.' Morgan offered a faint smile. 'Which is talking out of turn, but I know I can trust your discretion. Are you and his lordship friends?'

'We rub shoulders now and then,' Parnel Garrick said. 'And have done business together in the past. But our families aren't close.'

So that was something. 'Parnel, I see no point in unpacking my dispute with Lord Arkley. At best it's unreliable hearsay, and at worst tawdry gossip. But if it means you now mislike the match between myself and Maris, then—'

'Mislike it? Not at all!' Parnel Garrick said quickly. 'What man has never disagreed with another? Lady Garrick and I gladly bestow Maris upon you, Morgan.'

And just like that, so simply, even *carelessly,* his future was set in stone.

'Thank you, my lord.' He wanted to weep. 'Let me be comfortable with my father's condition and then I will return, so we might talk more thoroughly about this – this most pleasing arrangement.'

A flicker of uncertainty in Parnel Garrick's eyes. Did Maris's father sense his hesitation? Was he astute enough to see beneath the polite, polished mask?

*No matter if he does. He'll not rescind his welcome. They are ambitious, these Garricks. What I offer they'll not spurn . . . though Maris be made miserable because of it.*

Not that he intended to make Maris miserable. As far as he was able he would do what was right.

'Farewell, for now, Parnel,' he said, bowing, and then took his leave.

'Morgan . . . where have you been, boy? I was calling. A disobedient son, you are, not to come at once.'

Speechless, Morgan fumbled for his father's wasted hand. He'd only been away from the mansion a matter of days, yet his father looked to have aged thirty years. Scabbed, spittled and shrunken, he huddled beneath his blankets like a corpse.

'I'm here, my lord. What's this nonsense now?'

Wheezing, his father hawked and rattled the muck in his throat. 'Nonsense? I'll give you nonsense. Answer me. Where have you been?'

'Taking a little time with the Garricks, my lord. There was an invitation, do you recall?'

'An invitation,' his father mumbled. 'Yes . . . yes . . .'

Pother Ranmer stepped to the bed. 'Don't be alarmed, Councillor. His lordship's weak, and tires swiftly.'

'I have eyes, man. I can see that.'

'But in truth, sir,' Ranmer added, 'your father is much improved. Seeing you has strengthened him. You should take heart from that.'

Improved? Strengthened? Surely Ranmer had lost his wits. 'How do you explain this marked collapse in so short a time?'

'I'm sorry,' the pother said with care. 'I thought you understood that his lordship's condition is uncertain.'

He looked up, feeling savage. 'There's uncertain and then there's *this*. Do you tell me his deterioration is natural?'

'Councillor . . . death is a natural thing,' Ranmer said gently. 'Painful, but natural.'

Not always. Venette's angry warning sounded in his memory.

*'Did you honestly think Sallis wouldn't punish you for that challenge?'*

Sallis Arkley had connections, men and women who were in his debt or who looked to perform a service in the hope of future advancement. And there were ways other than magic to harm another mage.

*Could Ranmer be the cause of Father's falling away? No-one else is preparing his pills and possets.*

Standing, Morgan hustled Ranmer until the pother was backed into the corner furthest from the bed. 'I am not convinced that any of this is natural.'

'Sir,' the pother said, glaring. 'Do you think to blame *me* for his lordship's collapse?'

'Can you tell me where else I should look?'

'Be warned, Councillor Danfey,' Ranmer said, frigid with fury. 'Accuse me of incompetence – or worse yet, some deliberate *malfeasance* – and I will lodge a formal complaint with the Council. You have neither grounds nor proof to question my reputation. Furthermore, such an attack on my good name and competence will ensure that not only will *I* never set foot here again, you will struggle to find *any* pother prepared to take such a risk.'

Shaken, Morgan retreated. Was he wrong? Did his father's collapse have nothing to do with Sallis Arkley? Was he letting his rage at the man, his frustrations over Maris Garrick, his fear for his father, affect his judgement? Possibly. And if Ranmer were indeed blameless, to lose his skills now would be a disaster.

'Forgive me, sir,' he said hoarsely. 'I am not quite myself.'

Ranmer looked at him. 'No,' he said at last, unbending. 'Which is understandable. Councillor, do not let dismay overturn reason. Lord Danfey has rallied. And he'll gather even more strength from your continued presence, I'm sure. Assuming you will be here some goodly time?'

'Yes. I'm staying.' Morgan looked again at his father, stuporous beneath his blankets. 'But can you remain in the mansion tonight, Ranmer? I need you to see my father through this crisis.'

Ranmer shook his head. 'Alas, Councillor, I have several urgent cases come suddenly upon me. But I shall not leave until I am confident that Lord Danfey is in no imminent danger. And of course, should there be another crisis, I will return.'

It would have to do. In truth, he was fortunate Ranmer would do so much. 'Very well.' Morgan returned to the bed. 'My lord? I have good news that will cheer you.'

With an effort his father dragged open rheumy eyes. 'It's done?' he croaked. 'You're handfasted?'

Even were they alone, he'd not have confessed the whole truth of his time with Maris. Lord Danfey could be crude, but he had

331

old-fashioned notions. 'I have Parnel Garrick's consent. His daughter will be the next Lady Danfey.'

'Morgan . . .' His father's weak smile revealed bloodied gums and missing teeth. 'That is well done. I knew you'd not disappoint.'

'Sleep now, my lord,' he said, and kissed his father's clammy brow. 'I'll be here when you wake.'

Downstairs, he found Rumm in the foyer, exchanging old cut flowers for fresh. Seeing him, the master servant fumbled a dewy spray of violet goliffloss. 'Sir, his lordship?'

'Holds fast.'

A shuddering breath. 'I'm pleased to hear it.'

'I know you are, Rumm,' he said, and briefly clasped the man's shoulder. 'Tell me, where is Mage Lindin?'

'Sir?' For a moment Rumm looked puzzled, as though he'd never heard the name. Then his expression cleared. 'Sir, she's about. Somewhere. She knows her duties. I leave her to tend them. You'll find her dusting or polishing. Doing laundry. Or outside with the chickens. As I say, she's about.'

He needed to see her. It wasn't wise, but he didn't care. Venette was right, curse her. Barl Lindin and Maris could not live beneath the same roof. He'd have to send her away. But before he did . . .

'I'll have words with her, Rumm,' he said, cool and distant again, as was proper. 'If Ranmer wants me, see I'm told of it without delay.'

'Sir,' said Rumm, bowing, and took himself and his dying flowers away.

Morgan glanced after him, surprised by a sudden surge of affection. For a servant? He was doddled. Shrugging that aside, he reached out with his mage-sense, searching for Barl . . . and couldn't find her.

Though it was impossible, she was gone.

# CHAPTER TWENTY-ONE

Breaking Morgan Danfey's attic door ward was no more diffi-cult than unpicking the golden threads of his binding. Not now that she had his measure.

Even so, Barl couldn't help feeling a thrill as the last intricate counter-cant surrendered to her meddling. Nothing and no-one, unranked Barl Lindin, proving herself the best mage in Dorana. What a pity she couldn't shout her triumph from the rooftops. But this unlikely talent would have to remain a secret, even from Remmie.

She was meant to be in the poultry coop, scrubbing filthy perches. Doubtless she should feel ashamed, that she'd crept up here the moment word spread to the servants of Lord Danfey's collapse.

*Yes, I should. But I don't.*

She would never feel guilty about magework again.

Smiling, she eased herself into the attic and closed its door behind her, confident she could reactivate the ward once she'd poked about in the councillor's workroom. Probably she could even rebind herself . . . but she wasn't prepared to take such a chance. No, she'd run weeping to Morgan Danfey upon his return from the country. Show him herself how his binding had unravelled and beg him to reinstate it before the Council found out. He'd never dream it was her doing. She'd be perfectly safe.

Yes, and thinking of his return she had to remember that must be soon. Rumm would surely send word to him once the pother had been and given his opinion of Lord Danfey's health. Which meant she didn't have long before she risked discovery.

'So hurry up,' she muttered. 'Don't waste the little time you have.'

She thought the danger of being here was outweighed by what she'd learn. If she could unravel Morgan Danfey with a hair clasp, how much deeper could she plumb him by exploring his heart? And this attic was his heart, of that she was sure.

Same as his privy parlour, his workroom was ruthlessly neat, with shelving and cupboards and a long, wide workbench. He had crucibles and mortars in every possible size, lined up like Remmie's pupils before the start of class. One whole wall was shelved full of catalysts. Scores of them, with a jar or pot for every element, and every element in its place. Running her finger-tips along the rows, Barl marvelled at their variety. And the *cost*? After so many months of Arndel's moaning over the prices of even the most common tinctures and powders, she dreaded to think what the councillor had spent here.

And it wasn't just the amount of money spent that shocked her. He possessed catalysts far trickier than *gedlef* and *bidaline*. There was *susquinel* and *urvil* and dozens of substances she'd never seen before, that set her mage-sense on edge. What kind of magework was Morgan Danfey doing, that he'd need dangerous catalysts like these?

A pile of notebooks sat on the workbench. Acutely aware of time ticking by, she crossed to give them a cursory look. But when she flipped open the topmost journal and read the first neatly inscribed entry, describing the intricate theory behind a reworked elementary transmutation . . . time stopped.

His mind was beautiful. *Beautiful.* Clarity and precision and unfettered imagination, tempered by a dash of arrogant reckless-ness she couldn't help but admire.

Almost laughing, she turned the page. Quickly read the next entry, a notation upon travel, and then eagerly read on. A theoretical postulation regarding the nature of time. An argument in favour of single-helixed wards, though they were old-fashioned and long out of favour. An exploration of the relationship between harmonic incants and the sigils that triggered them.

Oh, he was bold. More than bold. He was *fearless*. Willing to run where most mages would not crawl.

*Being an incant for the creation of a fabulous cat . . .*

Seeing his witty sketches for an artisan cat toy complete with a rat to chase and a rusty, rumbling purr, she did laugh. How Remmie would love it. A perfect prize for his classroom.

There were other toys imagined in the notebook. A windless kite incanted to tamely follow its owner, a sailed riverboat that created its own breeze, a little girl's tea set, its transmutation incant designed to change cordial flavours with one word. Astonished, Barl tried to reconcile the mage who'd bound her with the man who could dream up such delights for the young.

Sketched in the margin of a page scrawled over with incomplete sigil designs, a small map of Dorana and its immediate neighbours. Scribbled beneath it a short, stark question. *Are we safe?* She frowned at it, startled.

*How odd. Of course we're safe. Why wouldn't he think so?*

She couldn't imagine a reason.

Several pages further on, past more partly worked-out sigils, six different variations of the one incant, scrawled through and scribbled over with countless pen – strokes, messy as chicken-scratchings in the dirt. Written underneath them, a revealing cry from the heart.

*Every attempt ends in failure. I begin to lose hope.*

Oh. He sounded so – so – vulnerable.

Moved, discomfited, she hastened through the rest of his notes.

At the back of the notebook she found another kind of incant entirely. A reworking of something called *Hartigan's transmutation*. She'd not heard of it before and wasn't certain she understood Morgan Danfey's intent in the way he wanted to alter it. What

335

she did see, almost immediately, was that it was a longer version of the incant that he'd so despairingly scrawled over.

And, now that she could read it properly, she could also see where he'd made his fundamental mistake.

But as she re-read his preamble, trying to fathom the new incant's purpose, the attic's closed door crashed open.

'*Mage Lindin?*' Framed in the doorway, Morgan Danfey stared in furious astonishment. '*What are you doing?*'

She had no idea how to answer. Took a prudent step sideways, away from his workbench and notes.

The councillor stepped over his own threshold and slammed the door shut. 'Who unbound you?'

Heart hammering, she met his blazing gaze. 'No-one. I dreamed again. It was terrible. As I came wake, screaming again, the incant unravelled.'

He shook his head. 'You're lying.'

If she looked away, if she so much as blinked, he'd be on her like a wolf.

'How else could the binding have broken?'

'And the warding on this attic? I suppose that unravelled too?'

Remmie liked to play spindle stones down at The Greased Pig. Sometimes he won the game and sometimes he lost, but he never risked a few cuicks. He always gambled with trins.

'*If you're going to wager,*' he liked to say, '*then best make it worth your while.*'

Barl lifted her chin. 'There was no ward, Councillor. And the door was unlocked. It's not strange you forgot to secure it, sir. There is much on your mind.'

'*What?*' Incredulous, he laughed. 'You must think me *Feenish*, that I'd swallow pap like that.' Then his angry amusement faded and he was staring again, his fingers clenching and unclenching, white-knuckled, by his sides. 'I want the truth, Mage Lindin. You'll not leave here until I get it.'

Her skin prickled with cold sweat. What remained of her breakfast churned in her belly like swill.

*He could kill me for this. He might kill me for this. At least,*

336

*he might try. Does he think I won't defend myself? Does he think I'll die without raising my hand?*

For all that she'd unravelled his magework and read through his notes, she didn't know him well enough to be certain of the answers.

*But I started this, didn't I? And now I must end it . . . one way or another.*

'The truth, Councillor Danfey? All right. I broke your binding. And I broke your ward.'

'Impossible.'

'You demanded the truth, sir. That's it.'

'*You* broke—' Half turning away, he dragged a hand down his face. A faint rasping sound, as his fingers scraped over stubble. Then he turned back. '*Why?*'

'Why do you care?'

'*Answer the question!*'

Let him shout and rage at her, she wasn't going to show him her fear. And she wouldn't spare him, either, this mage – this man – who had wrapped her in torments no civilised person should embrace.

'I had to,' she snapped. 'I did dream again. I did wake your binding. I was in agony, Councillor, and you weren't here to end it.'

He flinched. In his narrowed eyes, he flinched. 'You would make this my fault?'

'I didn't bind myself, did I?'

'The Council would say so.'

'And are you the Council, sir?'

He flinched again. 'And my ward? It was no threat to you. Why break that?'

'I was curious. I wanted to see where you worked.'

'Curious,' he murmured. '*Curious.* Mage Lindin—' Frowning, he pinched the bridge of his nose. 'So, now you are free, with powers even greater than I realised.'

'*Free?*' She laughed at him. 'Only you could think so, a man who was never constrained a day in his life. I am no more free now than I was the day I arrived. For all the good breaking my binding has done me, I might as well not have bothered. For even unbound, you have ways to hurt me. Why do you think I didn't break this estate's wardings and run? Until you and your precious Council decree I am punished enough I remain your prisoner. The power here is all *yours*.'

He was upon her in scant strides, the fingers of his right hand spread and pressing the flesh of her face against its bones, driving her backwards until her head struck the window. On a cry of pain she heard the glass crack.

'And you hate me for it, don't you?' he said, his voice low and unsteady. 'Lord Danfey. Is his collapse your doing? *Tell me!*'

Sharply hurting, she fought not to tug at his prisoning fingers. 'Is what my doing? I don't understand.'

'No more lies, Mage Lindin! I can rend you flesh from bone and I *will*, I swear it, if you—'

'I'm not lying,' she said, then gasped as his fingers crushed tighter. 'Not this time. Let go.'

He leaned so close she could have counted his eyelashes. 'Tell me what you did to my father or I will visit such pain upon you that—'

Had he gone mad? 'I've done *nothing* to your father! If there's magework behind Lord Danfey's strife, it's not mine.'

Head thrown back, he stared down at her. 'And why should I believe you? A mage who can break both binding and ward. A mage who should not exist . . . and does.'

'Because I'm telling the truth.'

He said nothing to that. His eyes, still furious, were narrowed to slits. But the pressure of his fingers eased.

And then he released her.

'So,' she said, touching the bruised places on her skin. 'You do believe me.'

'Yes,' he whispered at last. He sounded almost . . . defeated.

Letting her hand fall, Barl watched him walk to his workbench and return the notebook she'd been reading to its place on top of the others. His fingers weren't steady.

'Is Lord Danfey very ill?'

He tensed. 'Lord Danfey is dying.'

Oh, the desolation in his voice. *I don't care for his pain. I don't.* But even so, she felt something. She wasn't carved from stone. 'I'm sorry.'

'Are you?' Savagely he swung around. 'Mage Lindin, why—'

'I lost both my parents, Councillor, while I was still young. I'm no stranger to grief.'

Whatever he'd been expecting, she thought it wasn't that. His jaw tightened, muscle leaping, and for a moment his breathing hitched. 'You think to disarm me with sad tales of your youth?'

'No! I simply wanted to—'

'*You wanted,*' he said, scathing. 'Must the world always spin to your wanting, Mage Lindin? As far as I can see, *your wanting* has caused nothing but trouble!'

He sounded like Remmie. 'That is unfair.'

'*Is* it?' His hand slapped the workbench. 'Does that mean you don't expect me to hold my tongue on what's happened here? You don't expect me to pretend you didn't break my binding and the ward on that door? When both should be *impossible?*'

She felt her skin crawl with rewoken fright. 'If you tell the Council—'

'If? *If?*' Morgan Danfey slapped the bench again, and then started pacing. 'Mage Lindin, it is my *duty* to tell the Council what you've done. What you are.'

'And if you tell them, who can say what they'll do? Are you so resentful of my unusual talent you'd live the rest of your life with my blood on your hands?'

He swung round as though she'd struck him. 'I do not resent your talent!'

Was that true? She couldn't tell. 'Then you resent the inconvenience I've caused you,' she said, sure of that much. 'Doubtless I was selfish and short-sighted, not to let your binding kill me. It would've proven to the Council I am a mage misjudged, and they could have sent Remmie a brief note of regret.'

'Do not presume to tell me what I feel, Mage Lindin!' he said, furious, and closed on her. 'Trust me when I say you have no *notion* what I feel!'

She swallowed. He was like a caged desert cat, ready to lash out at the least provocation. 'I'm sorry.'

'And *that's* a lie,' he retorted, halting before her. 'Whatever you are, Barl Lindin, we both know you're not *sorry*. Not for bloodying Hahren or challenging the Council or breaking my binding or sneaking in here!'

'I admit,' she said, after a moment, 'I was wrong to break your ward and trespass in your workroom. But as for the rest—'

'You were wrong in all of it!'

'No, I was not! The College's ruling was unjust, Hahren laid hands on me, and if I hadn't broken your binding I would be *dead*.'

That halted him. 'Nonsense. My binding was not lethal.'

'I beg to differ. You saw what happened the first time your binding woke. Stand there and tell me to my face that my life then was not in peril. I dare you.'

Silence, as they stared at each other. Then he retreated to rest both hands on the attic door. His head lowered between his outstretched arms, and after a time he breathed out a long, slow sigh.

'How did you do it? How did you break my binding and ward?'

Still wary, she eased away from the wall and window and gingerly touched the back of her head. There was a bump, but nothing worse than that. Her fingertips remained dry. To make a point, to carve a little space and time for herself to think, she mended the cracked windowpane.

'Mage Lindin?'

She turned from the window to see that he was facing her again. Waiting. The power she'd felt in him at Winsun, that echoed around them now, was ruthlessly leashed. But she had no illusions. He could unleash it with a thought and destroy her for what she'd done . . . and not a mage on the Council would call it murder.

340

'I don't know how I did it.'

His fist struck the door beside him. '*Mage Lindin*—'

'I don't!' she insisted. 'Not to explain it, or show you. For some reason it seems I have an affinity for your magework. I can see the warp and weft of it and – and have it do as I bid.'

'I see. And how many other mages' incants have you interfered with?'

She almost said *none*. But then she sighed. Her life was already in his hands. Too late now to turn back. 'Only one. Baret Ventin's. When I saved Arndel's artisanry.'

'But for all you know,' he said slowly, 'you can override any incant. And if that's true there's not a mage in Dorana who's safe.'

'You mean from me?' she said, shocked. 'But I would never – Councillor Danfey, I *wouldn't*. And I'll prove it. Bind me again.'

His laugh was derisive. 'When you can snap your fingers and unbind yourself on a whim?'

'I won't. I promise.'

'And why should I believe you?'

She stepped closer, beseeching. 'Because I'm not lying! Can't you tell?'

He looked at her oddly, then. 'And what of your brother?'

Remmie? Why would he –

*Oh. Oh, no.*

She stepped back. 'Leave Remmie out of this.'

'How can I? He's your twin.'

'I never told you that!'

'You didn't have to. I met him, remember?'

'It doesn't matter we're twins,' she said, feeling so sick. 'Councillor Danfey, he knows nothing about this. And he's nothing like me.'

'And what if you're wrong? What if your brother possesses this same inconvenient quirk of talent? Have you any *idea* what—'

'You can't lift your hand to him!' She wanted to scream.

341

'Remmie's done nothing wrong, he's broken no law! If you perse-cute him for no better reason than he's my brother, I'll – I'll—'

Morgan Danfey raised an eyebrow. 'You'll do what, Mage Lindin?'

She had to blink and blink to defeat the stinging tears. 'I'll never forgive you.'

He stilled so completely she could believe she'd turned him to stone.

'If you don't want me here, Councillor, I'll understand,' she said, when he remained silent. 'You can send me away. Send me back to the Hall or give me to Lord Arkley for guarding. I don't care. I don't. Only please, don't hurt Remmie.'

Morgan Danfey breathed out a shuddering sigh. 'And I'm to accept your word, unproven, that he'll never use magic against another mage? That *you* won't, even though you've already done so?'

'Yes.'

'How can I?'

She shrugged. 'Because I won't.'

'Mage Lindin . . .' He sighed again, so harshly it was almost a groan. 'You seek to make this simple. But you are a complica-tion the likes of which I've never known.'

And if she was, she'd never wanted it. All she'd ever wanted was to be left alone to pursue her magework, and be fairly recognised for her achievements. Why was that so unreasonable? Why did she seem fated to encounter nothing but jealousy and meanness and people who would not rest until she was humbled in the dust?

Blinking back another sting of tears, she folded her arms. 'Very well. I'm a complication. Perhaps you're right, and I'm dangerous. So what?'

Instead of answering, he crossed to his workbench, picked up an empty crucible and with his back to her wrapped it in a heavy ward. Even distressed she could feel the stirring of his power, feel the binding threads he wrapped about the heavy stone. When he was finished, he turned.

'Break this,' he said, and threw the crucible at her.

Startled, she caught it, gasping as its weight sang a pained protest through her wrists and forearms. As his convoluted warding prickled over her skin.

His eyes were glinting. '*Break it*, Mage Lindin. And then I'll decide.'

She tried to ignore him as he prowled his attic, but it was impossible. In the confined space she found his woken power overwhelming.

'Well?' he demanded. 'Can you do it?'

'I can, yes, provided you stand still and hold your tongue!'

When was the last time an unranked mage had dared speak to him like that? From the look on his face, she suspected never.

*Too bad, Morgan Danfey. It's long past time you were spoken to like an ordinary man. And if you make a fuss, well, I'll keep to myself what I can tell you about your reworking of Hartigan's incant.*

And she could tell him a great deal. For where he was stumbling, she could see a clear path.

Still staring, he shook his head. 'Your impertinent arrogance knows no bounds.'

But he stopped prowling, as she'd known he would.

The weight of the warded crucible was making her arms ache, so she lugged it to the end of his workbench and let it drop with a thud.

*Break the ward. Break the ward. Of course I can break the ward.*

It was difficult to believe that this cold, uncompromising man was the mage who'd created a purring toy cat and a tea set to delight little girls.

*Because I broke his binding I thought that I knew him. I think I don't understand him at all.*

But she couldn't dwell on that. She couldn't let fear rule her. She had to protect Remmie. Nothing else could matter.

Closing her eyes, she sank into Morgan Danfey's magic.

\*     \*     \*

Watching Barl Lindin closely, Morgan wrestled his howling disbelief into submission. However ludicrous her claims might appear, there was no arguing with the evidence of his own eyes and senses. The ward protecting his workroom was undone. And the mage he'd bound so carefully stood before him now, unbound.

Why he'd even bothered to look for her up here, he couldn't say. He'd certainly not expected to find her. But he and Rumm had searched everywhere else, the other rooms in the mansion, the poultry coop and outbuildings, even the flower beds and manure pile. Desperation, not conviction, had sent him up the attic stairs.

And there she was.

Halfway up the final staircase he'd felt it, of course. The unravelling of his attic ward. The neat, precise severing of its threads and counter-threads, its undoing as accomplished as if he'd unwarded the door himself. The shock of it had nearly dropped him to his knees.

*Who is Barl Lindin, that she could break my ward, break my binding? Hide from me? What is she, this young mage, that I should look at her and feel . . . awe?*

Feel awe and despair, wretched and wracking, that he could not have her instead of Maris Garrick. For were he and Barl Lindin bound together, what magics couldn't they achieve?

*She's right. The Council cannot be told. Compared to Barl, Bellamie Ranowen is no more dangerous than a lamb. They will put her down if they learn what she's done. I'll threaten as I must to keep her compliant, but her gifts must remain secret. They must remain . . . mine.*

Which meant he couldn't send her away from the estate. There was nowhere else in Dorana he could keep her safe. And what Maris would say to that – what Venette would say – he shuddered to think.

*But none of that can matter. What is Maris to me, or Venette, compared to this?*

And *this* was the sight of Barl Lindin unravelling his warded crucible as easily as another woman might unpick a skirt's hem.

Astonished, he felt the shift in the shape of her magework, how she'd melted and moulded it to echo his own.

With a small, tight smile she looked up. 'There. It's done.'

Such arrogance. He could have slapped her. Wanted to kiss her. His coupling with Maris was a fast-fading dream.

Joining her at the bench, he took the unwarded crucible to examine it. No sign of his warding, the stone washed clean as a window in a rainstorm.

*I watched her do it, and it's still hard to believe. This girl is unranked. What kind of accident created her?*

'It might not just be me, you know,' Barl said, watching him. 'Perhaps any mage could do this, if they felt threatened enough. If they thought they would die if they didn't.'

If she threw his imminent murder of her at him *one more time* . . .

Throttling temper, he put down the crucible. 'That's most unlikely. Countless mages throughout history have felt threatened, Mage Lindin. The Council would know if they'd defended themselves like this.'

'Perhaps,' she agreed. 'Perhaps not. After all, how likely is it they'd tell you?'

*Arrogant . . . impertinent . . .* Glaring, he showed her a little of his temper. Smiled to see her see it, and see her bite her lip. Cheeks colouring, she clasped her hands behind her back.

'Councillor, I'll make a bargain with you. Leave Remmie be, and I'll show you where and why your reworking of Hartigan's incant has gone wrong.'

For a moment he thought he must have misheard her. But then he realised *no.* And for a moment found it very hard to breathe.

'I know it was rude,' she added, 'but I read some of your notes. You can't get the syllabic balance to hold, can you?'

He found his voice. 'My magework is none of your business. The incant is nothing. A theoretical puzzle to be solved, that's all.'

A scornful glitter in her eyes. 'Really? Now who's lying?'

She meant it. This girl, this unranked nobody, thought she had the skill to outmage *him*.

'You'd school me, Mage Lindin? When I am a dozen years or more your senior? College trained? Patented *and* the youngest mage ever appointed a member of the Council?'

She tilted her chin at him. 'Yes.'

She was *outrageous*. And also . . . magnificent.

'You take a grave risk, Mage Lindin. I could promise you anything and then carelessly betray you once I had what I desired.'

A pulse was beating at the base of her throat. Her slender, elegant, kissable throat. Beneath her crumpled linen tunic her breasts rose and fell as she breathed.

'If ever you betrayed me, I think it would not be careless,' she whispered. 'I don't think you've lived a careless day in your life.'

'And you've not lived a safe one.'

Despite her unease, she gave him a brief, mocking smile. 'Since when is magework safe?'

He was drowning in her blue eyes. His blood threatened fire. If she touched him he'd ignite. He thought he might die if she didn't.

*You're handfasted, you fool. You're to wed with Maris Garrick.*

Mere hours since he'd breached Parnel Garrick's daughter, and he couldn't remember the girl's face.

'Since you've read my notes, Mage Lindin, you know that aspects of my magework are . . . unorthodox.'

Her smile widened. 'You mean someone like Lord Arkley is bound to disapprove?'

'Not just Sallis.'

'*Good.*' She almost spat the word. 'I'm not inclined to court the approval of a man who wants me dead.'

He snorted. 'You and I both know you're not inclined to court anyone's approval.'

'And why should I?' she said, haughty and unsmiling now. 'I tell you, Councillor, my days of bowing and scraping before lesser mages are done with.'

346

'And are all the other mages of Dorana *lesser*, in your eyes?'

She looked at his notebooks. 'No, Councillor. Not all.'

It was a compliment, and it thrilled him.

'So, do we have a bargain?' she said . . . and couldn't quite keep her voice steady.

Let her know what she did to him, and he'd be forever lost.

'Not quite,' he said, showing her nothing but indifference. 'Prove to me this is more than desperate bravado. Prove to me you're as great a mage as you claim. Show me where I have misstepped with my incant . . . and I will keep your brother safe.'

Her shoulders slumped. 'Agreed.' Then she straightened again. 'And me? What will happen to me?'

'Never fear, Mage Lindin. I'll keep you safe too.'

'From the Council, you mean?'

*From everything and everyone who might dare to harm you.* 'Yes.'

'And when will I be released from your custody?'

'When the Council is convinced you've been punished enough.'

Grimacing, she turned away. 'In other words, never.'

'Have patience, Mage Lindin. Give their tempers time to cool.'

'Patience,' she muttered. 'Not one of my strengths.'

'Indeed,' he said, very dry. 'I would never have known.'

Cheeks flushed, she scowled at him. 'And my own magework? You'll let me pursue it?'

Ah. He had her. 'We will have to take precautions,' he said, hiding his jubilation. 'The servants. Lord Danfey. But yes. You'll have your magework.'

'And you won't bind me again?'

'Mage Lindin—' *Barl*. He gentled his voice. 'By taking precautions I meant allaying suspicion with the Council. If they should visit they must find you bound. But at all other times you will be free. I promise.'

He could see she was desperate to believe him, but couldn't bring herself to trust.

'I know you count me an enemy,' he said, cajoling. 'Because

I'm granted status and privilege denied to you and your brother. But a man is born where he is born and has no say in the matter. And if you let me, Mage Lindin, I'll prove an enemy can become a friend.'

'I don't have a choice, do I?' she said, after a silence stretching beyond bearable. 'If I hold my tongue on your magework, you'll harm Remmie.' Her fingers clenched. 'I *hate* this.'

'Then we have our bargain,' he said. 'And we will both keep our word. As for my stubborn incant—' He frowned at his notebooks. 'It will have to wait. I have matters requiring my attention. Stay behind a short time after I leave, then make your way downstairs and outside. I shall deal with Rumm. Meet me back here at midnight.'

Without giving her a chance to reply, not trusting himself to remain aloof in the face of her trembling relief, he left the attic.

'Sir!' Agitated, Rumm waylaid him in at the foot of the staircase. 'I have scoured the grounds *twice* and Mage Lindin is not to be—'

'Fret not, Rumm. I found her, and have dealt with her intransigence. Where is Ranmer? Still upstairs with his lordship?'

'No, sir. He awaits you in the library,' said Rumm. If he was taken aback, he was too well trained to show it. 'Shall I bring sherry?'

He could do with something stronger, but that would only make Rumm stare. 'Yes.'

Ranmer was dealt with quickly enough. After a closer examination, the pother could safely say that Lord Danfey's collapse had no obvious cause. Still, it should be remembered that a man in his doubtful condition was subject to relapse. The good news was that he rested comfortably, and there were new draughts and possets and herbals for him to take. He was to be kept quiet, no excitement. A few days rest should see some improvement.

It wasn't hard to hear what hadn't been said aloud. Smothering grief, Morgan kept Ranmer company with one glass of sherry apiece, then saw the pother off the estate and turned his attention to letter writing. A note to Parnel Garrick, explaining the situation, begging leave to delay further talk of a wedding until his father was more settled. Another to Maris, saying much the same. Courteous in tone. Regretful. No mention of what had happened between them in that closet. Such a mistake he'd made there. He'd been a fool to let himself be ruled by his body.

*I will be certain not to make that mistake again.*

With the notes sealed and set aside, he returned upstairs. Heavily dosed with soporific, his father heaved for air, his paper-thin eyelids lowered over sunken, restless eyes. Seated beside him, Morgan closed his own eyes and conjured Barl Lindin's arresting face to mind.

*She broke my ward. She broke my binding. She challenged me beneath my own roof and won. She is glorious. But can she do what she claims? Can she complete my reworking of Hartigan's transmutation? For if she can . . . if she can . . .*

Thud, thud, thud, boomed his heart within his chest. Blood heated. Desire stirred. Not the brutish, lustful passion he'd felt for Maris Garrick. Nothing so simple as the need to rut and fuck. This was sharper. Cleaner. Mixed pleasure and pain. This was – this was –

*Love.*

# CHAPTER TWENTY-TWO

'The flaw in your thinking is here.' Barl pointed at Morgan Danfey's scrawled sequence for the reworked incant. 'The flow of energy through the fourth to fifth syllabic vibration. On its own the incant keeps balance, but the second sigil – this one—' She tapped her finger to the page. 'It's counter-compatible. The energies work against each other, you must see it.'

Past midnight in his glimlit workroom. Below their feet, the mansion slept soundly. Standing beside her, the councillor shook his head.

'No, I do not see it. Nor do I find it credible that *you* see this apparent flaw, given all you've done is read my notes.'

She folded her arms. 'Just because you can't see what I see, is that any reason to call me a liar?'

His sidelong glance was skeptical. 'Others have thought so.'

Artisan Master Arndel. Would the old toad never cease troubling her? 'And others are wrong.'

'No, I think you're wrong,' he snapped. 'There is no indication of counter-compatibility. After some initial resistance the sigils coalesced to perfection. And I paid particular attention to that syllabic sequence when reworking the original incant.'

'I'm sure you did,' she said, striving for patience, 'but it doesn't matter how careful you were, does it? Not when the result is failure.'

Hearing his sharply indrawn breath, she remembered Remmie's oft-repeated complaint.

*Barl, Barl, it isn't what you say. It's the way that you say it.*

'Councillor . . .' With an effort, she sweetened her approach. 'I've no doubt that between us we can unpick this knot. But it would help if I could see for myself where you started.'

Muttering under his breath, he crossed to the attic's cupboard and took from it an old, rolled and tied sheet of parchment. Then he returned and spread it flat between them.

'You will see,' he said, acerbic, 'that in adapting Hartigan's original construction I have done everything in accordance with Cylte's rules of reworking.'

'Cylte?' She shook her head. 'I've not heard of him – or her.'

'No?' He feigned shock. 'You astound me. No intimate acquaintance with one of Dorana's greatest innovators? And yet you presume to know where my magework has failed.'

'I don't *presume* anything!' she retorted. 'I know, and if you'd climb down off your high horse, I'll show you! Or can't you bring yourself to admit when you're wrong?'

Another hissing, indrawn breath. 'Mage Lindin—'

'I'm sorry, I'm sorry,' she said, raising one hand. 'You're right. That was rude.'

'*Very* rude.'

'And I said I was sorry! What are these rules you've been following? Can I see them?'

With a glare and a finger-snap he summoned a battered book to his hand, leafed it open and thudded it to the workbench atop his notes and the old parchment, then paced the attic while she read through this Rubin Cylte's *rules*.

They were interesting enough. Most of his observations she'd already worked out for herself, as she made clocks for Arndel and new crystal for herself. Even in her early days as an artisan mage, serving her swift apprenticeship with Artisan Master

Fabien, it seemed she'd instinctively understood most of what Cylte had to say.

*Except here . . . this is interesting. This is something I'd never considered.*

A new way of looking at internal syllabic rhythms, a twist upon her own, small discovery of contrapuntal give-and-take. And how exciting. How high did her blood leap, reading this scholarly work and seeing a sudden explosion of possibilities?

*This is what the College would've been. This is what Arndel and Hahren and the Council deny me.*

She smothered the familiar surge of resentment. All the roads she could've travelled, all the great work she could've done had she even *once* been encouraged instead of pushed aside as unworthy.

*I'm going to read this Mage Cylte's book of learning. And when I've read it, I'll read every other book in Morgan Danfey's library. I'll make this mansion my college. I'll take for myself what they think they've kept from me.*

And then she'd teach what she'd learned to Remmie, and he'd teach his precious pupils, and the ranked mages' guarded secrets would spread until every unranked mage in Dorana knew what those selfish men and women had tried to keep for themselves.

'Mage Lindin?'

Halted, Morgan Danfey was staring, his lips pinched with impatience. Beneath that, he looked tired. His eyes were shadowed with grief.

*His dying father.*

Crushing unwanted sympathy, she pushed Rubin Cylte's rules aside and shuffled through the councillor's notebook of preliminary calculations until she found the page where he'd scribbled the shape of the sigil he needed. A moment's careful perusal gave her the answer she sought.

'Come and look,' she said, beckoning. 'And don't feel so fretted. What's gone wrong is as much Rubin Cylte's fault as yours.'

That made him laugh. 'You criticise *Cylte* now? Mage Lindin—'

'He didn't think far enough ahead,' she said. 'And neither did you.'

Joining her at the workbench, Morgan Danfey stood discomfortingly close. Even while it was sleeping, the power in him roiled her. Set her skin atingle and heated her blood.

She crushed awareness of that, too. Crushed awareness of *him*.

'Where is the final mapping of your sigils? I can't find it.'

A hesitation, then he shrugged. 'You won't. I did not commit the successful sigils to paper.'

'Really? I believe in making thorough notes, Councillor. What if you forget something?'

He looked down his nose at her. 'I won't.'

Ha. And he called her arrogant. 'If you say so.' She pulled an empty crucible toward them. 'Conjure the second sigil of your incant.'

He conjured it, then saw it caught safe in the crucible. Deeply impressed, though she'd rather cut her hand off than let him see it, Barl took a deep breath then opened herself to the sigil's volatile energies. Something sourly acrid caught the back of her throat.

'What's that?' she said, recoiling. 'It's disgusting.'

Councillor Danfey laughed again. 'So there is something you don't know? I count myself amazed.'

Let him scoff all he liked. He still needed her, whether he'd ever admit the truth or not. As fascinated as she was alarmed, she leaned a little closer to the sigil.

'What *is* it?'

'*Azafris*. Rare, expensive and unpredictable. Like you, I think, Mage Lindin.'

A note in Morgan Danfey's voice shocked her. Not scorn. Not impatience. Instead she heard *affection*. Startled, she looked at him . . . and felt her blood thicken like syrup. His face, his eyes, were unguarded, and in them she could now see something other than grief. Fresh heat flashed through her, dangerously close to pleasure.

*No.*

He had a beautiful mind to match his beautiful face, but if she let either seduce her then he would win.

She tapped his notes. 'I need pen and paper.'

He fetched them for her from the cupboard, and watched without comment as she fiddled his sigil's construction, feeling her way through the changes that were needed for it to perform in seamless tandem with the transmutation incant he'd reworked.

'There,' she said, breathless, when at last she was done. 'There's an odd gap that won't close, but even so it will hold. Although . . .'

'I know,' he said as she bit her lip, suddenly uncertain as she stared at her reworkings. 'There is a small instability within the harmonics.'

'One that might well cause counter-instabilities elsewhere,' she said. 'Have you considered that?'

'I have.'

'And?'

'And I think that just as a pond ripples then stills after a thrown stone, so will the syllabic harmonics smooth themselves out.'

'Hmm.' She tapped the notebook, thinking, then nodded. 'Yes. Doubtless, you're right. So. Remake your sigil, Councillor. And then we'll see, won't we, if I'm as good as I say.'

Her turn to watch, then, as he gathered the catalytic agents he needed for the task. Stepped well out of the way, she drank in his neat, precise ordering of the workbench. Shivered a little to feel the slow building of his power. She'd never constructed such a complex sigil before. Never thought to harness so many disparate elements and energies. What he was attempting . . .

*He's mad even to think of it. But it's a wonderful madness. I want to be mad like that.*

He laughed when the reworked sigil coalesced and hung in the air before him, shining. She'd never imagined he could sound so joyful or carefree.

'Now try the full incant,' she suggested. 'I think you'll find the sigils and syllables will mesh properly now.'

Nodding, barely aware of her, the councillor banished the summoned sigil and began the incant from its beginning. Inscribed the air with the first sigil. Watched it blossom and hold. Recited the first syllables of his new incant. Smiled as the sigiled air tightened, vibrating. He summoned the second sigil. Completed the incant.

And the tightened air rippled in a soundless explosion of power.

Gasping, Barl staggered. A good thing the attic was tightly warded, else the ignition of the incant would have rocked the mansion to its cellars. The councillor staggered too. But as the incant wasn't grounded in an actual working, the effect passed off swiftly.

He turned to her, his face so alight, so alive, she couldn't breathe. 'I don't believe it! How did you – how *could* you—'

Before she could answer, he kissed her.

His warm, slender hands, framing her face. His soft lips, his sweet lips, covering hers. Never in her life had she been kissed like this. She felt her arms drop to her sides, abandoned. Felt every muscle soften and go limp. Heard herself sigh her longing into his mouth. She dragged her eyes open so she could perish in his gaze.

Then swallowed a protest as he let go of her and stepped back.

'I'm sorry,' he said hoarsely. 'That was wrong.'

Yes it was, completely wrong. A terrible mistake.

*You idiot, Barl, you idiot. To let yourself feel for him? How much power over you does he need?*

Willing her heart to calm, she cleared her throat. 'It's all right, Councillor. You were caught up in the moment. We'll not regard it.'

He clasped his hands behind his back, as though they'd be safer there. 'No. We won't.'

Her kissed lips were aching. Her heart wouldn't calm. He had a beautiful mind and a beautiful face and he stirred something within her that she'd never known was there.

*But it doesn't matter. It can't matter. I'm here for me. For the magework. I'm not here for him.*

'So,' she said, and raised a deliberately provocative eyebrow. 'I was right. About the sigil and the syllables and Rubin Cylte being wrong.'

'Yes, you were right.' He offered a small, not quite mocking bow. 'Mage Lindin, you are an extraordinary talent.'

She could easily hate herself, that she cared for his compliment. 'Then perhaps you'll not be so quick to doubt me next time.'

'Next time?' he murmured. 'You think there'll be a next time?'

'I hope so. I live for my magework, as you live for yours. As different as we are, it's one thing we share. And it seems you and I work well together. It would be a shame to waste that.'

*And for as long as I'm kept prisoner here, I'll turn captivity to my advantage. I won't have had my life ruined for nothing.*

Silence, as they stared at each other. And then Morgan Danfey's expression chilled toward wariness. 'You do not ask why I am so determined to rework Hartigan's transmutation incant.'

'I'm curious, of course,' she said, shrugging. 'But if you wanted me to know, you'd tell me.'

'That seems unusually restrained of you, Mage Lindin.'

'I'm trying to turn over a new leaf.'

Eyes shadowed with more than grief, he smoothed a wrinkle in his sleeve. 'Not even my father knows what you've learned here tonight.'

'Is that your clumsy way of telling me I'm trusted?'

He slapped the workbench. 'Do not joke on this! It is no laughing matter!'

'I'm sorry,' she said quickly. 'Councillor, I do know what it means, that you've shared this work with me. You've given me a weapon. But I won't use it against you.'

He sneered. 'Because you want to save your brother.'

There was no point denying it. 'And because what you do here is marvellous. Your incants . . .' Her fingers brushed his notebooks. 'They're *marvellous*. I want to be a part of them. Is that so wrong?'

Without shifting his gaze from her face, he summoned to hand a newly plucked flower, intact from bud to root. From the garden bed by the stables, she thought. Tanamies grew in profusion there. The blossom's lightly fragrant, pale pink petals were brushed with droplets of dew. Little clots of damp soil rattled to the attic floor.

Gravely, he held it out to her.

'Go on,' he said, when she hesitated. 'It won't bite. And neither will I.'

Her fingers brushed against his as she took the flower. The touch shivered her, and rushed blood to her cheeks. She saw him feel it. Saw him smile. But before she could change her mind, give the flower back, turn away, he burned the air with sigils and trembled it with words.

The power of his transmutation incant roared through her like a storm.

'Oh!' she cried, delighted, as the tanamie quivered, and rippled . . . and *changed*. Became a flower of slender crimson petals narrowly striped with gold-edged purple, its fragrance deep and rich. '*Now* the incant makes sense. That gap between the ninth and thirteenth syllables, that's where you specify how the transmutation subject is to be changed.' Amazing. Inspired. His new flower was beautiful.

*His new flower* . . .

'I know,' he said, as she stared at him. 'The transmutation of living things is forbidden. But a flower isn't really alive, is it? And some rules must be broken for a greater good to prevail.'

She would never argue against that, but even so . . . 'Councillor, you play with fire.'

'Are you going to burn me?'

'I told you already. No.'

He was watching her closely, his eyes half-lidded. 'Compared to what I have done, your transgression is nothing. You'd be forgiven in a heartbeat if you brought my sins to light. You might even be rewarded with a place in the College. After all, we let Bellamie Ranowen teach there . . . and like you, she is unranked.'

She threw the flower at him. 'Yes, I'm unranked, but that doesn't mean I have no *honour*. I'm not in the habit of buying and selling other mages' secrets! And if you think I am, then—'

'Shall I tell you what I think?' Stooping, he picked up the thrown flower. 'I think that without you, Barl Lindin, my incant was doomed. I think we were meant to find each other. I think that together, we can remake the world.'

He was standing so close she could feel his power, hot as the sun. She could feel her cold, bitter memories thaw and warm and melt.

*I think that together, we can remake the world.*

Her cold, bitter memories were trickling down her face. 'Councillor—'

Smiling, beautiful, he pressed his palm to her cheek. She felt herself lean into him. Fall into him. Fall.

'*Morgan*. Barl, call me Morgan. Say it. I want my name on your lips.'

'Morgan,' she whispered. 'Morgan Danfey.'

'Louder,' he commanded. 'Shout it. Shatter the ceiling. The midnight sky.'

So she shouted it, laughing.

'*Morgan. Morgan. Morgan.*'

And knew, as he laughed with her, that there was no going back.


Not far enough past dawn, Morgan was roused from a pleasurable dream of crimson and purple flowers by Rumm, roughly shaking his shoulder.

'Sir – sir – come quickly. It's his lordship.'

Almost half an hour later, Pother Ranmer was in the mansion, shaking his head.

'I'm sorry,' he said, straightening. 'His lordship has indeed taken another turn for the worse.'

Savage with fear, Morgan stared down at his father, so still and sickly pale against the pillows. 'Thank you, I had noticed. The question is, Ranmer, how do you intend to fix this?'

Ranmer looked up from rummaging in his leather bag of pills and potions. 'Councillor?'

He jerked his head toward the chamber door. 'Outside.'

'Sir, I understand this is hard,' said Ranmer, once they were alone in the sitting room. 'You feel angry and helpless, which is only natural. But you must understand, sir, your father—'

'Is dying,' he said, crossing to the window and pulling back its heavy curtains. The sun was well-risen, and a day of obligations awaited. 'I know. But he must not die yet. It is his dearest wish to see me married and the father of a son. I would grant him as much of that wish as I can. So you will see that he at least stands at my wedding. Do I make myself plain?'

Ranmer snorted. 'Quite plain. And now I shall make my own position equally clear. I can make you no promises. I am not some Brantish charlatan, waving a bottle of coloured water claiming it comes from a secret spring and can defy the laws of nature. I will do everything in my power to help Lord Danfey, but *you* must accept that my power has limits.'

'I do,' Morgan said, and rubbed his burning eyes. 'Now return to him, Ranmer. I cannot stay, I have Council business. Leave your instructions with Rumm. He'll see they're carried out.'

'Sir,' said the pother, and did as he was told.

Swallowing a groan, Morgan slumped against the windowsill. How swiftly joy turned to misery these days.

*My lord, your timing is execrable.*

A door opened behind him. 'Sir?'

He bit back a curse. None of this was Rumm's fault. 'What is it?'

'A note's arrived, sir. From Lady Martain.'

Venette? But this was the last day of the Garrick house party. What could she want? Turning, he held out his hand. Rumm crossed the floor and gave it to him, his face schooled more severely than ever.

'If I might ask, sir. His lordship?'

Morgan shrugged. 'Ranmer's with him.'

He cracked the seal on Venette's note and flipped the folded paper open.

*Come early to the meeting. I would have private words.*

'Sir?' Ever alert, Rumm stepped forward. 'Is there trouble?'

So. She'd abandoned the Garricks too. He closed his fingers on the note, crushing it. 'No. Wait here for Ranmer's instructions, Rumm. I must leave for the Hall.'

'Of course, sir,' Rumm murmured. 'Was there anything else?'

Pausing at the door, Morgan half-turned his head. 'Mage Lindin. How is she occupied?'

'She is tending the poultry,' Rumm said, after a moment. Every word was ice-laden with his disapproval of her lenient treatment. 'Unsupervised. Sir.'

He gave the man a sharp look. 'Mind yourself, Rumm. Prisoned here or not, Barl Lindin is still a mage.'

And that was cruel of him, reminding Rumm of his failing, but Rumm was crippled. A servant. He could never be permitted to place himself too high.

'Sir,' Rumm said again, properly subdued.

'I'll be back later. You know where to send for me, should—' Morgan watched his fingers whiten on the door handle. 'You know where to send.'

He'd planned on riding into Elvado for the afternoon's Council meeting. Desperately needed the exercise and the solitude, but thanks to Venette he'd have to forgo the pleasure. Whatever she wanted it had better be important, or without compunction he'd take his fear and temper out on her.

After swallowing a hasty breakfast, he closed his eyes and reached out to Barl. And yes, there she was, surrounded by chickens. Glowing like a burning diamond. She'd promised not to hide from him again. It still amazed him that she could hide herself at all. Where had she sprung from, this fiery, potent young mage? Nothing in her bloodline so much as hinted at what she could do.

*She is a mystery.*

His mystery. After last night's magework he had no intention of giving her up. He and Maris would reach an agreement. After all, Parnel Garrick's fortunate daughter should be required to pay *something* for her imminent climb up the social ladder.

And if Maris refused to accept that, well . . .

*But she will accept it. She has to. I will rule my own life.*

Venette waylaid him in a Hall corridor, on his way to the Council chamber.

'Not in there. Brice is huddled with Sallis and Shari.' She beckoned impatiently. 'Step out to a balcony with me.'

She sounded as disapproving as Rumm. Even her attire was severe today, midnight brocade cut and stitched without embellishment. She wore her short golden hair slicked close, and her earrings were restrained rondels of striped moss agate.

Immediately wary, and not pleased by her tone, Morgan allowed her to hustle him out onto one of the Hall's sixteenth floor balconies overlooking the plaza. The fountain's leaping water dazzled in the sunlight, its frivolous mosaic designs a blur so far below. Elvado's bustle was muted up here, distance lending it dignity, the silence a solemnity. The stirring air was cool and clean, caressing his face like a lover.

'I did not look to see you here, Venette,' he said, making sure to keep his own voice friendly. 'Don't tell me you tired of the Garricks' hospitality.'

'Don't be ridiculous,' she snapped, oblivious to Elvado's beauty. 'I've come back early for Maris. Morgan, how could you of all people be so crude and clumsy? I wouldn't have believed it had she not shown me your note. Stars above, my dear fool, whatever were you *thinking*?'

'For one thing, that my correspondence with Maris is private.'

Venette flung up her hands, as though beseeching patience from a Trindeki god. 'Trust me, Morgan, I heartily wish it was! Then I'd not be subjected to floods of tears and grief-stricken prostrations! Have you no imagination? Did you not consider for even a moment how such a careless missive would be received?'

He had no desire for this conversation. He was tired, and more than tired, of Venette's meddling in his life. Glancing sideways, he tried to catch a glimpse through the Council chamber's window but the balcony was too far away.

'Tell me, why do Sallis and Shari huddle with Lord Varen?'

Arms folded, one hip leaning against the balcony balustrade, heedless of the sheer drop, Venette rolled her eyes. 'I'll give you three guesses.'

He needed only one. 'My pending patents. Lord Arkley's stirring trouble?'

'Did you think Sallis wouldn't use your absence to make mischief? I told you it was a mistake to threaten him, my dear.'

'Then why aren't you huddled with them, Venette? You have a say in the matter of patents.'

Venette poked his arm. 'Brice is well aware of my opinion on the matter. There's nothing more that I can add that won't harm your case instead of help it. Now stop changing the subject. I will have this out with you, Morgan. You left the house party because of your father. But if you're here for a humdrum Council meeting that means he's not at death's door. So why do you not return to the country to be with your bride?'

'She is not my bride yet.'

'You asked Parnel to grant her to you, and Parnel agreed! You're wed with her now, Morgan, save for the ring and a public declaration. That means your place is with Maris. *Go* to her.'

He raised an eyebrow. 'And am I answerable to you, Venette? Must I gain your permission before I live my life as I see fit?'

'Do not take that tone with me! Maris is *crushed*. You couldn't be handling this courtship less adroitly if you tried. Do you *want* to have her slip through your fingers?'

'Oh, so you do care what I want?' he retorted. 'This isn't simply about Maris Garrick, whom you think of as a daughter.'

'Somebody has to,' said Venette, close to scowling. 'Justice knows her mother is a ninny. It had to be *me* who—'

'Who what?' he prompted, when Venette turned to stare across the city as though seeing it for the first time. 'Venette . . . what did you do?'

Her cheeks were tinted deep pink. She didn't answer, or turn back.

'*Venette*,' he said, sharply enough to make her wince.

Wince, but not answer him.

A nasty, sneaking suspicion. A knifing twist in his guts. Maris, in the closet. So forward. So bold. Too bold for an unranked mage of gentle breeding. Enticing him. *Seducing* him.

*Oh, Venette. Say you didn't.*

'It was your idea?' he whispered. 'Her breaching? You're the one who saw me thrust between her legs?'

'She came to me,' said Venette, her voice low and unsteady. 'She asked me if I thought you desired her. She thought you did. She wasn't sure. She loves you, Morgan. She wants you, more than anything. I told her about Luzena. I said your heart was healed, but scarred. I told her to give you a new and kinder memory. I said nobody would know if she took her pleasure sooner rather than later. If you both did. And that *if* you did . . .'

'Our handfasting would be assured.' He let out a slow and shuddering breath. 'Well played, Venette. I must give you this game.'

She spun round. 'I wasn't playing! I just wanted to make certain. You carry Luzena's memory in you like a *shroud*. I wanted you free of her, Morgan. I wanted you for Maris.'

Venette and his father, both forcing his hand. Both of them claiming love for him, neither of them offering him the smallest respect.

'And what you want, naturally, must come before all.'

'Morgan—' She took a step after him, her footfall unsteady on the balcony's smooth tiles. 'Don't walk away from me. Don't—'

Ignoring her, he let the balcony door slam shut between them and made his way to the Council chamber.

'Morgan,' said Lord Varen, his tone mild, his eyes wary. 'You are come a little earlier than the allotted time.'

'My lord,' he said, with most of his attention given to Sallis Arkley and Shari Frieden, seated side by side at the chamber's table and smirking. 'Forgive me. I did hope for a privy word with Lord Arkley before the Council's business commenced.'

'No privy words are necessary,' said Sallis, relaxed as a cat. 'I have been discussing patenting business with Lord Varen. We know you're anxious for an answer on your magework, and now that a decision has been reached I'll gladly give it. Both your patents are denied.'

It took every lesson of self-restraint he'd learned not to wipe the smirk from Sallis's face with physical violence.

'Lord Arkley,' Varen murmured, reproving. 'There is no need to gloat. I agree with your decision, but do show some consideration for a fellow councillor's sensibilities.'

As Sallis made insincere noises of regret, Morgan stared at the floor. Varen was being too conciliatory for Sallis to have told him of their angry exchange of threats in the hot room. That meant the man's interference extended only to Parnel Garrick, an action that, if challenged, could be passed off as undeliberate.

*Which means I was right. Lord Arkley is vulnerable.*

But not so helpless that he couldn't strike a blow using his Council authority as a shield.

*I cannot swallow this without protest. To accept defeat too easily will be to invite further aggression.*

He looked at Brice Varen. 'My lord, I am not convinced of Lord Arkley's competence to judge my magework. Nor do I have faith in Lady Frieden. I request an impartial adjudication.'

Lord Varen silenced Sallis's gobblings, and Shari Frieden's shrill protests, with a sharp look and a raised hand. 'You're within your rights to do so, Morgan. But you'd subject all recent patenting decisions to scrutiny and doubt and thereby undermine confidence in this Council. Is that what you want?'

'I want justice, my lord. Am I to relinquish the rights granted to the least mage in Dorana for no better reason than I serve it as a councillor?'

Settling his clasped hands on the table, Varen took a moment to reply. 'Morgan . . . were you not listening? I said I concur with this decision. The incants you submitted are not worthy. There is a roughness in the syllabic harmonics. And none of us was convinced of their wider application. In truth, though it pains me to say so, those incants are far from your best work.'

Stunned, Morgan stared at him. Not worthy? His magework?

*Last night I transmuted a living flower. You doddering old fool, what would you know of worthy?*

'Brice is right, Morgan,' Venette said behind him, her entrance into the chamber silent and unobserved. 'You can do better. You *will* do better. And when you do, the work will be recognised. There is no vendetta here.'

Ah, dear Venette, meddling yet again. Assuming her unrequested opinion was welcome. He turned, letting his eyes inform her how far she had misstepped.

'No vendetta, Lady Martain? When Lord Arkley and Lady Frieden have done nothing but belittle me from the first day of my appointment? When they have snatched at any and every excuse to call for my dismissal? Are you *addled,* my lady? Are you—'

Varen slapped the table. 'Watch your step, Morgan. You forget yourself and the respect owed your seniors.'

'Respect is earned, not owed. Lord Varen, I do not accept the decision. It is my right to—'

'To hold your tongue before you talk yourself into real strife! As head of this Council, Danfey, I command your silence!'

'For pity's sake, Morgan,' Venette implored, taking his arm. 'Don't let our falling out goad you into folly.'

He shook himself free of her. 'Lady Martain, you hold yourself too lofty.'

'Morgan, that is *enough*!' Breathing heavily, Varen stood. 'I am gravely disappointed in you. I had high hopes when confirming your appointment, but now I am forced to wonder whether Lord Arkley and Lady Frieden weren't right after all!'

Venette stepped forward. 'Brice. Please, don't be too harsh. Remember that Morgan is under great strain.'

365

'You'd have him hide behind his father's bedpan?' Sallis snorted. 'Disgraceful.'

'That was uncalled for, Lord Arkley,' Varen said. Then he sighed. 'Lady Martain makes a salient point. No man can be temperate when faced with his father's demise. Morgan, I think it best we overlook this entire unfortunate conversation. Go home, where you're needed, and stay there until—' He hesitated. 'Until matters are resolved. It is unreasonable of us to expect reason from you while you endure such trying circumstances.'

Morgan swallowed. 'My lord—'

'No, Morgan. It's done.'

He was dismissed? Sent to his room like a schoolboy in disgrace? He looked at his fellow councillors' faces. Saw angry sympathy, naked hatred, sorrowed despair . . . but no hint of a reprieve. Sickened, he realised what he'd done.

*I'm a fool. I've let Sallis Arkley manipulate me.*

Any anger he felt was at himself, most of all.

'And as for your unwise prisoner,' Sallis added, freshly gloating, 'I think Mage Lindin must be—'

*Protected. My lord, do not test me on this.*

'She goes nowhere,' he said flatly. 'The girl is kept well occupied with chicken shit and dusting. In my custody she gives this Council no trouble. And as I am still a councillor, despite your best efforts, Lord Arkley? I see no reason to alter the arrangement. Unless you wish to accuse me of some malfeasance?'

'There is no question of malfeasance,' Varen said, silencing Arkley with a look. 'If you are confident you can keep her restrained while dealing with your father's illness, I see no reason to remove her. As far as other Council business is concerned, you'll be sent for if you're needed. But for now, Councillor Danfey, you are excused.'

# CHAPTER TWENTY-THREE

Morgan's return to the Danfey estate was so stormy that Barl, washing dishes, dropped a soap-wet tureen to the scullery floor where it smashed into glazed clay shards.

'*Mage Lindin!*'

On her hands and knees, picking up the pieces because Rumm couldn't know she was unbound, she winced. Of *course* the master servant had to be passing the scullery's open doorway at precisely the wrong moment.

'I'm sorry, sir.'

'I'm not interested in apologies!' Rumm snapped, glaring. 'Be more careful in future. I have no desire to present Councillor Danfey with a new list of household expenses!'

'Yes, sir,' she said, hastily scraping the shattered tureen into a prosaic dustpan. One piece missed. She reached for it and cut her finger. Blood welled, dripping. *Curse it.* Sucking the shallow, stinging wound, she could feel the master servant's unsympathetic regard like dragon's breath on the back of her neck.

'I notice you've still not taken the kitchen scraps out to the poultry.'

'No, sir. I'm sorry, I—'

'You will be if you don't complete your tasks in a more timely fashion.'

Biting her tongue, Barl tipped the bits and pieces of tureen into the scullery bin. Then, because life would be far simpler with Rumm on her side, she showed him her meekest face.

'I was wondering, sir, how his lordship's faring after the pother's visit.'

From the way Rumm tensed, she'd have to guess badly. His lips thinned. 'That's no concern of yours, Mage Lindin.'

'I'm under his roof, Master Rumm, so I think it must be, a little,' she said, daring. 'I've no wish to leave here. There are far crueller places for me to serve the term of my punishment.'

'Since you have no say in the matter, I don't see how it serves you to dwell on it,' Rumm said. 'Dwell on not breaking any more crockery, instead.'

And with that reproof delivered, he left her to the sink full of soapy water and dirty dishes.

She finished washing them without breaking any more, even though Morgan's distress still shivered through her. Next she dried the plates and pots and pans and put them away. With no further tasks to be done inside, she found some astringent ointment for her cut finger, then collected the scrap pail from the kitchen and resigned herself to an afternoon with the chickens.

Morgan found her in the poultry coop an hour later, sticky with feathers and sneezing as she emptied the laying boxes of their fouled straw and refilled them with fresh. Alone, save for the crooning, clucking birds, they stared at each other across the complicated distance between them.

*Last night he kissed me, and told me to speak his name. But now the sun's shining. Has anything truly changed?*

Not really. Even unbound, she was still a prisoner. Still dependent upon this volatile man's goodwill. And she'd be wise not to forget it.

'Something's happened,' she said at last. 'Can I help?'

Ignoring the cackling hens, the dusty air, the stink, indifferent to the muck smearing his tunic, Morgan turned to pace the cramped coop.

'My patents are denied. Sallis Arkley, he lives to thwart me. Made some nonsense claim that my magework lacks sophistication. He's a fool. I am three times the mage he will ever be and yet—'

A bubble of laughter escaped her before she could burst it. 'I'm sorry,' she said quickly, as he whipped round. 'Only, well, now you know how I feel.'

'You think your disappointments are comparable to *mine*?'

Irked by his dismissive scorn, she folded her arms. 'Yes, I do, Councillor. And why shouldn't I?'

Scowling, he looked away. A victory. Then he dragged a hand down his face.

'I challenged the ruling. There was . . . a dispute. Now I'm stood down from the Council. Sent home to rusticate.'

Two bruises to his pride with one well-placed blow. No wonder he was stormy. So stormy he'd not stopped to think. 'Perhaps Lord Arkley has done you a favour.'

The councillor scowled. 'How so?'

'Well, every hour you're not in Elvado, fretting over petty rules and getting into arguments, is another hour you can spend on your magework. And since he thinks you defeated, Lord Arkley will find someone else to upset. That's all to the good.'

He stared at her, an oddly arrested look on his face. And then his lips quirked in a brief smile. 'That's very true. How devious you are, Barl. I think I approve. And I told you to call me Morgan.'

It was dangerous, surely, to feel such pleasure hearing that. She did her best not to show it.

'Anyway, you shouldn't care what an old frog like Sallis Arkley says. Could he have reconfigured Hartigan's transmutation incant? Would it even have occurred to him that he could try?'

Morgan's face lit up with laughter, banishing the discontent, making him beautiful again. 'Devious and disrespectful. No wonder I—'

She waited for him to finish. When he didn't, she busied herself emptying the next laying box of fouled straw.

'Barl . . .'

He was right behind her. She didn't have to turn round to know it, she could feel him, his heat and power. Her lips tingled, remembering that fierce, devouring kiss.

*Don't be a fool. It meant nothing. It can't.*

'Barl, look at me.'

Reluctantly, she straightened and let the half-filled hessian sack drop to the ground. 'If I don't finish these boxes, Master Rumm will have my hide.'

'*Look at me.*'

Oh, he did love to bark orders, didn't he? As though he was the lord of her. As though she were still bound. She shifted far enough to see him from the corner of her eye, and no further.

'Barl, my circumstances are not . . . simple,' he said, all amusement fled. 'There is a woman I've been courting.'

'Maris Garrick. I know.'

'Of course you do,' he muttered. Then he sighed. 'But you should also know that whatever my privy domestic arrangements might be in the future, they'll have no bearing on my – our – magework. Nothing and no-one will interfere with that.'

*Our magework.*

She felt her heart thud with relief, and turned. 'Not even a wife?'

'*No-one.*'

Foolish or not, she believed him. And what Maris Garrick would make of that, she didn't want to think.

'Good.'

'And you're not to concern yourself with Rumm, either,' he added. 'Henceforth you are released from your menial duties. There is a guest chamber on the second floor. Consider it your own.'

No more sleeping in that pokey little cupboard? *Justice be praised.* 'What about the Council?'

370

'What about them? As far as those fools are concerned, out of sight is out of mind. Trust me, I'll not be missed. And what they don't know won't hurt them . . . or us. When the time is right, we'll reveal our work to them. Until then, though, to be prudent, we keep circumspect. Which means you can't contact your brother. I'm sorry.'

*Remmie.* She felt a twist beneath her ribs. He'd be fretting for her, but Morgan was right.

'No, I understand. Only . . .'

'What?' he prompted. 'Barl, our magework must be secret. That doesn't mean there should be secrets between us.'

It would be easier to remain aloof if he didn't say things like that. 'It's Maris Garrick. I can't imagine she'll be pleased to find me here. How can you be sure she won't complain to the Council? As your wife, she—'

'Maris Garrick and I aren't even formally handfasted yet,' he said, impatient. 'And until I can trust the excitement won't harm Lord Danfey, we won't be. Nor will we be married until Ranmer can swear my father is strong enough to stand witness. That could be weeks. Do not concern yourself with Maris Garrick. She doesn't matter.'

Didn't matter? And he was marrying her?

Morgan frowned. 'I don't mean to sound unkind. What I mean is that Maris will not prove an impediment. She perfectly understands the importance of my work.'

It was the height of foolishness, surely, to be jealous of a woman she'd never met.

'Then perhaps, when you're married, you'll want to share that work with her.'

'Instead of you?' He laughed. 'Don't be ridiculous. Now, the entire estate is yours to wander as you like. I've taken down the boundary warding. All I ask is that you go on avoiding my father's apartments. He . . . would not understand.'

She had no doubt of that. 'Does this mean I'm free to read the books in your library? There are so many I've never seen before. I want to catch up.'

Morgan grinned, disarmingly boyish. 'Read them to your heart's content. I can explain whatever you don't understand.'

'How generous you are, sir! But don't be surprised if I end up explaining a few things to *you*.'

'Get back to your chickens,' he said, still grinning. 'Your rule as lady of the manor doesn't start 'til the morning.'

After he left, she picked up the stinking hessian sack. But instead of emptying the next laying box she stood still in thought. The poultry coop echoed to the sound of hens, cackling. Her bundled hair and drab, rumpled linens stank of their shit. She could leave this behind, now. She could wash herself clean tonight and never think of hens again. After today her life would be naught but magework. Thanks to Morgan Danfey, she was about to become her best and truest self.

*But that means nothing. And I can't hope it ever will.*

Finished at last with the laying boxes, she returned to the mansion intending to scrub herself clean in the scullery before the servants' dinner. But as she reached the bottom of the staircase she saw Rumm, and he saw her, and the look on his face told her that Morgan had already taken him aside.

'Master Rumm,' she said, and offered him a tentative smile. 'Could we speak?'

Unsmiling, he nodded. 'I think we should.'

Because he was the mansion's master servant, he was granted the privilege of his own apartment below stairs. Closing the small parlour's door, Rumm indicated a chair.

'Please.'

She sat, and he retreated to stand with his back to the fireplace, his arms folded. 'I knew you were unbound.'

*What?* 'I'm sorry?'

A muscle twitched beside Rumm's right eye. 'I am no mage worth a damn, but I have a little sensitivity. As soon as I saw you this morning, I knew.'

'And said nothing?'

'It wasn't my place. I am instructed not to discuss Council matters with anyone.'

'Not even Lord Danfey?' *That's fortunate.*

'Master Rumm . . .' Barl let her hands lift and fall in her lap. 'I mean the councillor no harm. Nor his lordship. I only ever wanted to be left alone to learn.'

'The Council sees you as a threat.'

'And the Council is mistaken.'

Slowly, that twitching muscle fell quiet. 'I'm told you'll be mageworking with Councillor Danfey.'

Interesting, that Morgan had trusted this man with the truth. She nodded. 'I will.'

'Then I hope you're a better mage than you are a housemaid.'

'I believe I might be,' she said gravely, resisting the urge to smile at his tartness. 'Master Rumm—'

'Mage Lindin?' he said, perfectly polite.

'How soon, do you think, will Lord Danfey die?'

She saw anger leap in him, and grief. Watched as he wrestled both into proper, servantly submission.

'Too soon,' he said at last, his voice tight. 'Why?'

'There's something I'd like to do, Rumm. Before I fell foul of the Council I was an artisan mage. A clock-maker. I'd like to make Lord Danfey his funeral clock. But I'll need your help, for I have no money and no clock-making supplies.'

She'd startled him. Eyes intent, he tapped one forefinger against his lips. Assessing her.

'I will have money again, one day,' she said. 'And however you purchase what I need, I'll repay you. Or the mansion coffers. I give you my word.'

'And are you a good clock-maker, Mage Lindin?'

'Master Rumm, I am the best clock-maker in Dorana.'

He snorted. 'But not the most modest.'

Now she did smile. 'No, sir. Never that.'

'Very well, Mage Lindin,' Rumm said, nodding. 'Give me a list of what you require and I shall do my best to obtain it.'

'Without mentioning it to the councillor?' She stood. 'I don't wish to distress him.'

Did she imagine it, or was that approval in his eyes? 'A good master servant knows when to hold his tongue.'

Agreement, then . . . and maybe even a promise, that if anyone were to betray her, it wouldn't be him.

'Thank you, Master Rumm.'

'You're welcome, Mage Lindin.'

The next morning, after breakfast, she and Morgan hid the Danfey estate from prying eyes.

It wasn't a warding, not exactly. Instead they took a standard deflection incant, used by some considerate mages to keep from disturbing their neighbours with the more combustible magics, and . . . *enhanced* it. The rush of heat and power as they melded their mageworking was headier than the finest wine. When it was done, the estate guarded, they retreated to the mansion's attic, determined to forget the outside world.

First of all, just to make certain they'd not dreamed it, they invoked the reworked transmutation incant. Laughed to see yet another new flower created. Then another. And another.

'Stop!' Barl said at last. 'Morgan, no more, or we'll turn the workroom into a garden. Why don't you show me those incants the Council denied?'

So he showed her, and she risked his anger by half-way agreeing with Sallis Arkley, that he'd been hurried in his scholarship and careless in their execution. Surely he could see that if he'd taken a *little* more time he'd have realised that his incant for the more perfect distillation of temperamental Iringan sour-pips into a teeth-shuddering liqueur would in fact be better suited to the less inimical Brantish pea-currant. And *then,* by combining the distilled pea-currant with robust Doranen icewine, he could in fact create a new luxury tipple entirely.

As for his reworking of Beckins' privy ward, well, that seemed a waste of effort entirely. If he wanted to impress, why not create an incant that relied upon a mage's unique magical signature to keep it strong for years? The fact that such a ward had been tried already, only to fail, wasn't a good enough reason to abandon the idea. Especially if he paired *this* sigil with *that* one, and used syllabic harmonics vibrating in a different minor key.

Morgan called her rude names, then admitted she was right.

Entranced with each other, with the magework, they scarcely noticed the bright day dwindling toward dusk. Rumm appeared at intervals with hot food on a tray, which they devoured in haste so they could continue their discoveries. When Lord Danfey stirred, wanting company, Morgan reluctantly withdrew to sit with his father until the old man drifted back to restless sleep.

Not wanting to magework without him, Barl buried herself in the library, gleefully devouring scholarly works instead of cake. After supper they returned to the attic, taking some of the books with them, and Morgan assumed the role of teacher. But he learned as much as he taught, for her mind was a gift to him. A constant surprise. It was past midnight when they admitted exhaustion and retreated to their separate beds.

At the next day's dawning they rose . . . and eagerly lost themselves in magework again.


'Mage Lindin.'

Almost at the library door, Barl turned. 'Rumm? Is something wrong?'

'No.' Rumm came down the rest of the stairs, frowning as they both heard Dilys's tuneless humming along the other corridor. 'A privy word, though, if you've time.'

She held the door open for him, and pushed it shut after. 'There is something wrong. Is it his lordship? Morgan's just gone to sit with him.'

'His lordship's condition is unchanged,' Rumm said. 'Your clock-making supplies arrived while you and the councillor were in the attic. I've put them in your chamber.'

'Rumm, that's remarkable. It's only been four days. I thought it would take a week or two, at least. Some of the items I asked for are quite obscure.'

Rumm looked down his nose. 'I have long been in the habit of procuring obscure items for the Danfeys.'

And that was Mage Lindin put firmly in *her* place. 'Oh. I see. Ah—' Barl bit her lip. 'Did you have to spend a great deal?'

'Yes,' Rumm said. 'I slipped the final tally under your pillow. The supplies I've hidden beneath the bed. They should be quite safe there. Dilys only remembers to sweep the bits of floor she can see.'

He sounded so peevishly resigned she had to swallow a laugh. 'Rumm . . .' She shook her head. 'I don't know how to thank you.'

His guarded eyes warmed, just a little. 'You can thank me by making Lord Danfey the most beautiful funeral clock in Dorana.'

Accepting that she might well be alone for hours, as Morgan kept his father company, she'd intended to pass the time in study. Instead she turned her thoughts to Lord Danfey's memorial timepiece. Not knowing how many of her requested items Rumm could obtain, she hadn't let herself dream of it. But since he'd managed to find *everything* . . .

Alone again, she fetched paper, ink pot and quill and settled herself at one of the library reading tables to chart the initial design of the most spectacular clock crystal ever created.

His father had drifted back to sleep, so Morgan put aside the book he'd been reading aloud and let his own eyelids close. He was exhausted. Couldn't remember the last time he'd poured himself so passionately, so unreservedly, into his magework.

*Never. I never have done. At least not like this. I've never had to. There has never been anyone who challenges me like Barl.*

And if someone had told him there would be, he'd not have believed them. Because he'd never imagined a mage like Barl Lindin could exist.

Opening his eyes, he summoned to his hand the small wooden box she'd warded shut. Four days of trying and he still hadn't breached her seal. For a whole morning he'd watched as she broke every one of his wards, unstitched them, unravelled them, barely out of breath. And when she tried to explain how she did it, how she saw his magework, all she did was baffle him. She *baffled* him. It was an unsettling thing.

*But there is a trick to it, this unwarding business. And if she can learn it, so can I.*

The trouble was, of course, that he kept getting sidetracked by the sheer elegance of her magework. She brought an artisan's touch to the most prosaic of incants.

*If only, for one day, I could see through her eyes.*

In the bed beside him, his father stirred. Coughed. 'Morgan? Morgan, are you there?'

He sent the warded box back to the attic, then leaned forward in his chair. 'Yes, my lord. Here I am.'

'Good . . . good . . . I thought you'd gone.'

'No, my lord,' he said, and helped his father choke down one of Ranmer's strengthening possets. When that was done, he plumped the pillows. Stared down at the ailing man, feeling so helpless. 'Is there anything else you need?'

'A grandson,' his father grunted. 'When will you announce your handfasting, Morgan?'

Swallowing a groan, he dropped to the edge of the chair. If only his father would stop *carping*. 'When Maris wants me to, my lord. As I've told you, she feels that—'

'Ha!' Fretful, his father plucked at the counterpane. 'Curse her namby-pamby feelings! Are you a man or aren't you? What kind of a marriage is it going to be if the girl has her fingers wrapped round your balls already?'

Morgan bit his tongue. *Justice preserve me.* Easy for Ranmer to declare Lord Danfey too weak yet for any kind of celebration. Ranmer wasn't the one who had to make up lies.

'She's young and nervous, my lord, and if I push her, she might bolt. Trust me, I will bring her to heel in good time.'

Capricious in his sickness, between heartbeats his father shifted from anger to grief. 'I only want what's best for you, Morgan. You are my son. It's my duty to guide you.'

*Really, my lord? I thought your duty was to drive me to distraction.*

'I know,' he said, soothing. 'And I will be guided, I promise. My lord, if there is nothing else pressing I can do for you, I should return to my magework.'

His father turned his face into the pillow. 'Yes, yes. Your magework. Very important. You go. Send Rumm to me. He reads aloud better than you.'

Making his relieved escape, Morgan found Rumm and ordered him upstairs, then continued to the library. Barl was so engrossed in her reading she didn't realise he was there. Smiling, he leaned against the doorjamb and lost himself in the way she curled and uncurled a strand of hair about her finger.

When he couldn't stand not being seen by her a moment longer, he closed the library door.

'Morgan!' she said, startled by the thud. 'How is his lordship?'

Sometimes the urge to touch her stifled the air in his throat. One kiss, they'd shared. Only one. And that was supposed to sustain him for the rest of his life?

*It must. Do not do this. Only a fool torments himself.*

'His lordship is disgruntled,' he said, feigning lightness. 'I fail to meet his exacting standards.'

'What cause has he to complain of you?'

The indignation in her voice was a balm. 'It seems I don't read well enough. Rumm has taken over.'

She smiled. 'Well, he is quite remarkable.'

'Perhaps, but I'll thank you not to tell him so,' he said, sitting as close to her as he dared. 'He might demand an increase in salary.'

'If he does, you should agree to it. This mansion would fall down round our ears without him.'

Ignoring that, Morgan pointed. 'You're covered in ink, Mage Lindin. What have you been doing?'

She stared at her blotched fingertips. 'Oh. Nothing. Scribbling. Thinking aloud. Are you free now, Morgan? Can we go back to the attic?'

'We can, if you'd like. Or we can pause for a moment, and take a wander through the woods. I know I could use a breath of fresh air.'

She leapt up. 'Councillor, that is an *excellent* idea. And while we're walking I'll tell you about an incant I've thought of. A way to combine silk, gold and topaz into a new kind of fabric!'

Heart aching, he followed her out of the library.

*Justice save me, she is glorious.*

And because he could not have her, could almost wish they'd never met.


Orwin Martain stared more loudly than any man ever born.

Abandoning her cup of tea, Venette sat back in her chair. '*What?*'

'My dear, you know perfectly well,' Orwin said, infuriatingly placid on the other side of the solar's breakfast table. 'You should stop sulking and go to see him.'

'I am not *sulking*. I am giving Morgan time alone with his father . . . and a chance to reconsider his rash behaviour.'

Orwin pursed his lips. 'You've given him nearly three weeks. Which, I confess, is longer than I expected. But you're fretting, my dear. Don't pretend you're not.'

'*Maris* is fretting,' she retorted. 'She's not heard a whisper from him. But I am perfectly indifferent.'

'Venette.' Orwin reached across the table and covered her hand with his. 'Don't be silly.'

A lifetime of affection in that gentle reproof. Furious, she felt her eyes prick with tears. 'He's going to spoil everything, Orwin. Maris Garrick is *perfect* for him. Even if he can't see that, I can, and he has no business not trusting my judgement. I found the right matches for my nephews, didn't I?'

Orwin interlaced his fingers with hers. 'You did, my dear.'

'And as for baiting Sallis like that. How could he be so *foolish*? How could he not see that the rejecting of his incants was a *trap*? Now Sallis is insufferable. He and Shari have convinced themselves that Morgan is all but dismissed. And I fear they're right. Brice won't hear of recalling him, certainly not before Greve—'

She couldn't finish the thought. Greve was far from her favourite person, but even so . . .

'And that's why you should take the first step, my dear,' said Orwin, squeezing her hand. 'We both know Morgan is his stubborn father's son. *Go to him.* You'll not regret it. But the longer you let this silence drag on, the harder it will be to mend the breach. And if you leave it 'til it can't be mended, well. *That* you'll regret.'

'I'll see,' she said, not wanting to admit he was right. 'Perhaps I'll try talking to Brice again, first. It won't be called meddling if Lord Varen has a quiet word with him.'

Orwin disentangled their fingers, sighing. 'You'll do what you think is best, I'm sure.'

In other words, he thought she was wrong but had no desire for an argument.

Venette pushed her chair back and stood. 'I have that meeting to attend. I must get ready, I don't want to be late.' A glance through the solar window showed her blue sky and distant, lacy clouds. 'It's going to be a lovely day. I think I'll walk to the Hall.'

But she'd not gone more than a few steps from the town house's front gates when her name was called. Seeing who stood in the shadow of the large djelba shading the quiet street, she felt her eyes widen.

'Mage Ranowen?'

Dressed in a drab grey linen tunic, her head covered by a grey cotton shawl, the unranked College tutor glanced around them as though she were afraid of being seen.

'Lady Martain. Good morning. Have you a moment to talk?'

'Not really, no. I'm due at the Hall. You should make an appointment to see me there. Really, this is hardly—'

'I'm sorry,' said Mage Ranowen, stepping closer. 'I don't think it's wise for us to discuss this in . . . a formal setting. Not when you and I don't ordinarily cross paths.'

Perplexed, she stared at the inconvenient young woman. 'Mage Ranowen, I am a busy woman. State your business plainly or be on your way.'

Bellamie Ranowen pressed two fingers to her temple, as though she were in pain. 'I'm afraid there is something wrong in Dorana.'

'Wrong?' Out of patience entirely, Venette lifted her hand. 'I think perhaps you're unwell, Mage Ranowen. Seek a pother and do not—'

'*Please!* Lady Martain, you must hear me out!'

'Oh. Must I, indeed?'

'Yes,' the woman insisted. 'For all our sakes, *yes*.'

So much for a leisurely, pleasurable stroll to the Hall. 'Then I will listen to you as I walk to the plaza. And if that is too formal a setting for you, Mage Ranowen, then I suggest you unburden yourself to a tree.'

'I am sorry,' Bellamie Ranowen murmured, as they made their way side by side along the otherwise empty residential avenue. 'Believe me, Lady Martain, I'd not have accosted you like this if I didn't believe it was needful.'

'I'll be the judge of what's needful. Well?'

Bellamie Ranowen offered her a diffident smile. 'Yes. An explanation. Only first, might I ask when it was you last performed any complicated magework?'

To her surprise, Venette had to think before she answered. When *was* the last time? Goodness. It had been days. Perhaps a week before the Garricks' house party. And since then, of course, with so much upset over Morgan, well, she'd not been in the mood for anything more difficult than glimfire.

'A little time,' she said, cautious. 'Why?'

'It means there's no hope you've felt it too,' said Mage Ranowen, almost speaking to herself. 'Of course, that might not matter, since I seem to be the only tutor in the College who—'

'Felt what? I swear, Mage Ranowen, if you don't stop talking in riddles I won't—'

And then Bellamie Ranowen so far forgot herself as to take hold of a councillor's arm and tug her to a halt. Plain face drawn with tension, her eyes wide with distress, she seemed not to realise she'd just committed assault.

'Lady Martain, I feel magic the way others hear music. So if I say to you I can hear a discordant note in the choir . . . do you understand what I mean?'

Venette stared. Did Bellamie Ranowen intend to be insulting, or was she simply so distracted she'd not thought before speaking?

*This once, I shall give her the benefit of the doubt.*

Gently, she extricated her arm from the young woman's grasp. 'Are you suggesting there is a flaw in the fabric of Dorana's magic?'

Fear and relief flooded into Bellamie Ranowen's eyes. 'Yes. Lady Martain, that is *exactly* what I'm saying.'

'I see.' Venette glanced around still-empty Asvoden Way. No wonder the College's only unranked mage had wanted this to be a privy conversation. 'And you are the only mage in Dorana who can feel it?'

As though startled by the question, Mage Ranowen frowned. 'I have no idea. As far as I can tell I'm the only mage in the College who's noticed, but as to – oh.' She almost laughed. 'I see. You think I'm imagining things.'

'I think it's possible. I certainly think it's more likely than you being the *only* mage capable of sensing such a catastrophic event.'

'I never said I was!' Mage Ranowen said, close to snapping. 'And I think the only reason *I've* felt it is because I've been conducting some highly complex syllabic reconfigurations. That's why I asked if you'd done any difficult magework of late. Whatever this discordant note is, whatever it means, it's so faint I think it can only be sensed when a mage is deeply, *deeply* focused. And even then, perhaps not by many.'

'If it's so faint, indeed, so serendipitous, then how do you know you're not imagining it?'

Bellamie Ranowen leaned close. *'Because I know!'*

Justice save her, what an intense young woman. Perhaps the strain of teaching at the College was finally starting to show.

'Very well, Mage Ranowen,' Venette said, subtly easing aside. 'You have a concern and you've rightly brought it to a councillor's attention. You may return to the College, confident that your assertion will be investigated.'

Bellamie Ranowen looked at her, silent. And then she smiled, not diffidently at all. 'Confident. Yes. Of course.' She stepped back. 'Thank you for your time, Lady Martain. I am sorry to have disturbed you. I hope I've not made you late.'

Astonished, Venette watched the grey-clad mage retreat a short distance down the avenue, then slip into Nolin Lane.

'Extraordinary!' she murmured. 'Quite extraordinary.'

But as she made her hurried way toward the plaza, and the Hall, she thought she might . . . just *might* . . . do a little complicated magework of her own that evening. On the principle that generally it was better to be safe than sorry.

# CHAPTER TWENTY-FOUR

Barl stole every moment she could to work on Lord Danfey's funeral clock.

Morgan was too preoccupied to notice her theft. His father grew weaker every day, and every day demanded more of his time. He gave it, willingly, even though it meant less chance to magework. Even though it meant he left his father's chambers almost speechless with fear and grief.

Helpless to help him, Barl poured all her empathy into the clock. And then struggled to hide her exhaustion from him during their snatched time in the attic. She was hiding it now, as they took advantage of Lord Danfey's slumber to think of something other than illness and death.

After some tweaking and fiddling, the fabric incant she'd dreamed up had at last come out to her satisfaction. Wrapping herself in the silky, slithery golden material she'd created, she danced around the attic.

'I think every woman in Dorana would like to see herself dressed in this,' she said, smoothing her cheek against its cool elegance. 'I can make it work just as well with gold and ruby, or with silver and sapphire, silver and amethyst, bronze and citrine . . . Morgan, I believe the possibilities are *endless*!'

Leaning on the wall beside the attic window, arms folded, Morgan stirred himself out of melancholy and smiled. The side-ways-slanting light threw his face into sharp relief, merciless in its revelation of weariness and sorrow.

'I believe you're right. And I believe the outrageous cost of the base materials will be more than covered by the trading returns.'

*Outrageous cost.* Penitent, she stopped dancing. 'I was so caught up in creating this I forgot what you'd be spending on the gold and silk and topaz. Morgan—'

'You owe me nothing, Barl,' he said, still smiling. 'We can't act on this yet, but as soon as the Council deems you sufficiently punished we'll submit the incant for Guild ratification. And once it's ratified I'll talk with our man of business about its trading prospects. Within a year I'll wager you'll find rich women from Trindek to Vharne adorned in your glittering creations . . . not to mention every ranked mage in all fourteen districts.'

Struck silent, she stared at him.

*Just like that? He snaps his fingers and my dream of being the best-known artisan mage in Dorana comes true?*

Morgan raised an eyebrow. 'You don't believe me?'

'No, I do,' she said, dazed. 'Only . . . nothing in my life has ever been so *simple*. I'm not used to wanting and having standing close enough to hold hands.'

'There's no great mystery to it, Barl. The Danfeys have been involved in trading within and beyond Dorana for generations.'

And this was when, of a sudden, Morgan transmuted into a stranger. The things he took for granted. The easiness of his life. It wasn't his fault. Doubtless birds never noticed the air as they flew.

*But for those of us who are earthbound and gasping, the air is all we can think of.*

Smile faded, he was frowning now. 'If you mislike the notion, we don't have to—'

'Mislike it? No!' she said quickly. 'Thank you. *Thank you.*

385

But you may yet come to regret your generosity. Glossy material is but the start of things, you see. My head is stuffed full of ideas for artisan work!'

'As mine is full of . . .'

'Transmutations,' she said, when he didn't finish. 'I know. And we should work on that now, Councillor. You've indulged me long enough with my frivolous fabrics. We should have at least an hour before—' She faltered, seeing his imperfectly concealed pain. 'Or perhaps a little longer, if his lordship rests more comfortably this afternoon.'

She rarely asked how his father was faring. Left it to him to tell her what he could, when he could. He was pressured enough. He didn't need her to push him.

'Yes,' he said, straightening. 'That would be helpful.'

Laying her beautiful golden fabric aside, Barl watched as he assembled the tools he needed for his next experiment with the reworked Hartigan incant. His groundbreaking magework had suffered for lack of attention, and that was grieving him too. *Why* these transmutations were so important to him she still didn't know. Sometimes she thought her curiosity must choke her, but when the urge rose again to ask him what they were for, why they mattered, she gritted her teeth. He would tell her when he was ready. To push for more than he could give her would be to lose him. Of that she had no doubt.

*Like it or not, I am being forced to learn patience.*

And wouldn't Remmie roll his eyes, if he knew.

Muttering under his breath, Morgan picked up his sealed glass jar of powdered *orifim* and shook it. There was very little of the blue-grey catalyst left.

'But you can get more, can't you?' she said, picking up their conversation out of thin air, as often happened since they'd begun working so closely together. 'Or use a different element.'

He slammed the jar on the workbench. 'If I could use something other than *orifim* I would be using it, wouldn't I?'

She'd grown indifferent to his snappishness. 'I don't know. My magework has never required the use of *orifim*.' Or *azafris*, or *susquinel*, or any other of the potent elements he kept here. 'Can you not get more?'

'Not without difficulty. But I shall have to risk it,' he added, more to himself than to her. 'Sallis Arkley be cursed.' A finger-snap beckoned her. 'I need these four catalysts combined in the precise order I've placed the jars. One measure apiece. Be exact.'

'Where are you going?' she said, as he headed for the work-room door.

'To fetch something. I won't be long.'

Turning her attention to the four catalysts he wanted mixed, she hauled a heavy crucible close then one by one dropped into it an exact measure of each element. *Orifim. Barfloy. Yellow wort. Haginth.* Her eyes watered as she crushed each one to a finer powder. In the attic's warm air, a soft sizzle of potency.

The attic door opened, and Morgan returned carrying a large box and a fistful of ebony rook feathers. Something alive was scrabbling inside the box.

Slowly, Barl lowered the pestle into the mortar. 'Morgan?'

He put box and feathers on the workbench, inspected the finely crushed catalysts, and only then turned to look at her. His expression was almost grim.

'Do you trust me?'

'Do I – what kind of question is *that*?'

'An important one.'

'Do I *trust* you? Well, Morgan, given that my life sits precarious in your hands, if I *didn't* trust you I'd have to be a lackwit!'

*Scrabble scrabble scritch* went the prisoner in the box.

She pointed. 'And what is that?'

'An armoured beetle,' he said, frowning at the box. 'From Trindek.'

She stared at him. *No. Surely not.* 'Are you saying you want to transmute it?'

As self-contained as he'd ever been, Morgan folded his arms. 'In a manner of speaking.'

'Morgan . . .' She rubbed her forehead. *Perhaps lack of sleep has muddled his thinking.* 'Transmuting flowers is one thing. But a beetle is—'

'So close to a plant there's no discernible difference. You'd hardly call a beetle intelligent, or aware.'

'That might well be true,' she said slowly, 'but why do I suspect the Council wouldn't see it that way?'

'Since I have no intention of asking the Council to look, your suspicions don't matter.'

Like her, he never meant to be arrogant. Sometimes the words just came out that way. 'Morgan, do you intend to transmute the beetle or don't you?'

'Yes and no,' he said, picking up a rook's feather and threading it through his fingers. 'I want to see if we can imbue these feathers with an aspect of the beetle's armoured carapace.'

As a rule she could follow his thinking with ease . . . but not this time. 'Why?'

'Because Trindeki armoured beetles are unique. Their chitin has been known to turn aside a Vharne swordsman's blade.'

She felt her temper flare. Sometimes he forgot he didn't walk this tightrope alone. 'Don't be clever with me, Morgan.'

'Because it's important,' he said, and let the feather drop. 'To me. To Dorana.'

An answer that wasn't an answer. 'In other words, you want me to take this on faith?'

'Take me on faith. Yes.'

As he'd taken her. How unkind of him to use that weapon. 'And you won't tell me *why* it's so important?'

His sharp regard softened. 'Not won't, Barl. Can't. Not yet.'

Uneasy, she looked at the box. Listened to the scrabbling. 'I know it's just a beetle, Morgan, but still . . . it's alive. In a way all those flowers we've changed will never be alive.'

Morgan stepped close enough to touch her. Rested his finger-tips on her shoulder, briefly. 'You eat meat, don't you?'

'Yes, to live! Are you saying – Morgan, what are you saying?'

'I'm saying I need you to trust me.'

*No, you need me to kill that beetle. To break our most fundamental law, with only your word as surety.*

'I know you think you can keep the Council from interfering, but—' She shivered. 'If you can't, if they find out what we've done . . . Morgan, they'll not spare us.'

He smiled. '*When* the Council learns of it, Barl, when the time comes to tell them? Those haughty mages will fall on their knees in gratitude, and weep. Even Sallis Arkley.'

She wanted to believe him. Needed to believe him. No, she *did* believe him. Why would he lie?

*It's only a beetle. Hardly alive at all.*

'You promise this is to help Dorana?'

'Yes.' A note of pain in his voice. His beautiful eyes steady on her face. 'I swear it.'

'Then we should get started, Councillor. Time's ticking on.'

He wanted to kiss her again, she could see it. But he was handfast with Maris Garrick . . . and an honourable man. To spare both of them, she turned away.

'So, tell me how we begin.'

These past days of their mageworking, flowing into weeks, they'd discovered that together they could achieve things no mage could achieve alone. They complemented each other. Light to dark, shade to sun. Between them there was an instinctive comprehension, understanding without words. She found it more powerful, more perfect even than working with Remmie.

And though transmuting a living creature would be the hardest thing they'd ever attempted, she had no doubt that together they'd succeed.

Speaking quickly, his thoughts running ahead, Morgan explained his intent. It was to invoke the reworked transmutation incant on both beetle and feather together, using a bridging sigil enhanced with the catalysts she'd prepared, to make certain they did not fly apart in the moment of transformation. And in the incant's deliberate gap he intended to insert a sequence of syllables that would see the rook's feather imbued with the armoured character of the beetle.

'Wait,' Barl said, reading his scribbled notations. 'That's not right. Your harmonics are out of kilter.' Snatching the quill from his fingers, she scrawled over his neatly written syllables. 'See? Four beats, then two, then five. Not four and three and three. That will keep the harmonic ripples gentle. And not taking from Berring's Compulsion, either. That's too bullish. What do a feather and a beetle have in common? Not enough that we can shout at them. This needs to be a whisper.'

'Show me,' Morgan said, pulling the paper toward him.

Though he knew syllabic harmonics were her strength, he never would accept her corrections without first poking and prodding and twisting them about. His unwillingness to capitulate had irked her until she realised it was simply his way of making peace with imperfection.

By now used to waiting, she wandered to the attic window and gazed at the distant woodland. How long was it she'd been on this estate? Weeks, now. Had she ever stayed anywhere so long and never left it? No. And yet she didn't feel trammelled. She felt utterly free.

*If I'd listened to Remmie, been meek and apologetic, I would've missed this. Missed Morgan. Let that be a lesson. First and foremost, I must always trust myself.*

Dear Remmie. If her joy was marred it was marred by knowing he could know nothing of her life here. Not until she was freed by the Council. Then she'd send for him, and they'd celebrate, and he would marvel at what she'd achieved.

*He'll be so proud of me. We'll forget we ever had harsh words. And if Morgan's right and my artisan work makes me rich, then I'll buy him a cottage wherever he likes, even if it's pokey little Batava, and after Morgan's married maybe I'll live there too and maybe I won't . . . but he'll be happy. We'll be happy. Everything is going to be all right now. I know it.*

Behind her, Morgan slapped his hands to the workbench. 'Very well. Have it your way. Four then two then five. But if we can't use Berring's Compulsion, Mage Lindin, what do you suggest?'

A few weeks ago she'd never even heard of Berring's Compulsion. But the books in Morgan's library had taught her so much she sometimes thought her skull would burst. Hiding a smile, she turned away from the window.

'I thought perhaps Chalwyn's Quatrain? The alternating rhythms are compelling, but still subtle.'

Morgan considered her a moment. 'Elzear's Variation carries more weight. And this is a difficult transmutation.'

*Difficult* didn't begin to describe what they'd be attempting. And in truth, there was almost nothing to choose between the two incants . . . so surrendering with grace would do her no harm.

'Elzear's Variation it is, Councillor.'

Together they crafted the new version of the reworked transmutation incant. When at last they were satisfied, Barl retreated from the bench.

'You can deal with the beetle, Morgan. I don't like creepy crawly things.'

Which was true . . . but it wasn't the whole truth.

And Morgan knew it, of course. 'You still fret for the beetle's insignificant life?'

'No,' she said, lying. 'The work must come first. But in killing this beetle, though it be for a noble cause, we break our mage oath. I don't want us to overlook that because the life lost is so *small*.'

There was an intent, almost angry look in his eyes. 'You think I have no respect for the rule of law?'

'I think . . .' She swallowed. 'I think that when you believe you're right no law ever written could stand in your way.' *No law. No person.* 'I think I want you to think about that, before we do something that can't be undone.'

'I *have* thought about it!' he snapped. 'Would I cross this line if I didn't *know* I had to?'

He sounded hurt as well as angry . . . and why wouldn't he? He'd asked her to trust him, to have faith in him, and instead she was berating him with suspicion and doubt.

*Remmie would question if I can trust someone I've known only a handful of weeks. But he fell for that girl in Granley the first time he met her. And Morgan has risked so much for me.*

She managed a trembling smile. 'No, you wouldn't. I'm sorry, Morgan. I should be braver than this. I should be fearless.'

'You are fearless,' he said fiercely, and held out his hand. 'Is there another unranked mage who would have stood before the Council and demanded justice? Barl, I know this is daunting . . . but we'll do it together. And in times to come the mages of Dorana will know that *this* was the moment we saved them.'

Yes, but saved them from what? Before they went too much further with this, she'd insist that he tell her. But for now . . .

Breathing out hard, she took his hand. Felt its warmth. Its strength. Felt her blood leap at his touch. Watched his eyes widen as he felt it too.

*This is for Dorana. And it's only a beetle.*

'Very well,' she said, tightening her fingers before releasing him. 'Let's begin.'


Feeling nervous . . . and she *never* felt nervous . . . Venette sat in the corner of her town house workroom and waited for Brice to finish performing a difficult fourfold transmutation: silk to glass, glass to flint, flint to sand, sand to silk. She wasn't sure what she wanted to happen next. If Brice felt nothing out of the ordinary then she was made to look silly and gullible, hardly a welcome outcome. But if he did feel what she'd felt, after four days of searching . . .

*Then we are in a great deal of trouble.*

It had taken a certain amount of trial and error to hit upon the level of mageworking that let her feel what Bellamie Ranowen had felt. Well. *Claimed* she'd felt.

*I'm still not convinced either of us felt anything. We could both be suffering from overactive imaginations.*

Beyond her workroom window, dusk was slowly creeping through the streets of Elvado. Soon the glimlamps would ignite, casting shifting shadows over cobbles and walls, transmuting window after window of stained glass into darker, subtler, more mysterious colours. A kind of magic in itself, and only one of many reasons why she loved this city.

A shiver through her mage-sense turned her attention back to Brice. He was halfway through the transmutation now. Sweat beaded his brow and glistened at his temples as he took a moment to gather himself ready for the next step in the magework. Then with his left hand he inscribed a sigil on the air. The effort of it tremored him. Fresh sweat stippled his skin. The sigil ignited, burned dark green, then fitfully faded. Brice began the next sigil – and then stopped on a sharp breath.

*Oh.*

Feeling ill, Venette stood. Brice, his eyes closed, slowly lowered his upraised hand, fingers clenching to a fist. Tiny spasms of pain flickered over his face and his breathing, usually so controlled, became ragged.

*Oh, justice save us.*

With a grunt, Brice wrenched himself free. Blinking rapidly, in the workroom's soft glimfire his eyes were wide with shock.

Not needing to ask, Venette crossed to the cupboard, withdrew a bottle and a glass and poured him a generous helping of icewine . . . then raised an eyebrow as Brice tipped it straight down his throat.

'More?'

Coughing, he shook his head. 'As much as I'd like to drain the bottle, this is something best dealt with sober.'

'Really? I think I'd rather get uproariously drunk.'

His gaze met hers bleakly. 'Bellamie Ranowen was right.'

*On second thought, I'd prefer to look foolish.*

'Whatever this is, Brice, it must be spreading. Or deepening. You felt it more quickly than I did. It took me many mageworking attempts . . . and I got to the very end of my fourfold transmutation.'

'Whereas Bellamie Ranowen felt it before either of us,' Brice said, frowning. 'In magework that did not demand so much.

I know, I know, you've not been mageworking of late. But Venette, I have. I noticed nothing.'

And that realisation had shaken Brice to his foundations, something she had never thought to witness.

'Don't blame yourself. I doubt there's a mage in Dorana who could've imagined something like this.'

Banging his emptied glass to the workbench, Brice flicked her an impatient look. 'I am head of Dorana's Council of Mages. It is my *duty* to imagine something like this.'

'But Brice, truly, for all we know this – this – whatever it is – might have been present for months. Perhaps years. Just because Bellamie Ranowen stumbled across it a few days ago doesn't mean its origin is recent.'

'Venette . . .' Brice rubbed a hand across his face. 'Let's agree we'll not waste time attempting to make each other feel better.'

'Fine,' she said, a little stung. 'How then would you like to waste it?'

That earned her another look. 'The Council will have to meet at once. And I'll send for Bellamie Ranowen to attend.'

'What of Morgan?'

Sighing, Brice shook his head. 'No.'

'But Brice—'

'*No*, Venette. This matter is extremely grave. I've no desire for distractions.'

Cold with dread, she took an imploring step forward. 'Brice, please, reconsider. When Morgan learns he's been excluded from dealing with something this important he'll be furious. And rightly so. You said he'd be summoned if he was required to—'

'Precisely, Venette. *If he was required.* At the moment we have no idea what we're dealing with. So until we do, we're better off if he stays where he is.'

'You're being unjust,' she said, hearing her voice unsteady and not caring. 'Which isn't like you. First you condone Sallis's underhanded behaviour toward him . . . and now *this*? Brice—'

Brice snapped his spine straight. '*No*. I have it on excellent authority that Greve Danfey will very soon breathe his last.

Given that, not only would it be cruel to take Morgan from his side but even if I did, would his counsel be reliable with his mind mired in grief?'

Shocked, Venette retreated to her chair and sat. Greve was that far gone? Why hadn't Morgan told her? With an effort she smothered the swift hurt.

'You underestimate him, Brice. As much as Morgan loves his father, he loves Dorana more. If we truly are facing a disaster then—'

'Then there will be time for him to help avert it,' Brice said flatly. 'Venette, I'm in no mood to sit in a room listening to Morgan and Sallis bicker while Dorana's mageworking fabric unravels around us! And please, do *not* try to tell me there'll be no bickering.'

She wished she could, but of course he was right. 'Then exclude Sallis, not Morgan. He provokes most of the unpleasantness, you know he does.'

'Impossible,' said Brice. 'However provoking Sallis might be, he is the senior councillor and Morgan is already excused.'

She knew him well enough to realise that further argument was pointless. So she stood again, with all her dignity on show. 'As head of the Council your word is final, of course. But Brice, I warn you, *this is a mistake.*'

Brice offered her a wry, tired smile. 'And if it is, Venette, it's not my first and likely won't be my last. Come. We should make haste to the Hall.'

'Give me a moment,' she said, resigned. 'I'll need to tell Orwin I'm going out.'

'Then I'll see you in the Council chamber,' he said. 'But Venette, you cannot mention this discovery to your husband. *No-one* can know. Not until we know exactly what we're dealing with. And perhaps not even then.'

After nine years, dear Orwin was used to her keeping Council secrets. But even though she knew Brice was right, that news of Bellamie Ranowen's dreadful discovery could not be allowed to escape, still she found herself resenting the stricture.

She had a terrible feeling that this was one burden she'd soon be desperate to share.

'Barl. *Barl*.'

Moaning, Barl opened her eyes. 'Morgan?'

'Here,' he said, bending down and holding out his hand. 'Can you sit up?'

There was blood on his face. Why was he bleeding? And why did her ears ring as though her skull had been turned into a bell?

Then she remembered.

Gasping, she knocked aside his offer of help and scrambled to her feet. 'Did it work? I felt – I *thought* I felt—' Her tongue was stumbling over the simplest of words, and she could feel the salty tang of blood on her lips. 'Morgan, *did it work*?'

He was laughing, his eyes brilliant, hands clasped behind his back. 'Of course it worked!'

'And the harmonics are holding?'

'Of course. Why, did you doubt me?'

'Every good mage fosters a healthy sense of skepticism, Councillor. You know that.'

He laughed again, so excited. 'I know you'll have to say you're sorry!'

'Oh.'

She stared at the greeny-gold rook's feather lightly held in his fingers. It was oddly sheened, as the Trindeki beetle's armoured greeny-gold carapace had been sheened. Her gaze shifted past the feather, past Morgan, to rest on the workbench. Only a wet smear of the beetle remained.

*Funny. I thought . . . I hoped . . . it would vanish entirely. That way –*

Morgan stepped sideways, shielding her. 'Don't look. Don't spoil this. Barl . . . *we did it*.'

When she held out her hand, palm up, he laid the feather across it. The unexpected weight sang through her bones. It was still warm. Still alive with the power that had moulded and melded and made it something new.

*Something that has never before been seen in Dorana.*

'Try to bend it,' Morgan suggested.

She tried, but the feather remained straight.

'Now try to break it. Go on. Throw it on the floor and do your worst.'

'Morgan—'

'Go on!' he insisted. 'Try!'

So she dropped the feather, jumping a little as it struck the wooden floorboards with a clatter. And then she stamped on it, hard, with the sturdy heel of her shoe.

'*Ow!*'

Laughing again, Morgan retrieved it. 'You see? Didn't I tell you that—'

'*Councillor! Councillor!*'

And that was Rumm. Morgan's bloodied face went very still. Heart aching, Barl took the feather back from him.

'Go,' she said gently. 'I'll put this place to rights. But make sure to clean yourself. You don't want to frighten his lordship.'

As the attic door banged shut behind him, she laid the transmuted feather on the end of the workbench. Couldn't stop herself from flinching at the heavy, unfeatherlike sound it made. Flinched again as from the corner of her eye she caught another glimpse of those smeared beetle remains.

*This is no different than the rabbits used to demonstrate Mage Tranter's incant at Winsun. Besides, Dorana must come first.*

Quickly, efficiently, she cleaned up the mess. And after that she summoned the funeral clock to the attic. It was almost completed. Only one or two finishing touches required. She should do that now, just in case . . .

And if she kept herself busy with clock-maging, she'd have no time to think about transmutations. About how it felt to be the first mage in history to transmute a living creature. How the power of the incant had flooded through her like fire, like honey, like Morgan's lips in a kiss.

No, no, no. Best not think about that.

\*   \*   \*

397

'Councillor?'

Startled by the touch on his arm, Morgan jerked his head up. 'Ranmer. What time is it?'

'Some hours past midnight,' said Ranmer, bending low beside the bedside chair. 'And I must tell you there is now nothing more I can do.'

He couldn't bring himself to look at the bed. 'Then go.'

Ranmer hesitated, then straightened. 'I have other patients, Councillor. They—'

'*I said go!* And be certain you hold your tongue on this, Ranmer. If you don't I will hear of it . . . and I won't be amused.'

The pother collected his coat and leather bag and let himself out of the hushed chamber. In the hearth the fire crackled, obscenely cheerful, its scented logs not quite masking the smell of impending death.

Untouched by the flames' warmth, Morgan steeled himself then looked at his father, so frail beneath his burden of blankets. His life measured in embers.

*The end has come so swiftly. Ranmer said we'd have months yet. It seems the fool lied.*

The rise and fall of his father's chest, the flaring of his nostrils, were almost imperceptible. But then his head shifted on his pillows and he muttered something under his breath. Eyes burning, Morgan took his father's hand and felt the terrible, bone-deep cold stab through his trembling fingers.

'My lord,' he whispered. 'I'm here.'

His father's darkly veined eyelids fluttered open. 'Morgan.' A slow breath, rattling deep in the throat. 'New daughter. Where is she?'

His gaze flicked upward, toward the attic. And then he remembered. *No, he means Maris.* 'She's with her family, sir. She sends you her love.'

Which was true. Twice a week like clockwork, Maris Garrick wrote him letters. Good wishes for Lord Danfey mixed with inane gossip, always ending the same way: *I do hope to see you soon.* He made sure not to answer all of them. When he did reply, he kept it short. *His lordship slowly recovers. Your wishes are kindly received.* No more encouragement than that. How could he encourage her? His heart was full of Barl Lindin.

'Morgan.'

Leaning closer, he gagged. The oozing sores covering his father's face and scalp were odorous and putrid with pus. Nothing Ranmer had given the ailing man could keep the rot at bay.

'She should be here,' his father wheezed, clouded eyes alive with anger. 'Maris Garrick. You should be rutting with her. You promised me your *son*.'

'My lord, don't distress yourself. There will be a son, in time. I will—'

'*Too late*.' His father's voice broke. 'You've failed me, Morgan. Without an heir to follow you, the Danfey estate will go to your mother's cousins. The Jarralts will take all.' Blood-tinged tears leaked down his cheeks. 'Ah, what a ruination it is, to have a feckless son.'

The injustice of that was sharper than any uncivilised spear or sword. 'I am sorry, my lord, that I could not marry fast enough to suit you. But I have some good news. That incant I have been working on? I succeeded. Look.'

Releasing his father, he summoned to hand a potted lace-fern from the foyer. Considered its blueish-green foliage, imagined it different, and then told it to change. The chamber's warm air quivered. The lace-fern trembled and blurred. A silent explosion of raw power . . . and then he was holding a fern coloured violet and gold.

'You see, my lord? I have elevated transmutation to an art! And with this new incant I shall protect Dorana from all—'

But his father wasn't listening. Beneath his blankets he was shuddering, convulsions wracking him head to toe. Eyes straining wide, his face drained of colour, a strangled moan escaped his peeled-back lips. Black blood gushed from nose and mouth. Another shuddering convulsion, bowing him in two.

And then nothing . . . save silence.

Morgan stared. 'My lord? My lord? *Father!*'

The fern slipped through his fingers. He scarcely felt his knees crush it as he slid from his chair. Heedless of the blood, the pus, the stench, he gathered his father close and held him as he'd never once in his life held the living, breathing man.

Time passed. The world blurred. When he was again aware of himself, he realised he was standing in the corridor outside the attic. Though its door was warded, he could feel Barl within.

A muffled stirring. The ward collapsed, the door opened, and there she stood, his unranked mage, his miracle.

*My Barl.*

Her eyes filled with tears. 'Lord Danfey?'

Pushing past her, he almost stumbled into the attic. The airy space beneath the mansion's roof was bright as day with glimfire. And on the workbench . . . on the workbench . . .

'It's a funeral clock,' Barl said softly. 'I didn't know your father. But I know you, Morgan. I see him in you.'

Her creation was a fluid, frozen explosion of night-black crystal, dazzled through with tiny brilliant crystals, like stars. Its centre was hollow, and suspended in it the clock's workings, wrought in pure gleaming gold. Swirling around them a rich constellation of jewels: ruby, sapphire, ambrix.

Slowly, he shook his head. 'I don't understand. How did you – *when* did you—'

'Rumm helped me with what I needed,' she said, her gaze not leaving his face. 'And every day, while you sat with your father, I worked on it. Warded it in my chamber so you'd not realise what I was doing.'

He had to clear his throat. 'So you knew . . . you never believed . . .'

'I wanted to, Morgan. But no-one lives forever. And he was very ill.'

The clock was magnificent. Somehow she'd managed to capture his father's spirit, his austere, severe and elegant essence. His brilliance. In a clock she'd somehow captured him.

'Oh no, Morgan, don't,' she said, holding him as the tears came. 'He was suffering. It's better this way.'

He didn't mean to kiss her. His lips just . . . found hers. He felt her fingers thread through his hair, tasted her sweetness as she kissed him in return. His senses swam.

'Morgan,' she murmured. 'Morgan.'

Entwined with her, drowning in her, he let Barl pull him to the attic floor. Let her hands glide beneath his stained tunic. Didn't try to stop her as her fingernails scored his skin. Her touch flamed through him like wildfire. He gave her heat for heat, and smiled to hear her gasp. Tasted her again, her lips, her throat . . . and wondered if he dared taste any more.

She tangled her fingers in his hair and pulled his head lower. Looked into his eyes, smiling, her own eyes glimfire bright. 'It's all right, Morgan. It's all right. I'm not afraid.'

Maris Garrick had said that. But Barl wasn't Maris. She'd not been strumpeted to him by Venette. This time was different. This time he wasn't prey.

With his last coherent thought he summoned a feather quilt from his chamber. Rolled it beneath them . . . and murdered grief with love.

# CHAPTER TWENTY-FIVE

'I'm sorry, councillors,' said Bellamie Ranowen. 'But I have no idea what this phenomenon might be. At least—' She shook her head. 'Let me rephrase that. I know too well what it might – what is most likely is. What I don't know is why it's happening. Which means I don't know how to stop it.'

Sallis snorted. 'And you are held up as some kind of expert? The best mage to advise us the College can find?'

Not waiting for Brice to respond, Venette rapped her knuckles on the Council table. 'My lord, please don't vent your fears upon Mage Ranowen. Without her it's likely we'd still be ignorant of this strife.' She spared the younger woman an apologetic glance. 'Instead I suggest we consider what's to be done. It can only be a matter of time before this – this – *instability* comes to wider attention.'

As Sallis opened his mouth to reply, Brice glared. 'I warn you, Lord Arkley. I am not in the mood.'

Wisely, Sallis subsided. Beside him, as always, Shari patted his hand in consolation.

'Mage Ranowen . . .'

Bellamie Ranowen, less drab this time in muted blue, without a sheltering shawl, turned her attentive, carefully noncommittal face toward Brice. 'My lord?'

'For the benefit of Lord Arkley and Lady Frieden, who have not felt what you and I and Lady Martain have felt, explain what it is you think we are facing.'

Though it was the early hours of the morning, the young, unranked College tutor did not appear unduly tired. Perhaps she was used to working through the night. Venette, aware of a growing headache and her body's disgruntled need for sleep, clenched her jaw against a yawn and blinked to focus her eyes. It wasn't much consolation to know that Brice, Sallis and Shari looked as weary as she felt.

*You'd think stark terror would have us on the edge of our seats.*

But more than anything, she was filled with a numbing disbelief. This was all so improbable, so terribly *unlikely*. They had to be wrong. Didn't they? After centuries of untroubled magework, this couldn't actually be happening?

'Mage Ranowen?' Brice prompted, when the tutor's silence continued.

Standing before them as easily as she stood in a classroom, Bellamie Ranowen stirred out of thought.

'I'm sorry, my lord. I was trying to decide how best to answer.'

'Are you suggesting that we are somehow *simple*?' Shari demanded. 'Perhaps I should remind you, Mage Ranowen, of who in this chamber is unranked and who sits upon the Council of Mages!'

Four – nearly five – days ago, Bellamie Ranowen had seemed a woman in want of her wits. Watching her closely now, Venette saw that she had regained her poise and self-restraint. Looking at offended Shari, unintimidated, the young woman merely inclined her head.

'My apologies, Lady Frieden. Of course I am suggesting no such thing. Only I have been told that on occasion my explanations can veer toward the complicatedly theoretical. I investigate questions of magework as much as I teach, you understand. So I wish to avoid the need for tedious explanations when, with a little effort, I might express myself more plainly.'

403

'Very considerate of you,' said Sallis, unimpressed. 'Now do as Lord Varen bid.'

Another polite nod. 'Certainly, my lord. In its simplest terms, then, and begging your indulgence for a fanciful illustration, I would say that if Dorana were a tapestry, then some of its threads have come loose.'

Sallis and Shari exchanged looks. Then Shari pursed her lips. 'Yes indeed, a most fanciful illustration. But I find myself no more educated than I was before.'

'The warp and weft of magic that permeates the world, that the mages of Dorana can feel and manipulate to everyone's great advantage, has been damaged,' said Bellamie Ranowen. 'How, I cannot tell you. Not yet. But what I can say, Councillors, is this: until the cause of this disruption is found, we cannot continue our magework. If we do, we will only hasten the tapestry's unravelling.'

Venette closed her eyes. Though she'd fleetingly suspected that what she'd felt might lead to this, hearing the suspicion spoken aloud, so bluntly, made her feel ill.

Sallis was choking. 'You'd have us cease our magework? Woman, are you *mad*?'

'Mad?' said Bellamie Ranowen. There was an edge to her voice, as though she chided a rude student. 'No, my lord. But I am very frightened.'

'And would make cowards of *us,* to keep you company!'

'Lord Arkley, such invective serves no useful purpose,' said Brice. 'Mage Ranowen, you must understand such a suggestion is . . .' He frowned. 'Unprecedented.'

'What is happening is unprecedented,' said Bellamie Ranowen. 'And I would prefer to err on the side of caution.'

'No, you'd prefer to set Dorana in an uproar,' said Shari. 'Not to mention damage its standing in the wider world.'

His face so grave, so careworn, Brice braced his hands on the table and stood. 'Mage Ranowen, your advice is appreciated. Now wait outside, in the antechamber, while this Council considers what you've had to say.'

'There's nothing to consider,' said Sallis, belligerent, even as the door closed behind Bellamie Ranowen. 'At best she's an alarmist and at worst an utter charlatan. Where is her proof? I have not seen it.'

Seated again, Brice stared at him. 'So a sighted man says the sky is blue, a blind man says I do not believe you, where is your proof, and you would take the blind man's side? Is that it?'

'You're calling me *blind*?' Clumsy with anger, Sallis shoved to his feet. 'Because I am not so quick to believe the outlandish claims of an unranked, overweening young woman who—'

'Justice preserve me, Sallis!' Brice shouted. 'This is *not* about Nevin Jordane! Have you wax plugs in your ears? I felt this unravelling *myself*, mere hours ago. Venette has felt it and so has Mage Ranowen. It is *real*, not some fancy born of too much wine or mopeweed. And as the premier mages of Dorana we have a sacred duty to take whatever steps are needed to prevent a disaster!'

Venette watched as Sallis struggled to rein in his temper. 'Brice is right,' she said softly. 'You know he is, Sallis. But Brice—' She shook her head. 'Sallis has a point too. We might be reading these warning signs correctly, but we *cannot* suspend mageworking throughout Dorana. Not with such flimsy proof. And it *is* flimsy.'

'Nor can we impose such an edict without a thorough explanation,' Shari added. 'Which I'm sure we must be loath to give. Unless of course you are eager to see panic break out from one end of Dorana to the other?'

Brice flicked her an irritated look. 'Don't be ridiculous.'

'No, what's ridiculous is Mage Ranowen's suggestion!' Shari snapped. 'And do not for a moment think I will support it!'

'Nor will I, Brice,' Venette said, still feeling ill. Feeling like a traitor. 'Not yet. Not until I can be persuaded there is no other course to take.'

'And what will persuade you, Lady Martain? The wholesale collapse of our way of life?'

The pain in Brice's voice was shocking. Even Sallis was taken

405

aback. Sinking into his seat, he glanced at Shari then rearranged his face into an expression of solemn concern.

'My lord, of course I do not doubt your experience of this phenomenon,' he said, choosing his words carefully. 'And you may be assured that as soon as I'm able I shall seek to confirm its existence myself. But if it were a widespread problem we would know, for other mages would have brought it to our attention. They have not. This gives me some little cause for hope, that whatever this anomaly might be, it is yet in its infancy and so can be easily contained.'

Shari nodded. 'Well said. I agree.'

'And you, Venette?' Brice asked. 'Do you also agree?'

'I think I must,' she said, after a moment. 'It would be tragic indeed if in seeking to save ourselves from one disaster, we created another by acting in haste. Let this Council task Bellamie Ranowen to learn all that she can about Dorana's unravelling tapestry. And while she investigates, so can we. Let us make discreet enquiries in every district. Learn by diverse and unobtrusive means whether there are other mages who have felt anything . . . strange. Between us I've no doubt we can shed light on this mystery.'

'Very well,' Brice said at last. 'For now, that will be our course of action. But let me make one thing abundantly clear. This is now our greatest secret. We in this chamber and Bellamie Ranowen must be the only mages who know of it. Not a word, not a *whisper,* to anyone else.'

In other words, don't tell Morgan. Venette met Brice's cold stare with a coldness of her own, angrily aware of smug Sallis and Shari, gloating.

'What of the General Council?' she said. 'Do you mean to treat them with equal disdain?'

'Those fribbles?' Sallis snorted. 'Why would we involve them? Half their number at least is unranked. Their acumen is taxed enough with tariffs and petty lawbreakers. This Council has no need of their prosaic advice.'

'I'm sure Lady Brislyn would be edified to hear it!'

'Enough, both of you,' Brice said tiredly. 'The time may well come that we must inform the General Council. For now, with the rest of Dorana, they will remain ignorant. Sallis, ask Mage Ranowen to step back in. The sooner we start our investigations, the sooner we can put this distasteful business behind us.'

Morgan opened his eyes to the warmth of Barl curled by his side on the floor . . . and the freezing memory of his father's agonised death.

The sunlight shafting through the attic's window was pale. Insubstantial. So it was early, then. Not much above an hour past dawn. He'd have to go downstairs. The servants must already be stirring. They'd have to be told. And there were things to be done.

But all he wanted to do was stay here with Barl.

Breathing softly, he kissed her forehead. Knew that if he kissed her lips, tasted her again, he might not leave the attic for a week. Her golden hair was tousled, her innocent, exciting hands pillowed under her cheek. The faintest of shadows tinted the skin beneath her closed eyes. The lips he didn't dare kiss were bruised with last night's passion. But then, so were his bruised. For all he was the one with experience, they had fallen asleep as equals.

Abruptly, almost painfully, he wanted her again.

Holding his breath, he slid out from beneath the feather quilt. Barl murmured a little protest but didn't wake. His clothes were unwearable, so he gathered them up and went downstairs to his privy apartments. Cold water from the ewer doused passion and chased away the lingering remnants of sleep. Sober and heavy-eyed, he stared at his reflection in the mirror above the basin.

*Lord Danfey is dead. Long live Lord Danfey.*

He dressed in black silk brocade and went downstairs to the silent third floor. Stood outside his father's privy apartments, fingers resting on the door handle, and waited for the courage that would let him go in.

It didn't come. Perhaps if Barl was with him, then he could face –

Without warning the doors opened, revealing a grimly pale Rumm.

'Sir! I mean—' Rumm swallowed. 'My lord.'

*My lord.* Shuddering, Morgan stared at him. 'What are you doing?'

Instead of answering, Rumm stepped aside and held the door open. 'My lord.'

So now he had no choice. He had to go in.

Vaguely aware of Rumm following him, he crossed the hushed, empty sitting room and entered his father's bedchamber. Braced himself, as the door swung open on its oiled hinges, for the sight and stink of his father as he'd left him, bloodied and twisted and fouled in the final indignities of death.

'Rumm?' He turned. 'What is this?'

The master servant moved past him to stand at the foot of the neatly made bed, on which lay the bathed, dressed and peaceful body of Greve Danfey. The chamber's air was sweet again, scented with fresh flowers.

'This is the last service I could perform for your father, my lord.'

What could he say? He lacked the words. And even if he'd had them, he lacked a voice with which to speak.

Rumm's eyes were full of grief. 'My lord, I am so sorry.'

He nodded. Stood in silence for a time, looking at his father, feeling Rumm's sorrow like the touch of a friendly hand. Then he looked up.

'Do you intend to stay, now his lordship is dead?'

'What?' Rumm said, startled. 'Forgive me, my lord. I mean, yes. Of course. Unless . . .'

'No. You're invaluable. But I want the other servants released from their duties. Not permanently, although if they'd prefer that they are free to leave my employ. Otherwise send them home, to be called back in due course.'

'My lord,' said Rumm, severely noncommittal.

'You shouldn't be overburdened with work. There will only be myself and Mage Lindin to care for. And much of the time, we'll take care of ourselves.' Despite the pain, despite his dead father on the bed before him, Morgan smiled. 'I hope you know which end of a stable fork to use.'

Rumm's eyes widened, as close to a shout of surprise as he would come. 'As it happens, my lord, I do. And, if I might ask, should I also prepare for the arrival of Mage Garrick?'

*Maris.*

There was no point trying to hide the truth from Rumm. 'My courtship of Maris Garrick is ended. My affections have been engaged elsewhere.'

'My lord.' Rumm's gaze flicked ceilingward. 'Yes, my lord.'

He felt himself tense. 'You disapprove?'

'My lord, it is hardly my place to approve or disapprove,' said Rumm. 'But since you have broached the subject, I will say that it's clear Mage Lindin makes you happy.'

The man was astonishing. 'Yes. She does. Rumm, tell the servants they're not to speak of his lordship. If anyone asks, they're to say he rests comfortably. We will crypt him ourselves, tonight, in private.'

'My lord.'

'It is out of the ordinary, I know,' he said, hearing Rumm's unspoken disapproval. 'But I have my reasons. And if you wish to remain here, you'll not question them. Understood?'

Rumm bowed. 'My lord.'

Unable to bear the sight of his father's corpse any longer, Morgan crossed to the window and drew back its curtain.

'You must also know this, Rumm. Mage Lindin and I are engaged in magework crucial to the benefit and safety of Dorana. Some of this work is not, strictly speaking, sanctioned. You may see things, or hear things, that strike you as odd. If you feel unable to—'

'My lord,' said Rumm, 'say no more. I know you would die to protect Dorana, and that is all the explanation I need.'

A sting of tears. He blinked them away. 'This mageworking

means that, from time to time, I will be relying on you to assist me in obtaining what some might call . . . dubious supplies. Does—'

'My lord.'

This time Rumm sounded pained. 'I don't intend to take you for granted!' Morgan said, then looked over his shoulder. 'Speaking of supplies, Mage Lindin says you helped her with the creation of my father's funeral clock.'

Rumm looked down. 'It was nothing, my lord.'

'No, Rumm. It was something. And it won't be forgotten.' He turned back to the window. 'Now I'd like a little time alone. See to the servants, and then . . . do whatever it is that you do.'

'My lord,' said Rumm. 'Shall you and Mage Lindin be wanting breakfast?'

'Barl will, most likely. For myself . . .'

The thought of food had bile rising to burn his throat.

'My lord,' Rumm murmured, perfectly deferential, and withdrew.

In silence, for some time, Morgan continued to stare out of the window at the woodland, and distant Elvado. It was disturbing, knowing his father was behind him . . . and hearing only himself breathe.

*But he is dead. He is dead. And I must become accustomed.*

As he stood there, gazing at the estate that was now his, the pale morning light grew stronger and deeper. At last he stirred, and turned to the bed with its silent, stiffening burden.

'I'd have you understand this, my lord. I don't abandon Maris Garrick to spite you. I do not love her. I never did. And love matters to me. I know you thought me weak and foolish for that. You thought it was my mother's taint and so you did your best to rid me of it. You failed, my lord . . . and for that I am most grateful. If I dropped dead beside you now, in this moment, I would die a happier man for one night in Barl Lindin's arms than you ever were in the whole of your life.'

And having said that, he walked out.

\*      \*      \*

410

He found Barl in the library, dressed in her faded, favourite blue linens and deep in perusal of Thimbole's *Examination of an Incant*. Hearing his footfalls on the parquetry she looked up. Her eyes were shadowed, and grave.

His heart thumped, remembering. 'Are you sorry?'

'No,' she said. 'Are you?'

'*No*.'

She lowered the book to her lap, slowly. 'And what about Maris?'

He closed the library door. 'Maris who?'

'Morgan . . .' Her lips curved into a faint, kissable smile. 'Do you mean that?'

He didn't smile back. This was too important. 'My father wanted Maris. I make my own choices now. Barl, I choose you. I chose you, last night.'

Her fingertip smoothed the edge of one page. 'And I chose you, Morgan. But this is a new day. And before I choose you again, for good, I'd have something clear between us. *I want no more secrets.* No more half-truths. No more answers that aren't answers. Morgan, we transmuted a living creature. Everything is different now. And if you want me to follow you any further down this path, you'll tell me *why* we did that. Or you'll walk it alone.'

Step by step he closed the distance between them, and when he reached the chair he dropped to his knees.

'Barl, do you trust me?'

'Oh, *Morgan*.' Her face twisted. 'Did you not hear what I just said?'

Reaching over the top of the book, he seized both her hands. 'I *am* answering you. But first, answer me.'

'*Yes*. I *trust* you. I don't know why you keep asking. If I've not proven it by now then—'

'You have,' he said, and pressed her knuckles to his lips. 'The trouble is, I don't have a good reason to give you. I can tell you why, but that isn't the same. Because the why is nothing more than a feeling, *my* feeling, that Dorana isn't safe.'

411

'Not safe?' She frowned. 'I don't understand.'

'I don't either, sometimes,' he confessed. 'Thought about lightly, my fears make no sense. We are mages, gifted beyond the dreaming of any other race. We're respected, even feared, by every nation beyond our borders. While our neighbours make war on each other, we live in peace. While their rulers rise and fall in dynastic conflagrations, we conduct our affairs with consummate civility.'

'Really?' she said. 'I'd hardly call Sallis Arkley civil.'

'Sallis Arkley is a cantankerous old bastard, but that's not the point. Despite personal differences, our culture endures. It thrives.'

'And yet you say we're not safe?'

Letting go of her hands, he sat back on his heels and rubbed his hands across his face. 'No. I do not think we are. We might be mages, Barl, but we can still be pierced by a spear or slashed in two by a sword. An arrow can puncture our hearts. A rock can crush our skulls.'

'We have incants that can destroy weapons like that.'

'True,' he said. 'But what if we faced hundreds of them? Or thousands? We could never invoke those incants fast enough then. And don't forget the panic that would surely spread in the face of such aggression.'

Her eyes widened with disbelief. 'You think Feen or Trindek or Vharne or *any* of our neighbours would be so foolish as to *attack* us?'

'I don't know,' he muttered. 'When you say it out loud it sounds ridiculous. I see that. But Barl, the truth is that Dorana is defenceless. We abandoned martial magework nearly four centuries ago. Yes, the incants still exist, but they're warded deep below the Hall, never again to see the light of day. Beyond the Council, I'd wager every other mage has forgotten we ever used them. For all the good they could do us, they might as well have been destroyed.'

Barl swung her legs over the side of the reading chair and slid to her feet. 'But why would we need them? We're not at war,

Morgan. And whatever bickering exists between Feen and Manemli, or Trindek and Iringa, or Iringa and Vharne, it has nothing to do with us. It never has done. It never will. This is *Dorana*. We don't need martial magework. No other nation would dare raise its hand to us.'

He shook his head. 'You sound like Sallis and Shari.'

'And you sound mad!'

'I'm not,' he said, and unfolded to his feet. 'Barl, we are in danger. Even without proof of it, I know that as surely as I know I love you. As surely as I knew you were the only woman for me, the very first time I saw you in Hahren's antechamber.'

'Oh, Morgan.' She turned away, then almost at once turned back again. 'Wait. You saw me *then*?'

'I did. And sat through dinner with Maris afterwards, unable to see any face but yours.'

He'd surprised her. 'I had no idea,' she murmured. 'I was so upset that day, so *angry*.'

'A good thing, too,' he said. 'Else you might not have flown at Hahren . . . and we may never have met.'

She stared at him, fingers straying to her lips. 'You're quite sure you've no proof of this danger aside from your feelings?'

'None,' he said simply. 'Which is why this is about trust.'

'And I do trust you,' she said. 'Never doubt that. But Dorana in danger? Attacked? It sounds so *unlikely* . . .' Sighing, she turned to the nearest bookshelf and gazed at the titles before her. 'But let's assume you're right. What do our transmutations have to do with this?'

And now they'd reached the heart of the matter.

'Since we cannot defend ourselves, we need someone . . . or something . . . to defend us. Something that cannot be defeated by swords and slingshots and arrows. That will fight for us, and die for us, so that no mage of Dorana will be lost.'

'You want to create warriors?'

'I do.'

Hesitant, she turned back to him. 'Create them out of what? Trindeki armoured beetles?'

'Partly,' he said, and took a step toward her. 'But the Trindeki beetle was only the beginning. Once we have perfected the transmutation, we'll need to look further afield.'

Her eyes clouded. 'Use other living creatures, you mean?'

'I know,' he said. 'I find the notion distasteful, too. But how much more distasteful will it be if we do *nothing,* and Doranen mages end up slaughtered in their beds? Barl, could you forgive yourself if even one mage died when you might have saved him? I couldn't, so I *must* do this. And I cannot do it alone.'

Looking away, Barl let herself slump against the bookshelves. Morgan watched her, his heart pounding, so frightened she'd say no and walk out of his life forever.

*What will I do if she leaves me? How will I live if she's gone?*

'Barl—'

She held up a hand, demanding his silence. So he fell silent, and waited, sweat trickling down his ribs.

At last she straightened, and stepped close to him. Her hand, fingers spread, came to rest above his thundering heart. Lifting her head she stared at him, seeming to see right through his soul.

'Swear to me, Morgan, on the memory of your father, that everything you've said is true. That Dorana is in mortal danger. That there is no other way to save it but *this*. And that if we should learn we've made a mistake we will *stop* our dangerous magework . . . and destroy all trace of what we've done.'

He covered her hand with his. Lowered his lips to hers, and kissed her. Relief and joy and excitement were a bonfire in his blood.

'My love . . . my beloved . . . I do so solemnly swear.'

*'Promise me this, Barl. Promise me you won't die.'*

Lying in Morgan's bed as he slept restless beside her, Barl heard his anguished plea echo in her memory, and sighed. He was so powerful, and yet so afraid. She'd never expected that. The new Lord Danfey was such a contradiction. In his magework unassailable, but in her arms, as vulnerable as a child. And not simply because he mourned for his father. He was scarred more deeply than that.

Since the night of Lord Danfey's death, Morgan had laid his life bare to her. She'd wept with him as he remembered his mother. Held him tight as he shared his memories of Luzena, reliving his first love's cruel, untimely death. Watched him, close to tears, as he haltingly roamed his chamber, chivvied by Greve Danfey, that imperious, autocratic, demanding old man.

Four days had passed since his lordship's crypting, performed privily with only themselves and Rumm as witness. She'd helped Morgan with the preserving incants and the effigy for the tomb, lending him her magework when his own faltered beneath the burden of his overpowering grief. At first she'd been afraid her own memories of loss would render her useless to help him. Instead they'd given her strength . . . and he'd leaned on that strength as though without it he would perish.

'*Promise me this, Barl. Promise me you won't die.*'

And of course she'd promised. What else could she do?

'*Neither of us will die, Morgan. You and I will live forever.*'

Which wasn't true, and never could be. Of course they knew that. But for a small time they had to pretend it was, or be broken to pieces.

She hadn't known love would be like this. So consuming. So *liberating*. For the first time in her life she really was herself. Only now, with Morgan beside her, did she understand how caged she'd been. Remmie, dear Remmie, used his love like a tether, always *tugging* to keep her close to the ground. Remmie lived his life in fear. But Morgan . . . Morgan . . .

*Morgan gave me wings and demanded that I fly.*

And to think she'd cursed Artisan Master Arndel, when without his mean-spirited, short-sighted interference she and Morgan would never have discovered how perfectly they complemented each other.

*Like Hahren, without Arndel we would never have met.*

The moment it was safe to declare themselves in public, she'd return to Arndel's artisanry and thank him in person. And then she was going to laugh while he choked on his bile.

*Between us, there is no magic Morgan and I can't do. Together we will save Dorana. I think it's why we were born.*

Remembering that, it was growing easier to accept what must be done. Sometimes, caught up in the power of the transmutation incant as first they perfected the melding of armoured beetle with feather, then moved on to the next, even more challenging stage of their quest, it was even possible to forget that in her determination to save Dorana she was taking lives with magic. She welcomed that oblivion, even as she accepted Morgan was right. Small lives perished so larger lives could survive. There was no shame. It was simply the rule of nature. More fool her to ever forget it.

'Barl . . .'

She opened her eyes to find his heavy blue gaze upon her. Traced his smiling lips with her fingertips. Smiled as he kissed them.

'Good morning, my love. I slept well. Did you?'

Hoisting himself onto one elbow, Morgan smoothed her hair from around her face then slid his hand down further to pull sheet and blanket aside. He said he never tired of seeing her naked. His desire for her was bold. Invigorating. Unashamed. It woke in her a recklessness, so that she revelled in his regard.

'I slept perfectly,' he said, trailing his fingers from her navel, between her breasts, to the base of her throat. 'But now I'm awake.'

The day's new light, filtering through the window, gilded his face and all the muscles of his arm and chest. Lifting her head, she tasted him. Felt him tremble. Felt her power.

'So I see,' she murmured. 'And so am I.'

It was another kind of magic, their loving. Pleasure upon pleasure, so powerful that it hurt. There was nothing he could do to her she would not welcome. Nothing he could ask of her she would not give. And when it was her turn to demand, he gave without hesitation. They surrendered to each other. They both conquered. They both won. Her cry of release mingled with his sobbing sigh.

Sweat-slicked and sated, they clung to each other in the wreckage of his bed. A good thing they'd warded the chamber to silence, else they'd have Rumm banging the doors down in the belief they were being murdered.

Morgan kissed her, lightly, then rested his head on her breasts. She could feel his heart thudding, keeping time with hers.

'Barl . . . my beloved . . .' His sigh fanned her damp skin. 'I never knew how starved I was until you became my feast.'

She roamed her fingers down his spine, relishing the feel of taut skin and muscle. Breathing him in, she felt the slow burn of fresh arousal.

'And I was a paper woman, until you set me on fire.'

Quizzical, he shook his head. 'That makes no sense.'

'It makes perfect sense,' she said, laughing. 'I'm forged anew in your flames, Morgan. The old Barl Lindin is a drift of ash and I've taken her place. I am gold and iron. Everything that is made beautiful in conflagration, that's me.'

He kissed her eyes, her cheeks, her lips. Kissed her breasts and her belly. 'That's very true. Barl, thank you for my father's clock.'

It was the first time he'd mentioned it since that night. 'I was afraid that once you'd had time to consider what I'd done, you'd be angry. I thought you might think it an impertinence and punish Rumm for overstepping his bounds.'

'No. *No.*' Morgan stretched out beside her, entwining his fingers with hers. 'How could you think that of me?'

'How could I not think it? I didn't know you then.'

Rolling his head on the pillow, he stared into her eyes. 'And you know me now?'

'Yes,' she whispered. 'As I know myself.'

He raised their linked hands. Kissed each of her knuckles. 'I never knew myself until I met you. That other man with my face, he is a stranger.'

The simple declaration brought her to tears. When he pulled

her close she hid against him, undone by happiness. He loved her again, slowly, like a priest worshipping his goddess. Selfishly she let him, accepted each caress like a tribute, each gasping wave of pleasure as though it were her due. At last, when he'd wrung from her so many shudders she was sure she must die, he took his own shuddering release.

Humbled, she framed his face with her hands. 'I love you, Morgan Danfey. You are the lord of my heart.'

He stared at her, silent, as tears brimmed in his eyes. And then he smiled. 'And you are my lady . . . until time itself ends.'

For a moment, one single, terrible moment, she couldn't breathe through her fear. *Don't die,* he'd begged her, the night they crypted his father, and she'd promised she wouldn't, promised him knowing it was a lie.

*Unless . . . unless . . . is there a way to defeat death?*

She didn't know. But if there was, she would do her best to find it. Or create it. Because if anything should ever happen to him? Well. Living without Morgan would not be living at all.

# CHAPTER TWENTY-SIX

An hour later, Morgan considered his dwindling supply of catalysts, and frowned.

'I think we must soon send Rumm off with a fat purse and a long list.'

'How soon?' said Barl, as she scribbled notations at the attic workbench. 'And for how long? He must have time to bake us a pie before he goes, and he can't stay away more than one night, else between us we'll either burn down the mansion trying to cook dinner . . . or starve.'

If that weren't true, it might be amusing. Perhaps he'd acted a trifle hastily in dismissing all the servants. Of course, solitude and privacy were paramount so his mageworking with Barl might continue uninterrupted, but timely, edible meals were also important. He might have to consider bringing back the cook.

Barl set aside her quill and joined him to stare at the dozens of emptied and nearly emptied jars and bottles on the workroom's shelves.

'How difficult will it be to replace what's been used?'

He frowned again. 'Difficult enough. Though most of these catalysts aren't restricted, we have run out of so many that if we're not roundabout there may well be awkward questions asked. And

I have no desire to rouse Sallis Arkley's curiosity. Not when the Council seems to have forgotten our existence.'

'Then it's best Rumm makes his purchases from more than one supplier,' she said. 'He must become a busy little bee, dipping for nectar from a variety of blossoms. That way nothing he does will be remarkable – or remarked upon.'

And that was only one reason to love her. She had a quicksilver mind that was forever in tune with his.

'Morgan.' She touched her fingertips to the back of his neck, making him shiver. 'Speaking of the Council . . . it's a week since your father died. Ranmer has held his tongue so far, but we can't trust he'll not let slip the truth. Or if Lord Varen asks him directly how your father does, of course he'll answer.'

And if that happened, they'd have Varen and the others on their doorstep, overflowing with spurious sympathy and likely demanding his return to the Hall. He was surprised he'd not already had to fend off Venette. So much for her claims of affection and concern.

Barl slipped her arm through his. 'What are you going to do? If the Council recalls you to duty, will you go?'

'I won't have a choice,' he said, resentful. 'But never fret, my love. Our magework will continue. Not even Brice Varen can be allowed to interfere with that.'

She nodded. 'Agreed. Now come see what I've done with this next variation. I fear the transmutation will still be deadly, but I think I might now have found a glimmer of hope.'

For the next few hours they worked side by side, deconstructing Hartigan's reimagined incant syllable by syllable, searching for the elusive combination of paired harmonics that would let them create a transmutation without killing the subject. So far they'd had no success with that. And until they did, his dream of an invincible defender for Dorana would never be more than a dream.

The thought of failure was a constant haunting. If it hadn't been for Barl, he wasn't sure he could sustain his hope. But with her at his side, he could believe nothing was impossible. The sun would be his, and the moon, and the stars.

As the morning ticked its steady way toward noon, Morgan kept catching himself no longer working, just watching, entranced by the way his beloved lost herself inside her mind.

His father's last words to him were a wound yet to heal. If he still lived, Greve Danfey would claim his son's adoration of Barl Lindin was merely a childish rebellion. Greve Danfey would say that, a man who never loved his wife.

*He never knew what love was. He never loved me, I think, to want for me a loveless union like his.*

Tongue nipped between her teeth, Barl scribbled down more of her quicksilver thoughts. Then, feeling his regard, as she always felt it, she glanced up.

'What?'

Instead of answering, he kissed her. And in kissing her ignited his passion, which these days was insatiable, sleeping lightly beneath his skin. No need for words, for asking permission. If he wanted her, she wanted him no less fiercely. Ink, quill and scribbled incants were swept to the floor. A jar of *rathil* crashed after them, scattering glass splinters and expensive dried leaves. Pleasure was pain, and pain gave pleasure, and when he looked into her eyes he saw nothing but the future.

In the aftermath, replete and panting, she pushed back her tousled hair and laughed. 'Curse you, Morgan. Now I don't remember what harmonic key I wanted to use.'

'You will,' he said, sliding off the workbench. Then, as he put his clothing to rights, he smiled. 'Think about it while I fetch us lunch. Oh – and while I'm doing that, you might also tidy this workroom.' Glass cracked beneath his feet as he retreated to the attic door. 'Such a disgrace, these unranked mages. No sense of decorum, no notion of tidiness . . .'

Laughing, he closed the door on her outraged shriek.

But his amusement was short-lived. Rumm intercepted him on the third floor landing, his jaw tight, his eyes anxious.

'I'm sorry, my lord. I did my best, but . . . she was insistent.'

Morgan felt his cheer fade. 'Don't tell me, let me guess. Lady Martain? Well, I suppose it was only—'

'*No*, my lord. It's Maris Garrick.'

A shudder of revulsion. 'Maris?'

Very upright, very proper, Rumm clasped his work-roughened hands behind his back. 'If you recall, my lord, two days ago I did draw your attention to several letters received that you are yet to open.'

Letters from Maris. He'd lacked the stomach to read them. Had thrown them back at Rumm, now he thought of it, with a curt order to keep unwelcome missives out of his sight.

He sighed. Now was his hand forced. How easily he could hate Maris, for ruining his peace.

'So, Rumm. You are proven right, yet again.'

'I am sorry, my lord.'

In passing, he patted Rumm's dejected shoulder. 'No need for apologies. This is my doing.'

Because her arrival had unnerved him, or because he knew precisely how poorly she'd be welcomed, Rumm had left Maris to amuse herself in the foyer. Hearing footsteps on the staircase she looked up, her expression twisted between hope and annoyance. She was dressed with a restraint that belied her wanton nature, her cream silk tunic throat-buttoned, her skirts almost sweeping the floor.

'Morgan!' she said brightly, seeing him. Her eyes were cautious, her fingers tight. 'So you're not ailing after all. It's been so long since I've heard from you I was convinced you suffered an ague.'

He stopped on the fourth stair from the bottom of the staircase, hands clasped before him. His tunic was unbuttoned, his skin still damp with sweat and warm from the memory of Barl's fingers and lips.

'No, Maris. As you can see, I am well.'

A hint of puzzlement in her face. 'Yes. And your father? How does he go on?'

'Alas. My father is dead.'

Her lips parted. '*Dead?* But—' She frowned, the puzzlement growing. 'There has been no announcement.'

'I haven't made one yet.'

'Dead,' she said again. 'So that means—'

And if it was a pleasure watching Barl think, it turned his stomach watching Maris. 'Yes. I am now Lord Danfey.'

She took a step toward him, almost eager, then halted. 'Morgan, I am sorry. Why did you not send for me? It's not right, you shouldn't be alone with your grief. You shouldn't—'

'I don't care to discuss my grief, Maris,' he said. 'It's a private thing.'

'*Private?*' Breathing hard, her milky skin flushed, she stared at him. 'Morgan, what is going on? Why do you look at me so strangely?'

They had coupled in a closet, he and this girl. The tawdry memory shamed him. Felt like a betrayal of the woman he loved. Looking at Maris now, he was astonished at himself.

*Did I truly think I could marry her? Did I imagine I could ask Barl to live with being second-best? I must have been mad. Yes. I was out of my mind.*

Watching the colour fade from Maris's cheeks, he felt a vague wash of pity. True, she was cold and calculating . . . but in fairness, he'd been just as prepared to use her. Justice be praised he'd come to his senses in time.

Maris took another step forward. 'Please, Morgan. You're frightening me. Something else has happened, hasn't it? Tell me. Whatever it is, we can face it together.'

He offered her a small, regretful smile. 'You shouldn't have come here, Maris. Not without an invitation. It was unwise – and impolite.'

A breath of shocked laughter escaped her. 'Impolite? Morgan, has grief disordered you? We are *handfast*. How can you stand there and talk to me of *impolite*? If we must discuss a lack of manners, let us consider your disheveled appearance, shall we? To present yourself to me as good as half dressed, with your hair unbound and unbrushed? It is most unbecoming of you!'

'Unbecoming?' an amused voice said, from behind him. 'Oh, I don't think so. Myself, I think he's as comely as can be.'

*Barl.*

As Maris's face blanched snowish, Morgan held out his hand.

Smiled to feel his beloved's fingers slide over his. Through his. Tighten, until two were become one.

Maris was staring. 'Morgan, who is this – this—'

'Person?' said Barl, helpfully.

She bared her teeth. '*Whore.*'

'No, Morgan,' Barl said sharply, as he tensed. 'It's all right. The only thing we've left her is anger.' Slipping her fingers free of him, she continued down the staircase until she reached the foyer floor. Her tunic was fastened, but not every button was in its hole. 'I am sorry, Mage Garrick. But he was never really yours.'

Tears glittered brilliant in Maris's slitted eyes. '*Lord Danfey and I are handfast.*'

'No,' said Barl. 'You were. But his lordship has changed his mind.'

Maris gasped. '*Morgan?*'

He said nothing, content to let Barl and his silence speak for him.

'Think,' Barl said. 'If he loved you, could I – could anyone – come between you?'

Maris's glittering tears fell, raining rage down her cheeks. 'Who *are* you?'

'My name would mean nothing to you, Mage Garrick.'

Maris took a step back. 'You are *unranked*?'

'Ranked or unranked, what difference does it make?'

'What difference?' Maris shook her head, disbelieving. Shifted her gaze past Barl. 'Morgan—'

Impatient now, he trod the last four stairs lightly and stood beside Barl. 'If this discovery distresses you, Maris, you've only yourself to blame. I intended to withdraw my pledge to your father in a manner that would have shielded you. It was your choice to impose yourself upon me like this.'

She chewed her lip, gaze stabbing back and forth between them. 'I think . . . I think . . .' She breathed out, a snake hiss. 'The loss of your father has clearly unbalanced your reason, Morgan. And I believe it is not unheard of, in times of distress, for a man to seek solace in common female flesh. I will not judge you for it. No. I will forgive you. Especially since no-one need know of this . . . lapse. You can send this slut packing and we need never mention it again.'

'If I send any slut packing, Maris, that slut will be you,' he said, out of patience. 'Do you imagine I fucked you for any reason but filial duty? Do you think I don't know who it was sent you into that closet? It was *business*, Mage Garrick. And it happens I've decided to take my business elsewhere.' With a snap of his fingers he swung wide the foyer doors. 'You showed yourself in. You can show yourself out.'

She stood before him an ice maiden, still and cold as winter. And then, without another word, she left.

'That was unkind, Morgan,' Barl said, pressing her hand to his back. Hot and heavy it rested there, thawing his own icy rage. 'You can't blame her for being hurt.'

He waved the doors shut. 'She wasn't hurt, Barl. She was insulted. Maris Garrick never loved me.'

'But I do,' Barl whispered. Sliding her hand around him, she passed it softly over his face. 'And I always will. So no more frowning, Lord Danfey.' Her other hand slipped inside his tunic, shivering his skin. 'Let's eat, shall we, and then get back to work. We've incants to finish, and a shopping list to compile.'

He let her tug him to the stairs leading down to the kitchen, where they'd taken to eating their meals so there'd be less cleaning up for Rumm. Her loving comfort was a balm to his frostbitten soul. Thanks to Maris Garrick, their idyllic respite from the world would soon end. He could hate the bitch for that, if for nothing else.

*But I don't care who she tells, or how hard she stamps her feet. There is no law in Dorana that compels a mage to wed. A handfast is simply a promise . . . and promises are broken every day.*

Heart sunk almost as far as her silk slippers, Venette cast a resigned look at her husband.

'You'd best go, Orwin,' she murmured. 'I'm sure Maris will feel better with only another woman for company.'

Orwin nodded. 'Indeed,' he said, thankful, and made his escape.

She rolled her eyes. *Typical*. And then forgot him as she turned her attention to Maris.

Distraught, too angry to weep, though doubtless tears would come, the girl was batting her way around the town house parlour like an exotic moth trapped in a jar.

'Maris,' Venette said, yet again. 'My dear, you really must compose yourself. Please, do sit down, and tell me what's wrong.'

Although she was tolerably certain she knew the answer already, or part of it. *Morgan*. Only a man could put a woman into such a state.

Chalky pale, Maris whirled about, narrowly missing an exorbitantly expensive Feenish vase. 'Who is she, Venette? Who is the whore with her claws sunk into Morgan Danfey?'

The whore? What was the girl talking about? Who could – And then she realised. *Barl Lindin*. Flooding cold, Venette stared.

*Oh surely not, Morgan. Surely not, you fool.*

'Ah! So you do know her!' said Maris, angrily triumphant. 'Don't bother denying it, the truth is written all over your face.'

Venette sat a little straighter. Chilled her voice. 'Do be careful, my dear. I'm not in the habit of being spoken to like that.'

But Maris was too upset to notice her trespass. 'I don't understand, Venette! I thought you cared for me!'

'Don't be silly, Maris. Of course I care!'

'Then how could you push me into Morgan's arms knowing he already had a mistress? He *flaunted* her before me, Venette. I could smell the passion on them, they stank like alley cats. *Who is she?* I shall *ruin* her. I shall see that she is dragged through the mud.'

'You'll do no such thing,' she snapped. 'You will leave this to me.'

'To *you*?' Maris's laugh was almost hysterical. 'Venette, you are the *cause* of this debacle! I'm spurned. He's discarded me. For that nobody, that unranked mage, that thieving little whore!'

Much more of this unbridled hysteria and she'd be forced to

slap Maris's face. 'Mage Garrick! Control yourself! You *will* leave this to me!'

'Why?'

'Because I'm telling you to. Because the situation is more delicate than you realise. There are ramifications that—'

'Do not speak to me of ramifications!' Maris said, close to screeching. 'I *know* there are ramifications, Venette! What mage of rank will wed with me now? When news of this spreads, I—'

'Maris, it won't spread,' she said quickly. 'Between us we'll make sure of that. You'll not be humiliated.'

Maris snatched up a pillow and threw it, haphazard. '*You wouldn't say that if you'd seen them together!*'

She felt a wave of rage at Morgan so thick and hot that for a moment she couldn't breathe.

*Oh, Morgan, you thoughtless, selfish bastard.*

'Maris,' she said, fighting for composure. 'Please, my poor child, sit down so we can discuss this matter calmly.'

The tears came then, as she'd expected. She let Maris sob stormily for a few moments, then handed her a handkerchief.

'Dry your eyes, my dear, and catch your breath. You're upset, it's only natural, but I think you'll agree that Lord Danfey won't let Morgan do anything so crass as *spurn* you. I've known Greve most of my life, and while he might be unwell at present I can promise you he won't – what?'

Maris was staring again, her mouth almost comically open. 'You don't know?'

Another shiver of dread. 'Know what?'

'The old man's dead, Venette. Morgan is Lord Danfey now.'

*The old man's dead.*

She sat there, unmoving, not sure of what she felt. Shock, yes. Grief. Of course. But most of all she felt a fresh wave of searing anger.

*How could you not tell me, Morgan? How could you let me find out like this?*

'No,' she said, hearing her voice oddly distant. Detached, as though she'd never even met Greve Danfey. 'I hadn't heard.'

'He hasn't told anyone,' said Maris, sneering. 'He's been too busy fucking his whore. Venette, I'd be surprised if his father is even *crypted*.'

She shook her head. 'No. No. Not even Morgan at his most careless would leave his father to rot.'

Maris sneered again, trembling fingers twisting and untwisting the damp handkerchief. And then her sickly pale face crumpled. 'Oh, *Venette*. What shall I do?'

'Go home,' she said, wincing as a vicious pain stabbed behind her eyes. 'And stay there. Tell your parents what's happened, and then tell them they *must* speak to me before they say or do *anything*.' She raised a warning finger. 'I can salvage your pride, Maris. I can, with some wrangling, undo the damage Morgan has wrought. But only if you and your parents hold your tongues. Discretion is *vital*. Is that clear?'

Breathing quickly, Maris wrestled with that dictate. At last she nodded. 'But I want him punished, Venette. If he walks away from this unbruised, if he is allowed to insult the Garricks in such a fashion and pay no price, then I swear you'll see ramifications the likes of which Dorana has never known.'

'Have no fear, Maris. Morgan will not go unscathed.'

'And *her*?' Maris demanded. 'His whore?'

Barl Lindin. *Who I knew full well was trouble the moment I laid eyes on her.* 'You can leave her to me.'

Maris said nothing for some moments, her gaze narrowed. 'She was laughing at me, Venette.'

'I promise you, Maris. By the time I am done with that little bitch, laughter will be the furthest thing from her mind.' And then, as though she were seeing Maris for the first time, she frowned. 'My dear – how did you get here? Weren't you still at your family's country estate?'

'Yes,' said Maris. 'But I used a travel incant. How did you think?'

A travel incant, and over such a distance. What a mercy nothing had gone wrong. And it could have, easily. Bellamie Ranowen's latest report to the Council had warned them the mysterious instability was growing more marked. She'd urged them again, forcefully, to begin magework restrictions. She'd practically *begged* them to put a stop to incant travel. Brice had once more refused the College mage's request, but it was clear his resolve was weakening. Even Sallis and Shari were beginning to rethink their stance, because at last they'd felt the wrongness for themselves.

*And all of us know it's just a matter of time before we won't be able to keep it a secret any more. We might not have admitted it aloud yet . . . but we know.*

'Venette?' said Maris. 'Are you all right?'

With an effort she thrust the fear out of sight. 'Hardly, my dear. Your news has quite broken my heart. And now I'll ask a favour of you. Don't incant back to the country. I'll have my travelling carriage take you. Incanting such a distance when you're upset isn't safe. *Please,* Maris,' she insisted, as the girl began to protest. 'I'd never forgive myself if something went wrong.'

Sighing, Maris nodded. 'All right.'

Light-headed with relief, Venette summoned her master servant. 'Jarman, Mage Garrick is leaving. I want the travelling carriage put to so it can take her home. And while she waits, bring her refreshments.'

Jarman bowed. 'My lady.'

'I'll have to desert you now, I'm afraid,' she said, forcing a smile. 'You've brought me quite the knot to untangle and it's best if I get to work straight away.' She held out her arms. Maris hesitated, then went to her. Holding the girl tight, she kissed her damp cheek. 'You must not worry about this, my dear. I will make everything right, I promise.'

'I *told* you!' With rare, unchecked anger Sallis slammed both fists to the Council table. 'We had no business letting Danfey take that troublemaking mage out of here. Now, Brice, see where your soft-hearted pity leads us!'

Venette watched Brice's lips pinch bloodless, and held out a calming hand. 'Please, Sallis. Shouting recriminations at each other is hardly going to solve anything. Besides, it's not as if any law has been broken.'

'If you didn't think this was a disaster you wouldn't have called for an emergency meeting,' Sallis snapped. 'So kindly—'

'I called for this meeting because Greve Danfey is dead and Morgan has not seen fit to inform us of the fact,' she retorted. 'The death of a ranked mage is very much Council business. That one of our own is bereaved makes it doubly a matter of concern. As for this other unpleasantness—'

'Is that what you call it, Venette? When a ranked mage, a *councillor,* stoops to rutting below his station?' Shari Frieden tittered. '*Unpleasantness?*'

'It is highly unpleasant, I promise you, when a charming young woman like Maris Garrick is put in such an untenable position!'

Shari sniffed. 'A great pity you didn't seek advice when it came to pushing a match between the Garrick girl and Morgan Danfey. I could have told you it would all end in tears. The Danfey men's history with women is—'

'Not the point, surely. I don't see—'

'Of course you see,' said Brice, frowning. 'You simply chose to ignore your misgivings, Venette. As I chose to ignore mine when it came to allowing Morgan custody of Barl Lindin.' He shifted his dour gaze to Shari. 'But I suggest you reconsider your accusations, Lady Frieden. It might well be inadvisable for ranked and unranked mages to mingle, but doing so is not a legal transgression.'

'It is when she's a proven miscreant and he's her Council-appointed custodian,' said Sallis. 'Why are we even debating this, Brice? Mage Lindin must be retrieved, immediately, and put under a judiciary's lock and key. As for Morgan, well, I think he has more than made my argument for me. He must be expelled from this Council.'

'For what?' Venette demanded, before Brice could reply. 'Seeking an escape from his grief by dallying in the wrong bed?'

Sallis laughed, mocking. 'Of course you defend him. The sun

has yet to rise on a day in which you won't defend Morgan Danfey.'

'*Defend* him, Sallis? I could slap him until he begged for mercy! I am so angry I happily admit I agree with you in that Barl Lindin cannot remain where she is. But I won't support you in Morgan's expulsion. However distasteful we might find his behaviour, he isn't a miscreant. We don't have the grounds.'

'Lack of judgement is grounds,' said Shari. 'A resolution of no confidence is grounds.'

'You require a unanimous opinion for that,' she retorted. 'You don't have it.'

Flushed with temper, Shari leaned across the table. 'It seems to me, Venette, that when it comes to Morgan Danfey your judgement is equally lacking. Perhaps—'

'*Enough,*' said Brice, his voice heavy with warning. 'I will not preside over a catfight. We are in agreement on one thing. Barl Lindin must return to the Hall of Knowledge, after which time we will further consider her fate. To that end, I suggest we pay Morgan a visit.'

'Why should we go to him?' Sallis demanded. 'Like supplicants? Summon him to us, Brice. Let him answer for his gross behaviour here.'

'No, Sallis,' said Brice, shaking his head. 'I would not put him on the defensive. As Venette says, he is grieving. Let us show him some little mercy. Express our condolences for his loss, as is proper, then exert our influence as tactfully as we can.' He looked around the table, his lined face weary. 'Do you feel comfortable travelling by incant? I'd prefer no delay in this.'

If any of them were nervous, they weren't about to admit it. They incanted to the Danfey estate, and were greeted at the mansion's imposing front doors by its master servant.

With a glance, Brice ceded his authority for the moment. Grateful, Venette stepped forward. 'Rumm. We must speak with Councillor Danfey.'

Looking past her to Brice, the master servant hesitated then bowed. 'Councillors.'

Rumm's form of address wasn't incorrect, but it lacked a certain . . . deference. Uneasy, Venette looked at him more closely.

'We've heard your sad news, Rumm. You have the Council's sympathy.'

Rumm's eyes glittered, his grief close to the surface. 'Thank you, my lady.'

'Where is the councillor now?'

'His lordship is occupied with privy business,' said Rumm, a note of censure in his voice. 'I shall inform him of your arrival. Please come with me.'

As Rumm left them stranded in the foyer and withdrew to fetch Morgan, Brice gestured her a little aside. 'This is most odd. There is a powerful warding around this estate. Can you feel it?'

Of course she could. Morgan's country home dwelled within a cocoon. 'Yes.'

'Venette, I do not care for it.'

And neither did she, but if they didn't tread carefully this visit would end in disaster. 'I'm sure it's nothing nefarious,' she murmured, with a worried look at Sallis and Shari. 'Brice, please, one fight at a time. First let us settle—'

'More uninvited visitors?' a brittle voice said behind them. 'How irritating. I think I must consider some kind of lock on the gate.'

They turned. *Morgan.* Seeing the grief in him, feeling it, Venette bit her lip. Her anger still burned, but who could remain indifferent to such pain? A touch to her arm told her Brice was resuming his authority. She eased back, her heart pounding.

*Don't be a fool, Morgan. Please. Don't be a fool.*

'Councillor,' Brice said quietly. 'The Council extends to you its formal condolences on the death of Lord Danfey. All of Dorana shares in your loss.'

'You should have told us yourself he was dead,' said Sallis. 'Why didn't you?'

Brice turned. '*Lord Arkley.*'

Chastened, at least for the moment, Sallis stared at the foyer floor. Shari stepped closer to him, her inevitable allegiance truculently declared.

'Let me guess, Brice,' Morgan drawled. He was clad in indigo silk, unrelieved by jewels. The colour heightened his pallor, and all the planes and edges in his face. 'Maris ran to Venette, and Venette ran to you.' He laughed. 'And now you've run to me, doubtless with a list of demands. We'll make this quick, shall we? *You cannot have her.*'

Sighing, Brice clasped his hands before him. 'Morgan, you—'

'*Lord Danfey.*'

Risking Brice's displeasure, Venette took a step toward Greve's reckless son. 'Whether or not Maris should have involved me, Morgan, one thing is indisputable. Mage Lindin can't remain on this estate. You must see it's not . . . advisable. And quite apart from the social implications there is the brute fact that she's a miscreant. She belongs in a cell.'

'She belongs here. You wanted her punished? She was punished. And now she is with me.'

'Which is surely some kind of punishment,' said Shari, 'but not the sentence meted out by the Council.'

Morgan's eyes were so dark they looked like polished obsidian. 'The Council's sentence was that she be bound until she saw the error of her ways. She has seen it.'

'So you say,' Brice said, with admirable restraint. 'But that is not your decision.'

'Nor is it yours,' said Morgan, so haughty. 'You forfeited your power over her when you chose to treat her differently for no better reason than she is unranked.'

Sallis made a spitting sound of disgust. 'We're wasting our time, Brice. Unbridled lust has overturned his judgement.'

'And unbridled arrogance long ago destroyed yours!' Morgan stared at them, his thin face twisted with contempt. 'Who do you people think you are, to barge into my home demanding the life of a blameless young woman? *You cannot have her.* Whatever small mistake Barl Lindin made with Hahren is paid for and done. And if you think to force my hand on this, be warned. I will shout your

433

injustice into every corner of this land. I will see *you* bound, I swear it, with unbreakable chains of your own making. Have you forgotten that in Dorana we have *two* Councils? And that the General Council is the voice of the unranked . . . who outnumber us?'

Shari broke the shocked silence with a disbelieving laugh. 'You are threatening us? With a *rabble*?'

'No,' said Morgan, thinly smiling. 'I merely remind you of an uncomfortable truth. But if you're eager for a rabble, Shari, then all you need do is persecute Barl Lindin. You'll have your rabble then. I promise.'

Another silence. Then Brice sighed. 'Lord Danfey—'

Morgan folded his arms, so proud. So unapproachable. So like his dead father.

'Don't bother, Lord Varen. You can keep your Council seat. I have no further use for it. I have no use for you.' He flicked his fingers, and behind them the foyer doors swung open. 'My thanks for your condolences.'

For a moment Venette thought Brice was going to argue. Then he nodded. 'Farewell, my lord. For now. But we shall speak again. Soon. When you are less . . . distempered.'

He turned for the doors, and with a sharp look took sputtering Sallis and Shari with him. Venette stayed, waiting for Morgan to speak. When he didn't, she sighed.

'Well, my dear. This is something of a tangle.'

'For you, perhaps,' he said, shrugging. 'Not me.'

There had to be a way to reach him. 'You must know you've hurt Maris.'

He snorted. 'A pinprick. She'll live.'

'Morgan . . . what are you *doing*?'

'I'm following my heart.'

'Your *heart*?'

His laugh was bitter. 'What – you don't think I have one?'

'Don't be silly,' she snapped. 'I think—'

*I think Barl Lindin will ruin you. I think this is a mistake.*

And then she shook her head. What was the point? He had no intention of listening. His mind was made up.

'My dear, I am so sorry about Greve.'

His lips tightened. 'He's at peace now.'

Perhaps. If only she could say the same about his son. 'Morgan—'

'You should go,' he said, nodding at the doors. 'Or they'll be claiming I hold you here against your will.'

He really was unreachable. She'd never felt like that before. Despite Maris, despite her anger and disappointment, she was deeply grieved. Somehow, she'd failed him. She'd failed his mother, her friend. Close to tears, she nodded.

'Well, then. Goodbye, my dear.'

'Goodbye, Venette.'

But before she reached the foyer doors, she slowed then turned back. 'Morgan, why is the estate warded?'

'Why do you care?' he said, sneering. 'Or is it you'd like to add that to my list of transgressions?'

'Of course not. You've broken no law. Tell me . . . is it because you've been mageworking with Barl Lindin?'

'And if I have?'

'Then some might say that *is* breaking the law. She hasn't been formally released from her binding.'

He shrugged, faintly smiling. 'I released her. All perfectly legal, since I was a councillor at the time.'

Which was true. Conflicted, Venette bit her lip. She should say something of Bellamie Ranowen's alarm. But if Brice found out she'd directly disobeyed him . . .

*I must speak. Morgan's one of our best mages. And we need all the help we can get.*

'During your mageworking, you've not felt anything . . . out of the ordinary, have you?'

Morgan raised an eyebrow. 'Out of the ordinary?'

'Peculiar. Odd. You know. Unusual.'

'No, Venette,' he said, and gestured at the open doors. 'Goodbye.'

Defeated, at least for the moment, she left.

# CHAPTER TWENTY-SEVEN

Morgan didn't need to look round to know that Rumm had returned cat-footed to the foyer and was standing ready, the model master servant. Waving the open doors shut again, he considered his departed visitors.

'Do you think they will test your resolve, my lord?'

'I don't know, Rumm,' he said, after a moment. 'I hope not, for their sakes.'

'Yes, my lord.'

Turning, he offered the master servant a grim smile. 'It's not too late to find other employment.'

'Thank you, my lord, but I am perfectly satisfied in my current position.'

'Which now involves cooking, dusting, laundry, scullery, chickens, hounds and stables.'

Rumm's severely proper expression eased. 'I was developing a little paunch. Happily, it would appear that danger has been averted.'

'Very happily,' he said, and laughed, though his mood was so grim. 'Rumm—'

'It seems to me, my lord,' said Rumm, serious again, 'that though the Council of Mages must be honoured for its services to Dorana, that honour should not extend to giving it power over a man's heart, and upon whom that heart might be bestowed.'

'Rumm,' he said, after a moment. 'You should know I voted *aye* on the amendment that now prevents you from marrying.'

'I am not surprised to hear it. In almost all things, you are your father's son. But as you say, my lord.' Rumm smiled, very dry. 'There are two Councils in Dorana . . . and rules can be amended. Was there anything else you required?'

'Dinner, in due course,' he said, staring. 'And on the morrow there will be mageworking supplies to procure. I should warn you, that task will likely occupy the whole day and be something of an onerous undertaking.'

Rumm bowed. 'My lord.'

'Just so we understand each other,' Morgan said, as Rumm turned to leave. 'I meant what I said. I will start a civil war before I let Brice Varen steal Mage Lindin from me.'

Rumm's gaze was steady. 'Yes, my lord. I did take that to be your meaning.'

'That frightens you.'

'Yes, my lord. It does.'

'Let's hope it frightens Lord Varen, too. And Sallis Arkley.'

Rumm hesitated, then nodded. 'I'm sure it does, my lord. Just as I'm sure Lady Martain won't let things go so far. She's your friend. She'll speak up for you.'

*Venette*. A perpetual thorn in his side. He grimaced. 'She was my friend until I spoiled her plan for Maris Garrick.'

'No, my lord. She's still your friend.'

'Certain of that, are you?'

'Quite certain, my lord.'

And perhaps Rumm was right. Perhaps Venette would forgive him. Had already forgiven him.

*The question is, do I forgive her?*

'Very good, Rumm. You can go.'

In the library, waiting for him, Barl had pulled down almost a shelf's worth of books and was sat cross-legged on the floor, surrounded. Without looking up at his entrance she waved an impatient hand at him.

'At last! I thought you'd get rid of them much faster than that. Now come sit beside me, for I've found something here that might help us with our transmutations.'

Amused, he closed the door. 'You don't want to hear what our revered Council had to say?'

'No,' she said, glancing up. 'Why? Was it other than we expected?'

'It was not.'

'Well, then.'

'You're not interested in what *I* said?'

Now she smiled, brilliant. 'You said what I would've said, had someone come to threaten you. Go away or be very sorry.'

He laughed. 'Is that what I said?'

'Isn't it?'

'More or less. Though you should know, I resigned.'

'From the Council?' She blinked. 'For *me*?'

'And for me. I've had more than enough of their prosing interference.'

'Yes, but Morgan . . .' Troubled, Barl laced her fingers and stared at them. 'I do wish you hadn't done that. Not even partly for me. It's an important thing, a prestigious thing, being on the Council of Mages. Your father would never have wanted you to resign.'

Morgan joined her on the floor. 'Barl, there are many things I plan to do that my father would never have wanted. But I cannot live my life dancing to a tune played on a dead man's violin.' He touched his fingers to her knee. 'This was my choice, and I am content with it.'

She looked up. 'Truly?'

'Truly.'

'All right,' she muttered, and blew out a sharp breath. Then she thrust the book she was reading at him. 'See here. *Ollet's Compendium*. It's terribly quaint, isn't it? All these old-fashioned incants nobody uses any more. But I've found this one. What do you think?'

He looked where her finger pointed. *Being a rumination on a transmutation of intent. Recommended for the shifting of diametric oppositions.* Well . . . that was unexpected. Had he even known the *Compendium* was here?

*If I did, I'd forgotten. But trust Barl to find it . . . and to find the exact incant we must have to proceed.*

Taking his silence to mean disagreement, she wriggled a little and tapped the page.

'You said it yourself, Morgan,' she added. 'Every time we adjust the incant's base harmonics we seem to throw it out of balance somewhere else. I know I argued with you, but I begin to suspect you've been right all along. There is something askew in the fundamentals of the aspect enhancement. That's why we can't progress any further.'

She intoxicated him when she got like this. Leaning sideways, he pressed his lips to the pulse at the base of her throat. 'So I was right, was I?' he murmured. 'I think that means I deserve some kind of forfeit.'

'Yes, yes, later,' she said, impatient, and shrugged him away. 'Look, Morgan. Please. And tell me I've not stumbled across the perfect solution to our conundrum. I'll wager you can't, though. I'll wager I've solved at least one of our problems!'

Fingertip pressed beneath her chin, he drew her face toward him and took her lips in a swift kiss.

'You, my love, are the answer to every problem. Didn't you know it?'

She dimpled at him, wickedly. 'Well, yes, of course. But I was trying to be modest.'

'Really?' He widened his eyes. 'Why? You've never tried before.'

'Oh, Morgan. Do be sensible. Now let's go back up to the attic so we can—'

'In a minute,' he said, and took hold of her hand. 'But first . . .'

She stilled. 'What? Is something wrong? The Council. Did something else happen?'

'Something, yes. Perhaps,' he said slowly. There'd been such an *odd* look in Venette's eyes before she left. An improperly masked fear, that was very unlike her. 'As we've been mageworking, Barl, have you felt anything . . . untoward?'

'Untoward? What do you mean?'

He wished he knew. He wished he'd not dismissed Venette without first making her explain what she'd meant. But he'd been so angry.

'I think . . . Venette is worried.'

A shadow skimmed Barl's expressive face. 'Your dear friend Lady Martain has no love for me. Doubtless she's of the opinion I've ruined your life.'

'True, but that's not what I'm getting at.'

She looked at him, properly. 'Then what are you getting at?'

'I'm not sure,' he said, shrugging. 'She asked me if we'd felt anything out of the ordinary during our magework.'

'Out of the ordinary how?'

He shook his head. 'She didn't say. I didn't ask. I was eager for her to leave. But—' Frowning, he saw again that fearful glint in Venette's eyes. 'As I said. She was worried.'

'Well, my love, I've felt nothing to give me pause,' Barl said. 'And if I had, you'd know for I'd have straightaway told you.'

'And I'd have told you if I'd felt uneasy. And I haven't.'

'Exactly. And since if there *was* something wrong you and I would surely feel it . . .' Sliding the *Compendium* to the floor, Barl scrambled to her feet. 'Pay her no mind, Morgan. This is only Venette Martain seeking to cause trouble. She's trying to lure you back to the Council so they can crowd you into a corner and harangue you until you change your mind about me.'

Surprised, he watched her step over piles of books and cross to the library window. Stand before it with her back to him, her arms folded, her shoulders slumping a little as though she were burdened by some impossible fear.

'Barl? What is it?'

She pulled away from him a little when he joined her. 'Nothing.'

'*Barl.*'

'Well, it's the *Council,* isn't it?' she demanded, her voice unsteady. 'Morgan, they have so much power. And now that you're not one of them . . .'

'Not being one of them any more doesn't make me helpless,' he said, sliding an arm around her shoulders. 'Should they try anything foolish they would soon regret it. Barl, you are safe. *We* are safe. They can moan and mislike us to their heart's content but they cannot, they *will* not, interfere any more.'

She shivered. 'You sound so certain.'

'I *am* certain. I have not the slightest doubt that they'll leave us alone.'

Pulling away a little, she looked at him. 'What exactly *did* you say to them?'

He thought it might be best not to tell her. Not now, when she was feeling unsure of herself, and vulnerable.

'Nothing of which my father would have approved,' he said, and kissed the top of her head. 'Do not ask me to elaborate. I'd not sully your ears with language of that stripe. Now, what say we take *Ollet's Compendium* and—'

She pressed her palm to his chest. 'Yes, but first – Morgan, I've been thinking. There's something I need to do. *Want* to do. And I think I should do it sooner, rather than later.'

There was no need for her to tell him. He'd been waiting for her to speak on this. 'Your brother.'

Her eyes were tear-bright, and full of relief. 'Yes. I knew you'd . . .' Her fingers smoothed the front of his tunic. 'I have to go and see him. He must be sick with worry for me by now. I want to tell him I'm all right. I want to tell him goodbye.'

He felt an enormous blossoming of joy. 'Goodbye?'

'This is my home now,' she whispered. '*You* are my home. It's Remmie's turn to find his home. But he won't unless I tell him to his face that he must. My brother's a lovely man, and a jigget. This is the only way. Believe me.'

He stroked his fingertip down her cheek, across her lips. 'I do.'

'I won't be gone long. I'll be back in time for dinner.'

'You mean you want to go now?'

'I see no point in waiting.'

He gestured to *Ollet's Compendium,* abandoned on the floor. 'What of our mageworking?'

'I know, I know. After dinner?' She pulled a face. 'Or in the morning, if Remmie keeps me late. But that's all right, isn't it?'

'Yes. But you should know I resent every heartbeat you're away from me. I resent even a brother. I want you to myself.'

'And you have me,' she said softly. 'But Morgan, a part of me still belongs to Remmie. It always will.'

Yes, he could see that. And he could see that fighting Barl's brother for it would leave him the loser. So he smiled.

'You're family, and you love him. Go. I'll tender my formal written resignation to the Council. And then there's that list of catalysts for Rumm.'

'Speaking of which,' Barl said, brows pinching. 'Since he's going to be obtaining supplies. I think he should procure us some more chickens, Morgan. An awful lot have died, and we do need eggs.'

'More chickens,' he said gravely. 'I think that can be arranged. Anything else?'

'I don't think so,' she said, glowing like glimfire. 'And starting tomorrow, my love, with the help of *Ollet's Compendium,* we will take our recalcitrant transmutation incant by the scruff of its neck and shake it until it conforms most pefectly to our will!'

He watched her skim out of the library, so light and graceful on her feet. His Barl. His beloved.

*Bid farewell to her, Remmie. She's mine now. Not yours.*

When she walked into the schoolmaster cottage's kitchen she gave Remmie such a fright that he dropped his pan of mutton soup onto the floor.

'*Barl!*'

Oh, it was so *good* to see him. He was a jigget, and he tethered her, but she loved him anyway.

'Remmie,' she said, her voice breaking, and threw herself into his open, eager arms. Held him as hard and tight as he was holding her, half-laughing, half-crying, just like him.

'I can't believe it,' he said at last, pushing her to arm's length. 'Are you really here?'

'I'm here,' she said, smearing her cheeks dry. 'Remmie, the floor's swimming in soup.'

He looked down. 'Oh. So it is.' He put the dented pan in the sink then banished the mess with a quick chant and a sigil. 'Barl, *how* are you here? When Lord Danfey came to see me, he said you'd be gone a long time. And while it's *felt* like years, really it's only been weeks. Are you all right? What did they do to you? I mean, you look all right but—'

'*Remmie*! If you'd bite your tongue I could get a word in edgewise!'

He stared for a moment, then burst out laughing. 'Oh, Barl, I have *missed* you!'

'And I've missed you,' she said, grinning like a fool. 'Cut us some bread, pull out the butter, and I'll explain.'

'Still the same bossy Barl, I see,' he grumbled, but he did as she said and they settled down at the table with fresh bread and butter and cherry conserve between them. Still staring, Remmie reached out and poked her.

'What was that for?'

'Sorry,' he said, grinning like a fool himself. 'Just making certain you're real.' And then the grin faded. 'Tell me everything, Barl. Don't think to spare me.'

So she told him, and in the telling held back only her work with Morgan on the transmutation incants. It wasn't her secret to share . . . and besides, she knew her brother. She'd never be able to convince him she and Morgan were right.

It was harder than she'd expected, reliving the worst of the past weeks. The fear, the binding, the dread of being prisoned magickless for the rest of her life. Remmie listened without speaking, only his harsh breathing and his eyes revealing the depth of his pain. It wasn't until she told him about her and Morgan that he broke his silence.

'*What?*' Disbelieving, he sat back. 'You and Councillor Danfey?' He shook his head, seemingly unable to say it. As though the thought of his sister naked in a man's arms was more than he could stomach. '*Barl.*'

She wasn't sure what she'd expected. A little happiness for her, at least, after so much pain endured and survived. What she hadn't looked for was a stare of shocked disapproval.

*You were pushing me at Barton Haye, Remmie. If I'd not pushed back, where do you think I'd have ended up? I never imagined you could be such a prude.*

'He's Lord Danfey now, Remmie,' she said, nettled. 'His father died. And he's not a councillor any more, either. He resigned his appointment.'

'*Lord* Danfey? That's even harder to reconcile! Barl . . . what are you thinking? He's a ranked mage. And he's – he's—' Remmie pulled a face. 'He's so *cold.*'

'He's not cold at all,' she said, offended. 'You don't know what you're saying.'

'I certainly do! I met him, remember?'

'He was being a councillor then, on official Council business. That's all changed. He's different now.'

Remmie's eyes narrowed. 'Because he's resigned. And was that your doing?'

'No!' Then she wriggled a little bit, compelled out of habit to be properly truthful. 'Not exactly.'

'Then what exactly was it?'

'You're as bad as the Council,' she muttered, poking holes in her unfinished slice of bread. 'They don't approve of Morgan and me either. So he stepped down. But I *never* asked him to.'

'I swear,' Remmie said, marvelling. 'I never knew anyone who could find trouble the way you can.'

She glowered at him. 'Well, one thing's for certain. *You* haven't changed. Always convinced that I go *looking* for strife.'

'I'm sorry. Barl, what about your binding? It's not officially lifted, is it?'

'No,' she said, after a moment. 'But they won't try to bind me again. Morgan won't let them. And neither will I.'

'*You* won't . . .' He was staring again, aghast. 'Barl, do you *hear* yourself? Who do you think you are?'

'I'll tell you who I *will* be, very soon. Lady Danfey. And you'd best believe that while the Council might bully unranked Barl Lindin, they won't dare lift a finger against another ranked mage!'

'*Ranked?*' Remmie dropped his head into his hands. 'Barl, I think that binding must have addled you.' He looked up again. 'Handfast yourself to whoever you like, but to the Council and the First Families you will *never* be ranked. They won't accept you as one of their own. Why would they, when you've broken every rule in the book?'

'You make falling in love sound like a crime!' she said, indignant. 'Remmie, don't you *dare* be tiresome. I didn't have to come to see you, you know. I could have stayed on the estate and left you twisting in the wind!'

'Maybe you should have,' he said, slopping too much cherry conserve on a fresh slice of bread. Then he sighed. 'You must admit, none of this sounds very likely. A ranked mage, a lord, tumbling head over heels for you?'

Sitting back, she folded her arms. 'Such flattery, my dear! If you're not careful you'll turn my head.'

'You know what I mean,' he said, folding the bread in half, his boyhood habit. Rich red fruit oozed out of each end. 'I'm sure other ranked mages have dallied below them, but none of them handfasted with their fripperies! He's defying his peers, Barl. He's defying the *Council*.' Brooding, he shoved the folded bread into his mouth and bit it in half. Chewed, swallowed, and swiped conserve off his chin. 'Was this his idea, too? Like resigning? Or . . . you know.'

And to think she'd fretted herself sick about him, harrowed by the thought of him fretting for her.

'You mean did I look to seduce Morgan to save myself?'

Remmie blushed. 'Of course not. I know you wouldn't.'

Because she was so irked, she decided to shock him with more truth. 'Actually, if you must know, I might have. Since I was feeling quite desperate. Being bound, Remmie?' She shivered. 'Never again. I'd rather be dead.'

He was still holding his half-eaten slice of bread. Cherry conserve dripped onto his fingers. 'You don't mean that.'

'Don't I?' She treated him to a fierce smile. 'If ever you're bound, Remmie, you'll find that I do. It's the cruellest, the most inhuman, the most—' She had to clear her throat. 'Binding is wicked. And I'll see an end to it, Remmie. *Anyway*.' She reached for another slice of bread and began to poke little holes in that, too. Not hungry, just keyed up. 'As it turned out, Morgan and I seduced each other.'

Remmie swallowed the rest of his bread, then licked the drips of cherry off his fingers. His expression was muddled between dismay and resignation. And then he heaved another sigh.

'I suppose I shouldn't complain. Anything's better than you being bound. And at least this explains how you come to be dressed head to toe in fine silk.'

Oh. Yes. Her tunic and trousers. Beautiful. Expensive. A gift from Morgan . . . and his lost love, in a roundabout way. The fine clothes had once belonged to Luzena. He'd kept them, perfectly preserved, and offered them to her in place of her work-ruined linens. Just until other arrangements could be made.

*Only I don't believe I'll share that tidbit with Remmie.*

'Silk or linen or cotton, what does it matter?' she said, dismissive. 'It's only clothes. Just a way not to be naked.'

'That's true.' And then Remmie looked at her, his eyes cautious. 'This business of your magic, Barl. Unbinding yourself, and breaking Lord Danfey's wards. How do you explain it?'

She shrugged. 'I can't. And what does it matter? The point is, Remmie, I'm as good as I always said I was. In fact I'm better. And the things I'm *learning*. You should see Morgan's books. I've learned more in a few days of reading them than in my last three years of artisanry study.'

'That's good,' he said, subdued.

She leaned toward him. 'And I'm going to share what I'm learning with you. I'm going to copy out any incants I think are suitable and I'll send them to you, so you can teach your pupils and Barton Haye and *anyone* you think might like to learn them. So much fantastic magic, Remmie, that the ranked mages have kept for themselves. But their magic's mine, now. And I'm going to make it yours.'

'Barl . . .' Arms folded on the table, Remmie lowered his head. Shook it, very slowly. 'You can't.'

'Watch me.'

He looked up. 'No. You *can't*. What if you're caught? You think you're untouchable because you're bedding Morgan Danfey. And yes, all right, you're bedding him today. But what about tomorrow?'

'I told you. Tomorrow, or the next day, or in a week or so, I'll be Lady Danfey.'

'And you know that how? Because he told you?'

He'd told her many times since that night in the attic. Told her smiling, told her breathless, told her with tears in her eyes.

She lifted her chin. 'I suppose *you're* going to tell me he was lying?'

'Barl . . .' Remmie's eyes were full of fear for her. 'By your own admission he's already spurned one young woman, a mage ranked in the First Families. What's to say he won't grow tired of you in a week, or a month? And if he does, and he discards you, who'll protect you then?'

To her surprise, Remmie's harsh words didn't anger her. Instead, she felt sorry. He didn't understand.

She rested her hand on his arm. 'He'll not discard me, Remmie. And you'll believe that when you stand in the estate's gardens and watch Morgan and me handfast. You will come, won't you?'

He was smiling, shaking his head. 'Yes. I'll come.'

'I *am* untouchable, you know . . . but not because I share Morgan's bed.'

Smile fading, Remmie bit his lip. 'Because of your magework?'

447

'Yes. Magework is the only currency the ranked mages understand.'

Remmie's hand slapped the table. '*Exactly,* Barl! And that makes you a *threat.*'

'I don't have to be. There is no reason why the ranked and unranked mages of Dorana can't work together to make life better for *everyone.* All the Council and the rest of them need is some encouragement.'

'Oh, Barl . . .' He shook his head, affectionately exasperated. 'If you think your magework can make that happen, you're mad.'

She looked at him, frowning. Remmie's trouble was he thought he knew her . . . and he didn't. Not any more.

*I'll have to show him who I am now. Not all of it, but enough. Perhaps I can tell him the rest later. He's a talented mage. Morgan and I could use him once the transmutations get more complicated.*

Yes. She'd have to show him. Morgan would understand . . . if she told him.

Propping her elbows on the table, she frowned. 'Remmie, can I trust you? *Really* trust you?'

His eyes narrowed, warily. 'To do what?'

'Keep a secret. One that could hurt me, if you ever told another soul.'

'Yes, of course,' he said. 'But—' He rubbed his chin, his palm softly scraping the golden stubble. 'If it's so dangerous, maybe it's best you don't tell me.'

'But I want to. I *need* to. I need you to believe what I'm saying . . . and you never will, unless you know what I know.'

Shifting sideways in his chair, Remmie pulled up one knee and rested his forehead. Sighed. 'Am I going to regret this? I know I'll regret this. All right. Tell me. And if I change my mind I'll drink myself into a stupor down at the Pig. Wannet's cheap ale knocks a good day's worth of doings out of any man's head.'

Dear Remmie. Smiling, Barl snapped her fingers and plucked from her brother's vegetable garden a half-grown carrot. The rich dirt clumping its roots was damp and composty on her fingers, dribbling onto the scrubbled table and into her silk lap.

'Watch,' she whispered. 'And believe.'

Eyes half-closed, she drew the sigils, recited the syllables, and transmuted the carrot into a slender, fragrant lily. She heard her brother's choked cry as the power punched through her. Felt the red roar of it surge in her blood.

Remmie's eyes were so wide all the whites showed. 'That's *impossible*.'

'*Nothing* is impossible, Remmie,' she said gently. 'Not for me. Not now.'

'Where did that incant come from?' he said hoarsely. 'I've never – you shouldn't be able to – Barl, you – you – *jigget*! You just broke one of Dorana's most solemn laws!'

'I know,' she said, and laid the lily on the table between them. 'But I broke it for good reason. I can't explain why. But I will, when I can. Anyway, it's not important. What's important is that this lily is only the beginning.'

'The beginning of *what*?' he said, dazed. 'Barl—'

'A new Dorana.' And she wasn't lying. Part of its remaking had to do with warriors to protect them, yes, but she had far grander dreams than that. Dreams that would mean she hadn't suffered the torment of binding for nothing. 'Remmie, when Morgan and I are finished, there'll be no more ranked and unranked mages. There'll be no more selfish denials of *anyone*, just because of who they are – or aren't. He resigned from the Council because he doesn't believe in it any more. Doesn't need it. And as you can see, I don't need the College. I don't need anything but him.'

Remmie pressed shaking hands to his face, then after a moment let them fall. 'And you want to teach *me* how to do that?'

'Remmie, I want to teach you everything. I want you to know what true freedom feels like. And I want you to be madly happy like me.' Tears filled her eyes. 'I am *so* sorry that I spoiled things for you in Granley. You should go and find that girl. If you still love her, if you've not forgotten her, you should go. Tell her how you feel. Bring her back here, to Batava. Marry her and have a family and teach them all the wonderful incants you'll have learned.'

'I don't know . . .' Remmie was shaking his head again. 'You make it sound so simple.'

'It *is* simple,' she insisted. 'You decide what you want and then you *take* it.'

'Just like that?'

'*Just like that.*'

Lips twisting in a wry smile, he picked up the lily. Inspected it from every angle, wonder in his eyes.

'And just like you.'

'*Yes,* Remmie. Just like me. You *are* just like me, though you've never wanted to admit it. All the power that's in me, it's in you too. Only you've never been brave enough to accept that. Well, *get* brave enough. Because the ranked mages of Dorana have had things their own way for too long.'

Remmie slid from his chair and retreated to the kitchen window. Dusk had gentled the garden, encouraging the first shy stars to come out.

'So,' he said, over his shoulder. 'Are you really going to hand-fast with your fancy Morgan Danfey?'

She rolled her eyes. '*Yes*, Remmie. I really am. How many more times do I have to tell you?'

'A few more, I think,' he said, turning. 'Until it sinks in.' Then he scowled. 'Does it mean I'll have to call you *my lady* and bow and scrape whenever you deign to drop by?'

She grinned. 'If you know what's good for you.'

'What's *good* for me? Sister mine, shall I show you what's good for me?'

Before she could protect herself he'd summoned glimfire and was throwing it at her, little glowing fizzing balls that popped and sizzled harmless as they struck. Giggling, she struck back and within heartbeats the kitchen was lit up like a village green on New Year's Eve. Then Remmie leapt toward her and, shrieking a protest, she leapt out of his way. He chased her through the cottage then out into the garden, whooping and hollering, hurdling tomato vines and green beans and rows of potatoes. Squealing with laughter she gave as good as she got, until at last they collapsed side by side on the uncut grass down by the duck pond. Offended, the drake who lived there honked and paddled to safety.

'Stay for dinner,' Remmie panted, spread-eagled by her side. 'I'll grill sausages. Who knows when I'll see you again after you leave?'

She rolled her head to look at him. 'Don't be silly. Of course you'll see me. Not planning on leaving Batava, are you?'

'No. My life doesn't change, which is just how I like it. But yours? Barl, your life . . .' He laughed, disbelieving. 'I wonder if Mama and Pa ever imagined the kind of mage you'd grow up to be.'

'I don't know.' She shifted her hand until their fingers touched. Linked. 'I wish they weren't dead, Rem. I miss them so much.' Her voice caught. 'When Morgan's father died . . .'

'It's good that he had you with him,' Remmie said, very quiet. 'Nobody should have to grieve alone. Not for that.'

'You must come and stay with us once everything's settled. When school's out. You'll like Morgan, I know you will. Once you properly get to know him.'

'If he loves you, I must like him. Him loving you is the only thing that matters.'

The small, leftover cold knot under her ribs melted. 'What kind of sausages?'

'Wild boar and apple.'

She pretended to groan. 'Oh. Well. I suppose I could force one down. Or two. You know, if you made me.'

'Ingrate,' he said, snatched a handful of long grass and rubbed it in her face. Then he bounced to his feet. 'Come on, Lady Danfey. There's no sausage born I know of that's able to cook itself.'

On her return to the mansion she found Morgan in the attic, *Ollet's Compendium* open on the workbench beside him. His kiss was lingering, his look thoughtful as reluctantly they broke apart.

'You've eaten.'

'Remmie wanted to feed me. I couldn't say no.' She tapped the *Compendium*, pouting a little. 'You started already.'

He grinned. 'Serves you right.'

'And?' she said, ignoring the provocation.

Still grinning, he slid his notebook toward her. One glance at his scribbled notes and she was grinning too.

'Oh, Morgan. I think that's it.'

'I *know* that's it,' he said, and caught her in a crushing embrace. 'Barl, my beloved, we have saved Dorana.'

She wriggled free of him. Kept hold of his hand and looked at his notes more closely, seeing the incant come alive in her mind, in the way magic always did for her.

'Not quite yet,' she said, having learned caution these past few days. 'But we're closer. Although we'll have to expect some more failures before we can trust to reliable success. Best you instruct Rumm to buy lots and *lots* of chickens.'

And then she laughed, and flung her arms about his neck.

'Oh my love. You're right. We've saved Dorana.'

# CHAPTER TWENTY-EIGHT

B ecause she felt horribly responsible, that evening Venette risked the long travel incant to the Garricks' country estate and faced Parnel, his wife, and a tearful Maris in their drawing room. Broke the bad news, that Morgan had most definitely withdrawn his offer to handfast with Maris. Sat without protest as the storm of their displeasure raged around her, unabating. Maris wept until she made herself sick, then withdrew with her mother.

'This is a bad business, Venette,' Parnel said, breaking the uncomfortable silence the women left in their wake. 'Very bad. I suppose you'll tell me we've no recourse?'

She fiddled with her gold and ambrix wedding ring. 'There is always recourse, Parnel. But the question you must answer is: will the cost be worth it? Nobody save your family and I know how this affair has turned sour.'

'*He* knows.'

'Morgan has no desire to see Maris publicly humiliated,' she said, unblinking, and desperately hoped she spoke the truth. 'Besides, his unwise choice of a . . . companion . . . will keep him busy fighting his own fires. Trust me on that.'

'You think it's a case, then, of least said means soonest mended?'

'I certainly do.'

*And if you're wise, Parnel, you'll adopt the motto at once.*

He was a decent man. Perhaps a little too ambitious . . . but not a fool. 'All right, Venette. We'll keep Maris here with us until the gossip, if there's gossip, runs dry.'

She stood, feeling giddy with relief. 'Good. She'll repine a while, Parnel, but take no great harm from this, I'm sure. Maris is young and beautiful. The right mage will come along.'

Parnel, a doting father, tried to smile. 'Yes. Yes.'

*But it won't be me who finds him for you.*

'Now, if you'll excuse me, I should be on my way. Again, I am so sorry for this unpleasantness. I'm afraid that, like you, I was gravely deceived.'

Because he was a decent man, Parnel saw her to the front door. Courtesy dictated that she not incant from inside a host's dwelling, or in their presence, so she waited until the Garrick country house's front door clicked shut then, holding her breath, ignited an incant that would take her not home, but to Brice Varen's town house.

For the second time, she travelled without incident. Could that mean their alarm had in the end been for nothing?

*I can only hope so. I am tired of strife.*

'I was wondering if I'd see you again,' Brice said, and stepped back from his doorway. 'Come in, Venette. Go through to the parlour.'

Long widowed, like Greve Danfey, and like Greve not inclined to risk a second wife, Brice lived richly but simply. His parlour lacked the fussy ostentation of her own town house, painted in masculine shades of blue and cream. A lively fire danced in the hearth.

'Brandy?' Brice said, closing the door behind him. 'It's been that kind of day, I think.'

She laughed, unamused. 'Yes indeed, brandy. In fact, my dear, you can pour yourself a glass and hand me the bottle.' She rubbed her arms. 'I've just come from the Garricks.'

Brandy bottle in hand, Brice snorted. 'Where doubtless you

were called every name under the sun, Venette, and not without cause. Perhaps you'll think twice now before you indulge in any more matrimonial meddling.'

'Oh, don't you start!' she snapped, turning away. 'I've already had my ears chewed by Orwin, thank you. Him I must bear with, seeing as he's my husband, but you? You are merely the most important mage in Dorana.'

Faintly smiling, Brice handed her a generous glassful of brandy. 'So at last you admit it. Truly, a most remarkable day.'

'If not for the criminal waste, I'd throw this at you,' she said, waving the glass. 'Oh, *Brice*.'

'Oh indeed,' he said, nodding, then half-emptied his own glass in one deep swallow. 'Now do have a seat, my lady, and unburden yourself.'

She watched him fold into a comfortably shabby armchair, but was too keyed up to sit. Wandering the parlour, staring at its paintings and scattered figurines as though she'd never seen them before, she sipped her brandy and tried to order her thoughts.

'D'you know,' she said eventually, when the silence became oppressive, 'I incanted all the way to the Garricks' country estate, then all the way back here, as smoothly as ever. No hint of disruption.' She halted in front of the fire and swung round. 'No sense of anything amiss. What does that mean, d'you think?'

Brice shrugged. 'I don't know.'

'Well, don't you think it could mean that we panicked for nothing? It doesn't seem that anyone else has noticed there's a problem. Perhaps there isn't one, after all. Perhaps this is simply a – a – hiccup. That's a possibility, Brice, don't you think?'

'Venette . . .' He sighed, deeply. 'I suppose. Many things are possible. But I doubt it. I know what I felt. *You* know what I felt. And you heard what Bellamie Ranowen had to say. This is no hiccup. Something is gone far awry.'

Somehow his even, measured tone made things worse. He spoke like a man who had accepted the inevitable.

'I don't want it to be true,' she said, and gulped more brandy.

'But if it is, I don't want it to be something we can't *stop*. I don't want us to be *helpless*. Brice, I've been thinking. Have you considered that what's happening might not be . . . natural? That it's not some hitherto never-manifested imbalance of Dorana's magical plane? Do you suppose – have you considered—'

'That we're under attack?' Brice drank the rest of his brandy and put aside the glass. 'Yes, of course.'

'You have?' She stared at him. 'Why didn't you *say*?'

Another shrug. 'Because I dismissed the notion almost as soon as it occurred. We are the world's only mages, Venette. Who could attack us?'

'We're the only mages we know of,' she retorted. 'Perhaps the world contains mages we've never met.'

He lifted his eyebrows, gently mocking. 'In how many centuries? No. This is your trepidation talking, Lady Martain. There are no other mages. Dorana is safe . . . at least from a neighbour's aggression.'

'Then how do you *explain* it, Brice? There must be an explanation! Why don't we have one? Why hasn't that vaunted Bellamie Ranowen discovered the reason for this – this pernicious *unravelling*?'

Sighing again, Brice steepled his fingers. 'Bellamie Ranowen is doing her best.'

'And if her best proves inadequate? What then? We throw up our hands and say *Oh well, the world is ending but never mind, we did our best*?'

'Of course not,' Brice said, at last provoked to emotion. 'But Venette, we must accept that we might not find an explanation for this. Or a remedy. Consider the truth of our situation. We do not know magic's source. We do not know why our race and no other is able to use it. And we cannot explain why some of us are more gifted in its application than others. In short, magic is a *mystery*.'

'And that's *it*?' she said, staring. 'That's how you'd have me soothe myself? Brice Varen, are you mad?'

'What would you have me say?' Brice retorted. 'Would you

456

have me treat you like a child and declare that all will be well, when it might *not* be well? When there is a chance that our world *is* ending?'

She stabbed a finger at him. 'I want you to say that you've not given up hope! I want you to say that you'll fight to your last breath to preserve and protect Dorana and its mages!'

'And so I will.'

'Then *sound* like it, Brice! Don't you understand? I'm *frightened*. And though they'll never admit it, Sallis and Shari are frightened too. We look to you for guidance, for leadership. We need – *Dorana* needs – more than *magic is a mystery*.'

Brice's eyes in his seamed, aged face were shadowed and cool. 'What Dorana needs, Venette, should this unravelling persist, and become public knowledge, is a Council of Mages that is *not* afraid. A Council of Mages that is a beacon of calm. Without that beacon, we will surely be lost. So whatever your misgivings, you must keep them to yourself.'

'Of course,' she said, insulted. 'I'm not *reckless*. I don't need you to tell me what face I should wear in public. But we're not in public, are we? We're in your parlour, Brice, and I am confiding in you. Believe me, I'd much rather be confiding in my husband, but since you've made that impossible . . .'

'So it's my fault I'm being shouted at in my own home?'

She glowered at him. '*Yes*.'

'And do you intend to go on shouting?'

'Quite possibly. Yes.'

Brice stood. 'In that case, Venette, I require more brandy.'

He refilled his glass, and then topped up hers. She nodded her thanks and drank, wishing the leaping flames in his fireplace could chase away the chill of fear. When he was seated again, she fixed him with a baleful stare.

'And what are you going to do about Morgan?'

He sipped from his glass, eyeing her mildly over its rim. 'What do you mean?'

'Well, for one thing, you're not going to accept his resignation, are you? You must know he didn't mean it.'

'He seemed genuine to me.'

'Oh, yes, well, *seemed*.' She waved that away. 'You can't possibly pay any attention to *seemed*. He was angry. He's grieving. We shouldn't have gone in a group. We should have left Sallis and Shari behind. You should have let *me* go, Brice. Alone.' To her surprise, the parlour blurred. She blinked away tears. 'I can't believe Greve is dead. I can't believe Morgan didn't tell me.' She stared into her brandy glass. 'I can't believe he'd wilfully hurt me like that.'

'Which is why, dear Venette, I did not send you to see him alone.'

The sympathy in Brice's voice was a surprise, too. She looked up. 'Oh.' Terribly weary, of a sudden, she crossed to the parlour's other armchair and sat. Drank more brandy, then gave him a sideways glance. 'Does this mean you are going to accept his resignation?'

'I take it you think I shouldn't?'

'Absolutely! Brice, accepting his resignation would be a grave mistake. Not only do we need his talent during this crisis, if we don't keep him close to us we've no hope of influencing his erratic behaviour.'

Brice gave her a look. 'And you're of the opinion he's in the mood to be influenced?'

'Not just at the moment, I'll grant you,' she admitted. 'But once he calms down . . .' She bit her lip against a fresh surge of anger. 'Once he tires of that terribly tiresome Barl Lindin . . .'

'And you think that's likely? I think he meant what he said, about rousing Dorana against us should we interfere with him and the girl.'

'Oh, no. Surely not, Brice. He said that in the heat of the moment. Heat cools.'

'Not always,' said Brice, grimacing. 'Some fires burn hot. Some fires burn forever.'

*Luzena Talth.*

'But Brice, he's only known the wretched girl a handful of weeks,' she protested, not wanting to think that he might be right.

'Morgan *can't* truly love her. Why, she's entirely unsuitable. This is simply a childish rebellion against Greve.'

Brice put down his brandy, unfinished. 'Why can't it be both?'

'Both?' Disconcerted, she looked at him. 'Brice Varen, do not tell me you're a *romantic*.'

A long, thoughtful silence. Elbow propped on the arm of his chair, chin resting on his hand, Brice stared across the room at the fire.

'I am romantic enough,' he said, at last, 'to know that daring Morgan Danfey to prove his love for this unsuitable girl would be nothing short of folly. And while you might not be romantic, Venette, I think you know I am right. You can't challenge him over her.'

Yes, he was right, curse it. 'Fine,' she muttered. 'But what about his resignation?'

'There, I am inclined to take your advice. I think it's possible that when Morgan's temper cools, he might well regret offering it. So, at least for now, I will decline to accept it. As far as Council matters are concerned, as far as the rest of Dorana is concerned, the new Lord Danfey is on a leave of absence for personal reasons.'

Pleased, Venette savoured another small mouthful of brandy. 'Sallis won't like that.'

'Oddly enough, I don't make my decisions based on what Sallis Arkley will or won't like.'

Should she confess that she'd asked Morgan about Dorana's unravelling? No. Best not. That would only to lead to more shouting. But still, she should sound Brice out on enlisting his aid.

'Brice . . . even though you're content to let Morgan remain with Barl Lindin on the Danfey estate, that doesn't mean we can't make use of his talents. I know we've thrashed this out once before, but—'

'Venette, nothing has changed,' said Brice, with more forbearance than she'd expected. 'Indeed, he is more volatile now than he has ever been. No. Dorana is not in such desperate straits yet that we should risk his uncertain temper. Nor do we suffer such a dearth of talented mages that we must return to him on bended knees and beg for his assistance. We will continue to let him cool his heels while we wait to see how . . . or *if* . . . this unravelling continues.'

Venette sighed. 'All right, Brice. Only you'll need to keep Sallis on a very short leash. You and I both know he'll go to bed tonight celebrating Morgan's tumble from grace. And when Sallis learns that once again you've broken his fall . . .'

'Never fret,' said Brice. 'You may leave Sallis to me. Indeed . . .' He smiled. 'You may leave. No doubt Orwin is missing you.'

'Oh.' She stood. 'All right, Brice. If I'm boring you.'

'Venette, you are never boring.' Another smile, less gentle. 'As you well know.'

Complimented and insulted, she pulled a face and went home.

Nearly five weeks later, the first incidents of severe magical calamity were reported.

'*Mage-mist*?' Brice considered Bellamie Ranowen from beneath tightly lowered brows. 'That is what you've decided to call this – this phenomenon?'

The College tutor, wan with exhaustion and, Venette thought, thinner than she'd been the last time she stood in the Council chamber, clasped her hands behind her back. 'Yes, Lord Varen. I'm sorry. Is that too fanciful a term for the Council?'

'Watch your tongue,' growled Sallis. His temper had been wicked ever since he'd learned Morgan would one day return to claim his place at the table. 'This is no time for levity.'

Pointedly indifferent to his hostility, Bellamie Ranowen shrugged. 'No? At times like this, my lord, I find that levity is my only defence against hysteria.'

'Perhaps,' said Shari Frieden. 'But you'll find it's not much comfort when you're being marched into a judiciary!'

Keeping her gaze on Bellamie Ranowen, Venette snapped at Sallis's tedious echo. 'Shari, don't be a jigget. I doubt Mage Ranowen is the only one here who's feeling hysterical. Mage Ranowen, never mind what you're calling this perfidious substance. Can you tell us what it is? Can you tell us where it comes from? To the best of this Council's knowledge, it has never been encountered before.'

'Nor to the best of my knowledge, Lady Martain,' said Bellamie Ranowen. 'There is no record of it in the College's library or archives. And none of my colleagues can—'

'Your colleagues?' Brice drummed his fingers to the table. 'Do you tell us you have discussed your investigation of this new strife with other mages at the College? When you were expressly forbidden to—'

'I'm sorry, my lord, but given that not an hour ago I, and a number of other mages, witnessed a manifestation of mage-mist in the College's main quadrangle, I'm sure you'll agree that some discussion of the event was impossible to avoid!'

Silence in the chamber, as Bellamie Ranowen's heated words sank in.

'It manifested in the College?' Sallis said at last, fingers laced tightly before him. 'You're quite certain?'

Bellamie Ranowen looked at him, then turned to Brice. 'Lord Varen, since clearly I do not enjoy this Council's confidence, perhaps it would be best for all of us if you found another—'

'No,' said Brice. 'Your competence is not in doubt. But so we might be sure we are proceeding in the right direction, be so kind as to explain why you're convinced that what you saw in the College was, indeed, this *mage-mist*. Given that by the time you arrived at the location of the other manifestations, the phenomenon had dissipated.'

'The phenomenon, yes,' said Bellamie Ranowen, unmollified. 'But not its effects. There was the same charring of foliage and grass. The same damage to structures and unravelling of magework.'

'Was anyone injured?'

'No, my lord. Not this time. Fortunately it manifested when the quadrangle was empty. But there is no doubt this was mage-mist. What we saw matches what others saw in the Third, Fourth and Seventh districts.'

'Which brings us back to our reason for asking you here this morning,' said Venette. 'With your preliminary investigation of those manifestations completed, what conclusions have you drawn?'

'Conclusions? None,' said Bellamie Ranowen. 'I have a tentative theory. I have some suggestions. I have no definitive answers.' She shrugged. 'I'm sorry.'

Sallis turned to Brice. '*Now* will you agree that we should be seeking advice from a more competent mage?'

'There is no-one more competent,' said Brice, fingers pinched to the bridge of his nose. 'I have made extensive enquiries, and opinion was unanimous. Mage Ranowen has no peer when it comes to the theory of magework. Mage Ranowen—'

'My best explanation is that mage-mist is like a bleeding of raw magic,' Bellamie Ranowen said. 'Which is what I call the intangible substance that permits us, as mages, to do what we do.'

Venette felt herself shiver. 'So you're saying . . . Dorana is *wounded*?'

'Yes.' The College tutor took a deep breath, and steadied herself. 'And unstable. And now it would appear the instability is spreading.'

'And we repair it – heal it – how?' Shari demanded. 'Do you still claim we must cease all magework? That somehow *we* are responsible for our plight?'

'Lady Frieden, I never said we were responsible. I don't know that we are. I don't know why this is happening. All I know is that before things get better . . . *if* they get better . . . I expect they'll get a great deal worse.'

If Bellamie Ranowen had shouted the words, they might have hurt less to hear. But her soft grimness gave them a weight that threatened to crush any hope of hope.

'Mage Ranowen, I fear they have already begun to get worse,' Brice told her, equally grim. 'While you have been immersed in

462

your investigations at the College and elsewhere, this Council has been making discreet enquiries throughout Dorana, seeking to learn if the instability is widespread.' He looked down at his sheet of notes. 'Alas, the news is not encouraging. It seems that incants that should ignite without effort have been taking two and three attempts. Sometimes more. In some instances, the incants are refusing to ignite at all.'

'And when you say these incants should have ignited without effort, do you mean they were simple?' said Bellamie Ranowen. 'And the mages in question . . . how would you gauge their skill?'

Venette shook her head. 'The incants were not simple. Transmutations, deconstructions, third and fourth level enhancements. Challenging incants all . . . but well within the grasp of the mages who reported their difficulties with them.'

'According to their various testimonies,' Brice added, 'there was no ease, no suppleness, in the performance of their magework. The incants felt sluggish, the sigils reluctant to burn.'

Bellamie Ranowen tapped a finger to her chin. 'And where were these difficulties encountered?'

Brice consulted his notes. 'Here, in the First district. And in the Second. Also the Fourth.'

'Two days ago, in my own street,' said Shari, her face tight, her eyes anxious, 'three stained-glass windows of a neighbouring town house shattered. There was no reason for it that anyone could see. No children playing bat-a-ball. No wind to put a branch in the wrong place. The glass simply . . . fell apart. As though it had been clumsily unmade.'

'There have also been several instances of catalysts bursting into flame within their jars and bottles,' said Brice. 'Violent explosions. Four mages have been injured that way. One seriously.'

'I have combed through every last recorded note and journal in the Council archives,' said Sallis. 'There is no precedent for such events, Mage Ranowen. Since Dorana's first mage first commanded magic, never has it failed us.'

'Is that the extent of the trouble?' said Bellamie Ranowen. 'Or is there more?'

Scowling, Sallis dropped his gaze to the table. 'There might be more. Dorana has many districts. Our enquiries are ongoing.'

Slowly, as though his bones ached, Brice pushed his ornate chair back from the Council table and walked to the double doors leading onto the chamber's balcony. Flinging them open, he stepped into the clouded late-morning sunshine. Let the fresh breeze whip his hair around his sombre face, mould his silver-grey silk tunic to his gaunt frame. He was beginning to stoop, Venette saw, the weight of this mysterious, burgeoning crisis curving a spine that all his life had stood so straight.

Shaken, Sallis and Shari stared at each other, then at her. 'Well – don't just sit there, Lady Martain,' Sallis snapped. 'You know him best. Prod the truth out of him. Is there something else to do with this business that he's neglected to tell us?'

Prod the truth out of him? Just like that? How unlikely. But with a warning look at Bellamie Ranowen, who looked inclined to speak up, she followed Brice onto the balcony and even went so far as to rest a hand on his arm.

'What is it, my lord? You can't keep secrets. Not from us. Not now.'

Glancing at her, Brice shook his head. 'It's not a secret. I don't even know if it's relevant. More than likely it's a coincidence, nothing more.'

'I think you should let Mage Ranowen be the judge of that. You ask us to defer to her opinion in this crisis. Surely you can do no less?'

Sighing, Brice nodded. 'You're right.' His voice was low, guarded. 'But in truth, Venette, I fear to tell her. For if she says that this is relevant . . . that this is part and parcel of Dorana's strife, then . . .'

'Not so long ago,' she said, dropping her own voice to a near-whisper, 'you sat in your parlour and roundly scolded me for surrendering to my fears. Allow me to remind you of what you said, Lord Varen. You said—'

'Thank you, Venette. I remember quite well what I said.'

'*You said,*' she continued, 'that Dorana's Council of Mages must be a beacon of calm and that we, as councillors, should keep our fears to ourselves. So I suggest you take your own excellent advice, my dear. Because as *I* said, we are looking to *you*, Lord Varen, to lead us safely through these dark days.'

Behind them, the Council chamber was quiet. Out on the balcony the wind sighed and moaned. Far below them, the mages of Elvado walked the streets, unaware of the shadow slipping over their bright land.

Turning his head, Brice looked at her in silence. His eyes were very tired. And then he nodded. 'Indeed.'

Venette followed him inside, and waited for him to retake his seat before she slid back into her own.

'My late wife's brother,' Brice said, looking at Bellamie Ranowen but addressing them all, 'heads the Guild of Pothers. He came to see me last night. He was . . . ill at ease. Joryn Torvig's not one for panicking. Cannot abide histrionics and such nonsense. So when he raises an eyebrow I – well, I take him more seriously than most. He tells me the Guild's pothers have been talking amongst themselves. Some of their patients are dying unexpectedly, others are not recovering as quickly or as well as their maladies and injuries suggest they should. Joryn tells me the Guild's pothers are baffled . . . and growing concerned.'

'I don't know,' said Bellamie Ranowen, as all eyes turned to her. 'I'm sorry, I wish I could say with certainty that this is a separate matter, but I can't. It might be connected. Until I understand better the nature of Dorana's malady, it would be foolish of me to give you false hope.'

'What *do* you know?' Shari demanded. 'Anything? Or have you come here merely to impress us with your ignorance?'

Brice glared. '*Lady Frieden.*'

'No, my lord,' said Bellamie Ranowen. 'It is a fair question. Lady Frieden, I will tell you what I know. I know we can't keep this a secret any longer. Many things can be explained with a little clever sleight of hand. Mage-mist isn't one of them. Besides, it is *dangerous*. I suspect it might even be lethal. People must know how to protect themselves against it.'

'*Is* there protection?' said Sallis. 'You have not said so before.'

'I intended to, Lord Arkley. At the College this morning I banished the mage-mist in the quadrangle with a dispersal incant.'

'You'd use magework to fight magic?' Brice frowned. 'Is that wise?'

Bellamie Ranowen shrugged. 'I don't know how else we can fight it. Something tells me flapping our hands at it won't frighten the mage-mist away.'

'What else do you suggest?'

'That we limit the use of magework until this problem is resolved. Most particularly those incants that require complex syllabic harmonics and sigils.'

'You still think it's possible that somehow magework is the underlying cause of Dorana's wounds?'

'Lord Varen, it is still too early to say. I do not care to rule out any explanation. But it's my opinion that being cautious from now on can't hurt.'

'Agreed,' said Brice. 'Very well. This Council will issue an edict to that effect.'

Bellamie Ranowen almost smiled as some of the tension eased out of her body. 'My lord, given what happened at the College this morning, I would like to ask several of my fellow tutors to assist me in my investigations. I think I would arrive at the solutions you need far more swiftly if there were more of us asking the questions.'

For some time Brice sat silent. Then he looked around the table, one eyebrow lifted, inviting objection. When none came, he nodded.

'Very well. But choose your colleagues with care, Mage Ranowen. They must be sober and dedicated and able to keep their mouths shut. This is not an exciting opportunity. This is a grave challenge, with dire consequences should we fail. Understood?'

Bellamie Ranowen's eyes glinted, briefly, as though she found Brice's comment insulting. 'Of course, Lord Varen.' She stepped closer to the table and gestured at the ink pot, quill and paper by his right hand. 'May I?'

'By all means.'

Swiftly, she scribbled an incant then slid the sheet of paper toward him. 'This is how I dispelled the mage-mist. Every mage in Dorana should learn this incant by heart.'

'Our thanks,' said Brice, staring at it. 'With the General Council's assistance, we shall see that they do.'

'And given what Lady Frieden said about those shattered windows, I suggest that every mage sees to the protection of his or dwelling. And there should be mageworking of all public buildings. At the very least, a warding to keep people away if the incants needed to strengthen them are too deep for safety.'

Another silence, as the enormity of what they were facing rose to engulf them. Venette, looking at Brice's face, saw him grow haggard from one slow breath to the next. She felt her stomach clench, nausea roiling.

*Oh, my dear. Hold fast. Stay strong. I was not being fanciful when I said that we need you.*

'Yes,' he said, after a long pause. 'That is a wise precaution. Thank you, Mage Ranowen. Was there anything else?'

'Not of a useful or practical nature, my lord,' said Bellamie Ranowen. In her own way she was looking haggard too. 'If there is, of course I shall tell you. But there is one last thing I would say . . . even though I don't want to say it.'

Brice smiled, very faintly, as though he and the College tutor were sharing a joke. 'Of course. Speak your mind. Honesty is the only currency of value in this Hall.'

'Then, my lord, honestly? If we don't find a way to heal Dorana, and soon, I believe its unravelling will proceed apace. I believe there is the danger that it will spread first throughout every district, and after that beyond our borders. And if that should happen . . .'

She didn't need to say more. Venette, feeling her mouth dry, stared horrified at Brice.

*If that should happen, the whole world will be at risk.*

Ink-stained, her head pounding, Barl pushed aside her scribbled-in journal and pressed the heels of her hands against her dry, tired eyes. Frustration was a hot ball in the pit of her stomach, a creeping heat over every bit of her skin.

With a wordless cry, she leapt to her feet and stamped about the library.

'This is ridiculous! I *know* it's possible. *Anything* is possible. All I have to do is find the right incant to point the way!'

But she was beginning to suspect the right incant might not be here. Or, if it was, she had found it already, and already discarded it because she couldn't see what she needed to see.

*I promised Morgan we'd find a way to cheat death. I won't break my word to him. I won't. I can't.*

Because sometimes, in the middle of the night, as she lay awake beside him watching him sleep, he wept while he was dreaming . . . and begged her not to die.

She spun round at a knock on the library door. 'Yes? What is it, Rumm? What do you want?'

The door opened, revealing the master servant's very blank face. 'Mage Lindin. You have a visitor.'

Lady Martain.

'Mage Lindin,' the councillor said, sweeping in past Rumm. Her green silk tunic was rumpled. 'Am I disturbing you? I'm sorry.'

Barl looked at Rumm. 'Thank you. Don't bother with tea. Lady Martain won't be staying very long.'

As Rumm pulled the door closed, Venette Martain dropped uninvited into a chair. 'Where is Morgan?'

With a great show of indifference, Barl swept together her notebook and jottings and pushed them into a drawer.

'Asleep.'

'*Asleep?*' The woman stared out of the window. 'But it's barely past sunset.'

'He's been working very hard. And I'm sure it never occurred to him that he should ask your permission before retiring.'

Venette Martain's eyes narrowed. 'Mind your tongue.'

There was enough sharpness in the woman's voice to make her wince.

*Careful, Barl. You're not Lady Danfey quite yet.*

'Lady Martain, was there something you wanted?'

'I wanted to see Morgan.'

'Well, I'm not going to wake him.'

'He's been mageworking, you say? You both have?'

There was something oddly intent in the look Venette Martain gave her. 'A little,' Barl said, instinct prompting the lie. 'Hardly at all. Mostly he's been teaching me various theories of magework. Since I'm denied the College—' She flicked her hand at the book-lined room. 'This has become my new schoolroom. He's a very good teacher. I'm learning a lot.'

Venette Martain's lips pinched. 'Yes. I'm sure you are.' She stood. 'I came here out of courtesy, one friend to another, so do be sure you pass my message to Morgan. There will be an edict issued in the next day or two. Complex mageworking is to be restricted, by order of the Council.'

Barl stared at her. 'Why?'

'Tell Morgan if he wants to know more, he knows where to find me. Good evening, Mage Lindin. I'll show myself out.'

*Horrible woman.*

Alone again, Barl retrieved her notebook and notes. Slapped them down on the table and folded back into the chair.

*Complex magework to be restricted? What is the Council up to now?*

Then she shrugged. Morgan would find out. But anyway, it didn't matter. No Council edict would ever apply to them.

Frowning, she returned to her work.

# CHAPTER TWENTY-NINE

'So,' said Barton, his voice heavy with melancholy. 'That's it, then.'

Slumped on Batava schoolhouse's front step, Remmie nodded. 'Yes. That's it.'

Barton sat, keys dangling from his fingers. *Keys.* They needed Brantish locks to secure the schoolhouse's classroom doors because a warding couldn't be trusted to take, or last any length of time if it did.

'It's hard to fathom, Remmie.' With a sigh, Barton rested a hand on his shoulder. 'I never thought I'd live to see this. I never thought such a thing was possible.'

'Neither did I.'

They were surrounded by a dreadful silence. All the children had been sent home. The schoolhouse's classrooms and playground and field were empty, save for the random manifestations of mage-mist that had made them unsafe.

Barton heaved a sigh. 'So, Mage Lindin. What are you going to do now?'

'I'm not sure. You?'

'Remember my uncle, in the Third district? I'm going to him.'

Barton's uncle? Oh, yes. The baker. 'That's good,' he said,

trying to sound encouraging. 'At least you can make bread without magic. Yeast's a magic all its own.'

Barton heaved another sigh, then leapt to his feet as mage-mist thickened into existence halfway across the schoolhouse assembly yard. Cursing, he snatched up a pebble and threw it. The mage-mist spat and sparked and sizzled it to dust. Then it faded, capricious, as swiftly as it appeared. No need for the banishing incant that only worked one try out of three.

'I can't believe this,' Barton said, his voice shaking. 'Dorana's falling to pieces around us, faster and faster every day. And what is the Council of Mages doing to save us? *Nothing* . . . except take away more and more of our magework. All those high and mighty ranked mages and what use are they? *None!*'

'Steady on,' Remmie murmured. 'I'm sure they're doing their best.'

'It's not enough.'

No. It wasn't. 'When will you leave?'

'As soon as I can buy a seat on Benyt's wagon.'

Nib Benyt, who owned The Greased Pig. There was a man quick to take advantage of strife. With travel incants too dangerous now, he was running a wagon from Batava to Fothel, in the Fifth district. Not that he was the only one. Dorana's roads and byways had grown Brantish busy, crammed full of wagons and carriages and carts and horses.

'Remmie—' Barton stared around them. 'I know the District Council has said you're welcome to stay in the cottage, but you won't, will you? Won't you go to Elvado?'

Nearly four months ago, with too much of The Greased Pig's ale in his belly, he'd told Barton that Barl would soon be Lady Danfey. Had shown him the incants she'd sent him, the first of many . . . or so she promised.

But it hadn't quite worked out that way.

'Remmie?'

He looked up into Barton's puzzled face. 'I'd like to visit Barl, yes. Make sure she's all right. But I don't know if I'll stay there.'

He didn't know if he'd be welcome.

471

'Travel with me, then,' said Barton. 'At least as far as Fothel. I'd appreciate the company.'

'Yes. Why not?'

Another glum silence, as they considered their forlorn surroundings.

'Let's see Benyt now, then,' Barton said at last. 'Buy ourselves passage out of this cursed place.'

For one awful moment Remmie thought he might weep. He loved this schoolhouse. Had poured heart and soul and sweat and dreams into it. Remembering his pupils' faces, their cries of dismay as he told them there'd be no more classes until Dorana's troubles passed, he had to bite his lip.

'Come on, Remmie,' said Barton, sadly. 'Let's go.'

Nib Benyt sold them two seats on his wagon, leaving Batava on the morrow, at first light. Returning to his hushed cottage, Remmie picked himself some fresh beans from the garden then went inside to prepare them and make a small chicken pie. And after that, with supper cooking, he washed himself clean of pastry-makings and retired to the parlour, where he kept Barl's letters in a carved cherrywood box. Staring at the small collection of folded notes, he felt anxiety stir.

Almost three weeks had passed since he'd last heard from her. In the beginning, after her surprise visit and her even more surprising news, she'd written twice a week. Kept her word and sent him incants copied from Morgan Danfey's books. But then twice a week became once, and once a week became sometimes. When he'd heard nothing for twenty-six days, he wrote to her. Was something wrong? Could he help?

Her reply, when it finally came, was curt and hurtful.

*Stop bothering me. I'm busy. I've sent you plenty of incants. Amuse yourself for a while.*

His first instinct had been to turn up on her mansion doorstep demanding an explanation. But then he changed his mind. She'd not thank him for ignoring her. Besides, shouting at Barl never got him anything but a sore throat. Better to do as she asked and bide his time, trusting . . . hoping . . . that she knew what she was about.

Only now things were different. Dorana's troubles were deepening, swiftly. And he couldn't sit in Batava with no pupils to teach, not knowing how bad things were where she was, not knowing if she was in trouble. If Morgan Danfey still loved her.

*If he ever loved her at all.*

She'd sat in his kitchen and created a lily. Terrifying magework. Rules tossed aside. He had no doubt she was ignoring the Council's edicts, knew in his bones she was mageworking still. Then, it was a lily.

*But what is she creating now?*

If she was creating anything. What if the Council had found out she was defying them? What if Danfey had indeed tired of her and handed her back?

*Or what if she's still with him, and he's encouraging her, and something's gone wrong?*

Crushed with guilt, with fear, he slammed the cherrywood box's lid closed on her letters.

*I should've trusted my first instinct. I shouldn't have left her there alone. I promised I'd take care of her.*

And now that promise was as broken as Dorana itself.

His wagon trip with Barton could not come fast enough.


Venette looked up from pushing a wrapped packet of dried *burgot* leaves into the bag she'd already stuffed as full as she dared with catalysts. Orwin was staring again, shouting with his silence. As though he'd actually spoken, she shook her head.

'I'm sorry you don't approve, my dear, but I have no choice.'

'There is always a choice, Venette,' he said, standing in their town house workroom's doorway. 'Morgan made his weeks ago. The wrong one. There is no need for you to compound his mistake.'

'I am not compounding *anything*! I am trying to make the best of a *ridiculous* situation.'

Orwin slapped the open door with the flat of his hand, so loudly, so not like him, that she gasped and jumped.

'Venette, you are conspiring with Morgan Danfey to subvert the law in the midst of the gravest crisis Dorana has ever seen!'

'*No*, Orwin! I am aiding a fellow councillor in his attempt to *save* Dorana in the midst of its gravest crisis! Justice knows no-one else seems to be of any use!'

Including herself, but that thought was far too painful for any close examination.

'Venette . . . please . . .' His voice gentle, his own again, Orwin stepped into the room. 'Don't do this.'

She reached for the small jar of tinctured *bidaline* and pushed it into the bag's last nook. 'I wouldn't have to, Orwin, if Brice and Sallis and Shari weren't forcing my hand. But Brice is so overwhelmed, he's letting Sallis and Shari bully him. It is *madness* to keep Morgan from returning to the Council.'

'Morgan prevents his own return, my dear,' Orwin said wearily. 'All he has to do is renounce Barl Lindin and every objection to him will be dropped. But he won't.'

Finished lacing the bag shut, Venette hefted its long leather strap over her shoulder. 'And can you blame him? *I* can't. As much as I deplore his slutting with an unranked mage, I despise Sallis and Shari even more. That they would risk Dorana to pursue a petty, personal vendetta? It's *disgraceful*. And as for Brice's refusal to call their bluff? Well. He drives me to despair.'

'But Venette . . .' Orwin moved to stand between her and the door. 'You don't even know what Morgan wants with those catalysts. You have no idea what magework he performs!'

'I don't have to know the particulars. He's told me he works toward saving us, and I believe him.'

'*Why*?'

Sighing, she rested her palm above Orwin's heart. 'Because for all his faults, and justice knows they are many, Morgan loves Dorana. He always has. He always will.'

Orwin's kindly face was racked with anguish. 'If he loved Dorana he would discard that wretched girl!'

The bag of catalysts was cumbersome. Easing its weight on

her shoulder, Venette raised an eyebrow. 'And if you were Morgan, Orwin, would you discard me?'

An unkind question, but it had the desired effect.

'Go to bed, my dear,' she said. 'And I'll see you in the morning.'

She met Morgan on the empty Brantone road, beneath a night sky full of stars. Most of the day had been rainy. The open meadow on either side of her smelled of wet grass and burned mage-mist. Harnessed between her small buggy's shafts, her horse tossed its head, whickering, at the sound of another horse's approaching hooves.

Since not even glimfire could be trusted any more, she lit a torch and waited.

'Venette,' Morgan said, drawing rein just out of the flickering light's reach. 'You're alone?'

She rolled her eyes. 'Don't be ridiculous.'

'Not ridiculous,' he chided, nudging the stallion into the light. 'Cautious.'

She hadn't seen him for many weeks. He looked tired . . . but then, these days, who didn't? Beneath the weariness she thought she could see something else. An almost frenetic excitement, at odds with his usual reserve.

'Well? Did you bring them?'

She hefted the leather bag in her lap. 'Orwin thinks I'm making a terrible mistake.'

'And what do you think?'

'I think I'd like to know what it is you're doing.'

He shrugged. 'I told you. Magework to save Dorana. Did you remember the *azafris*? And the *susquinel*? I know they make you nervous, but they're vital. I promise.'

'What's *vital*, Morgan, is that I don't end up regretting that I've broken the law helping you!'

He smiled, and for an instant looked like his old, familiar self. 'There is only one law that matters now, Venette. The law of survival. I don't see that dying with our hands clean is anything to celebrate.'

And of course, he was right. Why else was she here?

As he took the bag of catalysts from her, he hesitated. 'How is Maris?'

'Oh, *Morgan*.' She could easily have slapped him. 'Don't pretend you care.'

'I do care,' he said, settling the bag on his hip. 'I am sorry she was hurt. No child should be a pawn of its parents' ambitions.'

She wasn't about to argue the matter. Not on the Brantone road in the middle of the night.

'The Garricks are like the rest of us in Elvado, Morgan. Frightened.' She leaned forward, feeling desperate. 'Promise me you can do something about that.'

'I can,' he said, that odd excitement flaring. 'And I will. I swear it.'

'*How*? Morgan, how is it you can keep mageworking when the rest of us are practically crippled? And what are you working on, that you're so certain will drag us back from the brink?'

His expression was smoothly unreadable. 'I still think it's best I don't say. Venette . . . either you trust me or you don't. I think tonight is proof that you do. And since you do, then *trust* me. I'm not a perfect man, but in *this*? I'll not lead you astray. People are frightened now, that's true. But the fear won't last forever.'

She felt sick, she wanted to believe him so badly.

*I have to believe him. If I don't, I'll be lost.*

'Can I rely on you to help me again?' he said. 'We run through our supply of catalysts very quickly, and with Sallis Arkley grown so vigilant I must be miserly in the use of my . . . irregular sources.'

*We.*

Her fingers tightened on the horse's reins. 'I wish you wouldn't magework with her, Morgan.'

'Or fuck with her?' He laughed, mocking. 'There isn't one without the other. And Venette, like it or not, you need the other. Without Barl Lindin, Dorana cannot be saved. Thank you for these supplies. I'll send word when I need more.'

As she sat in the flickering torchlight, listening to his horse's hoofbeats fade into the distance, mage-mist appeared in the meadow beside her. Her shouted incant dispersed it. A miracle. She watched it dissolve, and then was violently ill over the side of her buggy.

Churning with sickness and hatred, her mouth sour, tasting foul, she turned the buggy and headed for home.


Morgan found Barl in the library, reworking his next reworking of Hartigan's transmutation. Complementing his brilliance with her own. Hearing him enter, she looked up.

'Well?'

Every time he saw her anew he felt his bones turn, just for a moment, to water.

He sighed. 'My love, if you don't trust Venette, then at least trust me. Yes. We have more catalysts.'

Frowning, she abandoned her work and went to him.

'You look tired, Morgan,' she whispered, combing her fingers through his unbound hair. 'You're not sleeping enough. Isn't it time you told me what you work on, once I've gone to bed?'

He should have known he'd not keep that a secret. Brushing his fingertips over her breasts, he enjoyed the little catch in her throat, the shiver his touch always sent through her body.

'I will. Just . . . not yet.'

Her fist spread to fingers. Tangled in his tunic and tugged his lips down to hers. 'Don't be too sure of that, my lord.'

'My lord!'

He let his forehead thud gently to the top of Barl's head. 'Rumm, I swear. I am going to put a bell on you.'

'My lord, Nydd is here.'

*Nydd?* He turned, baleful. 'It's past midnight.'

'Yes, my lord,' said Rumm. 'He's says he'll not leave until he's seen you.'

'It must be urgent, my love,' said Barl. 'I'll take myself up to the attic and finish my work there.'

As she left, notebook under her arm, he frowned at Rumm. 'Show him in.'

'Lord Danfey!' Nydd said, almost scuttling into the library, far from his usual composed, dapper self. 'I apologise for the late hour, but this could not wait.'

'For your sake, Nydd, I hope that's true.'

Nydd eased a finger between his neck and the high collar of his sober linen tunic. 'Yes. My lord, as far as I can ascertain, what I am about to tell you is not common knowledge. Perhaps the Councils know. I cannot speak to that. But I believe the rest of Dorana is ignorant. Although that surely won't remain the case for much longer.'

'Nydd.'

Nydd let out a shuddering breath. 'Forgive me. I am quite overturned.' With a shaking hand he pulled a sheaf of papers from his satchel and held them up. 'As you know, my lord, I maintain a comprehensive network of subordinates, overseers and other functionaries to keep me apprised of your family's business interests. They report to me on a regular basis so that I might report to you on the state of your affairs. And this afternoon I received some *very* disturbing news, from three different sources.'

News that warranted an intrusion like this? With a shiver of apprehension, Morgan clasped his hands behind his back. 'Tell me.'

'My lord . . .' Nydd groped within his tunic for a handkerchief and dabbed dry his sweaty forehead. 'Whatever is afflicting Dorana, I regret to tell you that it has spread. Mage-mist has been encountered at your Brantone vineyards, and on the suswill farms in Trindek *and* Manemli. In all three cases your properties lie close to the Doranen border. This suggests that the trouble has not spread far, but—'

'But it has spread.'

'I fear so.'

'There's no doubt it was mage-mist?'

'None, my lord. The descriptions tally in every respect.'

'I see. And who else have you told?'

'Who else?' Perplexed, Nydd stared at him. 'No-one, my lord. Of course.'

'And the subordinates who sent you these reports?'

'They've been told to hold their tongues, on pain of severe retribution,' said Nydd. 'But chances are they're not the only witnesses. Chances are the mage-mist will be seen elsewhere, and reported on. There will be panic, my lord, which does not bode well for your interests.'

It did not bode well for a number of things. *Curse it.* Showing nothing but a restrained concern, he nodded.

'You were right to bring this to my immediate attention, Nydd. Now go home and steady yourself with some brandy. If you receive any more reports of mage-mist beyond our borders, inform me at once. And above all else, maintain your excellent discretion. Not a *word* of this is to pass your lips. Understood?'

'Of course, my lord,' Nydd murmured. 'I will leave these reports with you, that you might peruse them at length.'

As soon as the library door closed, Morgan sat at the nearest reading table and frowned at the smears his dragging fingertip left on the polished wood. Frowned at the letters Nydd had left behind.

*Mage-mist in Brantone? In Manemli and Trindek? I did not anticipate that.*

He hadn't anticipated the depth of Dorana's disruptions, either. Still, the trouble was temporary. Everything would return to normal once his transmutation work was complete. If he was certain of anything, he was certain of that. Everything he understood about syllabic harmonics confirmed it. Neverthless, this spreading of the mage-mist was a most inconvenient development. If Venette lost faith in him, she'd withdraw her assistance.

*There is only one remedy. Barl and I must redouble our efforts. We're in a race against time now. A race we must win.*

'What did Nydd want?' his beloved said, when he joined her in the attic. Her eyes were heavy with weariness, her cheeks pale from lack of rest. 'Is everything all right?'

He'd decided not to tell her how disruptive their more

complicated transmutations were proving. He did not doubt her resolve, but preferred to let her remain undistracted. If she thought her brother was in peril, she'd leave. Fortunately she was so engrossed in their magework she had no interest in the world beyond their heavily warded estate . . . and with Rumm warned not speak of what was happening in Dorana, she remained comfortably ignorant.

Which was for the best.

'Morgan?'

'A mine collapse in Trindek,' he said, and kissed her. 'Some deaths. Very sad. He thought I should know of it without delay.'

She stared. 'In the middle of the night? That's hardly considerate. It's not as if there's anything you can do.'

'True,' he said. 'But Nydd is nothing if not conscientious. My love, are you too weary to keep on working? For if you're not I'd like to finish this incant before we sleep.'

'Too weary? Never,' she said, then stifled a yawn. 'Here. See what I've done?' She pushed the notebook toward him. 'I think *this* reworking of the second stanza will allow us to transmute the armoured carapace into flexible scales without any more suffocations.'

And of course, she was right. A flame of excitement, leaping. Familiar heat in his blood. Underneath that, a tiny prickle of resentment, swiftly quashed. But oh, sometimes it was hard to accept how easily she reworked him. How she could look at his incants and see at once where he'd misstepped.

*And after all this time, I still cannot break her wards.*

'Morgan?'

He kissed her, deeply, smothering pettiness with pleasure. 'Yes, my love. That's it exactly. Let's go through the whole incant again, to be certain . . . and on the morrow, we'll test it.'

But on the morrow, Morgan received a note, by extremely roundabout means, from one of his mysterious catalyst suppliers.

'More bad news?' Barl said, as they shared breakfast in the

mansion's bread-scented kitchen. 'Please don't say we'll have only Lady Martain's goodwill to sustain us from now on.'

Folding the note, Morgan shook his head. Then he slipped it inside his tunic. 'No. But I will have to meet with him.'

'Here?'

'*Never* here. I'll be gone several hours. You'll manage on your own?'

She threw a toast crust at him. 'Mind your manners, Lord Danfey, or you'll be tidying your own incants.'

He still looked tired, but his smile was as dazzling as ever. 'Yes, my lady.'

*Yes, my lady.* He often said that, to tease her, but it was just a tease. They weren't handfasted yet. Of course they were very busy, the magework had to come first. And of course he loved her. That hadn't changed. But now and then she couldn't help wishing . . .

'Will you indulge me, my love?' he said, standing. 'Will you leave the testing of that incant until I return?'

*Oh.* 'Must I?'

He came round the table, bent down and kissed her. Slid his hand behind her neck and held her, in the way she liked best. 'Please,' he said against her lips. 'If we were still transmuting chickens I'd be easy. But we're not, and I'm not.'

When he asked her like that, how could she refuse?

'Yes. All right. But you won't be gone all day, will you?'

He kissed her again, on the forehead this time. 'Not quite all, no. I promise.'

Because poor Rumm was run off his feet these days with a whole mansion to care for, after Morgan left she cleared up in the kitchen, took the new bread from the oven and set it on racks to cool, peeled potatoes for lunch, hauled washing out of the laundry tub and wrung it sloppily dry, then traipsed upstairs to the library. If Morgan was going to be gone several hours, here was a chance to break her stalemate with the incant she'd promised him. The incant she'd promised herself.

Nearly two hours later, chance became reality.

Trembling with excitement, she stared at the latest variation of sigil and syllables designed to cheat death. And felt that funny *click* when all the pieces fell into place and the rightness of the magic turned her blood to liquid light.

'Oh, Morgan,' she whispered. 'Oh, my love.'

*I did it. Justice save me. I really am a brilliant mage.*

But she wouldn't show it to him yet. She'd save it as a surprise. No, a *wedding gift*. What could be more perfect than that?

Alone in the library, she danced a silly jig of joy. Oh, she'd forgotten how it felt to be carefree, after so long in the attic workroom and the poultry coop, the kennels and the stables, struggling with transmutation after transmutation. Failure after failure. Grieving for the ruined animals. Watching Morgan's fear and impatience wear on him. Feeling her own fear steal her breath. Knowing, always knowing, that every day brought Dorana's unknown danger one day closer.

But she wasn't going to think about that now. She'd done something extraordinary. She was going to enjoy that for a while.

*Only first I have to hide this incant . . . and not only by stuffing it into a drawer.*

So she incanted the incant to change her handwriting, and then inscribed the notebook with another mage's name. Finally she shoved it amongst the magework books dealing with childhood ailments, tolerably sure Morgan would never rummage through those.

And then she took herself outside for a days' long overdue breath of fresh air.

Someone was walking up the long estate driveway. For one heart-stopping moment she thought it was Morgan, thrown from his horse or in some other way hurt. But when she looked again she realised she was wrong. But even so . . . the walk was familiar. And then she recognised who had turned up, unannounced.

'Remmie?' she said, staring. Incredulous. 'Oh, for pity's sake. Will you *never* even *once* do what I ask?'

As soon as he set foot on the Danfey estate's driveway, Remmie could feel that something had changed. There was magework here, clean and powerful, as he'd not felt it for so long. He could feel Barl in it. Feel someone else too, Lord Danfey most like. Their combined talent was . . . formidable.

*I don't understand this. How can they magework, and nobody else?*

Tired, hungry and unkempt after six days cooped up in various wagons, he tramped the long stretch of gravel. Not as well-kept as he'd expected. There were weeds, and bare patches. There was a beautiful silence, though. A sense of sweetness and harmony. No sense of the wrongness he could feel everywhere else. The woodland ringing the Danfey estate seemed to keep out the world.

*No wonder Barl likes living here. I think I'd like it myself.* And speaking of Barl . . .

There she was. Standing up ahead of him, in the middle of the driveway, sunlight sheening her head-to-toe blue silk. Golden head tilted, hands fisted on her hips, and he didn't have to be any closer than this to know that her eyes were narrowed with annoyance.

'Remmie!' she said, when he was a stone's throw away. 'What are you doing here? Have you gone quite mad?'

Relief had him stumbling. He slowed and slowed and halted and drank the sight of her, whole.

'You're all right,' he said, hearing his voice crack round the edges. 'I was so worried. The whole journey here, the things I've seen. The things I was imagining . . . Barl, it's good to see you.'

She was staring at him as though he'd grown another head. 'Remmie, weren't you listening? *Why are you here?*'

'They closed the schoolhouse,' he said, and had to fight a fresh surge of grief. 'I had nothing else to do, so I came to see if you were all right.'

'Closed the schoolhouse? Why?' And then she was shaking her head, not giving him a chance to answer. 'Oh, *look* at you. When was the last time you saw soap and water? And a razor?'

'Last night,' he said vaguely. 'I've taken a room at the Shooting Star. But it's a long walk from Elvado. Lord Danfey likes his solitude, doesn't he?'

'Come on,' she said, and took his arm. 'You'd best come inside. I can't *believe* you're here. It's a good thing Morgan's ridden out on business, for if he hadn't we'd be mageworking and I'd have no time for you at all.'

Remmie fell into step beside her, and they tramped along the driveway toward the imposing stone mansion.

'I felt something . . . odd . . . as I crossed the estate boundary. Some kind of—'

'It's a warding incant,' she said, glancing sideways. 'Morgan and I are as fond of privacy in our magework as we are of solitude.'

'A ward? And it's holding?'

She gave him another baffled look. 'Yes, of course it's holding. Why wouldn't it?'

'Barl—' Stopping, he caught hold of her wrist. 'I know you get blinded by your magework, but . . . you do *know* what's happening in Dorana, don't you? The mage-mist?'

'Mage-mist?' she said, suddenly wary, and tugged her wrist free. 'What do you mean?'

A cold slap of understanding stole his breath. 'Justice save me. Is Danfey keeping you a prisoner here, *still*?'

'No, of course not! Remmie—'

Heedless, he took hold of her shoulders. Shook her a little, staring into her face. 'Barl, when was the last time you left this estate?'

This time she didn't pull free of him. 'Why?'

'Just answer me.'

'When I came to see you. *Why*?'

Letting go of her, turning away, he pressed the back of his hand against his mouth, breathing hard. When he could trust himself, he turned round. Rage was coursing through him, bitter and hot.

'So you don't know. Which means Danfey's been lying to you. I'll wager *everything* he's ever said is a lie.'

'*That's* a lie!' Barl retorted. 'You don't know what you're talking about!'

'And *you* don't know Dorana is falling apart!'

She stepped back. 'Falling apart? Don't talk nonsense.'

'It's not nonsense,' he said. 'Something's gone very wrong. I can't believe you don't *know*.'

She was standing still and straight, her fingers clenched by her sides, all the colour drained out of her cheeks.

'Then it's happening,' she whispered. 'What Morgan's feared for so long. But why didn't he tell me? We're not ready, and it's my fault. I can't keep the transmutations consistent. Every time we use the incant, it warps the syllabics and the magework fails, horribly. And then we have to go back to the beginning and start over, again and again. Oh, why didn't he *tell* me? I'd have done more, I'd have tried harder, I—' She squeezed her eyes shut, her face a mask of distress. And then she looked at him, her wide eyes filled with a sudden dawning hope. 'Oh! But Remmie, now *you're* here. You can help. You might be out of practice after all that stodgy teaching, but you'll find your feet quickly enough. What a mercy the schoolhouse closed. You've got here just in time!'

The flood of words left him feeling battered and dazed. 'Barl, what are you—'

She snatched his arm again and started for the mansion, dragging him with her. 'You remember the lily?'

How could he forget? The flower was still in the cottage kitchen, air-dried in a jar.

'What does your irregular flower have to do with any of this?'

'Everything,' she said. 'I'll show you.'

In horrified silence, he stared at the chickens huddled in the corner of the coop. Well. The things that used to be chickens. He didn't know what to call them now. Barl's mood had lightened, bringing him here. She was talking about the transmutation incant that had altered the birds, changed their feathers to living armour, their stubby beaks to living swords, their harmless scratching chicken feet to wicked, tearing talons. Telling him how difficult it had been to get the sigil and syllables balanced just right, how so many chickens had died before the first one lived and thrived.

If anyone in their right mind could call such a miserable existence thriving.

'Of course,' she added, 'they're not really good for anything. I mean, what we end up with won't be based on a chicken. Mainly we were trying to perfect the melding of carapace and feather. For protection. You understand?'

*No, Barl. None of it.*

But he couldn't trust his voice, so he nodded instead.

'We tried to change the hounds, but that didn't work at all,' she said, frowning. 'So we're trying something else now, something much closer to what Dorana needs, but it's not right. Not yet. I'll show you, Remmie. Only I'll warn you it's a bit upsetting. All right?'

No, it wasn't all right. None of this was all right. She'd kept calling him mad, but he thought she was the one whose reason had flown.

*She's transmuting living creatures. Deforming and killing them by the dozen . . . and she doesn't seem to care.*

This wasn't his sister. This wasn't the Barl he knew.

*I will murder Morgan Danfey. This is his fault.*

'Remmie?' Barl touched his arm. 'It's out here, on the other side of the coop.'

*It* was the most appalling thing he'd ever seen . . . and after seeing the corpse of a woman caught in mage-mist just outside Fothel, he'd not imagined there could be anything worse.

The dead calf's body was covered in grey scales, like a lizard. Scales crusted over its eyes and nose and mouth. Wicked spurs, like a fighting cockerel's, jutted from its spindly legs. A single horn, like a Trindeki spear, thrust out of its forehead.

Remmie felt his empty belly roil. No. No. This had to be a dream. 'You did this, Barl? You made this?'

'Morgan and I did, yes.'

'Why?'

She stepped closer, so intent, and took hold of his arm. 'Because Dorana is unprotected. Because our neighbours do not love us. Because something *terrible* is coming, Remmie . . . and only Morgan and I know.'

Remmie felt his eyes burn with grief.

*Oh, Barl. Something terrible is here . . . and I think it's you.*

'So you can see why we need you, Remmie,' she said, unheeding. 'The magework is so difficult. If there were three of us . . . if you and I could work together, the way we used to . . . I think then it would hold. Will you stay? You must stay. You must help us save Dorana.'

# CHAPTER THIRTY

Before he could stop himself, Remmie stumbled backwards.
Shook his head. Swallowed the bile surging into his throat.
'I can't.'

Barl's eyes widened. 'But you have to!'

A kind of sick fascination dragged his gaze back to the
monstrosity at their feet. The poor little thing. How the calf
must have suffered as it died. Suffered as she and Morgan Danfey
changed it.

His fingers shaking, he pointed. 'Barl, *nobody* has to do this.
Nobody *should* do this. What is *wrong* with you? What you've
done here is an abomination! It breaks the laws of common
decency, let alone magework. What were you thinking? And how
could you think *I* would want anything to do with it?'

Barl's pale face had flushed with hectic colour. 'Remmie Lindin,
don't you *dare* lecture me, you – you *hypocrite*. Yes, that's a
dead cow. Well, you eat cows, don't you?'

'I eat them, yes. But I don't torture them first!'

This time it was Barl who stepped back. 'You think I *like*
killing these creatures? I'm doing this because I *have* to, because
Dorana *needs* me to. Because Morgan asked me to help him save
us, and he can't do it alone. It's sad the calf died. And sad it

won't be the last one. But Remmie, I will kill a hundred calves, a *thousand,* to keep Dorana safe. If I don't, if I stop now . . . then I'll have done this for *nothing*!'

He stared at his sister, this stranger, his heart pounding against his ribs. In the poultry coop beside them he could hear the horrible, heavy thunking of the mageworked chickens' feathers as the deformed creatures struggled to move beneath the unnatural weight.

'Barl . . . let's go,' he said. 'While Danfey's away. However awful things are beyond this estate, they're worse here. Please.' He held out his hand. 'Let's go.'

She knocked his hand aside. There were tears in her eyes. 'You *are* mad! And you should never have come. How can you be so selfish, Remmie? What are your squeamish feelings compared to countless innocent lives?'

'If you care so much for countless innocent lives,' he retorted, his own eyes burning, 'then why don't you poke your nose off this privileged estate and see what is happening beyond its warding! Whole villages, swallowed by mage-mist. Crops ruined. Livestock rotting in ditches. Misery like you wouldn't believe. People are *terrified,* you stupid, ignorant girl. Thanks to the mage-mist, they're *dying.* If you want to use your magework to save Dorana, Barl, save it from that! Don't use it for *this*!'

'But *this* is what's going to save us, Remmie! Why are you arguing with me when we're on the same side? You just said it yourself, Dorana is under attack, and *I'm* saying that what Morgan and I are doing, what we're creating, will be our only hope!'

'You haven't heard a word I've said, have you?' Overwhelmed with angry disgust, Remmie fastened his fingers to his sister's arm and dropped to his knees beside the scaled calf, dragging her down with him. 'Look at this thing you've created, Barl. *Look at it.* This is not hope. This is cruelty and despair. It's *wrong,* you know it is, and while you might've convinced yourself to look the other way as you create these monsters, you will *never* convince me!' Panting, he flailed onto his feet. 'Now I'm going back to Batava. Come with me or don't. That's up to you. But if you stay here, Barl? If you choose to keep doing *this*? Then I never knew you. And I never want to see you again.'

She shouted after him as he walked away. Shouted pleas, shouted threats, shouted 'til she was hoarse. He didn't stop. He didn't listen. He could hardly see for tears.

*I'm sorry, Mama. I am. But there are some things I won't do. Not even for you.*

Because she was obliged to set an example, Venette ignored Orwin's objections and made her way from their town house to the Hall of Knowledge on foot.

She'd not walked more than three streets' distance before she was regretting her choice.

So deeply alarmed, so uncertain, were the people of Elvado now that they did not fear to accost her. But worse than their jostling, pointing, barging and weeping was the inescapable evidence of Dorana's dreadful decline.

*How did we come to this? Where did we go wrong?*

She didn't know. None of them knew. But as she stood in the middle of Asvoden Way, staring over the crowd at her neighbourhood's buckled walls, its cracked windows, the boarded-up gaping holes where stained glass once glittered, the oddly melted roof tiles and uneven front paths, she accepted – for the first time – that unless the Council and the College performed a miracle, and quickly, this city would fall to ruin . . . and after it, all Dorana.

Shaken, she looked at the waiting mages around her. A scant handful she recognised. The rest were unknown. But they all knew her, because she was Lady Venette Martain, Councillor. Too important to bother . . . until today.

'I know what you want to hear,' she said to them, raising her voice. 'And justice knows, I want to say it. But if I did, I'd be lying. All I can do is ask for your patience.'

'We've been patient!' an angry voice in the middle of the crowd retorted. 'It's not helping!'

A ripple of muttered agreement. Every face she looked at was unfriendly.

The angry voice wasn't familiar. 'Whoever you are, sir, do me the courtesy of showing your face.'

The unhappy crowd parted. A slender mage of middling height shifted through the space made for him and stood before her, belligerent. The right side of his face was puckered scarlet, the wound reaching past his hairline into his scalp. His hair had been shorn close, revealing one ruined ear.

'Mage-mist,' he said, sneering. 'Caught me unawares. And I'm not the only one who's been afflicted, Lady Martain.'

She swallowed. 'I know. The Guild of Pothers keeps the Council apprised of such unfortunate incidents. I am sorry, Mage—'

'Garven.' The man's right eye, its drooping lid bubbled, leaked a blood-tinged tear. 'My daughter Tiva was with me. Not yet twelve. A pretty child, with a great touch of talent about her. She's not expected to live.'

If she touched his arm in sympathy she thought he'd spit on her. 'I'm sorry. I had a narrow escape myself, the other night. Terrible.'

'And that's meant to lull us, is it? Make us believe you share our sufferings?'

The speaker this time was a woman, as unfriendly as Mage Garven. She wore plain, drab green linen. A servant's garb. What was the woman doing causing trouble in the street? Surely she had shelves to dust or boots to clean?

'Lulling you is not my purpose,' she replied. 'I merely point out that rank is no protection.'

'Your rank is meant to be *our* protection,' said Mage Garven. 'You mages on the Council, aren't you meant to have the answers? You lay down the law to us. Tell us what magics we can and can't have. There's a price for that, Lady Martain. Why aren't you paying it? Why are we the ones paying for what you can't do?'

Sparked tinder to dry grass, his demand whipped through the

491

pressing crowd. Loud voices echoed him. The day darkened with rising fear.

'All you've done is ban the use of magic!' a second man complained. 'You've made our lives even more of a misery and we've got nothing to show for it!'

Venette pointed at him. 'For shame, Mage Tolomew. How many times have you drunk my wine at one of our parties? You know better than anyone that I don't look to burden you. And not all magic is banned, only such incantery that isn't needful. Do you say a Brantish farmhand is more capable than a Doranen mage?'

Humiliated by her open scorn, Tolomew mumbled something then looked away. Not liking his swift capitulation or a harshly spoken truth, the crowd started muttering again.

Then another shout. '*Mage-mist! Run*!'

As the resentful crowd scattered like startled mice, Venette watched the drifting dazzle of raw, unrestrained magic. Afraid and furious, she stood her ground. Dared it to come nearer, to disfigure her. To kill her. The mage-mist drifted closer. Closer. So close she could feel its unbridled heat crisping her skin.

'*Bas'fana!*' she shouted, clapping her hands. '*Bas'fana disnoi!*'

In a shower of sparks it collapsed and vanished. Her breathing ragged, Venette pressed trembling fingers to her to lips. Held back the sobbing relief that did not become a ranked mage, let alone a councillor. Then she glared at the few mages still scuttling away. *Ungrateful jiggets*. For days she'd foregone comfort, Orwin's company, her own bed, decently cooked meals, fresh clothes and a bath, just so she could remain at the College to work with Bellamie Ranowen toward finding the key to their saving.

*What more do they want from me? Shall I slit a vein in my wrist and bleed for them? Take a knife and cut my own throat? Must I die for Dorana to prove I'm trying to save it?*

Asvoden Way was deserted now. Taking advantage, she hurried to the towering Hall of Knowledge. At least it was still intact, its stained-glass windows unsmashed, its framework unbuckled.

Every mage residing there worked night and day to keep it that way. The Hall was Dorana's greatest symbol. If it should fall . . .

*But it won't. It can't. Stop thinking like that.*

Hurrying into the Council chamber, she hurried into another storm.

'Lord Varen! Is it possible you do not fully comprehend the extreme gravity of this alarming situation?'

Halted in the open doorway, unnoticed, Venette winced as Brice surged to his feet, both fists striking the Council table as though he wished it were someone's face.

'No, Lady Brislyn, that is *not* possible!' He gestured at Sallis and Shari. 'Are these the faces of mages who fail to comprehend our plight?'

Lady Dreen Brislyn, recently appointed head of the General Council, sat back in her chair and folded her arms. 'It is well known to those of us who refuse to be browbeaten by certain elements of Doranen society that mages who achieve a place on *this* Council have raised dissembling to an art form. Why should I trust what your faces have to say? Indeed, why should I trust—'

'One moment,' Brice said curtly, and turned. 'Lady Martain, you are late.'

Not appreciating his tone, Vanette took her customary seat. 'I was delayed by a group of concerned citizens.'

'You were confronted? In broad daylight?' Sallis gaped. 'Tell us you did not lower yourself to converse with a rabble!'

'*Rabble?*' Lady Brislyn demanded. 'Don't you mean a group of frightened fellow mages seeking leadership? That you would heap scorn upon them Lord Arkley, speaks volumes of your failures. You wonder why the rest of us have lost faith in this Council? Look in a mirror!'

'Mind your manners!' Sallis spat. 'I won't be lectured to in this Hall by a second-rate mage with less than half my years in her dish, whose family clings to its ranking by a fingernail!'

'*Enough*!' Brice shouted, his face burnished dark red. He sat again, heavily. 'Conduct yourselves with dignity, all of you, or be expelled.'

Waiting for Sallis and Shari to stop their spluttering, Venette studied Dreen Brislyn from the corner of her eye. Young and lowly ranked she might be, but no mage became head of the oft-contentious General Council lacking political skill and a spine of steel forged as hard as a Vharne swordsman's blade.

'My purpose here is twofold,' Lady Brislyn declared, before Brice could speak again. 'Firstly I am come to determine what, in exact detail, this Council and the College of Mages is doing to undo the—'

'It's not your place to question us,' Shari snapped. 'The General Council devotes itself to such matters as are contained within its charter. *Not* contained within its charter is the right to—'

'Lady Frieden, our current circumstances *give* us the right!' Dreen Brislyn said, glaring. 'Three days ago the General Council received formal declarations from the rulers of Brantone, Feen, Trindek, Manemli *and* Ranoush. In other words, the rulers of every sovereign nation that sits upon our borders. Doranen magemist has been seen in their lands, and as you can imagine, *they are not amused.*'

Stunned silence. Chilled, Venette looked at Brice, then Sallis and Shari.

'Is there proof?' Brice said at last, hoarse with dismay.

Lady Brislyn lifted a leather satchel onto the table, withdrew a sheaf of papers and handed them to him.

'They have provided various eyewitness accounts, from nine different locations. There are also reports of inexplicable warpings and disruptions of buildings. Buckled roads. Suddenly unsafe bridges. Livestock suffering ghastly hurts with no cause apparent.' Daring any of them to challenge her, she looked around the table. 'In other words, they are suffering what we suffer.'

'Impossible,' said Sallis, as Brice quickly scanned the copied letters. 'Our borders are warded. No magic escapes them.'

'Our borders are *failing*,' Dreen Brislyn said, her face fierce. 'For centuries Dorana has lived in peace with its magickless neighbours because we have found a way to comfortably coexist.

494

Because we have never been a threat. Well, my lords and ladies, we are a *great* threat now!'

Venette leaned forward, capturing Dreen Brislyn's attention. 'Do you mean to suggest that these insignificant nations might inflict violence upon us?'

'Suggest?' The woman laughed. 'Lady Martain, I tell you outright, for that is what has been told to me. These princes and potentates, whose nations are *far* from insignificant, believe we are a danger to their sovereignty and safety. And being, for the most part, of warlike dispostion, some of them go so far as to accuse us of attacking them. So discarding old enmities, they have signed a treaty amongst themselves. Even now their various warriors gather along our mutual borders. They have told us, in no uncertain language, that we must control these rogue magics . . . or pay the price.'

This time it was Sallis who thumped the table. 'Then they are fools! They should fear what we'll do if they raise so much as a bread knife against us!'

'And what is that, Sallis?' Venette asked, with a rolling-eye glance at Brice. 'Stamp our well-shod feet and wave our impotent fists in the air?'

Silencing Sallis with a look, Brice tossed the copied letters onto the table. 'How has the General Council responded?'

'We have given them assurances that the matter is being dealt with,' said Lady Brislyn. 'More than that we were not inclined to say before consulting with this Council, bearing in mind that your purview is limited to the business of magic within Dorana's borders.'

'Obviously that purview must be expanded,' Shari said, her eyes narrowed. 'Given these unprecedented circumstances, the Council of Mages must—'

'Must not use this calamity as an excuse to expand its authority. You wield enough power, Lady Frieden. Any attempt to wield more will not be viewed kindly by the General Council.'

Ivory pale with temper, Shari turned to Brice. 'This cannot be tolerated, Lord Varen. We are none of us naughty schoolchildren to be treated to such scolds. The General Council is an undisciplined collection of lowly ranked mages and shopkeepers. For this woman to presume she—'

'Be quiet, Lady Frieden,' Brice said, sounding weary beyond bearing. 'Be quiet all of you, that I might think.'

Alarmed, Venette watched Brice retreat to his favourite brooding place, the Council chamber's balcony. It wasn't safe out there. If mage-mist manifested itself or, justice forbid, should Dorana's magical instability break through the workings on the Hall, he might plunge to his death. But as she opened her mouth to call him back, a knock on the closed chamber door distracted her.

'Councillors, my apologies for the interruption,' the day's duty mage murmured. 'But there is an unranked mage here, most insistent that he be given leave to address you. He says his name is Rem—'

'Have you lost your wits?' Sallis demanded. 'We are in emergency session! Get rid of the fool!'

The duty mage hesitated. 'My lord, I—'

'Get rid of him, I said! Tell him to make an appointment to see one of the administrators. *Go*.' As the chamber door closed, Sallis grimaced. 'And why that prim face, Venette? Have you not had your fill of rabblesome complaints today?'

'I have,' she said mildly, ignoring Dreen Brislyn's disapproval. 'Just as I've had my fill of bluster. Lady Brislyn is right, we must work together to overcome this crisis.'

Dreen Brislyn nodded her thanks, then linked her hands before her on the table. 'Councillors, the General Council expects me to take the truth back to the Second district.' One by one she looked at them, her light green eyes wide and unblinking. '*Can* this crisis be overcome? You and the College's best mages have been seeking a solution for weeks, yet you are no closer now than when you began. Meanwhile, Dorana unravels around us. How long before it unravels entirely and we are left to the mercy of nations who have long looked upon us with envy and suspicion, even as they benefited from our magework? We are vastly outnumbered and we have no warriors. For centuries our magic has been our shield. Bereft of that, what shall we do?'

'An excellent question, Lady Brislyn,' Brice said, rejoining them. 'What do you suggest?'

Her lips thinned in a wary smile. 'What do *I* suggest? Do you say my suggestion would carry any weight?'

Brice matched her thin smile with one of his own. 'As much weight as I decide it deserves to bear.'

Taking a moment to fiddle with the ruby ring on her forefinger, Dreen Brislyn let her smile fade. 'I do have a thought to share. Perhaps it has been thought of already, and already discarded, but . . .'

'Go on,' Brice invited. 'I am interested.'

'If Dorana is unmaking itself, then I believe our only course of action is to summon to the First district every ranked and unranked mage of talent, and under the auspices of this Council and the College, strive to save it in a working. Our many voices of healing must be raised to drown out the lone voice of disease, before we all perish . . . and take the wider world with us. Or before the wider world decides it can live without us.'

'It is an intriguing notion,' Brice said slowly, looking round the table. 'Venette, has Mage Ranowen, have any of the College mages, suggested a similar approach?'

'No,' she said, still looking at Dreen Brislyn. 'They – we – have been focusing on the cause of the problem, assuming that no answer is possible before that cause is understood.'

Dreen Brislyn frowned. 'Has there been any glimmer of understanding so far?'

'To an extent,' she admitted. 'The damage to the magical plane, for want of a better description, is not constant or consistent. It breaches, it ripples then cobbles together, only to breach in a new harmonic key, and ripple there, and finally cobble again. Mage Ranowen and her colleagues and I have had some small success healing, let's say, a few of these breaches, but . . .' Painfully reminded of recent frustrations and despair, she had to clear her throat. 'To borrow Mage Ranowen's fanciful analogy, if Dorana is a tapestry, then something is wildly dashing about with a sword, slashing holes in the fabric . . . and we, its mages, dash from slash to slash with needle and thread so we might stitch it back together before the whole collapses entirely.'

Eyes alight with eagerness, Dreen Brislyn leaned forward. 'Then surely you can see that my suggestion is most timely! I say we give you and the College's mages *thousands* of needles!'

'What say you, Venette?' Brice prompted. 'It sounds like a possible answer to me.'

She was tempted to retreat to the balcony herself, just to escape the pressure of everyone's stares. Even Sallis and Shari seemed impressed with Dreen Brislyn's suggestion.

'Sounds like, yes,' she said. 'And yes, it might be possible. But I caution against taking my analogy too literally. Until we know *why* these tears and instabilities are occurring, it could be very dangerous to throw so much magic at them at once. Instead of healing Dorana, we could destroy it ourselves.'

'That's true,' Dreen Brislyn said. 'But will you at least take my suggestion to the College, Lady Martain? Today? If its mages deem there is some merit to my suggestion, it will take time to organise. And I'm not sure how much time Dorana has. Quite apart from our dilemma, our neighbours are impatient . . . and not much inclined to give us the benefit of the doubt.'

Venette looked to Brice. 'There can be no harm done asking Bellamie's opinion.'

'Agreed,' said Brice. 'You should both go and sound out the College on this notion. But first, Lady Brislyn, we have privy matters to discuss. Perhaps you'd care for some refreshments? The duty mage will gladly escort you to the dining hall. Lady Martain can find you when our business is concluded.'

Dreen Brislyn stood, and offered them a brief nod. 'Lord Varen. Councillors. The General Council thanks you for your time and co-operation.'

'Arrogant wench!' Shari spat, once Dreen Brislyn was gone. 'I don't care how clever she is, that lowly ranked upstart needs putting in her place. She—'

498

'*Putting in her place,* Shari? Really? The head of Dorana's General Council?' Disgusted, Venette shook her head. 'D'you know, I might well have had my fill of the rabble but when I hear you say things like that, I'm forced to admit they might have a point!'

'Do not start your bickering,' Brice snapped. 'But instead consider the news Lady Brislyn has brought.'

Sallis's eyebrows lifted. 'You take this threat seriously, Brice?'

'You do not?'

'If you mean do I fear a rabble of unwashed, stick-wielding Trindeki plainsmen then the answer is most emphatically *no*.'

Brice sighed. 'Then you prove yourself a greater fool than ever I imagined, Sallis. Lady Brislyn is right. Without magic we are as lambs before a wolf pack . . . and with the magickless nations ranged against us, outnumbered.'

'Or do you believe that your sharp tongue alone can save you from a murderous Trindeki?' Venette said, poisonously sweet.

Sallis shut his mouth with a snap.

'Brice . . .' Bracing herself, Venette turned to him. 'I know you won't want to hear this, but it's time we brought Morgan back into the fold. Whatever his transgressions, surely—'

'Surely he has demonstrated he's not to be trusted!' said Shari.

'You want to worry about his sexual peccadilloes, Shari, with Dorana falling apart and five warlike nations baring their teeth in our direction?'

Shari's lips thinned to a stubborn line. 'A man careless and unthinking in his privy life will be careless and unthinking in his magework. At which, I say again, he is *not* so remarkably gifted!'

'He was gifted enough to be granted a seat on this Council, Shari! Either its mages are the finest in Dorana or they're not! Which is it?'

'Even this Council can make a mistake!'

Her hand itching to slap the stupid woman silly, Venette turned to Brice. 'I want this matter decided, Lord Varen, once and for all. I want *you* to rule on Morgan's position. I'm tired of you letting Sallis and Shari decide for you.'

Brice's eyes glinted. 'Be careful, Venette.'

'I *have* been careful! And I've been patient! For weeks now I have waited for you to do the right thing. Well, my lord, I am tired of waiting. I'm tired of listening to Sallis and Shari malign one of our own, knowing that you'll not lift a finger to stop them!'

'Very well, Lady Martain,' Brice said curtly. 'Here is my ruling. The fact that Sallis and Shari dislike Morgan does not mean their concerns lack credence. The harsh truth is that no matter his talents, which are many, I grant you, Morgan Danfey is unstable. There is an inconstance revealed in him that I fear one day will be his undoing. A mage and his magework cannot be taken apart. Who we are, *what* we are, informs everything that we do. You rail at me for not making my ruling sooner? Well, I have been waiting too. Waiting for him to come to his senses and ask me for the chance to prove his worth. Instead he remains on his estate, sulking and fucking. That is not the conduct of a councillor, Venette.'

She thought she might drown in Sallis and Shari's gleeful smugness. She thought she might weep, because Brice was wrong . . . and she could say nothing. Confess that Morgan was mageworking, and that she abetted him, and she'd be censured. Likely stripped of her position. And if she wasn't on the Council, she couldn't help Morgan at all – or Dorana.

So, with teeth gritted, she accepted what she could not change. 'Lord Varen.'

With a sharp nod, Brice looked to Sallis and Shari. 'You are unwise to dismiss our neighbours as beneath contempt. For countless generations they have known one thing above all else: the mages of Dorana are untouchable. But now *this* generation has seen us stumble. And though we *shall* regain our feet, it will be a long time before they forget what they have seen. They might even be emboldened to test our resolve. Therefore you'll retire to the archives and read every history book, every note, every scribbled scrap, in search of magics that we can use to defend ourselves should this generation seek to press their advantage.'

They sat, grimly silent, contemplating a future they did not wish to face. Perhaps did not even know how to face . . . though not a one of them would admit it. At least not yet.

Venette turned her shoulder to Sallis and Shari. Lowered her voice. 'Brice . . . will you at least let me be the one to tell Morgan?'

'Very well,' he said. 'But after today, Venette, I will not discuss him again.'

And that was that.


Nearly two hours after Remmie's furious abandonment, Rumm found Barl weeping outside the poultry coop, slumped on the grass beside the dead, ruined calf.

'Mage Lindin!'

Humiliated, she scrambled to her feet. 'Oh, *Rumm*. Morgan's right. He should put a bell on you!'

The master servant, thinner and far less immaculate these days in trousers and shirt sleeves, no buttoned tunic, took a prudent step back. 'I'm sorry. When I called you for lunch and you didn't answer, I became concerned.'

'Lunch?' Squinting, she glanced at the sky. And there was the sun, slid past its high point on its lazy glide toward the horizon. 'Oh.'

'Are you hungry? I've made some pea soup.'

'No. Yes. Perhaps.' She dragged her silk sleeve over her wet face, and when Rumm clicked his tongue at that gave him a look. 'Careful, or you'll be wearing those soupy peas.'

'Mage Lindin,' he said, very correct.

She watched him as he tried not to look at the dead calf. All the terrible things Remmie said came back to her, and she lifted her chin.

'Well? Go on, then, Rumm. Tell me I'm cruel. Tell me I make monsters. Tell me how much I enjoy killing helpless beasts like this.'

Shocked differently now, his gaze shifted back to her. 'I would never say any of those things, Mage Lindin. Much of your work is distasteful, but it's for the greater good.'

He answered to Morgan, not her, but she'd chance a question anyway. She had to know. 'Is something wrong in Elvado, Rumm? Something Morgan's told you to say nothing about?'

Rumm's eyes flickered. Seeing it, Barl felt her insides twist. So Remmie was right? Morgan was keeping things from her? She wanted to weep again, but managed to hold the tears at bay.

'What's gone wrong, Rumm? *Tell me!*'

'What makes you think anything's wrong, Mage Lindin?'

She slapped him. '*Stop* it! Don't you dare stand there treating me like a block of wood, you stupid man. My brother was here. He says Dorana's falling apart! *Is it?*'

Rumm's cheek was marred by a red mark where her hand had struck. 'And was it your brother who said those hateful things, too?'

'Being hateful doesn't make him a liar! Rumm, so help me, I won't ask you again!'

'Mage Lindin, I'm sorry. You'll have to take this up with his lordship.'

'*You're* sorry?' She pressed her trembling lips together, hard. 'I'm going inside,' she said, when she could trust her voice. Then she kicked the dead calf's spindly leg. 'Burn this. Or bury it. I don't care, only get it out of my sight.'

Rumm bowed. 'Mage Lindin.'

'And so that we're clear? I'd drink rat poison before I touched your pea soup again. It's horrible. It always has been.' Not waiting for him to answer, she turned on her heel and marched away. Only got a few steps before she thought to turn round. 'And if you dare tell Morgan that Remmie was here, I'll make *you* drink rat poison. Don't think that I won't.'

As she often did, she waited for Morgan in the library. But for the first time since she'd set foot in the splendid room, it gave her no pleasure.

*Morgan lied. He lied.*

Or held back the truth from her, which amounted to the same

502

thing. She was too angry for more weeping. Not even Remmie's hatefulness had hurt her like this.

*How can he love me, and lie to my face?*

He came home just on sunset, with the clear sky streaking mauve and gold. Strode into the library smiling, jubilant, a heavy satchel on his shoulder.

'My love! Good news! I have *azafris,* I have—'

'*One* chance to explain, Morgan, why you've been *lying* to me!'

He checked like a deer struck through the heart by an arrow. 'Lying? My love—'

'Don't!' she said, sliding out of the chair and lifting her hands. 'I'm warning you. *Don't.* What's mage-mist?'

'Oh.' Slowly, he let the heavy satchel thud to the floor. '*Rumm!*'

Snatching up a cushion, she threw it at him. 'You leave Rumm alone. He's got nothing to do with this. Morgan, when were you going to tell me that things in Dorana had turned so bad?'

'I wasn't,' he said, watching her carefully. 'At least, not until I had no choice. Barl, who told you about mage-mist? Was it Venette? Has she been here?'

She didn't know whether to weep or scream. 'No, it wasn't Venette, it wasn't Rumm, it doesn't *matter* who it was! What *matters* is that you lied to me. Why would you *do* that?'

'To protect you, my love.'

'Protect me? When have I ever asked you to *protect* me?'

His face was pale, his eyes distressed. 'You don't have to ask, Barl. I love you. I will always protect you.'

'Not by lying to me, you won't! *What is mage-mist?*'

'Oh, Barl.' He closed the distance between them, pulled her to his chest and rested his cheek on her hair. 'Mage-mist is a leaking of raw magical energy into the air. It's unpredictable and destructive and it's causing some problems.'

She didn't put her arms around him. Her insides were twisting anew with a terrible foreboding.

'Morgan . . . is it because of the transmutation incants? The shifting syllabics? Is this trouble our fault?'

He sighed. 'And this is why I didn't tell you. It might be. I don't know. But even if it is, what Dorana will gain from our magework far outstrips this tiny tempest.'

She tried to pull away, but he tightened his arms. Held her prisoned against him, and kissed her. And because he was a fever in her, because she needed Remmie to be wrong, she kissed him back. Nipped his lower lip to blood, though, because she was still angry.

'You had no right to keep the truth from me. Say you're sorry. Say you'll never do that again.'

'I'm sorry.' He dipped his head. Bit her breast through her silk tunic, not quite gently. 'Never again. Forgive me.'

His contrition and the small pain ignited a firestorm of pleasure. But she couldn't let that distract her. Shuddering, she ignored it.

'Morgan, if this trouble is our doing, then we must undo it.'

'And we will,' he said, his hands busy. 'When we finish what we started, all will be well again. You'll see.'

He had her blood thundering. It was hard to breathe. 'Morgan, I want to know what we're creating. All of it. Not just hints. I want to know what you've been working on without me.'

He groaned against her. 'Not yet. Soon.'

'You keep *saying* that, but—'

'Barl . . .' Pulling his head back, he looked down at her, his eyes almost blind with pleasure. 'My love, don't you trust me?'

'You know I do,' she said, hearing her voice hitch. 'But Morgan—'

His lips stole whatever she'd wanted to say. 'Then *trust* me.'

Those busy hands were driving her out of her mind. Taking them, she pressed him to her, high and low, letting out a soft cry as he did what she wanted.

'All right. All right.' The words escaped her in swift, breathless pants. 'But Morgan, we have to hurry. We can't let Dorana suffer. And I think it's time to step out of the shadows. We've worked in secret long enough.'

He groaned. 'Soon, my love. Soon.'

'No, Morgan. Now. *Now now now now.*'

Laughing, his eyes blazed at her. 'You want now? All right. *Now.*'

He dragged them both to the carpet. Stripped her bare, and made her scream. It wasn't what she'd meant, and he knew it.

But it would do . . . for now.

# CHAPTER THIRTY-ONE

Lying in bed beside Morgan, head turned on the pillow to watch him sleep, Barl marvelled at the moonlit planes of his face. She thought she could stare at him for hours, for ever, and never grow weary of his cheekbones, his lips, his nose. His hair was unbound and silver gilt, spread like spun silk on the pillows between them. Unfurling her fingers she stroked it, and felt her skin shiver. She loved his hair. She loved him. Even when she was angry with him, still she loved him. The simplicity of that stole her breath. The power of it sustained her. If they had to live apart on this estate for the rest of their lives, she didn't care. For where they loved, they would endure.

*So long as Dorana endures.*

'You mustn't fret, my love,' he said, not opening his eyes. 'All will be well in the end.'

Because he was awake, she slid her fingertips down his arm. 'I know.'

'And don't think I am crushed by the Council's rejection. I outgrew those fools some time ago.'

Venette Martain had brought them the news, not long after they'd sat down to their supper. She'd been so upset she'd actually deigned to join them at the kitchen table and let Rumm feed her plain mutton stew.

'I know that too. But Morgan . . .'

Venette Martain hadn't only told them about the loss of his position. There was worse news, that had killed appetite stone dead.

'Barl.' Morgan took her hand. 'What have we been preparing for, if not the predations of our neighbours?'

She hid her face against his shoulder. 'Yes, Morgan, I know. But we're not ready for them, are we?'

'We will be.'

'Oh, *Morgan*.' Letting go of him, she sat up. 'Must we have this argument again? So soon? You are *not* confident, my love. You're as worried as I am. Put on a brave face for Venette Martain and Rumm, if you must, but don't try to cozen me.'

He opened his eyes. 'All right.'

'So . . . what are we going to do?'

'We're doing it, Barl. We are creating the magework that will save Dorana. Provided we hold our course and keep our nerve, we will prevail. Do not doubt that for a moment. And I am *not* cozening you,' he added, pressing a finger to her lips as she began to protest. 'I believe it, wholeheartedly.'

She could see that he did. *If only I could believe it.* 'Morgan, how is it our magework is unaffected when the rest of Dorana is in such a state? Even Lady Martain seemed baffled.' She pulled a face. 'Relieved, too, curse her, but baffled.'

'Don't curse Venette,' he said, frowning. 'She's been a good and loyal friend.'

'To you. Me, she'd happily see broken-legged in a ditch!'

'Her loyalty to me extends to you, Barl. We are one and the same. Venette understands that.'

Uncertain, Barl dabbled her fingers on the sheet. 'You're so sure we can trust her. But Morgan, while she doesn't know everything, she knows enough to do us great harm.'

'Not without harming herself as well,' he said, faintly smiling. 'Trust *me*, my love. Venette is nothing if not a survivor. We are quite safe.'

He'd known Venette Martain his whole life. It was hardly surprising, she supposed, that he'd trust her, defend her, even when they were at odds and she made it plain she cared not at all for some of his recent choices. The same way she trusted Remmie, even though they were at odds.

*Remmie.*

The look on his face, in his eyes, as he'd shouted. He'd often been impatient with her. But disgusted? Never. Not until now.

*Well, so am I disgusted. He wants the protection of magic without paying the price. He really is a hypocrite. Give me the roast beef, he says, but don't show me the slaughterhouse. And under no circumstances invite the slaughterman to tea.*

'Barl?' Morgan took her hand again. 'What is it?'

Scant hours ago she'd railed at him for lying . . . or at least, withholding the truth. And now here she was with a secret of her own.

*Speaking of hypocrites . . .*

'It was Remmie who told me about Dorana's strife,' she said, frowning at his fingers, wrapped around hers. 'And the mage-mist.'

Morgan shifted a little more upright. 'I wondered when you were going to tell me.'

She looked at him. 'You knew?'

'I guessed.'

'We had a terrible fight. He's gone back to Batava.'

'You're sure of that?'

'He said he was going. And while we are very different, in one respect we're the same. We say what we mean, and we mean what we say.'

Morgan let go of her hand and stroked his fingers down her cheek. 'He hurt you.'

'He was angry.'

'*He hurt you.*'

'And if he did, it's my problem,' she said sharply. 'It's got nothing to do with you.'

His eyes glittered. 'I beg to differ.'

'*Morgan.*' She raised a warning finger at him. 'No. He's my brother.'

'Mine also, if you and I now count ourselves family.'

'Really?' She snorted. 'Then what does that make Venette Martain, I wonder? My stepmama?'

That surprised laughter from him. 'She would be alarmed to hear it.'

Barl lay back down beside him. Rested her palm on his chest. She could feel his heart beating, drumlike, through his skin. 'Please, Morgan. Leave it be. We have enough to deal with.'

Morgan didn't answer. When she glanced up at him, she saw he was frowning. She felt her own heart thud harder.

'He won't betray me, Morgan. He won't betray *us*. I promise.'

Still, he didn't answer. In the moonlight his face was suddenly cool and remote. *Thud thud thud* went her unsteady heart.

'Morgan, you have to trust me on this, just as you expect me to trust Venette Martain on your say-so.'

'Your brother lacks Venette's incentive to keep his mouth shut.'

'He doesn't need an incentive! He loves me. That's enough.'

Morgan looked at her. 'Are you sure?'

'Yes, I'm sure! How can you—'

'*Are you sure?*'

Remmie's sickened anger. The disgust in his eyes. Mouth dry, eyes burning, she nodded . . . and lied.

'I told you. I'm sure.'

'Very well,' said Morgan, after a moment. 'But for his sake, my love, let us hope that you're right.'

She didn't want to talk about this any more. Desperate for a change of subject, she returned to a different fear.

'This notion of a grand working, to heal Dorana's breaches. Do you think it will succeed?'

'I don't know,' said Morgan, shrugging. 'It might.'

'If it doesn't, do you think the General Council will do more than make assurances? Try to appease Trindek and Feen and the rest to keep them from crossing over our borders?'

His eyes darkened. 'Play the role of meek supplicant, you mean?

Kneel in the dirt at their feet mewling *Please, please, we'll do anything you say? Put your spears down, don't hurt us?*'

'My love . . .' Hesitant, she pulled a little away from him. 'Can we blame them for their anger? If our magework endangers them, then—'

'*Endangers* them?' In one swift movement he rolled out of the bed, to land lightly on his feet and start pacing their moonlit chamber. 'Our magework *enriches* them. These petty, complaining nations have grown fat on Dorana's magic. We sell them our incants and our expertise, we save them from pestilence and provide them with luxuries and all it costs them is coin while we *bleed* for the knowledge that fattens them. And you think it's *right* that we kneel?'

'Not right,' she murmured. 'But prudent. At least until Dorana is healed. But if you mislike the notion so much, perhaps we should rethink our part in this.'

He turned. '*Our* part?'

'You said it yourself, Morgan. These breaches could be our doing. If we ceased working on these transmutations, if we—'

'Are you *mad*?' he demanded. 'Our mageworking is all that stands between Dorana and its destruction at the hands of these lesser nations. Great working or not, Dorana will heal itself soon enough. But even if it healed itself tomorrow, it would be too late. You know what the Feenish say about unseeing the seen. We have never appeared weak before . . . but thanks to the General Council, we appear weak now. And every potentate and princeling, every merchant, every peddler, will look at us differently until they are given a reason not to. Until they are reminded of their proper place in the world.'

He was right, of course he was right, only . . .

'My love, I'm not certain they'll be reminded by transmuted chickens and hounds and calves.'

Rage was smouldering in his eyes. 'They will have far more to fear than that, Barl.'

In the silvering moonlight his naked body was beautiful. But for once it didn't stir her. Fear smothered desire.

510

'I don't – Morgan, what do you mean?'

'I mean to save Dorana. I'll need the attic to myself for a few days.'

To *himself*? 'Morgan—'

'When I'm ready, I'll show you what I'm working toward. In the meantime, you'll have the library. There are books you've not yet read.'

That was true. There were dozens. But since they'd found each other, Morgan had laid his heart and soul bare to her. He'd wept in her arms and shuddered his pleasure there, with abandon. She knew him better than any man alive, better even than Remmie, and Remmie was her other self.

*Why then do I look at him now and see a stranger?*

'Barl . . .' Morgan smiled, but the rage in his eyes still smouldered. 'Please. Don't be cross. This is nothing nefarious. I just need . . . a little time. I need you to trust me.'

He was Morgan, her beloved. She had no reason to fear. She was being foolish. Girlish. She knew better than that. Morgan deserved better.

'Of course,' she said. 'Morgan, of *course*.'

He leapt to the bed, laughing . . . and the stranger disappeared.

Venette drove her buggy to Brice's town house, to tell him of the previous night's meeting with Morgan before going on to the College to spend another miserable day working with Bellamie Ranowen.

The sun was barely an hour risen. Elvado's residential streets were empty, not only because it was early, but because the city's mages had begun to fear leaving their homes. Even Orwin had started to find reasons for dallying indoors. It broke her heart. Her husband was no coward . . . but the ever-present, ever-growing threat of mage-mist had beaten him. It was beating everyone, bruising all of Dorana with blows of dread. Yesterday, as they'd travelled from the Hall to the College, Dreen Brislyn had been unsparing in her descriptions of what Dorana's other districts endured. Also unsparing was her silent contempt, that the Council of Mages stayed safe in Elvado . . . for the most part not having to face the suffering visited upon everyone else.

She wished she could summon up some righteous, indignant anger. But Dreen Brislyn had good reason for her disdain. Between her and Morgan . . . and what she'd found at Morgan's estate . . . she had passed an uncomfortable night.

The flower she'd stolen sat on the buggy seat beside her, pink and cream and blue-striped . . . and *wrong*.

Brice opened his door to her wrapped in a quilted dressing gown. 'Venette.' Pained, he looked past her at the pale morning sky. 'I should be surprised, I suppose. However—'

'Let me in, Brice,' she said, and pushed the door. 'I don't need long and besides, the horse loathes being tied up while it's harnessed to the buggy. If I'm here more than ten minutes it'll pull free and trot home.'

With a sigh Brice stood back, one hand gesturing her inside. 'By all means.'

He kept her standing in his town house lobby, and did not offer her tea. 'I'm to take it you've already spoken to Morgan? How did he receive the news?'

It would serve Brice right if she told him the truth, that Morgan had laughed, genuinely disinterested in the Council's opinion of . . . well, everything. But since that might cause trouble for Morgan, she was tactful.

'He is disappointed.'

'Disappointed enough to mend his ways, do you think?'

'Alas.' She sighed. 'He is still besotted with the girl. Until his infatuation dies, Brice, there is nothing to be done.'

Brice grunted, then considered her with tired eyes abruptly sharpened with suspicion. 'Venette, do I need to remind you where your loyalties lie?'

That alarming flower was still in the buggy. Almost she'd brought it in with her, so Brice could examine it, so the burden of its existence might rest with someone else, but . . .

*I was friends with Morgan's mother years before my first smile at Brice. I'm not about to throw her son to the wolves. Not if I don't have to. And not if I can somehow save him from himself.*

'Of course you don't, Lord Varen. And it's insulting that you'd ask.'

Brice's eyebrow lifted. 'My apologies, Lady Martain.'

'I also wanted to let you know that, after careful consideration, Bellamie Ranowen feels a great working might be of use. Assuming, of course, the incants can be persuaded to take. There's every chance they won't. But just in case, since time is not on our side, I gave Lady Brislyn the Council's permission to begin sending the right mages here from the other districts.'

'I see,' said Brice. 'And if I dispute that decision?'

She raised an eyebrow at him. 'Then, Brice, you'd be a fool.'

Instead of answering, Brice moved to the front door and held it open. 'I'll warn those at the Hall who need to know that Elvado is about to be overrun with visitors.'

'Thank you,' she said, as she passed him. 'If you need me, my lord, you know where I'll be.'

Returned to the College, so eerily empty of students, Venette found Bellamie Ranowen in her cramped privy workroom and handed her the flower taken from Morgan's estate.

'Bellamie. What do you make of this?'

Haggard of face, like every mage in the College who toiled to save Dorana, Bellamie inspected the incanted bloom.

'It's not a natural flower,' she said at last, her voice gravelly with exhaustion. 'It's been transmuted.'

Venette felt her skin crawl. *Oh, Morgan.* 'Are you sure?'

'Quite sure,' said Bellamie, running her fingertips over the flower's pretty petals. 'The incant's imprint has faded, but it's quite unmistakable.'

And horribly distinctive. Morgan's signature was all over it. She'd felt it as she walked into the mansion and saw the vase of fresh flowers on the small table beside the staircase. Felt it again as, seeing herself out, she'd taken one and hidden it inside her tunic.

513

Bellamie was shaking her head. 'Even attempting this kind of transmutation is against the law, of course. Every mage knows that. And I am *horrified* that someone would so blatantly ignore the restriction.'

'*But,*' Venette said, and couldn't help a grim smile.

'Oh, yes, *but,*' Bellamie breathed, very close to admiration. 'The magework is extraordinary.' She looked up. 'Where did you get this? Who made it? Do you know?'

'It . . . came to me in the course of my Council duties,' Venette said, after a moment. 'More than that I cannot divulge.'

'Of course. I understand,' said Bellamie, still examining the flower. '*Extraordinary.* According to every authority on trans-mutation that I've read, this kind of magework is held to be impossible.'

*Justice save us all, Morgan. What were you thinking?*

'Well, it would appear that every authority is wrong.'

'Yes,' Bellamie said slowly. 'Venette, may I keep this?'

There was an odd note in her voice now. A tension in her haggard face. Her fingers had tightened on the flower's slender stem.

Venette felt a fresh thrill of alarm. 'Bellamie?'

'I'm sorry. It's just—' She shook her head again, sharply this time. 'No. I'd rather not speak without being certain. Look, do you mind going to help Jerot? He's mixing catalysts. I'll come and find you when I'm done.'

'Done with what?'

'I told you, I'd rather not say!'

Not so long ago, she'd have crushed an unranked mage who dared speak to her like that. But times had changed.

*And not for the better.*

'All right,' she said, at her most reasonable. 'How long before you can say?'

Bellamie tossed the flower onto the nearby workbench, as though its stem had stung her. 'I don't know. I'm not sure. It might be several days.'

Several days? *Oh, what have you done, Morgan? What has*

*she found?* 'Very well, Bellamie. I'll be with Jerot, if there's anything I can do.'

Pacing the attic, Morgan stepped over his makeshift mattress, heedless of thirst, of hunger, of all bodily cravings. Four days since he'd bathed or shaved or slept in his bed. Touched Barl. Eaten food at a table. It didn't matter. He needed none of those things. He had all he needed: an obliterating rage. That they would *dare* to threaten Dorana, these foreign, magickless princelings and potentates. Their audacity left him breathless.

His workbench was covered in pages of scribbled notes. Yet another reworking of Hartigan's reworked incant. Its ultimate reworking, the dream he'd been dreaming every since the thought had first crept into his mind.

*We are not safe.*

What he attempted was beyond anything he and Barl had achieved so far. Complex and dangerous, it would test him to his newly found limits. But to protect Dorana, to strike down these belligerent, *ungrateful* little nations, he would gladly bleed himself almost dry.

But not Barl. He wouldn't risk her. Besides, she'd already done her part. She had been his catalyst. He was a mage remade because of her.

*Catalysts.*

Frustrated, he swung about and glared at his many empty glass jars and bottles. He ran through his supplies so quickly now. And until they were replenished he was at a standstill. Unable to risk Venette again, he'd tasked Rumm to part with any amount of coin, meet every demand his source might make, no matter how outrageous.

*I will spend myself to poverty, if that is what it takes.*

Fired with fresh resolve, he returned to his workbench. Gathered his sheets of notes and prepared to go through the reworked incant again, step by step, in search of the slightest imperfection.

*We have so little time left. I cannot, must not, fail.*

\*     \*     \*

Barl didn't need Rumm to tap on the library door or clear his throat for her to know he was standing there. Cat-footed or not, she could always sense his presence.

Sighing, she paused her pen in mid-syllable. Didn't look up. 'Yes?'

Rumm took the question as leave to enter. 'Mage Lindin. I'm sorry to disturb you.'

'But?'

'But I was wondering if—'

'*No*, Rumm. He's not come down and he won't until he's finished.' With another sigh she did lift her gaze, to see Rumm's ordinarily disciplined face creased with worry. 'You know as well as I do, he'll go his own way and there's nothing you or I can say about it.'

'Yes, Mage Lindin. It's his own way that concerns me.'

She put the pen down. That was as close to criticism as she'd ever heard Rumm tread. 'Aren't you used to this by now? How long have you been in the Danfeys' service?'

'Since I was fourteen,' Rumm said. 'So there's nothing you can tell me of him that I don't already know. Mage Lindin, these catalysts he's got me chasing. Some of them – I've no idea what incants he's brewing and it's not my place to ask, only—' He shook his head. '*Azafris* is bad enough. But this time he's after *domish* too, and *gribb,* and crushed *crulin* leaf. I might not be a mage, but I've made it my business to learn a few things. I tell you, this concerns me.'

One of the first books she'd studied was Banlid's *Complete Guide to Catalysts*. Rumm's list was indeed alarming. *Domish, gribb* and *crulin* leaf were even more volatile than *azafris*. Banlid warned that their use should be avoided if another catalyst could be used. Their use had, in some cases, led to mental instability and a disordering of the wits.

*But those affected were lesser mages. Not Morgan.*

Besides, he would never forgive her if she sided with Rumm in his doubting.

'You've no reason to fret,' she said, schooling herself to

516

careless confidence. 'His lordship is more than capable. Now go find a length of banister to polish, or something.'

Rumm's expression chilled to its customary servant's mask. 'Mage Lindin.'

As he reached the door she added, 'Rumm. These catalysts. I know they're quite rare. Have you managed to procure them?'

'Of course I have, Mage Lindin. I expect their arrival within a day.'

'Good.'

Alone again, not needing to dissemble, she sat back in her chair and stared at the ceiling.

*Morgan . . . Morgan . . . what are you doing up there?*

The catalysts arrived.

'And I am to tell you, my lord,' Rumm said, frowning at the wrapped and warded boxes on the workbench, 'that this is the last of them. No amount of money you could offer will compensate for—'

'It doesn't matter,' Morgan snapped. 'I have what I need.'

'My lord . . .' Rumm cleared his throat. 'Mage Lindin and I were wondering—'

'If you value your life, Rumm, do not finish that sentence! *This work comes before all.* Now get out. And tell Barl to stop her nagging. She will have me between her legs again when I am done here, and not before.'

A shocked silence.

Shamed, Morgan pressed a hand across his eyes. Justice save him, he was so *tired.*

'Of course you can't tell her that. Rumm, tell her – tell her—' He shuddered his way through a yawn. 'Tell her something. Just – not that.'

'My lord,' Rumm said quietly, and withdrew.

His hands not quite steady, Morgan unwrapped his precious supplies. Last of all, unwrapped the four smallest boxes, worth more than all his other catalysts combined. Worth a future. Worth every sacrifice he must make.

Heart pounding, blood racing, anticipation washing away fatigue, he assembled the other catalysts for this, the greatest magework ever attempted. Lined up his crucibles. Pushed aside the sheets of notes, save one, the single piece of paper on which he'd recorded the syllables and sigils that would save Dorana from its enemies. Remake the world.

*Prove me the greatest mage who ever lived.*

No time for doubt. No room for it. He must be magework made man. Fleetingly, he thought of his father. What a shame Greve Danfey had died before learning the truth of the son he'd accused of betrayal. Of failure. Of sullying the Danfey name.

*You were wrong, my lord. I do not sully us. I glorify us. I will be remembered for this until the last star burns to death.*

Smiling, invincible, he set about proving his dead father a liar.

*Azafris.* Tinctured *susquinel.* Powered *vilys* root. Crushed *crulin* leaf. *Tilatantin. Domish* and *gribb,* ground into a paste. A pinch. A dribble. A touch. A drop. The balance exquisite, like Barl's lips on his skin.

Binding them together . . . his own hot, red blood.

The sigils bloomed like wildflowers in the heat of the summer sun. Immaculate and indestructible, they formed above their crucibles. Each matrix held with a shimmering solidity, as though they'd been painted on the air. Remembering his struggles with those first reworked sigils, he laughed. Then he wept. With a single word and burst of power he confirmed them.

And then he whispered the syllables of the transmutation incant.

'You should be alive, Father,' he said, as the sigils and syllables merged, seamless, like the workings of Barl's clocks. 'Were you alive I'd have you apologise to me.'

The incant was a success. All it needed now was to be spoken. But that could wait. Would have to wait, because he was swaying on his feet. The attic was blurring, spinning madly around him.

He was tired. He was so tired. The strangest roaring in his head.

Before he saved Dorana, he needed to rest.

A tentative knocking on the attic door roused him.

'My lord? I've brought you some supper.'

Cross-legged on his makeshift mattress, spine pressed to the attic wall, Morgan opened his eyes. Supper? He glanced at the window, and the night sky beyond it. Well, then. Yes. Supper.

He watched Rumm set the tray on an empty corner of the workbench. Chicken soup and hot buttered bread. Not very exciting.

'Your meals have been so irregular, my lord, and your work habits so excessive, I thought it best not to assault your belly with anything rich,' Rumm said, turning. 'And I shall stand here until you finish this. After that you may dismiss me from your service, if you like.'

A sick, sad roiling through him. Some sacrifices were so hard. 'No, Rumm. I'll not do that.'

Vaguely aware of hunger, he ate the soup and the bread. Dabbed his lips clean on the napkin Rumm had so thoughtfully provided. He was a thoughtful man. A good servant. He would be missed.

'Wait,' he said, as Rumm moved to collect the tray. 'There is something I'd ask you, Rumm.'

'My lord?'

*Say it. Just say it.* 'You said once that you served the Danfey family in all things. You remember?'

Rumm nodded. 'I do, my lord.'

'You spoke the truth?'

'Always, my lord.'

'In *all* things?'

'Yes, my lord.'

'And do you love me?'

'As a man loves his brother? Yes, my lord. I do.' Rumm swallowed. 'An impertinence, perhaps. But there you have it.'

An impertinence, yes. But also a relief. For when a man loved his brother, there was nothing he wouldn't do.

'*Reb'nes tev*, Rumm,' he whispered, and froze the servant where he stood.

And then he closed his eyes . . . and began the transmutation.

Taking a turn about the mansion's transformed gardens, needing cool, fresh air and a respite from thought, Barl felt the staggering punch of twisted power like a thunderclap in her blood. Shocked breathless, she spun round to stare up at the attic. Saw through its uncovered window a terrible scarlet glow. Even as she watched, the glow faded, leaving behind it a dreadful, plunging darkness. Every hint of glimfire in the mansion had burned out.

'*Morgan*!' she screamed. '*Morgan!*' Summoned more glimfire, and ran.

The attic door was warded. Stupid, *stupid* man. She smashed through his magic, not even needing to think. Summoned more glimfire and flung the door wide.

'*Morgan!*'

Chalk white and silent, adrift on his feet in the middle of the floor, he didn't look up. Just kept staring at – at –

'Justice save me, Morgan,' she said, doused ice-cold with horror. 'What have you – what is *that*?'

'I don't understand,' he murmured, sounding plaintive. Like a small and disappointed boy. 'It was right. The incant was right. The sigils held. The syllables balanced. So why did it *fail*?'

Her heart was beating so hard and fast she thought she'd be sick. 'Why did what fail, Morgan? What were you trying to do?'

He didn't answer.

Arms folded tight to her ribs, she made herself look again at the thing on the gore-splattered attic floor. It was unlike any creature she'd ever seen outside the pages of a children's darkly fanciful storybook. There were flaps of leathery skin, like enormous bat wings. There were long teeth, like fangs. Long, strong fingers ending in talons. Thin strands of pale hair straggled across a blood-smeared, leathery scalp.

*Hair? But only people have hair.*

She stepped back. Saw, properly saw, the supper tray on the bench. Looked around the glimlit attic. Looked at Morgan, still so stunned.

'My love?' She had to wet her lips, her mouth had gone so dry. 'My love, where is Rumm?'

Morgan spat a vile curse and leapt to his workbench. 'This is *ridiculous*. I know I reworked the incant correctly. Barl, don't just stand there.' He snapped his fingers at her, familiarly impatient. 'Come, come. We have to get this right. Dorana's safety depends on it.'

'Depends on *what*, Morgan? Before I help you, you'll have to explain yourself.'

'There's no *time*!' he said, turning on her. 'Will you wait until this mansion is overrun with Feenish warriors?'

'Morgan . . .' She raised her hands. 'Please. You're frightening me.'

His eyes were terrible. 'My love, don't be silly. What in this world can frighten us?'

'That!' she said, pointing at the monstrosity on the floor. 'Morgan – is that *Rumm*?'

'Yes.' Tears spilled to his cheeks. 'I don't understand why the incant failed.'

Appalled, she pressed her fingers to her lips, holding back an anguished cry. What she'd done to the chickens and the hounds and calf had been terrible. For the greater good, but terrible. Still, they were animals. Only animals.

*But that was Rumm. Oh, Morgan.*

'I think we should go down to the library, my love,' she said carefully. 'It will be easier to work our way through what went wrong if we—' *Don't have to look at that hideous thing on the floor.* 'Can sit comfortably and perhaps seek for guidance from one of your books.'

'Aren't you listening?' he snapped. 'Barl, there's no time.'

'We needn't take long. And I'll make us some tea. Hot tea with plenty of sugar is restorative when you've had a nasty shock.'

He stared at her, glassy-eyed. Haggard and pallid and so clearly wallowing in the dregs of his strength. To do such a terrible thing . . .

*This is my fault. I shouldn't have let him lock himself away up here alone. I shouldn't have let him use those catalysts. Oh, Rumm. I'm so sorry.*

Resentful, but in the end unresisting, Morgan let her take him downstairs. She left him settled in the library, on the sofa, then retreated to the kitchen and made the tea. Dosed his cup with the powerful, leftover sleeping herbs Rumm had used on Greve Danfey, at Pother Ranmer's insistence.

'Here, my love,' she said, returned to the library. 'Drink this. You'll feel better soon, I promise.'

He took the cup and drained it. 'Thank you.'

'Of course,' she said, soothing, and perched on the sofa's edge beside him. 'Now, my love, can you tell me what you were trying to do?'

His eyelids were already drooping. 'Armoured beasts won't be enough to protect us. We need true warriors, that can stand against the warriors of Feen and Trindek and the rest.'

'Warriors.' She shifted a little beside him, cold again. Couldn't help glancing at the ceiling, seeing again that ruined man on the floor. 'Morgan . . . do you mean people? You think we should be transmuting *people*?'

'We have to,' he said, his voice slurring. 'But not mages, of course. The magickless. They serve little other purpose. And we have enough cripples in Dorana that the few we'd take won't be missed.'

*Cripples.* Turning away from that word, for she couldn't bear to look at it, not now, Barl smoothed Morgan's tangled hair. It felt like straw, not spun silk.

'Morgan, we don't need to do that. All we need do is destroy the mage-mist. Restore Dorana's balance. Then the other nations will leave us alone. You and I, we are Dorana's greatest mages. We can do that. Let's do that. All right?'

Morgan smiled at her, slowly. Even exhausted, he was beautiful. Even so dreadfully misguided, she loved him.

'My love . . . it's too late.'

She felt the tears come. Felt them spill to her cheeks. 'Don't say that. You could be mistaken. It might not be too late.'

But it was, and she knew it.

'Oh, Morgan,' she whispered. 'What are we going to do?'

His hand fumbled, trying to stroke her face. The herbs were working on him now, swiftly. 'We're going to make Dorana safe, my love. We're going to give it an army. Rumm did not die in vain. He was but the first to give his life for the country he loved.'

She could argue, but she knew he'd not listen. He wasn't ready to hear that he was wrong. Heartbroken, she sat beside him and watched him slide into sleep. When she was sure he wouldn't stir she settled him on the sofa, with a pillow and a blanket. The herbs and his own exhaustion would keep him unstirring here for hours. Enough time for her to do what she had to, though the thought of his hurt and anger made her weep anew.

To make certain of him she warded the library's windows and door. Felt a wrenching flood of gratitude that he'd never learned to break her magework. Then she changed into fresh clothing and went to find the only person she could trust.

# CHAPTER THIRTY-TWO

Asleep in his room at Elvado's modest Shooting Star inn, Remmie startled awake to find himself no longer alone. Tangled in his nightshirt, he struggled to sit up.

'*Barl?*' The fitful glimfire she'd conjured showed him her unexpected, distraught face. 'How did you—'

'Don't be stupid, Remmie,' she said. 'Why are you still here if you didn't know that I knew you never meant to go back to Batava without me.'

He dragged a hand down his face, feeling the scrape of stubble. 'But I did mean it. I was going to leave days ago, only there's word of a great working meant to banish the mage-mist once and for all. Elvado's crowded to bursting with mages. I stayed to help.'

'Oh. So you really were going to—' Her lips trembled. 'Oh.'

Seeing her standing there, he wasn't sure how he felt. Every morning he woke, thinking *this* would be the morning he'd go back to the Hall of Knowledge and find someone who'd listen to what he had to say. And every morning he shrank from doing it. The first time, when they sent him away unheard, he'd been so angry with Barl he could barely think straight. Condemning her then had felt easy. Had felt just.

It wasn't easy any more. His blood had cooled, and instead of anger he felt guilt and grief.

'Remmie . . .'

Never in his life had he heard her sound so small. So frightened. Never had he seen such a dreadful look in her eyes. He kicked the thin blankets aside and slid out of bed.

'What's wrong, Barl?'

She gave an odd little hiccup. '*Everything.* Remmie, I know I was horrible. I know I've been arrogant. But you can't let that matter. Not now. You have to help me.'

She was his sister and even when he was furious he loved her, but hurt was muddled with disappointment and an old, stale resentment. She never changed. She did what she wanted then afterwards said sorry. It was a familiar dance and he was tired of it.

'Barl—'

With a sparking splutter the ball of glimfire died.

'No, don't try to reignite it,' he said, reaching for the sparker and bedside candle. 'This isn't your cleverly protected Danfey estate.'

'Sorry,' she said, as the candle flame created meagre light and deep shadows. 'I forgot.'

Dropping to the end of the bed, resigned to at least hearing her out, he patted the blankets beside him. 'Tell me.'

Sitting, she released a shuddering breath. Then she started to talk, her voice low and shaking. As her dreadful tale unfolded, her hand crept toward him and he took it, even though she'd stirred him to anger again. Her trembling fingers were cold. He ought to feel more pity for her, but his anger burned too hot.

'Rumm's death was an accident,' she said at last, exhausted. 'Morgan never meant to murder him.'

'For pity's *sake*, Barl!' Letting go of her, Remmie leapt up. 'The *incant* is murder. And don't you dare pretend he didn't know it!'

'I don't know what Morgan knew,' she said, hands in her lap now, twisting her fine silk tunic. 'He was exhausted. He wasn't himself. I'm telling you, Remmie, he's not evil. Could I love an evil man? Do you believe that of me?'

Staring at her, he shook his head. 'Barl, I don't know what to believe. Before I saw what I saw at the estate, I'd have said *no* without hesitation. But now? Now if you told me the incant had been your idea, I—'

'No, no, no,' she said, her eyes wide. 'Don't say it. *Don't.*' She sobbed, once. 'Remmie, please. It was never meant to be like this. All the good we meant to do and it's all gone so *wrong*. I never—'

'You never *thought*,' he said, brutal. 'You just rushed ahead, blindly, because you felt slighted and wanted to prove the Council wrong. Just like you wanted to prove Arndel wrong before that. You haven't changed, Barl. You just stumbled across someone stupid enough to encourage you. You call it love? I call it madness. You found the one man who could be trusted to bring out the worst in you. Not the best.'

Hands sheltering her face, she fought a silent battle. When at last she lowered them he saw that her eyes were dry.

'When this is over, Remmie, if you want to disown me, I won't argue. But for this to be over, I will need your help.'

'And what is it you expect me to do?' He folded his arms. 'I won't kill him for you.'

'I don't want you to,' she said, shocked. 'Remmie, I don't want Morgan dead. Like it or not, I *do* love him. He needs help.'

'He needs stopping, Barl. That's all the help he'll get from me.'

'Fine. Then help me stop him, *please,* and afterwards we can go our separate ways.'

She sounded so defeated it hurt. And though he'd wanted her defeated, wanted her humbled, made painfully aware of every bad choice she'd made, every flaw . . .

*She's my sister. I can't destroy her.*

Looking at him, knowing what he'd decided, knowing him, she tried to smile. 'You'll need to get dressed. There's someone we have to see . . . and then we need to talk to the Council.'

'There's no point in that. I tried, the day I saw you. The Council turned me away.'

She blinked at him. 'You went to the Council? Knowing what they did to me before?'

He didn't answer. After the dead calf, and ruined Dorana, he owed her no apology for that.

'Never mind,' she muttered. 'Remmie, they might have turned you away but they will see me. Especially after I've seen Venette Martain first. Now, please, get dressed. We haven't much time.'

'Fine,' he said, standing. 'But either close your eyes or turn your back, because I'm about to be naked and we're not little children any more.'

'I can wait outside.'

'No. You can wait here.'

Hurt, she looked up at him. 'Does that mean you don't trust me?'

'It means you're Barl Lindin,' he said, after a moment. 'And whether I can trust her, well, that remains to be seen.'

Faced with yet another pair of duty mages, these ones guarding the Council chamber's closed, imposing doors, Barl took hold of her fraying temper and for the fourth time repeated her claim.

'I am Barl Lindin, with urgent news for Lady Martain. I am told by her husband she is here, in Council session. Let me pass.'

'Barl Lindin?' The duty mage on the right narrowed his eyes. 'The same Barl Lindin who—'

'Yes. Let me pass.'

The duty mage's chin jerked at Remmie, who stood beside her silent and watchful and just a little bit unnerved. 'Who is he?'

'My brother.' She smiled, not quite pleasantly. 'You know who I am. You know what I did. Do you think I'll not do it again if you persist in this obstruction?'

After an exchange of glances, the two duty mages stood aside.

'Enter the chamber at your own peril, Mage Lindin.'

Ignoring them, she looked at Remmie. 'Don't forget, these

527

councillors aren't our friends. Don't speak unless you're spoken to. Don't give them any excuses. They'll bind you as soon as look at you, just because we share the same name.'

The duty mage who'd recognised her swung open the doors. Barl took a deep breath and led the way into the chamber.

*I'm not afraid. I'm not. These mages do not frighten me.*

But her heart was beating too fast, and she was glad that Remmie walked with her. Even a Remmie whose faith in her she'd destroyed.

The whole Council was there, seated around the book-scattered table, and with them two mages she'd never seen before. Both women, both powerful. One was quite young, weary, her linen tunic stained with a rainbow of catalysts. The other not yet middle-aged, dressed in fine silks and jewellery, and her plain face was stamped with authority and a formidable intelligence.

As the doors closed behind her and Remmie, Lord Varen stood, his aged face darkening with anger.

'What are you doing here? How did you gain admittance to the Hall, let alone this Council chamber?'

'It doesn't matter why she's here, Brice,' said Sallis Arkley, almost shrill with fury. 'If you don't bind her, I will. She cannot be permitted to leave the Hall, ever again.'

As Remmie opened his mouth to protest, she touched his arm. 'No. Don't.'

It was hard to look at these important, arrogant mages. To meet their eyes and see such fear and loathing and contempt in them. Lady Frieden was shaking, fingers curled almost to talons.

*No. No. Don't think about talons.*

'Mage Lindin,' said Venette Martain. She looked as exhausted as Morgan had, deep lines of sleeplessness grooved into her face. 'Despite what you might think, despite my colleagues' under-standable disaffection, it's good that you're here. We've been talking about you, as it happens. And there are a few things we'd like to know.'

On principle, because this woman loathed her for no better

reason than Maris Garrick's disappointment, Barl lifted her chin. 'Such as?'

Reaching amongst the scattered books, Venette Martain produced a flower. Slender-stemmed. Pink and cream petals brushed with blue along their edges. Morgan had laughed as he'd made it, created beauty out of a poor, plain daisy.

'Such as, how long you have been corrupting Dorana with forbidden magework?' Venette smiled. 'And corrupting Morgan Danfey with it. Let's not forget that.'

Before she could stop him, before she could remember how to speak, Remmie pushed forward. 'She didn't corrupt him. Morgan Danfey corrupted her. The transmutation incant is his doing. Barl would never have sullied herself with this *filth* if he hadn't—'

'You're her brother?' said Venette Martain, eyebrows lifting. She let the flower drop. 'Remmie, isn't it? Yes. Morgan mentioned you. The resemblance is remarkable . . . in more ways than one.' She glanced around the table. 'You all feel it?'

'Indeed, Lady Martain,' said the younger of the two unknown women. 'Extraordinary.'

Lord Varen, seated again, rapped his knuckles to the table. 'You seem well-informed, Mage Lindin. Tell this Council everything you know about your sister and her doings with Morgan Danfey.'

Remmie shook his head. 'Not before you promise me she won't be bound again.'

'You are in no position to make demands!' said Lady Frieden. 'Answer his lordship or be bound yourself and taken to a cell.'

Barl winced. Her brother was no fool. As a schoolteacher he was used to summing up others quickly . . . and recognising genuine authority when he met it.

It was one of the worst things she'd ever lived through, listening to him tell the Council first what he'd found at Morgan's estate, and then what she'd told him at the Shooting Star. Because he had a generous heart he tried to go gently, this time, but his rage and disgust were too deep, too heartfelt, to remain hidden.

The one thing he didn't speak of was Rumm, and how he died. But why? To spare her? Or to punish her, by making her be the one to tell that tale? She didn't know.

When Remmie finished he was near to tears. 'That's the truth, my lords, my ladies. I swear to you, in the name of justice, Morgan Danfey is the cause of this.'

'He is part of it,' said Lord Varen coldly. 'But according to your testimony, by her own admission your sister is the one who enabled him to perfect his transmutation incant. She has performed it with him, over and over again, and in doing so has brought Dorana to the brink of utter destruction!' He nodded at the younger woman. 'Mage Ranowen, here, of the College, has closely examined this abominable flower and proven that beyond all shadow of doubt. The magic that created it is unravelling us. Can you truly think this Council will do no more than say tut-tut and let her go her merry way?'

Remmie hung his head. 'No.'

Leaning forward, Venette Martain tapped the table. 'Mage Lindin. Where is Morgan now? How is it you come to be here without him, weeping and wailing and beating your breast in an orgy of contrition that may or may not be genuine.'

*Rumm.*

This wasn't going as she'd planned, and now there was nothing she could do to soften the consequences of her actions, and Morgan's actions, and the harm that they'd wrought.

The other woman, still unnamed, was staring at her intently. 'There's something they've not told us,' she said, her mellow voice clipped with distaste. 'A piece of this ugly puzzle is missing.'

'Well, Mage Lindin? Is Lady Brislyn correct?' said Lord Varen, and when she didn't reply, banged his fist to the table so hard that all the heavy books on it jumped. *'Answer me!'*

'Morgan is in the mansion, asleep,' she said, dully. 'I drugged him and warded him inside the library.'

Venette Martain didn't even try to hide her shock. *'Why?'*

Barl felt Remmie shift closer. Felt the sorrow and sympathy muddled in with his anger. So. He'd been trying to shield her.

Perhaps, when this was over, they'd have something to salvage after all.

'Answer Lady Martain, Mage Lindin.'

Brice Varen's harsh, imperious tone made her flinch. Breathing hard she looked up.

'He used a transmutation incant on his master servant, Rumm. It failed. The man died.'

A chorus of gasps. From the sudden pallor in his cheeks, not even Sallis Arkley had expected to hear such a thing.

'But why would Morgan do something so – so *monstrous*?' Shari Frieden whispered, her voice shaking. 'He is arrogant and unapproachable but he has never been this *misguided*.'

'He thought – he wanted—' Barl's throat closed, and she could hardly breathe, let alone speak. All she could see was Rumm, ruined and dead on the attic floor.

'Dorana has no warriors,' Remmie said, stepping closer again. 'He thought to rectify the lack.'

Lord Varen was the only councillor who'd kept himself in hand. 'Into what form did Morgan attempt to transmute his unfortunate servant?'

'I'm not—' She had to swallow. 'Lord Varen, it's hard to say. I saw wings. Like a bat. I saw fangs. His fingernails . . .' She couldn't stop her voice from failing. 'Nothing human.'

'Something our superstitious neighbours would see as demonic, then,' Varen murmured. 'The better to strike fear into their bellicose hearts.'

'I think so. My lord—' Remmie would be furious if she tried to defend Morgan, but how could she not? When she understood what drove him, even as she had to condemn what he'd done? 'You have to know he did it for Dorana.'

'I hope you cannot think his motive will excuse this vile act?'

Not a mage at the table tried to hide his or her revulsion, for Morgan, for her, for the things they had done.

'No,' she whispered. 'I don't.'

Venette Martain's eyes were bright with tears. 'Is this my doing, Mage Lindin? Did I get poor Rumm killed?' She looked

531

at Brice Varen. 'You might as well know, my lord, that when I told Morgan of his dismissal from this Council, I also told him of the news Lady Brislyn brought us. He knows about the threat of war from our neighbours.'

Lord Varen's eyes turned icy. 'That was most foolish, Lady Martain.'

'Well, what do you expect?' Sallis Arkley demanded. 'Where Danfey's concerned she is nothing *but* a fool!'

As Lady Frieden opened her mouth to join in Lord Arkley's attack, Barl stepped forward and slapped the table. 'Oh, stop your bickering! What does it matter now who said what to whom? All that matters is that we help Morgan . . . and find a way to help Dorana before the mage-mist destroys it, or our frightened neighbours attack. That's why I'm here. I might only be a lowly, unranked mage, but—'

'You want to *magework*?' said Lady Frieden, incredulous. 'After your crimes? Girl, are you—'

'Forgive me, but you shouldn't be so quick to spurn her offer,' said Mage Ranowen. 'Mage Lindin might be unranked, and her judgement appalling, but she is one of the greatest natural talents I have ever seen. I've no doubt she'd be an asset in the great working.'

'And Morgan Danfey?' said Lord Varen, very dry. 'What have you to say of him?'

'Sadly, I think Lord Danfey must be deranged.'

Lady Brislyn sat back in her chair. 'As head of the General Council, Mage Lindin, I will not presume to comment on matters of illegal magework. I want to know only one thing. *Do* you possess the skill to turn back the tide of destruction unleashed upon us by you and Lord Danfey?'

Another cold silence. Another onslaught of hostile stares. Barl felt her eyes sting.

'I don't know, Lady Brislyn. But I want the chance to try.'

'As do I,' said Remmie. 'I'll do all I can to help put right what's gone wrong.'

'So.' Sallis Arkley drew the word out. 'Remmie Lindin. Are we to take it, then, that you do not approve of your sister?'

Remmie looked at Lord Arkley steadily, as he'd so often looked at a pupil who'd said something crude. 'My lord, I love my sister. A man may love with all his heart, yet have that heart broken by a foolish, thoughtless act.'

'In other words—' Sallis Arkley was sneering now. 'You'd have us believe she acted without malice?'

'Completely without malice. On that you have my word.'

'Then how do you explain her destructive behaviour?'

'I don't, my lord,' said Remmie, curtly. 'Not here, and not to you. I won't read this Council a shopping list of my sister's faults. I don't see that as a provident use of my time.'

Lord Arkley's face flushed. 'You're as arrogant as she is.'

'And you, my lord, seem intent upon proving her right about ranked mages.'

'That's enough,' Lord Varen said, forestalling Sallis Arkley's furious reply. 'Mage Lindin is right about one thing, at least. We have not assembled here to indulge in petty brawling. Now, I think that before anything else is decided, we must hear what Lord Danfey has to say for himself. This time, however, we will not go to him. Mage Lindin—'

Still surprised by Remmie's defence of her, sick with fear that he'd made of himself a target for Sallis Arkley's revenge, Barl looked up.

'Yes?'

'You say you left Lord Danfey warded in his mansion?'

'I did, yes.'

'You'll provide me with the unwarding key, then wait in the Council's antechamber with your brother while Lord Danfey is sent for. Neither of you will speak of this. Is that understood?'

She nodded. 'Yes. My lord.'

For a moment he looked at her, his sickened, tired eyes searching. Then he sighed. 'I wonder, Mage Lindin, if you truly comprehend what you've done?'

More tears gathered, desperate to burst free. There was a terrible pain in her chest, as though guilt and grief were grinding her heart to a pulp. 'I do, my lord.'

533

He grunted. 'So you say. But that remains to be seen. The unwarding key?'

At his gesture, she fetched pen and paper from the chamber's cupboard and wrote out the sequence of sigil and syllable that would free Morgan from the library. Taking it without thanks, Lord Varen looked at Remmie.

'Escort your sister to the antechamber and wait there until you are summoned.'

'Yes, my lord,' said Remmie, and led her from the room.

It was Remmie who spoke first, breaking the long and miserable silence.

'It's been nigh on two hours. Do you think he'll come?' he murmured, mindful of the duty mages standing close by. 'Or will he – resist?'

Barl stared at the floor. 'He is devastated about . . . what happened. He won't hurt those mages the Council sent to fetch him.'

'I hope you're right.'

His disappointment in her was unbearable. 'I am. You'll see.'

Remmie's deep sigh was shatteringly sad. 'I don't know. Barl, I don't know what to think any more.'

His sorrowful declaration broke her. Folding over herself, she surrendered to the grief that was tearing her apart. Dimly, she felt his arm slide round her shoulders. Collapsed against him and sobbed without restraint. Wept as she'd never wept, not even when their parents died. When she sat up at last, emptied of tears, she saw that Venette Martain and Lady Brislyn were seated on a low padded bench opposite. Raised voices from within the Council chamber turned her toward its closed doors.

'They're arguing the finer points of Mage Ranowen's deconstruction of your magework, Mage Lindin,' Venette Martain said, sounding exhausted. 'I did suggest they ask you to adjudicate but alas, I was ignored. Oh. And Sallis has just been sent word from his mysterious informer. It seems Morgan's the one who's been bringing in all those dubious catalysts. Which of course you already knew.'

Barl shrugged. 'I know a lot of things, Lady Martain. Of course, it's not always easy to decide what's important, and what isn't. What should be spoken of . . . and what's best forgotten.'

They looked at each other in silence. Then Venette Martain smiled. 'Well, my dear, I'm sure that whatever you speak of, you'll keep everyone's best interests in mind.'

Lady Brislyn spared her an impatient, puzzled glance then turned. 'Mage Lindin. It's clear that even though Dorana is blighted with strife, your mageworking talent thrives while the rest of us wither. Can you explain that? It seems the Council of Mages is at a loss.'

Feeling ill from weeping, Barl shook her head. 'No. Not for certain. It might be the way Morgan and I magework together. We enhance each other's strengths to an amazing degree. It might be the shielding incant we placed over the estate. It might be serendipity. I'm sorry. I can't say.'

'Lady Brislyn—' Remmie cleared his throat. 'If I might ask . . . the danger from Dorana's neighbours. Is it real? You truly believe they intend to harm us?'

'Mage Lindin . . .' Lady Brislyn's lips thinned. 'I think if we cannot solve this crisis, our neighbours will do their best to slaughter us all.'

'*Which is why I did what I did. So our neighbours would fail.*'

Startled, they all turned. Stared. Flanked by the duty mages sent to retrieve him, Morgan stared back. Unsmiling. Very cold.

Barl shook off Remmie's fiercely restraining hand and crossed the antechamber, her eyes never leaving his haughty, beautiful face.

'Morgan.'

He touched his lips to hers, lightly. 'Barl.'

Palm resting on his silk-clad chest, feeling his heartbeat and his warmth, she looked up into his eyes. Saw something in them that made her skin crawl, and her blood chill.

'I love you.'

'You drugged me,' he said, faintly smiling.

'You were exhausted. You needed to sleep.'

'True. And I did sleep. But now I am awake.'

She watched her fingers slowly close until they were clutching his dark green tunic. 'It's gone too far, Morgan. *We've* gone too far.'

His mild gaze shifted past her, to fall on Remmie and Venette Martain and Lady Brislyn. 'Is that what they've told you?'

'No, Morgan, it's what *I'm* saying.' She shook him, just a little bit. 'I need you to hear me. What happened to Rumm – what you did to Rumm – what *we* did—'

'It upset you,' he said softly, his hand covering hers. With a sigh he lowered his forehead until it rested on the top of her head. 'I am sorry. I never wanted you to see that. And you have my word you'll never see it again.'

'So we can stop now?' she whispered. 'No more changelings like Rumm? We can work together to heal Dorana? I know you think it can't be done, Morgan, but there's nothing we can't do when we join our hands and our hearts.'

'Barl, Barl . . .' His warm breath sighed over her hair. 'You never said a truer thing.'

His lips captured hers, entreating, demanding. She felt her bones turn to molten gold, felt passion's dizzying rush.

'Lord Danfey,' said Brice Varen's cold voice, behind her. 'The Council awaits you.'

With a groan he lifted his head. Rubbed his thumb over her lips. 'Wait here for me, my love. I won't be long.'

She watched him walk to the Council chamber, to Brice Varen who stood in the wide open doorway, his lined face stiff with disapproval. His lordship stepped back, in a parody of hostly invitation, and Morgan swept past him with an elegant disdain.

Without warning, almost painfully, she was swept head to toe by a dreadful, dark foreboding.

'No. Wait,' she said, as Venette Martain and Lady Brislyn moved to follow him into the chamber. 'Please. Just . . . wait.'

Impatient, Venette Martain glanced at her. 'For what? Mage Lindin, sit with your brother and be quiet.'

She felt so sick with dread now she had to blink to see. 'Remmie—' She could hardly hear her own voice. 'No, Remmie, stop them – don't let them go—'

A terrible scream. And then another. A bilious surge of raw power. An odd twisting sensation. A brittle shattering of glass. Muffled shouting somewhere. A sickening shudder through the Hall.

Morgan appeared in the chamber doorway, a quizzical look on his face. Then a small smile replaced it, and as it widened he snapped his fingers.

'Justice save us,' croaked Lady Brislyn. 'You really *are* deranged.'

With a leathery rustling of skin flaps, four inhuman creatures with two arms and two legs gathered at Morgan's back. In their bestial, fanged faces, nothing of Brice Varen, Sallis Arkley, Shari Frieden or Bellamie Ranowen remained. Only the ragged remnants of their clothing made it possible to guess who had been whom.

'*Extraordinary,*' Morgan drawled. 'You know, Barl, I can't believe it. It was the segue between the third and fourth syllables. That's where I went wrong with Rumm. It catches me *every* time.'

The two duty mages, stunned into staring immobility, found their wits – lost their wits – and stupidly made a move toward him.

Three swift sigils. Eight syllables. The duty mages . . . *changed.*

Tears ran unheeded down Venette Martain's snow-white face. 'Oh, Morgan. Oh, my dear.'

The monstrous things that moments ago had been human, clicked their talons in confusion and hissed through their sharp fangs. The transmuted councillors hissed with them, uneasily shifting from side to side.

As Morgan looked at her, one eyebrow lifted in fastidious derision, Barl risked turning to Remmie. He was sickly pale too, but his eyes were determined. He gave her the smallest nod, his faith in her returned.

*But I don't know what to do, Remmie! I don't know what to do!*

Sickened almost to heaving, panic threatening to overturn reason, she struggled to think. They needed to get out of this antechamber. Out of the Hall. They needed somewhere safe to hide where Morgan didn't know where to look. Remmie's room at the Shooting Star. It would have to do.

*Only we'll need to incant to it. All of us, at once. Am I strong enough?*

There was no point wondering. She'd have to try it, and find out.

Because he was her brother, her other self, and he knew her so well, Remmie risked Morgan's fury by taking Venette Martain and Lady Brislyn by their arms and easing them back. Easing them together.

Morgan tipped his head to one side. 'Are you feared I'll transmute you, Remmie? You needn't fret on it. I love your sister, remember? We're near as brothers, you and I.' He smiled. 'It might be nice to have a brother. What do you think?'

Letting Remmie distract him with a rambling reply, Barl summoned to mind a broad travel incant that would take them to the Shooting Star . . . if her magework was reliable. If she didn't kill them instead.

*Oh justice, please, don't let me kill us.*

She drew the sigil behind her back, breath held hard, terrified Morgan would feel it. But he seemed drunk on power, on the success of his dreadful incant. The creatures he'd created hissed and shuffled and clicked their talons. Waiting to be commanded. His gaze kept sliding to them and he smiled, as though he were proud. With the sigil drawn and burning she whispered the travel incant in her mind. A shiver. Some resistance. And then the magic caught.

Morgan's head whipped round. 'Barl? Don't you do it – don't you leave me – *Barl*—'

With a despairing cry she leapt for Remmie, who'd not let go of Venette Martain or Lady Brislyn. Venette Martain flung out her hand, fingers desperately reaching. Morgan shouted again. The nearest hideous creature threw its head back and howled, then flapped toward them.

Her hand caught Venette Martain's . . . and the antechamber vanished.

Safely hidden in Remmie's room at the Shooting Star inn, they waited in the darkness, not daring to light a single candle, and listened to the distant screams and the beasting of Elvado. Flinched at the sound of glass breaking, walls buckling, roof tiles falling and smashing to shards. Winced as they felt the burning echoes of mage-mist, encroaching.

'This can't be happening,' Venette Martain said, yet again, her voice dull and cracked with disbelief. She was slumped on the bed, shivering. She'd not stopped shivering since they stepped out of the Hall. 'It simply can't.'

Remmie leaned against the wall beside his pokey room's little window, curtain tugged aside far enough for him to see into the narrow side-street that ran behind the inn.

'It'll be dawn soon,' he said tiredly. 'He'll stop then.'

Seated beside Venette Martain, Lady Brislyn looked up. 'How do you know?'

'He'll be vulnerable in daylight. I think he'll return to his estate, barricade himself behind the strongest wardings he can contrive . . . and plan what he means to do next.'

'Well, then.' Her head viciously aching, desperately hoping that the warding they hid behind would hold, Barl dropped into the room's spindly chair. 'I'll wander out there and pay him a visit.'

Remmie let the curtain drop, then lit his candle so she could see his face. 'No. You won't.'

'Be quiet,' said Lady Brislyn. 'If you can't be a Doranen before you're her brother, best you not say anything at all.'

Barl looked at him, pretending they were alone, in the cottage. 'He won't hurt me, Remmie. And I'm the only person he'll listen to.'

'Barl . . .' Remmie shook his head, helpless. 'You *can't* go to him. Look what he's *become*. Can you honestly say he's the man you fell in love with?'

'Yes. I can. Remmie, if Morgan has lost his reason it's because he's beside himself with guilt for what's happened. In his own way, he's still trying to save Dorana.'

'*How?*' Remmie cried. 'By turning every last one of us into *monsters?*'

'*Please,* Remmie. *He's not evil.* Lady Martain, tell him.'

With a shaking sigh, Venette clutched her hands together in her lap. 'This is Greve's fault. That cantankerous, snip-pursed old man, he saw love as a weakness. Never praised his son if there was a chance to berate him, or point out a fault. Never ceased his droning on the greatness of the Danfeys and how it was Morgan's duty to elevate them. Never once said to Morgan, "*My dear boy, I love you.*"'

'He ruined Luzena's locket,' Barl said softly. 'Threw it into the fire. I don't think he cared that his son was lonely, and desperate to be cherished.'

In the hush, in the candlelight, she exchanged glances with Venette Martain . . . and for the first time saw approval in the older woman's eyes.

Dreen Brislyn was staring at them. 'You would pity him, when he is out there turning people into beasts? When he has brought Dorana face-to-face with destruction?'

Barl met her hot stare steadily. 'He didn't do that alone.'

'No, Mage Lindin, he didn't. Which is why you *will* go to his estate and convince him to stop this madness before it goes any further.'

Remmie's fist thudded against the wall. 'And who are you to demand that she endanger her life by—'

'She's endangered *our* lives!' Dreen Brislyn retorted. '*Every* life in Dorana is at risk, thanks to her. And I should excuse it because

540

she was *in love*? Because an older man seduced her? Because she lost her wits when she lost herself in magework?'

'Don't, Remmie,' Barl sighed. 'Besides, you agree with her.'

'That's different. I'm your brother.'

'And she is the head of the General Council.'

The meagre candlelight showed her his eyes, too bright. 'Barl . . .'

Moving to him, she kissed his cheek, then turned away. 'I'll go now, so I'm there waiting for him. And if I don't return?' She shook her head. 'I don't know. Throw Dorana on the mercy of our neighbours, perhaps? Ask them to help us? Brantone and the rest might be our only hope.'

And with a shrug she left them, before Remmie could weep openly, or anyone could wish her luck.

# CHAPTER THIRTY-THREE

Morgan came home a scant hour after sunrise.

Waiting for him in the library, having put the time to good use, Barl sat on the sofa with her spine straight and her hands folded, a careful smile pinned to her lips. Her courage faltered as she heard the leathery *flap flap* of wings. The scraping click of talons. A chorus of sighing, hissing cries. How many of those ghastly things had he brought with him? It sounded like *dozens*. Horrible. So horrible. But when at last the library door opened, she was in control again. Brave again.

Well, as brave as she could be.

Silent, Morgan stared at her. Heart racing, Barl stared back. He seemed . . . different. Oh, the familiar desire for her was there. That never left him. But laid lightly over it was a different kind of hunger. Burning within him, a different kind of power. As though the night he'd spent transmuting mages into monsters had transmuted him, too.

But into what?

He closed the door, gently, and wandered to the nearest book shelf. Trailed an idle finger along the old leather spines. 'You left me.'

'Yes,' she admitted, showing him only her regret. 'But I came back.'

His face twisted. *'You left me.'*

'Morgan . . .' His pain was genuine, and it hurt her. How could it not, when despite everything she still loved him? She held out her hands, inviting. 'I am sorry. I was wrong.'

He took her savagely, on the carpet, ripping silk, tugging hair. Biting her. Bruising her. Weeping as he battered his way inside her. She didn't fight him . . . and for the first time since their first time feigned passion and pleasure.

Lost in desperation, *different,* he didn't notice.

When he was finished, still lying on top of her, pinning her, crushing her, he held her face between his tender hands and scattered kisses over her skin.

'Why, Barl?' he whispered. There were tears in his eyes. 'Why did you leave?'

He was breaking her heart. *How did we come to this? How could I have let things go so far awry?* 'I don't know.'

'Yes, you do, my love. Tell me.'

'You'll be angry.'

'I won't,' he said, and kissed her again. 'I promise.'

He'd know if she was lying, so she'd have to chance the truth. 'You frightened me. I thought you'd hurt Remmie.'

'I said I wouldn't. Don't you believe me?'

'I believe—' *That you believe it. For now.* 'Yes, Morgan. I believe you.'

Smiling, his altered eyes soft with love, he rolled onto his side and pulled her against him. If the hard floor beneath their half-naked bodies bothered him, he didn't show it.

'My poor beloved,' he murmured, his fingertips slowly trailing up and down her spine. Once his touch had thrilled her. Now it made her feel small. Vulnerable. 'I never wanted to distress you. Will you feel better if I swear to you, on my father's tomb, that I will only change as many people as we need to defend Dorana?'

Her heart was a lump of ice in her chest. 'Much better.'

'Then I swear it.' He kissed her breast, lips warm and soft and loving. 'That many and no more.'

Because he'd wonder if she didn't, she idled her fingers through his hair. 'And once we have our army? What then?'

He laughed. 'Then we teach our neighbours a lesson.'

'A lesson?'

'Barl . . .' He slapped her bare buttock, chiding. 'Come, my love. Don't be slow.'

Somehow, she managed a seductive chuckle. 'I'm not slow. You've worn me out. Tell me everything, Morgan.'

Half beneath him, half beside him, Barl listened in growing horror as he daydreamed aloud about the world he wanted to create. A world in thrall to mages, ruled by mages. Ruled by him. And her, of course. She'd be his consort, splendid in her finery like a Ranoushi concubine.

'And we'll have sons,' he said, sighing. 'As my father wanted. We will found a dynasty of mages, and live forever, and be in love.'

'It sounds wonderful,' she whispered. And as she smiled and kissed him, summoned to mind the binding incant she'd taken from one of his books and altered while she waited. Traced the sigils on his drying skin, four with her fingertips, two with her tongue. Drugged with pleasure, this time, he growled low in his throat. Laughed, not listening, as she whispered into his ear.

And didn't feel the magic catch fire until it was too late.

'Barl?' he said, his beautiful eyes filling with hurt and dismay, as the binding strands of the incant began to tighten around him. 'Barl? What are you—'

She stopped his question with a final kiss, tears spilling. 'I'm sorry. I'm so sorry. I know this mess is my fault as much as it's yours. But I have to do this, Morgan. You're so lost. You need time to find your true self.'

'Barl . . .' His eyes widened and then he shouted, a dreadful cry of rage and pain as the barbs of her binding sank deep into his soul. 'My love, how could you do this? You bitch, you slut, you treacherous whore . . .'

Watching as he fought in vain against her magic, as his will was consumed, rendered impotent by hers, Barl felt coldness seep through her like the slow encroachment of winter. If the night's horrors had changed him, then they'd changed her as well. This binding of him changed her. She, too, was remade.

*And if he's been made a monster, then what now am I?*

A monument to remorse. The embodiment of regret. A mage with but one purpose: to undo what she'd done.

When the sun finally rose, sullen and cloud-veiled, Venette ventured out of Remmie Lindin's room at the Shooting Star inn to see for herself what fresh calamities the new day had brought them. Dreen Brislyn ventured with her. They left Barl Lindin's silent brother behind to wait for his courageous, catastrophic sister.

'I pity him,' Dreen said, as they made their way through the hushed, seemingly deserted inn. 'He loves her, and would defend her, but it isn't possible to defend the indefensible – and he knows it.'

Venette pushed open the inn's heavy front door. 'You must live a very . . . uncomplicated . . . life.'

'Lady Martain, you astonish me,' Dreen said, staring. 'You'd *still* defend Morgan Danfey? Even now?'

She didn't answer. She had no interest in discussing Morgan, at least not with this young woman . . . and besides, the sight that greeted her beyond the doorway robbed her entirely of speech.

'Justice preserve us,' Dreen whispered, her voice colourless with shock. 'And how are we to mend this? Surely all of Dorana is suffering the same fate.'

Venette felt her belly churn. *Orwin.* But she couldn't afford to think of him . . . or the rest of their scattered family. Not yet.

The narrow street on which the Shooting Star sat was riddled and warped and blighted with mage-mist. The filthy stuff clung like fruit-rot to the buildings and the cobblestones, shattered stained glass or turned it to melted slag, poisoned the bright flowers and the spreading, shading trees. Floated malevolent through the air, bright and deadly in the growing sunlight.

Dreen pointed. 'Is that – are those – *bodies?*'

A stench of death and too-rapid decay clogged their throats as they picked their cautious way along the street. The silence was eerie. Unsettling. Broken only by the distant, staccato sounds of glass smashing to shards.

The corpses of two men and a woman huddled on the sidepath. She had perished from mage-mist, her face bubbled into obscurity. But the men – the *men* –

'It must have been those *things* that Lord Danfey created,' Dreen Brislyn said, her voice shaking. 'These wounds – only talons could make them.'

Nodding, Venette forced herself to look at the spilled entrails, the splintered bones, the punctured, rended flesh. 'And fangs.' *Oh, Morgan. Morgan. My dear, you are lost.* 'I wonder if there's any chance that Mage Lindin could—'

Above their heads, a slow, dry, leathery rustle of bat wings. And then a thud, a thud, and a thud amidst a clatter of loosened roof tiles.

'Do not move, Lady Drislyn,' Venette breathed. 'Do not even blink.'

Shadow by swallowed shadow, the rising day crept along the empty street. They waited, unmoving, muscles aching and trembling, breathing in the sour stink of spoiling blood and emptied bowels and viscera strewn like discarded fish guts at the markets.

After some endless stretch of minutes, with hissing cries and a lazy slap-slap-slap of the air, the three creatures perching on the roof above them flew away.

Dreen Brislyn's face was so pale it was almost translucent. 'After what we heard last night, Elvado is surely infested. And if Danfey is not stopped, the same fate awaits the rest of Dorana. Lady Martain, we can't live with those monsters among us!'

Venette sighed. 'Call me Venette. Under these circumstances, formality seems absurd. As for Morgan's *pets* . . .' She felt herself shudder with revulsion. 'I don't much like our chances of hunting them down, Dreen. Not without the aid of magic.'

Dreen tried to summon glimfire, but only succeeded in scorching her hand. Stung with pain, she stared at the empty sky. 'So we're at the mercy of Barl Lindin's powers and her intermittent conscience? Is that it?'

'It would appear so.'

'Wonderful. I don't suppose you can explain her magework, Venette?'

'No. Doubtless Bellamie Ranowen would have puzzled out the truth of it.' But the once-maligned mage was wings and fangs and talons, now. *Poor Bellamie.* 'If I had to guess, I'd say it has something do with the fact that her magic, and Morgan's, are responsible for these disruptions.'

'And you're probably right.' Dreen laughed, bitter. 'Seeing as his magework is also in fine working fettle. Oh, Venette. If only—'

'What?' Venette said, when Dreen didn't finish. 'If only we'd realised what was going on right under our noses, and put a stop to it before any of this could happen?'

Dreen's lips trembled, then firmed. 'The General Council trusted you. Every mage in Dorana trusted you. The Council of Mages' *purpose* is to keep us safe from magework run amok.'

And the Council of Mages had failed. Searingly aware of her own part in that, Venette folded her arms. 'I appreciate your dismay, Lady Brislyn. However—'

With a shrieking, groaning crash a fabric shop three doors along from them collapsed to splintered ruins. Tension forgotten, they stared at the destruction – then ran as the air began to thicken with mage-mist.

Instinct and desperation sent Venette towards Elvado's central plaza and the Hall of Knowledge, for so long her touchstone and her second home. They helped her keep to the vanishing shadows, avoid the treacherous drifts of mage-mist, the gaping holes in the streets where magic's fabric was giving way. Dreen kept pace with her, grimly panting.

As they ran they saw more bloody, mutilated bodies, but no other living soul.

Reaching the edge of the plaza, they stumbled against one of the pillars supporting the general library's grand portico. Blotted sweat from their faces and heaved air into their burning lungs. In the smothering hush, the central fountain's splashing water sounded loud and obscenely playful.

Venette looked past the fountain, across the expanse of the plaza, through more idly drifting mage-mist. Refused to dwell on the dead mages scattered over the cheerful mosaics. If she looked at their faces she had no doubt she'd know some of them. She had no intention of looking. Not now. Perhaps later. Instead, she stared up at the Hall of Knowledge and felt her heart shrivel in despair. Dozens of Morgan's inhuman creatures perched on its lofty roof and many balconies like diseased, deformed ravens brooding in a tree.

'And so the mages of Dorana are become nothing but carrion-eaters,' Dreen said dully. 'I think this is the end of all we have known and loved.'

Though she could easily weep enough tears to make a second fountain, Venette pushed away from the pillar and forced herself to stand straight.

'Enough, Lady Brislyn. Self-pity will not serve us. I am the last surviving member of Dorana's Council of Mages. You are the head of its General Council. Which means, for better or worse, you and I must lead our people out of this morass.'

Dreen sneered. 'Noble sentiments. But unless you stumble across a way to knit together our unravelled magework and destroy *those* monstrous things—' She pointed a shaking finger at the incanted creatures clinging to the Hall. '—then I fail to see how—'

In a leathery fluttering, in a parody of stooping flight, one by one Morgan's creations plummeted from their perches to the plaza below. As they stared, bewildered, another creature landed with a soft thud almost at their feet.

'It's not dead,' Breen said, kneeling beside it. 'I think – it seems . . . *entranced*.'

Staring down at the thing, revolted, skin crawling, *Did I know this mage before Morgan's meddling? Was this once someone I called my friend?* Venette felt instinct stir again.

'This is Barl's doing. It must be.'

Grunting a little, Dreen pushed to her feet. 'If you're right, it means we've been granted a welcome respite.'

'But for how long?' Venette murmured. 'Come. We should get back to the Shooting Star. This is no place for the making of difficult decisions.'

They returned to the inn, not stopping to speak with the dribs and drabs of mages who by some miracle had survived the dreadful night to emerge, dazed and shattered, from their hiding places. Their stories would have to be heard, of course . . . but that could wait.

It took them some time to reach the Shooting Star. The haphazard drifts of mage-mist were increasing, forcing them to detour time and time again. And everywhere they turned, every side-street and alley they hurried along, they saw Morgan's slumbering beasts . . . thick as fleas on a cur dog.

Wan and exhausted, changed into fresh silk tunic and trousers, Barl Lindin looked up from the old book she was reading as they entered her brother's unwarded room.

'It's done,' she said, letting the book fall to her lap. She was sat on the edge of the bed, more books piled beside her. 'Morgan's bound, and his creatures are bound with him. There's something in his magework that ties them together. They won't break free.'

Her brother stood by the window, his similar face hardened into deep and difficult lines. 'So you claim,' he retorted, as though he'd said it before and was tired of repeating himself. 'But you can't promise that, can you?'

Barl looked at him, her eyes cold. 'Yes. I can.'

'Your magework continues unaffected, then?' Dreen asked, sounding brittle.

'Apparently.'

549

Dreen held out her scorched hand. 'Then you must be the only mage in Dorana so favoured.'

An uncomfortable silence, thick with pain and anger and unspoken recriminations. Then Barl put the book aside.

'With Morgan and his creatures bound, we're safe. So we must—'

'*Safe?*' said Dreen, incredulous. 'We're all the rest of us turned into cripples, Elvado – *Dorana* – is rotten with mage-mist and our belligerent neighbours even now sharpen their swords! How is that *safe?*'

'She's right, Mage Lindin,' Venette said. 'My magework might be doubtful, but I can still feel the spreading rot beneath Dorana's surface.'

'A rot I can heal,' said Barl. 'But not on my own.' She gestured at the books around her. 'And these grimoires I took from Morgan's library won't be enough assistance.'

Her brother stared at her, then laughed. 'You're mad, Barl. He is bound and he is *staying* bound. But I fear even that might not hold him. You should wall him up in his family's tomb and ward the entire Danfey estate untouchable until the end of time.'

'Which would be even crueller than killing him,' Barl said sharply. 'And if you think I could do that, then you don't know me at all.'

'Barl—' His face anguished, her brother sounded close to naked grief. 'He's not a man any more, he's a beast – as dangerous as those monstrosities he created. We can't take the chance he'll—'

'*No*, Remmie!' Barl said, her voice ragged. 'Justice save me, how often must we argue this? Until we can no longer look each other in the eye? Until I hate you, and you hate me, and we have turned each other into orphans?'

Remmie Lindin was the first to shift his gaze. Seeming heart-broken at her victory, Barl turned to Dreen. 'With the Council of Mages all but destroyed, the General Council is Dorana's only hope of leadership. I can take you home, so you and your colleagues can quell any panic.'

Dreen cleared her throat. 'I don't know if that's possible, Mage Lindin. We can't quell the mage-mist, which is the cause of our panic. We can't keep it from spreading further beyond our borders, or prevent our neighbours from making good on their threats.'

'No,' Barl said slowly. 'But I can . . . provided you can hold back Brantone and the others for just a little longer.'

'How?' Venette demanded. 'You're a talented mage, I grant you, but there are limits, Mage Lindin. This is no time for arrogant boasting or vainglorious dreams. False hope is worse than no hope at all.'

'I can – I *think* I can – raise a warding on our borders,' Barl said, after a moment. She was staring at the book she'd set aside. 'One strong enough to contain Dorana's unravelling within it.'

'And then what?' said Dreen. 'We slowly but surely perish, trapped and swallowed by mage-mist and justice alone knows what other calamities?'

'Of course not. With the immediate danger of our angry neighbours averted, I can work towards healing Dorana.'

Remmie Lindin snorted. 'By yourself?'

'No,' she said, carefully. 'With Morgan's help, I hope.'

'Your brother's right,' said Dreen, shocked. 'You're mad.'

Barl held up an entreating hand. 'Please, hear me out. I won't deny Morgan's lost his reason. But it's my hope that with this binding, with this chance to rest, he'll return to himself. And if – *when* – he does, I know he'll want to make amends. I know he'll help me turn back this dark tide.'

Venette shook her head. 'That's if it can be turned back. I'm not sure that's possible. We never got the chance to start the great working, and now with so many of Dorana's best mages perished . . . and worse . . .'

The pain of that threatened to choke her. They'd come to Elvado on her authority, trusting in her and the Council. Now they were dead or beasted or in hiding, their lives a stinking ruin around them.

'We won't know what's possible until we try,' said Barl, standing. 'And we have to try. With or without Morgan's help, we have to. We can't cower here, weeping and wailing and wringing our hands, waiting for foreign warriors to slaughter us.'

Exhausted, Venette pressed dirty fingertips to her eyes. 'I fear there's little the rest of us can do, Mage Lindin, with our mage powers denied us.'

'We can still attempt a great working,' the girl said, so stubborn. 'Remmie can lead in that. It might not succeed, but we won't know for sure until it fails. And until Morgan's well again *you* can help me, Lady Martain. Your mage powers are uncertain but your experience and knowledge, those aren't diminished. You can help me with the theory of what I'll attempt. And when we're satisfied we've found the answers, I can put them into practice. Without Morgan, if I have to.'

'Ward the whole country,' Remmie Lindin muttered. 'Barl, you can't.'

'We won't know that, either, until I try.'

'And likely *kill* yourself trying!' he protested. 'I won't let you do it.'

Barl shook her head. 'It's not your decision, Remmie.'

He turned his back on her, his tired, handsome face twisting with grief. Sparing him a sympathetic glance, Dreen straightened her shoulders and lifted her chin.

'As leader of the General Council, I will have a say in this. And I say it is a plan worth pursuing. If you're ready, Mage Lindin, I'd have you return me to Basingdown. It would seem my colleagues and I have a raft of diplomatic missives to compose.'

After they left, Venette waited some time for Remmie Lindin to speak. When he didn't, just kept staring blindly out of the small window, his fingers clenched bloodless holding its curtain aside, she breathed out a deep sigh and sat on the bed.

'You blame yourself.'

'It's my fault.'

'No, Remmie. It isn't. No more than it's mine because I am Morgan's friend. She is a woman grown. She made her own choices. He made his. The fault is theirs.'

Releasing the curtain, Remmie dropped to the other end of the bed. Morgan's books bounced and overbalanced and slid to the floor.

'She's a talented artisan. She made beautiful clocks. But they were never enough for her. She always wanted *more*.'

Like the College of Mages. Remembering that confrontation, as though it had been a dream, Venette felt her mouth dry.

*And if we'd not denied her that, would we be in such dire straits now?*

A terrible question to ponder. She didn't think she could bear to.

'It does no good to dwell on the past, Remmie. Let go of your anger. She's going to need you in the days ahead.'

'And I'll be here,' he said bitterly. 'I always am, Lady Martain.'

'Venette.'

Startled, he stared at her. And then, slowly, he smiled. 'Very well. Venette.' Just as slowly, the smile faded. 'But so we understand each other? I still think Morgan Danfey should die. Until he is dead, the world will not be safe.'

She wanted to hate him for saying it. She wanted to rant at him, and curse. But how could she when every instinct was screaming he was right?

'I need to go home,' she said. 'I need to see that my husband has survived the night. And then I must be seen on the streets of Elvado. Dreen Brislyn has her tasks . . . and as the Council of Mages' last mage, I have my mine.'

He nodded. 'I'll leave a note for Barl and come with you. If I'm to lead those of us who are left in a working, I shouldn't be a stranger. Besides, with so much fear and uncertainty to contend with, you might not be safe alone.'

Once more, he was right. Not safe alone . . . not safe with Morgan living. As they left the inn, she couldn't help but wonder.

*Will any of us be safe anywhere, ever again?*

It took them nearly three hours to reach her once-peaceful, once-beautiful neighbourhood. Remmie's first sight and smell of the night's carnage bent him double, gagging. But after that he was stoic, his grief and horror contained. Soon he passed Morgan's entranced creatures, the shattered dwellings, the bloodied corpses, with little more than a sharply indrawn breath and a repressed shudder.

When they weren't evading mage-mist, they were struggling their way along rubble and glass-strewn streets or stopping to encourage the mages they found who'd lived through the night. Some were dreadfully wounded, by mage-mist or falling debris. Others seemed witless, their reason fled in the face of unrelenting horrors. After listening to their near-incoherent tales of survival, Venette told them to gather in the central plaza, where they might find friends and family and perhaps even a pother. Promised that help would come, soon, and urged them not to abandon hope. Dorana's Councils were working to see order restored.

'If these poor wretches are the best of us now,' Remmie muttered, as they left yet another gaggle of weeping mages in their wake, 'then I hold little hope of a working's success.'

He was likely right, but she couldn't afford to let him despair. 'Do not count your fellow mages so lightly, Mage Lindin. The best steel is forged in the hottest fires, remember.'

Close to noon, they finally reached her town house. Its wrought iron gates hung bent and crooked on their hinges, and the wide front doors had been splintered to kindling.

'Wait here,' said Remmie, his hand gently restraining. 'I'll see if there's anyone—' He bit his lip. 'Wait here.'

She wasn't brave enough to argue. Waited on the mosaiced front path, shivering, as Barl's brother entered the house. When at last he emerged, she took one look at his pale face and felt her knees buckle.

'I'm sorry, Venette,' he said, crouching beside her on the path. His left hand was cold on her shoulder. The fingers of his right hand unfolded, revealing a red-smeared gold ring set with diamonds and sapphires. 'Was this your husband's?'

She couldn't speak. Could only nod. Orwin's wedding ring sat on Remmie's palm, bloodily reproachful.

'He wasn't beasted,' Remmie said, his arm sliding around her. 'I think he must've fought back when the creatures Morgan sent here tried to take him.'

Any lingering affection she'd felt for Haeth's son died in that moment.

'I want to see him,' she said, struggling to her feet. 'I want to see my husband.'

His eyes brilliant with grief, Remmie took hold of her shoulders. 'No, Venette. You don't.'

Silenced, she looked at him. Thought, *I am a widow*. And then the tears came. She sobbed in Remmie's compassionate embrace until her throat was raw, her head aching. Some time after she was empty, she pulled free of his arms.

'Your sister should be back by now,' she said, and was shocked by how she sounded. 'We'll return to the inn, Remmie. There is a great deal to do.'

The days that came after blurred swiftly one into the next, until weeks had passed with hardly any good news to be found.

Morgan slept in his mansion, shifted from the library onto his bed. Every day, Venette checked on him. Not once did he stir, still and quiet as an effigy upon its marble tomb.

Scolding, cajoling, encouraging and pleading, Dreen Brislyn rallied the shaken General Council. She and her colleagues crafted their missives to the princes and potentates belligerent at the borders, and in return wrung from them a suspicious, reluctant respite. The cursed mages of Dorana had the span of two full moons in which to undo the creeping damage their magic had caused. But if, following two full moons, Dorana's innocent neighbours still suffered from Doranen magic, then the mages of Dorana would tender payment in blood.

Dreen and her General Council kept that ultimatum secret from all save Venette Martain, Barl Lindin and her brother, and devoted every hour they could find to the succouring of Dorana. Travelling laboriously by carriage, they visited every district, meeting with civic leaders, struggling to allay fears, instil confidence, and show by example that the mages of Dorana could, for a little while, live a magickless life. The people should not lose hope. Their magework was not gone from them forever. There was to be a working in Elvado, and a plan was in place to rid Dorana of mage-mist.

With Venette's guidance, Remmie by her side, Elvado's frightened survivors were shepherded to a fragile calm. The first thing they did was gather Morgan Danfey's bound beasts in the central plaza, nine hundred and ninety-six of them all told. Remmie tried to kill one, but no sooner had his dagger plunged hilt-deep in the monstrous thing's heart than the blade was spat out again, rejected. So the creatures were piled into the lightless chambers below the Hall, and Barl was called from her magework to ward them within.

'You know what this likely means, don't you?' she said to her brother. 'If you try to stab Morgan, you'll get the same result.'

Remmie wanted to call that wishful thinking on her part, but since Danfey and his creatures were indisputably linked . . .

'Yes,' he said curtly. 'And given what's happening, you shouldn't look so pleased.'

After that, Remmie rarely saw her. She shifted the books she needed from Morgan Danfey's startling library to the College of Mages, where she and its remaining tutors studied them, and she ate, slept and breathed outrageous magics. Argued the finer points of warding incants. Created and discarded scores of different wards. It was thought, for a few hopeful moments, that because Remmie and she were twins that he'd be able to magework like her. But like every other mage, his magework remained sporadic. Unreliable.

That didn't stop him from leading a series of workings, though. He claimed that practice made perfect, and with the workings to think about the mages of Elvado would not dwell on their grief. After four days of mass funerals, they needed something to distract them. And though the workings consistently failed, *Maybe next time* became their stubborn song.

Barl paid his doings scant attention. Wouldn't let him tell her the names of who'd lived, and who'd died. She didn't need to know. Sickeningly aware of the ultimatum they were facing, she drove herself without mercy to find a way to ward Dorana. Snatched sleep when she had to. Dreamed of Morgan then, and wept.

As instability spread inexorably through Dorana's frightened districts, as more and more dwellings and buildings became unsafe, as the scourge of mage-mist swallowed more villages, and looked likely to swallow whole towns, mages of every ranking, made equal at last by the loss of their magework, abandoned their familiar lives and sought shelter in Elvado. The city was swiftly overrun. Makeshift encampments sprang up in every open space, filled parks and streets and laneways and spilled into the surrounding countryside.

At the second full waxing of the moon, Barl told Dreen Brislyn to beg their angry neighbours for more time. Knowing a personal appeal might be their only hope, Lady Brislyn and her Council sued for a face-to-face meeting and returned from Brantone shaken, with a stark, unyielding message.

*The mages of Dorana have one more moon, and no longer.*

'Tell me you can do this, Mage Lindin,' Dreen Brislyn said, meeting with Barl in the College. 'Because I've seen the intransigence of the nations ranged against us, and how many swords and spears and bows stand ready to chastise Dorana. It will be a slaughter. There is no forgiveness in these princes for what we have done. Their people suffer as ours suffer and they demand a swift, rough justice.'

So weary she could barely speak, Barl pushed a note-covered sheet of paper across her workroom table. 'This is the warding, Lady Brislyn. The College's surviving mages and I have spent nearly two weeks pulling it apart for flaws. We can't find any. In theory, we believe it will work.'

'In theory,' Dreen Brislyn murmured, frowning over the incant.

'Theory is all we have, until I put it into practice.'

Dreen Brislyn looked up. 'I have never seen an incant so complex. It seems to me impossible.' She sat back, shaking her head. 'Can you do this?'

'I can try.'

'Mage Lindin . . .' Dreen Brislyn slid from her chair and paced the confines of the workroom. 'When do you begin to construct it?'

'Tomorrow.'

'You have everything you need? All the catalysts? Enough crucibles strong enough to contain these magics?'

She'd scoured the College for every last pinch of *azafris, susquinel, tilatantin* and *zife*. With Venette Martain's assistance had emptied every ranked mage's home of their myriad supplies also. And every College crucible, warded to protect it from violent, dangerous magework, was stacked in the distant workroom she'd chosen for this task.

'Yes, Lady Brislyn.'

'Can you – should you – attempt this alone?'

She was mad to be attempting it at all. 'Remmie has agreed to help me.'

'Your brother.' Dreen Brislyn sighed. 'No-one else?'

'No-one else can be spared. If I should fail, if something goes wrong . . .'

'I understand. Well, thank you, Mage Lindin. On behalf of the General Council, I wish you good fortune. I'll look to Venette to tell me how you get on.'

As soon as she was alone again, Barl returned to the Danfey estate. Before going upstairs to Morgan, she visited Rumm in the Danfey family crypt. Venette Martain had seen him interred there, his plain, unadorned stone coffin a silent, painful reproach.

'I'm sorry, Rumm,' she whispered, her hand flat to the coffin's lid. He deserved his own effigy. When this was over, if she survived, she'd make him one. It was the least she could do. 'We never intended any of this. You were a good man . . . and Morgan loved you.'

*Morgan.*

She couldn't linger. If she was going to face him, she had to do it now.

Dusk's shrouding gloom lifted by glimfire, she retreated to the mansion. Climbed the stairs one by one, heartsick and light-headed. Pushing their – his – privy chamber door open, she saw at once that Venette Martain had already been and gone. An oil lamp burned a little distance from the bed, lifting the sumptuous room out of a growing darkness.

She hadn't seen him since that terrible day in the library.

*'My love, how could you do this? You bitch, you slut, you treacherous whore . . .'*

Her betrayal of him was a brand seared into her soul.

He looked so peaceful, lying there. Venette had seen him stripped of his passion-wrecked clothing and dressed soberly, properly, in dark blue silk. His arms lay quietly by his side. The magic that bound him was as fierce now as in the moment she'd trapped him in it.

Leaving the glimfire to hover in the doorway, she crossed to the bed. Sat gently beside him and took his lax hand in hers. It was warm, the fingers pliable. His broad chest moved up and down. His unbound hair, like spun silk, drank the lamplight and glowed soft gold. His beautiful eyes were hidden from her. He couldn't see her. He didn't smile.

After tonight, she might never see him again. All the things she'd come here meaning to say. The apologies. The excuses. The fervent declarations of love.

She kissed him once, lightly, and left him to sleep.

# CHAPTER THIRTY-FOUR

Next morning, after a painfully restless night, Barl wasn't sure Remmie would come to her at the College, even though she'd asked him nicely, and even though he'd said he'd be there. Such a chasm had opened between them, anger and hurt and disappointment scouring away all the common ground of childhood and their years of sharing a home. It seemed he could not forgive her for Morgan, even though he'd forgiven her for so much else.

In her smaller, petty moments she thought his resentments sprang from jealousy. He'd turned his back on love, for her sake, only to see her find a love larger than he could hope to dream of. So of course he resented that. Resented her. Of course he was bitter. At least, she told herself that was the reason when he mostly ignored her during her hasty meetings with him and Venette Martain and sometimes Dreen Brislyn, why he didn't reply to her notes, and avoided every chance of seeing her in the scant, scattered moments they had to themselves.

But in her heart she knew better, and always regretted the harsh thoughts afterwards. If Remmie was wounded, she had wounded him, and he had every right to his pain and carefully guarded distance. Besides, it wasn't only his reluctance to face her that kept them apart. He was as busy as she, working hand in glove with Venette to keep the surviving mages of Elvado from drowning in dismay, or succumbing to hopelessness and surrendering to fear. In leading great workings in the most vulnerable areas of the city. The workings' successes were few and haphazard, Dorana's unravelling a stubborn foe, but even a tiny glimmer of progress kept hope alive.

But although she was doubtful, her almost estranged brother did come, soon after sunrise. For a long time he stood silent in her College workroom, staring at the jars and bottles of catalysts, at the strict rows of crucibles, and her careful notes outlining the theories behind her warding incant's creation, and the incant itself.

Slumped behind her small desk she watched him, and felt her heart stutter at his appearance. So thin now, so pale, with a weariness ground bone-deep into his body. His hair was longer, and untidy, and though his faded blue linen clothes were clean they lacked his familiar jaunty flair. He looked older, and sadder, as though he'd given up the notion that the world could be a kind and joyful place.

*I did that to him. His unhappiness is my doing.*

But if she tried to apologise again, she'd only make him angry. He'd lost patience with her sorrow. These days he cared only for deeds, not hollow words . . . and it was hard to blame him for that.

At last he stirred, and ran a hand down his face. 'Barl, this is madness,' he said, turning. '*Forty-nine sigils?* For a single incant? It's too many. The strain will kill you.'

She made herself smile at him. 'Nonsense, Remmie. I'm far too busy to die.'

'Don't joke,' he said, folding his arms. His eyes were shadowed. 'I'm frightened for you.'

Was it wrong, to feel such pleasure hearing that? Probably. But it was the kindest thing he'd said to her in weeks. She had to cherish it. 'I know. And I'm sorry. But that's what the warding incant demands.'

'Then concoct a different incant!'

The rawness in his voice had her lacing her fingers together to still their trembling. 'I can't. There's no time. Anyway, this is the right incant.'

He shook his head. 'There has to be another.'

'You mean you want there to be,' she said, gently. 'But there isn't. I've not been twiddling my thumbs, Remmie. I have exhausted every other imaginable possibility. You know that as well as I do, so let's not waste time arguing.'

He glowered at her, hating that she was right, then tapped the single sheet of paper on which the incant was neatly written. 'Who else has seen this?'

'Lady Martain. Lady Brislyn. The College's remaining mages.'

'And they all agree this is the only way?'

'Yes.' With a lot of arm-twisting. But she wasn't about to tell him that. 'Remmie—'

Turning away, he dragged his hand down his face again. 'And what if they're wrong? What if *you're* wrong? You are the only mage we have whose magework is reliable. If we lose you to this madness—'

'You still have Morgan.'

She waited for him to shout at her for that, but he only sighed. 'That's a dream, Barl. Forget it.'

'You always said that me setting foot in this College was a dream, too, and look! Here I am, with my own privy workroom and more magework to occupy me than I know what to do with!'

He spun round, his pained eyes wide with disbelief. 'You can *joke* about this?'

'Remmie . . .' Bracing her hands on the desk, she pushed achingly to her feet. 'If there is a joke here, you have to see it's on me. You have to see *I'm* the joke. A bad one. Please, let's not fight any more. I asked you here because the warding incant is ready, but I don't dare attempt its creation on my own. And there's no-one else I want beside me as I do.'

*Except Morgan.*

The tightening of his lips told her he knew she'd not spoken the entire truth, but instead of challenging her on it he crossed to the workroom's small, stained-glass window and stared down into the empty courtyard below. There'd been a garden there once, but mage-mist had ravaged it to rotting slime. Every time she felt like giving up she made herself look at it. Made herself remember the ruination that was Rumm, and the sound of talons clicking on the Council chamber floor. Reminded herself, forcefully, that she didn't have the luxury of giving up.

'D'you remember when we were five, and you tried to incant your way off the roof?' Remmie said eventually, his back still turned. 'You mistimed the sigil and knocked out two front teeth and Pa was so angry over you disobeying him that once he was certain you'd not really hurt yourself he paddled your behind until you shrieked the leaves off the trees in the front garden.'

'Yes, Remmie. I remember,' she said, pulling a face. 'Thank you so much for reminding me.'

Unsmiling, he looked over his shoulder at her. 'Do yourself a mischief over this incant and *I'll* paddle you, Barl. I swear it.'

Eyes stinging, sick with nerves, she moved to the workbench. *Forty-nine sigils.* No mage in history had ever attempted to create so many for a single incant. Well, she'd spent her life claiming she was a great mage.

*And now the time has come to prove it.*

Forty-nine sigils. Their completion took her nearly three days and in nearly three days Remmie did not leave her side. She cursed him. She cuffed him. Once she threw a crucible at him. It made no difference. 'Do your worst. I'm not leaving,' he said, and kept his word, and stayed. Did her bidding like an apprentice, kept anxious Venette Martain and the College's mages at bay, brought her food and drink, listened as she cursed the difficulties of her enormous task and encouraged her in those moments when she thought she'd have to admit defeat.

He wanted her to rest after the forty-ninth sigil was confirmed, but she couldn't. How could she? The spreading mage-mist had beaten Dorana to its knees, and all along their borders the warriors of Ranoush and Trindek and Brantone and Manemli and Feen waited with their sharp spears and swords. She could feel Dorana's time running out, running down like a clock whose central incant was failing.

Besides, she was so weary now that if she stopped, she might never start again.

The warding incant she'd devised contained one hundred and sixty-eight syllables. Three layers of harmonics. Fourteen bridges. Eight reversals. It took the principles of eleven different warding incants she'd found in Morgan's library and knitted them together with seven the College mages had shown her, and five from the Hall of Knowledge's archives. With forty-nine sigils to ignite and then bind the incant, the inherent power contained within her creation was more devastating than that of any incant ever before devised. She was mad even to attempt it. Mad to think she could ward an entire country. Mad and arrogant . . . which, according to Remmie and Arndel and the rest, were her two defining features.

So how could she fail?

Weaving sigil and syllable into an indivisible whole took her another two days and many, many false starts. When at long last she felt the warding incant coalesce, she burst into tears then fainted. But only for a few moments. She woke to find herself on the workroom floor, with Remmie shaking her and shouting.

'Oh, hush,' she croaked, shakily sitting up. 'I'm fine. Go and fetch Lady Martain. She'll want to see this for herself.'

'Rest first,' he said, smoothing the tangled hair from her face. 'We've waited this long, we can wait a while longer.'

Heart thudding unsteadily against her ribs, she covered his hand with hers. 'No, Remmie. We can't.'

His eyes darkened. 'I suppose not,' he said, and pulled back. Levered himself to standing, the strain of the past days making his movements stiff and ungainly, turning him into an old man. 'Well . . . bathe yourself, at least. Find clean clothes, and brush your hair. The state you're in, Barl, you hardly inspire confidence.'

It was a callous sort of kindness, but she was feeling too

bruised, and too grateful, to object. When he returned not quite an hour later, their dire predicament slowing everything down, she'd managed a hasty sponge bath and dragged on a peach-coloured silk tunic that wasn't too badly the worse for wear.

'Mage Lindin,' said Venette Martain, entering the workroom. 'Remmie tells me you've succeeded in creating your incant.'

The loss of her husband had marked the elegant, self-possessed councillor. Her hair was clean enough, but lank. Her slender frame had thinned to scrawny. And her eyes, once so swift to fill with scornful disdain, now filled with tears at unexpected moments. She wore dead Orwin's ring on a chain around her neck, and could not know how often her fingers strayed to it when her mind was occupied with other things. Between her and Remmie there had grown a comfortable rapport. He called her Venette, and never hesitated to disagree with her if he felt disagreement was warranted.

'Lady Martain,' Barl said, nodding. *I'm not jealous. I'm not.* 'Yes, the incant's completed. But whether it's a success or not remains to be seen.'

Venette Martain glanced up from the map on the workbench, which after days of deliberation they'd marked with the intended locations of the border incant's wardstones. 'I received word from Dreen Brislyn last night. The General Council is on its way to Elvado, along with as many families as they could convince to leave their homes.'

'Things are so bad in the Second district?' said Remmie, leaning against the wall, arms folded, his expression brooding.

Venette Martain sighed. 'They are. Of course, they're not much better here, and we're already woefully overcrowded. But I could hardly tell the General Council it's not welcome, could I?'

'Perhaps it's for the best,' said Remmie. 'Lady Drislyn can take my place in leading the workings.'

'Why? Where will you be?'

'With Barl. She can't ward Dorana on her own, Venette.'

'Of course she can. She has to. There's no other mage to ignite the incant.'

Relegated to the role of lamp post, Barl watched them stare at each other.

'That's true,' Remmie said, straightening. 'As far as it goes. But Dorana is dangerous. She'll need another pair of eyes while she's mageworking.'

'Even if she does, they don't have to be yours!'

'No, but I want them to be. Venette, she's my sister. I don't care to trust her life to anyone else.'

'And I don't care if you do or don't,' Venette Martain retorted. 'You are needed here, Remmie. The mages of Elvado see you and they feel heartened. I can't afford to have them lose heart in your absence.'

Barl smiled to hear the woman's praise, even as Remmie dismissed it with a scowl. She might be the better mage, but Remmie was the one who'd been gifted with a knack for wrangling people. It warmed her to find he hadn't lost it, to know that he was important, and needed, held in such great esteem.

'The same could be said of you, my lady,' Remmie said, in the tone of voice that should have warned Venette Martain that the argument was already lost. 'As the Council of Mages' last mage, your authority is trusted and absolute, your lightest word the law.'

'Then do as I say!'

'I can't. Venette—' Unfolding his arms, Remmie took a step towards her. 'Don't you understand? The last time I let her out of my sight she fell in with Morgan Danfey.'

'Thank you, Remmie,' Barl said sharply, rapping her knuckles to the workbench to ensure their attention. 'I'm not a wayward child you need to keep on a leash.'

'Exactly,' said Venette Martain, leaping in uninvited because it suited her purpose. 'You're being quite—'

'I'm being a good brother!' said Remmie, not appreciating her interference either. 'I'm honouring my word! Don't waste your breath, Venette. You'll not push me aside on this.'

Now they glared at each other, and if she'd not been annoyed by Remmie's high-handed bossiness Barl would have laughed at the thwarted look on Venette Martain's face.

She rapped the workbench again. 'The choice is mine, you understand? Since I am the mage tasked with warding Dorana, I will be the mage who decides how that warding will be done. And if you don't like it?' She spread her hands, tightly smiling. 'Then by all means, find yourselves another mage.'

Oh, and her brother and his new friend didn't care for that. But she was beyond caring for what they did and did not like. There was an excellent chance that the warding of Dorana would kill her . . . or at the least leave her badly debilitated. It was a sacrifice she'd make, if not happily, then willingly. She owed that much to every mage who suffered now because of her mistakes.

*But it doesn't mean I'll be bullied. They need me more than I need them and for once I'm not inclined to let them forget it.*

Venette Martain's shoulders slumped. 'Fine. The choice is yours. But I implore you, Mage Lindin, let Remmie stay here. Elvado needs him. *I* need him. There are mages here aplenty who can serve as your guardian.'

True enough. But no matter how badly Elvado and this woman needed her brother . . . she needed him more.

'I'm sorry, Lady Martain,' she said, doing her best to sound sincere. 'It's not simply a case of needing a second pair of eyes to watch for mage-mist and other calamities. Remmie knows this incant and my magework. He is my other, better self.'

'Venette . . .' His eyes soft with compassion, Remmie crossed to Lady Martain and slid his arm around her. 'I'll be back before you know it. You'll hardly notice I'm gone. And I do need to do this. Keeping Barl safe is more important than anything.'

'I know, I know,' Venette Martain murmured, and patted his cheek. 'Don't mind me, Remmie. I'm weary, and full of dark fancies.'

Moved by the undeniable affection in the woman's face, her voice, Barl scowled at the workbench. She didn't want to be moved. She didn't want to feel sorry for someone whose arrogant selfishness had helped push her towards disaster.

'When will you leave, Mage Lindin?'

Looking up, she saw that Venette Martain was holding fast to her husband's ring, drawing strength from the memory of the man Morgan had destroyed. Another inconvenient rush of sympathy warmed her. For better or worse, Remmie had stepped into that void. And she didn't have to like the woman to acknowledge the good she was doing, how hard she was working, and how much worse things would be if she'd not survived.

*Or how big a part Remmie plays in giving her the strength she needs to face each day.*

'At first light, my lady,' she said. 'The sooner Dorana is warded, the sooner we can pour our hearts and souls into its healing.'

Venette Martain closed her eyes, briefly. 'You still believe it can be healed?'

'I have to,' she said, after a heart-thudding moment of silence. 'For if I didn't . . . I couldn't go on.'

After a night of poorly-snatched sleep, and a plain breakfast, she and Remmie left the College at first light. If he was afraid of travelling by incant, she couldn't tell. Perhaps it helped that before she took him to their first point of warding, she took herself there, alone, then returned to the College unharmed. She felt ill, of course, afterwards . . . but whether that was simply her usual travel sickness, or a result of Dorana's unravelling, she couldn't tell. She said nothing, only chewed a handful of runip berries, made certain again of the map, the wardstones and her notes in the stout leather satchel slung over her shoulder, took one last look around the mage-misted College grounds – a home of nightmares now, not dreams – wrapped her fingers around his wrist . . . and recited the incant.

Stepping out of the air into a field on the outskirts of ruined Hoysten hamlet, which sat a stone's throw from the border with Brantone, Remmie blinked to clear his travel-blurred vision, then gasped.

'I know,' said Barl, following his shocked gaze to the row upon row of tents lined along the Brantish side of the boundary, and the gathered warriors beyond them. 'Despite Lady Brislyn's vivid description, seeing it somehow makes the danger more real.'

The cool morning air rang with the chilling sounds of swords, clashing, and the steady drumming of horses' hooves as their riders practised killing passes with their lowered spears. Underpinning that, the *thock thock thock* of arrows striking straw targets.

'If this warding doesn't work . . .' said Remmie, sounding strained. 'Barl, we have no hope of defending ourselves against them.'

'You think I don't know that?' she said. 'Why do you think Morgan and I—'

He turned away. 'Don't. It's because you and Morgan broke the rules that we're in this mess. You created what he feared would come to pass.'

As if she'd not already thought of that. As if she'd not lost countless nights of sleep, tossing and turning over that very notion.

'Come on,' she said, in that moment close to hating him. 'The sooner we start, the sooner you can get back to Elvado and your dear friend, Lady Martain.'

He gave her a sharp look at that, but didn't reply.

Mouth dry, palms sweaty, Barl struck out towards the border. The original boundary warding was mostly unravelled, but just enough of the incant remained to guide her to the precise place where Dorana ended and Brantone began. Falling into step beside her, Remmie roamed his gaze around them, seeking the first sickening signs of mage-mist, and danger. After fifty paces he took hold of her arm and halted them both.

'Let this be close enough. I don't want to stir any trouble with our neighbours.'

She resented being handled, but he did have a point. They'd not been noticed yet . . . and it would be best if they were never noticed at all.

Sinking to her knees, she fumbled the first wardstone out of her satchel. Dug a shallow hole in the sparsely grassed dirt before her, half-buried the marble-sized chunk of dull grey crystal, then took a few deep breaths to compose herself.

'All right, Remmie,' she whispered. 'Cross your fingers.'

To be sure, she recited the incant from her notes, not trusting to memory. As the weight of potent syllables gathered, she felt the sluggish rise of power in her blood. Felt her fingertips tingle as she inscribed the morning air with sigils. So many. Her head started to spin.

When the last syllable was uttered and the forty-ninth sigil burned the air, she fell forward onto her hands, gasping. Remmie dropped to a crouch beside her.

'Did it work? Barl, did it—'

'I don't know,' she said hoarsely. 'And I won't, not for certain, until the last wardstone is set and I try to trigger the incant. But . . .' Shaking, she sat back and blotted her sweaty face with her linen sleeve. 'I think it's all right. It felt smooth enough, and all of the sigils caught.'

He handed her a kerchief. 'Your nose is bleeding.'

'Oh.' She dabbed, then looked at the red spots on the blue cotton. 'Well. I suppose it could be worse.' After handing back the kerchief, she let him help her to standing then stared down at the incanted wardstone. 'So. One down, twenty-four to go.'

'Barl . . .' Remmie's hand came to rest on her shoulder. 'Can you do this? Are you strong enough?'

Glancing at him, she saw the genuine concern beneath his brittle, not quite friendly exterior. Made herself smile, though she could more easily weep.

'There's only one way to find out, Rem. Come on. Let's get out of here before those warriors look over their shoulders and realise they're not alone.'

As the sun climbed the sky, then slid down it, they made their slow way around Dorana's edge, embedding the wardstones with painstaking care. Soon enough Barl could recite the incant from memory . . . and everywhere she looked she found evidence of her folly. Dead, rotting livestock, killed by mage-mist. Rotting crops in the fields. Fresh graves. Abandoned farmhouses. Entire empty villages. Lives cut short, abandoned, all because she fell in love. Remmie didn't reproach her. Said nothing at all. But by the time they'd embedded the twelfth wardstone, the pain in his face forced her to speak.

'This isn't your fault,' she said, as they stood side by side in yet another blighted field. 'You tried to tell me.'

He shook his head, despairing. 'I should've tried harder. I should've known what to say.'

'Remmie, don't.' She pressed her hands to her face, hiding from the destruction. From him. 'How much worse do you want me to feel?'

'I'm not trying to punish you.'

She let her hands drop. 'Really?'

Bending, he touched a mage-misted stalk of wheat and watched it crumble to stinking ash. 'You don't think you deserve punishment?'

'*I did none of this on purpose!*'

'I know, Barl,' he said wearily. 'But still. You did it. Now come on. We're only halfway done.'

And because there was nothing she could say that would make the slightest difference, to anything, she took them to the next place marked on the map.

It was dark when they returned, exhausted, to the College. Venette Martain and Dreen Brislyn were waiting for them in the workroom. Like Morgan's inconvenient friend, Lady Brislyn showed the brutal fingerprints of Dorana's misfortunes. Pale and thin, her eyes haunted by sights no-one should witness, by fears and threats that daily seemed more and more likely to come true, she stood as they entered.

'Is it done?'

Barl looked at the woman, her head viciously aching. 'Would I have come back if it wasn't?'

'I warn you, Mage Lindin, do not try me!' Lady Brislyn

snapped. 'Not tonight. I lost two members of my Council to mage-mist on the way here.'

Pushing her aside, Remmie stepped forward. 'We're sorry for your loss, my lady. It's a tragedy.'

'For all of Dorana. They were good men,' said Lady Brislyn, her voice cracked with grief. 'Remmie, are we warded?'

'Almost,' he said. 'All that remains now is for the incant to be ignited.'

'You haven't ignited it?' said Venette Martain, torn between surprise and displeasure. 'Dorana *isn't* warded? Why not?'

Barl let the emptied satchel slide from her throbbing shoulder and dropped onto the nearest stool. 'Because if I'd died igniting it on the border, Remmie would've been stranded out there. If I die here he'll not be inconvenienced. You of all people should appreciate that.'

'Barl,' Remmie said softly. 'Don't.'

Venette Martain exchanged a glance with Dreen Brislyn, then nodded. 'Yes. All right. But can you ignite it now?'

'Surely we can wait until the morning,' Remmie protested. 'Barl is worn out. She—'

Lips pinched bloodless, Dreen Brislyn stared him down. 'We are all of us tired, Remmie. And we are out of time. You do know that people are sickening faster than ever? Dying from the slightest of ailments? You know we face the prospect of famine? And if this warding does not succeed, then—'

'*He knows!*' Barl said, leaping up. 'And *I* know. We've just come back from seeing the damage I've done to Dorana. If you think I need a sharper goad, Lady Brislyn, think again!'

'Enough, Dreen,' Venette Martain murmured. 'Your anger is justified, but not helpful. Mage Lindin, ignite the warding. Please. We *must* start Dorana's healing. Even an hour might make the difference.'

And so, though it made her eyes and nose bleed, threatened to crumble her bones to dust, felt like it came perilously close to killing her . . . she ignited Dorana's warding.

'Justice be praised,' she heard Venette Martain say, as Remmie gathered her close and held her hard against the wracking shudders and the pain. 'We're saved.'

For nearly three weeks, Barl thought that was true. The General Council dispatched a flurry of letters to the waiting princes and potentates, assuring them that Dorana's rancid magics were now contained. Believing them, their neighbours did not attack. With fresh hope, Remmie led the mages of Elvado in more great workings, which achieved little in practical terms but helped keep spirits high. She joined him once . . . but an unpleasant and unexpected encounter with Maris Garrick and her family sent her back to the College, where she could work alone, without screaming insults, on repairing Dorana's fraying magical fabric.

For nearly three weeks, she thought the worst was behind them.

'Barl, *wake up*. It's important.'

Dragged resentful out of sleep, she blinked at her brother. 'Remmie? Oh, go away. I spent all day and half the night shoring up the Hall and I've only just—'

And then she felt it. The absence of magework. Heard silence, when for days she'd heard, deep in her mind, like a lullaby, the distant thrumming hum of the impossible ward she'd created.

'Get up,' Remmie whispered, flickered with candle light and crouched beside the cot in her workroom. 'The warding fell almost an hour ago. Venette says we must meet with Lady Brislyn and the General Council.'

'What do they want from me, Remmie? That incant was the best I could do. I gave it *everything*. I have nothing left. So unless you agree to release Morgan, there's no more I—'

'No,' he said, and pressed his fingers to her lips. 'We can't risk that. As for what they want, Venette wouldn't say.'

Rolling away from him, she pushed her face into the pillow.

*Go away, Remmie. Leave me alone. I've wrecked Dorana and I can't fix it. Leave me alone.*

Ruthless, he stripped off the blankets then hauled her from the cot.

'I don't care what you're feeling,' he said, his fingers cruel on her arm. 'When this is over, however it ends, you can crawl into a hole if you like and never show your face again. But right now, Barl, we are going to see the General Council.'

Shocked, she stared at him. Searched in vain for her brother. Saw only a stranger with cold, fathomless eyes.

'Now get dressed,' he said. 'Quickly. We've wasted enough time.'

By some miracle, and a great deal of magework, the Hall of Knowledge still stood . . . while many of Elvado's other beautiful buildings were ruined.

Declining the offer of a seat at the Council table, Venette instead stood by the chamber's boarded-up window with Remmie Lindin, and watched the faces of Dreen's councillors as the unpalatable truth sank in. There should have been fifteen of them, some ranked, some not – but death had thinned the herd to eight. Nine, counting Dreen.

'You can do *nothing*?' Councillor Horbeck echoed, staring at Barl Lindin. From the baggy fit of his clothing, the Fourth district's representative had been a robust man, once. Now his tired silk tunic hung in limp folds. 'Nothing at all?'

Hunched in her own chair, barely respectable in stained, patched linens, Remmie's sister looked like a chastened child.

'No, Councillor. I'm sorry. Ever since the borders were warded I have been working, almost without respite, to knit together Dorana's tattered magic. I've had a little success, it's true, but not enough. What Dorana needs is time for the imbalance to right itself, which it will do. I am sure of it. Only time is the one thing we don't have any more.'

'No, no. You must be mistaken,' Horbeck persisted, sweating. 'You are Barl Lindin. There must be *something* you can do!'

Venette felt Remmie flinch. For everyone's sake, not least his sister's, though some might say she deserved no such consideration, none of the councillors had been told of her part in their strife. All they knew was that Mage Lindin retained her magework, and that she'd used it to ward Dorana's borders and save them from a bloody invasion.

'I'm sorry,' Barl said again. 'I know you don't want to hear this, but there's no point giving you false hope.'

'Mage Lindin is right,' Dreen pointed out over the dismayed mutterings of her Council. 'And I asked her to address this gathering so there might be no doubt. Councillors, the time has come for us to make a difficult decision.'

Horbeck and his colleagues exchanged alarmed looks. 'And what does that mean?' he said. 'Lady Brislyn, if you've something to say, best you come out and say it.'

Nodding, Dreen steepled her fingers. 'Here then is the bald truth. With Dorana undefended, and the mage-mist uncontained and worsening, soon we will come under attack from our neighbours. You know as well as I that their patience is long since exhausted.'

'So what do we do?' asked Lady Marnagh, of the Fifth district, her eyes wide, her voice unsteady. 'Wait for them to come and kill us in our beds?'

More dismayed outcry, louder this time. The shock was wearing off. Soon raw terror would prevail.

'No, of course not!' Dreen said loudly, banging the table for silence. 'Anticipating the worst, I have given this a great deal of thought. And once you've heard my proposal, I think you'll agree that it must be our only chance of survival.'

Venette closed her eyes. She and Dreen had discussed this, at great and secret length. And while the idea repulsed her, horrified her, she could not argue against it.

'Justice save us all,' Remmie murmured, leaning close. 'She wants to abandon Dorana, doesn't she?'

Of course he'd guess. Barl Lindin's brother was an astute young man. She silenced him with a warning glance.

Lord Atheling, now representing the Seventh and Eleventh districts, looked down his high-bridged nose and sneered. 'Speak plainly, my lady,' he said, flirting with insolence. 'These riddles of yours grow tiresome.'

Unintimidated, Dreen gave the man stare for stare. 'Plainly, then, my lord, I say that every mage in Dorana should pack as much as he and she can carry, and retreat to a safe haven beyond our borders until the magical instability subsides.'

A heartbeat of shocked silence, and then the chamber erupted in protest. Unsurprised, Venette watched Dreen let the furious shouting wash over her . . . for a time. And then she slapped both palms hard to the table and pushed to her feet.

'Control yourselves!' she said loudly. 'This caterwauling helps *no-one*.'

Raggedly, the dismayed councillors let their tongues run dry. One by one Dreen looked at them, her eyes icy with disdain.

'This is a terrible thing, I know, but the harsh truth is now staring us in the face. We flee . . . or we perish. Which shall it be?'

D orana's General Council chooses to flee . . .
    The choice is not made easily, nor swiftly, nor with any
kind of joy. Nor does every mage in Dorana agree with the
Council's decree. Father turns on son, mother on daughter.
Brother and sister fly at each other's throats. Husband and wife
clench their fists and turn away, unforgiving. Ravaged by terror
and mage-mist, Dorana falls apart. No Council can hold together
what blind arrogance has destroyed.

Unchecked, the mage-mist creeps across Dorana's unwarded
borders. The princes and potentates of the magickless nations
regard the blight with furious dismay. The mages of Dorana
have proven themselves false. Now countless lives are on the
brink of ruin.

They send their warriors into blighted Dorana.

Word of this disaster reaches Elvado. The warriors of
Brantone and Trindek and Ranoush and Feen and Manemli are
chanting Death to all mages! as they ride with drawn swords
and spears ready to kill. In their wake they leave bodies, and
silence.

At last run out of time, Venette Martain and Dreen Brislyn
accept they cannot wait until every mage agrees to abandon
their home. Those who would run will run . . . and those who
cling stubbornly to denial of Dorana's dire predicament, or who
simply cannot face the terrible unknown, will remain to take
their chances against the swords and spears and blight.

'I cannot tell you where we will fetch up,' Venette Martain
tells the anxious crowd crammed into Elvado's central plaza. 'Or
how long it will take us to get there. I can only tell you what I
believe . . . that we will find a safe haven. And that once we are
far enough from Dorana our magework will return to us, and
when it does we will find a way back and heal what is so sick.
This is not the end. Dorana will rise again to greatness.'

Barl wants to take Morgan with them. She is shouted down,
loudest of all by her brother. Defeated, Barl falls silent. She
cannot stay behind, for her magework is needed. She agrees to
abandon her love.

577

*But she weeps when she is alone, afraid she will never see him again.*

*Though she wears a bold face in public, in private Venette is also afraid. She fears the angry princes and potentates will not relent until every man, woman and child of Dorana is dead. She fears there might be no safe place where its mages can catch their breath . . . and that even if they do find a haven, by then there will be no Dorana left to heal.*

*Confiding in Dreen Brislyn, she learns her fears are shared. And so they decide they must take as much of Dorana with them as can safely be carried: books and scrolls of magic, of history, seeds from their most precious and beloved plants, paintings and other artworks, squares of stained glass. Representatives from each First Family that has decided to leave are called to a privy meeting and asked to help the General Council bear this grave burden. If each trusted mage carries a little, then a great deal can be saved.*

*The First Families agree.*

*The General Council convenes for the last time in swiftly decaying Elvado's beautiful Hall of Knowledge. The mages of Dorana cannot flee north, for beyond the northern borders of Brantone and Feen there is naught but wilderness, bleak and inhospitable. They cannot seek safety beyond the east or west coasts, for Dorana is landlocked with no tradition of the sea. Nor will they find comfort in the lands of their immediate neighbours, whose warriors ride towards them with innocent blood on their hands. Dorana's mages have but one choice: they must flee south. In fleeing south, only Manemli will stand between them and the unblighted lands of Vharne, Iringa and mysterious Benbarsk. In one of those three nations they will surely find respite.*

*The terrible exodus begins.*

*Within a day, they are dying from mage-mist. There is no time for funerals. The dead are left behind. Thousands of mages struggle and straggle across blighted Dorana, bewildered by these unimaginable events. Their bludgeoning fear is a blessing. It makes them docile, and easier to lead.*

*Soaked in grief and guilt, Barl rides in a pony cart, desperately working on the magics they will need to escape, letting her brother and Venette Martain and Dreen Brislyn and the General Council shepherd the frightened mages of Dorana towards the unknown.*

*The princes and potentates command many warriors, but not enough to encompass Dorana's entire border. Imperfectly shielded by Barl's blurring magics, the fleeing mages cross into northern Manemli, where blight has chased the inhabitants south. The General Council decides they will seek shelter in Vharne. Though its people are warriors, they are kindlier than the Iringans. Surely they will understand the mages of Dorana mean no harm.*

*But the very old, the very young, the sick and infirm, they travel too slowly. The princes and potentates' pursuing warriors find them before they reach the border with Vharne. Terrified, the mages try to defend themselves with magework. Blood is spilled on both sides.*

*And in spilling warrior blood with magic, Dorana's mages seal their fate.*

*Chased and chivvied and harried, they are scattered like pigeons by the falcon as it stoops to strike. With wildfire word spreading of the warriors killed by magework, warriors of Vharne and Iringa sharpen swords and spears and join the hunt. Every hand is raised against Dorana's mages. No kindness, no mercy, no impulse to forgive. They have proven themselves the enemy. Nothing Doranen can be trusted. The only good mage is a dead mage . . . and mages can die.*

*In the weeks that follow, Dorana's homeless are hunted out of the lands that once welcomed their magework and paid good coin for the privilege of its possession. The weakest perish, the strong survive. They are a proud people reduced to beggary, to*

579

the startlement of rabbits. They are hunted into Benbarsk, where
the princes and potentates fear to tread. Benbarsk is a harsh
land, as deadly as any sword or spear. Its reclusive people are
unfriendly, suspicious of the outside world. Vharne and Iringa
know better than to rile them.

So the princes and potentates reach an agreement: warriors
of every nation will line the Benbarsk border, keeping the hated
mages safely penned. Let Benbarsk finish what they were forced
to start. Let Dorana die there, in that strange, brutal land.

Let it be forgotten . . . and good riddance.


One by one, in the brutal aftermath of flight, the trapped mages
of Dorana find each other in Benbarsk's wilderness. Thin and
ragged, they come together to count the cost of their flight. So
many left behind. So many dead. But they have their magework
and their memories. Not all is lost.

They look to Venette Martain, Barl Lindin, her brother
Remmie and Dreen Brislyn for leadership. They despair of ever
seeing Dorana again. They look around them at the rich emptiness that is Benbarsk, and wonder. Could this be their new
home? Could Dorana be reborn here?

And then Barl has a dream . . .


Snared in his beloved's perfidy, trapped by her poisoned love,
Morgan pursues his escape with a bitter, dogged patience.
Though he is trapped, cocooned in magic, bound and bound
again, still there are tears in him. Still he can weep. He weeps
when he's not screaming. He screams when he can no longer
weep.

You left me. You left me. Barl, my love, how could you? You
bitch, you slut, you treacherous whore.

He can feel her, of course. There is nowhere beneath the sun
that she can run to where he'll not feel her. Won't find her. Will
fail to know. And when he breaks free of her binding . . . when
he is once more a man . . .

You will say you're sorry. You will . . . apologise . . . to me.

*Through Barl's fading incants he can feel Dorana's writhing, rotting anguish. The unbalanced magics lash like a wounded snowcat's tail. But he can use them. They feed him. They make him stronger with every slow breath. In binding him, Barl has freed him. In being bound, he's found himself.*

My love, without meaning to you have done me a favour.

*But that does not mean she is forgiven. Oh, no.*

*Nursing his strength, coddling his fury, Morgan pursues his escape.*

581

# CHAPTER THIRTY-FIVE

Brimful of foreboding, unable to sleep, Jervale left his wife snoring and slipped outside their crumbling mud brick cottage to wait for dawn. Lur's night sky was cruelly clear, not even a hint of cloud . . . and no moisture in the air, either. Underfoot, the dead grass made a helpless, crackling sound. Three years, was it, since the last spit of rain had fallen on the cottage's roof? No. Longer than that. Closer to four, by now. Must be. He'd given up properly counting. Too sad a pastime, that was. Not that he had any right to complain. Other hamlets had been rainless almost twice as long. In these dry, dispirited days his wet childhood felt like a dream.

As he pottered down the starlit cart track to his favourite rock by the good-as-dead creeklet, passing his neighbours' unlit mud-brick dwellings, he caught the low, fretful wail of Tam and Rinna's new baby. Poor little mite. It'd be dead soon. He'd seen it. But he'd not told Tam and Rinna, for what was the point? Knowing wouldn't save their baby. There was no medicine could save a sickly life born too soon. Besides, like most folk, Tam and Rinna wanted to live in hope.

Grunting only a little bit, surefooted in the near dark, he climbed the weathered lump of sandstone that was the best fishing vantage point above the creeklet. Used to be, anyway, back when there was water. And fish. Twice a man's height, in daylight it let him see all the way down to the creeklet's lazy bend on the hamlet's western edge. Looking t'other way, with eyes shaded he'd see east to the cliff above Fogget's ravine.

Settling his bony arse onto the rock, he shivered. The cliff. Eleven days since Ma Gammil had pitched herself off it, to smash herself to pieces at the bottom. Why hadn't he seen that coming? He'd have stopped her jumping, if he had.

But no. Aside from a quick glimpse of that poor little baby, all he'd seen for weeks now was the starved, terror-pinched faces of the strangers with pale yellow hair, who climbed over the mountains dragging death behind them. The strangers he'd dreamed as a small boy, who he'd not dreamed again 'til three round moons ago.

Now he dreamed them every night, snatches and flashes of other lives, other places. He dreamed a beautiful city fallen into decay. Terrible winged creatures with eyes that used to be human. A young woman and an older man, their long hair sunlight golden, their eyes startling blue as they pulled fire from thin air. He wept when he dreamed them, for the love and the loss.

His belly rumbled, complaining. He ignored it. What kind of father filled his own belly and left his child's empty? Tilda was a growing girl. They'd buried three babes before she was born. He and Bene were agreed. No matter what they suffered, their daughter would survive the grinding hard times that had Lur beaten to its knees and whimpering.

*She has to survive. For she's like me, my Tilly, and Lur needs her to live.*

He couldn't say why he was so certain of that. He only knew he was, that the feeling was a lot more than a father's love for his child . . . and that if he ignored his quiet, insistent, inner voice he might as well pitch himself off the cliff.

The waning night was so silent. Lur's drought had killed a lot of birds. It was slowly killing everything. He didn't need his dreams to know that. He was an Olken, born hearing the earth's song . . . and the earth had stopped singing. It was weeping now. Wailing. And not even Lur's best earth-singers knew a lullaby to soothe it.

*Why can't I dream a lullaby, instead of these strangers?*

As he sat on his sandstone rock, waiting for the future to become the present, he watched the stars fade and the sun rise. Looked down into the parched creeklet, counting skeleton fish and dry rocks. Last of all he looked north, to the smudge of mountains on the distant horizon. He'd dreamed them, too. Dreamed them shimmering and golden, filled with a power that stole his breath. They didn't have a name. They were simply *the mountains*. No-one knew what lay beyond their high jagged peaks. No-one cared to find out. The Olken weren't an adventurous people. They lived small and peaceful lives.

*At least we used to. But that's about to change.*

He might not know exactly how, but he was certain it would be soon. The crawling sensation between his shoulder blades never lied. The leaping pulse of his blood, that was a truth-teller, too. Lur was about to get itself tipped topsy-turvy. As fervently as ever he wished for rain, he wished he was wrong, but he wasn't. The things he saw came true. Always. That was his curse.

Tilly laughed when he walked into the mud brick cottage's kitchen, and waved her little spoon at him. The old whittled wood was yellow with egg.

'Pa! Pa! There you are, Pa!'

'Yes, there you are, Pa,' said Bene, half-smiling, half-frowning, seated beside their daughter at the weathered wooden table. 'And where have you been?'

As always, his heart skipped when he saw his wife. Twenty-one summers had passed since the first time, at the winter fair the year he turned nineteen, but he still felt like a young lad tumbling headfirst into love. It upset her when he slipped away while she slept. His dreams upset her. It was hard for her, knotted with a man who oft could see what would be more clearly than what was. He'd long ago told her what he waited for. He and Bene had no secrets. But Tilly was a bright child, and he didn't want to alarm her.

584

'Counting crickets,' he said lightly, and kissed Tilly's cheek three times, noisy fat splutters that made her kick and squeal. 'Is there egg for me?'

He and Bene shared a small, scrambled yolk, and drank hot potle tea. Tilly guzzled goat's milk, coaxed from the hamlet's little flock. A good thing goats were hardy. The last milkless cow had been butchered weeks ago, for its stringy meat and thin blood.

A knock on the cottage's front door just as breakfast finished had Tilly squealing again. It was Fern, Mag's youngest, who minded the hamlet's little ones during the long, hot days while their parents toiled to keep everyone alive.

'Jervale?' With Tilly safely gone to play with her friends, Bene stopped pretending. She dropped their spoons in the drawer then folded her arms. 'Is it happening? What you've been dreaming? Is that why you couldn't sleep?'

Feeling wretched, he tipped grease-stained scouring sand out of the fry pan and into its wooden pail on the end of the kitchen bench. 'I reckon so.'

Her brown eyes wide with trepidation, Bene sat on the rickety kitchen stool. 'Oh, Jervale. What are you going to do?'

He'd been thinking about that. He wasn't ready to tell anyone else what he knew. They'd never believe him . . . and even if they did, it wouldn't make a difference. He was bound up in this, as a bone was bound in muscle. The dreams were his. And so was the saving of Lur.

'Well,' he said slowly, knowing Bene wouldn't like it, 'when word comes from the Black Woods that these yellow-haired folk have appeared, there'll be a call to council. I'll put my hand up to speak for the hamlet. It's a long cart ride to the mountains. Merrin won't want to go.'

'So you'll go?' Bene twisted her fingers in her lap. 'And then what? Jervale, what can you do about these folk?'

Dropping to a crouch before her, he gave her knees a comforting pinch. 'I don't know. But I have to do this, Bene. I'll be needed there.'

Her lips trembled. 'You're needed here.'

She understood how important this was. She wasn't really trying to stop him. He kissed her fingers, then her trembling lips. 'We've a little time yet. I'll work hard 'til then, I promise. I'll make this up to you, Bene. I won't leave you wanting.'

Her laugh had weeping in it. 'Jervale, you always leave me wanting. Too much of you is never enough.'

Suffocated with love for her, he crushed her close to his chest. And then they joined their friends and neighbours in the hamlet's struggling fields, where they foraged and toiled and charmed survival from the weeping land.

Three days later, the hamlet's elder, Merrin, called everyone to the hall.

'Something's happened,' the old man said, his voice quavering. 'There's word come through the stone.' His gnarled fingers touched the chiming crystal that kept Lur's far-flung hamlets and villages connected. 'Strangers have come into Lur, from over the mountains.'

Theirs was a small community. One hundred and twelve folk didn't quite fill the meeting hall . . . but they made a lot of noise when they were taken by surprise. Seated two bench rows from the front, Jervale took Bene's callused hand and dropped a kiss to Tilly's dark head.

'Settle now, settle,' Merrin said, waving them quiet. 'And I'll tell you what I'm told. They've travelled a long way, these strangers, from far, far to the north. Their homeland fell into a sickness, worse even than our drought. If they wanted to live, they had to flee. So they did. Now it's our help they're asking for.'

Murmurs and mutterings as the hamlet's folk shifted restless in their seats. Lur was a land apart, and the Olken liked it that way.

'Are they saying there ain't other folk beyond the mountains to lend a hand?' That was Mag, ever the first to speak. 'Sounds odd to me, that does. And how did they cross the mountains, Merrin? Everyone knows they ain't passable.'

Troubled, Merrin rubbed his chin. 'Seems these strangers found a way. Seems . . .' He shook his head. 'They call 'emselves *mages*.'

Blank stares around the hall. More lively discussion.

'What's a mage?' said Tam, whose baby was going to die. 'And who's telling us all this, Merrin? D'you say these *mages* speak our tongue? How likely is that?'

'I'm told this by Elder Chaffie of Gribley village, in the Black Woods. As to how she knows their story, I couldn't say. But she ain't a liar.'

And neither was Merrin. Since they all knew that, Tam said nothing more.

'Chaffie's sent a call to every hamlet and village,' Merrin added. 'There's decisions to be made, she says. So one of us'll have to go.'

'To the *Black Woods*?' said Mag, shocked. 'Are you sunstruck?'

No lively discussion this time, just an uproar. The furthest anyone in the hamlet ever travelled was four days to reach the winter fair at Bram. It had taken the best part of a year before folk stopped marvelling that Jervale was come from Tabstock, and that *two weeks* away.

Beside him, Bene sighed. 'Go on, then,' she murmured. 'I know you have to.'

He smiled, loving her, then wriggled out of his seat. When he couldn't make himself heard, he climbed onto it and waved his arms till Merrin noticed and banged the meeting gong.

When the uproar was died down to mutters and murmurs, Jervale climbed down off his seat. 'I'll go to Gribley, Merrin, and speak for the hamlet.'

Merrin nodded, pleased. 'And a fine speaker you'll make, Jervale. You'll take a chiming stone so we can talk on things, and the best cart, and the two strongest donkeys. As much food as we can spare you, which means you'll need to eat but once a day.'

He wasn't eating much more than that now. He'd manage, and eke extra on the road. 'Yes, Merrin.'

'Chaffie's all a-bustle. You'll want to leave at first light. Bene, you'll bide with this?'

Bene held his hand, hard. 'I'll bide with it, Merrin. For I know Jervale will do the right thing.'

Everyone clustered around him and Bene and Tilly, after.

Slapping his shoulder. Wishing him luck. The shock of the news was yet to fade. It was a wonder the hall's roof didn't fall in, there was so much loud chatter. As they were leaving, at last, Merrin pulled him aside.

'You be careful, Jervale,' he said, his expression serious. 'Ask lots of questions. It's a boggling thing, what's happened, and a sad story these *mages* have told, right enough, but like our Mag noticed, it's a story with holes in it.' He grimaced. 'And I ain't fond of holes.'

Feeling a warm rush of affection, Jervale patted the old man's arm. 'Never fear, Merrin. I've my Tilly to think on. I'll not bare our throats to any wolves.'

Not if he could help it, anyway. Not unless his dreams told him to. And even then, not without a fight.


Leaving Bene and Tilly was a misery. The whole hamlet gathered to see him go, and most everyone pressed a little something into his hands. A shrivelled apple. A boiled egg. A few elderly, withered carrots. Food they could hardly spare, that he couldn't refuse for fear of hurting them. Tam and Rinna gave him a flask of precious barley wine. Kissing his wife for the last time, Jervale murmured into her ear.

'Stay close to them, Bene. They'll need you soon.'

She pulled back, her eyes full of grief and understanding. Three babes, they'd lost. This was Tam and Rinna's first.

'Pa! Pa!' Tilly held out her arms, bouncing on Bene's hip. 'Kiss me, Pa! Kiss me!'

He kissed his daughter, holding her tenderly and tight. She patted his cheek with her grubby little hand.

'Go see the people, Pa. They've got yellow hair, like straw.'

His heart thudded hard, sickening, but only Bene had heard. 'Yes, Tilly, that's right,' he whispered. 'But never say that again. Never talk about the people. They're our special secret.'

'Pa,' she said, and hugged him. 'Come home soon, Pa.'

He drove out of the hamlet with his head high and his back straight, and didn't weep 'til he was well out of sight.

\* \* \*

Almost halfway to the Black Woods he joined up with two others making the same long trip. It was good to have company after nearly three weeks on the road with only the donkeys to talk to, his dreams to steal sleep and Lur's suffering lands to fret him. So far now from the hamlet, he'd hoped to see a sign that there'd been a little rain *somewhere*. That the long drought was easing. That the threat of famine was in retreat.

But no.

'I don't recall things ever being so grim,' said Bannet of Salting village, astride his dusty, ribby horse. 'These *mages* come to us for help? We can't help ourselves. We can't hardly feed our own children. What makes 'em think we can feed theirs?'

Jervale slapped his reins against the donkeys' peaky rumps. 'Salting village thinks to turn 'em away?'

Bannet shrugged. 'Salting village wants to know more about 'em.'

Riding a spit ahead of them on her own underfed nag was Del, from the southern fishing village of Westwailing. She was a comely lass, with a bright flirting in her eye. Something about her made Jervale stare. He couldn't hammer a nail into it. He only knew that his bones jumped every time she spoke.

'Lur's fishing folk don't much care for the notion of feedin' strangers,' she said, scornful, shifting round in her saddle. 'Every elder I'm speakin' for told me to tell these mages the same thing. *Go back where you came from. Lur's got fratches of its own.*' She shrugged. 'So that's what I'll tell 'em. Too sinkin' bad if they don't like it.'

'Jervale, your face says you reckon they won't,' said Bannet, uneasy. 'What are we riding into, d'you say?'

He found them companionable, but he wasn't about to trust them with his dreams. 'I try not to think on it, Bannet. We'll learn what's what when we get to Gribley.'

Three of them travelling together found it easier to forage food. Their earth-singing was stronger in a chorus, their inter-weaving voices helping to drown out the earth's piteous groans. They charmed rabbits and wild pigeons and even fish from a puddling lake. But even so, they could feel Lur's changes, a slow dying beneath its parched, brown skin. It seemed likely these strange *mages* would end up sorry they'd come.

*I know we will*, Jervale thought morosely, woken yet again out of violent dreams.

And that was the worst of it. Huddled on the cold ground under his blanket, listening to Bannet snore and Del stir restless on his other side, and the donkeys and the horses rattling their hobbles, he tucked his fingers into his armpits and tried to forget what he'd seen.

*But how can I forget all that blood? How am I meant not to remember black hail and crimson lightning?*

He didn't know. He only knew he had to stop it from happening. Or else why did he dream?

*'My love, how could you do this? You bitch, you slut, you treacherous whore . . .'*

Anguished, Barl twisted and moaned on her rough, lonely cot.

*'This binding won't hold me forever, Barl. You know I'll break free of it. You know I will find you.'*

Sobbing, breathless, she hid her face in her hands. 'If I can't see you, Morgan, then you can't see me.'

It was a child's way of thinking. She heard him laugh, vicious with pain. *'You cannot hide from me. I live in your soul.'*

'No,' she said, weeping. 'That's not true.'

*'You left me, Barl. You left me.'* He sounded heartbroken. Bereft. *'How could you do that when I love you more than life?'*

'I didn't have a choice.'

*'We all have a choice, my love. And every choice has a consequence. You're going to learn that, soon enough.'*

'No!' she shouted, tumbling out of her makeshift bed. And then she gasped as glimfire ignited, leavening the dark.

'Morgan again?' said Remmie tiredly, ducking inside her tent. The glimfire came in with him, cheerful as a firefly. 'Barl, you should take a sleeping posset.'

She shook her head. 'I tried. It doesn't help. He still finds me.' A shudder. 'He always finds me.'

The first time, in Benbarsk, she'd thought it was a dream. But then she'd heard him while she was waking . . . and realised no, it was real. Somehow he'd found a way to cross the vast distance between them. Her warded binding was weakening. One day, he'd break free.

*And when that day comes . . .*

He was mad now. He was a madman. Whenever his mind touched hers she could feel its warped twisting. Those terrible catalysts he'd used to create the beasting incant. The night he'd spent using it, killing all those mages and his soul along with them.

*Our magic destroyed him. Justice save me, he's past saving.*

If she'd been alone, she'd have howled her grief aloud.

Remmie eased her back onto the cot, then sat cross-legged beside her on the felt matting floor. 'It'll be light soon. Or as light as it gets in these sun-forsaken woods. You're tired, Barl. Rest.'

Yes, she was tired. But how could she rest when she was so heartsick it was hard to breathe?

*Remmie and I, we are two of only one thousand, seven hundred and sixty-four living Doranen, that we know of for certain. Before we abandoned Dorana there were at least a hundred times as many.*

Memory taunted her with the faces she'd never see again. Ibbitha. Master Arndel and his artisans. Lady Grie with her careless favours. Barton Haye and Remmie's pupils. All left behind or dead or swallowed by the hostile lands beyond Dorana.

But her sorrow was nothing compared to Remmie's. Poor Remmie. Having found his Irielle, he'd lost her again. The girl from Granley had perished in the slaughter near Vharne. He never spoke of her. Whatever grief he felt remained locked in his heart. But despite that, somehow he'd forgiven her, for everything. Irielle. Morgan. All their dead and maimed. The nightmares. The hauntings. The loss of home and hope.

Overwhelmed, she let the tears fall.

'Don't, Barl,' Remmie said gently. He was her other self, and always knew. 'What's done is done. And you know, I've been thinking. We've been gone a long time now. Dorana could be

591

healing. It might not be ruined after all. And a lot of people stayed behind.'

The horror of the dream – or whatever it was – crashed over her. 'To face what, when Morgan is free? Remmie, when he breaks my binding he'll—'

'You don't know he'll break it,' Remmie said quickly. 'Barl, don't—'

'But I *do* know,' she said, shivering again. 'Why else did I push Venette until she agreed we should keep running, risk those terrible mountains, if I wasn't *sure* he was a danger?'

Remmie dropped his gaze. And because she was *his* other self, and always knew, she knew what it was he'd not allow himself to say.

*Why did it take you so long to see the truth of him? Why did so many of us have to die before you'd believe?*

The answers were a whip, flogging her. She couldn't bear to give them a voice. Instead she touched his knee.

'You should be in bed, Remmie. You're as tired as I am.'

'I was helping Pother Ranmer. Barl . . .' He looked up. 'Someone else has died.'

She should weep for the loss. But after so many deaths her soul felt as dry as this dry land they'd stumbled into.

'Who was it?' she said at last. 'Don't say another child.'

Because too many children had perished already. Dorana's sad future, buried in tiny little graves.

'It was Councillor Horbeck.'

Oh. Well, yes. Once blood-rot set in, there was little anyone could do, even a skilled pother like Ranmer. Ever since the councillor fell off that treacherous mountain ledge, she'd known it was simply a matter of time. And with Horbeck dead, so too died the General Council. Dreen Brislyn had perished in Benbarsk. Mauled by a bear. Perhaps when they were settled in their new home they'd create a new council. That was what civilised people did, after all.

'But I'm not going to fret on it,' Remmie added. 'We still have Venette to lead us. The Council of Mages lives on in her. And we have you, Barl.'

'No, we have you. How many times must I say it, Remmie? Don't look for me to play councillor. I'm not about to tell other mages what to do. Not when—'

*Not when I'm responsible for their plight.*

'All right, all right,' he said, hands lifting. 'I'm too tired to argue.'

Fine. Then they could talk about something that had been puzzling her.

'Remmie. This place. *Lur*. There's another power here, in the bones of the land. Separate from the power we feel everywhere else, as mages. And it's not like anything I've ever felt before. When I touch it I feel . . . *different*.' But that sounded like nonsense. She scrubbed her face with her hands. 'Oh, I don't know. Perhaps it's all in my mind.'

'No, I feel it too,' said Remmie, sighing. 'And so does Venette, I think. Maybe some of the others, though many of us are still so ill and injured and weak, it might be weeks before we can be sure.' He bit his lip. 'What d'you think it means?'

She frowned. 'I don't know. But I'm going to find out. We ran from Dorana because of my mistakes, Remmie. And we're in Lur because Venette – because *everyone* – trusted me. I won't have brought us here to die.'

'You can't think this power is dangerous. Not to *us*.'

'Why? Because we're the vaunted mages of Dorana?' She snorted. 'Now who's being arrogant? Surely I've proven we're as vulnerable to magic as any magickless race.'

His lips pinched at that. 'Barl, if we're in danger here it's the same danger the Olken face.'

And that much was true. Nearly all the talk of the Black Woods villagers was about Lur's drought, its worsening famine, the growing fear that rain might not fall again before it was too late. True, there were underground springs but they were starting to run dry. Even the abundant Black Woods were showing the strain . . . especially now, with so many Doranen mouths to feed.

But if she thought about that, about a natural calamity she had no power to undo, she'd curl into a ball and weep herself into oblivion. She considered another puzzle instead.

'I wonder how it is these Olken don't realise they're mages?'

'But they aren't,' Remmie said, surprised. 'They have no mage-work. Not even glimfire.'

'They have an affinity with the land. You must have felt that, too. Doesn't that make them mages?'

Stifling a yawn, he shook his head. 'No more than a fly having wings makes it a falcon.'

And perhaps he was right. But she couldn't shake the odd feeling that there was something important in this. Something she shouldn't ignore.

'Go to bed, Remmie. You need sleep.'

He stood, laboriously. Stared down at her, his brows pinched. 'So do you.'

He was so thin. So unlike his Doranen self. The Olken had scrounged clothes for him, tatty roughspun and tanned hides. The trousers were too short. These Olken weren't a tall people. His pale, bare ankles looked so vulnerable. Easy to snap. His face looked vulnerable, too. Months ago he'd hacked his hair short because, in the wilderness, long hair got in the way. A fading pink scar ran in a puckered line from the corner of his left eye down his cheek, where a Feenish warrior had caught him with the tip of his sword. And coming over the mountains he'd missed his footing and nearly plunged to his death. The fall hurt his hip, and now he walked with a limp. And his eyes . . . they were so sad. Crowded with the things he'd seen, and memories of the people he would never see again.

'Sleep through the day, Rem,' she said, her throat tight. 'You might as well. We've nowhere to be.'

'I will if you will,' he retorted, and left her.

Since he'd taken his glimfire with her, she conjured her own. Then she rummaged in her satchel for the battered diary she'd kept during their flight from Dorana.

It was a rambling, disjointed thing. Odds and ends of obser-vations as they fought their way south. A scribbling of incants and sigils that she didn't want to forget and hadn't been able to carry with her in books or scrolls. Old, obscure warbeast incants she'd found in papers taken from the Hall by one of its archivists. Caught alone, once, she'd used them in Manemli. Dreadful things. *Dreadful*. With the archivist spitted on a Trindeki spear, she'd copied the incants to the diary then burned that page without compunction. She trusted herself with destructive magework. Nobody else. On other pages she'd scribbled ideas for new incants. Not because she thought she'd have the chance to create them, but because it was one way to stop herself from going mad.

Most helpful of all, the ancient incant used between races so that strangers might speak. That one she had from a College scholar. She was dead now too. Snake bite in the mountains. The Black Woods' villagers already had the benefit of the incant, and in time every Olken in Lur would receive it. There could be no misunderstandings between the Doranen and their hosts.

Using borrowed ink and quill, she made a note of her thoughts about the power she felt in this land. About the Olken and what she could feel in them. Then, suddenly restless, she tossed the diary aside. Slid off the cot, tugged back the felt matting between herself and the ground, and stretched out with her palm pressed lightly to the dry dirt. Straight away she felt that humming of unfamiliar power. Sighed as it whispered through her flesh and bones. It was warm. It was gentle. Not like brash Doranen magic. But still, there was a depth to it. A strength. A *promise*.

But a promise of what?

*What if I could find a way to meld Doranen and Olken magics? Would that give me enough power to keep Morgan at bay?*

She didn't know. But it was an idea she had to explore, because Morgan was coming. She knew it with a suffocating certainty. A smothering dread. And she knew that without help, she had no hope of defeating him.

When at last she stirred out of thought, her mind whirling with an idea so fantastic she wondered if she'd gone mad, tree-filtered daylight crept through the tent's drawn flap and she could hear the rise and fall of adult voices in their makeshift camp. The higher, welcome voices of the children who'd survived. Stiff and hungry, she picked herself up and went in search of an unused privy hole.

Walking back through the close-pressing trees afterwards, she came face to face with Maris Garrick. Felt herself tense, with dislike and resentment.

*Of course she had to survive. Why her, and not Irielle of Granley? Or Dreen Brislyn? Or any other mage?*

But that was a horrible thing to think.

'Wait,' she said, as sneering Maris turned away. 'Have you handed over any books or pamphlets or old scrolls of incants still in your safe-keeping?'

Maris was dreadfully thin now, her hair dull, her face drawn. But though she'd suffered, she'd lost none of her haughtiness. 'Ehrig and I didn't bring any,' she said, looking down her nose. 'Our parents had them.'

And their parents were dead.

Barl winced. 'I'm sorry, I didn't mean to – Maris, *wait*.'

Breathing harshly, Maris stopped. 'What?'

'I know we can't be friends, not after—' She felt a surge of belated shame. 'Only . . . Maris, there are so few of us now. Can't we put aside our differences and work together, for the good of—'

'*No*,' said Maris, coldly. 'Don't speak to me again.'

Disappointed, but not surprised, Barl made her way to the camp's communal area, where several mages and a handful of youngsters were eating an early breakfast. Small bowls of honey-sweetened porridge. Tart berries and apples. A meagre offering of eggs. Compared to the paucity of the mountains, it was plenty . . . but remembering Dorana's bounty made the meal harder to accept.

Venette sat on a roughly sawed log, sipping sour Olken tea from a wooden mug. She seemed content, which was remarkable for a mage who'd spent her life drinking vintage icewine out of jewel-crusted gold cups.

'Barl,' she said, faintly smiling. 'Join me.'

She was the highest-ranked surviving mage and the only councillor they had left, and she took both responsibilities seriously. Working almost without respite from dawn to dusk and later, cooking and cleaning, helping their three pothers, easing the hearts of orphaned children, the grief of mothers who'd lost their children and wives who'd lost husbands, she never complained or shirked no matter her exhaustion.

Barl shoved another rough log closer.

*I hated her once. How times have changed.*

She should tell Venette about the dream. If she didn't, Remmie would. And she should confide in her the thoughts she'd had about protecting them from Morgan. But they were only half-formed . . . and the magework she'd need didn't even exist. Not yet, at least.

*And it might never exist if I fail to create it.*

Venette lifted an eyebrow. 'Barl?'

'I saw Maris,' she said, to divert her. 'She says they have no books for our library.'

'Yes, she told me the same thing,' said Venette. 'And it's hardly a library. A motley collection of mostly useless information is what it is. Or will be, when I've done nagging everybody.'

But it was all they had left of Dorana, so it was precious. 'You know about Councillor Horbeck?'

Sighing, Venette rested the emptied mug on her thigh. 'I do. But on the other hand, my dear, four of us are pregnant. Relief, it seems, is a potent aphrodisiac.'

'*Pregnant?*' She stared. 'I suppose that's good. Isn't it?'

'Is it?' Venette murmured. 'Let's hope so.'

'It must be, surely. When so many of us—'

And then she stopped, because here came Chaffie, the wizened elder of the Black Woods' village they'd stumbled into three-quarters dead, nearly two months ago.

'Good morrow to you, mages,' the Olken greeted them. 'The last of our people have arrived in Gribley to hear your story. We're in the hall, gathered and waiting. Can you come?'

# CHAPTER THIRTY-SIX

It was the oddest thing, Jervale thought, to find himself staring at the face of a stranger he knew so well from his dreams.

*Mage Barl Lindin.*

She was young . . . and at the same time, dreadfully old. What she'd endured had aged her. It had aged her brother too. And the woman standing beside him, Lady Venette Martain, her eyes were as old as time itself.

These Doranen had suffered. It was harder to fear them, feeling their pain. But he couldn't let sympathy soften him. Suffering or not, they were dangerous.

Nearly one hundred of Lur's hamlets and villages had answered Elder Chaffie's call and sent someone to Gribley. Sitting with his new friends Bannet and Del, crowded into the village hall to hear the mages of Dorana tell their sorry tale, Jervale traced his fingertips over his still-tingling face, where Remmie Lindin had soaked magic into his flesh.

*They're speaking Doranen and I understand them. That seems unnatural. These are unnatural, powerful folk.*

Which begged the question . . . how in the name of all things green and growing was he supposed to stop them from destroying Lur? The task seemed impossible. He quailed at the thought.

*But if not me, then who? There ain't nobody else.*

Which hardly seemed fair.

Barl Lindin was into the meat of the Doranen's story now, fear and bloodshed and desperate doings, and her captivated Olken audience was aghast. Some of the women were weeping. All the poor little children. The cruelty of death.

But the Doranen mage was telling them lies.

Or not lies, exactly. Just . . . not the whole truth. She was leaving things out, things he'd seen in his dreams or simply *knew*, when he looked at her. The handsome mage who terrified her. The dreadful thing she'd done, that helped bring about the fall of her people. And she'd done something. He could feel it, like a sharp knife carving in and out with his breathing.

Del of Westwailing leaned close. 'You all right there, Jervale?'

'Fine,' he whispered, and willed his pounding heart to ease.

Del didn't seem to notice the lie.

At last Barl Lindin finished her terrible story. Glanced at her brother, and Lady Martain, then turned back to the hall.

'Good people of Lur,' she said, sounding weary and sad, 'I know we must seem strange to you. Perhaps frightening.'

With a snap of her fingers she summoned fire from thin air, hovering it in a glowing ball above her outstretched palm. Jervale felt his heart pound even harder. It was just like his dream.

'Sink me,' muttered Del, beside him. 'That ain't right.'

She wasn't the only one who thought so. Around the hall, gasps and a rising tide of unease that could easily wash away sympathy.

Barl Lindin closed her fingers around the ball of fire, snuffing it out. 'And I know our magework must seem like a threat,' she added. 'It's not. But if you choose to disbelieve me, if you don't want to help us, we will leave your land peacefully. Only—' Her voice shook. 'I am begging you. *Do not turn us away.* For if you do we will perish to the last man, woman and child. The mages of Dorana will become bleached bones and scraps of faded linen. We do not deserve that.'

As the gathered Olken turned to each other to comment, Bannet leaned close. 'Mayhap they don't, but do we deserve to starve faster, with all of them to feed?'

'There ain't so many of 'em,' said Del, staring narrow-eyed at the mages. Staring longest at Barl Lindin's brother, a small, appreciative smile quirking her lips. 'Enough to fill a few villages, and a hamlet or two.'

Bannet grunted. 'Until they start breeding. D'you tell me they won't?'

'You'd drive them away so they can die?' Del frowned. 'That's harsh, that is.'

'Eh?' Bannet gaped at her. 'You're the one said there'd be no helping them.'

'The fishing village elders said that,' Del said, shrugging. 'But I've seen 'em now, ain't I? I've heard their sad story.'

With another grunt, Bannet folded his arms. 'Got yourself an itch for that scarred mage, you mean. Hussy.' Ignoring Del's protest, he jerked his chin. 'Jervale, what's your thought?'

Not one he could share. 'That we've a lot of talking ahead of us, and—'

'Mage Lindin,' said Elder Chaffie, sitting in the crowded hall's front row, as was proper. 'We're not heartless, but Lur's got its own strife. There's crops failing. Rivers running dry. Skin and bone livestock dropping dead and still-birthing their young. If our woes keep on, could be we'll need to escape over the mountains ourselves.'

Again, Barl Lindin looked at the other mages. Then she took a step closer to Elder Chaffie. 'You mustn't,' she said, her eyes terrible. 'For one thing, the crossing will kill you, as it killed many of us. Those mountains are treacherous. Unforgiving. Believe me, you don't want to watch your loved ones plunge to their deaths, as we have. You don't want to sit helplessly beside them as they die in agony from snake bite, or because they ate a poison berry.' She took a deep breath, shuddering. 'Besides, as bad as things are in Lur, beyond the mountains they're worse. Those lands are blighted by rogue magics and fear, and their princes and potentates are no friends to strangers. Whoever survives the mountains will be slaughtered without mercy.'

A frightened silence followed her stark words.

'But hope here is not lost,' Barl Lindin continued. 'I know things are dire, but the mages of Dorana can help you. All we need is your trust.'

Watching closely, Jervale saw her brother and Lady Martain fail to hide their surprise. And that surprised him.

*So she's keeping more secrets? What's she got up her grubby sleeve?*

Elder Chaffie found her feet. 'Posing riddles ain't the way to win us over. Plain speaking, Mage Lindin, if you please.'

Barl Lindin smoothed the skirt of her roughspun dress. 'Plainly speaking, Elder Chaffie, I'm not ready to say. But when I am, I—'

With a sharp look at his sister, Remmie Lindin stepped forward. 'Elder Chaffie, I think we've already given you a great deal to think on. We'll withdraw now, so you can talk about us freely. Thank you.'

Before Barl Lindin could object, her brother was hustling her from the hall. Lady Martain followed them, her expression unreadable.

Elder Chaffie turned to face everyone. 'Right, then. Let's mingle a while and talk this over.'

A shuffling of feet amid excited chatter. Jervale looked at Bannet and Del. 'Need to water a tree,' he muttered. 'I'll be back by and by.'

Under cover of the noisy crowd, he slipped from the hall. Saw Remmie Lindin and Lady Martain walking towards the mage camp, slowly, on account of his limp. But where was Barl Lindin?

A flash of movement turned him towards the northern edge of Gribley village. Yellow hair and a straight back clad in ill-fitting roughspun. Remmie Lindin's untruthful, surprising sister. He plunged after her.

The Black Woods swiftly swallowed them. A scritch-scritch of squirrels dancing in branches overhead. The low, plaintive *bo-bo-no* of a wood pigeon. A breeze soughing through dry leaves. Brooding unseen above them, the might of the mountains.

The slight shift of her head showed that Barl Lindin knew she was being followed, but she didn't stop until the village was merely a murmuring hint behind them. Then she turned.

'If you're worried I'll lose myself, you needn't be,' she said, raising her voice. 'The mages of Dorana don't get lost.'

Once they were close enough for comfortable talking, Jervale slowed to a halt. Thought of fire plucked from thin air, and straightened his shoulders.

*She won't hurt me. She can't. Lur's not done with me yet.*

'Are you sure, Mage Lindin? You look mighty lost to me.'

Her clear blue eyes, beautiful as a summer lake, sharpened with suspicion. 'Who are you?'

'My name's Jervale,' he said, politely enough. 'Mage Lindin, you know he won't rest 'til he's found you.'

She was already pale from her long ordeal, but her face drained so colourless he thought for a moment she might faint. Still, he couldn't let that put a bridle on his tongue.

'You did your best to fettle him, but he's stronger than you thought. Isn't he?'

'What d'you—' Her voice cracked. 'I've no idea what—'

He raised a finger at her, as though she was his Tilly. 'Tell another lie and I promise, there'll be mischief.'

'*Another* lie? I haven't lied. Everything I said in that hall is true.'

'Sometimes a lie gets told by leaving things out.'

Baffled, she folded her arms. 'Who *are* you?'

'I told you. Jervale. And I know things, Mage Lindin.'

Surrounded by the hushed woods, she stared at him, uncertain. He remembered her in his dreams, dressed in fine clothes, and laughing. A younger Barl. A happier Barl. This Barl Lindin's spirit was maimed.

He closed his eyes and heard the flapping of large, leathery wings.

'Mage Lindin,' he said, looking at her again, battered sick with dream memories. 'What d'you reckon'll happen when he

602

finds you? What d'you reckon'll he'll do to the woman who left him, and the folk who gave her shelter?'

Her eyes glittered in the shafting sunlight. 'You can't know this. How do you *know* this? And who have you told?'

'No-one,' he said, stepping closer. 'Yet. As for how I know, that don't matter. Just tell me, Mage Lindin. How can you keep us safe from a man who can do what he's done? You can't, can you? You did tell a lie.'

She flung up one hand in protest, or self-protection. Fearing fire, he leapt back and they stared at each other, breathing harshly.

'I wasn't – I'm not going to *hurt* you, Jervale!' She sounded shocked. 'Do you really think I'd—' And then, when he let his eyes speak for him, she pressed shaking fingers to her lips. 'Oh.' There was a fallen pitty-pine nearby. She sidled to it and sat on its trunk, heedless of creepy-crawlies and fungus. 'I don't understand,' she whispered. 'How do you *know*?'

He shrugged, in no mood to talk of his dreams. 'I just do. What's his name, Mage Lindin?'

For a long time she didn't answer, simply breathed in the sweet, living silence of the Black Woods.

'Morgan,' she said at last, her voice full of grief and longing. 'Morgan Danfey.'

'And you love him.'

She looked away. 'That's not your concern.'

Except it was. 'He loves you too. And he hates you. Love can turn to hate quick as a wink. You know that.'

'I don't—' She bit her lip. 'You knowing things. It's Olken magic, isn't it? Clearly, Jervale, you're a powerful mage.'

Surprised, he shook his head. 'I ain't a mage.'

'Of course you are,' she said, impatient, then stood. 'Show it to me. Your magic. I need to feel it, I need to know if—'

'If what?' he said, wary. The glitter in her eyes now wasn't unshed tears.

Arms folded again, tight to her ribs, Mage Lindin turned to stare into the woodland's depths. 'I didn't lie, Jervale. I do think I can save your people. And mine. But first I need to understand

Olken magic. I need to know if what I'm thinking is even *possible*. It might not be. And if it's not . . .'

Then the man she loved would find her . . . and Lur would be deafened by the sound of leathery wings.

She looked at him, her face naked. 'Will you help?'

Barl Lindin was the most dangerous creature he'd ever met. How could he help her, when helping her meant ruin for Lur? But that driving voice inside him was driving him now to say yes. He didn't understand.

'Please,' said Barl Lindin.

He knew so much about her . . . and knew nothing at all.

*If I trust her, and I'm wrong, Lur's ruin'll be my doing. And if I don't . . .*

If he didn't, and he was wrong, then that would mean ruin too.

Without warning the hushed Black Woods blurred, and he was thrust into the midst of a waking dream. Instead of crowding trees and leaf-filtered fingers of sunlight he was staring at Lur's heartland, the gently rolling hills covered in long, rich grass, the flat plain in ripening grain. The pasture was a lush, brilliant green and the ripening grain was turning gold like the sun. He could feel the sun gently warm on his face, not scorching, feel the gentle caress of a breeze, smell the richness of damp earth. And in his bones he could hear the damp earth's voice . . . but not as he'd ever heard it before. Now he could hear two voices singing, the sweetest of harmonies, the sweetest of songs. And he knew without knowing how that this was the magic of the Olken and the Doranen mingled, singing together for the plentiful bounty of Lur.

Gasping, he blinked . . . and was in the Black Woods again.

'What was that?' Barl Lindin demanded. 'Jervale, what just happened?'

He waved a hand at her for silence, and took a moment to breathe in and out, breathe hard, shake himself free of the vision.

*A vision which makes no sense at all. On the road I dreamed crimson lightning and black hail. Death and destruction for Lur. But now there's this – this bounty . . . and what does it mean?*

He didn't know. He didn't *know*. All the things he knew . . . why couldn't he know this?

'Jervale?' Barl Lindin almost sounded nervous. 'Are you ill?'

*Trust yourself,* Bene would say. *You always do what's right.*

Heart thudding, sweat trickling, Jervale shook his head. 'No. Just weary. It was a long road here.' He blotted his forehead on his sleeve. *Trust myself.* 'In Lur we don't call it magic. It's just – it's singing, to us.'

Her smile was swift and trembling. 'Then sing for me, Jervale. I have to hear you sing.'

There were foxes in the Black Woods. He coaxed two out of hiding, a vixen and her half-grown kit. Their pelts glowed brownish red in the dappling sunlight, eyes in their dark masks shiny and unafraid. Barl Lindin stared at them, silent. He held them in thrall for only a few moments, then released them.

'Well?' he said, when she didn't say a word.

Her beautiful eyes were wide in her thin, pale face. 'What else can you do?'

So he told her how the Olken lived in harmony with the land. How they sang the seeds in springtime, nurturing new life. Sang their crops to harvest in summer and autumn. How they hunted fish and game with kindness, never wasteful or cruel. How they felt the seasons, shifting, and the coming of the rain.

Or used to, before Lur's long and dreary dry spell.

'And can you feel the drought?' she asked, when he was finished. 'Does the earth's song sound different because there's no rain?'

She might be a great mage, but was she a lackwit too? 'Of course I can. Of course it does. Lur's in pain. We can feel it.'

'Strange,' she murmured. 'I can't. But even so, you can still . . . sing?'

'Yes, but it's harder. And it leaves us feeling sour.'

She looked at him intently. 'And if I could ease Lur's pain, Jervale? How would you feel about me then?'

She was a dangerous mage, he knew that much for certain. But even so, she wasn't wicked. She wasn't mad, like her Morgan

Danfey. And she could ease Lur's pain. He'd seen it, hadn't he? He'd felt the land's joy in his brief, waking vision.

*So she's our ruin and our saving? How can that be?*

He'd thought this was going to be simple. See the yellow-haired strangers for himself and speak out against them. Save Lur from the trouble they brought with them over the mountains.

*And now it's all got complicated. Bene, I wish you were here.*

'Well,' he said, cautious. 'I'd say you'd be owed something, Mage Lindin. If you could ease it.'

Up went her chin, so haughty. 'I can.'

'You say you can.'

'*I can,*' she insisted. 'I am a great mage. And if you know so much, you should know that.'

Trouble was, he did know it. Trouble was, he knew too much. Feeling sick, he nodded. 'Then I reckon you should save us.'

Her thin face lit with a fleeting smile. It made her beautiful. But then her eyes darkened with shadows, and before he could shift out of reach she wrapped her fingers round his wrist.

'You mustn't breathe a word of this, Jervale. Not to *anyone*. You must keep my secrets *secret*. Lur's safety depends on that. The life of every Olken and Doranen depends on it. Swear you won't repeat what you know, that you won't betray me. *Swear* it!'

He pulled himself free. 'I won't be swearing anything to the likes of you, Barl Lindin! Who are you to ask me to hold my tongue?'

'I'm the mage who wants to save Lur from the drought . . . and from Morgan. Would you be the mage who lets Lur wither, and bares its parched throat to his blade?'

The sharp question stabbed him. The weight of Lur and every Olken on his shoulders . . . he'd *never* asked for this.

'I told you,' he said, scowling. 'I ain't a mage.'

'Whatever you are, Jervale, you stand at a crossroads,' said Barl Lindin. Her eyes were glittering again, shadows chased away by purpose. 'And the fate of your people turns on this moment.'

She was so young. How could she be so dangerous and so *young*?

*The fate of my people . . . and her people . . . and the world.*

He felt his head swim. His blood thunder. He felt the ground tilt beneath his feet. Saw again that lush green farmland, and heard the twinned joyful voices singing in his bones. Instinct stirred again, sharply prodding.

'All right,' he muttered. 'I'll hold my tongue. For now. But if it seems to me you're rushing us down a road as'll lead nowhere but trouble, then I'll speak up. I'll have to. And if that time comes, you'll show us all what kind of mage you are. What kind of folk you are.' His belly twisted. 'You Doranen.'

And with that, he turned his back on her and walked away. What happened next would happen. He'd wait and see what else his dreams had to say.

Alone in the woods, Barl slid from the fallen tree-trunk to the cool, leaf-littered woodland floor and opened herself completely to the land of Lur. Watching the Olken, Jervale, as he'd summoned the foxes, feeling the way Lur's unique magic moved in him, moved him, feeling it suffuse her blood, she'd begun to see her way. Had seen, in brief glimpses, how she could weave Doranen and Olken magics together . . . or, at least, how it was possible. But whether she was mage enough to achieve such a feat was another question entirely.

*But I have to be. To fail is to condemn all of us to death.*

She had to keep reminding herself of that. It would be too easy to let fear incant her into a coward, if she didn't.

Surrendering to the power humming deep in the earth beneath her, she closed her eyes and breathed in the richness of the Black Woods. Breathed in hope. Breathed out fear. Breathed in the future. Breathed out the past. Drifted her mind through the books she'd studied in Morgan's library, incant after incant, her thoughts and the thoughts of Dorana's greatest mages shifting and coalescing into something uniquely her own.

The clock behind her eyes ceased its ticking. She was adrift in this new land, untethered from time, and only the whispering feet of a millepede running over her lax hand brought her back to bare earth and shafts of sunlight and the dark, dreadful feeling that once again, their time was running out.

She returned to her tent in the makeshift camp at the edge of Gribley village, and settled herself on the cot with her diary and a pen. Writing things down always helped her clarify a problem. Remmie found her there soon after, barging into the oiled-felt tent to glare down at her, his hands tight fists upon his hips.

'Where have you been?'

She put the pen down, left the diary open in her lap. 'In the woods. Walking.'

'Avoiding me, you mean.'

She shrugged. 'If you like.'

'No, Barl, I *don't* like!' Remmie retorted, his temper ragged. 'You shouldn't wander alone in those woods. Remember Benbarsk? Remember Dreen? This is a strange land. It could be dangerous.'

*Dreen.* Hunched on her cot, Barl squinted up at her brother. Pain spiked behind her eyes as she remembered torn flesh and splintered bones and the last agonised moments of a dying woman. A friend.

'I'm sorry. I didn't mean to worry you.'

'Oh, well, then,' he said, scornful. 'That makes everything all right.' He shoved his hands into the baggy pockets of his rough-spun trousers. 'If you're interested, Elder Chaffie says she can't say yet if we can stay. It'll take some time for her people to make up their minds about us.'

'I'm not surprised. We're asking a lot of them.'

'She was curious about one thing. She's wondering how *we* can help *them*. Funnily enough, Venette and I are wondering the same thing. *And* we're wondering why you lied to the Olken. There was no civil war. Mage hadn't turned against mage. We *ran*, Barl. We escaped the ruin you and Morgan created. But you didn't mention that, either.'

'No, I didn't!' she snapped. 'We want the Olken to help us, not turn away in fear and horror.'

'They'll turn away when they find out you lied!'

'But they won't find out, Remmie. Not if you don't tell them. And you won't.'

His shoulders slumped. 'No. I won't. *We* won't. But Barl, this other business . . .'

'Morgan is coming,' she said, with a shiver. 'And if I do nothing else, I'm going to keep this land and all of us safe.'

Groaning, Remmie rubbed at his eyes. 'You can't tell the Olken that. You don't even know for certain it's true. You've no more proof than a few dreams.'

She had Jervale. But even as she opened her mouth to tell Remmie what the Olken had said, what he knew, what she'd seen him do in the Black Woods . . . instinct had her shrinking.

*I need Olken magic to stay secret a little longer, even from Remmie.*

'Barl?' he said, exasperated now. 'I'm right, aren't I?'

Hurt, she closed the diary and smoothed its scarred, mottled leather cover. 'I thought you believed me.'

'I believe you believe it,' her brother said, after a moment. 'And I believe Danfey's wicked enough to hurt you, if he could. But Barl . . . Dorana is *months* behind us. And you think that's really him, talking to you? No mage is that powerful. Not even Morgan Danfey.'

'That's not what you said last night. And it's not what you said in Benbarsk.'

He grimaced. 'I wanted us out of Benbarsk. If we'd stayed there we'd have all died, for certain. Its people are as deadly as its bears.'

'So . . . what? You've been humouring me?'

'No,' he said, after a long silence. 'I wanted you to be right. And wrong. If that makes any sense.'

It made perfect sense. He was afraid she was losing her mind, so he wanted Morgan to be real. But if he was real, then they were in danger again . . . and he didn't want that.

'Yes,' she sighed. 'It does.'

'Barl, I know you think you're right about Morgan, but you mustn't forget you're exhausted.'

'Exhausted or not, I *am* right,' she said. 'But to be honest, Rem, I don't care if you don't believe me?'

Uncertain, he bit his lip. 'And what's that supposed to mean?'

'It means that sooner or later we'll both learn the truth. And in the meantime, I don't want to fight.'

'Neither do I,' he said. 'So you can stop hiding in here and come and help me with class. It's past time the children got back to their lessons, before they forget what it means to be a mage.'

'I can't. I'm busy.'

Remmie made a little growling sound in his throat. 'What could be more important than making sure Dorana's children—' And then he frowned at the diary. 'Barl? What maggot's in your brain now?'

He'd never leave her alone if she didn't satisfy him with a plausible answer. 'Should the Olken let us stay, we'll suffer the drought and famine with them,' she said. 'And Remmie, I can't bear the thought of watching any more of us die. I think there might be a way for our magic to ease Lur's suffering. So that's my maggot. I'm trying to save us from the drought.'

It was true. And if she was trying to do more than that, well, he didn't need to know. Not until he believed the threat from Morgan was real.

Remmie's eyebrows lifted. 'With magework?'

Oh, why was he so determined to be difficult? 'If we can cure renna blight, then why can't we – oh, I don't know – coax more of Lur's springs to the surface, say, or create a crop that needs less water to thrive, or—'

'*No*,' Remmie said, his face thundery. 'Are you mad, Barl? More transmutations? After what happened at home?'

She stared. 'Of course not! I'm talking about commonplace magework. All we need do is show these Olken that we can make their lives better, easier, and they'll let us stay. I know they will.'

Turning away, Remmie pulled back the heavy tent flap and stared across their camp, towards the village of Gribley. 'I wish I knew it, Barl. I tell you, I think we're on the knife's edge – which is why you can't breathe a *word* about Morgan. You were right about one thing, I think. Give these Olken an excuse and we'll be homeless again.'

Not even during their dreadful mountain crossing had she heard him sound so dispirited, so afraid. Had he reached the end of his strength?

*He can't have. Not Remmie. How will I do this if he loses heart now?*

'I promise, I won't mention him,' she said, trying hard to be gentle. Not to show him her fear. 'Now you should go. Your pupils will be waiting. And I need to work.'

'Barl . . .' Turning, he showed her a face full of doubt and hope. 'They've waited this long. They can wait a few days longer. Whatever you're doing, I can help. Let me help. You shouldn't be doing difficult magework on your own. You're too tired.'

All their strife, all their arguments, and she couldn't breathe for a moment, she loved him so much. And because of that love she could never involve him in her plan. He'd lost Irielle because of her. He'd lost Dorana. She wasn't about to let him lose anything else.

She stood and went to him. Pressed her palm against his thin, scarred face. 'I need to work through this alone. If you really want to help, go. Bring me some porridge and a mug of water every now and then. And trust me. Please? *Trust me.*'

Deeply distressed, he left her. Guilt mingled with relief. She could hardly think straight in the face of his fear. Could hardly think straight in the face of her own.

*I'm mad. I must be. I failed to ward Dorana. What makes me think I can ward Lur?*

Only Lur wasn't Dorana . . . and that was why this was possible. Not only was this place not blighted with mage-mist and instability, it was soaked in its own magic, potent in its own way despite its gentle malleability. Potent because of the Olken's affinity with their land.

*And that's the key. Lur's malleable affinity. If I can meld its soft singing with Dorana's strident, martial cry I can create a barrier that not even Morgan will breach.*

Only . . . the cost of it. The terrible cost. If she was right in what she suspected, in a way she'd be destroying the Olken.

*But it's the only way to save them. And I have to believe*

*they'll think it's worth it. I have to believe they'll give up what little they have to gain so much more.*

Provided, of course, she could see her way through the maze of magework her idea demanded. Provided the smattering of catalysts that had survived the flight from Dorana were enough. Provided – provided –

*Remmie tells me I'm arrogant. I tell myself I'm great. I'll need to be both if I'm to save two innocent races.*

Frightened, she pressed her hands to her face. If she thought about this too closely she'd never do it. She'd lose faith.

*Stop snivelling, Barl. You can do this. You have to. And that's that.*

Left unsettled by his encounter with Barl Lindin, Jervale walked the woods on his lonesome for a time, enjoying the solitude after the bustle of crowded Gribley, welcoming the chance to breathe dampish air and listen to birdsong and the hidden business of woodland creatures. It made a sweet change from his dry, sadly silent hamlet of Toblin . . . but it made him miss Bene too, and his little Tilly. They'd love it here in the Black Woods' sun-dappled stillness and peace. Thinking of them, he was roiled giddy with homesickness and wept a little, wanting them. Wept for himself, too, because the burden thrust on him was heavier than ever he'd imagined. It made the coming death of Tam and Rinna's baby seem light . . . and he'd never thought that could be.

To cheer himself, he picked a handful of yellow woodland daisies and a scarlet bibiloo, to press dry and take home to his girls.

When at last he returned to the village, he decided to wander for a while to hear what folk had to say about the Doranen. He was yet to chime Merrin and tell the old man of the day's doings, since Toblin's elder was a man who wanted to know first what others were thinking before he said his own piece.

Besides . . . his nagging inner voice was on the nudge again, pushing him to mingle with more folk than Bannet and Del. Why that mattered, beyond being friendly, he couldn't tell. But he'd long ago learned to be nudged, so he mingled.

The Olken who'd travelled so far to hear the pleas of Dorana's mages had mostly met in Gribley as strangers . . . but were fast becoming friends. Some sleeping in makeshift tents, like the Doranen, others taking a bedroll on the floor of a Gribley villager's modest cottage, they gathered at the alehouse and in the village square and outside the bakery to trade stories and spin endless wonderings about the strangers who'd asked to make Lur their new home.

It was no hardship, Jervale thought, chatting with folk. Only reason he'd kept so much to himself was on account of his dreams and knowings. He'd worried someone would notice his unease and ask awkward questions.

But now he had to, and wasn't sorry for that. He found great pleasure in hobnobbing with folk from pockets of Lur he'd heard of, but never seen. The Olken lived scattered, separate lives. Funny how that struck him so hard now, after hearing the Doranen talk of *Iringans* and *the Brantish* and the warlike folk of *Feen*. Their lives were full of people, full of travel and differences and new sights and change. Not like the Olken, whose lives were tiny set next to theirs. If the Doranen stayed, they'd change that, most likely.

And it might not be a bad thing. Could be Lur's folk might not be suffering the drought so hard if they were in the habit of reaching out instead of pulling in.

Well, that was what *he* thought. His fellow Olken weren't so sure. What he learned in his mingling was that while sympathy for the Doranen remained, there was uncertainty too. Fear. Change came hard to the Olken, especially change that struck like lightning out of a clear sky.

He ate his supper early, sitting comfortable with Bannet and Del, then turned in to his tent and chimed Merrin. The old man listened, grunting now and then, and said he'd talk things over with the hamlet. Weary, Jervale rolled into his blanket and plunged swiftly into sleep . . .

. . . to wake startled at sunrise, visited by a dream that left him fuddled and more afraid than ever that he'd fail.

# CHAPTER THIRTY-SEVEN

'She's up to something,' said Remmie, morose. 'I know she is. But she won't tell me what and she won't let me help. Venette, I'm telling you, this will all end in tears.'

Venette eyed her sour porridge, swallowing nausea. If she never ate another bowl of Olken porridge in her life, she'd die happy. Not that she complained, of course. As the last surviving member of the Council of Mages, it was her duty to set an example. So set an example she did, always smiling as she graciously thanked the Olken for their generosity . . . and ate the dreadful porridge to the very last smear in the wooden bowl.

'Venette! Are you listening?'

She looked across the narrow, rough-hewn wooden table at the young man who'd become like a second son to her. The good son. The honourable son. The son who'd never hurt her. He was so decent. Everyone liked Remmie. Even Maris liked him, though her hatred of his sister continued undimmed.

'Of course I'm listening, my dear. I'm just not sure what you want me to do.'

'*Talk* to her! Make her tell you what she's thinking, what she's doing!'

Another rule she'd made for herself was that she must always take her meals in the camp's small, root-knotted central square. That no matter how sad or weary or defeated she felt, she could never retreat into solitude, into the privacy of her tent. The exiles of Dorana must see her every day, brave and determined and undefeated by their tragedies.

Which meant that on this one hundred and twelfth morning in Lur, she ate her breakfast with Remmie in full sight of their fellow mages. The few who'd braved the sunrise, at least, aside from those whose turn it was to cook. Hayne Jarralt, Tarlin Amsher, Vonie Trevoyle and her young son, Abbet. Most everyone else stayed late abed, though, these days . . . and while she deplored sloth, she found it hard to lay blame. With nearly all magework forbidden for the time being, so as not to alarm the Olken, there was little for the weary, heartsick mages of Dorana to do.

Hearing Remmie's raised voice, those hardy few early risers cast surreptitious glances at them.

'Now, now, Mage Lindin,' she murmured, reproving. 'I'll have no ructions causing dismay.'

Glowering, he pushed aside his half-finished porridge and leaned forward. 'Are you going to talk to Barl, or not?'

'Remmie . . .' Venette sighed. 'I've already talked to her. Well, I tried. She's no more forthcoming with me.'

'And that doesn't alarm you?'

Of course it did. But she saw little purpose in telling him so. He was on edge enough already. 'My dear, your sister will confide in us when it suits her, and not a moment before.'

Remmie grunted a grudging acceptance, then ran a hand down his lightly stubbled face. 'Will you speak to Elder Chaffie today? See if the Olken are any closer to a decision?'

'Yes. But doubtless she'll give me the same answer. Until your sister can explain what she meant by us helping them, they can't be expected to say one way or the other.'

'Which is why you should make Barl tell you what she's doing,' said Remmie, retrieving his porridge bowl. 'Venette . . .' He swallowed another mouthful of the unpalatable mush. 'We did the right thing, didn't we, leaving Benbarsk? Coming here?'

615

A question she'd asked herself every day since they began their terrible struggle over the mountains. And every death in those jagged peaks, every broken bone, every bloodied scrape and bruise, had served only to gouge her deeper with doubt.

But she couldn't tell Remmie that, either.

'Yes,' she said firmly. 'Here, with the Olken, we have a chance to rebuild our lives. To rebuild Dorana, after a fashion. Benbarsk would have become our tomb. For certain, Remmie, we did the right thing.'

'Even with the drought that's gripping this land?'

'Droughts end. Rain returns.' If they'd been alone she'd have touched him. Perhaps stroked his hair. But because others were watching, she had to content herself with a smile. 'And don't forget your exasperating sister, my dear. We must have faith that what she's working on will help.'

He didn't smile back. Birdsong from the surrounding trees lifted the woodland gloom. No bears here. No Iringan spears, no swordsmen of Vharne. Things weren't perfect, that was true . . . but they could be much worse.

'She's still convinced Danfey is a danger, you know,' he said at last. 'She says she still dreams him.'

Venette looked away. *Morgan.* She did her best not to think of Haeth's son. When she thought of him, she thought of Orwin . . . and then she wept herself sick.

*Orwin. Brice. Bellamie. Even Sallis and Shari. And all those other mages, most of whom I never knew.*

How many wounds could a heart bear, before it tore apart completely?

'Morgan is the past, Remmie,' she said, standing. 'He is caged, and will stay caged. We are safe here, I'm sure of it. And I'm sure that in their own time, the Olken will decide we can stay.'

Staring at her, his eyes troubled, Remmie tapped his whittled wooden spoon against his porridge bowl. For a moment she thought he was going to argue, but then he sighed.

'I'm teaching, later. Will you come?'

'Of course,' she said warmly. 'And perhaps you could ask

Maris to help? She's good with children. Perhaps you've seen her with her nephew? And I know she'd like something useful to do.'

Remmie gave her a look. 'Yes. I suppose I could.'

She knew better than to push any harder than that. 'Good. Now, my dear, I must spread myself about a bit. I'll see you in class.'

And leaving him to think about Maris, she hoped, she joined Hayne Jarralt and the others, whose enthusiastic greeting chased away the shadows of pain . . . for now.


Nine days after hearing the Doranen's sorry tale from Barl Lindin, and then not another word nor even a glimpse of them, the Olken gathered in Gribley were starting to get restless. Elder Chaffie had already broken apart two brawls, and was threatening to send the next troublemakers back to their home villages.

Nursing a half-mug of cider in a corner of the village's smokey alehouse, Jervale let his head rest against the wall behind him and drifted his eyes nearly closed. Nine days since he'd confronted Barl Lindin in the woodland. Nine days since he'd dreamed . . . or slept well, because of it.

'Jervale! There you are.'

And that was Bannet, shifting his way through the midday crowd to join him. Bannet, a good man, a new friend, who was part of his last dream. The only part of it he recognised. The five other faces he'd dreamed . . . he didn't know them. He'd seen them round about, they'd all come to Gribley from villages scattered the length and breadth of Lur, but he didn't *know* them. Not to trust. And yet there he was, dreaming them, and his nagging inner voice wasn't nagging any more, it was *shouting*.

*These folk are Lur's future. And when it's time, you'll know.*

But time for what? He didn't know that. He wasn't even certain he wanted to. He was tired of secrets. Even more tired of waiting. And as for his dreams . . . He felt sick to his stomach.

What was Barl Lindin doing? What was taking her so long? Should he go and find her? Perhaps she needed his help, perhaps for all her fancy Doranen magework the magic of Lur was too wild for her taming.

*What am I meant to do? I don't know what to do!*

'Jervale?' Bannet slid onto a stool opposite, and thumped his own mug of cider on the rough bench between them. 'Is aught amiss? You look like a man with a mortal bad bellyache.'

Should he confide in Bannet now? Was this the right time? He didn't know. His inner voice was silent.

*Best I follow Bene's favourite saying, then. When in doubt, don't.*

He picked up his mug and took a comforting swig of strong cider. 'Nothing's amiss, Bannet. Save I'm weary of being such a long way from home. It'd be easier to bear if the chiming stones were more reliable, and I could have a word with my Bene and Tilly.'

But that was proving nigh impossible. Gribley was so far away, and there were so many of them trying to chime home at once. Lur's troubles meant their stones stuttered and would not hold their notes.

'I hear you,' said Bannet, who was missing his own wife and two sons, back in Salting. 'And I can tell you, we ain't the only ones put out. There's folk mighty grumped on all this thumb-twiddling, and starting to lose any kindness they might've felt for these mages. If they don't answer their own riddles soon, then—'

'Hey-de-ho!' said a cheerful voice, and there was Del of Westwailing come to sit with them. She carried a tray with three bowls of what smelled like bean stew, and her own mug of cider. 'Make room!'

So they shifted about, and Del settled at the bench. After taking a mouthful of stew, she sat back and grinned.

'You'll not believe it. I've come from talkin' with that mage, Barl Lindin.'

Bannet snorted. 'Hope you told her we've got better things

to do than sit on our arses waiting for her to show us her magic tricks.'

'As a matter of fact, I didn't,' said Del. 'Seein' as how I ain't a sinkin' fool.'

Hiding a smile in his mug, Jervale once more felt the odd, inner tugging that told him this young woman was important. He'd given up trying to figure out why. Neither dreams nor instinct would tell him – and there was no point pushing for an answer. He'd know when he needed to know. If he needed to know it.

'What did Mage Lindin want of you, Del?'

Del hunched a little, and beckoned them close. 'She wanted me to tell her about the coast,' she said, near to whispering. 'What the weather was like southwards. What storms rolled in and when. Did we ever set sail on the open ocean? And when I told her about the bits and pieces left of the reef? She went very quiet. And there was a look in her eyes . . .'

Despite himself, Bannet was intrigued. 'Why? What do storms and an old reef matter?'

'I don't know,' said Del, shrugging. 'But if she took time to ask me, then I reckon they must. That handsome brother of hers came along while I was with her, but she sent him away with a flea in his ear.'

'*Handsome?*' Bannet stared. 'Young Del, what did I tell you about the folly of Olken lasses mooning after strangers with blond hair?'

Del flushed bright pink. 'I ain't mooning! He's handsome, is all.'

'Now you listen to me. If they stay here, there'll be no good come of us and them getting tangled,' said Bannet, crossly. 'Besides, you said on the road you were promised to a lad in Restharven.'

'Aye, that's right, I'm promised to Bede. But I can still look at a pretty face, can't I? Ain't no rule against *lookin'*.' Aggrieved, Del dug her fork into her bowl of stew. 'So, Jervale, what d'you reckon Mage Lindin's wonderings mean?'

There was little he could say that wouldn't reveal the things he knew . . . and Del of Westwailing wasn't one of the Olken he'd dreamed.

'I reckon we'll find out when we find out. Don't borrow trouble, that's what I say.'

'Oh, sink you,' said Del, and fell into more cosy brangling with Bannet.

Content for now just to listen, Jervale busied himself with his stew.

*It comes down to Barl Lindin. As soon as she breaks her silence, that's when I'll know what to do.*

Thirteen days after learning the truth of the Olken from Jervale, Barl sat in her stifling tent, cold to the marrow, and went over and over and over her magework. Perhaps she'd made a mistake. Perhaps she was wrong, and her mad plan wouldn't work after all.

Except she wasn't wrong, and she knew it.

*I can keep Morgan at bay forever. I can preserve what's left of Dorana, and save the Olken people from a slow, tormenting death by drought and famine. I can turn their little land into a paradise. And all I have to do is . . . die.*

Unless the convoluted syllables and sigils of her incants could be combined in a kinder, gentler, less murderous way. Could they? Had she missed a different method of melding Doranen and Olken power so they would break the drought, heal the ailing land and seal the Doranen and Olken safely behind Lur's towering mountains?

Hours later, sweating, shivering, she threw aside diary and pen and pulled her knees to her chest. No. Try as she might, she couldn't escape the stark truth. The final incant she'd need to coalesce the disparate Doranen and Olken magics, to create an impenetrable barrier around Lur, marrying safety and weather into a perfect, seamless whole, would simply . . . *unmake* her.

After a time, her shivering stopped. Then, feeling strangely calm, she went in search of Remmie and Venette. Found them sitting in the camp's square with Maris Garrick. The faint dawn daylight was surprising. Yet again she'd worked through the night.

Remmie took one look at her face and dropped his mug of tea, splashing, to the ground. 'Barl? What is it, what have you—'

Ignoring him, she nodded to Maris. 'I'm sorry, Mage Garrick. Would you excuse us? I have something privy to discuss. Remmie? Venette? Walk with me.'

Leaving Maris to complain about certain people's lack of manners, she led Remmie and Venette away from the barely stirring camp and into the surrounding woodland. Summoned glimfire to dispel the swiftly descending gloom and kept on walking the narrow, winding tracks, though there was muttering behind her.

'All right, Barl, we've gone far enough!' Remmie said at last, catching her arm. '*Stop.*'

She'd not spoken properly with either of them for days. Hadn't spoken to anyone, save for that Olken girl from the coast, and Elder Chaffie. But that had been on purpose. She'd been afraid that if she let herself dwell on family, on friends – though it still felt odd to think of Venette Martain as a friend – she might surrender to cowardice and turn away from her task. She was afraid of that now. The fear in Remmie's wide-eyed stare threatened to curdle her blood.

Venette sighed. 'What have you done, Barl?'

Shifting her gaze from Remmie, she lifted her chin. 'I've found a way to keep us all safe. I'm not finished, there's a great deal of magework to complete, but – I have the bones of it. And the bones of it are sound.'

'That's for us to decide,' Remmie snapped. 'This isn't something you'll do on your own.'

Of course it was. It had to be. But he'd need time to accept that.

The hushed, glimlit gloom of the Black Woods cradled them. The ground beneath their feet thrummed softly with Olken magic, that strangely gentle power that was the key to all she would do. Jervale had said the land was wounded. She still couldn't feel it. Had to trust that even if he was right, it wouldn't make a difference.

*Doranen magic is stronger. Ailing or not, I can bend the Olken's magic to my will and purpose.*

'Come, Barl,' Venette said, coaxing. Not sounding at all like the arrogant mage she used to be. 'You've brought us out here to tell us.'

So she told them of the magework she'd imagined, the syllables and the sigils that would entirely change their world. And when she was finished, found a fallen tree and sat, exhausted.

'I . . . don't know what to say,' Venette murmured. 'Truly, Barl. You have astonished me. And to think you are an unranked mage.'

She felt a prickle of temper. *That's the Lady Martain I remember.* 'And *I* think we need to leave that kind of nonsense on the other side of the mountains, Venette. What I want to know is if you think the notion wise.'

'Wise?' Venette laughed. 'My dear, it is the most magnificent folly. I can't think of a single mage in our history who would even dream up such a thing – let alone possess the talent to create it.'

'I do.'

'Yes, most likely, *and* the arrogance to accompany it.'

Barl looked at Remmie. 'You're very quiet.'

He shrugged. 'Like Venette, I am astonished.'

'Remmie—'

He threw up his hands and half turned away. 'What? What would you have me say? Your plan is brilliant and demented. And if the Olken agree to it – if they agree to do everything you ask—'

'We won't be trapped here forever,' she said softly. 'Morgan is powerful and angry but he's still just a man. Forty years from now, fifty, the warding can be released. And if the world beyond the mountains has healed itself . . . and I must believe it can and will heal itself . . . then Dorana's mages can go home.'

Shifting round, Remmie stared at her, the puckered scar on his cheek livid against his pallor. His eyes glittered in the glimlight, brightly sheened with grief and pain. And then he walked away.

'Give him a moment, my dear,' said Venette, holding out her hand. 'This magic of yours . . .' She cleared her throat. 'You ask a great deal of him.'

Only what she asked of herself. And if she could face this, then so could he.

'You do realise everything depends on the Olken?' Venette added. 'Your magnificent folly will come to naught if they choose to stay as they are.'

'Yes, but why would they?' she said, baffled. 'When I am offering them abundance and prosperity and an end to their troubles. This land is *dying*, Venette. I can't believe they'll not save themselves.'

Venette shook her head, wondering. 'Magework to rule both weather and ward. To think I've lived to see such a thing.'

Barl smiled, wryly. 'You haven't seen it yet.'

'And I won't, Barl, if you don't convince the Olken to help us. The time's come to talk to them. I know you think the choice is obvious, but I suspect that getting their consent for this won't be a swift or easy matter.'

'Fine, fine,' she said, knowing Venette was right. 'Can you ask Elder Chaffie to have everyone gather in the hall after supper? I'd like to rest for a few hours, before I speak to them.'

Venette nodded. 'Of course.'

'Thank you.' She glanced at her brother, standing a long stone's throw distant with his back turned and his outstretched arm braced against a tree. As though he'd fall in a heap if it didn't hold him up. 'Can you find her now? I'd like a moment alone with Remmie.'

'My dear,' said Venette . . . and shockingly, bent and kissed her cheek.

'*Don't*,' Remmie said, when they were alone and she'd walked slowly, her heart unsteady, to stand behind him. 'There is *nothing* you can say that will make this all right.'

She felt a rush of tears. Blinked them back. 'You could finally say *I told you so*. That might help, Rem.'

On a choked sob, he shook his head. 'If you do this, it'll kill you.'

'You don't know that for sure.'

'Oh, *Barl*,' he said, and spun round. His cheeks were wet. 'Don't insult me. I'm not some ignorant Olken.'

'They're not ignorant, Remmie. Just different. And a bit like children. Simple.'

His face twisted. 'And yet you'd give your life for them?'

She wanted to touch him, to hold him, but she feared they'd both shatter if she did. 'Not for them. For us.'

'For no *reason*!' he cried. 'When you've no sure proof that Morgan Danfey won't stay warded in Elvado until the end of time!'

He *still* refused to believe her? 'Remmie—'

'Go away, Barl. Leave me be.'

'No, Remmie, I—'

'*Leave me be!*'

His anguish echoed through the woodland. Startled birds leapt to the air, wings clattering.

Defeated, she left him.

Alone with his rage and pain, Remmie wandered the gloom of the Black Woods, raggedly circling the remote village of Gribley. Feeling the drag of his hurt hip. Hating it. The silence should have been soothing, but instead it mocked him with the silence of the dead he'd left behind. For months he'd pushed away all thought of what he'd lost. Irielle dead. Barton Haye. All his pupils, not just in Batava but his other schools as well. Of course, there was a chance they weren't all perished. They could be living still, trapped in Iringa or Manemli or Vharne or Benbarsk, hunted like animals, struggling to survive.

*So many dead and missing. Our race is practically extinct. And now Barl would die to save what's left?*

He should love her for it, but he didn't. He was tired of

sacrifice, tired of putting on a brave face for the mages who now looked to him for answers. For relief.

He was tired.

Eventually his aimless wandering returned him to the crowded village. The Olken stared at him, nudging and whispering as he passed by. Because the Doranen needed these odd, rustic little people he nodded pleasantly, and smiled, but inside he was raging.

*And if she does this thing, my sister, will you care what it cost? Will it matter to you that a stranger died to give you so much, asking so little in return?*

'Mage Lindin,' said Elder Chaffie, looking up from stirring a large pot of soup. Crowded around her in the village bakery's lean-to, six more pots simmered over open, wood-fueled flames. So many bellies to fill, thanks to his people. The old woman looked weary enough to weep. 'I've seen Lady Martain. She says there's news to share.'

'There is,' he said, nodding. 'But I'll let Barl speak of it tonight. I was wondering . . . do the Olken drink ale?'

Elder Chaffie's eyes were sharp and knowing. 'They do,' she said, after a moment. 'Got a thirst, have you?'

A thirst? No, he had the driving need to drink himself blind. To numb the pain and gift himself with an hour or two of forgetfulness.

'I could swallow a drop, if you can spare it.'

She rested her wooden spoon on the battered cook top. 'I'll spare you a jug, Remmie Lindin. The misery in you is enough to break this mother's heart.'

He took the stoppered jug she gave him and retreated to the woodland. Found a fallen log and settled himself against it, feeling the bark hard against his spine and the aching muscles of his back. Unstoppered the jug, sloshing it. His empty belly rumbled.

*See what you've done, Barl? You've driven me to drink.*

Olken ale was rich and potent, making him gasp at his first mouthful. Gasp again at the second. But by his fifth swallow he was smiling . . .

The jug was a drop from empty when he heard a twig snap. Peering over the log he frowned, muzzy, at the Olken girl who'd found him.

'Sorry,' she said. 'Didn't meant to fright you.'

She was slender. Nearly pretty. She had dark eyes and dark hair. He pulled a face. 'You didn't.'

She came a few steps closer. 'I saw you leave the village. You looked sad. I thought . . . well.' She dimpled, a hint of mischief. A tease of flirting. 'I thought I could give you a mite of cheer. My name's Del.'

'Is it?' he said. 'Mine's Remmie.'

'I know,' she said, folding to the ground beside him. Rested her hand on his thigh, and smiled. 'Hello, Remmie.'

He felt his blood pound and his head spin. Reckless, angry, he tossed the jug aside and kissed the Olken girl. Fingers busy, she kissed him back. Giggled into his panting mouth. Heart racing, he stared into her dark eyes. Felt his hand on her small breast, where she'd put it, and started to pull away.

'No – we shouldn't—'

'Why shouldn't we?' she demanded. 'We ain't hurtin' anyone.' She nuzzled him, lips seeking. 'Remmie, you look so sad.'

His blood was full of ale and fire. They burned away his grief. Burned caution, burned common sense, burned everything but desire.

*All I feel these days is pain. I want to feel something – anything – else.*

'Don't be sad,' the girl whispered. 'For a little while, don't be sad.'

'All right,' he said. 'I won't be.'

And let desire have its way.

*'Barl, my love . . . what mischief are you planning?'*

Twisted in restless sleep, Barl heard herself moan. 'Go away, Morgan. You're a dream. You're just a dream.'

*'You're planning something, my love. I can feel it. There is a fire in your mind.'*

Was he free? Had he freed himself? Weeping, she tried to feel him as he could feel her. But all she felt was rage and grief. Were those passions his . . . or hers? She couldn't tell.

'*You are mine, Barl. For ever and always. Come home, my love. I'll keep you safe.*'

'You won't. You can't. Oh, Morgan, don't you know what you've become?'

'*Of course, my love. I am the greatest mage the world has ever known.*'

'The greatest murderer,' she told him, still weeping. 'The greatest monster. You should've told me what you were planning, Morgan. I could've stopped you. I could've saved Rumm. And now it's too late. You're lost.'

His fury drenched her dreamworld scarlet. '*Lost? Not lost, you foolish girl. Found. And when I find you, you'll find—*'

'You'll never find me, Morgan. Not in the flesh. Not in the world. Soon I'll be gone from you, far, far away, and the mages I stopped you from killing, they'll—'

She felt him strike her, as though they raged at each other face to face. The pain was shocking.

'*You will not leave me, Barl! I forbid it! You bitch, you slut, you treacherous whore! You will not—*'

'Barl! Barl! For pity's sake, wake up!'

She opened her eyes, panting, fingers pressed to her wet, burning cheek. On his knees beside her cot, Remmie snatched her wrist and pulled her hand away. Turned milk-pale, staring, then slumped on his heels. Released her. His breathing in her small tent sounded ragged and loud.

'There's a handprint on your face,' he said dully. 'So it's not just a dream, is it? Somehow he's really found you.'

His pain hurt more keenly than the blow from Morgan's mind. 'I tried to tell you, Remmie.'

'Yes,' he whispered. 'You did.'

Weeping again, she sat up and reached for him. 'Don't be afraid. He's not free yet. Maybe he never will be. My binding could still hold.'

Remmie shook his head. 'You don't believe that. If you believed it, you'd never—' His voice broke. 'Prove you believe it, Barl. Abandon this mad plan.'

She let her hand fall. 'I can't, Remmie. I can't take that chance.'

'Yes, you can,' he said harshly. 'For me, you can. Barl, you owe me that much. For Irielle, you owe me.'

And that was a second blow, even crueller than Morgan's. '*Remmie.*'

His eyes flint hard, he pushed unsteadily to his feet. 'But you won't. Because you're Barl Lindin, and you have to be right.'

She scrambled off the cot. 'I *am* right! Remmie, d'you think I'd do this if—'

'You've slept the day away,' he said, stepping back. 'The Olken are gathering now. I'll go and tell Venette and Elder Chaffie you're coming.'

'No, Remmie, wait, I—'

The tent's door flap fell closed behind him.

Shaken, Barl stared blankly at the drab, oiled-felt wall. Felt her fingers creep up to touch where Morgan had struck her.

*Oh, Remmie.*

Sat in Gribley's crowded hall with Bannet, Del nowhere to be seen, Jervale watched Barl Lindin and her brother and the other Doranen mage, Lady Martain, enter with Elder Chaffie. The look on Remmie Lindin's face chilled him.

*Something's wrong.*

He tried to catch Barl Lindin's eye, but the mage was inward-looking, her face paler than ever. There was a faint red mark on her right cheek he'd not seen before.

'Hush now,' said Chaffie, her hands raised. 'Mage Lindin has some things to say.'

As Chaffie took her seat, and voice by voice the hall fell silent, Barl Lindin stepped forward. 'My dear Olken friends, I must ask your forgiveness. When I first told you our story, there was a part I left out. I didn't think you needed to know it, but

I was wrong. So now I must tell you, for it will explain why I need you to do what *you* must do, so we all can be safe.'

A buzz of consternation. Bannet leaned close. 'I don't like the sound of this.'

Jervale swallowed, churned with unease. 'Nor do I.'

'There is a mage I have not mentioned,' Barl Lindin said, her blue eyes haunted. 'He was a friend once, but no longer. His magework corrupted him. He became a great danger. And when Dorana began to fall apart, we left him behind. But now he's looking for us, and I fear that if he finds us he will wreak a terrible vengeance. Not just on the Doranen, but on the Olken as well, for helping us.'

Chaffie stood. 'Why would he come looking?'

'Because he loves me . . . and because he thinks I betrayed him.'

'And did you?' said Chaffie.

In the hall's ordinary torchlight, Barl Lindin's eyes shone with tears. 'Yes.'

Uproar. Loud voices, stamping feet, folk leapt up with fists waving. The mages stared at each other. Lady Martain said something, her voice smothered by Olken anger.

Giddy with dismay, Jervale sat unmoving, his rudely woken instincts clamouring as loudly as his fellow Olken. Even Bannet was protesting. Lur's green and growing future was set to go up in flames. If he didn't do something, say something . . .

Ignoring Bannet's cry, he shoved his way along their row of seats and joined Barl Lindin at the front of the hall. Waved his arms and shouted for folk to hear him. But no-one was listening. He turned to her, despairing.

An explosion of glimfire silenced every raucous voice.

'Listen to her!' Jervale said loudly, before Chaffie or anyone else could speak. 'If you love your families, *listen*.'

'I understand your disappointment,' said Barl Lindin, into the shocked hush. 'But I promise, I have no more secrets. And I promise this, too, that even if Morgan did not pose a danger, *still* the people of Lur would be in dire peril. But with your help, I can save you.'

'So you claimed before, Mage Lindin,' said Chaffie, sharply. 'Now you'd best explain.'

Nodding, Barl Lindin clasped her hands before her. 'With Doranen magework I can create a wall around Lur that will keep Morgan, and all those other warlike nations, at bay. And with that same magework I can tame the weather to my hand. I can make sure your land never suffers drought or famine again.'

Jervale startled, pricked by memory. A wall around Lur. *That golden shimmer in the mountains.* And the lush, green hills, the fields heavy with grain.

'She's telling the truth,' he said quickly, before there was more shouting. 'I've seen it.'

Chaffie stepped forward, waving at everyone else to keep them quiet. 'Jervale, isn't it? From Toblin hamlet, out to the west?'

He swallowed, his mouth dry. 'That's right.'

'And you've *seen* this? *How* have you seen it?'

'I . . . don't rightly know, Elder Chaffie.' He could feel the Doranen mages looking at him, and the amazement of his fellow Olken. 'I've been this way my whole life. I see things, dream them, then they happen. I've seen Lur more lush and bountiful than it's ever been, *safe*, and I know it's because of these mages. I know we have to trust them, for if we don't, there'll be strife.'

Chaffie looked him up and down. 'You know that, do you? You'd risk your life on it?'

He made himself look at wide-eyed, staring Bannet, and then searched for the other five Olken he'd seen in his dream. Finding them, one by one, he felt that odd, inward *click* that told him *yes, don't be frighted, you tread the right path.*

'I would, Elder Chaffie.'

Chaffie snorted. '*You* would. And tell me, Jervale . . . why should any of us believe you?'

# CHAPTER THIRTY-EIGHT

Jervale wanted to look at Barl Lindin, but didn't dare. Instead he looked at the crowd of Olken gathered to hear the Doranen. Felt the dizzy twist that told him another knowing was on him, and pointed at a woman seated a handful of rows behind Bannet.

'You there. You weren't s'posed to speak for your village, but the man who was chosen upped and broke his leg.'

'Is that true?' said Chaffie, her thin, worry-worn face sombre.

The woman nodded, wary. 'Aye. But I've spoke on it. This Jervale could've heard mention.'

'I didn't.'

Chaffie folded her arms. 'Can you prove it?'

No. He couldn't. For the first time in his life, he willed his inner voice to whisper. Waited . . . waited . . .

'You,' he said, pointing again. 'Have you and me chinwagged since I got to Gribley?'

The man he singled out shook his head. 'Just to say good morning.'

'Your wife's nibby-cakes give you a gripe but you ain't got the dibble to tell her.'

A ripple of nervous laughter, as the man's mouth dropped wide. Looking again to Chaffie, Jervale felt his eyes drift almost closed.

'When you were a tiddy girl in Crick hamlet, Elder Chaffie, your best friend paid no never-mind to her mama and she drowned down the well.'

Chaffie gasped. 'I've not told a soul in Gribley of that.'

'I could spend half the night plucking folks' secrets,' he said, suddenly weary. 'Can't see what good I'd do. Either you believe me, or you don't. But ask yourself this. I'm Olken. Why would I lie for a Doranen mage?'

The other Olken murmured, heads nodding. Pursing her lips, Chaffie turned to the Doranen. 'You've not put him up to this?'

'*No*,' said Barl Lindin. 'We will have your help honestly, or we'll not have it at all.'

With a glance at the crowd, Chaffie sighed. 'We'd help if we could, but we ain't got magic.'

'No,' said Barl Lindin, carefully. 'But you do have your singing. That's what I need.'

'Our singing?' Chaffie looked taken aback. 'How d'you know about that?'

Jervale bit his tongue. If Barl Lindin answered truthfully, she'd likely land him in such strife . . .

'I'm a mage, Elder Chaffie,' she said, grave. 'I know many things.'

Elder Chaffie swallowed. 'And our singing's all you want?'

'Yes. That's all.'

As relieved muttering broke out, Jervale felt a nasty prickle of foreboding.

*No, that ain't all. Here's where things start to turn rotten.*

But before he could sound a caution, Barl Lindin's brother gave her an almost unfriendly look and stepped forward. 'I'm sorry, Elder Chaffie. My sister does not make herself clear. She needs you to *abandon* your singing. She needs to take Lur's power, and use it, and leave none of it for you.'

Fresh uproar, filling the hall to its rafters. Staring at Barl Lindin, Jervale saw that her brother was right . . . and in that heartbeat every dreadful dream of black hail and crimson lightning and calamity battered through him.

632

*We can't let her do that. If we give her our earth songs we'll be jumping ourselves off a cliff, just like poor Ma Gammil.*

He didn't know the how of it. He didn't know the why. He only knew this meant disaster, just as he knew that back home, Tam and Rinna were mourning their dead son.

'*Please!*' Barl Lindin shouted. 'Hear me out!'

But no-one was listening . . . so again, she used her glimfire to stun the hall into silence.

'I'm sorry,' she said, sweeping them with her piercing gaze. 'I must ask this difficult thing, because Morgan *is* coming and you *are* dying from drought. I can save Lur. *I can.* But not without you.'

Lady Martain stepped forward. 'People of Lur,' she said, breaking her silence for the first time since she'd told them her name. 'This Morgan we speak of? He murdered my husband. And I tell you he would see *every* woman in Lur widowed. Every man bereft of his wife and every child made an orphan. I loved him like a son, once. But if I could, now I'd kill him. Do what we're asking. It is your only hope.'

Looking around the hall, Jervale saw Lady Martain's words strike every Olken like blows. And he knew she spoke the truth. He *knew* Morgan Danfey was Lur's bitter death . . .

*But so is Barl Lindin. They're forever entwined.*

'Jervale . . .'

And that was Chaffie. Sickened, he turned to her. 'Yes?'

'What do you say? What do you *see*? Will Lur's drought end on its own?'

More than anything, he wanted to lie. But if he lied, he'd twist his gift. If he lied, he'd not be able to face his Tilly.

'No, Elder Chaffie. I don't see that.'

'And this mage they speak of. Have you seen him?'

His heart was breaking. He was weeping inside. 'I have, Elder Chaffie. He's as wicked as they say.'

Chaffie shuddered. 'And what else do you see?'

'I – I—' He pressed a fist to his breast, feeling a pain there as cruel as a knife. 'I see our ruin if we don't help them. And I see our ruin if we do.'

'So we are ruined regardless?' Chaffie shook her head. 'You are no help to me, Jervale.'

'I'm sorry,' he said, desperate. 'What I mean is, we must help them. Only we *can't* abandon our singing. If we do, we'll rue the day.'

'And if you don't, I can't save you,' said Barl Lindin. 'The incants and sigils of my magework are powerful and dangerous. Should your earth-singing disturb them, the consequences will be calamitous.'

'Not as calamitous as giving up our songs!' he said, but even as he protested he knew he was wasting his time. He was smothered in foreboding now. Could hardly draw a breath.

*Oh, Bene. I've mucked this up. I've made everything worse.*

'Good people of Lur,' said Barl Lindin, ignoring him, 'think what this will mean. No more drought. No more famine. Your children won't go to bed hungry, and you won't weep because there is nothing to feed them. The Doranen know how that feels. We'd spare you such pain. Join with us in this great magework and there will be food enough for every belly, for ever and ever. *That* is the power of Lur's magic when matched with Doranen magework. So, in a way, you won't have lost your earth songs. You'll be singing them differently, that's all. And don't you see? You'll be *safe*.'

Despairing, Jervale watched his fellow Olken fall under her spell. And when he couldn't bear to watch any more, he left the hall.

Not a soul called him back.

Outside, he wandered the torchlit village, breathing in the cool night and trying to calm his disordered mind.

*I can mend this. I have to. There's Bannet and the others, they've a part to play yet. I just have to –*

He heard footfalls behind him, and turned. It was Del of Westwailing, wandering dreamlost out of the woods. She looked tousled and replete, with a lingering memory of pleasure in her eyes. Torchlight sparked along a golden hair on her sleeve.

Seeing it, he was abruptly pummelled with knowing . . . just as he'd been pummelled when Bene fell with their Tilly. He could feel the bright humming inside this careless fisherfolk lass. A new life just starting. A frail seed of hope.

*In the Final Days shall come the Innocent Mage . . .*

'Jervale!' Del said, noticing him. Surprised and suddenly wary. 'Sink me, what are you about, lurking in the shadows?'

In the Final Days? An Innocent Mage? Where had that come from? And what did it mean? 'You know there's a meeting in the hall, Del? Where've you been?'

Her fingers strayed to her lips, tracing a swift and secret smile. 'I was in the woods. I fell asleep.'

*No, girl, you tumbled with Barl Lindin's brother.*

But instinct urged him not to say that aloud. 'Come along, lass,' he said, and took hold of her arm. 'There's important doings in the hall. Best you get in there.'

After they withdrew so the Olken could talk among themselves, Remmie glanced at Venette, a warning, and walked with Barl back to their camp. She was quietly triumphant, on fire with purpose, seemingly oblivious to what her likely victory meant.

But he was all too aware of its meaning. He didn't know whether to rage at his sister, or weep.

'Let me see your notes,' he said, when they reached her tent. 'I want to check your magework.'

She lifted an eyebrow. 'Don't you trust me?'

'Please.'

On a grumbling sigh she held the tent flap aside for him, then tossed several balls of glimfire into the air as she followed. Sat on her cot while he sat on the felt mat flooring and read her notes, read her incants and their sigils, and broke his heart anew over what she'd achieved.

'It's too late to stop me, Remmie,' she said. 'The Olken will agree to my proposal.'

As if he didn't know that. As if he hadn't watched her enchant them with her gilded promises and smiles.

He looked up. 'I know you have to do this – but you needn't do it alone. If we work the incants together, and the blending, and the bindings, if we – if we share the final transmutation we'll share the danger and then maybe the spill of energies can be contained, maybe—'

'Oh, *Remmie*.' She shook her head. 'You know better.'

His eyes were stinging. 'We sprang from the same womb, Barl. We're not so different.'

'We're different enough. It won't work.'

'You don't know that.'

'I can't risk it! We have one chance, Remmie. Just one. And it's going to be hard enough to juggle all the syllables and sigils by myself. I could never do it with another mage.'

He met her eyes, breathing harshly. 'Not even with Morgan Danfey?'

Her gaze softened. 'Not even with you.'

'Oh, Barl.' The sorrow was overwhelming. 'How I wish you'd never met him.'

She made a small sound that was half laugh, half sob. 'But I did.'

He had no more strength left for fighting. She'd made her choice. Now he had to make his. On his feet again, he bent down and kissed her hair.

'I love you, Barl.'

She smiled up at him. 'I love you too. Now go and get some sleep. We'll talk again in the morning.'

'I'll sleep if you will,' he retorted. 'You go first.'

'Bully,' she said, yawning . . . but didn't complain when he plumped her thin pillow, and tucked the coarse blanket round her once she lay down.

And waited, patient and heartsick, until she fell asleep.

Venette waylaid him as he headed into the woods.

'And where d'you think you're going, young man?'

She wasn't his mother. Could never replace his mother. But in the strangest way, he'd come to love her like an older sister.

Wise and sarcastic, purposeful and brave, during the last long months Venette Martain had become important.

And so he wouldn't lie.

'I was mistaken,' he said quietly. 'Morgan Danfey isn't a wild fancy. Just before the meeting, I saw him strike Barl across the face.'

Glimfire showed him Venette's eyes widening in shock. 'That's not possible.'

'Not in person,' he added. 'But with his mind, he struck her. She was right. He's found us. And he will come after her. You know that, Venette.'

Venette was silent, fingers worrying Orwin's ring on its chain about her neck.

'What you said to the Olken. About Danfey. I know you were simply supporting Barl, then. But now that you know he really is a threat . . . I have to ask. Did you mean it, about wanting to kill him?'

Her fingers closed hard. 'Yes, I did. Why?'

Instead of answering, Remmie tipped his face to the night sky and rested his tired gaze on its unfamiliar stars. Remembered Batava's schoolhouse, and clever Rine Grovsik's pleasure as his constellation incant held.

The unfamiliar diamond pinpricks high above him blurred.

'Remmie, you're frightening me,' said Venette. 'What is this about?'

Slowly, he looked at her. 'Barl's magework is in two parts. There's the weather magic, to end the drought and ensure Lur's bounty . . . and then there's the warding, to keep it safe from the world. Her magework's only lethal if the two parts are combined. But if the warding wasn't needed? If she only had to break the drought?' His voice caught. 'If that was all of it, Venette, she wouldn't have to die.'

Venette was too intelligent not to grasp his meaning. Orwin's ring slid through her fingers as she gasped, and stepped towards him.

637

'You think to go *home*? To rid the world of Morgan? Remmie, you *can't*. You'd never survive the journey.'

'Not on foot, no,' he agreed. 'Besides, I'd never get there in time. But if I incanted . . .'

'To *Elvado*?' Incredulous, she laughed. 'Remmie—'

'It's not as mad as it sounds. Maris told me her uncle Arlin once incanted from Elvado to Iringa.'

'Did she also mention the state he was in when he got there?'

'I gather he wasn't a pretty sight,' he said. 'But Venette, if you helped me . . . if we did a working on the strongest travel incant we know . . .'

Shaking her head, Venette turned away.

'Or doesn't it bother you, that Barl is about to kill herself to save us?'

And that spun her back to him, her eyes in the glimfire sparking with temper. 'That's a *wicked* thing to say. Of *course* I am bothered. But what you're suggesting – my dear, it's *madness*.'

He managed a crooked smile. 'Not if it works.'

'And if it works, how will you get back to us?'

A good question. 'Now, now, my lady. One conundrum at a time.'

'Remmie . . .' Venette pressed trembling fingers to her lips. 'Please. Don't ask me to do this.'

'I have to,' he said simply. 'It's Barl's only hope.'

'And what of hope for *you*?'

He thought for a moment before answering. 'My mother loved Barl, but she knew her daughter well. Before she died, I promised her I'd see my sister kept out of trouble. And though I've done my best . . .' He grimaced. 'My best was never enough. Perhaps this time, it will be.'

Tears welled in Venette's eyes. Spilled. Impatient, she brushed them away. 'And if I say no?'

'Then you say no,' he said, shrugging. 'And I'll incant home the long, slow way, in stages. Cross my fingers I don't step into the middle of a Feenish war camp.'

638

'Now *that* is playing dirty!'

He shrugged again. 'I'm desperate.'

A long silence, and then she sighed. 'How d'you plan to kill him?'

Remmie reached inside his roughspun shirt, and pulled out the knife he'd carried since the day they left Elvado. 'With this. And if that doesn't work, if Barl's binding hasn't made him vulnerable, well . . . I'm sure I'll think of something.'

Despite everything she'd said about Danfey, Venette flinched. 'I see.'

'Venette . . .' He took her hands and held them. They were cold, and felt small. 'Please. Help me.'

She tugged free. Folded her arms. 'And how will we know if you succeed, and Morgan dies?'

'Barl will know,' he said, reluctant. 'They're connected. If he dies, she'll know.'

'And if you die?'

'She'll know that, too.'

Staring at him, Venette blinked away more tears. 'Remmie Lindin, I could hate you for this.'

'I'm sorry.'

'Are you *sure* there's no other way?'

He kissed her cheek. 'You know there isn't.'

'I could go.'

Loving her, he shook his head. 'No, you couldn't. You're the last of Elvado's Council of Mages. You're needed here, far more than me.'

'I beg to differ.' Her eyes narrowed. 'And so would Maris.'

Maris Garrick? She really was thinking to push him into that girl's arms? *Oh, Venette.* And then, remembering the Olken girl in the woodland, he felt his face heat.

Misreading him, Venette smiled. 'Ah. I knew you liked her.'

There was no time for contradictions. Besides, he didn't have the heart. Let Venette cling to her daydream. One way or another it would never come true.

'Venette, if I'm going to do this, I have to do it now,' he said. 'So are you going to help me or not?'

She sighed, shuddering. 'Yes. I'm going to help you. But why must it be *now*?'

'Because if Barl sees me, she'll know something's wrong. She'll try to stop me . . . and I don't want to hurt her.'

'You don't want to—' Bemused, Venette stared. 'And you don't think *this* will hurt?'

'This is different,' he muttered. 'Please, Venette. Let's go.'

Abandoning argument, she let him lead her into the Black Woods. And when at last they stopped, beneath a bobbing of glimfire, and debated the best travel incant to use, she gifted him with magework from the Hall's most secret archives. They worked the obscure incant together, drawing even more strength from Lur, and felt the incant's power like a waterfall thundering through their blood.

'She'll be furious with me,' he said, before Venette triggered the final sigil. He held his knife tightly, fingers cramping on its hilt. 'Barl. She'll need you, Venette. Don't let her turn you away. Help her, however you can.'

Her fingertips traced the scar on his cheek. 'I will, my dear. I promise. Just finish this, I beg you. For your sister. For Orwin. For everyone we've lost.'

*Irielle.* He nodded, his vision blurring again. 'Venette, tell Barl—'

'I will,' she said. 'Now go, my dear. *Go.* Before I change my mind.'

The night air burned with magic . . . and the Black Woods disappeared.

When at long last the meeting in Gribley's village hall broke up, Jervale loitered a little distance from the doors until he saw Bannet come out, a subdued Del by his side. Catching sight of him, Del's cheeks pinked. She murmured something and slipped away.

Paying no attention to the curious glances thrown in his direction, Jervale waved to catch Bannet's eye.

'Thought you'd come back in,' said Bannet, joining him. 'There was a lot of lively talk, after you left.'

He could imagine. 'I said my piece, Bannet. But I've more to say to you. Are you willing to listen?'

Bannet's eyes narrowed in his plain, weathered face. 'You're set to tell me something hacklesome, ain't you?'

'Something . . . heart-thumping,' he said, not smiling. 'But for all our sakes, Bannet, it's got to be told.'

'I can see that.' Heaving a resigned sigh, Bannet nodded at the Olken leaving the hall and milling in the narrow street. 'They chose to side with the Doranen, Jervale. Every last one of 'em's said they'll chime home to say it's best.' Another sigh. 'And who can blame 'em? Lur's in a bad way.'

'I know. For better or worse, I'll be chiming home the same thing.' Jervale touched his arm. 'We'll go back to my tent.'

Bannet took the news of being dreamed about without fuss. When the telling was done with, he sat silent on his tree-stump stool, scratching his raspy chin and watching the excited comings-and-goings of the other Olken who'd travelled to Gribley.

Jervale eyed him, nervous. 'Bannet, reckon I know how this sounds. And you ain't known me long, so—'

'Reckon I've known you long enough,' said Bannet. 'And it's funny.' He frowned. 'Now you've told me? What you say about these Doranen . . . it feels right, Jervale.'

Dizzy with relief, he clapped his new friend on the knee. 'Means a lot to hear you say that. Means more to know I'm believed.'

'Good to know I'm useful,' said Bannet, almost amused. 'But what else I can do, I ain't sure.'

'You can sit by while I find the others I dreamed. For I won't rest easy 'til this is settled.'

'Settled how?'

He frowned. 'I don't know. Not yet. Will you stay? Could take me a while.'

'I'll stay.'

So he left Bannet to his own musings and went in search of those other Olken, folk his instinct told him would help save Lur. Searched for them, found them, learned their names and then persuaded them to meet him at the eastern edge of the village, at first light. Just like Bannet, they seemed strangely unsurprised. And with every nod, every tentative smile, Jervale felt that odd twist of rightness.

*Could be I've not mucked this up after all.*

He returned to his tent, light-headed with the first hope he'd felt for days.

'Done?' said Bannet.

He nodded. 'Done. We'll talk it over in the morning.'

'Then best we get some shut-eye,' said Bannet, standing. 'I'll wish you pleasant dreams.'

And some time in the night he did dream, a blizzard of faces and knowings, so when he woke before dawn . . . he woke knowing what to do.

Barl startled out of sleep to the torment of Morgan's lips soft on hers. To the echo of his mocking voice, his breath sighing against her skin.

*'My love, my love, don't worry. We'll be together soon.'*

She sat up, heart pounding. 'No!'

The tent flap was pulled open. She never left it that way. And then, in the dawn gloom, she realised she wasn't alone.

'It's all right!' Venette said swiftly. 'It's me, Barl. Not – it's me.'

'Venette? What are you—'

'I've something to tell you. About Remmie. He's—'

'*Gone*,' Barl whispered, feeling his absence like a limb cut off, and snapped her fingers for glimfire. The light showed her Venette, somehow elegant in her roughspun shift, cross-legged on the tent floor. Her eyes were hollow, and haunted. 'Oh, my lady. What have you done?'

Waiting for Bannet and the others, Jervale felt oddly serene. Bad times were coming to Lur, he knew that without a doubt. But he'd not live to see them. And before the bad times, there'd be good times. Years and years of them, he knew that too. Which, also oddly, was a comfort.

*And as it stands, I'll take what comfort I can find.*

One by one, the Olken he'd dreamed of joined him, bleary-eyed in the early woodland light. Bannet came last, still lacing up his shirt.

'Right, then,' Jervale said, nodding. 'Let's find us a place to chat.'

He led them into the woods until he was certain they were deep enough they'd not be stumbled on, and overheard. Stopped, he had them introduce themselves so they weren't entirely strangers any more.

The oldest of them was Phryn of Tanny hamlet, on the eastern edge of the Black Woods. Bushy grey eyebrows pulled low, he worried the wattles on his neck.

'So, Jervale. What is it you want to say?'

Bannet gave him a small, encouraging nod. Warmed by it, Jervale cleared his throat. 'First of all, I want to know if you believe the things I said in the hall last night.'

'Say we do,' said Neese of Dellin, once she and old Phryn and the others finished exchanging cautious glances. 'So what?'

'You want us to chime our elders to say we were wrong, the Doranen should be sent back over the mountains?'

And that was sharp-faced Boyde from Jerring village.

Jervale pulled a face at him. 'No. Truth is, like I said, Barl Lindin's magework will save us from drought and famine and worse.'

'Then what are we doing here?' said Eryn of Sapslo, sounding plaintive.

'We're here 'cause there's *another* truth,' he said gently. Was she too young for this? He feared so, but had to follow his dream's prompting. 'There'll come a day when the Doranen are helpless . . . and then it's an Olken as will save Lur.'

Comfortably middle-aged Emmie from Hoyne, near the Flatlands, made a disbelieving sound. 'Helpless? How could these Doranen ever be helpless?'

'They're flesh and blood,' said Bannet. 'They make mistakes. Had to run, didn't they?'

Old Phryn snorted. 'Pity they had to run here.'

'Not if they save us from the drought, it's not,' Emmie

643

muttered. 'There's nine dead of it already, in Hoyne, and a score of others mortal sickly.'

'Last night, Jervale,' said Boyde, before a brangle could start, 'you were hard set against us giving up our singing. But what can we do if the Doranen want to magic it away?'

'That's a fair question,' said Bannet, as the others shared dismayed looks. 'Ain't none of us strong enough to stand against those mages. And I don't know about you, but I wouldn't know where to start.'

'I might have an answer to that,' Emmie said slowly. 'Born on the coast, I was. Bibford. Lived there half my life. Every season the fisherfolk gather to sing the sea. It's a powerful song, and when you sing it with so many folk, you can get into strife. There's a herbery most everyone drinks. Keeps the singing from sinking into you, doing all kinds of nasty mischief. Could be there's a way to make it even stronger. Strong enough to fuddle a Doranen mage. I'm a herbery woman. I know about these things.'

Looking at her, Jervale felt a great surge of affection. Felt it for all of them, these men and women he'd dreamed, who'd trusted him because he asked it . . . and for no other reason.

'Before I drink any herbery muck,' said Boyde, 'I want to know what you want of us, Jervale. You dragged us out here for a reason. Time to tell us what that is.'

Even Bannet was nodding. And he couldn't blame them.

'I know things,' he said, after a moment. 'But not everything. I can't see every twist and turn in the road. But I know this. *I know it*. You and me, we were born to be the secret keepers of Lur's magic. I know we're tasked with the saving of this land. I know the day will come when what we know, what we've held onto, will make the difference between life and death for the Olken.' One by one, he looked at them. 'And in your bones, I think you know it too. Why else did you let me drag you out here?'

Silence, as they thought about that. As he thought about the other things he'd learned from last night's dreams, that instinct told him they weren't ready to hear of, like the other ways Lur would change and the other sacrifices they'd be making.

*Like the Innocent Mage.*

Oh, yes. He'd keep *that* truth to himself a good while yet.

It was Bannet who spoke first. 'That's a mighty heavy burden, Jervale.'

'I know. I'm sorry.'

'And counting you, there's only seven of us to carry it. That ain't what I'd call a lot of folk to save Lur.'

'Seven's enough to start with,' he said. 'But don't fret. In time, we'll have more. In time our Circle will have all the folk it needs.'

Old Phryn rolled his eyes. 'Our circle?'

'The Doranen have their Council. And we'll be a circle, so strong the strongest Doranen magic will never break it. No matter what.'

'To our Circle,' said Emmie of Hoyne, and held out her hands. An acceptance. A challenge. A promise to stay true.

Holding hands with them, in a circle, Jervale blinked back tears.

*I've done it, Bene. I ain't mucked it up. Come what may, we'll survive.*

At breakfast, Maris asked after Remmie.

'He's feeling poorly this morning,' Venette said, and patted her hand. Years on the Council kept the truth out of sight. 'He's staying abed. But I'll tell him you were asking, my dear. That's bound to cheer him up.'

And Maris, for whom life had become such a wretched disappointment, nodded, believing her, and chatted with Mage Jarralt's son instead.

With her porridge bowl bravely emptied, Venette next took a turn about the camp. Not simply because she was avoiding Remmie's sister, but because it was important Dorana's mages knew she thought of them all the time. So she wandered and chatted and cuddled children and comforted the sad. Made a note of what her people needed, so she could approach Elder Chaffie later and ask for more help.

So *galling*, to be made beggars. How she longed for it to end.

The other reason to be social was to fill her mind so full there was no room in it for Remmie. No time to berate herself, wondering *Did I do the right thing?* She'd done what he wanted. She owed no apologies for that.

Returning from the camp's sick tents where a handful of mages still languished, recovering from the mountains, she saw Elder Chaffie hovering on the path between the village and the camp.

'Lady Martain,' the Olken greeted her, with a small, respectful nod. 'You look weary.'

'As do you, Elder Chaffie,' Venette replied, feeling her blood leap. 'I hope nothing is wrong.'

The little Olken woman shifted her gaze to the makeshift camp, where all that remained of Dorana ate and drank and murmured . . . and lived.

'We have made up our minds, Lady Martain. The mages of Dorana are welcome in Lur.'

'Oh,' she said faintly. 'Really? Well. That's good. You've decided much faster than . . .' She cleared her throat. 'Yes. That's good.'

To her surprise, Elder Chaffie laughed and patted her arm. 'It ain't a wonder you're fuddled. Truth be told, I'm fuddled too. We'll have a proper chinwag on it later. For now, I'll leave you be.'

If he'd been here, she'd have told Remmie first. But Remmie was gone . . . and so she went to tell his sister.

Like a marble effigy, Barl sat silent and stonelike in her tent. Venette entered without asking, then dropped to a crouch beside the cot.

'Barl? We have a new home. The Olken have said we can stay.'

Not even a flicker of eyelash suggested Remmie's sister had heard.

'*Barl!*'

646

The girl stirred. Looked up. Her eyes were full of contempt. 'How can I ward Lur when Remmie's not here? You *fool*, Venette. We suffered it all for *nothing*.'

Stung, Venette took Barl's shoulders and shook. 'Not for nothing. *Never* for nothing. Besides, there's time yet. If Remmie were stood beside me right now, you still wouldn't be ready. So do what you have to do . . . and trust in your brother. He'll come back before time's run out. I know he will. And so should you.'

'Don't you *dare* tell me what I should know about Remmie!' said Barl, wrenching herself loose. 'Get out of here. Get *out*, Venette! The sight of you makes me *sick*!'

Shaken, Venette did as she was told, and left the girl alone.

Two days after the Circle was formed, overcrowded Gribley began emptying of its extra Olken. Asked by Elder Chaffie to leave their chiming stones behind for the Doranen, Jervale and his new friends split theirs in two, gave half to Chaffie then cracked the other half into pieces, for swapping, so the Circle would remain unbroken. With that done, Jervale bid them farewell. Promised he'd chime them when he knew what next to say. What the Doranen planned to do. What that was he hoped to find out by speaking with Barl Lindin, before he left for home.

Bannet decided to ride for a time with Boyde and Emmie, wanting a chance to know them better. 'So it's peace to you, Jervale,' he said. 'Never doubt you've done what's right.'

'I don't,' he said, returning his new friend's hearty clap on the back. 'And I thank you. I'd have walked a lonesome road, I reckon, without you at my side.'

'And I'd have lived the rest of my life dull,' said Bannet. 'Funny, ain't it, how things turn out.'

Halfway to the Doranen camp, Jervale crossed paths with Del of Westwailing. The tiny life within her set his instincts freshly ablaze.

*In the Final Days shall come the Innocent Mage . . .*

'I'm off,' she said, and gave him a friendly peck on the cheek. 'Take care of yourself, Jervale.'

It was in him to warn her, but instinct stopped his tongue. Del was promised to a boy in Restharven. Folk would think the babe was early. No-one would know.

*Except for Tilly. When the time comes I'll tell her. She'll inherit my task.*

'Ride safely,' he told Del, and waved the lass out of sight.

Then he went in search of Barl Lindin, but instead of finding her, he found Lady Martain.

'I'm sorry,' the mage said. 'She is busy. Good day.'

There was no arguing with a Doranen. They were a haughty, arrogant lot. Never mind. He could wait. Barl Lindin was staying put, wasn't she? He'd talk to her some other time . . . once Lur was safe, and green.

Whistling, dreaming of Bene, he harnessed his donkeys and pointed their long, grey noses towards home.

# CHAPTER THIRTY-NINE

The impossible travel incant from the Hall of Knowledge's most secret archives spat Remmie out a stone's throw across the border into Dorana's First district. Spat him out of its mage-work to sprawl in a pool of his own blood-tainted vomit. Dazed, racked with pain, he lay beneath the fading sky and tried to pull the pieces of his shattered mind together.

*Venette . . . Venette . . . what did we do?*

He had no way of knowing for certain, but it felt as though he'd been travelling for days. *Days* in the suspended otherness of incant magic. No wonder he felt pulverised. No wonder he felt half dead. Venette was right. To attempt this had been madness.

*But what a wonderful madness. To reach for something no mage has ever done before. To reach . . . and grasp it. This must be how Barl felt.*

Understanding that, he wept a little. Because now, for the first time, he truly understood her.

*And if I'd understood her sooner, would I be lying here now?*

Lying in an open field, beneath a fading sky, in a land still torn and twisted with blight.

Although . . . not as badly as it was twisted when the Doranen fled their home. Despite the pain in his abused body, he could feel that much at least. Barl was right. Dorana was healing. In time its mages would be able to return.

*Provided I can kill Morgan. Provided he doesn't kill me.*

His fingers were still wrapped about the hilt of his knife. Amazing. He tried to lift his arm, to look at the blade, but his bones had turned to straw and the straw was catching fire. Giving up in the face of such hot torment, he closed his eyes again and waited for it to pass.

The next time he looked at the sky, it was morning.

Damp with dew, skin chilled and muscles stiff, he fought to sit up. Won that small battle, and groggily looked around. Yes, he was still in an open field. Aside from grass and trees, he was the only living thing in it. But if he squinted north . . . if he strained his eyes . . .

*That glitter on the horizon. I think that's Elvado.*

He heard himself groan. It was a long way to walk. And once he'd reached the city, he had further still to go before he reached the Danfey estate.

*Perhaps I'll find a horse. It's only been a few months, I can't have forgotten how to ride.*

But until he found his horse, he'd be walking. And to do that, he had to stand.

Swaying on his feet, head swimming, Remmie groaned again. He was hungry. But at least his time in the wilderness had taught him how to hunt and forage. Whatever else happened, he wasn't going to starve.

And if he thought about that, about hunting and foraging and filling his empty belly . . . then he'd be too busy to think of anything else.

Like his sister. Like Danfey. Like dying here, alone.

*I had to do this, Barl. When you calm down, you'll know I had to. I promised Mama I'd keep you safe, remember? And I always keep my word.*

Barl's rage at her brother was so consuming, she wrote him out of her diary. Used an expunging incant on her scribblings to make it seem he never was. And if he came back . . . *when* he came back . . . she'd show him his absence. Thrust the diary beneath his nose and shout, *You see? You weren't missed!*

Because she missed him so badly, she woke in tears with every dawn.

*How could you, Remmie? How could you do this to me?*

She'd made her peace with Venette. Beneath the pain, she knew this was Remmie's fault. Not hers. He'd have done this with or without the councillor's help. At least with it, he had a chance.

*To get there in one piece. But how will he get back? If he survives the incant . . . the blight . . . Morgan . . . how will he get back in time?*

And that was the crux of it. As ever, for her, it came down to time. The Olken were running out of it. The drought was tightening its grip. And if she broke its stranglehold on Lur without raising the wall, then the warding incant she'd created would never see the light of day. The magics wouldn't permit it.

*Which means if I break the drought first, and then Remmie fails, there will be nothing to stop Morgan . . . and all of us will die.*

And though she could hardly bear to think of it, there was a chance he'd fail.

*So now I must hope my brother murders the man I love. Loved. The man whose madness I helped create. The man who loves me, though his heart is made barren and his brilliant mind a ruin.*

And so, hoping, she would wait. Wait as long as she could. And while she waited, continue to create Lur's future. The future she wouldn't see if Remmie failed to murder Morgan . . . and, out of time, she was forced to raise the wall.

With the inciting weather magic incants perfected, she turned her skills to what came next, the incants and protections that would keep Lur's weather tame, the land in precarious balance, the warding powerful enough to hold Morgan at bay for the years it would take him to die of old age.

Because she knew, oh she knew, that until time claimed him he would stop at *nothing* to reach her. Though for some reason his dream sendings had ceased of late, she didn't need them to know.

There was also the question of who would magework the weather day in and day out, once the warding wall was raised. But the answer was obvious. She chose Venette as the weather magic's first guardian. Who followed next would be Venette's choice, in consultation with the new Council, when it was formed.

Since the weather magics were too dangerous to leave unguarded and easily absorbed, she used Olken crystal as a repository for the incants and sigils and protected them with copious wardings. Drove herself to the brink of breaking, for the powerful incants resisted their caging.

After careful thought, she crafted another incant, this one to let a mage see through Lur's wall, once it was raised. For a locked room without a window was not a safe thing.

As she laboured over her legacy, waiting and hoping for Remmie to return, she left Venette to take charge of everything else. The forming of a new Council. The finding of a place for the Doranen to create their own township. The creation of the incant that would blank the Olken's magic from their minds and memories, as though it had never been. A difficult decision, that was . . . but Lur was better safe than sorry. There was the code of justice that would allow Doranen and Olken to live side by side in peace. And a second code, the Doranen code, that would ensure no ruinous magics would ever be used again. That meant they must sift through their history of mageworks, deciding what to discard and what to keep.

And in their careful sifting, become better mages than they had been.

All of that, Barl left to Venette. Trusting her to do what was right, as she was trusted to make them safe. She worked, she ate, and in brief snatches she slept. Because time was running out, Morgan still lived, she was sure of it . . . and Remmie hadn't returned.

\* \* \*

*Bound in Barl's magic, bound with cruelty and failed love, Morgan turns his swiftly growing strength to the destruction of her warding. It is almost completed, his ruin of her plan to hold him, constrain him, deny him what is his. Every thought turns towards freedom. He has no time to touch her mind. But he can wait. He is patient. A pleasure deferred is a pleasure prolonged. It is a lesson she has taught him, a lesson he has learned –*

The shock of the knife sliding into his chest was so great, Morgan almost lost his grasp of Barl's final, frayed binding incant. The invading blade was long and narrow and brutally sharp. He'd felt a blade like that before. Once. A lifetime ago, it seemed. When someone had tried to murder his darling. His *dravas*. The mageworked child of his heart.

Now, as then, he repudiated the insult. Used Dorana's tainted, transformed magics to heal his rudely pierced flesh. And as he did so, rage surged through him.

*Who seeks my life? Who dares raise a hand to Morgan Danfey?*

The fury released him. Burst him free of Barl's restraint. Burst his *dravas* free of bondage with him. He felt them stir and wake. Heard a wild shout of triumph. Felt the blood pump through his veins. A flare of light as his eyes opened. A hoarse gasp as he breathed free air. Sickening confusion. Where was he? And then he recognised the curtains. The chamber. This was the Danfey estate. His mansion. His bed.

*And that is my beloved's brother. Remmie Lindin. Holding a knife.*

With an oiled ease that pleased him, no harm taken from his captivity, he rolled from the bed and onto his feet. Noted that he was dressed in silk, but barefoot. Felt the new length of his hair. Barl's would-be murderous brother was staring, shocked eyes wide in his pinched, bloodless face. He was very thin, and he favoured one leg. His face was scarred, a line of pink, puckered flesh spoiling the beauty he shared with his sister.

*My, my. How long have I been bound?*

'Barl said you were breaking free. I didn't want to believe it.'

Barl's brother sounded hoarse, shattered with surprise. With grief. But surely if anyone deserved to be griefstruck, it was Morgan Danfey. Betrayed. Abandoned. Discarded by the woman he'd loved more than his life.

He raised an eyebrow. 'Well, Remmie. You stayed behind to kill me?'

'No. I came back.'

'Came back?' He smiled. 'From where?'

Remmie's jaw clenched. He was frightened, but not running. That was, of course, preferable. The killing of cowards was no sport at all.

'I won't tell you that, Danfey.'

Of course he would. But there was time. 'You look a trifle ragged, Mage Lindin. Has life been unkind?'

Tears sprang to Remmie's eyes. 'Dorana is dead. It might be healing, but it's still dead. Its mages are slaughtered. Elvado's a deserted ruin. Worse. A graveyard. All of Dorana's a graveyard. I've walked for days to get here, and hardly saw a living soul. And those I did find have gone half-mad from hunger, and fighting the blight, and each other. What you did, Danfey.' His harsh breathing harshened further. 'With your cursed magework and ambition. What you *did* . . .'

'What your sister and I did,' he said, amiable, and laughed when Remmie flinched. 'Speaking of Barl, how is my beloved? Do you know she weeps for me, in her restless dreams?'

'She weeps for ever knowing you,' said Remmie, sneering. 'She never loved you, Danfey. That was a lie.'

'It was *not* a lie!' he shouted, rage surging again. And then he laughed, because he saw that was the truth. Though Remmie tried to hide it, Barl's love was in her brother's eyes.

He felt a rush of heat, seeing it. Was scalded by memories of this chamber, that bed, her heated flesh heating him. Desire. Longing. Regret. He doused them all with rage.

*She bound me. She left me. That is not love.*

'Where is she, Remmie? You must know she's mine. You must know we belong together. Have you ever loved? If you had, you'd not stand between us. Please. Stand aside.'

654

'*Please?*' Remmie's fingers were bloodless on the knife's hilt. 'And is that what those poor councillors and the mages of Elvado said before you beasted them? *Please?* You were a man, once, Morgan. You were human. But now? I don't know what you are now.'

He laughed. 'Magnificent.'

'If there is a trace left in you of the man my sister knew, for her sake, in her memory, let me—'

He snapped his fingers. '*Be quiet.*'

Silenced, caught between heartbeats, Remmie Lindin held his breath. Smiling, Morgan indulged in a luxurious cat-stretch, then stripped off his tired tunic and dressed himself as befit a lord. Silk brocade and supple leathers. Jewels in his ears. With his long hair brushed and neatly braided, he turned back to Barl's brother. The *dravas* incant came easily, his fingers dancing through the sigils, its syllables tripping off his tongue. Once changed, Remmie would obey his every whim. Would remember enough to remember Barl . . . and swiftly take him to her.

*Be patient, my love. It won't be long now.*

He released Remmie from his thrall so the *dravas* incant might take effect.

And then a shock. Remmie was *fighting* him. He was resisting the incant's changes . . . and because he was, after all, Barl's twin brother, monstrously, terribly, he was winning a reprieve.

Snarling now, not smiling, Morgan opened himself to the darkness that was Dorana. Felt its tainted power flood him. Pain flooded after it and he cried out, protesting. Cried out a second time as he imposed his implacable will. Panting, he straightened. Invoked the *dravas* incant again.

Barl's brother screamed as his body began its remoulding. Eyes wide with the searing pain, the bones beneath his skin contorting, his pale, scarred skin thickening, teeth lengthening to pointed fangs, fingers curving into claws, breath by breath he changed.

'*No!*' howled Remmie Lindin, and plunged the knife he held into his own throat.

Linked by the *dravas* incant, Morgan felt the blade sink hilt-deep. Sank to his knees, screaming, as Remmie Lindin sank before him, the hot blood pumping with every beat of his dying heart. Rage thundered, fury shook him. To be bound, and escape the binding? To triumph over Brice Varen and Sallis Arkley and Shari Friedin, and then *die*?

*At the hands of a treacherous whore's brother? Never! Never! I am Morgan Danfey!*

So he fought to live as Remmie Lindin slowly died. Sprawled on his chamber floor and watched the tide of blood flood towards him. Felt it soak him in its heat. Breathed in its salt sweet stench.

*I will not die. I will not die. I am magnificent Morgan Danfey. I will not die.*

Toiling over the creation of her weather incant's final, most important piece, Barl felt a searing pain shaft through her. Crying out, she staggered then slumped to the floor of Gribley's village hall.

*Remmie. Remmie. Oh, no. Remmie. No.*

Pain blazed in her throat, in her bones, in her blood. There was a filthy taint inside her, a grotesque twisting in her mind. A cruel, familiar presence, crowing even as it screamed.

Dimly she heard the hall's door bang open. Heard panicked footsteps racing over the wooden floor.

'Barl? Barl! Justice have mercy, what's wrong?'

Venette. Of course Venette. She couldn't play a part in the weather map's creation but still she insisted on remaining close by. Just in case.

*She'll never let me forget she was right.*

'Barl!' Venette shouted, dropping beside her. 'Is it Remmie? My dear, please tell me it's not Remmie!'

Her throat hurt too much for speaking, but the truth must have shown in her eyes. Venette sobbed once, wildly, hands flying to her face.

'Oh, no. Oh, no. I should never have helped him!'

She wanted to scream, *No, you shouldn't, Venette! This is your fault!*

But it wasn't, and she knew that, and to say so would be cruel.

After Dorana, after the things she'd done, she'd sworn she'd never be cruel again.

Remmie was dying. She could feel it. His life was ebbing fast. She could feel his tears. They were her tears. They were weeping together now.

*I took you out of my diary, Rem. I'm so sorry. I shouldn't have done that.*

And now it was too late. There'd be no time to put him back.

How far away was he? So far . . . and slipping further. They were twins. She could feel him. If she reached out with her mind . . . with her broken heart . . . would he feel her? Could she touch him? Was there enough time left to –

'*My love, my love, your brother's dead. I'm sorry. It wasn't me. I promise. Poor Remmie killed himself.*'

Morgan. Unbound.

Shuddering, she felt herself roll into a ball. Felt Morgan's roaming lips on her, felt his hands caress her skin.

'Barl! Barl, for pity's sake, what's happening?'

She couldn't answer Venette. Her skin was crawling, her mind whirling, she wanted to scream and sob and retch.

'*My love, my beloved, I know where you are. Remmie told me. Such a little scamp. I was in his mind as he died. Beyond the mountains. A land called Lur. Full of simple, ignorant people. They will make such beautiful* dravas. *A thoughtful gift, my love.*'

'No,' she moaned, writhing. 'Remmie . . . Remmie . . . no . . .'

'*Wait for me, my beloved bitch, my treacherous slut, my whore. For I know where you are, Barl, and you have no place left to run!*'

With a horrified cry, Barl opened her eyes and sat up. Clutched at Venette, who was clutching hard at her.

'Morgan, it's Morgan,' she gabbled, almost choking with fear. 'He's free, Venette. He's coming. He knows where we are. Oh quick, there's no *time.*'

The weather map. It wasn't finished. She had to finish it, or the magic would fail. No tamed weather, no shielding wall, and Morgan loose among the Olken.

*Remmie.*

She pulled free of weeping Venette and staggered to her feet. 'Get up. *Get up!* We have to hurry. I don't know what power's in him now. I don't know what he can do.'

Tears slicked Venette's blanched cheeks. The haughty councillor was gone. 'Remmie's dead? Barl, is he—'

'*Yes*, Remmie's *dead*!' she said, and shook her. 'Mourn him later, Venette, when I'm gone. But if you don't help me now, we'll all be dead. Understand?'

On a shuddering breath, Venette regained her self-control. 'Yes.'

'*Yes*. Now run to my tent, and bring my big leather satchel to me. *Hurry*.'

As Venette ran, Barl flung herself back to the weather map. So nearly done, so nearly, *surely* she had time . . .

The world blurred around her as she finished her crucial task, embedding the remaining incants in the model of Lur carved by loving Olken hands. The details could be finished later, after she was gone, but the magic couldn't wait. It had to be finished *now*.

Lost in desperate magework, she was vaguely aware of Venette's return, of Elder Chaffie and Maris Garrick and some others on the new Council, all come to the village hall to see . . . whatever they saw.

And then she was done, she was *done*. The incants ignited. The weather map came to life, humming with potential. Waiting for the wall.

She looked at Venette, sweat dripping down her face. 'My satchel. Quickly. And send everyone else away.'

Of course Maris protested, but she couldn't care about that. Upending the heavy leather satchel, she showed its scattered contents to Venette.

'My diary. You keep it. Read it, by all means, but never let it out of your sight. There's an incant in here . . . I finished it early this morning.' She felt herself shiver. 'Venette, it's for an unmaking. The worst you'll ever see. Don't use it unless you have to. It's for a last resort. Understand?'

Venette's eyes brimmed with tears. 'Yes, my dear. Yes.'

'This? Take it. This is a warding. My own personal seal. When the time is right build a library for the books and scrolls of magic you think should be kept secret, and ward it. It's the only way to be sure.'

Nodding, Venette looked at the seal. 'Of course.'

What else . . . what else . . .

'Here's the orb with the weather magics,' she said, holding up the crystal sphere, 'and all the notes on how to use it.' Pages and pages of them, littering the floor. 'I know I've only explained it once, but once will have to be enough. And remember, taking the magics will be painful. I'm sorry. There's nothing I can do about that now.'

Seemingly bewildered, Venette was shaking her head. 'Barl, my dear, take a breath. Slow down. Surely—'

'I can't slow down!' she said, shaking. 'Didn't you hear me? *He's coming!* Now quickly, quickly, help me fill the satchel.'

So Venette helped her shove the notes and the diary and the orb back in the leather satchel. And as she laced it tightly closed –

*'Barl, my beloved . . . wear flowers in your hair . . .'*

Her bones shuddered, her heart quailed, and she sank moaning to the floor.

*Remmie . . . Remmie . . .*

'Barl, please,' Venette begged her. 'Please, you have to stop this, you have to—'

Somehow, from somewhere, she found the strength to stand. 'I can't. There's no time. Venette, I have to go.'

'But the warding's magework, Barl!' Venette protested. 'The weather magic's incants! The syllables and the sigils, this is a complicated working. Where are your notes? You can't remember—'

'Yes, I can.' She tapped her temple, then her breast. 'The magic's inside me, Venette. It always was. Didn't you know?' She held out her hands. Took hold of Venette's wrists, and pulled her onto her feet. Kept holding, because these were the last hands she'd ever hold, this the last face she'd ever see.

*And they belong to Venette Martain. Well, I suppose it could be worse. They could belong to Maris Garrick.*

Venette's hair was in disarray. Trying to smile, Barl smoothed it. 'Stay here, my lady. You've done all you can. What's left to do is up to me.'

'Oh, Barl . . .' Venette whispered, weeping. 'Oh, my dear. You'll not be forgotten, I swear it. Every mage born shall know what you've done. What you've sacrificed. What you're owed. Yes, and every Olken too. *We will not forget.*'

Bemused, Barl shook her head. Had they hated each other once? She and Venette? It seemed a long time ago. Hate and love. Love and hate. What did that odd little Olken man say? What was his name? Jervale?

*'Love can turn to hate quick as a wink. You know that.'*

Well, if she didn't know it before . . . she certainly did now.

'Goodbye, Venette,' she said, smiling. 'And good luck.'

And before things became impossible, she turned and hurried from the hall, past Maris Garrick and Elder Chaffie and the other mages whose faces were too blurred for her to see, past Gribley's surprised villagers . . . who'd become monsters if she failed.

Once she reached the edge of the village she broke into a run, and kept running, faster and faster, feeling Morgan's hot, hungry breath on the back of her neck. Ran until the birdsong gloom of the Black Woods swallowed her completely. Until her mage-sense stirred and told her: *Here, Barl. Here.*

Panting, exhausted, with Morgan outrun for the moment, she dropped to the cool, damp, leaf-littered ground. Felt the mountains, towering above her. Felt the gentle song in Lur's bones. Felt the magic, waiting inside her, desperate to burst free.

And then she felt a strange peace wash over her, like the brief touch of a gentle, loving hand.

'Yes, Remmie,' she whispered. 'I'm ready.'

And drew her first blood-red sigil on the cool, waiting air.

# ACKNOWLEDGEMENTS

Tim Holman, Bernadette Foley, Mary GT Webber, Glenda Larke, Mark Timmony, Elaine and Peter Shipp, Ethan Ellenberg, Abigail Nathan, David Wyatt, Peter Cotton, the Orbit Team.

# extras

www.orbitbooks.net

# about the author

**Karen Miller** was born in Vancouver, Canada, and moved to Australia with her family when she was two. Apart from a three-year stint in the UK after graduating from university with a BA in Communications, she's lived in and around Sydney ever since. Karen started writing stories while still in primary school, where she fell in love with speculative fiction. She's done a variety of interesting jobs, but now writes full time. For more information, visit www.karenmiller.net

Find out more about Karen Miller and other Orbit authors by registering for the free monthly newsletter at www.orbitbooks.net

if you enjoyed
A BLIGHT OF MAGES

look out for

THE HEIR OF NIGHT

by

Helen Lowe

# CHAPTER ONE

## *The Keep of Winds*

The wind blew out of the northwest in dry, fierce gusts, sweeping across the face of the Gray Lands. It clawed at the close-hauled shutters and billowed every tapestry and hanging banner in the keep. Loose tiles rattled and slid, bouncing off tall towers into the black depths below; as the wind whistled through the Old Keep, finding every crack and chink in its shutters and blowing the dust of years along the floors. It whispered in the tattered hangings that had once graced the High Hall, back in those far-off days when the hall had blazed with light and laughter, gleaming with jewel and sword. Now the cool, dry fingers of wind teased their frayed edges and banged a whole succession of doors that long neglect had loosened on their hinges. Stone and mortar were still strong, even here, and the shutters held against the elements, but everything else was given over to the slow corrosion of time.

Another tile banged and rattled its way down the roof as a slight figure swarmed up one of the massive stone pillars that marched along either side of the hall. There was an alarming creak as the climber swung up and over the balustrade of a wooden gallery, high above the hall floor – but the timbers held. The climber paused, looking around with satisfaction, and wiped dusty hands on the seat of her plain, black pants. A narrow, wooden staircase twisted up toward another, even higher gallery of sculpted stone, but the treads stopped just short of the top. She studied the gap, her eyes narrowed as they traced the leap she would need to make: from the top of the stair to the gargoyles beneath the stone balcony, and then up, by a series of precarious finger- and toe-holds, onto the balcony itself.

The girl frowned, knowing that to miss that jump would mean plummeting to certain death, then shrugged and began to climb, testing each wooden tread before trusting her weight to it. She paused again on the topmost step, then sprang, her first hand slapping onto a corbel while the other grasped at a gargoyle's half-spread wing. She hung for a moment, swinging, then knifed her feet up onto the gargoyle's claws before scrambling over the high shoulder and into the gallery itself. Her eyes shone with triumph and excitement as she stared through the rear of the gallery into another hall.

Although smaller than the High Hall below, she could see that it had once been richer and more elegant. Beneath the dust, the floors were a mosaic of beasts, birds, and trailing vines; panels of metal and jeweled glass decorated the walls. There was a dais at the far end of the long room, with the fragile remains of a tapestry draped on the wall behind it. The hanging would have been bright with color once, the girl thought; the whole hall must have glowed with it, but it was a dim and lifeless place now.

She stepped forward, then jumped and swung around as her reflection leapt to life in the mirrored walls. A short, slightly built girl stared back at her out of eyes like smoke in a delicately chiseled face. She continued to stare for a moment, then poked her tongue out at the reflection, laughing at her own fright. 'This must be the Hall of Mirrors,' she said, pitching her voice against the silence. She knew that Yorindesarinen herself would have walked here once, if all the tales were true, and Telemanthar, the Swordsman of Stars. But now there was only emptiness and decay.

She walked the length of the hall and stepped onto the shallow dais. Most of the tapestry on the rear wall had decayed into shreds or been eaten by moths, but part of the central panel was still intact. The background was darkness, rimmed with fire, but the foreground was occupied by a figure in hacked and riven armor, confronting a creature that was as vast as the tapestry itself. Its flat, serpentine head loomed out of the surrounding darkness, exuding menace, and its bulk was doom. The figure of the hero, dwarfed beneath its shadow, looked overmatched and very much alone.

The girl touched the battered figure with her fingertips, then pulled back as the fabric crumbled further. 'The hero Yorindesarinen,' she whispered, 'and the Worm of Chaos. This should never have been left here, to fall into ruin.' She hummed a thread of tune that was first martial, then turned to haunting sadness as she slid forward, raising an imaginary sword against an unseen opponent. Her eyes were half closed as she became the fated hero in her mind, watching the legendary frost-fire gleam along her blade.

Another door banged in the distance and a voice called, echoing along silent corridors and through the dusty hall. 'Malian! Mal – lee-ee – aan, my poppet!' The Old Keep caught the voice and tossed it into shadowy corners, bouncing echoes off stone and shutter while the wind whispered all around. 'Where are you-oo-oo? Is this fit behavior for a Lady of Night? You are naught but an imp of wickedness, child!'

The door banged again, cutting off the voice, but the damage was done. The bright figure of Yorindesarinen faded back into memory and Malian was no longer a hero of song and story, but a half-grown girl in grubby clothes. Frowning, she smoothed her hands over her dark braid. The hero Yorindesarinen, she thought, would not have been plagued with nurses when she was a girl; she would have been too busy learning hero craft and worm slaying.

Malian hummed the snatch of tune again and sighed, walking back to the stone balcony – then froze at a suggestion of movement from the High Hall, two storeys below. Crouching down, she peered between the stone balusters, then smiled and stood up again as a shimmer of lilting sound followed the initial footfall. A slender, golden figure gazed up at her through the twilit gloom, his hands on his hips and his sleeves flared wide, casting a fantastic shadow to either side. One by one the tiny golden bells on his clothes fell silent.

'And how,' asked Haimyr, the golden minstrel, the one bright, exotic note in her father's austere keep, 'do you propose getting down from there? Just looking at you makes my blood run cold!'

Malian laughed. 'It's easy,' she said, 'especially if you've been trained by Asantir.' She slid over the balustrade and made her way back down the finger- and toe-holds to hang again from the gargoyle. She grinned down at the minstrel's upturned face while she swung backward and forward, gaining momentum, before arching out and dropping neatly to the stairs below. The staircase swayed a little, but held, and she ran lightly down, vaulting up and over the second balcony, then scrambled through its wooden trusses to descend the final pillar. The minstrel held open his golden sleeves, scalloped and edged and trailing almost to the floor, and she jumped the last few feet, straight into his arms. He reeled slightly, but kept his balance, catching her in a brocaded, musical embrace. A little trail of mortar slid down the pillar after her.

'I had no idea you were due back!' Malian exclaimed, her voice muffled by the brocade. 'You have been away for-*ever*! You have no idea how tedious it has been without you.'

Haimyr stepped back and held her at arm's length. His hair was a smooth curve along his shoulders and no less golden than his clothes, or the bright gleam of his eyes. 'My dear child,' he said, 'you are entirely mistaken. I have every idea how tedious it has been, not to mention dull and entirely unleavened by culture, wit, or any other redeeming quality. But you – I go away for half a year and you shoot up like a weed in my absence.'

She shook her head. 'I'm still short, just not *quite* as short as I was.'

'But,' he said, 'every bit as grubby and disheveled, which will not do, not if you expect to embrace me in this wild fashion.' He looked around with the lazy, lambent gaze of a cat. 'This is a strange place for your play, my Malian – and what of the danger to your father's only child and heir, climbing about in that reckless manner. What would any of us say to him if you were to fall and break your neck?'

'Oh, he is away at present, riding the bounds and inspecting the outposts,' said Malian. 'You would all have time to run away before he got back.'

Haimyr regarded her with a satirical eye. 'My dear child,' he said, 'why do you think your good nurse and the maids are all out hunting for you, high and low? Your father is back.' Mockery glinted in his smile. 'On the whole, my Malian, I think that it would be better for you and your household if you were on time for his returning feast.'

Malian pulled a face. 'We all thought the patrols would be away another week at least,' she said, with feeling. 'But thank you for coming in here after me. You're right, I don't think anyone in my household would brave it, even to prevent my father's anger.' She grinned again. 'That's why I like it, because no one else ever comes here and I can do what I want. They think it's haunted,' she added.

'I know,' said Haimyr. 'They have been telling me so since before you were born.' He shrugged, his tall, fantastic shadow shrugging with him on the wall. 'Well, folk have always liked to frighten themselves, by daylight or by dark, but they may be partly right about this place. The shadows of memory lie very thick here.'

'It is a strange place,' Malian agreed, 'but I don't think it's dangerous. It seems sad to me, because of the decay and the silence, rather than frightening. And the memories, of course, are very bitter.'

The minstrel nodded. 'All the histories of your people are tragic and shot through with darkness. But the memories here must rank among the darkest.'

'You are not afraid to come here, though,' she said.

Haimyr laughed, and the sound echoed in the high stone vault overhead. 'Afraid? Of the past's shadows? No. But then, they are not my shadows. They are your blood heritage, my Malian, not mine.'

Malian frowned. 'I am not afraid either,' she declared, and Haimyr laughed again.

'Of course not, since you choose to come here,' he said. 'And rather often, too, I suspect.'

Malian smiled in response, a small secret smile. '*Quite* a lot,' she agreed, 'especially when you and Asantir are away.' She drew a pattern in the dust with her foot. 'It has been very dull without you, Haimyr. Six months was far too long a time.'

He smiled down at her. 'I apologize for condemning you to a life of tedium. Will you forgive me if I say that I have brought back something you value, to make up for my neglect?'

Malian considered this. 'New songs and stories?' she asked. 'Then I may forgive you, but only if you promise to teach me every one.'

Haimyr swept a low, extravagant bow, his sleeves tinkling and his golden eyes glinting into hers, one long slender hand placed over his heart. Malian smiled back at him.

'Every one, remember,' she said again, and he laughed, promising nothing, as was his way.

It was only a few hundred paces from the old High Hall to the gate into the New Keep, which was barred and soldered closed, although there was a locked postern a few yards away. Malian's customary means of coming and going was a narrow gap between the apex of the gate and the corridor's arched roof, but she was resigned, rather than surprised, when Haimyr took the postern key from his pocket. 'Oh dear,' she murmured, 'now I am in trouble.'

Haimyr slanted her a mocking smile. 'Didn't you hear poor Doria, calling to you? She summoned the courage to put her head around the postern for love of you, but even a lifetime's devotion wouldn't take her any further. Nhairin, of course, is made of sterner stuff, but we agreed that I was better suited to hunting you out.'

'Because you could hope to catch me if I ran?' she inquired, with a smile as sly as his. 'But I cannot see you scaling the walls, Haimyr, even to save me from my father's wrath.'

He closed the postern behind them, locking it with a small, definite click. 'You are quite right. Even the thought is an abhorrence. The ghosts of the past are one thing, but to scramble through the rafters like an Ishnapuri monkey, quite another. I would have absolutely no choice but to abandon you to your fate.'

Malian laughed aloud, but sobered as they turned into the golden blaze of the New Keep. Darkness never fell in these corridors and halls where jewel-bright tapestries graced the walls and the floors were patterned with colored tiles. Pages sped by on their innumerable errands while soldiers marched with measured tread and the vaulted ceilings echoed with all the commotion of a busy keep. Malian's eyes lit up as the bustle surged around them. 'It's always like this when my father comes home,' she said. 'He sets the entire keep in a flurry.'

Haimyr's laugh was rueful. 'Do I not know it? And now I must hurry, too, if I am to prepare my songs for the feast.'

'Everyone will be eager for something new,' Malian agreed. 'But only after you have sung of the deeds and glory of the House of Night – for are we not first and oldest?'

'Oldest, first, and greatest of all the Derai Houses on the Wall, in deeds and duty if not in numbers,' a new voice put in, as though reciting indisputable fact. A spare figure rose from an alcove seat and limped forward. She was as dark and reserved as the minstrel was golden and flamboyant, and her face was disfigured by the scar that slashed across it from temple to chin.

'"*For it is the House of Night that holds the Keep of Winds,*"' Malian chanted in reply, '"*foremost of all the strongholds on the Shield Wall of Night.*"' It was you who first taught me that, Nhairin.'

The newcomer's dark brows lifted. 'I have not forgotten,' she said, taking the postern key from Haimyr. She had soldiered once for the Earl of Night, until the fight in which she gained both limp and scar, and she liked to say that she soldiered still in the Earl's service, but as High Steward of the Keep of Winds, rather than with a sword. 'I do not forget any of the few lessons that did not have to be beaten into you,' she added meditatively.

'Nhair-*rin*!' said Malian, then a quick, guilty look crossed her face. 'Have I caused you a great deal of trouble, having to look for me?'

The steward smiled, a slight twist of her mouth. 'Trouble? Nay, I am not troubled. But I know who will be if you are not clean and in your place when the feast bell strikes.' The smile widened at Malian's alarmed look. 'That bell is not so very far off, so if I were you I should be running like the wind itself to my chamber, and the bath that is waiting there.'

Haimyr clapped Malian on the shoulder. 'The good steward is right, as always. So run now, my bold heart!'

Malian ran. Her father held strict views on the conduct appropriate to an Heir of Night, and exacted the same obedience from his daughter as he did from the warriors under his command. 'We keep the long watch,' he often said to Malian, 'and that means we are a fighting House. The Wall itself is named for us, and of all the fortresses along its length, this one stands closest to our enemy. We cannot let our vigilance or discipline waver for an instant, and you and I must be the most vigilant of all, knowing all others look to us and will follow our example, whether good or bad.'

Malian knew that upholding discipline included being on time for a formal Feast of Returning. Her nurse and the other maids knew it, too, for they did not stop to scold but descended on her as one when she ran through the door, hustling her out of her grimy clothes and into the tepid bath-water. Nesta, the most senior of the maids, caught Malian's eye as she opened her mouth to complain, and Malian immediately shut it again. Nesta came from a family that had served the Earls of Night for long generations, and she held views on the value of discipline, tradition, and truancy that were remarkably similar to those of Malian's father.

Doria, Malian's nurse, was more voluble. 'An imp of wickedness, that's what you are,' she said. 'Running here, and running there, and never in sight when wanted. You'll be the death of me yet, I swear – not to mention the wrath of the Earl, your father, if he ever finds out about your expeditions.'

'We'll all die of fright on that day, sure enough,' said Nesta, in her dry way, 'if nothing worse happens first. But will our fine young lady care, that's what I ask? And none of your wheedling answers either, my girl!' She struck a stern attitude, with arms akimbo, and the younger maids giggled.

'Well,' said Malian meekly, 'it hasn't happened yet, has it? And you know I don't mean to be a trouble to you, Doria darling.' She hugged and kissed her nurse, but poked her tongue out at Nesta over Doria's shoulder.

The maid made a snipping motion with her fingers, imitating scissors. 'Ay, Doria knows you don't mean to cause her trouble, but it won't stop trouble coming – especially if we don't get you down to dinner on time.' She held up an elaborate black velvet dress. 'It had better be black, I suppose, since you welcome the Earl of Night.'

'Black is good, thank you,' agreed Malian, scrambling into it. She waited, as patiently as she could, while Doria bound her hair into a net of smoky pearls.

'You look just like the ladies in the old tapestries,' the nurse sighed, as her fingers twisted and pinned. 'You are growing up, my poppet. Nearly thirteen already! And in just a few more years you will be a grand lady of the Derai, in truth.'

Malian made a face at the polished reflection in the mirror. 'I do look like a scion of the oldest line, I suppose.' She kicked the train out behind her. 'But can you imagine Yorindesarinen wearing anything so restrictive?'

'That skirt would make worm slaying very difficult,' Nesta observed, and Malian grinned.

Doria, however, frowned. 'Yorindesarinen is nothing but a fable put about by the House of Stars to make themselves feel important.' She sniffed. 'Just like the length of their names. Ridiculous!'

'They're not all long,' Malian pointed out. 'What about Tasian and Xeria?'

The nurse made a sign against bad luck, while Nesta shook her head. 'Shortened,' the maid said. 'Why should we honor that pair of ill omen with their full names?' She pulled a face. 'Especially she who brought ruin upon us all.'

Doria nodded, her mouth pursed as if she had filled it with pins. 'Cursed be her name – and completely beneath the attention of the Heir of Night, so we will not sully our lips with it now!' She gave a last tweak to the gauze collar, so that it stood up like black butterfly wings on either side of Malian's face. 'You look just as you should,' she said, not without pride. 'And if you hurry, you'll be on time as well.'

Malian kissed her cheek. 'Thank you,' she said, with real gratitude. 'I am sorry that I gave you all so much trouble.'

Nesta rolled her eyes and Doria looked resigned. 'You always are,' she said, sighing. 'But I don't like your gallivanting off into the Old Keep, nasty cold place that it is. Trouble will come of it – and then what the Earl will do to us all, I shudder to think.'

Malian laughed. 'You worry too much,' she said. 'But if I don't hurry I really will be late and my father will make us all shudder, sooner rather than later.'

She blew a butterfly kiss back around the door and walked off as quickly as the black dress would allow, leaving Doria and Nesta to look at each other with a mixture of exasperation, resignation, and affection.

'Don't say it,' the nurse said to the younger woman, sitting down with a sigh. 'The fact is that she is just like her mother was at the same age – too much on her own and with a head filled with dreams of glory. Not to mention running wild, all over the New Keep and half the Old.'

Nesta shook her head. 'They've been at her since she was a babe with all their lessons, turning her into an earl in miniature, not to mention the swordplay and other skills required by a warrior House. I like it when she acts like a normal girl and plays truant, for all the anxiety it causes us.'

Doria folded her arms across her chest. 'But not into the Old Keep,' she said, troubled. 'That was her mother's way, always mad for adventure and leading the others after her. We all know how that ended.' She shook her head. 'Malian is already too much her mother's daughter for my comfort.'

Nesta frowned. 'The trouble is,' she said, pitching her voice so that no one else could hear her, 'does the Earl realize that? And what will he do when he finds out?'

Doria sighed again, looking anxious. 'I don't know,' she replied. 'I know that Nhairin sees it, plain as I do – and that outsider minstrel, too, I've no doubt. It's as though the Earl is the only person who does not see it.'

'Or will not,' Nesta said softly.

'Does not, will not,' replied Doria, 'the outcome is the same. Well, there's nothing we can do except our best for her, as we always have.'

'Perhaps,' agreed Nesta. Her dark eyes gazed into the fire. 'Although what happens,' she asked, 'if your best is not enough?'

But neither the nurse nor the fire had any answer for her.